"Ambush! Alarm!" The shouts came from the mounted archers who served as advance guard for Rick's party. There were insistent hoof beats from the road ahead. A dozen horsemen, lightly armed, had burst past the advance party and were charging directly at Rick, sabers raised high, the nearest not a hundred yards away.

"Kill the traitor!" "For the glory of Vothan!" "Vothan calls!"

"Dismount to receive cavalry!" Bisso shouted. "Jamiy, look to the Colonel!"

Jamiy spurred his horse to get between Rick and the charging enemies. He was only just in time before the raiders were on him. One engaged him. The others charged past, ignoring the orderly, their eyes fixed on Rick.

"Vothan calls! Kill the traitor! Vothan calls!"

Rick fumbled at his shoulder holster. His pistol was buckled in, his shield hung on the cantle of his saddle. Jamiy had bought him a moment, but only that. The nearest enemy was no more than five yards away, saber raised high—

Bisso must have been just behind him. His H&K battle rifle sounded like the crack of doom. Rick's ears rang with the muzzle blast, but the first enemy screamed in pain. His saber dropped. Bisso fired again.

# MAMELUKES

### ✠ BY ✠

# JERRY POURNELLE

With contributions by
## David Weber & Phillip Pournelle

BAEN

MAMELUKES

Copyright © April 2020 by the Estate of Jerry Pournelle, Phillip Pournelle, and Words of Weber, Inc.

A Baen Books Original

Baen Publishing Enterprises
P.O. Box 1403
Riverdale, NY 10471
www.baen.com

ISBN: 978-1-9821-2537-0

Cover art by Dominic Harman
Map by Randy Asplund

First printing, June 2020
First mass market printing, May 2021

Distributed by Simon & Schuster
1230 Avenue of the Americas
New York, NY 10020

Library of Congress Control Number: 2020008743

Printed in the United States of America

10 9 8 7 6 5 4 3 2 1

Dedicated to the fans, whom Dad loved.

## ⊹⇒ EDITORIAL NOTE ⇐⊹

Many years ago, Jerry Pournelle wrote the novel *Janissaries*. I was a graduate student at the time, working in military and diplomatic history, and an avid science fiction reader, so *Janissaries* was right in my wheelhouse. I loved the original book and both of the sequels—*Clan and Crown* and *Storms of Victory*—and one of my deep regrets was that the series hadn't been continued. One thing that I did not know at the time, and learned only recently from Phillip Pournelle, was that Jim Baen had been instrumental in creating the series by challenging Jerry to write a book explaining why aliens might be visiting Earth covertly, rather than announcing their presence. Knowing Jim the way that I did, I can just hear the conversation, and I found it very…satisfying to discover that he'd had a hand in creating a novel and a series I liked so much long before he and I had ever met.

Fast-forward twenty-one years, and I'm sitting in the Baen Books office in North Carolina reminiscing with Toni Weisskopf about my favorite, unfinished series, and *Janissaries* came up.

That was when I found out that Jerry had been working on the first new *Janissaries* book in twenty years when we lost him, that the manuscript was mostly completed, that he had left detailed notes about how he had intended to finish it, and that his son Phillip had undertaken to complete his dad's final book. And, by the way, would I be interested in lending a hand?

The answer is the book you hold in your hands. Phil and I have tried very hard to maintain his father's voice in what both of us regard as a labor of love. We aren't Jerry. We are simply his son and a writer who loved his books, and we hope we have done right by him in completing the task he left unfinished.

—David Weber

# GLOSSARY

# DRAMATIS PERSONAE

❧━━❧

**The Galactic Confederation** is a loose federation of nonhuman races, governing Earth's region of the spiral arm of our Galaxy. Its member races include the **Shalnuksis**, the **Ader'at'eel**, the **Fusttael**, and the **Finsit'tuvii**. The **Council** is the supreme governing body of the Confederation; the **High Commission** is a subordinate body, in charge of relations with nonmember races, particularly humans.

## TRAN

**The Five Kingdoms** is a confederation of northern kingdoms (including Ta-Boreas [Kingdom containing the seat of the High Rexja], Ta-Meltemos, Ta-Lataos, Ta-Kartos, and Ta-Merga) under a High Rexja.

**Drantos** is an independent kingdom under its own Wanax, although it has been claimed by both Rome and the Five Kingdoms. **Chelm** is part of Drantos.

**Rome** is a (self-proclaimed) empire, descended from Romans of the time of Septimius Severus (c. AD 200) brought to Tran by the **Shalnuksis**.

**The City-States** are an array of independent cities lying south of Drantos and southwest of Rome. Their most prominent members are **Vis** and **Rustengo**.

**The Sunlands** is the general term for everything south of the City-States.

**The Westmen** are nomadic horse barbarians from beyond the High Plains, ultimately descended from Scythians.

# DRAMATIS PERSONAE

## THE GALACTICS

**Gregeral**—One of Inspector Agzaral's trusted aides.

**Inspector Agzaral**—Confederation High Commission law enforcement officer.

**Jehna Sae Leern**—Courier for the Ader'at'eel.

**Karreeel**—**Shalnuksi** merchant, in the Tran trade.

**Les**—Human pilot in **Shalnuksi** service; Gwen Tremaine's husband.

*Wilno*—Retired Confederate naval officer; classmate of Agzaral.


## THE STAR MEN

*Private Jack Beazeley*—Mason's right-hand man.

*Sergeant Harold Bisso*—Elliot's right-hand man.

*Private Alexander Boyd*—Gengrich's chief of staff.

*Sergeant William Campbell*—Professor of Engineering at the University.

*Sergeant Lance Clavell*—Rick Galloway's ambassador to Nikeis.

*Sergeant Major Rafael Elliot*—Topkick of the mercs; Provost of the University.

*Rick Galloway*—Captain, U.S.A.; Colonel of Mercenaries, Eqeta of Chelm, Captain General of Drantos, War Leader of Tamaerthan.

*Corporal Arnold Gengrich*—Formerly leader of mutinous mercs and Lord of Zyphron. Now stationed in southern Chelm to protect the border.

*Private Clarence "Jimmy" Harrison*—Clavell's right hand man.

**Corporal Alan MacAllister**—Expert sniper.

**Sergeant John McCleve**—Medic; Professor of Medicine at the University.

**Major Art Mason**—Rick's right-hand man; Marshal of the Captain General's Household.

**Sergeant Ben Murphy**—Bheroman of Westrook.

**Private First Class Arkos Passavopolous**—"The Great Ark"; machine-gunner.

**Technical Sergeant Harvey Rand**—Former scout/assassin for Gengrich, now prison trustee foreman at madweed farm.

**Private Lafferty Reznick**—Murphy's partner. Killed in battle with Westmen.

**Corporal Mortimer Schultz**—Formerly Master of Foot in Rustengo, now publisher at the University of Tran.

**Gwen Tremaine**—Rector of the University.

**Corporal Jerzy Walinski**—Balloon crewman. Blinded in one eye from an arrow wound.

**Warrant Officer Larry Warner**—Chancellor of the University.

# THE ALLIANCE

**Ajacias**—Former Bheroman of Drantos, in the Sutmarg. Betrayed Drantos to the Five Kingdoms and is now deposed.

**Apelles**—Son of Lykon; Priest of Yatar.

**Balquhain**—Drumold's son and heir.

**Camithon**—Deceased Lord Protector to Ganton until the young Wanax reached age of majority. Killed in battle against the Westmen. Ganton's battle-axe was Camithon's.

**Corgarff**—Subchief to Dughuilas.

**Caradoc**—A lord of Clan Tamaerthan; rescuer of Tylara from Sarakos in *Janissaries*. Deceased husband of Gwen. Assassinated on orders of Tylara.

**Drumold**—Mac Clallan Muir; Tylara's father.

**Dughuilas**—Chief of Clan Calder.

**Enipses**—Bheroman of Drantos.

**Ganton**—Son of Loron; Wanax of Drantos.

**Hilaskos**—Bheroman of Drantos.

**Mad Bear**—Chief of the exiled Silver Wolves clan of the Westmen (the Horse People).

**Maev**—Merchant's daughter; handfasted to Apelles.

**Monira**—Leader of the war-trained Children of Vothan.

**Morrone**—Son of Morron; companion to the Wanax Ganton.

**Pinir**—Son of the smith; Master Gunner in the Royal Artillery of Drantos.

**Rudhrig**—Eqeta of Harms.

**Lady Siobhan**—Art Mason's fiancée and Gwen Tremaine's office manager.

**Teuthras**—Colonel of First Tamaerthan Hussars.

**Traskon**—Son of Trakon; Bheroman of Drantos.

**Tylara do Tamaerthan**—Rick Galloway's wife; Eqetassa of Chelm and Justiciar of Drantos.

**Yanulf**—Highpriest of Yatar and Chancellor of Drantos.


## THE ROMANS

**Flaminius Caesar**—Former Emperor of Rome, deposed.

**Titus Frugi**—Commander of Flaminius' legions against the rebellion.

**Titus Licinius Frugi**—Legate, commanding the Fourth Legion.

**Lucius**—Freedman and confidant to Marselius.

**Gaius Marius Marselius**—Former Prefect of the Western Marches; now Emperor of Rome.

**Octavia Marselia**—Publius' daughter and now wife of Ganton.

**Archbishop Polycarp**—Founder of the movement for the united worship of Yatar and Christ.

**Publius**—Marselius' son and heir.

**Marcus Julius Vinicianus**—Exiled Roman nobleman and former chief spy for Gengrich.


## THE ENEMIES

**Ailas**—General in service to Issardos, currently in command of a Five Kingdoms army occupying part of Chelm.

**Prince Akkilas**—High Rexja Toris' sole surviving legitimate son.

**Issardos**—High Chancellor of the Five Kingdoms.

**Laërtes**—Wanax of Ta-Kartos.

**Neleus**—Wanax of Ta-Merga.

**Matthias**—Highpriest of Vothan.

**Phrados the Prophet**—Religious fanatic opposed to the united worship of Yatar and Christ, assumed deceased at the Battle of Vis.

**Crown Prince Strymon**—Heir to Ta-Meltemos.

**Prince Teodoros**—Strymon's younger brother.

**Toris**—High Rexja of the Five Kingdoms.

**Volauf**—Captain General to Matthias.

**Walking Stone**—Paramount war chief of the Westmen.

# MAMELUKES

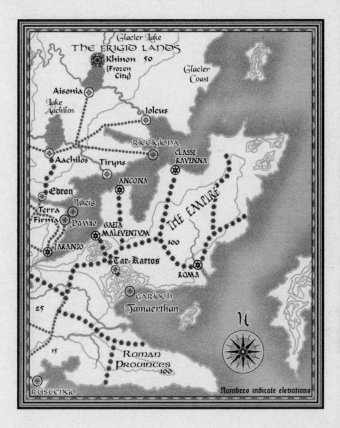

Glacier Lake

THE FRIGID LANDS

Rhinon 50
(Frozen
City)

Glacier
Coast

Aisonia

Lake
Aachilos

Ioleus

Ricciglona

CLASSE
RAVENNA

Aachilos

Tiryns

ANCONA

THE EMPIRE

Edron

Nikeis

Terra
Firma

Pavino

GAETA
MALEVENTVM

100

Taranto

Tar-Kartos

ROMA

GARIOCH
Tamaerthan

25

15

Roman
Provinces
100

RUSTENGO

Numbers indicate elevations

# PROLOGUE

During the height of the Cold War the United States Central Intelligence Agency sent volunteer US military units to Africa to aid anti-communist insurgencies against regimes which the USSR supported with Cuban mercenaries. One such unit was headed by Captain Rick Galloway, a track-star ROTC officer who had intended to be a history teacher. Although he believed in the liberation effort, he was never quite certain why he had volunteered to go to Africa. He was discerning enough to realize that he was sent in large part because he was expendable; the Regular Army was being held to fight the coming big war in Europe when Russian divisions would pour through the Fulda Gap in a race to the Rhine and beyond. His unit was hardly elite, made up of troopers of varying experience.

Rick's second-in-command was Lieutenant André Parsons, a soldier of fortune whose background was obscure but almost certainly included a hitch in the French Foreign Legion.

1

Rick's company was surrounded and under attack by Cuban-assisted forces that greatly outnumbered Rick's light infantry unit. Someone in higher headquarters had called off the rescue attempt, and it would be a matter of hours at most before Rick's surrounded force would be killed or captured. The unit had been warned of the doctrine of plausible deniability, and someone in the government had decided to deny Rick's unit had any legal US status. Thus, surrender meant trial as mercenaries and probable execution.

They escaped when an alien spacecraft landed in their midst. Rick thought it might be an experimental US craft, but all doubts were gone when he was invited aboard and met three Shalnuksis, humanoids but certainly not human. This was an alien spacecraft, no matter that Rick did not believe in flying saucers.

The aliens invited Rick to bring his men aboard, and urged haste, as the Cubans must not see the spacecraft. Rick persuaded his men to board. They were taken to a base on Earth's Moon where they met a human who claimed to be a police inspector for a multiracial interstellar Confederation. Inspector Agzaral wanted to be certain that they had been rescued from a hopeless situation, not kidnapped. Rick convinced him that this was true. Agzaral then told them they would never be allowed to return to Earth. However, the Shalnuksis, the alien merchant race that had engineered their rescue, wished to employ them as mercenaries on Tran, a human-inhabited planet with a civilization comparable to Earth's Middle Ages. Their task would be to assure the growth and processing of a crop of rare recreational drugs much prized in the Confederation. The Shalnuksis would purchase the crop and give them ammunition and some modern conveniences in exchange.

Their only other alternative was to be wards of the Confederation—wards who had refused employment. Inspector Agzaral made it clear that this would not be pleasant.

❖ ❖ ❖

When they landed on Tran, Rick was astonished to find that there had been another American aboard the starship that transported him and his troops from Earth's Moon to the colony world. Gwen Tremaine, onetime student at the University of California at Santa Barbara, had become the mistress of Les, the ship's pilot, and was pregnant. When she would not consent to abortion, Les had no choice but to abandon her and the baby. He explained that the Galactics would routinely execute the child; breeding of the human servants of the Galactic Confederation was carefully controlled. He left her on Tran with Rick.

❖ ❖ ❖

Immediately after landing on Tran, Rick was deposed as leader in a revolt led by André Parsons, who persuaded the troops that he was more qualified than a college boy. Corporal Art Mason was permitted to accompany Rick into exile. Gwen Tremaine chose to go with Rick rather than stay with Parsons.

On the road east Rick met Tylara do Tamaerthan, heirless Dowager Countess of Chelm and daughter of a highlander clan chieftain. The clans of Tamaerthan were menaced by a reconstituted Roman Empire, and the County of Chelm was under invasion by another empire,

the northern Five Kingdoms. Chelm's Castle had fallen.
Tylara was treated as spoils of war by the invaders, but had
been rescued and taken out of the dungeons by one of her
father's Tamaerthan henchmen. As they traveled they fell
in love, and were married in her father's highland
stronghold, making Rick the Eqeta—Count—of Chelm,
and obligating him to reconquer her dower lands.

Rick gradually pieced together the history of Tran.
Every six hundred years or so a group of Earth soldiers
had been brought to the planet. Each group was used to
secure local power and grow crops in one particular region
of the planet. Each group founded a culture which
diffused into the surrounding cultures without replacing
them. The result was a variety of governments. In every
case the intrusions corresponded with what local legends
call "the Time," when the seas rose, there were storms,
and the weather got increasingly hotter.

Rick deduced that the Romans were late eastern
empire when heavy cavalry dominated and infantry was
despised; sometime after Constantine and Adrianople, but
before the Fall. The Tamaerthan clansmen, probably
Welsh, were menaced by the Roman Empire, and faced
hunger or starvation unless new sources of food could be
found. The clansmen were already excellent archers but
had no tactics to use against the Roman heavy cavalry and
combined-arms army. Rick taught the clansmen the use
of pikes, and by using pikes and bows in combination was
able to defeat a Roman provincial army and levy tribute
on Roman provinces. This led to a revolt in the Empire.
Marselius, formerly a provincial governor, declared
himself the new Caesar, and negotiated a peace treaty

with Rick and Tamaerthan, thus pacifying the eastern part of the planet's major continent.

André Parsons, as leader of Rick's former troops, had sold his services to the Five Kingdoms. Five Kingdoms forces had already overrun Tylara's County of Chelm, and were about to conquer all of the Kingdom of Drantos. Tylara owed allegiance to the Kingdom of Drantos. Rick's marriage to Tylara automatically put Rick at war with Parsons and his employers.

Parsons had not proven to be a good leader, and many of the mercenaries had deserted him. Most of the others were disloyal. Parsons tried to kill Rick during a truce conference, but Tylara, armed with a pistol Elliot had given her, killed Parsons. The remaining mercenaries returned their allegiance to Rick and named him their colonel.

Due largely to Rick's reputation derived from defeating a Roman army, Rick and Tylara became the guardians of Ganton, the boy king of Drantos. By combining the forces of the Tamaerthan clans, the mercenaries, and the Drantos feudal army, Rick was able to defeat the remnant forces loyal to Flaminius Caesar and thus unite the Roman Empire under Marselius. One result of this alliance was the formation of an international university at the Tamaerthan border, with Gwen Tremaine as Rector.

Rick then used the alliance forces to halt the Five Kingdoms invasion of Drantos and begin the work of reconquest. He was also able to begin production of the recreational drug crops for sale to galactic merchants. This convinced the alien faction which had taken him to the planet that he would continue to produce the desired crops in profitable quantities, and ammunition and supplies purchased on Earth were traded for his initial drug crop. The Drantos-Tamaerthan-Roman alliance was able to beat back a number of threats, including an invasion of the high plains nomads known as Westmen, probably descendants of Scythians. There were many other threats, and Rick was feeling overwhelmed.

Unknown to Rick, Tylara formed an intelligence and assassination corps of war orphans known as the Children of Vothan. They were raised in crèches and taught personal devotion to her. She used her assassins to remove a former ally who had become a mortal threat to Rick, but Rick knew none of this. The strain of keeping secrets and Tylara's jealousies led to the estrangement and informal separation of Rick and Tylara. Tylara in particular was consumed by guilt for deceiving her husband. Rick, having learned of Tylara's trained assassins, was afraid of his wife. They remained polite, but drew farther apart, and spent little time in each other's company. Their two children, Makail and Isobel, were to be heirs to the County of Chelm, but affairs of state occupied both Rick and Tylara, so that the children were largely raised by governesses and bodyguards.

The Five Kingdoms began a new invasion of Drantos, a main attack through Chelm and a second attack in the east exploiting disloyalties of certain Drantos border lords. Tylara attended Morrone, the King's Companion, in the battles to the east, while in the west Rick held Chelm despite being outnumbered. When Tylara was captured by Prince Strymon, heir to one of the Five Kingdoms and nominally in the service of the High Rexja of the Five

Kingdoms, Rick turned over control of his army in the west to his second in command, and rushed to her rescue. He arrived in the middle of the battle of the Ottarn River during a storm. Rick discovered Wanax Ganton was holding steady on the threatened right wing of the army, but no one was effectively in overall command. Rick quickly organized a flanking maneuver against the forces attacking Ganton. While this did turn the battle, Rick quickly became the target of a charge led by Matthias, Highpriest of Vothan and Marshall of the Great Host of the Five Kingdoms. Just when Rick thought he would be killed, Tylara appeared like a Valkyrie out of the gloom and struck down Matthias.

# PART ONE
# TREASON

# ⊱⊰ CHAPTER ONE ⊱⊰
## VICTORY

The rain had slacked off to drizzle, leaving the battlefield wet with both water and blood. There were screams of dying men, horses, and centaurs, but the thick rain and fog softened these if not the sudden crack of a .45 pistol. The smell of blood hung heavy in the air, bright copper smells mingled with the muskier odor of centaur blood. Neither sun was visible for long through the gray clouds, but the True Sun shone through near the horizon for a moment as it set. The dimmer Firestealer made a bright spot two hours high, and through the clouds lit the grisly battlefield with a dull gray light.

Rick Galloway, Colonel of Mercenaries, Warlord of Drantos, Eqeta of Chelm, and one time Captain, United States Army, rode painfully after his wife. There was no way to catch her, not with his horse blown from three days hard travel and a day of fighting.

A hard day of fighting. Rick had arrived unannounced

in the middle of a major battle between Ganton's royal army and invading forces from the neighboring Five Kingdoms. King Ganton was somewhere in the thick of the fighting. Prince Strymon, formerly an enemy and now inexplicably an ally to Ganton, was in charge of the army but was unsure where the forces of Drantos were engaged or how the battle was progressing. No one was in effective command.

*And I took charge and won the battle. Luck*, Rick thought. *Blind luck*. He had just enough information to form a battle plan. More a scheme than a plan, he thought, but it had worked. Rick took charge of all the idle forces he could round up and led them in a flanking maneuver that gave the enemy the choice of trying to fight through the one Drantos formation that held steady under Wanax Ganton, or run away in disorder. The fog of war— more literally heavy rain, which silenced Rick's gunpowder weapons but blinded the enemy as well—had done its work. Taken from flank and behind by Rick and his star weapons, the Five Kingdoms invading forces had fled in panic.

*Victory*, Rick thought. But it was a near thing. He felt the weight of his armor dragging at him, and he ached all over.

He looked up to see Tylara racing ahead. His heart sang. *She's alive, unhurt, safe!* And the darkness had lifted from her soul. She rode laughing through the rain, the war axe hanging from its strap on her pommel. It was forgotten now, but moments before she had been swinging that axe about her head, charging like a Valkyrie into a battle that seemed all but lost. Now they rode through the aftermath of battle and victory. More horses screamed in pain, men wandered aimlessly with haunted eyes. A few peasants had already crept out to rob the dead and dying. Rick turned to give orders, then shook his head. Let others take charge now. The battle was won.

*And I have my wife back!* Rick grinned widely.

Tylara do Tamaerthan, Eqetassa of Chelm, High Justiciar of Drantos, and the loveliest girl Rick had ever seen, looked back to see that Rick was falling behind. She reined in. "You said you would race!" she said. "You forfeit!"

"I love to hear you laugh," Rick said. "Tylara—I thought I'd lost you."

She waited until he reached her, then rode on beside him.

"I was lost, my husband. My love," she said in a lower voice. "And I may yet be, there is much you do not know."

"I think I do. If you mean the Children of Vothan."

"My assassins. That is not the worst. I killed Caradoc," she said. "My most loyal man, my rescuer, and I sent the Children to kill him like a dog in the streets."

Rick glanced around. MacAllister was twenty paces behind. Jamiy, his orderly and shield bearer, had lost his horse and was farther back still waiting another. A few troops rode ahead with Padraic, his Guards commander, but there was no one to overhear.

"I know that, too," Rick said. *And I know why. I would never have done it, but something had to be done—*

"And you forgive me?" She pulled gently on the left rein and guided her horse to meet his until they were riding side by side, close together.

"I could forgive you anything," Rick said. "Would, and do."

"Would I could forgive myself," Tylara said. "But I never will. Rick, I thought I did right. And there was so little time to decide."

"I know. Tylara, when I heard that Caradoc was dead in a street riot, dead before he could return to what he thought was his home, I thought it was divine providence. It was the only way! Alive he would have entangled us in war with the Galactics. And with good reason, too. I was glad he was dead. But I thought it good fortune, luck, not—later I learned better. You should have told me."

"It was an act of dishonor. Should I have dishonored you as well as myself? But all seemed lost—my husband, My Lord, we will speak more of this another time," Tylara said. "I am glad you know. I brooded—"

"I know. I didn't know why, and I thought it was me."

"I am sorry, my love. I was afraid. And you were cold, and I thought I had lost your love—"

"And I thought I'd lost you. It's done and over," Rick said. "We stand together now, now and forever. And whatever there is to fear, Tylara, we face that together."

She smiled and reached for his hand.

"Now and forever," she said, so low that he barely heard her. "Yatar and Christ be thanked." They rode on in silence.

"I think the king does not know any of this." Tylara gestured ahead. Ganton, Wanax of Drantos, stood by the banner of the Fighting Man, golden helmet under his arm. His helmet was dented, and his armor was stained with blood, but he stood proudly enough, with a dozen dead

enemies at his feet, hundreds more in front of his position.
He looked much older than his years, a man now rather
than the boy he had been when he came to the throne, even
if his years were not yet those of a man. A score of the
chivalry of Drantos stood around him to shout his praises.

"Victory!"

"A victory for Drantos alone! Without Roman aid!
Ganton's victory," someone shouted.

"Ganton alone! Ganton Imperator! Ganton the Great!"

The shouting quieted as Rick and Tylara rode up.

"Lord Rick," Ganton said. The triumphant grin faded.
"I had heard that you were here." Suddenly he looked
smaller and younger, as he might have when Tylara was
his Guardian and not his Justiciar; a teenaged boy for a
moment before standing straight like a king again.

"Aye! Majesty! He was here in truth!" Three lords of
Drantos appeared out of the rain. "The battle was lost, we
knew not where you were, where our troops were! The
rain silenced the Great Guns, clouds and rain hid the
enemy. The armies of the Five rallied to the attack. All
seemed lost, and then Lord Rick came! In an hour he had
taken command, led us across the field to fall upon the
enemy! Did you not know? You were near lost, Majesty,
the day was near lost, the enemy was upon you when Lord
Rick fell upon them from behind!"

Ganton turned to his lords. "Is this true?"

Some shrugged. One or two said, shamefacedly, "Aye,
Majesty. It was a near enough thing."

"So it was none of my victory," Ganton said. "Well, a
day. A victory none the less. And I have not greeted you
properly, Lord Rick. Welcome!"

"I think little good will come of this," Tylara muttered.

Rick painfully climbed down from his horse to kneel in greeting.

"My thanks for your welcome, Majesty."

"So you arrived just in time," Ganton said. "To save me yet again. Stand up, Warlord. I must think of a suitable reward."

Rick got to his feet. He felt unsteady, as the fatigue of his forced marches followed by a day of battle caught up with him.

"I need no reward, Majesty. I have only done my duty."

"Yet, I recall, we had agreed that your duty was to hold the West against the invaders there," Ganton said.

"They are held," Rick said. "Held and more than held. And when news of this day comes to them, they will likely fall back to their own lands."

"News of this day," Ganton said. "News of your victory."

"Not mine, Majesty. Yours. You commanded here."

Ganton gestured around him, at heaps of dead and dying men and horses. Some of the dying stirred feebly, and here and there a horse screamed in pain. The bright blue and yellow of the priests of Yatar moved among the wounded.

"Commanded. I stood my ground, here, and we held," Ganton said. "We held. I thought to let them come to me and break their teeth."

"Aye! Nobly done!" one of the knights shouted. "A thousand fell before you! Nobly done!"

"Aye, say nobly done," Ganton said. "Say bravely done, but say stupidly done as well, since I left no one in command able to exploit our deeds." He lifted his palms and face to the sky, then grinned. "And Yatar and His Son Christ have rewarded me, for in my hour of need came once again Lord Rick and Lady Tylara to win the day for me. Well done, Lord Rick. Well done, and welcome."

Rick and Tylara exchanged glances.

"Without your anvil, my hammer would have fallen on empty fields," Rick said. Which was true enough. Ganton had stood like a rock in the middle of the tide of battle. "The bards will sing of your victory." *Or I'll have their heads...*

"Tell me of the west," Ganton said.

"Majesty. Dravan and Chelm hold fast for you, though Captain General Ailas with twenty thousand holds the plains north of Castle Dravan for the Five Kingdoms," Rick said. "I could have hoped the Five would send a less competent general. Ailas is well dug in, and has learned the use of scouts. His light cavalry is as good as ours, he's built fortifications, and from somewhere he has learned camp sanitation. He is well supplied from the north."

"He learned what you call sanitation from you. And he is supplied from harvest off your lands," Ganton said dryly.

"Yes, Majesty. But the upshot is that it would take a frontal attack against fortified positions to dislodge him. That would lose so many we could not defend against the next onslaught. So I've sent pandours into his backfield—"

"Pandours, My Lord?"

"Light cavalry raiders. Live off the land. Guerrillas, we sometimes call them. They'll harass him, intercept supplies, generally give him problems."

"That cannot force him to withdraw," Ganton observed.

"Perhaps so, perhaps not, Majesty, but they'll surely make him less likely to advance until he hears of the progress of his cause in the east. What he will hear is of your victory here."

"Ah. And who leads these—pandours?"

"Lord Murphy," Rick said. Murphy, a merc who'd got lucky, and was now a Drantos lord in his own right. Another complication in Rick Galloway's command structure. Did Murphy obey Rick as Colonel of Mercenaries, as Eqeta of Chelm, or as Warlord of Drantos? It might make a difference . . .

One of the junior lords in Ganton's train thrust forward. "Majesty, during the battle a message arrived from Lord Murphy. I had not time to tell you before. It is directed to Lord Rick. The messenger learned from a semaphore station that Lord Rick was coming here, and has come looking for him."

"A message," Rick said.

"Bring it," Ganton ordered. "Bring it here. It may be important."

✚ ✚ ✚

There were two messengers, one a sturdy burgher from a town near Tylara's Castle Dravan, the other a kilted clansman of Tamaerthan. The burgher carried a small cask, the clansman a shield wrapped in leather. Both wore sashes and armbands in the household colors of Chelm. When they saw Rick, Tylara, and Ganton together they hesitated.

"You have a message," Ganton said. "From the Bheroman Murphy."

"Majesty. We were directed to Lord Rick." The young

clansman indicated his armband. "As you see, we are in the service of the Eqeta and Eqetassa of Chelm."

"Then give it to them," Ganton said.

The clansman glanced at Rick, who nodded. "Out with it."

"Lord," the messenger said. "Lord, two hundred stadia northwest of here we came upon a caravan. We attacked it and captured much plunder. The leader of the caravan was killed in the battle. This is his shield."

He gestured, and the other messenger helped him to unwrap the shield with a flourish.

"Defaced, argent, a rampant griffin sable crowned Or," someone muttered.

"Akkilas?" Ganton muttered. "The heir?"

"We believe so," the messenger said. "This is his head." He opened the cask and poured out alcohol. His companion laid out a cloth, and the head rolled onto it. Sightless eyes stared up. The alcohol had preserved it well enough.

"Griffin earring," Ganton's herald muttered. "It could well be him."

"Does anyone here know Prince Akkilas?" Ganton asked.

"No, Majesty."

"My compliments to Prince Strymon, and if he pleases could he come," Ganton said. "Surely he'll know him."

"At once, Majesty."

"Akkilas," Tylara said. "Brother of Sarakos."

"The late and unlamented Sarakos," Ganton said. "And this is the Heir to the High Rexja."

"Formerly the heir," one of Ganton's lords said excitedly. "Now, Majesty, you are heir!"

"He is," the herald shouted. "By the same claim that the High Rexja held himself entitled to Drantos. Hail Ganton, heir of the Five Kingdoms!"

✤ ✤ ✤

Strymon, Crown Prince of Ta-Meltemos, was tall and serious, well known as a man of high honor and quixotic chivalry. Heir to one of the Five Kingdoms, he was allied with Ganton and Drantos, but subject to neither, and what he would do if there came a direct order from his father to abandon that alliance neither Rick nor Ganton knew. Strymon stared down at the head on the cloth.

"It could be him," he said. "I have not seen him for years."

"Akkilas is dead!" one of the lords shouted. "Ganton is heir! High Rexja Ganton!"

"High Rexja is elective," Strymon said. "Surely all know that."

"But it has been within the House of Sarakos for four generations," the herald protested. "The Five have always elected an heir to Radalphes the Great."

"There has always been a direct heir to Radalphes," Strymon observed dryly. "Until now. Majesty, I believe your claim is through your mother?"

"Yes. I take it you do not accept."

Strymon smiled thinly.

"I am Prince of Ta-Meltemos, not Wanax, and were my father dead and my inheritance secure I would still be one vote among five. It is not for me to accept or deny, Majesty."

"Yes." Ganton looked around at the aftermath of battle. "It grows late, and I confess I am weary."

"Well earned, Majesty!" several lords shouted.

"Earned or no, I need rest. Let us resume this another time. Prince Strymon, my thanks for your aid in this battle. Lord Rick, a splendid victory. We shall think how best to take advantage of it. And how to reward you. Good evening, Prince, Lady Tylara. My Lords. You all have my leave."

Rick limped to his horse and let Jamiy hold it for him.

"I can do with a bath," he said. "For all that I did more riding than fighting."

"And that is the best victory of all," Strymon said. "Fewer killed than might be, and I believe Drantos is safe enough for the moment."

"With no small aid from you," Rick said. "My thanks for that. And I will not forget that you returned My Lady unharmed."

"We were much pleased to have her as our guest," Strymon said. "What I gained in healing knowledge alone is worth far more than any ransom." He paused. "You have no camp here, and the Wanax has forgotten to provide for you. You are both welcome guests in my camp. It is a soldier's camp, but perhaps more than you brought on your march."

"I had expected to stay with the clansmen," Rick said. "But your offer is generous. Tylara?"

"My father must needs be told, but I think we have much to speak of with Prince Strymon," Tylara said.

Rick was unsurprised to see that his orderly had found a new mount.

"Jamiy, my respects to Mac Clallan Muir, and we beg his forgiveness for the night. See that he is informed," Rick said. "Prince Strymon, if your hospitality to your guests is as gracious as My Lady tells me you give to your prisoners, we would be fools to decline."

"Good. I will ride ahead to order preparations," Strymon said. He spurred his horse.

"Jamiy," Tylara said. "Inform my father that I will join my husband for the night as guest of Prince Strymon. And you may remain in the clan camp, we will not need you before morning." She waited until Jamiy had ridden off. "Prince Strymon wants to speak with us alone."

"You know this?"

"Was it not obvious?"

Rick shook his head. It hadn't been obvious to him.

"What will he want to speak about?"

"Ganton's claim, where this army goes, the war with the Five Kingdoms," Tylara said. "And he would learn more of the Galactics."

"How much did you tell him?" Rick asked.

"Little, my love. Only that you are a great warrior from a far place, brought here by men of great power but little courage."

"An interesting summary," Rick said. "True enough."

"My husband, Strymon for all his chivalry is Prince Royal of Ta-Meltemos, undisputed heir to one of the Five Kingdoms, and has as good a claim to be High Rexja as Ganton. His interests were ours when the armies of the High Rexja stood in Drantos, but now? I cannot think he will be pleased to see Drantos armies march past our northern borders no matter where they head."

## ⊰≈ CHAPTER TWO ≈⊱
# THE PRINCE ROYAL
# OF TA-MELTEMOS

Strymon's accommodations were military rather than luxurious, but comfortable enough. Tylara pointed out a field hospital. Priests of Yatar bustled about among the wounded. Acolytes tended fires and boiled cloths for bandages. Priest surgeons scrubbed meticulously before and after tending the wounded, and the dead were carried far downwind from the hospital.

"He has learned fast," she said.

"Your teaching while you were his prisoner?"

"Yes, My Lord Husband. Was that not proper? You have told me that knowledge is not to be hoarded."

"Indeed, my most wise lady wife. It was very proper to teach the germ theory of disease. My surprise is at how fast he's learned."

"Cleanliness has always been pleasing to Yatar," Tylara said. "His priests needed little persuading."

*And there are priests of Yatar in both armies*, Rick thought. Judging by the small red crosses on the shoulders and left breast of their blue and yellow robes, nearly all the priests of Yatar in Strymon's force were converts to the New Faith, which accepted Christ as the Son of Yatar. What that would do to Tran politics was likely to be more than Rick could guess.

But at least there was enough hot water for a bath. When they reached the tent assigned to them he was delighted to see there was a large tub to soak in. Hot water and a tub! And Tylara was smiling, enjoying their renewed friendship. Like falling in love all over again! He thought of inviting Tylara into the bath with him, but that might shock Strymon's servants. Prince Strymon had no male heirs and was twice a widower, but unlike his young brother was rumored to be somewhat prudish in both habits and speech. And Tylara had her own bath. *But by God we'll sleep together*, Rick thought. For the first time in months...

✢ ✢ ✢

Rick's pistols and sword were missing when he emerged from his bath. So was his armor. A page explained they were to be cleaned.

"Prince Strymon has ordered they be returned to you so soon as you need them," the boy said. His voice was strong, but Rick thought he saw fear in the boy's eyes. As well he might. The boy indicated new clothing laid out on the bed. "And if you and your lady will come to dinner when you are dressed?"

Rick dressed in silence. There would be no point in complaining to a ten-year-old boy, and there was no one else he could speak to. *May as well play this one as it lies . . .*

Guardsmen held umbrellas to protect them from the rain as they were conducted to Strymon's command tent.

"My pistol's missing," Rick muttered.

"As well mine," Tylara said. "Likewise my dagger."

"What the hell?"

Tylara nodded.

"Prince Strymon's honor and chivalry are known everywhere, and I have more than enough reasons to know those stories are not false," she said. "Whatever his reason, we will know in good time. I am certain he means us no harm, and I think we would do best to trust him."

"Trust is fine," Rick thought. Then he laughed.

"My husband?"

"I keep thinking how Mason would have fits if he knew," Rick said.

"Ah." Tylara grinned. Art Mason would never let Rick go out in public without full armor, chain mail over flak jacket, pistol in shoulder holster, short sword and dagger, and a full escort. And here they were both in garta cloth robes and slippers, while their armor was away to be polished and oiled and their weapons were God alone knew where.

"And Major Mason is not without his reasons," Tylara said. "Yet I feel safer here than I would in similar conditions in the camp of our own Wanax."

"You know something I don't?"

"Know?" She shook her head, a slight gesture that still said volumes.

Rick frowned. Ganton had seemed friendly enough.

But Tylara understood Tran dynastic politics far better than Rick ever would. Relax and enjoy it, Rick thought. Nothing else to do.

✢ ✢ ✢

Rain drummed on the tent roof, and sometimes a gust of wind shook the walls. For the most part Strymon's tent caravan was proof against the weather. A long trestle table had been set up, with an almost white tablecloth, and pewter dishes. A cheery fire blazed in one corner of the tent. Rick inspected the portable fireplace with approval, and made a mental note to have one made for his own travel caravan: an open-faced Franklin stove, with sections of chimney made of some kind of ceramic and held together with metal collars. He had seen nothing like it in Drantos. The Five Kingdoms pretended a superiority that Drantos didn't admit. Could this be evidence that it was more than pretense?

Dinner was far more than Rick had expected, and Strymon's troops had liberated a store of wine from the enemy's camp. Like most of the wine on Tran, it was thinner and more tart than Rick liked, but it was strong enough and left a good aftertaste. When Rick drained his cup it was filled again without his asking. He caught Tylara's eye. She grinned slyly, and Rick asked for water as well as wine. After that he was careful not to drain his wine cup again. Tylara thought he drank too much, and when he was being reasonable he knew that was true. And tonight he would need his head clear. Strymon was no fool.

Strymon drank plentifully but from a different jug. Tylara watched, saying nothing, until after dessert was served and the dishes cleared away. Strymon dismissed the servants.

"It is odd that you are here," Strymon said.

"I came for my wife," Rick said simply. Tylara beamed. She looked happier than she had since they were first married. It must have been terrible, a secret like that with no one to tell it to, he thought. *And that won't happen again. I nearly lost her!*

"I did not mean here at this battle," Strymon said. "All her time when she was my captive your lady promised me that you would work the most terrible revenge if any harm came to her, until I thought to see you come out of the mist at any moment. No, My Lord, I mean that you won the battle today. Much as I am pleased to have you here, you should be the honored guest of the Wanax, not of his ally."

"So should be you," Tylara said simply.

"He was exhausted," Rick protested.

Strymon politely ignored him.

"Then you believe as I do?" he asked Tylara.

"Yes."

"What are you two talking about?" Rick demanded.

"Oh. My husband is a direct man," Tylara said. "Quick to trust, and never thinks another may harbor ill thoughts. My Lord Husband, we mean that with Akkilas dead, the world has changed a very great deal for the Wanax Ganton, and he was hardly too exhausted to know that. Or to know who won his battle for him." She smiled. "You 'saved his bacon,' I believe your Major Mason would say."

"I do not think that head was Akkilas," Strymon said.

"What? But why did you not say so, Prince?" Tylara asked.

"I cannot be sure, and would I be believed? Wanax Ganton is aware that my claim is as good as his. He would wonder if I played for time. And it might well be Akkilas."

"If it's not him, who is it?" Rick asked.

"His tanist," Strymon said.

Rick frowned the question.

"A custom no longer followed in southern lands. Nor indeed in all of ours, but it is invariable in the High Rexja's household," Strymon said. "As the prince comes of age, a young man of good family who closely resembles him is selected. He is trained as companion, advisor—and possibly as target for assassination. Akkilas was fortunate. His tanist was a young man of ability, a good advisor and a better student of war than Akkilas ever was."

"Who'd know the difference?" Rick asked.

"Any who knew them well, I suppose. The birthmarks are only similar, not identical, and the tanist was a year older than Akkilas—"

"Ah." Tylara nodded understanding. "My Lord Husband means that it may not matter whose head that is, if there exists someone of ability who can claim to be Akkilas."

"Indeed," Strymon said. "One more complication. Among many. Lord Rick, what does your Wanax Ganton intend now? Whoever leads, whether Akkilas or his tanist or the Honorable Matthias of Vothan's Temple, these invaders will retreat well into the Five Kingdoms before they can regroup. They may again become a formidable force, but it will take time, even without the pursuit you are in no condition to make. When word of this defeat reaches Chancellor Issardos, Captain General Ailas will be recalled to the defense of the realm. He will abandon your lands in the west. The invasion of Drantos is ended."

Rick nodded agreement.

"That's the way I read it. The war is as good as over."

"For now, certainly," Strymon said. "So what will Ganton do?"

Rick frowned as Tylara and Strymon looked at each other. Clearly they understood each other better than Rick did. *The war's over*, Rick thought. *The peasants can go back to their fields, I can go back to Armagh and work on increasing the surinomaz crop for the Shalnuksis, and we can send our best diplomats to the Five Kingdoms to settle the matter. If Issardos is smart he'll put Strymon on his negotiating team, only he can't as he has already charged Strymon with treason. Now who can we send?* He looked from his wife to the prince, and saw only frowns. Tylara was thinking hard. On what? Would she want to be a negotiator? She should be . . . .

The silence lasted half a minute.

"He will press forward, I think," Tylara said finally. "Left to himself I think Ganton would return to his home and his Roman queen, that was a true love match for all that it was arranged, but his barons will demand otherwise. The nobility of Drantos smarts under remembered grievances. The inclination will be strong to press forward, seize lands in compensation for what was lost in these wars. And Ganton's claim to the throne will be strongest if he stands with an army at the Capital of the Five Kingdoms! My Lord, I weary of war, but did I not know that My Lord Husband would never approve, I would myself be among those clamoring for Ganton to press his claims. My own county of Chelm has lost much to the Five, to Sarakos when he came—"

She shuddered, and Rick reached to take her hand. The memories of what Sarakos had done to her would never leave her.

"And to Ailas," she continued, calm enough that only Rick heard the tremor in her voice. "My people should have some recompense." She turned to Rick. "Oh, I know, I have heard you say often enough that I have come to believe it, in a well-managed land plunder is no substitute for production, labor spent planting and building and trading will bring more reward than looting. I know this, I believe this, but I do not feel it. And Ganton's bheromen do not even know what I know. Depend upon it, they are even at this moment clamoring for him to press his claims."

"That was my thought," Strymon said. "And I cannot permit it." He poured himself another cup of the thin wine. "I was never in favor of invading Drantos, and I will not say I was unhappy when circumstances made me ally to Ganton in resisting the invasion. But I cannot remain his ally when his armies march into the Five Kingdoms!"

"You'd come to the aid of a king who's charged you with treason?" Rick asked.

"I would not come to the aid of the High Rexja or his false chancellor, but I would act to spare the lands of desolation by the greedy bheromen of Drantos, particularly in light of the warning of the Time."

"But if Ganton comes as the High Rexja of the Five?" Rick asked. "If the Five Kingdoms become Six, as I am told they once were?"

"There is an election to be held," Strymon said. "And I do not think Ganton will win. Certainly if he comes as legitimate monarch I will accept him, but that is not likely."

"So what will you do?" Rick asked.

"Go home," Strymon said. "Go home and prepare. Prepare for a war that I hope is not against you, and mostly prepare for the Time."

"And your father the Wanax?" Rick asked.

A look of pain crossed Strymon's face. "Did not your lady tell you? My father the Wanax Palamon is vigorous, but he has the mind of a child."

"Oh." *I may have known that and forgotten it. What else have I forgotten that may get us killed?*

"And his chief advisor Rauros is a tool of Chancellor Issardos," Tylara added.

"On your lady's advice I have sent my brother home to guard our family's honor," Strymon said. "He is a better soldier than statesman. As am I, but I am the oldest, and now I must return, and organize defense of the borders. Quickly, before the Wanax Ganton can lead his troops northward."

Rick nodded slowly.

"He can be decisive."

"You taught him that," Strymon said.

"I did." Rick bowed his head. "It was my duty."

"Which you have discharged well," Strymon said. "And I know you have taught your young king of the Time."

The Time. The Demon Sun approached the planet of Tran, changing climates and seasons. Thrones, Dominions, and Powers were shuffled like a pack of cards every six hundred years or so, and while that happened the agriculture of the planet changed as well. And the Time was upon them.

"We've taught him," Rick said. "Whether he's learned is not so clear. And certainly many of his lord's advisors have not."

"But it is true?" Strymon asked. "Not a stratagem your lady devised to win me over?"

"It's true enough," Rick said. He grinned. "Tylara can charm anyone, but in this case she was telling the exact truth."

"Truth as I learned it from Rick," Tylara said. "The Priests of Yatar tell of the Time, when the seas shall rise and the lands shall scorch—of course you have heard those stories. But My Lord Husband knows why the tales are true."

"Ah. And can you tell me?" Strymon asked.

"I can try," Rick said. "But at the risk of insulting you, I must ask what you know of suns and stars."

"I have been told that the suns are great masses of flaming gas, and stars are distant suns," Strymon said. "I suppose I believe it, but I must confess it is not a matter of great importance to me. Should it be?"

"In this instance, yes," Rick said. He looked around the room. It was a tent, floored with rugs, and there were no solid walls. "I'll need a charcoal from the fire," he said.

Tylara went to the fireplace and returned with a cold ember.

"Will this do?"

Rick nodded.

"I'm going to draw on your tablecloth," Rick said. "This

circle represents the True Sun. Tran is a world, round, a ball—I suppose you know this?"

Strymon grimaced.

"Again, I have been told this, but it does not seem reasonable. Yet, if the world is flat, what is on the underside? I am willing to believe it is a ball. I am told you have seen it as such, that your ships go"—he pointed up—"up beyond the sky, above the Vault of the Sky, above the realm of the Day Father. I confess this disturbs me. If you have been beyond the sky, to the realms of endless day, you must have seen God."

"I've been there, but God hides Himself," Rick said. "Not even the Galactics have seen Him."

"And yet they believe in Yatar?" Strymon asked.

"He is not known by that name, but yes, many believe in the Almighty," Rick said. *And how did Agzaral put it? "The dominant religion of the Confederation is not inconsistent with the great Monotheisms of Earth." Something like that.* "But yes, I have seen this world as a single ball in space." He drew a circle around the dot of the True Sun. "And this is the path this world takes around the True Sun. And now, well out beyond this world, moving in a greater circle around Tran and the True Sun alike, is a second sun that you call the Firestealer." He drew another circle enclosing the first. "When the Firestealer is on the other side of the True Sun, it's moving farther away from Tran, because Tran is moving much faster than the Firestealer. The Stealer appears to grow dimmer and dimmer because each day it's farther away, until it passes behind the True Sun. Then each day it becomes brighter again as Tran grows closer to it." Rick illustrated on the tablecloth. "Eventually Tran passes between Firestealer and True Sun and we have the high summers, warmer with the night lit by the Firestealer."

Strymon stared at the tablecloth.

"If you say so," he said finally. "I confess uneasiness. When I was a child I believed True Sun and Firestealer were gods. Then I found not even the priests believed this. The gods live in the realms of endless day beyond the vault of the sky, or so it is said, but you have been there and did not see them. But what has all this to do with the Time? Every year there comes a time when the Firestealer stands in the night sky. It is always thus."

Rick drew a large arc on the tablecloth.

"There is a third sun," Rick said. "Red. It is smaller than either True Sun or Firestealer, and its path carries it so far away that you don't see it unless you know to look for it. But every three hundred fifty-three of your years it comes closer, close enough to bring heat and light and chaos. It is coming now."

"The Demon," Strymon half whispered. "We see it. It grows brighter. But you say it is no more than another sun? But the Honorable Matthias said—" Strymon frowned in thought for a moment. "I suppose it is no matter what the priest of Vothan said. This is no speculation. You have seen all this. You know."

"Yes, Highness," Rick said.

Strymon laughed.

"Highness. You have been higher than ever I shall be, but you call me Highness. Welladay, Lord Rick. Your lady's stories of the Time are true, then. The seas will rise, the days grow longer, the summers hot. Waves of refugees will come from the south. The icy plains will melt, grass grow on the tundra. All this."

"All this," Rick said. "This and more."

"And your part?" Strymon asked.

"I beg your pardon?"

Strymon stretched his feet out under the table and lifted his wine cup.

"My Lord, I am a simple man, soldier not diplomat. So, I think, are you. You will do well all the tasks that the gods give you, but you are not ruled by ambition. So. As one soldier to another, what will you do? What are your preparations for the Time? I freely confess I would copy you."

Rick smiled thinly.

"Fate has given us different roles, I think," Rick said. "My part is different from yours. Give me a moment." Rick drained a water glass and stared into the fire. "Highness, you've heard stories of the sky demons."

"Yes. They are part of the legends of the Time. Do you say, then, that all the old legends are true? The seas rise, the land burns, crops fail, and evil gods rain *skyfire* across the land." Strymon shuddered. "The sky demons bring the skyfire."

"They do," Rick said. "More than once in Tran's history. And that is my part, Highness, to prevent the skyfire if I can."

"How will you do this?"

"I may not be able to," Rick said.

Tylara took his hand.

"If anyone can, you will, My Lord Husband."

"I hope so. Highness, the sky demons are real. They

are not true demons, they are creatures of flesh and blood, but they were not born of human women. They see this world and all its people as you or I would see a herd of sheep, useful in potential, valuable even, but of no great importance. They want only one thing from Tran."

"And that is?"

"The essence of the plant we call madweed. They use it for pleasure, and they are willing to pay well for it."

"Ah," Strymon exclaimed. "That explains why you grow madweed at Castle Armagh! When it was told to me I could not believe it, yet my agents were trustworthy."

"Trustworthy and very adept," Rick said. "I had no idea you had agents watching Armagh. My security officers must not be as careful as I thought."

Strymon smiled coyly.

"We can discuss this another time," he said. "But you grow madweed for the sky demons?"

"I do."

"And in exchange they bring you new charges for your star weapons." Strymon's tone was emphatic. He reached into a sleeve pocket and retrieved a .45 ACP cartridge. "Like this."

"Like that," Rick agreed.

"When I was taken prisoner they naturally took my weapons," Tylara said. "The pistol among them. Later, after the attempts on my life, Prince Strymon was honorable enough to return the pistol to me for my protection."

Rick nodded.

"Less one cartridge. That much was in your letters," Rick said. "Now he has all our weapons."

"Only for the moment, My Lord," Strymon said. "Only

for the moment. They will be returned to you long before you have need of them."

"All right, we'll leave it at that for now. Prince, my wife tells me you became her friend before you ceased to be her jailer. I have great regard for Tylara's abilities. Her father once asked me who last fooled her, and I had no answer. It's because of your kindness to her and her good opinion that I speak this frankly with you."

Strymon spread his hands, fingers apart.

"Thank you. I believe I deserve your trust."

"So do I," Rick said. "Despite this mystery of our weapons. So. You know what I must have from the sky demons, and why the Armagh madweed farms must be my first concern. Now I tell you that it is Armagh that will most likely suffer skyfire. With luck it will be only Armagh."

"Luck and the favor of Yatar and Christ," Tylara said.

Rick nodded. Tylara's sudden conversion to the new Unified Christian Church had been a surprise, but it was no surprise that her conviction was deep. *She's never been a shallow person*, Rick thought. *And who am I to encourage cynicism? Maybe it's all true, here anyway. Maybe God lets us create Him. I'm no preacher.*

"To business, then," he said. "You have a treaty with Ganton. May I know the terms?"

"Certainly. I would gladly tell you, but perhaps—yes." Strymon clapped his hands. "My compliments to My Lord Father Apelles, and we request his attendance," he told the servant who answered.

"My Lord Father Apelles?" Rick said.

Tylara smiled.

"He has risen since you saw him last. Justifiably.

Highpriest Yanulf and Archbishop Polycarp have decreed that he be raised to bishop as soon as sufficient prelates may be gathered to consummate his elevation."

✢ ✢ ✢

Apelles was robed in blue garta cloth and wore a large pectoral cross topped with the sun disk of Yatar, as befitted a bishop-designate of the Unified Church, and he hardly resembled the young swineherd turned clerk that Rick remembered. *He can't be thirty yet, doesn't look twenty-five.* Rick stood and bowed. It never hurt to show respect to the clergy.

"My Lord Father Apelles. It's good to see you again."

"And you, Lord Rick. My Lady."

*Learned some courtly manners, too*, Rick thought. *Respectful, but mindful of the dignity of his offices. Odd how quickly they pick that up . . .*

"Lord Father, Lord Rick has requested to know the terms of my treaty with Wanax Ganton. As you were one of the witnesses, I thought it best to have you recite it," Strymon said.

"As you will, Highness," Apelles said.

"It will be dry work," Rick said. "Perhaps My Lord Father would care for wine?"

"A small glass only," Apelles said. "It is a short treaty. Ta-Meltemos withdraws from the invasion of Drantos, will assist in the expulsion of all enemies from Drantos for the period of one year, and thereafter will aid Drantos in war against any power other than the Five Kingdoms for five years. In return, Drantos imposes no demand for reparations, and for five years will aid Ta-Meltemos against enemies other than Rome. Furthermore, as soon as Prince

Strymon and his army have departed from Drantos, I am to share with him all I know of the Time, including what I know of sky demons, skyfire, and the box that speaks to the stars. Prior to that I am free to share what I know of the healing arts, and to preach the True Religion of the Unified Church of Yatar and Christ." Apelles raised the palm of his right hand. "That latter is not formally part of the treaty, but it is an understood condition of my accompanying his Highness to the Green Palace."

Rick frowned.

"I heard nothing to prevent Wanax Ganton from pressing a claim to the throne of the High Rexja."

"Nor I, Lord," Apelles said. "Of course at the time the treaty was made, there was no serious thought of such. Am I to understand that the head was that of Akkilas?"

Rick looked to Strymon.

"I am not sure," Strymon said. "I suppose I should not be surprised that you know of the head."

Apelles bowed slightly.

"Highness, I would be astonished if there were any man in the army who does not know of it. Your own soldiers rejoice that you have as good a claim as any, now that the heir is dead. I make little doubt that Wanax Ganton's men feel much the same about his claims."

"And the treaty says nothing of any of this," Rick observed.

"More to the point," Strymon said, "my chief benefit from this treaty was to be knowledge. Knowledge I do not receive until I have brought my army back to Ta-Meltemos. Ganton has reaped the benefits of this agreement. I have not."

"That is a matter of time only," Apelles said. "I certainly intend to fulfill my part of the bargain."

"Until Ganton orders you otherwise?" Strymon suggested.

Apelles' expression didn't change.

"Highness, I was given an order by a king in regards to a treaty. The Wanax swore to that treaty, and I swore as a sacred witness. No order from the Wanax can change that." He shook his head side to side gravely. "I do not say what I might do if I received a decree from Patriarch Yanulf nullifying the treaty, but I hardly consider that a likely event. My future seems clear enough. I shall be your advisor until am released. I expect I will also be appointed the Patriarch's Nuncio. The arrangement is not uncommon."

"With the clear implication that my interests and those of the Patriarch are the same."

"Are they not?" Apelles asked.

Strymon nodded.

"I suppose, I have no reason to think otherwise. Assuming that what I am told of the Time to come is true."

"I am convinced that it is true," Apelles said. "I believe Lord Rick and Lady Tylara are convinced. I know that Patriarch Yanulf is, for he speaks of little else by his own choice. Preparation for the Time should be the highest consideration of everyone to whom God has given authority. So says the Church. Heed that advice, Prince, and you will do well by the people God has entrusted to you."

Strymon sat nodding to himself for a moment, then stood in decision. He bowed.

"My thanks. You are welcome to join us for the rest of the evening, My Lord Father, but I suggest your time would be better used preparing to march. We depart immediately for Ta-Meltemos. I hope to have my entire army on my home soil by dark two days hence. Earlier if possible. We march."

"You said immediately?"

"Yes. I have already given orders to my officers. Now I inform you."

"There are wounded that should not be moved so soon," Apelles protested.

"Yes, I had thought of that. My Lord Rick, regarding any of my troops who must be left behind, I release them into your service and custody. When they are recovered they should be escorted to our borders, or they may remain in your service if they so choose. I pledge to pay any expenses you may incur by this. My Lord Father Apelles, will this fulfill the conditions of the treaty?"

"My Lord Rick remains Warlord of Drantos?" Apelles asked formally. "Then all is well, and we may consider leaving wounded soldiers under the orders of a Great Officer of Drantos to be a fulfillment of the treaty requirement that all Ta-Meltemos troops return to their own soil. My Lord Rick, I will leave suitable medical officers to attend the wounded and explain to them their new status. I think you will not need a large escort to guard them. All that I know of are converts to the True Faith, and their word will be good."

*He says that with a straight face*, Rick thought. *I suppose he believes it*.

"And with your Highness' leave I will see to my

preparations," Apelles said. He bowed and left. They could hear him speaking urgently to his assistants the moment he had left the tent.

"A young man who will go far," Rick said.

"He already has," Tylara said. "And did you know he accompanied me into captivity? Of his own free will, he surrendered in order to care for me."

"I'd heard. We owe him," Rick said. "I will think on suitable rewards."

"I would guess that you are too late," Tylara said. "I doubt he would set much value on any reward you or I could give him now. He looks elsewhere for his rewards."

Rick nodded understanding.

"So. Highness, you honor me with your trust, but I think I need to consult with Wanax Ganton on this request."

"And I think I cannot allow that," Strymon said. "I don't know if Ganton would try to stop me from leaving, but I do not intend to find out. With luck, the first he will know of our plans is when he finds my camp empty at dawn."

"And us?" Tylara asked.

"You must pardon me," Strymon said. "I regret that you must remain my guests until I have begun to march. Otherwise, honor would require you to warn Ganton, and that I cannot have."

"You do yourself little honor to make prisoners of your guests," Tylara said.

"My Lady, I would hope you would not put it that way. Say rather that you remain my guests."

"Until Ganton has our heads," Rick said. "Better to be your prisoners."

"That had not escaped me," Strymon said. "It is fortunate that proper care of your weapons will require my armorer pages to work through the night until morning. I would not have them returned to you in less than perfect condition, nor can I hospitably allow you to depart without them. You will have all you brought here when you join me for breakfast."

"Oh." Rick looked to Tylara and saw she was grinning faintly. So she'd understood all this long before. "I trust your pages will not harm themselves," Rick said. "Handling star weapons can be tricky."

"As well we know," Strymon said. "They will have a care."

"Until morning," Rick said.

Strymon nodded. "We began preparations an hour after the battle ended. My main body will be on the road before first light." He smiled. "Wanax Ganton's army may be efficient, but I doubt he can march soon enough to catch us."

"He has also the services of Sergeant Bisso and his star weapons team."

"Who are unlikely to do much without direct orders from you," Strymon replied, and Rick dipped his head in agreement.

"I suppose that's true enough," he said.

"And, My Lord," Strymon said, "fortunately we are in border country that I know better than Ganton. Or you, if it comes to that. If I cannot take my army home I am a poor captain indeed."

*And he's anything but that*, Rick thought. *So now what?* He looked to Tylara, but got no answer.

# ✦ CHAPTER THREE ✦
# PARLIAMENT

Rick and Tylara watched as the last of Strymon's rear guard vanished over the hill. The True Sun brightened the east but was not yet visible above the wooded hills that shadowed them. There was enough light to see by from the evil red Demon Star. Rick felt no real warmth from the Demon, but that would change. Even now it had increased the illumination falling on the planet by at least a full percent, perhaps more. He didn't need to feel it, the warmth was real enough. The seas were rising. Climates changed. Rain fell on the lowlands and coastal plains but not on the high pampas above the Greatscarp. A great *Volkswanderung* was beginning, tribes migrating from the deserts, while civilizations drowned in the south, growing seasons longer but fields flooded. The southerners fled northward. Confusion everywhere, and it had just begun.

His reverie was disturbed by two pages, boys no more than eleven years old, who rode back from Strymon's rear guard. Behind them walked an older man Rick recognized as one of Strymon's personal attendants, a grizzled old veteran with a distinct limp. The boys dismounted to kneel in front of Rick. One spread open a cloth to reveal Rick's pistols and sword. The other opened a bag containing Tylara's pistol and dagger. The older of the boys clapped his hands, and the older man stepped forward.

"Your armor," the boy said. "Handral will assist you."

"I should arm now?" Rick squinted at the brightening east. "We've hardly had any sleep—"

"My husband, I think sleep the least of our needs at this moment," Tylara said. "My guess is that even now Ganton's ushers seek us. It will do no harm to be armed before they find us."

✢ ✢ ✢

The messenger carried a black wand. His voice was just short of disrespectful as he shouted.

"My Lord Eqeta and Eqetassa, I have been commanded by Wanax Ganton to conduct you to him, instantly upon my finding you."

"Black Rod Usher," Tylara muttered. "He has sent a Black Rod Usher to summon a Warlord and Justiciar. An insult."

"Not if we refuse to take it as such," Rick said.

"You are too forgiving," Tylara said. "But I think we have no choice."

"No more do I," Rick said. "Good morning, gentleman usher. We were detained by Prince Strymon through a misunderstanding which now has ended." Rick turned to Handral and the two pages. "My compliments to Prince Strymon. Tell him I say you have served him well."

"One more strap," Handral muttered. He pulled hard and fastened the buckle on Rick's shoulder holster. "That's done it." He handed Rick his Government Model Colt.

"Thank you." Rick checked the loads and holstered the weapon, then took a silver coin from his pouch and gave it to Handral. "Give the boys what you think they merit."

"Thank you, My Lord."

The boys rode north, followed by the older warrior. Tylara waved, and one of the boys waved back.

"His Majesty was impatient before I left," the usher said. "My Lord, My Lady, I urge haste."

"Coming, gentleman usher. As you see, we are armed. Have we not time even to dress properly?"

"I urge haste," the usher repeated.

Rick held Tylara's stirrup while she mounted. There was no one to hold his, and swinging into the saddle with full armor was difficult. Rick painfully lifted himself into the saddle and felt sharp pains as he always did. Did the old heroes have piles?

*And now what?* Rick thought. Mostly he wanted a bed and a long sleep. They followed the usher towards Ganton's camp three kilometers away, but where the road forked the usher led them to the east, towards the Ottarn battlefield, rather than west to where the main encampment would be. Rick and Tylara exchanged glances. There was nothing to do but follow.

✢ ✢ ✢

Ganton, Wanax of Drantos, had built a stage on the hill overlooking the Ottarn River battlefield. He sat on a high dais. His Council was grouped around him one step below, and on the steps below that his Lords and chief knights sat in full array. All were in full armor. Ganton was wearing the battle crown of Drantos, but his golden helmet was carried by a page who stood on the left side of the throne. The Sword of State was held by an esquire on the right. Below and around the king were the officers of the army, and to one side an assembly of the priesthood.

"A full Parliament," Tylara said. "Lords spiritual and temporal, and commons."

Rick nodded agreement. A Parliament summoned to meet overlooking the field of a victorious battle. In tradition and fact such Parliaments enjoyed special powers, including both the high and the low justice. Rick was glad of his armor. He looked behind him, to see the assembled clan chiefs of Tamaerthan, and with them Sergeant Bisso and the Earth mercenaries. A dozen men. Three mortars, and there was Passavopolous with the light machine gun. Not enough, not nearly enough . . .

The sky remained overcast, but there was no more rain. Chill winds whipped across the hills. They smelled of the swamps below, but there were odors of the battlefield as well. Beyond the assembly of the officer corps, troops worked to count the dead, recover weapons, and clean up the litter of battle. All but the Wanax's personal guard. Every one of them attended the king.

As Warlord and Justiciar respectively, Rick and Tylara should have been seated with the great officers of state at the king's feet just below the throne and a level above the Council. Instead the usher halted to place them at ground level in front of the entire array, looking upward to the Wanax and Parliament, their backs to the officers and clansmen and Rick's own troops. Rick looked for friendly faces in the assembly. There were few enough. And Rick and Tylara stood outside the Parliament, though they should have held a great place within it.

"I've got a bad feeling about this," Rick muttered. Tylara made a short chopping gesture with her left hand to quiet him. Rick noted that her right hand was in her sleeve.

"The Lord Rick and Lady Tylara," the gentleman usher announced. "My Lord Speaker, I found them at the empty encampment of Prince Strymon."

"Empty," the Speaker said. "The reports are true, then. Strymon has marched north without any word to us of his departure."

"It is true enough, My Lord Speaker. Regarding the Lord Rick and Lady Tylara, they came immediately upon summons."

"That's in their favor," someone muttered from among the lords.

"We greet you," the Lord Speaker announced formally. "Majesty, the Lord Rick and Lady Tylara. My Lord Rick, a question. You did not think it meet to inform the Wanax that Prince Strymon departed like a thief in the night?"

"Very meet, right, and our bounden duty," Rick said. "Were it possible. But Prince Strymon made it clear enough that we would not be permitted to do so."

"You were armed," Lord Enipses shouted from his place just below and to the left of the Wanax. The place that should have belonged to Tylara.

"In fact we were not," Tylara responded. There was ice in her voice as she spoke to the man who sat in her place.

"The fiction was made that our weapons and armor were being cleaned, but they were certainly not available. We were said to be guests, and we acted like guests. We did not think it seemly to begin hostilities which could only end badly no matter who the victor. Think, My Lord Enipses, if you can: Would you have open war between Drantos and Ta-Meltemos? Hostility between Wanax Ganton and Prince Strymon? At the moment the treaty holds. Did we resist, it would be broken."

"By Strymon," a councilor said. "No bad thing."

Tylara looked to Rick and nodded.

*No bad thing,* Rick thought. *He said that, and no one corrected him. It's come to this already?*

"And what do you know of this treaty?" another lord demanded.

"More than you daft lot!" someone roared from the assembled clansmen nobles who stood behind Rick and Tylara.

Tylara's father, Rick thought. As Mac Clallan Muir, leader of the Garioch Clans of Tamaerthan, he had been a witness to the treaty, and one of its negotiators.

"Cheeky bastard." There were other mutters from the star men mercenaries who stood with the clansmen.

"Quiet in the ranks." Corporal MacAllister spoke in English. "At ease."

"Prince Strymon told us of the terms of the agreement," Rick said.

"And of course he told the truth!" one of the lords shouted. There was more clamor from the Tamaerthan ranks now, and a scattering of obscenities in English. Rick looked sternly at his mercenary troopers. Strymon had made himself popular with the troops during his period of close alliance with Ganton.

Sergeant Bisso broke the silence.

"Ten-hut! Corporal, next man that speaks, take his name."

"You note that the Wanax says nothing," Tylara said under her breath. "He can yet disclaim any of this."

"But he does nothing to stop it," Rick said.

"There will be worse," Tylara muttered. She struck a pose and declaimed, "The terms were recited by My Lord Father Apelles, a sworn witness to the treaty. Unless, Lord Epimines, you question his word, as well as that of Prince Strymon. Do you so? Perhaps we should have a trial by battle? I am certain Prince Strymon would choose to act as his own champion." Everyone there had heard how Strymon in single combat had bested and captured Morrone, Champion and Companion to Wanax Ganton.

"I meant no dishonor to His Highness," Epimines protested.

"I had not heard the terms before, and I listened carefully," Rick said. "And we heard no terms of the treaty that forbade Prince Strymon from returning in haste to his own lands. Indeed, all we heard urged him to do so." Rick purse his lips and paused for a moment. "The treaty required him to depart, and he was departing. I saw no need to interfere."

Ganton nodded solemnly and spoke for the first time.

"Indeed, that was the chief requirement of the treaty. Of course that treaty was made before we knew of the death of Prince Akkilas. Still, it must needs be honored.

My Lord Rick, did His Highness tell you aught of his plans?"

Rick didn't need Tylara's nudge to warn him to be careful. Ganton wasn't asking for information. If he wanted information he'd ask for it privately. This was clearly a show staged for the great lords of the realm. But why? What did Ganton want? One thing was certain, Ganton would not easily ignore the advice of his lords. His father had done that and had lost his throne, and that was a mistake Ganton would never make.

"Majesty, he said he would return to his capital to prepare for the Time," Rick said. That at least had the merit of being true . . .

"And you believed him?"

Rick spread his hands widely.

"I had no reason not to. Certainly all his questions were directed to the Time. He asked lessons in astronomy, that he might understand what is coming."

"Which you gave freely to a rival!" The shout came from the councilors.

Rival. Of course. They saw Strymon as a rival claimant to Ganton's rights as heir to the High Rexja of the Five Kingdoms.

"Yes, My Lord Enipses, freely I received that knowledge, and freely did I give it. As I have always done," Rick said. "To all who have asked."

There were mutters of approval from the ranks of the priesthood.

"The Time comes!" a thin priestly voice shouted. "Be wary, great Wanax! God humbles the proud and the unbelievers!"

And that would be treason from anyone not in holy orders, Rick thought. Close enough even for the priests.

"We met in Council during the night," Enipses shouted. "Warlord and Justiciar were summoned but did not attend. The Council met anyway."

*So that's where this is headed*, Rick thought.

"The War Council of Drantos has advised His Majesty to claim the throne of the Five Kingdoms," Enipses continued. "We meet now in Parliament to confirm that decision. Lord Rick Galloway, Warlord of Drantos, have you advice to offer this Parliament in this matter?"

"My Lady Tylara is High Justiciar," Rick said. "She speaks before me. As well you know."

"And I say that Toris High Rexja lives a widower, and while he is elderly, he may yet take a queen and produce an heir," Tylara said. "In the hills we know better than to count any man heirless until he is dead. Not even then. And are we certain that was the head of Akkilas?"

More shouts among the councilors.

"Strymon said so."

"I heard he has doubts," another shouted.

"Aye," Tylara said. "The prince expressed his doubts about that head. It may have been that of the tanist. So Prince Strymon said to us."

"My Lady, your pardon," Lord Arandos said. "But is it not true that Tamaerthan has good reason to wish Drantos and the Five Kingdoms wary of each other?"

"I am Eqetassa of Chelm and a loyal peer of Drantos! And High Justiciar to the realm," Tylara shouted. "I give the best advice I know, without fear or favor."

Enipses stood, turned to Ganton, bowed, and received a slight nod. He turned to face Rick and Tylara.

"I am commanded to say that His Majesty no longer requires service as Justiciar from Tylara do Tamaerthan said to be Eqetassa of Chelm."

It took a moment for Rick to understand that Enipses had actually said that. *He can't be acting on his own,* he thought then. *This is staged, and for a reason. Ganton is allowing this. But why?*

"Said to be!" Drumold, Mac Clallan Muir, High Chief of the Garioch Clans, but first of all Tylara's father, shoved his way forward from among the clansman chivalry drawn up behind Rick and Tylara. "Said to be! Who dares say she is not?"

"At ease!" Bisso shouted to the mercs. "But it sure don't hurt to have your powder dry," he added in English.

"Gently, Mac Clallan Muir," Enipses called to Drumold. "You are allies, not members of this Parliament. Therefore—"

Whatever he was about to say was cut off by Drumold's roar.

"You would deny my daughter her titles! You would reject her advice? Wanax Ganton, is this your will? Barach gui haigh!" The clansmen stirred. Two young dunie wassails left ranks to run towards the Tamaerthan camp.

*Jesus, he's warning the clansmen to be ready for battle!* Rick thought. *I don't suppose any of these Drantos ironheads know what he said, but they have to be able to guess. And once the gullfeathers start flying . . .*

"Father, Father, it is enough," Tylara shouted. "Let be,

let be. Balquhain, be kind enough to go look after those young hotheads. See our people do nothing rash."

"Aye, Tilly," her brother called. He looked to their father for consent, and got a nod. Balquhain was frowning deeply as he loped off after the young warriors, and Tylara turned to Ganton.

"Majesty, is this true? You seek not my advice, because it is your will that I quit the office of Justiciar?"

"Trial!" someone shouted. "Court of Chivalry!"

And was answered by another, "How can there be trial when the Justiciar is not fit—"

"A woman as Justiciar when the Wanax is no longer a minor!" someone else shouted.

*Jesus,* Rick thought. *Now they're saying she isn't fit to head a court of chivalry.* There could be many reasons for them thinking that way, but one would be a disaster. Did they know of the Children of Vothan and how Caradoc came to die? *How much of that story has got out? But the clans aren't reacting, they're supporting her, so they can't be thinking of her as Caradoc's murderer, they're loyal. Now. But for how long? What in God's name—*

Senior Warrant Officer Larry Warner had been moving slowly towards Rick. "Colonel, I couldn't get to you earlier. While you were in Strymon's camp last night, the barons and old Drumold had a hell of a fight over this High Rexja thing. The clans think if Ganton becomes High Rexja, he won't need the Tamaerthan alliance."

"Not true," Rick said.

"Maybe you know that, but the clansmen don't. Hell, Skipper, there was talk about pressing the old Drantos claim to all the Tamaerthan lowlands. A couple of the border lords got liquored up and said Drantos writ used to run through the Garioch, even, and—"

"Bloody hell," Rick muttered. "No wonder Drumold's upset."

"There's more. There were rumors flying about Lady Tylara and assassins."

"Specifics?" Christ, Warner knew all about Tylara and the Children of Vothan. He was one of the group that uncovered that secret!

"Nothing specific. It's pretty clear they have maybe fifth-hand information. The only name I heard was Dughuilas, and nothing certain about him."

Dughuilas was supposed to have been murdered by a prostitute's daughter. Few mourned him. But still too close to home, Rick thought. Too close indeed. It was a near certainty that he had been brought down by one of the Children of Vothan who took orders from Tylara and no one else.

"Thanks, Larry."

"There's more, Colonel, but maybe it'll wait."

Someone else was shouting "Trial!" as another was drowned out by Drumold's roars in the Old Speech. Everyone began yelling.

"Treason! Woman Justiciar! Lord Rick brings us victories! Beargha hai! Long live the victorious Lord Rick! Conflict, conflict—" Half the councilors and most of the clansmen were shouting. Some councilors sought Rick's eye before shouting the names of battles he had won. It was clear enough he had support up there, but how much?

"Who can I count on?" Rick asked.

"All of us, that's for damn sure," Warner said. "But there's more to that story, too."

*The mercenaries and the clansmen. For now. Enough to get out of here alive, unless Ganton takes a hand.* For a moment Rick regretted giving Ganton a Browning pistol. *How much practice has he had with it?*

The group fell silent as Ganton stood.

"Enough," he said. His voice was low but clear. "My Lady Tylara, Eqetassa of Chelm, we are more than aware of the service you have given us. You came to this great office during our minority. You held it during the critical years when few sought any office I could bestow! You have held this burden long. Long enough, long enough! Now you have duties to your own family. Your children grow up without you. Surely this is a burden you would willingly lay down?"

"I have offered to do so many times," Tylara said. She didn't sound very eager.

"And this time your offer is accepted," Ganton said. "I mean no more than that. Lord Enipses, it was not well said to question My Lady Tylara's right as Eqetassa, and whoever advised you to do so is no friend to you or to the realm!"

"Majesty, if Tylara is to be dismissed, then perhaps it's time I laid down my offices as well," Rick said. "With peace to the north, Drantos no longer needs a Warlord."

"That was no part of this plan!" Lord Enipses shouted. "Lord Rick, we meant you no disrespect."

"No disrespect? You dismiss My Lady wife, you question her titles, and you say you mean no disrespect to me?!" Rick began removing his gauntlet. *By God I'll challenge him!*

"They'd heard all wasn't good between you and Tylara," Larry Warner said urgently. "Hell, Colonel, I thought that myself! They thought they were helping you. Take it easy, Sir!"

"Easy! By God—"

"Hold!" Ganton shouted. "My Lord Rick, clearly some here have been misinformed."

Rick looked around for friends. There were a few among the Drantos lords. Bisso and the mercs looked steady enough. And the clansmen were fidgeting. Drumold had stopped shouting, but his face was red and contorted. There was a stir in the Tamaerthan camp where Balquhain had followed the dunie wassails. They'd be stringing bows. Balquhain should be able to control them. *Should be. But what in hell is going on here?* He dropped his voice to a near whisper.

"Tylara, what do we do?"

"I think I see the pattern," she said. "Will you trust me to deal with this?"

"Thank God. Yes, of course."

"Majesty," Tylara said. "You have won a great victory, yet the armies of the Five Kingdoms remain in the west. Will you send my husband to deal with them? Naturally I will accompany him. I have not been home to my children since this war began. And as there are matters of import to be decided at Court, matters that admit of no delay, I willingly return the office of High Justiciar to Your Majesty to dispose of as you will." She removed the chain of office and handed it to a frightened page. "Take this to the Wanax," she said.

"We accept," Ganton said. "You have my thanks and

gratitude for your service to the realm, and to me." He turned towards Rick. "Lord Rick, Warlord, we charge you to return to the west and expel all foreign armies from our lands. We will next see you at a Great Council of the Realm, where we shall consider all these matters. Warlord of Drantos, you have my thanks. You have good leave to leave us."

"Majesty." Rick backed away two paces and turned. "Let's get the hell out of here," he muttered.

## ⇥ CHAPTER FOUR ⇤
# MOVING OUT

It was as near noon as anything was on Tran. The True Sun stood an hour past overhead, while the Firestealer had an hour to go. Rick had learned that sun time has a different meaning when there is more than one sun.

Rick sat in the vestibule of his command tent. All around him the army was packing gear. Knots of men stood near the battlefield, gesticulating wildly as they tried to make an even division of the spoils and trophies of the battle. Beyond them at the central encampment there were shouts and curses as each group tried to claim what it thought was a fair share of supplies and provisions, wagons and packhorses. Nothing was packed and ready to go.

"So just how long until we can get on the road?" Rick demanded.

Sergeant Bisso shook his head.

"We're ready, but as to the others, damfino. Jesus,

Colonel, what a mess, never thought there'd be this much trouble just breaking camp!"

"In war, everything is very simple, but the simplest things are very difficult," Rick said. "Clausewitz, who knew what he was talking about."

"Whole damn army's coming apart," Larry Warner said. "And I have a message from Lady Tylara. She says the Second Light Cavalry from Chelm wants to go with you."

"Why not, they're from the Littlescarp," Rick said. "That's their home, and Tylara's their colonel—"

"Sure, Skipper," Warner said, "but Ganton wants them with him. Ordered Lady Tylara to turn over command to one of his barons. Can't blame him much, he's learned how bad he needs scouts and those nobles don't like the job."

"Only his barons never did like having peasant-class horsemen with the army," Bisso said. "And peasant-class officers they hate like the plague. Which brings us to the artillery and cannon company."

"Oh," Rick said. The light cavalry officers were yeomen freeholders. Not quite peasants, but the Tran aristocracy tended to regard them as no better. Worse, from their view, if an able man showed enough initiative, Tylara had learned that it was better not to inquire too closely into his father's status. Born bound or born free, good officers were hard to find. And all of the artillery troops, whatever their rank, were from the cities, free men, middle class. Of course that wasn't the term the nobility used. They'd talk about townsmen and burgher, when they were being polite. Usually they had ruder terms. Tylara's clansman background gave her a different attitude from the other great lords of Drantos, but it had taken even her a lot of effort to accept the notion of middle-class officers mixing with the hereditary baronage.

"The nobility hasn't ever liked the gunners to begin with," he said.

"Can't blame them," Warner said. "Those ironheads aren't that stupid, they can see that middle-class gunners are their class enemy."

Rick nodded.

"'Nay, said the cannoneer, firing from the wall. For iron, cold iron, shall be master of you all.' A lesson the Drantos chivalry hasn't quite learned, but they're beginning to get the picture. So what's the problem? The scouts and gunners want to go home, and the Great Lords of the Realm don't want them in the army in the first place. Sounds like the problems solve themselves."

"Yeah, except you taught that kid king of theirs too well," Sergeant Bisso said. "He knows damn well he's never going to beat the Five Kingdoms with heavy cavalry alone. He hasn't got enough to begin with, and it's odds on the Five Kingdoms troops are every bit as good as his. Better if Strymon leads them."

Warner nodded agreement.

"If Wanax Ganton is going to win this new campaign the barons have their hearts set on, he'll need a combined arms army. Only he hasn't got one. Drumold's taking the clansmen home, you're taking the scouts and gunners—what's he got left besides the chivalry? Some of his native pikes, some hired crossbows, and the Royal Guard, but hell, even they look to you for leadership."

"Here she comes," Bisso said.

Tylara rode up, her expression grim.

"The Wanax demands use of our Chelm Light Cavalry," she said. "Rudhrig's son Guy is to command."

"Good choice," Bisso said.

"Sergeant, I agree that Guy is as suitable as anyone, but these are Chelm troops!"

"Yes, Ma'am," Bisso said.

There was a tiny twist of a smile on the sergeant's lips. *So how much does he know?* Rick wondered. *Warner knows it all, but Bisso was never in on the full story of Tylara and her child assassins. He has to have guessed some of it. And I don't dare ask.*

"How did you leave this?" Rick asked Tylara, and she frowned.

"It was a direct order from the Wanax," she said. "I did not think it wise to defy him, so I said nothing and came to you."

"You know better than that," Rick said. He thought of the phrase about rape and inevitability, then caught himself before he could say it. Tylara had been raped, and worse, by Sarakos, and while she might agree with the vulgar phrase— "You taught me better."

"So we submit? And thus I am to be gracious?" she demanded.

"Do we have a choice?" Rick asked.

"Yes," Tylara said. She looked to Warner and Bisso. "Do you not agree? You are all the counsel we have. Advise us."

"I ain't no officer, Ma'am," Bisso protested, shaking his head. "Skipper, tell me who to shoot, and I'll get the job done, but don't ask me!"

"It won't come to shooting," Larry Warner said. "Lady Tylara's right about that. If you refuse this request, the Wanax will find a reason to withdraw it. The problem won't come today, it'll be the long-term relations with the Wanax you'll have to worry about. Chelm, you're okay there, that's damn near self-sufficient and you've got enough to defend it. But I can tell you this, an open break with Ganton would sure cause problems for the University."

Tylara put her hand to her mouth as if in surprise. It was a gesture Rick had never seen her use before, but it reminded him of someone. Gwen Tremaine sometimes did that. Thinking about the University could naturally lead to thoughts about Rector Gwen Tremaine, but why imitate her? Now what was Tylara up to? Or maybe her subconscious was sending a signal?

"I had not thought of that," Tylara said. There was no need to talk about the importance of the University. Everyone there was long ago agreed on that. But the University was in a critical location, in the hills where the borders of Drantos, the Roman Empire, and the Tamaerthan clan territories came together. It was nominally in clan commons land, but it would be no great trick for either Rome or Drantos to find precedent for a claim. So long as Rick's alliance of Rome, Tamaerthan, and Drantos held, that had been the right place, but now—

"What about the clans?" Rick said. "What does an open break with Ganton do to Tamaerthan?"

"No great harm, I think," Tylara said. "The clans have never had lasting alliance with Drantos. The new plows are bringing in greater harvests, and this when the growing seasons will be longer due to the Demon.

Independence from Drantos lowers trade but it is no great hardship so long as there is peace with Rome. My Lord Husband, my father tells me some of the Drantos lords have been boasting of past conquests within our borders. Lord Warner, you were present, I believe."

"Yes, My Lady," Larry Warner said. "It was mostly just talk. By nobody important."

"But the Wanax allowed it," Tylara said. "He did not forbid it."

"No, Ma'am, he didn't," Warner said. "He let them babble on."

"Including a boast that Drantos once ruled the Garioch as well as the lowlands?"

"Yes," Warner said. "And that's one thing that's got me worried about the University."

"Christ on a crutch," Rick said.

"Do not blaspheme. And Ganton is married to the Roman heiress," Tylara said. "Drantos alone is no great threat, but the clans have ever had one fear, that Rome and Drantos would unite against them. Now—"

"All the more reason not to cause an open break, I'd say," Rick said. "Right now Ganton needs us, and it's not going to make him need us less to let him borrow our light cavalry troops."

Bisso nodded.

"Time's on our side, Skipper. And we're running low on ammo; if we have to fight I'd sure rather do it after the next supply shipment from Earth. So would the troops."

Rick nodded.

"Tylara, you wanted advice, I think you just got it. We do what it takes to avoid an open break with Ganton."

It was her turn to nod.

"I will ride back and be gracious," she said. "And endure the smiles and winks." She mounted, waved, and rode off, a dozen household troops falling in behind her. She didn't need the protection here, but a great countess required an escort, even in camp.

"So what happens when the king asks for us?" Sergeant Bisso said. He gestured to indicate the Earth mercenaries taking their ease next to their packed-up gear and weapons. "He will, you know, and pretty soon, too. He's going to need his star weapon troops if he expects to get anywhere invading the north."

Rick nodded.

"I know. But not yet, not until we run Ailas off."

"Maybe," Warner said. "And maybe he's just working up his nerve. He's still a little scared of you."

"Of Tylara, more like," Rick said. "So what other problems have we got?"

"What don't we have?" Warner said as he looked through his notebook. "Let's see. We assumed Sergeant Clavell was with the Nikeis forces when they arrived. Turns out he's not."

Rick frowned.

"Where the hell *is* Clavell, then? And what about Private Harrison? Didn't we send him with Clavell?"

Sergeant Clavell and Private Harrison had been sent as ambassadors to Nikeis as part of a "medicine show" routine to spread the word about hygiene and sanitation. When reports came back about crop yields on the island, Rick had them arrange for shipments of seagull guano to the University.

"Yes, Sir. We did. This whole battle was thrown together in confusion, particularly after your wife was captured. I wouldn't be surprised if Clavell and Harrison are still back in Nikeis. I don't know if there was time for troops to come from the island. It's been a while since we heard from them, though. I'll look into it, but I suspect the halberdier regiment was from their colony on the coast, Terra Firma."

"Please do," Rick replied. "We can't afford to lose track of our people."

"It gets weirder. The Nikeisian infantry marched off in a huff, something about unequal division of the spoils. Rudhrig claimed they didn't do enough fighting to warrant a full share per man, and the last I saw their captain was shaking the dust off his feet in the general direction of Ganton. After he did it, all his troops did too."

Rick frowned.

"Does that have the Biblical meaning in Nikeis?"

"The Nikeisians are Christians," Warner said. "Claim they always have been. From what I can see they're pretty straightforward Roman Catholic. No pope, of course."

"So we can guess where they got that ritual," Rick said. "But despite the new Unification religion, there aren't many Bibles in Drantos."

"Yeah, and they're all in Latin," Warner said.

Rick didn't ask how Warner knew that. Back in Africa the troops had called Larry Warner "Professor" and that stuck well enough that he was now Provost of the University when he wasn't called into active duty. It would be like Warner to know.

"So Ganton won't know they've just cursed him?"

"Not sure they have," Warner said. "But it looks like that's what they meant. They sure went away mad."

"Christian," Rick mused. "Allied to Rome, then?"

"No," Warner said. "They've got their own Patriarch, and from what I heard their chaplain wasn't all that thrilled about the new Unification. They're nominal allies of Drantos, but they trade with Rome and the Five Kingdoms and everybody else, and they seem willing to let their trade partners think part of the trade is tribute if that makes people feel better."

"Who the heck are these people?" Rick asked, and Warner looked to the sky for answers.

"I never thought about it a lot, Skipper, but if I had to guess I'd say Crusade-era Venice. Probably pretty late Crusade era, from the little we know about their government's setup. Maybe early thirteenth century?"

Rick frowned.

"Does that fit? There wasn't a Demon Star passage in crusader times, was there?"

"Well, that's not the only anomaly," Warner said. "Been meaning to talk to you about that—"

"Not to interrupt a good conversation, Colonel," Bisso said. "But it's getting late, and we got problems a lot closer to home."

Rick nodded.

"Okay. But get messages off to our people in Nikeis and find out what's going on and what they've been up to. I want a report as soon as possible, and they're authorized to use the semaphore and message riders to speed it along." When Bisso nodded, Rick said, "And what other cheerful news do you have for me?"

"Drumold," Bisso said. "Your father-in-law is fit to be tied. Claims he's getting the short end of the stick on rations. Not enough to get home, he said."

"And you know what that means," Warner said. "Them clansmen sure as hell won't starve."

Not going home through the wealthiest section of Drantos, they wouldn't. Borderer clansmen were quite adept at foraging for themselves. Surely Ganton knew that?

"Do you think this is deliberate?" Rick asked. "Put them in a situation where they have to steal to live, and then accuse them?"

"Skipper, it sure don't make sense to goad the clans into a fight," Warner said as he shook his head. "He's going to need those archers and pikemen every bit as much as he needs us."

"Some of the barons think they'll get them as conscripts," Bisso said. "Conquer the clan territories, and conscript the troops. Cheaper that way."

"Jesus, are they that stupid?" Rick asked. "Conscript archers?"

"Yeah, some of them ironheads are dumber'n a box of rocks," Bisso said.

"Ganton isn't."

"No, Sir, maybe not, but then we don't know what his game is," Bisso said. "He sure wasn't acting too bright this morning."

"Or maybe he was," Warner said. "And we just don't know what he was after."

"It's a damned dangerous game," Rick mused, and Warner laughed.

"Skipper, tell me what we do that won't fit that description?"

"Yeah. Okay, let's get our troops on the road. The longer we stay here the better the chance our young Wanax will decide he wants something else we can't give him," Rick said. "We'll deal with Drumold's rations later. Get 'em saddled up."

Warner grinned.

"Yes, Sir. Head 'em up, move 'em out."

"Rawhide," Rick said. "And which one of us grows up to be Dirty Harry?"

# CHAPTER FIVE

# THE RUINED CHAPEL

There was a chapel at the crossroad. Most crossroads in Drantos had some kind of shelter. There was usually a cistern, and always at least a stoneheap to revere the conductor of the dead. This was a stone building with tiled roof, as large as a village church, as befitted the crossing point of two major roads, one leading south to Armagh and on to Edron, the other west to Chelm. Rick wondered idly why the roads led through a place unsuitable for a village. The church was on a small hillock but the land around it was low and swampy. There was just enough dry land to allow a small garden and churchyard. The village this church served was nearly a mile away on higher ground.

Probably just happened, Rick thought. Cows wandered through and made a track. People used it, and crossroads are so holy in this part of Tran that no one dared move either road to better ground.

Warner squinted up at the suns.

"Got about three more hours of real daylight," he said. "And some of the clans got a late start. They'll be streaming in until after dark. Think we ought to stop here?" He indicated some low hill land west of the crossroads.

"Good place to make camp," Rick agreed. "This is where we part company, and we still have things to talk over."

"That we do," Warner said. "The stream looks all right, but better avoid that well. Ground's low, and I know there's a village up on that ridge."

He pointed. The village would be a mile away, but it was as likely that the sewers drained down this way as to the other side. The Unified Church now knew the germ theory of disease, but that hadn't spread to all the country parishes, and many places were still devoted to the old religions of Yatar and Vothan.

*Cistern, not well,* Rick thought, but it wasn't worth correcting Warner on the difference. It was unlikely to be biologically isolated from the swampy ground water.

There were no villagers in sight. That was to be expected. People in border villages tended towards thin loyalty to either side, and mostly hoped to be ignored by foraging parties. These would be lucky. Rick's supply wagons were full.

The church building itself seemed intact, but the doors stood ajar and the site was deserted. He looked inside.

"Pretty well looted out," he said. "Nothing much left."

"Furniture went for campfires," Warner said.

Tylara rode up in time to hear Warner's speculation.

"Who would dare despoil a temple?" she demanded.

"Both sides been through this crossroads more than once, My Lady," Warner replied. "Not much dry wood in the swamp and that's all stripped out. Could have been almost any outfit short on firewood. At least they didn't burn the place down."

Tylara went inside to look. She returned looking less upset.

"It was a Temple to Yatar," she said. "Not yet converted to the new Christian faith. There is no hint of a crucifix or Stations of the Cross." She turned to Rick. "With your consent I will see to arranging a Mass, and perhaps we can find someone to attend this place until the regular clergy return."

"With my consent?"

She smiled thinly.

"We are not in Chelm, My Lord. And I am no longer Justiciar. I have no authority here that you do not give me."

*Never stopped you before*, Rick thought.

"Whose county is this?" he asked.

"Lord Ajacias was Eqeta here. Of course the title and all his lands are forfeit for treason," Tylara said. "But this was Church property, and should be returned to the Church in any event. I know no one who has the benefit of bestowing this parish. Ajacias or one of his minions, but that would likely be forfeit with the titles."

"Ah." So whatever clergy were installed during this lawless time would probably keep it. Some lord would end up with jurisdiction here, but he'd be unlikely to turn out an established pastor. And Tylara would have favorites among the converts to the Unified Church. "Then, my love, take possession for the Church, and do whatever pleases you with this place, with my blessings," Rick said. He looked around for his orderly. "Jamiy."

"Sir."

"My compliments to our unit commanders, and they can circle the wagons. We'll camp here for the day. And get my caravan set up. Oh and tell our corpsmen they can house the wounded of Ta-Meltemos here after the Mass."

*So another village is converted to the Unified True Church*, Rick thought. No one was consulting the villagers. Tylara certainly wouldn't. The old pagan cults of Yatar and Vothan had initiates and a priesthood, but they weren't an orthodoxy and didn't think about heresy. The new Church didn't either. Yet. Rick had heard rumors of resistance to the new Unified Church, mostly from the Five Kingdoms. Combine patriotism and religion and you could get nasty persecutions. Heretics became traitors and vice versa.

*God save me*, Rick thought. *I don't want to bring the Inquisition to Tran. But what can I do?* The traveling medicine shows taught the germ theory of disease, and the Unified Church had adopted that as revelation. That helped because simple sanitation worked what looked like miracles compared to what they'd been doing.

*Science and religion. Have to see they don't conflict. One more damned job I don't know how to do. And I don't have time to think about it.*

✣ ✣ ✣

Rick laid out the map on his field conference table. Unlike most maps on Tran, this one was accurate over reasonably long distances: Rick had drawn it on a tracing from a photograph taken from orbit. Mapmaking had never been a high art on Tran, and even Roman maps became distorted when they covered more than a few days' marches. Roman cartographers were vaguely aware of the problems associated with different map projections, but they had never worked out what to do about them. Roman maps were good locally, but could be misleading over large distances. Maps drawn by anyone but Roman engineers were hopelessly distorted.

*One reason they think I'm a military genius,* Rick thought. *Amazing what a good map will do. Couple it with a compass and a magnetic field which nearly matches the planet's rotational poles and I don't spend a lot of time getting lost.* Rick remembered one of Warner's lectures on how there had to be a magnetic field for life to survive here.

The others filed into the caravan. Rick's traveling command post was built up from two wagons placed side by side. It was large enough to hold the conference table and had whiteboard walls for diagrams. The only problem with it was that even broken into four wagons, two for the post itself and another two for maps and furniture and supplies, the command post moved slowly on Tran's primitive roads. The headquarters was often several days behind the commander. This time it hadn't arrived at the battlefield before Rick was headed home, meeting it on the way and turning it around.

Rick took his place at the center of the table. When he first did that it shocked Tylara, who expected a commander to sit at the head of the table, but it hadn't taken her long to see the advantage of being in the middle of things. Now she sat next to Rick and watched closely.

Tylara's father Drumold sat across from Rick and Tylara. *He looks tired*, Rick thought. *Can't be too surprised at that, he's got to be past sixty. That's old on Tran. Life in the saddle ages you fast.*

"My son sends his regards, and begs to be excused," Drumold said. "He's out hurrying along stragglers."

Rick nodded understanding. The clansmen were more disciplined than Drantos nobles, but that wasn't saying much. The Romans seemed to have the only really disciplined native forces on Tran. Except for the Nikeisian infantry, Rick amended. The Nikeisian axe and halberd men had fought in orderly ranks, and consequently took few losses, which may have been why the Drantos lords thought they hadn't contributed enough.

"So where do we stand?" Rick said.

"With the Wanax?" Tylara said. "Not high."

"Colonel's still Warlord of Drantos," Warner said.

"Aye," Drumold said. "And will be so long as Ganton finds it useful to have him so. But not a moment longer, to my way of thinking."

"And how long will that be?" Rick asked.

"He needs you to chase that Five Kingdoms army back home," Drumold said. "After that, you can hold the west as Eqeta, and there won't be an enemy standing on Drantos soil. Where's the need for a Warlord? Unless you'll lead his armies north. Will ye? Will you be bringing your star lords to fight when the Wanax invades the Five Kingdoms?"

"I sure hadn't planned on it," Rick said. "We don't want

the Five Kingdoms! Not now, anyway." Rick pointed to the map. "Look, this climate change is getting whole nations on the move. Southerners streaming north, and from what I hear the whole high plains is going to be a dust bowl. Whatever's up there will come down."

"Westmen already have," Bisso said. "Tough little buggers."

"What scares me is there may be people up there tougher'n the Westmen," Larry Warner said.

"What makes you think there is anyone tougher than the Westmen?" Bisso asked. "Please tell me you made that up! The Westmen damn near killed us all at the Hooey River!"

"Just a hunch," Warner said. "They've got legends about their paradise being west of where they live, but they never go there. Maybe somebody's keeping them from going?"

"Interesting," Rick said. *There was a time when I'd be the one to know that sort of thing. Now all I do is pee on fires.* He shook his head. "But the important point is, there'll be lots of people trying to settle in Drantos. Too many to support. We can't keep them out, so what do we do with them?"

"Hell of a lot to kill," Bisso said. "Not enough bullets."

"Leaving aside the ethical problems," Rick said. "So if we can't keep them out and we can't kill them, the only thing left is to move them on to somewhere else. The easiest place is the Five Kingdoms, but we can't push the refugees in there if we own the joint!"

"Actually, we could, Colonel," Bisso said. "Easier, really, if nobody's trying to keep them out."

"Good point," Warner said. "Hmm. You know, Colonel, maybe he's got something there. Hard cheese on the Fivers, but hell, it's going to be tough on them anyway. Not that you need reminding, but the important thing is to keep those damn madweed farms producing. First crop of refugees, we can put to work in the fields. Promise them safe passage north if they work hard and don't cause trouble. If we hold the Five territory, we could do that. Send them north and give them land to settle on."

Rick frowned.

"You're proposing that we help Ganton with this conquest?"

"Rather have the Fivers unhappy with us than have our own Wanax hate our guts! Sure, why not?"

"We don't have enough troops to do all we have to do now," Rick said. "Let alone this. It was all we could do to keep the Five from conquering us, now you want to go the other way?"

"We still have that problem," Warner said. "It won't get easier. Skipper, we got long-term problems, too. Bisso can tell you, the troops are getting restless."

Rick looked the question to Bisso.

"It's true enough, Sir. We don't know where we're going. Look, Murphy was a private soldier. Now he's set up as a great lord all on his own, with wives and kids and land. Mason's an officer, marrying into the nobility. Warner's got his University. What have the rest of us got? More'n that, what do we look forward to, Colonel? We got no lands, most of us have concubines but not real families, we can be called out to fight any time. Hell, Colonel, Chelm yeomen have more rights than we do!"

"I've never heard you talk like this before," Rick said.

"Never had the chance, what with Sergeant Major Elliot and all. Colonel, I'm not saying anyone's muttering about mutiny. We know what happens! Warner got sold into slavery, Gengrich damn near lost his whole command. Only good things that happened to us were after you took over. I'm just saying we don't see where we're going. We trust you, but frankly, Sir, when I hear you talk like you don't know what we're doing either, it scares hell out of me!"

Tylara was about to say something. Probably to protest the sergeant's tone, Rick thought. And that wouldn't do.

"So, just what do you want out of all this, Bisso?" Rick asked before she spoke.

"Me? Retirement to a gated post with a good pension, with grandkids coming to visit on holidays. I reckon there's others with more ambition, but that'd suit me just fine."

"And the others?"

"Like I said, Sir, there's others with more ambition, 'specially when they see how Murphy's set up. But I reckon being retired on good pay in a safe place wouldn't be the least of what they want."

Rick nodded.

"A military colony in a safe place. Training a new regiment. Might surprise you to know that's always been what I had in mind for the company, Bisso. The big problem is making things safe enough. Right now—"

"But right now, there's no place on this planet safe. Skipper, I know that, Elliot knows that, most of the men know that. But you did ask."

"I did indeed. Okay, Warner, you think the best way to get a peaceful old age is to install Ganton as High Rexja of the Five Kingdoms. Maybe so. So why does Ganton think he can do it now?"

"He has this claim," Warner said. "Lady Tylara can tell you, the Wanax thinks he'll get allies in the Five. Legitimists. Isn't like this never happened before."

Tylara nodded agreement.

"My Lord Husband, you have yourself said that sometimes when you have enough problems, they solve each other. Could this be so now? Our Wanax has ambitions, but he also has claims that will win him support in the North. We need a place to send the refugees from the south. If we help Wanax Ganton, we will have such a place."

"I need to think on it," Rick said. *The problem is, they may be right. But I'm tired! I don't want to fight anymore.*

"Perhaps God wills it," Tylara said. "That we bring the true religion to the heathen."

*And she means it*, Rick thought. Of course true religion brought benefits like hygiene.

Bisso looked uncomfortable, but Warner nodded.

"There's already Unification converts in the Fiver armies," he said. "Maybe they'll defect to us. Some already did. It's always been uneasy between Yatar and Vothan up there."

"There have never been religious wars on Tran," Rick said. "And I sure don't want to be the cause of one."

"All due respect, Skipper, how do you know?" Warner demanded. "History on Tran means what your grandfather told you, plus maybe some legends like the Time and Skyfire, and damned little details of those. For all you know they've had religious wars out the wazoo."

"Do you know what you're starting?" Rick asked.

"No, Sir, and neither do you," Warner said. "But after watching that Parliament, I think Ganton's going to try no matter what you do."

Rick looked to Tylara and got a confirming nod.

"He is a Wanax determined to satisfy his nobles, particularly when they urge him towards what he wants to do anyway," she said. "Yes, he will press his claim."

"Will he do it well?"

Tylara sighed.

"On that matter you have as much knowledge as I. He is young and vigorous and has charm. His men will follow him and he is not a lackwit."

"But will he win?"

Tylara's shrug said volumes.

"So the question is, how are we better off, helping him or dragging our feet?" Warner demanded. "We help him and he wins, maybe he resents our help, but that's the worst of it. We drag our feet and he probably loses. He'll blame the loss on us. He's not going to like it much, and we still have to save the bacon depending on just how bad he loses. We sure won't be better off than we are now. He wins without us, he's going to be pissed off and have the strength to do something about it. Either way isn't much of an upside, is it?"

"So just how do you propose we conquer the Five Kingdoms?" Rick demanded.

"I don't know, Colonel, but if anybody can do it, you can."

Tylara nodded.

"I have not always agreed with Lord Warner," she said.

"But you have always said he is right more often than he is wrong. And he is not wrong in this, My Lord Husband. If it can be done, you will do it. And what choices have we? We cannot retire to our estates and pretend there is no world outside our walls! The world is all around us, inside our very keeps! You explained that very well to Prince Strymon. The Time is upon us, and we each do what we must, and on you lies the heaviest burden of all."

"Oh bloody hell, I don't want to fight anymore," Rick said.

"Seem to remember you telling us that what we want isn't always a factor," Warner said. "Skipper, would you get mad if I tell you to shut up and soldier?"

# ← CHAPTER SIX →
# AMBUSH

The scene at the Ottarn battle camp wasn't much different from what it had been hours before when Rick led his troops southward after Ganton's abrupt dismissal. The King's officers had made little progress in forming up a route column, and now it was too late in the day to begin travel. An advance guard might make it onto the road before dark, but the main body of the army and all the supply trains would be here at least another night and probably longer.

"Stinks here," Bisso said.

"There isn't enough wood to burn the dead," Rick said. "There'll be plague if they don't get out of here pretty soon."

"What you reckon they'll eat?" Sergeant Bisso asked. "This area's been picked over by three armies." He glanced at Jamiy, Rick's Tamaerthan orderly, and cocked one eyebrow. "Think even the clans could find enough to eat here?"

Jamiy shook his head, pleased to have been brought into the conversation by the star lord. Sergeant Bisso had a reputation for being surly.

"I would not think there is enough to support field mice, much less an army."

"Maybe they'll eat mice," Bisso said.

"It's happened before," Rick said.

"Can't say much for their security," Bisso said. "Nobody's said boo to us."

"As if they knew we were coming," Jamiy said.

"Think so? Nah, they just know who we are," Bisso decided. "Anyway, there's a royal page. You! Lad! Please run to the Wanax, and give him Lord Rick's compliments. The Warlord of Drantos requests a meeting."

"The Warlord of Drantos requests audience with the Wanax of Drantos," the page said formally. "It shall be told." He paced off, not quite running, conscious of his dignity.

"With luck I'll catch Ganton alone," Rick said. "Jamiy, when I go into the Royal tent, you wait outside in case we need anything. Bisso, I'd appreciate it if you'd nose around, see what rumors you come up with."

"Sure, Colonel. There's enough owe me, least I can get is a drink. Maybe some information too. Jamiy, I'll be hanging out with the Mounted Archers."

"Given they're not so happy at staying behind, maybe they don't know so much as other outfits," Rick said.

"Yeah, maybe, Colonel, but whatever they do know I'll find out for sure."

Rick dismounted at the royal tent. Four sentries stood outside. None left his post to help Rick dismount. Jamiy waved one of Rick's Tamaerthan bodyguards to hold Rick's stirrup as the royal sentries watched dispassionately. Long cry from the Battle of Vis, Rick thought. At Vis the entire army had refused to move until Rick was out of danger.

*And maybe that's the problem*, Rick thought. *Ganton knows a lot of his troops think more of me than of him. Maybe that's it. But it sure feels cold here . . .*

The page looked out from the tent flap, waited until Rick was dismounted, then opened the tent entrance.

"The Warlord of Drantos," he said formally.

"Lord Rick, I had not expected to see you so quickly." Ganton was standing at the other end of the command tent. With a wave he dismissed three courtiers who had been engaged in earnest conversation as Rick came in. They left without acknowledging Rick in any way.

"Nor I you, Majesty, but I think the matter urgent. My greetings."

"Greetings. An urgent matter, you said, and as you see I have dismissed my advisors. Tell us."

"Majesty, your Parliament has urged you to press your claim to be High Rexja."

"As you know. You were there."

"And you accept that."

"Yes. I am no longer accustomed to being examined as I was when I was a pupil, Lord Rick. Were we not so close, I might resent your tone." Ganton spoke evenly, and in low tones, but Rick wondered if any of the guards and nobles in and out of the command tent would hear.

"Your pardon, Majesty, but I must be certain of your intent," Rick said. "The matter is one of both importance and urgency."

"That is twice you have mentioned urgency. How so?"

"If you intend this course, our best chance is now," Rick said.

"*Our* best chance. You believe I cannot win without you?"

Rick spread his hands.

"Do you, Sire?"

"I confess uncertainty," Ganton said. "But only to you. It would hardly do to let my doubts become public."

"Agreed. Doubly agreed," Rick said. "More. You are able, and you learn fast. I think you could win without me. I also think it would take you much longer, and cost much more."

"Then let us heartily agree, for I said the same thing to the Lord Speaker not three hours ago," Ganton said. "So. I take it you have plans. But first, surely, you will return to your own lands to drive out Lord General Ailas and his army."

"No. We want that army there," Rick said. "Sire, an army in Chelm isn't defending the capital of the Five Kingdoms. Which is where we shall be as quickly as we can travel there."

"But our forces are not yet assembled—"

"And theirs are worse scattered," Rick said. "Strymon returns to the Green Palace with all the force he can muster. That is a long way from Aachilos. Whatever he finds there, it will take time to sort it out, and he won't be looking for trouble. True, he may not respond to a summons from the High Rexja to defend the realm, but he will probably defend the realm against predations, even against you. Then again if Toris has his wits, or

Issardos does, they'll pardon Strymon and summon him. All that will take time. So if we strike fast and hard, by the time he can arrive you will be host to an Electoral College. Called by you, to chambers you control, in Aachilos where the elections are always held. It is but a short step from there to having that College name you High Rexja."

"You would kill Rexja Toris?"

"No, but I have no hesitation in deposing him," Rick said. "For cause. Incompetence for one."

"He may be even less competent than you know," Ganton said.

"I've heard those rumors too. If so, all the better. Leave him the throne. The College meets, and we say we have no designs against the High Rexja, but the realm must be governed. We pray the College will proclaim you, as both heir and regent. And we lock the old man in a place of comfort where the only women he can father children on will be whores."

"That would have been more pleasing to Prince Sarakos than to Toris. But what if Akkilas lives and that head was indeed that of the tanist?" Ganton asked.

"We deal with that when the time comes. If we have to, we shoot him."

"And the religious wars? Chancellor Issardos supports Vothan. We have converts among Strymon's army because Ta-Meltemos has long been a land where Yatar prevails, but the Five Kingdoms officially rank Vothan at least Yatar's equal, and the priests of Vothan hold by far the most influence in the capital."

"The best way to win converts from a religion is to show it is a religion for losers," Rick said. "When you hold

Aachilos you may build a great cathedral to Yatar and Christ, and that, I think, will be the end of the matter."

"I do not understand you, Lord Rick. You were no enthusiast for my claims as High Rexja."

"I am no enthusiast for more war, Sire," Rick said. "But on reflection I believe it best for all if we unify the realms of Drantos and the Five, with Drantos in the lead. We will endure the Time better. I should think you would be pleased of my aid, Majesty."

"Why? Was there doubt that it would be offered?" Ganton asked. "I am pleased to have your aid, Warlord, but I shall be more pleased to have it when I am ready to make use of it. Did you think I had not considered pressing forward instantly? Do you believe yourself the only strategist in Drantos? No, no, My Lord, I have looked at these possibilities as carefully as you, and with better counsel.

"You wish me to press onward, with the enemy's best army to my southwest. On your land, but without you to oppose it there is nothing to prevent Ailas from marching swiftly to the defense of his capital. And there is another army between us and Aachilos."

"Scattered in defeat, Majesty," Rick said.

"Scattered and dispersed, but even as we speak it is called to muster again by Matthias, a competent enough general. Then to the east there is Strymon with all his force. Strymon who will have left spies to watch us and who will know our every move. Strymon, the best general on Tran it is said, with his army intact and ordered well enough that he was able to march homeward while we squabble over meager spoils! No, My Lord Rick, I think not. It is well to be bold, but it is another matter to be foolhardy.

"Return to your lands. Expel Ailas while I gather the strength of the realm and see to my borders. Time enough to press this claim when that is done." Ganton smiled thinly. "I am always pleased to see you, Lord Rick, but I do not expect to see you again while Ailas is entrenched in our County of Chelm. My thanks for your suggestions. Good day, My Lord, I will not detain you longer."

✢ ✢ ✢

The True Sun was down, and the Firestealer was making long shadows into the thickets. Rick rode along the darkening road in silence. Jamiy and his guards had not spoken a word since they saw his mood after his interview with the Wanax.

*Handed me my head*, Rick thought. *I suppose I should be gratified, we tried to teach him to think independently. But not independently of us!*

The worst of it was that Ganton might be right. It was a chancy business, charging forward without supply lines. Not as chancy as Ganton thought. Murphy's raiders were operating ahead, and the private reports Murphy sent to accompany his grisly trophies made it clear the Fiver armies were scattered and no organized force stood between the border and the capital. *Should I have told him that?* But Ganton was in no mood to listen.

*A strange meeting*, Rick thought. *As if he expected me to come, and had his answer ready. But how would he know I was coming? Or what I would propose?*

"Ambush! Alarm!" The shouts came from the mounted archers who served as advance guard for Rick's party.

There were insistent hoof beats from the road ahead. A dozen horsemen, lightly armed, had burst past the advance party and were charging directly at Rick, sabers raised high, the nearest not a hundred yards away.

"Kill the traitor!" "For the glory of Vothan!" "Vothan calls!"

"Dismount to receive cavalry!" Bisso shouted. "Jamiy, look to the Colonel!"

Jamiy spurred his horse to get between Rick and the charging enemies. He was only just in time before the raiders were on him. One engaged him. The others charged past, ignoring the orderly, their eyes fixed on Rick.

"Vothan calls! Kill the traitor! Vothan calls!"

Rick fumbled at his shoulder holster. His pistol was buckled in, his shield hung on the cantle of his saddle. Jamiy had bought him a moment, but only that. The nearest enemy was no more than five yards away, saber raised high—

Bisso must have been just behind him. His H&K battle rifle sounded like the crack of doom. Rick's ears rang with the muzzle blast, but the first enemy screamed in pain. His saber dropped. Bisso fired again. The man stayed in the saddle, but he rode past without striking. Bisso fired a new burst, and the charging group parted, flowing around them. A saber grated on Rick's chain mail, then they were past.

His ears rang. Someone shouted, but he couldn't make out what was said. Jamiy was down, out of the saddle and sprawled on the ground. His bodyguards were scattered. Then he saw dust rise ahead, and a dozen new shapes in the gloom. More enemies! Grimly he drew his pistol, but there was no one between him and the new force. This was defeat.

Dimly through the ringing in his ears he heard "For Yatar and Christ!" The newcomers were his own advance guard, turned to pursue the enemy that had broken past them. Now other mounted archers came up to form beside Jamiy and shield their commander. He heard new battle cries.

"Tamaerthan! For Lord Rick!"

And as suddenly as it had begun, the attack was over. More assassins rode past at a gallop. Two were down. The others escaped.

"Pursue!"

"Hold!" Bisso's shout stopped the pursuit before it began. He looked to Rick for instructions.

*You handle it,* Rick thought. *You or somebody. Not me, I don't even know what just happened. I'm too damn old for this, I never was a good tactical commander and I'm dead tired—*

Bisso frowned, then rose in his stirrups to shout.

"Let 'em go. You, Cambyrly, take five more Tamaerthans and scout ahead. You'll be safe enough, they're after the Colonel, not you. Adams! Take your partner and play connecting file between us and the advance guard. Now who's got the best horse here?"

A young Tamaerthan lord limped up. "I do."

"Yeah, Sean, but you're hurt."

"Not badly, and my horse not at all."

"Good man. Okay, you go with the advance guard there and when they get far enough out, leave 'em behind you and ride like hell to the camp. Come back with Balquhain and some reinforcements. And make sure Lady Tylara knows the Colonel's okay. Colonel, you all right?"

"I'm fine, Sergeant. Jamiy!"

His orderly was down, but he seemed able to sit up.

"Medic!" Rick shouted.

"None with us, Colonel," Bisso said. "Jamiy, you bleeding?"

Jamiy nodded dully.

Bisso dismounted.

"God Almighty, no wonder you're bleedin'," he said. "Hang on, I got to tie that off. You two, see he gets to the surgeon as soon as we get to camp. Colonel, all due respect and we need to get movin' before those creeps come back with an army. My Lord Dugready, is there some reason you're not riding to camp?"

"On my way, Lord Bisso."

Bisso nodded acknowledgment.

"Okay, Colonel, let's get moving."

"I'm worried about Jamiy—"

"Yes Sir, and if you get killed, we all go. The troops will get him back to camp, and there's nothing you can do they can't. He's got a hell of a slice on his shield arm, and he needs sewing up, but neither one of us is going to do that. So let's get the hell out of here."

"I suppose."

"Suppose hell, Colonel. Okay, troops, move out."

Rick let himself be led away, towards the camp and safety.

✚ ✚ ✚

Warner inspected the dead attacker.

"Looks like a Fiver to me, Sir. And you say they were shouting about Vothan?"

"Sure were," Bisso said. "'Favor of Vothan!' That sort of thing. And 'Kill the traitor,' who I reckon is the Colonel here. That's sure who they were after, Mr. Warner."

"The interesting thing is, how did they know to be there?" Warner asked, and Rick nodded.

"That's been bothering me, too."

"Pity they didn't leave anything but dead behind," Warner mused. "Bad luck, that."

"Nope," Bisso said. "Not luck, Mr. Warner. They led their wounded off, and this guy they finished off. The bullet didn't kill him, it was that arrow that done it, and one of his own shot that from one of them small crossbows."

"Kill their wounded rather than let them be captured," Warner said. "Tough bunch. Did you go through his things?"

"Yeah, mixed bag, the kind of stuff you'll find on any trooper after a few weeks on campaign. Loot, this and that. But nothing pointing to where he came from, leastwise nothing I get any feeling from."

"I'll go over it later," Warner said. "Religious objects?"

"Both Vothan and Yatar stuff," Bisso said.

"But no cross? Nothing Christian."

"No, Mr. Warner."

Tylara burst into the command center.

"My Lord. They say you are all right—"

"I'm fine, sweetheart. Not a scratch on me."

"Christ be thanked. Sergeant, I am told there were a dozen, in ambush, and that they made directly for My Lord Husband, to kill him."

"I'd say that was an accurate picture, Lady Tylara," Bisso said.

"A dozen, in hiding and waiting. Did you ride slowly from your meeting with the Wanax, then?" she demanded.

"No, Ma'am, we wasn't at forced march or anything but we weren't dawdling either."

"If they had set out when you left the Wanax would they have been able to get into position and hide before you encountered them?"

"No, Ma'am," Bisso said. "Not easily, anyway. I see where you're goin', and I don't like it much. I don't know, My Lady. Maybe, but it don't seem too likely. They sure wouldn't have had any extra time."

"So," Tylara said. "A dozen enemy soldiers are concealed near Wanax Ganton's camp. They remain undetected until by happenstance they see Lord Rick and a small party set out on this road. They immediately form a plan and ride away at the gallop, still undetected. They ride past two small crossroads until, again by happenstance, they find a good place of concealment. There they lie in wait for Lord Rick. Do you believe this, Sergeant?"

"Now you put it that way, not a bit of it, My Lady," Bisso said.

"And you, My Lord Husband?"

"No. And I'll give you another one," Rick said. "I think Wanax Ganton was expecting me, and knew precisely what I was going to say."

"I'll buy the part about expecting us," Bisso said. "I thought it was funny at the time, the way the Wanax's guards didn't challenge us, and that page was right there, ready to go announce us. Didn't wait for a tip, didn't protest about going in to the Wanax without permission, just took off. Skipper, I'd bet he was waitin' there for us all along."

"I sent you to talk with the Mounties," Rick said. "Learn anything?"

"No, Sir, and I don't think they was hiding anything. They was surprised enough to see me. Thought we'd rode off into the sunset. Some of them was grousing about a long campaign coming, but they didn't seem to know anything special about it."

"You know what this means," Rick said.

"Certainly." Tylara's voice was firm and assured. "We have a traitor within our camp. Someone who warned Wanax Ganton you were coming, and for what purpose. Someone who deserves to be hanged."

"I think we might have trouble justifying that," Rick said. "Hanging a man for loyalty to the Wanax. Okay, I buy it that Ganton has a spy in our camp. But on our staff? Hell, we've got agents in his army, too, but not high up enough to overhear his council meetings."

"Didn't need to be so high," Bisso said. "Hell, Skipper, we didn't make any secret of what we were going to propose to Ganton. I'd reckon half the officer corps and all of the sergeant's mess knew every bit of that before we rode out of camp. What else would you be doing, riding back while the troops sit here?"

"Okay, not necessarily so high up," Rick said.

"But more than Ganton's spy," Tylara said. "He will not hang for loyalty to the Wanax, but disloyalty!" She jerked her thumb towards the dead ambusher. "A spy for the Five Kingdoms as well."

"Yeah," Rick said. "Treason. That's all we bloody need."

"Treason to whom?" Tylara said aloud. "It is not treason to obey the orders of the Wanax, even if those involve dressing as an enemy."

Rick gasped. *She understands this stuff,* he thought.

"You think Ganton sent those ambushers?"

Tylara shook her head.

"It will not matter. The traitor, if we find him, will hang as a spy for the Five. In fact I do not think our Wanax would treat us so. But are you certain he did not?"

⁜ ⁜ ⁜

There was stew for dinner. Rick had eaten stew for a week now, a routine broken only by the more varied fare served in Strymon's camp.

"I weary of stew," he announced, and Tylara grinned.

"Then let us hasten to be home where there is something else."

"Not sure I should go home just yet," Rick said.

"And where shall we go in preference?"

*We,* Rick thought. *She likes being with me. As I with her. Thank God we're back together again. But—*

"Not us, me. You're needed at home. The kids need you. I think I have to go to Armagh."

Tylara frowned. She wasn't the kind of woman who pouted, but Rick could sense her disappointment.

"And why Armagh?"

"Ammunition," Rick said. "All our spares are at Armagh. If I get there before the Wanax, there won't be any trouble about gathering everything and taking it with us to Chelm. If Ganton gets there first, he may wonder why I want it all."

"And you think it is time we took control of our resources," Tylara mused. "After your treatment today, I agree. But I hate being parted from you."

Rick grimaced at a spoonful of stew. It tasted of rabbit, but there was a gamier flavor Rick was afraid to ask about. Earth wildlife had been released on Tran over the centuries, and most of it thrived without natural predators, just as most native Tran species were poison, or indigestible, to humans. Over centuries human cooks had found a few Tran species edible and even nourishing, but none of those were very attractive for the appetite. Neither were the Terran rats which seemed to have taken over half the planet, but armies often ate them.

"I hate leaving you, too. But it's the same with the surinomaz, I—we—need control of that as much as we need the ammo. I don't know how much Harvey Rand has collected, but any is better than none, and if I've got it I've got something to trade with the Shalnuksis. Also I want some seeds, and some of the crop foremen, too."

"You will raise madweed at Chelm?"

"Not at Chelm, but not too far away, either," Rick said. "Someplace we control. Tylara, I'm getting scared. That crown business changes everything. Ganton's acting independent—"

"That is the way of a Wanax," Tylara said.

"Yeah, but it scares me the way he's acting. I'll feel a hell of a lot better if we have our ammunition and all the star troops near enough that I can control them. Same with the surinomaz."

"I agree regarding the ammunition. But, Rick, you have

placed the surinomaz cultivation and the visible signs of your actions at Armagh so as to draw attention away from Chelm," Tylara reminded him. "You feared skyfire, and thought better it fall at Armagh than at our home. And I agreed, and I still believe that important."

"Yeah, and now I'm not sure which is the bigger threat, Ganton or the Galactics," Rick said. "The Galactics are an unknown."

"Are they?" Tylara asked. "My Lord Husband, if there is one thing certain about the history of this realm, it is that skyfire falls when the sky demons come. It was you who put names to the demon lords, but our grandsires knew of them before ever you arrived. Wanax Ganton was our ward, and owes us, owes you, more than he can ever repay. Agreed that it is dangerous to have a Wanax in your debt. But whatever we apprehend from the Wanax, ill will and skyfire from the demon lords is certain!"

"I'm not so sure," Rick said.

"You put your hopes on that policeman?" Tylara asked.

"Yeah, I suppose I do pin a lot of hope on Inspector Agzaral," Rick said. "But nobody, not Les or anyone else, seems to know what the Shalnuksis are really up to this time. Just that things are different, and Agzaral has made the difference. Anyway, it's getting close to periastron. The legends say the Demon has grown dim before skyfire falls, meaning it has finished its track through this system and is on the way out again. That's years we've got. It's pretty clear the Shalnuksis delay their skyfire as long as they can in hopes of getting more product. Inspector Agzaral said most of their motives were commercial." Rick spooned up something indescribable, let it fall back into the stew, and brought up a carrot. "I want to string things out as long as possible."

"Keep this new activity far from Castle Dravan, then," Tylara said. "Your reasons for not attracting attention to our home remain strong. In the High Cumac, perhaps?"

"Not enough rain, not usually—"

"My love, there are strong legends of skyfire in the High Cumac," Tylara said. "And of dealings with sky demons. You have said that rainfall changes at the Time."

"By the Lord, I think you have something."

"Do not blaspheme," she said automatically.

"Your pardon. Tylara, I think you're right, every place we know of that has legends of local star demon activity had the right soil for madweed even if there's not enough rain. There are streams we can dam, for that matter. With the Littlescarp to the east the High Cumac ought to be easy enough to defend from refugees. Or Ganton if it comes to that. Defending to the west is another matter."

"Westmen," Tylara mused.

"And worse, if Warner's right," Rick said. "We'll need to look to defenses, and good stockpiles. But nomads don't have any use for madweed, and if we don't grow anything else up there they won't be interested. Nothing to steal. It does mean we'll need good transportation and supply. And fortifications. Magazines. Damn. That means logistics, and we've just sent our best bureaucrat off with Strymon."

"My Lord Father Apelles has trained apprentices," Tylara said. "I am told that several show great promise."

"Good. Get them on it. We'll want to put a dozen square stadia in cultivation. I don't know how many farmers and troops that will take, but I'll find out when I get to Armagh and send that information along. It's going to take a big effort, Tylara, but I think it's worth it."

She nodded sagely.

"As do I. But must you go to Armagh yourself? Your children will miss you." She smiled. "As will I."

"I've seen them since you have," Rick reminded her. "They need you more than me, and I won't be any longer than I have to be. But yes, for something this drastic, I better go myself. Ganton isn't going to like this, you know."

"There seems little we do that he does like," Tylara said. "And I fear that will become worse, not better."

# ⊰═ CHAPTER SEVEN ═⊱
# THE QUEEN'S BANNER

**One week after the Battle of the Ottarn River**

They traveled fast towards Armagh.

Rick sent his office caravan and most of the baggage west with Tylara. A bodyguard of his mercenaries accompanied her. "Godspeed, my love," she called as Rick, Warner, Bisso, and an escort of Tamaerthan mounted archers rode southward towards Castle Armagh, the strongest fortress of Drantos.

He had a new orderly, a young Tamaerthan squire named Haerther. Choosing him had been easy enough. Haerther was cousin to Tylara, and at the proper age for the position. It was more difficult leaving Jamiy behind. Jamiy was a crofter's son, not born to be a squire, but he had been faithful in his duties.

"Lord, I regret that I can no longer be your shield," Jamiy had said. "It was my life to follow you. What will become of me now?"

"You'll be on sick leave at least half a year with that arm," Rick said. *And probably lose it if I don't authorize penicillin. Maybe even after I do.* "At full pay, of course. After that, we'll see. Would a place in the Chamberlain's staff be to your liking?"

"Lord, I cannot read."

"So you have a year to learn," Rick said. "It's time my children started reading. As soon as you're able, learn with them. I can use a reliable man to help watch over them. Yeah." He waved to Tylara to come join them.

"My love, Jamiy is worried about his future now that he can't carry my shield."

"I saw him save your life in the battle at the Ottarn," she said.

"Not for the first time. Nor even the last," Rick said.

Tylara nodded significantly at Jamiy's bandaged arm.

"Then we are his debtors."

"Agreed, so I had an idea. With your consent I'll appoint him an officer of the bodyguards for the kids. That way he can be with them in their lessons. Learn to read himself. Good thing, knowing how to read."

Tylara smiled.

"A splendid suggestion. Jamiy, does this please you?"

"With all my heart, My Lady. If I cannot guard My Lord Rick, at least I can help to keep his children safe. My Lord, you are most generous."

*Generous*, Rick thought. *Take a kid with a plain case of hero worship, get him maimed, and have him grateful for a sinecure. Hero worship, with me as the hero! Damn flattering. The worst of it is, there really isn't anybody else who can do what I'm doing. Well, that's one less thing to*

*nag me. Jamiy's smart, and God knows he's loyal. I can
stop worrying so much about Makail and Isobel when I'm
away. At least I've gained that much.*

✧ ✧ ✧

Armagh was a stark castle in a stark land.

Before they reached it they passed through the
madweed fields. Work in those marshy fields was hard and
dangerous, and Rick knew of few volunteers. Many died
of rabies or other infections from the crazed animals that
lived in madweed patches. Prisoners earned double time
served for work in the fields and even then had to be
forced to it. When there were too few prisoners, there was
no alternative: peasants and serfs became temporary
slaves, paid well—Rick insisted on that—but guarded by
soldiers and forced to their work. It was bad enough that
there were other soldiers to watch the guards.

The scent of the fields was palpable. It reminded Rick
of a combination of a locker room and a slaughter house.
As they rode past, sullen heads rose from the madweed
patches to stare curses at those free to ride through
without stopping. Rick felt their eyes on his back as he
rode on. They hated him, and with good reason. And what
could he do about it?

*I wouldn't blame the slaves for running. Cultivating
madweed's hard work. Dangerous, too. But if we don't
grow the stuff, we'll have nothing for the* Shalnuksis, *and
they'll bomb the planet just to keep it in the Stone Age.
And if I tell myself that often enough, maybe I'll believe
it's all right to be a slave master. Maybe.*

✧ ✧ ✧

Trumpets sounded as they rode up to the long

causeway leading to the castle. Armagh stood high on a mound above a fully moated bailey laid in a swamp, and the approach was well defended by water and quicksand. Rick looked up at the banners above the main gate.

"Bloody hell, that's the Queen's arms! Warner, last I heard, the whole damn Royal Court was at Edron."

"Yes, Sir, they sure were there when we set out north."

"Well, she's here now."

"Sure looks that way, Colonel."

"Hmm. It's my castle—"

"Yes, Sir. But don't I remember you advising the Wanax to take refuge at Armagh if things got sticky?"

"I suppose I did."

"So he took you up on it and sent the court here. If he'd sent you a message, and I'm betting he did, you'd have been already on the way east before it got to Dravan." Warner turned the palms of his hands upwards. "I doubt anyone back in Chelm thought it was important enough to chase you down with it by semaphore. You were on the way to a battle, Colonel, and moving like hell. To rescue your wife. Why would anyone think you gave a hoot about where the Royal Court was?"

"And it never came up when the King and I met? Yeah, I suppose it could have been that way. I expect it was," Rick said. "All right, they're invited. But it still makes them my guests. Not the other way around." *And why do I care that her banner is higher than mine? Like King Richard in* The Talisman . . .

"Maybe not," Warner said.

"Eh?"

"Sir, lots of places have laws making the queen the

official hostess any place she's at. Wouldn't surprise me if Drantos is one of them. For sure she'll be the highest ranker in the joint. Not to mention her father's connections."

Her father. Wanaxxae Octavia's father was Publius, son of Marselius Caesar, and likely enough to be Caesar in his own right in no great amount of time. An educated and pleasant girl with good manners, Rick thought, but she'd grown up in a Roman household, well accustomed to intrigue and politics. She'd be better at those games than the Wanax himself, and it was best not to forget it.

"Who comes?" a warden shouted.

"Open the gates for the Warlord of Drantos," young Haerther shouted.

"Approach and be recognized."

"Hell, you see it's us," Bisso shouted. "Rand, that you? Open the bleedin' gates!"

"What the hell is Rand doing on guard duty?" Rick muttered.

"Elliot's testing him, would be my guess," Bisso said. "You can be pretty sure Sergeant Major isn't going to take any big chances. We weren't expected, but even so there'll be somebody watching him."

"I suppose."

"Come forward alone, if you please, Colonel."

*By the book*, Rick thought. *Make sure nobody's holding a knife in my ribs*. It also made him a perfect target.

There was a small door, just large enough for one man to pass, set in the main gate. It opened slowly. Rick had to dismount and lead his horse to get inside. *I could send someone in first. Just to test things. Sure, and show my troops I'm getting paranoid about my own men.*

He stepped forward through the gate without visible hesitation.

"Welcome, Colonel."

"Thanks, Henderson." Rick was relieved to see Sergeant Henderson at the end of the gate passageway. He shook off the feeling of suspicion. "All's well. You can let the others in."

"Yes, Sir." Henderson gestured, and the main gates swung open. "Good to see you, Sir."

"Good to see you, too."

Everything seemed in order. Henderson held Rick's stirrup so that he could remount. Warner rode up alongside him.

"Colonel," Warner said. He pointed through the gates to the outer courtyard beyond.

"Romans," Rick said. "Well, that's no big surprise." Marselius had sent a detachment of Romans as personal bodyguards for Octavia. They were rotated periodically.

"Yeah, Colonel, but that's no ordinary Roman trooper," Warner said. "That's a Praetorian officer. Damn all, First Cohort, First Praetorian Legion."

"Marselius Caesar's guards? He can't possibly be here," Rick said.

"No Sir," Warner replied. "I wouldn't think so, but— Hah. The rest of them are Second Praetorians, Publius' guards."

"A lot of them," Rick muttered. "First Cohort of the Second, so Publius himself must be here. But what's a Tribune of the First doing here? I can't believe Marselius Caesar is here. For that matter, what the hell is Publius doing here?"

"I can go back and ask Henderson," Warner said.

"No point. We'll find out soon enough," Bisso said. "They ain't exactly putting out the welcome mat for us, Colonel. It's your castle, and here we come with news of a victory, but nobody's rushing out to meet us. We rode fast getting here, but I bet messages have arrived from the Wanax before us."

"Well that makes sense," Rick said. "He'd want the Queen to know he was safe. Of course the Wanax wouldn't have any reason to know we were coming here."

"Maybe he wouldn't have any reason, but it sure looks like they knew you was coming," Bisso said. "And he'd sure know the Queen was here."

"And you'd think the Queen would want to know details, no matter they know the king's safe," Warner observed. "Colonel, Sergeant Bisso's right, they knew we were coming."

"And we still get a chilly reception," Rick said. "In my own damned castle."

They rode in silence across the outer courtyard to the main gates. The drawbridge had already been let down. The guards removed their hats in salute as they rode past into the inner bailey. Grooms waited there. So did Sergeant Major Elliot.

Elliot saluted as Haerther leaped down to hold Rick's stirrup. Rick could feel eyes watching him from the castle walls.

"Report, Sergeant Major."

"Sir. Welcome to Castle Armagh. Thirty-eight days ago we received messages to the effect that the Queen and the entire Royal Court had been instructed by the Wanax to take refuge here. The Queen and court, including your people from Edron and the University, arrived eight days later. Having no instructions to the contrary I admitted them and assigned them the most suitable quarters available."

"Which means my suite," Rick said.

"Well, yes, Sir. I did hold on to your office and the sleeping room next to it, but the Queen and her people have the big master suite, and that whole south wing for that matter. I'll have to put you in a west wing guest suite."

"I'll just move into the sleeping room next to my office. Nothing else you could have done, Sergeant Major. Approved. Who all came with the Lady Gwen?"

"McCleve, Sir. Lady Siobhan. Couple of Drantos scholars and apprentices, but they've gone on to their homes. The Tamaerthan faculty members can fade into the hills if they have to, so they stayed behind. So did the Romans. Campbell's in command there. He stayed to try to keep the place going. He's got a garrison of Roman troops and clansmen working together. I've got his reports in the orderly room, Colonel, being copied before I sent them on to you."

*Copies*, Rick thought. *Bureaucracy, and it's needed*. He looked around at a growing number of castle functionaries.

"I take it I'm expected," he said. "How?"

"Eight days ago we heard by semaphore you were headed east to rescue your wife," Elliot said, in a low voice that wouldn't carry. "Nothing after that until a Royal Messenger got in about five hours ago, Colonel. Went straight to the Queen. I waited to hear, but I got no word for a couple of hours. Then one of the Romans came to say you were expected sometime this afternoon."

"A Roman. Not one of the Queen's people?"

"No, Sir, and that bothered me enough I put Rand and O'Brien with Henderson at the outer gate, and formed the rest of the troops here. I tell you, I was relieved when your lad there announced you as Warlord. I'd about half decided the Wanax tried to fire you or something."

"It's or something, Top," Rick said. "But let me get this straight. There was a messenger from the Wanax, but he reported to the Queen. Not to you."

"That's it, Sir."

"But you're the castellan."

"Me or Henderson, depending on which hat I'm wearing, but yeah, Colonel."

"So you don't know about our victory?"

"Not details, Sir. The Roman officer said the Wanax had won a glorious victory at the Ottarn Ford, and would be coming here with the army in a bit more than a ten-day. Then he said, sort of like an appendix maybe, that you'd been at the battle and could be expected shortly, probably today."

"And you haven't had any formal notice from the Queen's people?"

"No, Sir, not unless you count a Roman officer as being a queen's messenger."

"Bloody hell. She might think that way. She is Roman after all, but—. Okay, about the Romans. We saw Praetorians. Publius is here?"

"That he is, Colonel, and whatever's the problem with

the Queen, his officer sounded glad enough you're coming. You're invited to dine with him after you make your respects to the Queen."

"Then I'd better get to that. Who else is here?"

"The civil cabinet, the treasury lords, the ladies of the court, like that. But Lady Gwen's here with some of the University people," Elliot said. "If anybody knows what the Queen's thinking it'll be her."

"Right. And Romans? Warner spotted a First Praetorian officer."

"That'll be the escort for Lucius," Elliot said.

Lucius. Marselius Caesar's freedman, and probably his best friend.

"If Caesar sent Lucius, it's going to be important. Any idea of why he's here?" Rick asked.

"No Sir, not a bit."

"How long has he been here?"

"About three days longer than Publius, Colonel. He got here first, about two weeks ago. Wanted to see you or the Wanax or both. When we told him the Wanax was north with the army and you were back at Dravan, he dithered about which way to go, and while he was dithering Publius came up with his Praetorians. He never said what he was doing here, either, but given the Queen's his daughter I sure wasn't going to question his right."

"Where did you put them?"

"Sir, I pleaded there was no suitable room left in the castle, what with the Queen here and all, and Publius allowed as how his troops would get by fine camping in the outer bailey. Which suited me just fine, too." Elliot lowered his voice. "Didn't much suit some of the ladies of the court, though. Little hard to have secrets when everybody's got to pass two sets of guards."

"All right. Well done." He looked out at the castle troops, mostly sword and crossbowmen old enough to avoid field duty, and a few musketeers training cadre. "You can dismiss the troops, and I'd better get cleaned up. Do whatever formalities it takes to get me a gracious audience with the Queen. And everybody's to be on their best and most formal behavior, Sergeant Major."

"Yes, Sir. Trouble with the Wanax?"

"It looks that way. He was losing that battle when I got there."

"And you won it for him," Elliot said.

"He sees it like that. It may be simple jealousy, may be something more serious. Anything else I need to know?"

Elliot frowned.

"Madweed production's well above normal. Rand's done a damned good job on that, Colonel. Looks like he was the right man to put in charge of it."

"Interesting." There was no need to say that Rand had been given the assignment as a punishment.

"But it may compound your problem with the Wanax."

"How is that?"

"It didn't become clear to me until I talked to Rand after he was living with the inmates working on the madweed. Turns out a lot of our prisoners are actually refugees picked up for petty theft, cattle rustling, that sort of thing. Stuff people who are starving do."

"How is that a problem?"

"We treat them too well."

"What do you mean?"

"So look at it from the perspective of a peasant refugee. Even before the Demon Star appears, they'd be worried about crop failure, plague, being overcharged for taxes, or just being molested by the local lord. Then the Time comes and the water goes away. Either they starve or, if they're working good land, the local warlord kicks them off it and then they starve.

"So they hear things and head up here, where we've got fertilizer, irrigation, and iron plows. We've got great crops, so no one starves. We've got cotton to export, bringin' in quite a bit of cash. We've got good hygiene and medicine, hell we have a population explosion here, Dravan and Ferdon. Lots of kids who normally wouldn't have made it through childhood are alive and thriving. Meanwhile, you've set the example for governing without corruption, so your people don't get hit with the usual shakedown and backsheesh.

"Now growin' madweed ain't no joke, but it's a lot better than choking on dust in the south and Rand's worked out procedures to minimize the risks.

"Meanwhile," Elliott continued. "Lewin and Apelles have moved forward with the Hestia fertilizer water."

That had been a battle. The first time Sergeant Lewin had smelled ammonia rising up from the caves under the castles, he had suggested using it as fertilizer. The problem was that it came from the Protector plant whose roots made ice in the caves and were used to preserve food for the Time. The plants were sacred to the priests of Yatar and the new Church. Rick had had to convince Apelles that in order for them to fill the caves with food they'd have to get a better crop going and that took fertilizer. Then it became a question of balancing growth with necessary storage. At least it was easy to convince the local farmers to use ammonia diluted in water by naming it after Hestia, goddess of family and fertility, known as the Mother of Christ in the new faith. If this batch worked out, Rick intended to send a search party to the Littlescarp and look for caves where the Protector plant was growing.

"Between the Demon Star," Elliot went on, "Hestia water, seagull crap, irrigation, and iron plows, we've doubled the plantings this year and bumper crops in each."

With Tran's long years, almost seventy percent longer than Earth's, growing seasons were almost twice as long as on Earth. The problem was that in normal times the winters were *more* than twice as long. Now winters were steadily shorter and the growing season was increasing in length but storms were ruining crops.

"Okay," Rick replied, "I'm still not seeing the problem."

"Colonel, our prisoners live better than most serfs. Our peasants live better than most yeomanry. Add in the fact you recruit and reward merit in business and the army regardless of class and no wonder we've got a population explosion. Did you know prisoners are volunteering to come here? Many who've completed their sentences are choosing to stay on as sharecroppers in the cotton fields. Some are even volunteering to come back to work on madweed 'cause they know you'll pay them."

"What about those sullen faces I saw in the madweed fields?" Rick asked.

"They know you're a softy," Elliot said with a chuckle.

"Ever know anyone who's happy to work someone else's field? Besides it's still dangerous and backbreaking work. But word's spread and the bheromen are worried that some of their serfs are leaving their fields for ours. Even if that ain't true, you've got the richest county in the kingdom, probably all of Tran, and getting richer steadily."

"I have enough trouble with the Ironheads as it is," Rick said. "I knew raising our new model army from the peasants and middle class was troubling them. I didn't realize until now I was threatening their livelihood so directly."

"On top of that," Elliot continued. "Word's gotten out that we're actually seeking the advice of the village elders and councils and stuff like that."

*What seems to be natural to us is threatening the whole political system*, Rick thought. *I wanted to avoid the whole chapter of wars related to industrialization, but I just don't see how we can survive the Time without these reforms . . .*

"Okay. No contacts with the Galactics, or you'd have told me. Anything else?"

"Nothing that can't wait a few hours. Pile of reports over the semaphore from Major Mason. There's more Westmen coming down the passes, but nothing he can't handle, or he says it's not. Of course, last he knew you were on the way to join the Wanax, and he might not be sending me everything he knows. And the Romans have been getting official messengers all week, Colonel. *Frumentarii*, I'd guess."

"Nothing they cared to share with you?"

"Not yet."

"You got any feelings about that, Top?"

"Not really, Sir. Them Roman intelligence officers do a good job of reporting once they put things together, but they do take their own time digesting stuff. Never known one of them to leak a report until he thought he had a good picture. Not to us, anyway."

"Careful about not blowing their sources," Rick agreed. "Okay. I'm off to the baths. Get a semaphore off to Mason telling him we won at the Ottarn, and I'm here, details to follow. Oh, and priority: Lady Tylara is on her way home to Dravan."

Elliot nodded and didn't say anything.

*Of course*, Rick thought. *Elliot knows all about Tylara and Caradoc and—*

"It's fine, Top," Rick said. "Tylara's my wife again."

Elliot nodded again.

"I'd guessed, Colonel."

"How?"

"It's the first time I've seen you look happy in a year," Elliot said. "By your leave, Sir." Elliot turned and walked swiftly towards the orderly room.

✢ ✢ ✢

Rick lay on his belly while two bath attendants pummeled his sore muscles. *One advantage to having the Queen come from Rome*, he thought. *Roman baths go where she goes*. They hadn't had a chance to build a real bathhouse, but they'd rigged up a pool and hot and cool rooms. Roman baths had done wonders for hygiene. Not to say comfort, Rick thought.

His reverie was interrupted by Haerther's apologetic cough.

"Your pardon, My Lord, but the Lady Gwen waits in the outer apartments."

Gwen. There was only the one bath, and bathhouses were an exception to the local nudity taboos. The Romans would rather mix the sexes than go without their baths . . .

"Tell her I'll be dressed shortly. Is she alone?"

"No, Lord, the Lady Siobhan is with her."

*That settles one question. She won't be expecting me to invite her to join me. Alone. Thank God. The last time we were alone together*—he fought off the memory. A little too disturbing.

"I'll be along presently."

*Siobhan*, Rick thought as he dressed. *An Anglo-Norman name, probably fourteenth century. Just what was the makeup of the expedition that brought an Irish girl with an Anglo-Norman name to Tran? I'll have to set Warner thinking about it.* Lady Siobhan was Mason's betrothed, an arranged marriage. Be a good match for his second-in-command.

✢ ✢ ✢

Gwen Tremaine looked older.

*She's got every reason to*, Rick thought. *Three kids by two husbands in a land without anesthetics. One husband dead, the other God knows where off in the galaxy. It's a long way from a Southern California university. Still a fine looking girl. Teeth and skin still good. Short, but you forgot that soon enough. William James wrote that Mary Ann Evans, sometimes known as George Eliot, was short and had bad teeth and half an hour after he met her he was in love with her, and so was every man she ever met.*

Maybe Gwen wasn't quite in that league, but she had

a good start. And was the only Earth woman within twenty light-years or more. That made her even more attractive.

"My Lady Siobhan. Gwen, it's good to see you. Both of you."

"You too," Gwen said. She hesitated. "Have you heard anything? From the Galactics?"

Rick shook his head. "You'd be more likely than me. I take it you've no word from Les?"

"No, but when they said you were here, unexpectedly, I thought maybe—I mean, you do keep your transceiver here, and—"

"No, nothing. Which reminds me, I'll be taking that west when I go. Bloody shame your set and mine won't talk to each other." Communications equipment was the one glaring lack in Rick's organization. Rick had set up a semaphore system to send messages throughout the kingdom, but he had no better way than his enemies did to transmit orders in battle.

"Maybe this time the Shalnuksis will bring me some decent radios. Or Les will. I still don't know what happened to the HF radio set we brought with us from Africa. It disappeared along with the lawnmower and the coffee maker when Parsons was in charge. I suspect one of the missing mercs took them when they deserted."

The last radio message Rick had received was to surrender to the Cubans. Then the set went dead when the flying saucer appeared.

"I told Les we needed radios before he left," Gwen said. "But he didn't make any promises. I suppose he'll want to check with Inspector Agzaral."

"I wish I could do that," Rick said.

Gwen frowned questioningly.

"Check with Agzaral."

"Not much chance of that, is there?" Gwen asked.

"Only through Les. But Gwen, Agzaral didn't warn me about hiding technology."

"He didn't warn me, either."

"More to the point, Les didn't warn you either, and given he loves you and you've got his child, you'd think he would if that was important. You had to work that out on your own."

"Yes, and it wasn't easy. But Rick, skyfire isn't a legend! Every time there have been technology advances here, it's been bombed back to the Bronze Age. It's the only explanation for why Tran hasn't advanced beyond medieval technology. Anything higher gets bombed. Every time!"

"And you've been scared, and I don't blame you, but we're way past the less spectacular technology, like better candles and better plows. Change was inevitable once you taught your students how to think for themselves and other people started looking at the advantages we have. Like gunpowder. We had to have it, and there was no way to keep it secret once I used it."

"And I get frightened every time I think about it. But gunpowder could have been discovered by Tran people."

"While for damn sure the Shalnuksis would know where we got radios," Rick agreed with a nod. "It doesn't matter, it's not like we can build them anyway. Bloody hell, what did Marconi use for receivers?"

"I don't know, but it wasn't very portable," Gwen said. "Wasn't that before vacuum tubes? Crystals?"

"Could be. We don't have anyone who knows vacuum tubes, either. Transistors and integrated circuits are way beyond us, but I could make vacuum tubes if I knew what to do with them. There's a filament that's negative, and a plate that's positive, and a negatively charged grid in between that you can use to control the flow of electrons to the plate, and I don't remember where I learned that. What I need's an old ham-radio manual from the 1940s."

"A power source wouldn't hurt either."

"Well, yeah. Fat chance I'll get anything like that from the Shalnuksis, but I know the principles. We can make generators. All we need is time with some peace and quiet."

"There are a lot of things we could do with time and some peace and quiet," Gwen said. "Including building one of those vacuum tubes you just described and setting Warner to fooling around with it."

"The fooling around would require building meters," Rick said. "We don't have the tools, or the instruments to tell us how to build the tools or—oh hell. It would be fun to try, but I don't suppose I'll ever have any time for that kind of thing. Pity you didn't get to do a week's technology shopping before Les brought you here! Anyway, Gwen, the situation here in this castle—hell, in Drantos—is a bit complicated."

"Yes. I've spoken with Larry Warner."

"Ah. Good." So she'd know about his problems with the Wanax. Better still, Warner would have told Gwen about the reconciliation with Tylara. One less complication to worry about. "Are you still friends with the Queen?"

"As much as she has friends," Gwen said. "She's in a tough spot."

"Tell me about it." Rick clapped his hands. "Tea," he said. "Or would you prefer wine?"

"You have a good sherry in your cellars," Gwen said. "Hunter's. Perhaps a glass of that with tea?"

Rick nodded to the steward.

"Let it be so." He waited until the servants had left. "We'll see what he brings. I don't know how much English these people have picked up," he said.

"Not much," Lady Siobhan said. "Not as much as I."

"Yeah, but you're getting pretty good at it, My Lady," Rick said. Siobhan was tall and fair, brown eyes and long hair the color of honey. She was younger than Gwen but older than most unmarried ladies of the court. At the University she functioned as Rector Gwen's office manager, and unofficially as dean of female students.

She blushed slightly. "Thank you. I am glad to see you, My Lord, but I had hoped for another . . ."

Rick nodded understanding.

"I had to leave Lord Major Mason in command at Dravan so I could come rescue my wife. I'm sure he's as disappointed as you are."

"Or perhaps he's forgotten me. I have heard nothing from him for a long time."

*Fat flipping chance*, Rick thought.

"He spoke of you daily, and how would he know you were here, My Lady? I didn't, until I got here today. I thought all the Court was in Edron. And he isn't comfortable sending messages to you by semaphore. I think you need have no concerns about his continued regard for you." That got him a smile and a slightly darker blush. Good.

"The move was sudden," Gwen said. "Morrone's scouts said there were enemy light cavalry operating in the University area, and I decided this would be a good time to visit the Court in Edron. We hadn't been there long when we got messages of enemy action not far away. We were making preparations to defend Edron when word came from Wanax Ganton that we were to move the entire court to Armagh at once. There was something about accepting your invitation. Didn't he send you word at the same time?"

"No. Of course he had no way to know I'd come east. If he'd sent me a messenger at the same time he sent you orders to move, I should have got it before I left, but maybe not. Was there some immediate threat to Edron?"

"None I heard of," Gwen said.

"Curiouser and curiouser."

"We didn't find it particularly curious," Gwen said. "Morrone had lost a major battle, half the border lords had gone over to Strymon, and Strymon's army was moving south faster than it had any right to. Tylara was captive, and you were way back west. This is the strongest fortress in the realm. Rick, I don't see anything more sinister than simple prudence."

"You're probably right." Rick nodded. "Only why didn't he tell me when I saw him at the Ottarn? Oh, well, he's a bloody king. He doesn't have to."

"And he does have a lot on his mind," Gwen said.

"So. And you don't find any of this odd? Everything all right with the Queen?"

Gwen shook her head.

"No, it's not. It's nothing I can put my finger on, but I used to be her closest friend. Now I never see her alone, and while she's friendly enough, we never talk about anything important."

"And all that started when you moved here."

"Yes. And she has no reason to be suspicious of me. Or of us. Or does she?"

"None I know of." Rick shook his head. "Is it possible it's the other way around? She's ashamed because she knows we have some reason to be suspicious of her. Or maybe worse, of her husband? Or her father for that matter."

"Rick, I never thought of that," Gwen said. "Funny, I never thought of you being more nasty suspicious than I am."

"Didn't used to be. Command does that to you," Rick said. "Now what are the Romans doing here? Both of them, Publius and Lucius?"

"Damned if I know." She shook her head. "Lucius showed up, clearly not expecting the Court to be here, hoping to see you."

"To see me."

"Yes. His official story was either you or the Wanax, but he didn't make much effort to find out where Ganton might be, and he was about to set out west to Dravan when he got a message and decided to wait."

"Message from whom?"

"I'd guess Publius. It was brought by a Second Praetorian officer."

"Okay. So Publius sent him word to stay here and wait for him."

"That's certainly my guess. Rick, Lucius is friendly, and I love to chat about history with him, but he sure hasn't let me in on any secrets."

"Think he knows any?"

She chuckled.

"He came here for something, and since he's been here the *frumentarii* have been flowing in. They may or may not see Publius, but they always spend hours with Lucius."

"So he's looking for me, gathering information by the ton, but he won't talk to you."

"Yes. Not about anything serious, anyway."

"And Publius?"

Gwen looked away.

"He came looking for Lucius, but he knew the Queen would be here," Gwen said. "She was surprised to see him."

*And I think she's blushing. Curious.*

"Does any of this make sense to you?"

"No."

"Me either. Okay, it's time to see the Queen."

"Just you," Gwen said. "I wasn't invited."

## +≒= CHAPTER EIGHT =≒+
# LONG LIVE THE QUEEN

The audience with Wanaxxae Octavia was formal, held in the Great Hall—*his* Great Hall, Rick reminded himself. Although it was now fitted out as the Queen's receiving chamber.

The interview was short.

"Welcome, Warlord Rick," Octavia said. "You are well?"

"Very well, Majesty," Rick said. *And I'll keep it to myself that you're welcoming me to my own castle.* "Your Majesty is well?"

"Just so," Octavia said.

"And Prince Adrian?"

"Well enough, My Lord."

"That's good."

But no pleasantries, no stories about the young heir, none of the usual chatter from a young mother about her first born. No questions about Makail and Isobel, even though when they were older they would probably be sent to the royal court for their duties as page and lady apprentice. Interesting.

"Has your Majesty any estimate of how long we will enjoy her visit?" *With your train of servants and courtiers eating me out of house and home.* Rick had been appalled at the costs. The local treasury was nearly dry, and he would have to send money from Chelm to make up arrears in the pay of his castle guards, not to mention settling accounts with local merchants who were happy to extend him credit at exorbitant interest. It would take a lot of money . . . .

Elizabeth Tudor had used that technique, state visits to annoying subjects. They could hardly plot treason while she was there, and they generally didn't have enough money to do anything at all after she had left. *And I taught that to Ganton, and now he's using it against me*, Rick thought. *Well, we'll see about that.*

"That must depend on the will of the Wanax," Octavia said. "Now that the campaign in the north is ended doubtless he will return, but whether here or to the capital is not decided. Or not made known to me, in any event. My last instruction from the Wanax was to await him here. So I wait, My Lord. With patience."

"To be sure, Majesty," Rick said. *With patience. With patience. By God I'll give you patience.*

The rest of the interview was much the same. She was polite, thanked him for the use of the castle, and assured him she wouldn't keep him from his important duties.

✛ ✛ ✛

Rick fumed as he strode to his study behind the

conference room Elliot insisted on calling the Orderly Room.

"Get me Elliot," he said to the clerk on duty. "Fast."

"Yes, Sir!" The young local ran out, and Rick chuckled to himself. *No good scaring my own people to death, but—*

"First Sergeant reporting as ordered."

"Come, in, Top."

"Sir. Colonel, you pardon my saying so, you don't look happy."

"I'm not. Just how long has the Queen been putting on airs?" Rick demanded.

"Few days, Colonel. Before that she was polite as anything, apologetic about being here, offered to cover expenses."

"She did, did she? Good. We'll take her up on it. I want a bill for everything it cost to put her up. Prepare it and send it on to the Treasurer. Another thing. From now on, anything we requisition for the Queen or the Court, pay for it with a warrant on the Royal Treasury."

"Can we do that?"

"I can. Sign it by order of the Warlord of Drantos."

"Yes, Sir. Reckon the Wanax will pay? Hate to lose all the credit we've built up with the local merchants."

"I don't care. We're abandoning this place," Rick said. "Get ready. We'll pull everything we have back to Chelm. Heavy weapons, mercs and their families, loyal auxiliaries, ammunition, refined product, seeds, trained madweed farmers, draft animals, plows, anything. Everything we need to set up operations in the west. Leave what you can of the madweed operations going here, and we'll put the best local we can find in charge, just in case they can produce anything. We can use all they can grow, but I can't count on it any longer. We'll need a local to be castellan, too. There must be a retired old soldier you can promote. But all our mercs and their families come out. I'm not leaving anyone I care about as a hostage."

"Jeez. Yes, Sir."

"You're not going to ask if I know what I'm doing?"

"Colonel, if you don't know what you're doing, we're all in big trouble," Elliot said. "Of course, *I* don't know what you're doing, but I assume the Colonel will tell me what I have to know."

"Well, ostensibly I'm carrying out the orders of the Wanax," Rick said. "He told me to clear the Fiver armies out of Chelm. I'll be doing just that. My story is that I need everything I have to defeat the Fivers."

Elliot nodded.

"Mostly, though, I don't like the way our little King is acting, and the Queen's attitude hasn't made me feel better about it. And then there was something Bisso said," Rick went on. "Got me to thinking. As long as our interest and the King's ran together it was fine, but my first obligation is to our own troops, mercs and locals both, and it looks like a conflict coming."

"Yes, Sir. Colonel, this is going to be expensive. Hell of a lot of transport involved."

"I know that, Top. Do what it takes."

"Yes, Sir, but there are priorities to worry about," Elliot said. "You want everyone out, that's fine, but that's hard to do fast."

"But if it's not fast we may not be able to do it at all,"

Rick replied. "I don't want to disobey a direct order from the Wanax, and I'd like to get all this done before he sends one telling me not to do it."

"Yes, Sir. What about the communicator?"

Rick frowned, puzzled by the question.

"Of course we have to take it with us."

"Wouldn't surprise me if the Galactics had some way to locate it. From space."

*Oh.*

"I'm sure they do. But without it we don't have any way to talk to them."

"And with it, they know where we are," Elliot said. "I'll keep it close to hand, Colonel. Always do. But you do need to think about this. Wouldn't be surprised if that's how they know where to bomb when they're done with us."

Rick nodded.

"Me either. I agree we have to worry about the Galactics, but just now the Wanax is closer, and there's something gone wrong in that relationship."

"Just like a marriage. Yes, Sir. So the top priority is, everything and everyone out fast."

"Correct. It's important that the madweed crops continue to grow here, but first priority is to get everything and everyone important to us out of harm's way before we get a direct command from the Wanax. I don't want to be in open defiance, I just want to have our resources where I can control them."

Elliot nodded again. His look was thoughtful. "Sir."

## ✦ CHAPTER NINE ✦
# THIS MEANS WAR?

Publius seemed genuinely glad to see him. Too glad, Rick thought. Why? Although the Romans were willing to consider star men as civilized, Rick earned little status as principal advisor to a barbarian king, even a barbarian king married to Publius' daughter; and to Publius as to many of the Romans, status was all.

"Hail, Heir of Caesar."

"Hail, Colonel Rick. Hail, Lord Warner. Colonel Rick, I would welcome you, friend to my father," Publius said. "But that it is your castle, and not mine to make you welcome in. Still, welcome to whatever comforts our Roman camp can provide. Will you and your officer dine with us?"

"Thank you," Rick said. "I think that would be well. As you say, it is my castle, but with the Queen your daughter present—"

"And acting the great lady," Publius finished. "Yes. Doubtless on instructions from my son-in-law, who ought to know better. As should she. I am a soldier, I can't always fathom the ways of royalty." He sighed and shook his head. "Welcome, then. We have plain soldiers' fare, but there is plenty of it. And we have much to discuss."

"Thank you," Rick said. *Publius playing plain soldier and questioning royalty? I wish Tylara were here. She might understand all this.*

"Lucius will join us," Publius said. "He comes on Caesar's orders, prepared to find you even if that required a journey to Dravan. For his sake I am glad he is spared that."

Rick nodded. Lucius had been tutor to Publius and if there was one person in the world other than Marselius Caesar that Publius respected, it was his father's freedman. His concern for the health of the aging scholar would be quite genuine. Actually, when you thought about it, Publius was quite generous with his own people. It was his allies he tended to be suspicious of. Allies and converts from the previous Caesar . . .

"Do you know his message, then?" Rick asked.

"Yes. And we have more to add to it," Publius said. His voice fell. "Dangerous times, Colonel Galloway. Dangerous times." Publius nodded to Warner. "As I am sure you both know."

Rick suppressed a grin at the pronunciation of "colonel." It was interesting that Publius would use that title, rather than Warlord. *Or Caesar's Friend. Tylara understands these nuances. I don't.*

"Dangerous indeed, Heir of Caesar," he said.

Two civilian servants entered without knocking. Their status would nominally be slave, Rick supposed. The

Church disapproved of slavery, but Roman policy prohibited indiscriminate manumission. If you freed a slave you had to provide for him. By keeping him in slavery, you could at least get some work out of him, although the Church's deacons were charged with preventing cruelty and overwork, and many were honest enough in carrying out that duty. Publius tended to keep elderly retainers who had been with him a long time. They would probably be miserable if he told them their service was no longer wanted. For all his faults, Publius did have some good qualities. He was certainly loyal to his subordinates.

And of course what some considered faults, others considered a mark of pride. Publius made no more secret of his conquests than had Don Juan, and while he probably didn't have a book recording so many—Mozart's Don Juan had a thousand and three in Spain alone!— there had been enough.

*Including Gwen?* Rick wondered. *Why not?* The thought disturbed him. But really, why not? Publius was a widower and given the number of his conquests without issue, obviously sterile. For all that Les was the father of Gwen's first child and was possessive when he was on Tran, the Galactic pilot wasn't really a husband and didn't expect fidelity when he wasn't around. Publius had certainly tried to bed Gwen. He tried with everyone. And Gwen was a modern girl who enjoyed— He pushed the thought and the uneasy feeling away. *Gwen's sex life is none of my business. If she's managed an assignation with Publius, neither one of them is talking about it, and that's all that matters. But to be honest it may be the main reason I don't like him.*

"Wine?" Publius asked. "It will not be as good as what my daughter served me from your cellars, but it should serve."

"Thank you," Rick said. *I suppose I'd better take inventory. Just what do I have left?* Fortunately, weapons and medicines were in Elliot's care. Octavia couldn't requisition those as easily as his pantry and wine cellar.

"And here's Lucius," Publius said.

"Ah. Well met again, Sage," Rick said.

Lucius limped in slowly. He carried a stout staff which he gave to an attendant when he was seated. He seemed frail, but his manner was energetic.

"Well met, Caesar's Friend," he said. "You are well? And the Lady Tylara?"

"Well indeed," Rick said.

"She is none the worse for her captivity, then?"

Rick hesitated.

"No. Prince Strymon is an honorable man," Warner said.

Lucius nodded, and nodded to Warner as if seeing him for the first time.

"I had heard such. It is good to know that some of our enemies have honor." The elderly scholar sighed. "But of course you know I have come to tell you of grave matters."

"I guessed as much," Rick said.

"There are matters of immediate concern," Lucius said. "But first, know that Marselius Caesar has appointed me Principal Scholar of Rome."

"My congratulations."

"Thank you. The title is flattering, but the duties have been severe. It has been my task to winnow through the oldest records in the Roman archives, records long sealed by generations of Caesars and bishops."

"Back to the Time?"

"And beyond, to Times before the last. Lord Rick, we have good reason to believe that the lowlands around the city of Rome will be flooded, to a depth allowing ships to pass between the Empire and Drantos. Rome and the Latin provinces will be an island! Tamaerthan another! Ships will come from the south, ships bearing plague. Rome's western provinces will be isolated, victims to barbarian migrations, unreachable by land from Rome. All this and more, and what is astonishing is the speed at which it will happen. No more than a year will pass before the only communications between Rome and Drantos will be by ship! Already the roads are mud, and the low valley fields have become salt swamps!"

Rick had never seen the old man so excited. Of course he had reason to be.

"Icecaps melt," Rick said. "Glaciers flow into the sea. Sea level rises during the Time. I'd heard this, but I never knew by how much or how quickly." The Shalnuksis had told him almost nothing about their previous visits to the planet. His brief look at Tran from space had revealed extensive ice caps at both poles and extending well north and southward. Enough ice, Rick supposed, to raise the seas if melted, but there was no way to find out. Local records were all he had to go on, and few of those were reliable. Perhaps the Roman records were better.

"This castle is set in a swamp," he said. "Will it be flooded?"

"The bailey, almost certainly, but I think not the castle

itself," Lucius said. "It remains on the ancient maps. But an arm of the sea will reach far inland, perhaps to the very gates. And the caves below may flood."

"Jeez," Warner said.

Interesting that Lucius knew about the caves. That was supposed to be Yatar's secret. With this move to unify the Roman Christian Church with the worship of Yatar, there would be precious few secrets of that kind for much longer. As to flooding, it would be unlikely, Rick thought. The passage under the castle to the caves would flood, but the caves themselves were largely set in limestone hills a mile south of the castle, and were probably higher than the castle courtyard itself. But without a survey there was no way to know. Something else to do . . .

"The madweed fields," Warner said. "They're mostly above the swamps, but how far above? I sure don't know."

Rick nodded.

"And the croplands at swamp level will certainly flood. We'll have to find another base for that operation." *Which I'm doing now, but no need to tell the Romans. Still, it's another damn thing to worry about.* He'd hoped to get another ten years' crops out of this place. Without a continuous supply of madweed, the Shalnuksis wouldn't put much value on Tran. *Then what?*

"We will require a navy," Lucius said. "We have a small war fleet, but we have always relied on Nikeis to provide most of the shipping in the Great Bay, and our southern provinces provide their own navy. At Rome proper our ships are old. We think little of the sea."

"And Rome has few forests near the coasts," Publius said.

"But perhaps near what will become coasts," Lucius mused. "We would be grateful for any information your University can provide."

"Of course." *And life here goes on, unless the Shalnuksis decide to finish us off once and for all. We have to be prepared for what happens if they don't.* "Look to your early records, Scholar. On Earth, Rome was a considerable naval power," Rick continued. "So much so that the Roman navy was largely without a history once the pirates were suppressed. The Mediterranean became *mare nostrum*, and Roman fleets dominated the seas. Have you no such traditions here?"

"No," Lucius said. "And it is odd, because I have found designs for ships in the archives. Some match ships we have. Others are for larger craft than any in our present fleet. But no, we have no history of naval power."

Rick nodded.

"Neither does Drantos. Nor do we have forests near the coasts." He tried to imagine where the high water would reach. *If the stories about flooding between Rome and Drantos were true, then this might be a rise of forty or fifty feet! A lot of water.* "Except possibly here. We'll need to study maps and get some accurate measures of terrain elevations. Warner, that will be your job. You're going to invent surveying."

Warner looked thoughtful.

"If I ever get back to the University, Sir, I can set some gadgetry students to making a surveyor's transit. I think I can do that all right. Then we can send some teams out . . ."

"Do that, Mr. Warner. As a high priority job. If the seas are rising we need to know where they'll go."

"Sir."

"Indeed, I have begun mapping," Lucius said. "Drantos has few seacoast forests and no tradition of shipbuilding. Tamaerthan has few forests, but does build coastal and fishing boats, much as Rome does. The Five Kingdoms have extensive forest in the eastern provinces. They have ships, and their fleets have raided south far enough that we have fortified most of our ports. There is one place that has always been active on the seas, however. Nikeis. They have always had shipyards, and the coasts around their island city are covered with hardwood forests."

"Ah. Nominal allies of Drantos," Rick said.

"Perhaps," Publius said.

Perhaps. That word said volumes.

"You know something?"

"Their council has expelled or imprisoned all foreigners and ambassadors. Including the star lords. Shortly thereafter the city was sealed. No word comes in or out. I do not believe this bodes well for your future relations."

"Expelled? Or imprisoned? My people?" Rick slammed his fist on the table. "Why wasn't I told? We can't have this!"

"First I've heard of it, Boss," Warner said.

"Lucius?" Rick demanded.

"Gently, Friend of Caesar," Lucius said. "I have known of this only a few days, and I did not know where to find you. It is not news to be given out lightly! And we know only that Nikeis is sealed, and Romans expelled. We know nothing of your people."

"Warner."

"Sir?"

"Warner, I sent messages weeks ago asking for reports from our people in Nikeis. Have we heard anything?"

"Nothing, Sir," Warner said. "With your permission I'll ask Elliot to look into it. There's been long enough for a message to get there and back. Of course the reply might be chasing you down, since you told Bisso you wanted it personal."

Rick nodded.

"Make it so. Maybe we should have heard from Nikeis and maybe not. Would they harm ambassadors? Star lords?" he asked.

"It is unlikely, I think, but I cannot say for certain," Lucius responded. "They have long been our trading partners, effectively allies, but they keep their own counsel. They are a nation of traders, mostly, and they share little knowledge—none that they think might give them an advantage. As to this latest matter, we have no full reports. One messenger, with what he was told. We believe some of our agents were forewarned and escaped. We have heard no more about yours, but we await news."

"Clavell and Harrison were in Nikeis," Warner said. "Part of the medicine shows and the whole seagull guano experiments. I know they took their sidearms and battle rifles, but I don't remember them having any other equipment. Colonel, this could mean war."

"Yeah," Rick said. *One more bloody thing to worry about!* "But why would they do that?"

"The records show they have been a great power in the past," Publius said. "A naval power, mostly, but a great power. Perhaps they feel they can do as they like. Perhaps they believe your star weapons will not reach to their city. It is certain you have shown no inclinations to build a navy."

"And their captain left the Ottarn battlefield angry with Drantos," Warner said.

"We have heard that it was with reason," Lucius said.

"You've heard about that? Sheesh, what else have you heard?" Rick asked.

"Much," Publius said. "Much that I do not care to discuss anywhere we can be overheard. Come to dinner. There is much we must tell you."

✢ ✢ ✢

Rick had never got used to dining in the Roman manner, guests reclining on couches. Not only did it seem decadent, but it was hard to eat properly unless you encouraged one of the many retainers to feed you. Warner seemed to have no trouble with that. For a moment, Rick envied Warner's easy rapport with the serving girl he would undoubtedly meet later in the evening. Then he remembered Tylara.

*Strange to feel married again*, he thought. *But good. But good . . .*

Over dinner Warner told them about the departure of the Nikeis captain.

"And he shook the dust off his feet at us," he finished.

"Certainly a curse," Publius said. "One I've used

myself. The bishops tell me the original apostles could call fire down on people that way. Never saw that happen myself, but you never know."

Warner nodded sagely.

"What's the status of the Nikeisian Church, then?" Rick asked.

Publius looked to Lucius.

"They are accepted as Christian, but uneasily," Lucius said. "We do not share clergy, but Rome recognizes their sacraments as valid. Certainly as valid as the new Unified Church."

"You don't accept the validity of the Unified Church?" Warner asked.

"I am a scholar, perhaps a philosopher," Lucius said. "But certainly not a theologian. If Polycarp can accept the new and unified religion, I will certainly find no quarrel with it. There is much to recommend it."

*He's an agnostic. Stoic, probably. Weaseling just like I am*, Rick thought.

"So the Nikeisian Church is valid. Orthodox," Warner said, and Lucius frowned.

"It is not a word we use, but I divine its meaning, and perhaps it is applicable here. Like Publius I have never seen a curse call down fire on an enemy, but if it can be done, the Nikeisian clergy might have as much power as any Roman clergy."

*Skyfire*, Rick thought. *They know it's possible, so why not as a result of a curse? Being absolutely certain that miracles can and do happen will change your religious views a whole bunch.*

"Yeah, well these weren't clergy exactly," he said aloud.

"That I know of. They were soldiers. Pretty good ones, I was told."

"Nikeis has warrior orders," Lucius said. "Their officers may be ordained."

"Maybe these were, then," Rick said. "I never asked before. I didn't see much of their fight myself, but by all accounts their company gave a good account of itself in the battle. So Nikeis is likely to be important now?"

"They have a long tradition as seafarers," Lucius said. "And a reputation for importance greater than the reality. But as you can see from the maps, they are bottled up in the Great Bay. They have holdings along the west coast of the bay. They call that Terra Firma, and there is much dispute over those. City-states, Drantos, the Five Kingdoms, the Grand Duchy, the Ganvin pirate nation—"

"Pirate nation?" Warner asked.

"As good a name for the Ganvin as any. They inhabit a chain of islands and a strip of the mainland along the northern tip of the Great Bay, and they raid the coasts for slaves. It is because of the Ganvin that Rome maintains an alliance with Nikeis."

"An expensive alliance," Publius said. "We have twice in my lifetime sent a legion to their aid against the Five Kingdoms. Legions are expensive."

Lucius nodded.

"So is a navy, Heir of Caesar. And now, I fear, we will need both in the Time ahead."

"So you've sent troops to help Nikeis," Rick said.

"Mostly to maintain their hold on the coastal forest strips. They have great need of those forests. For ships, but also for charcoal for their foundries. Nikeis has excellent foundries, as good as any in Rome. We buy from them."

"Bronze or iron?" Warner asked.

"Both, Lord Warner."

"Guns," Warner said. "May not be why they sent that company to join Ganton, but no soldier in his right mind could see Ganton's Great Guns and musketeers without realizing the significance." Warner suppressed a grin. "I'm certain the Roman officers didn't."

Lucius said nothing.

"I'd be astonished if Rome doesn't have foundries as good as any in Nikeis by now," Warner said. "Bronze and iron. And most of the students at the University know the formula for gunpowder."

Rick frowned.

"You never said anything about that—"

"It's not the kind of thing you can keep secret," Warner said defensively. "Colonel, you made barrels and barrels of the stuff! There must be four hundred craftsmen who've worked in powder mills. Hundreds more were out harvesting saltpeter from manure piles. Two squadrons of dragoons guarded sulfur mines. Charcoal is easy to make. Colonel, probably a quarter of the students at the University want to learn how to make proper gunpowder. They already know the formula. They make songs about it."

"And Roman *frumentarii* are very efficient," Rick finished. "Yeah. I've been expecting this." *Just not so soon. And I've been running around pissing on fires, no time to think about any of this. Wonder if Lucius has figured out that his new navy is going to need guns and powder and lots of both? If he hasn't, somebody has. But Lucius will certainly understand, and Marselius probably has foundries building cannon in Rome right now.*

*Which means there's no way to hide widespread technology advances from the Shalnuksis. Not with ships carrying cannons all over the planet . . . What comes after gunpowder? Smokeless powder. Strong water. Nitric acid and guncotton. And I don't know how to make them. Maybe Warner does?*

Lucius resumed his rambling account.

"The Nikeis influence to the south has been limited by the long sailing times around Rome's Latin provinces. They have leased bases along the Roman eastern coast, but we maintain Roman garrisons in those fortresses. With a water passage separating Rome and Drantos opening a direct route to the south—" He shrugged "I would expect that to make a great difference."

"Even as it is, they have factoring posts all over the south," Rick said. "We got some of our information about southern conditions from Nikeis. Shame to lose them as allies over some battlefield slight."

"What happened?"

"I never really understood it," Rick said. "I got to the battle, found out Ganton was in the thick of it rather than directing all his forces—"

Publius nodded.

"My son-in-law has always been wont to command more like a centurion than a legate. It is good for morale, but a dangerous practice."

Rick paused, expecting a remark about barbarians, but Publius said nothing more.

"But Julius Caesar himself fought in the ranks when he had to," Warner said, and Lucius nodded.

"So it is recorded. A great inspiration to the Legions."

"Yeah." Rick leapt in before they could begin a new conversation that left him out. "Anyway, I got there to find there wasn't really anyone in charge of the battle, and half our forces were standing their ground waiting to be told what to do. With Ganton holding like a rock in the center and everyone eager to pound at him it was no great trick to swing around and take the enemy from behind. Visibility was bad so we were able to surprise them. I don't know where the Nikeisian contingent was during all this. Certainly not in my force. But come the next day, they were unhappy, about the division of the spoils, and how they were used, and everything else, and they didn't even want to discuss it. Seemed a pretty trivial thing, but they shook the dust off their feet in our direction and went on their way. Now you tell me the city has imprisoned my ambassadors?"

"Imprisoned or expelled yours and everyone else's," Publius said. "And closed the city for good measure." He frowned and shook his head. "And that is all we know until more detailed reports arrive."

"All that over one regiment of troops getting shorted on the loot?" Rick said, and Publius smiled thinly.

"Friend of Caesar, I doubt much that anything done at the Ottarn had one whit to do with this. Indeed, I think it the other way. The Nikeisian commander may have been ordered to find cause to leave you and found it simpler to simulate anger than contrive a better story. Much that happened in Nikeis was done before the battle of the

Ottarn. It is difficult to determine times precisely, but we
believe a week before that battle. Perhaps longer."

*Week*, Rick thought. Rome used weeks, like most
Christian nations, so Nikeis probably did. In Drantos they
used ten-days. The seven-day week wasn't much used,
although with an increasing number converting to the new
Unified Church of Yatar and Christ they probably would
take to it. *Hard to worship on Sunday using a ten-day week.*

"They closed the city before the Ottarn battle?"

Publius nodded confirmation.

"I believe so."

Lucius was more certain.

"The time cannot be fixed exactly, but yes, I believe
these events took place shortly before that battle."

"What events? And do we know why?"

Lucius sucked his teeth.

"Possibly. Understand, Lord Rick, we had more agents
in Nikeis than you, but no great number, and few have
returned to us. But from what we discern, there was some
great discovery made in a forest on the mainland facing
the island city. There were rumors. Lights in the sky.
Great men of the city taking a ship to the mainland, while
cavalry patrols swept the area for spies. There were
rumors of strangers, a courtesan from the stars, and of a
black man. Our *frumentarii* spent freely but this was all
they could learn before all foreigners were expelled from
both the city and the neighboring Terra Firma, and the
city sealed to traffic.

"Caesar's swiftest messengers came to Rome to report,
and it was then I appreciated the importance of the
references to the rising sea." Lucius was very serious now.

"We have sent additional *frumentarii* to investigate, but there are few reports as yet. The last thing we know of internal matters in Nikeis is that they have opened the Arsenale, their great shipyard, and they are sending agents to recruit every shipbuilder they can locate. They offer wealth and status to master shipwrights, and good pay to journeymen. My agents on the mainland report they are logging great trees. They know their coming destiny, Lord Rick. The intriguing question is, how did they find it out? For certainly they did not act as if they knew prior to the lights in the sky."

Publius had been watching carefully.

"It appears this is as great a surprise to you as to us," he said.

"Indeed," Rick said.

"You will understand, we had hoped you had some explanation," Publius continued.

"No," Rick said. "I'm worried about my agents in Nikeis. They should have reported by now. But I'm as concerned as you are about lights in the sky." *Maybe more*, Rick thought. *Maybe more.* "I will have to do something about this. We cannot allow mistreatment of Drantos ambassadors. Particularly not star men! But what are we up against?"

"Jeez, Colonel," Warner said. "Shalnuksis bringing in a new force?"

"Shalnuksis," Publius said. "That is the name you give to the starfarers who brought you here."

"Yes, how did you know?"

Publius looked to Lucius.

"We learn when and where we can, Lord Rick," Lucius

said. "As needs must. In this case I believe we learned from our agents in Nikeis."

"Clavell," Warner said. "He always was a blabbermouth when he had too much wine."

"Which means Nikeis knows at least that much?" Rick asked, and Lucius nodded again.

"And more. Lord Rick, it seems to us there is great dissension among the star kings, the kings and great lords of the stars who in power are to you as you are to us. Is this so?"

*Blunt question. Sudden. No time to think, and no point in lying. I wish Tylara were here.*

"Actually," Rick said, "dissension is a mild term for it. There are factions among the stars and some hate each other. As to power, I believe they have weapons that can kill every soul on this world."

"Skyfire," Lucius said firmly.

"And worse. Much worse."

"Theomachy. Wars among the gods," Lucius said. "In such wars humans are always harmed. Even if these are no true gods."

"One thing," Warner said.

"Yes?"

"Whatever these new star lords brought—"

"It's not clear these are star lords," Rick said.

"No, Sir, but it's likely. Assume it for a moment. Whatever they brought, it's not decisive in itself. They need local assistance, why else would Nikeis open up the Arsenale and start cutting trees?"

"Good point, Mr. Warner," Rick said.

"Another thing, Sir. We're going to need ships, too. If

Nikeis is recruiting the master shipwrights who could build them for us, we need to stop that, and now."

"Just so," Rick said. "Make it so, Mr. Warner."

"Sir."

Publius stood.

"Duty Tribune!" he shouted.

A young Roman officer wearing two gold rings and gilded muscled armor came in.

"Aye, Heir of Caesar!"

"No shipwright master or journeyman is to leave Roman lands without permission from Rome," Publius said. "Send word to my father. There will be a detailed message from Scholar Lucius soon, but send messengers immediately to Rome and to the frontier posts. Have the border guards stand by for other such orders. What forces have we available here?"

"Two cohorts of cataphracts, Heir of Caesar. Two centuries of cohortes equitates."

"Have them make ready to march. We may need them shortly. Lucius, have you further orders?"

"Not at present. I will write my letter to Caesar before lunchtime tomorrow."

Publius nodded.

"Dismissed," he told the tribune.

"Aye, Caesar." The officer hurried out and Publius turned back to Rick.

"Our course is plain," he said. "We must build a navy. Romans have done that before."

"My course is plain also," Rick said. "I'll have to organize a punitive expedition to demand the return of my men."

"Your honor is no more precious to you than the honor of Rome is to Caesar," Publius said. "We will aid you. I will send those cataphracts to aid you."

"And alert our ships and marines," Lucius said. "We are not entirely without maritime resources in the Great Bay. We have a small fleet. In itself it is no threat to Nikeis, but with your star weapons it might be more formidable than they imagine. But we must know who we face."

"It would be well to know," Publius agreed. "But gods or men, we will face them like Romans."

Lucius nodded assent.

"Organize your force, Son of Caesar. Send your cohorts to Taranto. Send word to have all available ships and marines meet them there. But it would be ill advised to march against an ally on the strength of rumor. You do not know what has happened to Rome's citizens, any more than Lord Rick knows the fate of his ambassador. Prepare to march, yes, but wait until we know more. That is my advice."

"Mine too, Colonel," Warner said.

"Harrison and Clavell," Rick said. "If they were expelled, what would they do?"

"We'd know it by now," Warner said. "Clavell's a pretty good man, drunk or sober. If he could get word to you, he would."

"That was my thought," Rick said. "So we'll have to rescue them. Only we haven't got anyone to send. We'll have to go ourselves. Heir of Caesar, I ask that you tell your cohorts I will meet them in Taranto. Perhaps by then we'll know more."

# CHAPTER TEN
## LOYALTIES

Dinner was long over. Rick suppressed a yawn.

"It's been a long day for me," he said. "With your permission, I'll turn in."

They all rose. As Rick and Warner neared the door, Lucius said, "A moment, Lord Rick? I wish to show you something that will not be of interest to Lord Warner."

Rick and Warner exchanged glances, and Rick nodded.

"See you in the morning, then."

"Sir. I'll see to those orders." Warner left with an amused smile.

"I am at your bidding," Rick said.

"Please sit down." Lucius spoke urgently, his voice full of concern. "Heir of Caesar, will you speak now?"

"In a moment," Publius said. "First, your message from my father."

Lucius drew in a breath.

"There is no easy way to say this. Lord Rick, Marselius Caesar has not long to live."

*I knew it*, Rick thought. *I could see it coming. But not yet*—

"Surely the Legions will follow Publius," Rick said. "There will be no war of succession."

"We hope for none," Lucius said. "But we must be honest. Publius Son of Caesar has never been as popular as his father. There are those who would have another as Emperor."

"You know Titus Frugi, once a legate and prefect under Flaminius the Dotard," Publius said. "What will he do?"

"He will follow you," Rick said. "He has no ambitions for himself, and he is desperate that Rome have no more civil wars. He remained loyal to Flaminius until it was clear Flaminius had lost. Since then he's been loyal to your father, and he will be loyal to you."

Lucius smiled.

"You see, Heir of Caesar. And though Lord Rick does not say it, you will do well not to give Titus Frugi cause to fear your accession. He is a capable and popular general. Rome has need of men of his abilities."

Rick nodded. *But is Publius wise enough to follow that advice?*

"Many empires have fallen because the emperor was afraid of competence among his generals," he said.

"And some have been lost because the emperor was too little afraid," Publius said.

Lucius gave Rick no chance to speak.

"But Lord Rick, there are those in the Army who would have your Wanax Ganton as Caesar. What think you of that?"

"What can I say to that? He is my Wanax," Rick said.

"A Wanax who treats you as a subject, not as a friend," Publius said. "Marselius Caesar has been your friend."

Rick nodded agreement. There was a long silence.

"Are you asking for my support against Wanax Ganton?" he asked finally.

"Marselius Caesar asks that you consider it," Lucius said.

*Sheesh. No wonder they didn't want Warner listening in! This is an invitation to treason.*

"Or at the least, that you not use your troops and skills to oppose Publius," Lucius continued, and Rick nodded slowly.

"That would be an easier promise to make," he said. "Wanax Ganton has no claim on Rome."

"None beyond his acceptance by the legion commanded by Titus Frugi," Publius said sourly.

"I wasn't there, but Lord Mason assured me nothing was meant by that acclamation beyond respect for a battle hard fought and well won," Rick said. "The impetus to hail him as Imperator came from the legion, not from its primus pilus or from the legate." He paused for a moment. "And you must understand, it is not my custom to act without the advice of My Lady Tylara. Doubly so in an instance that must affect Tamaerthan."

"A wise man listens to his wife," Publius said unexpectedly. "I would that mine had lived to advise me in this time. I cannot fault you for wishing the counsel of Lady Tylara. We have all come to respect her abilities."

*And not a trace of sarcasm*, Rick thought. *I think he means it.*

"But I don't need her advice to know that I have never

doubted that Publius would be the worthy successor of Marselius Caesar," he said.

"So," Lucius said. "And even that is not my worst news. Surely all have long known that Marselius Caesar is ill. And old like me, as well."

"And your worst news?"

Lucius looked to Publius.

"I have had my own warnings from God," Publius said. "I do not expect many years as Caesar even if the succession is tranquil."

"Perhaps my physicians—"

"I appreciate the offer and I accept eagerly," Publius said. "I need not tell you of the need for discretion. This news would be welcome in many places."

Rick nodded.

"I am flattered that you entrust it to me." *But of course you'd have to tell me if you want McCleve to look at you. And just maybe it's something we can cure. VD?* That existed on Tran, although the most virulent forms of syphilis didn't seem to have traveled from Earth.

*I think we have enough antibiotics. Do we want to cure him even if we can? I'm sure we do, but I've got to discuss this with Tylara.*

"But we must prepare for all events," Lucius said. "All. And Lord Rick, while you can hardly be expected to say treason against your Wanax, from what we have heard you would not count it such a great thing for Ganton to be emperor as well."

"Yet unification of the Five Kingdoms, Drantos, and Rome under one ruler would make for a peaceful world," Rick said.

"And how possible is that?" Lucius asked. "It would take a hero out of legend to impose such a solution! The Five Kingdoms under the High Rexja have ever had their civil wars, and are about to have a war of succession. Your own County of Chelm is as powerful as any two of the Five Kingdoms, and has not always been content with the taxes imposed by Edron. Succession in Rome is never certain. And as to Tamaerthan, there is neither unity there nor any pretense of it, nor would your father-in-law willingly submit to either Drantos or Rome. Especially to a Rome with Ganton as emperor." Lucius chuckled. "'Barach gui haigh!' was, I believe, one of Mac Clallan Muir's comments when last he met with the Wanax. Hardly a shout of loyalty."

"Your sources are good," Rick said. "You must know what else transpired at that High Council."

"And more," Lucius said. "Roman *frumentarii* are well trained, and we have sent them far and wide recently. And it is clear that all is not well between you and your Wanax, nor do I believe you would rejoice to see him in a purple-bordered toga. You need not answer that."

"So what do you want me to do?" Rick demanded.

"Marselius Caesar wishes a pledge from his friend," Lucius said.

"A pledge," Rick said. "What pledge would that be?"

"Of support for his heirs," Lucius said. "For Publius, although that will not likely be needed. And for Prince Adrian and the children of Queen Octavia."

"Even against her husband?"

"If Ganton remains her husband, there may be no conflict, although the temptation of the purple has set father against son before. But if Ganton casts her aside in favor of a daughter of the Five, as well he may, then there would be new heirs. And Ganton Caesar might well prefer the new to the old."

"This seems a bit farfetched," Rick said. "Pardon me for speaking bluntly."

"I prefer blunt," Publius said. "Friend of Caesar, you and I have never been close, and I know you have said hard words about me. Yet I never heard you say I am unworthy of the purple."

"Nor have I," Rick said. "I always thought you would be your father's heir, and that you would rule long and well."

"Thank you. To rule well I can hope for. Long is in the hands of God, and He may not have given me all the time I would like. The marriage treaty provides that the firstborn son of the union of Ganton and Octavia will be educated in Rome. If I survive long enough that Prince Adrian is of age, I will adopt him and associate him in the purple. Ganton can hardly object, and the succession will be as secure as any Roman succession can be, no matter who proves to be Ganton's true heir in Drantos. But in these perilous times I cannot put purple diapers on the prince. The legions will never accept a child as emperor."

"I must think on all this," Rick said.

"You have not heard all," Lucius said. "Marselius Caesar is aware that he asks much. He is prepared to hear your requests in return. One benefit he gives freely, whether you pledge or not. Hail, Rick, Patrician and Citizen of Rome. Hail to your Lady, with the same titles. Hail to her father Drumold, Patrician and Citizen."

Patrician and Citizen. It didn't mean a lot to Rick, but Drumold would be pleased. For all the enmity between Tamaerthan and Rome, there was considerable envy as well.

"We are prepared to offer all of Drumold's clansmen the status of Friends of the Roman People. Which will confer immunity from slavers, now and perhaps forever," Publius said.

"Generous of you." Rick didn't bother to disguise the sarcasm in his voice, and Publius nodded.

"At the moment, tribute flows from Rome to Tamaerthan, and it is true Tamaerthan has bested legions in the field. It is true that led by you they may do so again and again. But you will not always be there to lead, and Rome is large, and Rome endures. Rome will last longer than you or I. So long as Marselius Caesar, or I, hold command Tamaerthan will be safe whether you are present to assist Tamaerthan or not, but the status of Friends will be a powerful argument no matter who commands."

Rick nodded.

"I appreciate that. And so will Drumold. Our thanks to Caesar."

"We have more to tell you," Lucius said. "You do not know that Wanax Ganton even now rides to the northwest."

"To Aachilos?"

"Aye."

"To seize the crown?"

"It would seem so."

"But—"

Lucius nodded.

"I know. You recently attempted to persuade him to do just that, and were rebuked." He looked down at the table. "It seems he has accepted your advice but not your aid."

*How do you know all this? But that's one question I better not ask.*

"So he may be High Rexja before he returns to his capital," Rick said. "I have to admire him. A bold course."

"Overly bold without your aid, I would say," Publius said. "It is a great thing to seek a crown, but seeking is not always attainment."

"Do we know his progress?" Rick asked.

"No. He cleverly paused at the Ottarn as if in confusion and doubt, while he gathered strength and supplies. He sent you away, the best ruse yet, convincing all he would never march north. Then when he marched out, he marched quickly. The Queen has not heard yet, although she may have known her husband's plans before he acted. But I doubt that Prince Strymon knows as yet, nor the Chancellor in Aachilos. Your Wanax has taken all by surprise, I think. We have only today heard, and our messenger foundered two horses in his haste."

"And rejecting me was part of his stratagem," Rick mused. "Well done, Ganton." *Well done indeed. And all the more reason for me to make haste in clearing out of here.* "Thank you."

"And our request? For now Caesar asks only that you do your best to protect his heirs," Lucius said. "We understand that more may not be possible. But we ask that much."

*What the hell should I do? Tylara would know. But I can't stall.*

"That much you have," Rick said. "I've always accepted Publius as heir to Marselius. I continue to do so, and I will do what is in my power to protect Prince Adrian. This I can do without any disloyalty to Wanax Ganton. Beyond that I will have to consider the matter."

"We thank you," Lucius said. "Caesar will be pleased."

"And I thank you, Lord Rick," Publius said.

"How soon will your troops be at Taranto?" Rick asked, and Publius looked thoughtful.

"I would say before you can be there," he said. "Particularly if you intend to abandon this castle and move all your holdings west."

"You do have good sources," Rick said. "All right. What about ships?"

"At least one small squadron with a quinquireme flagship will be there now," Lucius said. "I will send word that it is to be made ready, and if there is not a full complement of marines now there will be when you arrive. Messengers will go to the other ships of the Inner Sea to converge on Taranto. I take it you wish to appear formidable when you visit Nikeis."

"Appear and be," Rick said. "I'll load enough star weapons to make your quinquireme invincible, and put musketeers in one of the other ships. But I still can't figure what made Nikeis decide to shuck the alliance."

✦ ✦ ✦

Rick lay down in his bed in the alcove off his study. He was grateful to be sleeping in an actual bed, even a small one, inside and not in a field cot or worse on the ground.

*If only Tylara was next to me*, Rick thought to himself. *There is so much I need to talk to her about. Not to*

*mention I've gotten used to sharing my bed with her
again . . .*

His mind raced as he thought about all of what Publius
and Lucius had shared. *What am I missing about Nikeis?
How far will the waters really rise? Do we really need to
continue fighting the Five Kingdoms?*

Eventually exhaustion caught up with him and he
drifted off.

⁂

Rick stood on the great redoubt on the hill near Vis.
He peered into the billowing clouds of smoke created by
the burning of white phosphorus. Screams of agony and
fear came from the cloud.

What was left of a man shuffled out of it. Smoke rose
from burning phosphorus covering his body. Black burnt
flesh and clothing sloughed off, revealing bones and
internal organs. Even as his body burned and shriveled,
the figure kept walking towards Rick. Finally it looked up
at Rick. The face was mostly gone, leaving the grin of a
human skull behind. The eyes were burning coals. Rick
could feel the rage in them—rage directed at *him*. He felt
frozen in place. And then charred hands reached out.
They gripped his throat. He began to choke, unable to
breathe.

He awoke from the nightmare gasping for breath.

# PART TWO
# THE EDUCATORS

# ☞ CHAPTER ONE ☜
# SAN FRANCISCO

"Change? Spare some change?" Bart Saxon's upper lip curled in self-contempt even as he shook the two quarters and a dime that rattled in the Styrofoam cup. He'd pocketed nine dollars, mostly in quarters. It hadn't been a very good day, but it was a lot better than some had been this last year.

The November sky was dark. He shivered as a cold wind drove a light drizzle into every corner and doorway on his side of the street. The wind smelled musty, not fresh like rain at all. Momentarily the rain fell more heavily and obscured the tall column across the street in Union Square. Then it slacked off to drizzle again. It was a miserable day to be on the streets in San Francisco, but for nearly a year every day had been miserable for Bart Saxon. This one wasn't a lot worse than most. Just worse weather.

The cable cars were almost empty, and the wind and rain kept the few tourists scurrying past Saxon's doorway to their expensive hotels. Sometimes bad weather helped. Saxon had taken the corner doorway usually occupied by a younger and stronger man Saxon called Lenny after the Steinbeck character. Lenny hadn't showed up today. He didn't often come when the weather turned this nasty. Lenny had a car, or access to one. Someone drove Lenny to within a block of his regular corner on Union Square. Not today, though.

Four tourists got off the cable car. They had already turned up the collars of their overcoats. They dashed for the Hyatt.

Saxon rattled his cup.

"Change? Dollar for a place to sleep?"

The knot of tourists hurried past. It was easy for them to avoid eye contact in this weather. If you didn't get eye contact you didn't have a chance.

"Spare some change for a veteran?" Saxon wasn't a veteran, but it made a good line, and he might have been one. Too young to have been in 'Nam, and he hadn't even considered volunteering after they ended the draft.

He had the timeless but aged look of one habituated to the streets. That bothered him, sometimes, when he let anything about his present situation bother him. He hadn't been out here that long. Long enough, though. Long enough.

The tourists dashed onward. Stingy bastards.

"Got a minute?"

Saxon turned away from the futile task of watching the tourists and imagining how much they might have given him. A man was standing quite close to him, too close, within his personal space, and Saxon had never

heard or felt him coming. He was a little shorter than
Saxon's six feet. Clean shaven, at least on the upper part
of his face. The London Fog raincoat and Burberry scarf
hid everything below the chin. The brim of a London Fog
tan rain hat didn't quite hide the eyes, which were a light
brown, almost yellow, and looked vaguely Oriental.

"Change?" Saxon asked.

"You looking for work?" the man demanded. There was
a tiny accent, but nothing Saxon could identify.

"What kind of work?"

The man eyed the Styrofoam cup.

"I'll give you fifty dollars and a pint of Scotch for the
afternoon. If things go on past six I'll buy you dinner."

Saxon thought for a moment. He could sure use fifty
dollars. And whiskey, not cheap wine! But—

"What things? What kind of work?"

"Talk. Fill out some forms. Take a test."

Saxon grinned wryly.

"You from Berkeley?" This man looked old for a student.

"UCLA. We're doing a comparative study. Look, it's not
far. I'll give you twenty just to get out of the rain while we
talk about it."

Saxon felt a twinge of hunger as he contemplated what
he could do with twenty dollars, but tried to feign
indifference.

"Sure. Where to?"

"This way."

✢ ✢ ✢

The man led off at a rapid pace down Mason, then
around the corner past Lefty O'Doul's, a cafeteria and bar
where Saxon liked to eat when he had money. They

scurried past the Hilton, and into the tenderloin district. A
block past the Glide Memorial Church the man turned into
a doorway between two sex shops. He used two separate
keys to open the outer door, then led up two flights of badly
lit stairs into a dingy hall that smelled of urine. He needed
two more keys to open a door marked 3B.

The room inside was neat and freshly painted. There
was a bay window, partly hidden by soiled lace curtains.
The window was protected by iron bars. An open door to
the left led to a tiny kitchen, where he could see a
refrigerator. To the right was a bathroom, clean and white,
with what looked like a new linoleum floor. Clean towels
hung on towel bars.

There was a large couch against one wall. Across from
it was an oak veneer fiberboard computer desk holding a
Dell desktop personal computer. The logo on the front
said "Intel Inside." There was an animated *Star Trek*
screen saver on the seventeen-inch monitor screen: Mr.
Spock being gassed by a flowering plant. In the middle of
the room was a table and two wooden chairs. Another wall
held ceiling-high bookcases, with a rolling ladder attached
to a rail at a little below eye height. There was room for
an entire library, but most of the shelves were empty, no
more than a dozen books in all that shelf space. One was
a new biography of Virginia Woolf. The rest seemed to be
computer reference books.

All the furniture looked new, and clearly came from
one of the discount furniture houses that advertised in
inserts to the comic pages of the Sunday paper: sturdy,
neat in appearance, good value without big expense.

"Familiar," Saxon said. "I once had a study furnished just

like this." *Except there was a lot more clutter, and it was mine, the only room in the house that I could clutter up . . . .*

"Did you now?" the man said. He indicated one of the chairs at the table. "Coffee?"

"More books, though. I'd rather have that whiskey."

"After we talk."

Saxon nodded.

"What do I call you?"

"Dr. Kroeber will do."

"Yeah, sure."

"Problem?"

"I don't believe you. Not that it matters, call yourself anything you want."

"I'm more interested in why you don't believe me?"

"Come on. Kroeber was the best known anthropologist America ever produced. I know he had a daughter, but I never heard about sons. Anyway. You don't look like him, and you don't look like you ever had any ancestors named Kroeber." Saxon sniffed dismissively. "Maybe a coincidence, but I doubt it."

"All right. Call me Dr. Lee, then. Or George will do for that matter."

"George Lee." That name was probably as phony as the other, but maybe not. Lee might fit, provided you thought of Lee as an Oriental name. Saxon took a closer look at the man and thought he looked vaguely Oriental. Eurasian, probably. "All right, Dr. Lee, you said twenty bucks up front."

"I did say twenty, didn't I? All right, you've earned twenty. You can earn thirty more—"

"And a pint of whiskey."

"And a pint of Scotch whiskey," Lee said.

"What do I do?"

"Start with this." He sailed some papers across the table.

"Raven's Progressive Matrices," Saxon said. "An IQ test? You want me to take an IQ test?"

"Yep."

"Why?"

"What do you care? Actually, we want to get a handle on just what kind of people end up in the streets."

"People down on their luck," Saxon said reflexively.

"Right."

"Real down. You know I've taken this test before," Saxon said.

"Have you now? Any idea of how well you did?"

"No."

"Just a minute," Lee said. "Before you start, want some coffee?"

"Sure, since you're making me wait for the whiskey."

"Back in a minute." Lee went to the little kitchen.

It was still raining outside. Saxon looked at the test booklet. It was warm and dry here, and even twenty bucks was more than he usually made. Lenny did a lot better than that, but Lenny was aggressive in a way Bart Saxon never could be, although he'd tried. Saxon thought about how to drag things out past dinner time—

Assuming that Dr. George Lee would keep his word about dinner. Or about anything. Saxon hadn't seen any money. His head hurt, and he wasn't likely to do well on this stupid test, which he remembered as one of the hardest he'd ever taken. Or thought he remembered.

He'd spent the best part of a year trying to forget that he'd ever seen a college or an IQ test. Now here he was in a room with a college professor—anthro or sociology? But what the hell, at the worst he'd get a cup of coffee and be out of the wet for the afternoon, and maybe the son of a bitch would give him the fifty bucks.

"When do I start?"

George Lee came back with two cups of instant coffee.

"After you've finished this." He opened a brief case and took out a sealed bottle. "Thiamin and B-complex. Want some?"

Saxon thought that over. Why not? It might help clear his head. Thiamin was supposed to be the sobriety vitamin. Or at least B deficiency was part of a hangover. Did he want to be sober? But again, why not? There would be a bottle of Scotch later.

"Sure," he said.

Lee went to the kitchen and came back with a glass and a bottle of Évian bottled water. Fancy, Saxon thought. He opened the vitamin bottle and shook out two capsules, saluted Lee with the glass, and downed the vitamins. He handed the bottle to Lee, but Dr. Lee shook his head.

"Keep them. They may come in handy."

"Thanks." Saxon sipped at the coffee. It wasn't as good as the real coffee in Lefty O'Doul's, but it would do. Taster's Choice. Not as romantic a situation as the TV ads for Taster's Choice. He'd seen those on the TV in the Glide Memorial lounge. Outside the wind came up and rain spattered on the bay window. Saxon sipped at the coffee again.

✢ ✢ ✢

The test was harder than he remembered it. There would be a series of figures, abstract shapes, and he was supposed to guess which one would be the next in the series. Some were easy, simple alternations of circular and square shapes. More were hard. Some were damnably hard. Eventually he was done.

George Lee took the score sheets and fed them into a scanner. The PC screen flashed a couple of times. Lee cleared it before Saxon could read what it said.

"How'd I do?"

"Well enough," Lee said. "Not quite so good as you did the first time, but within the limits of test reliability—"

"Did the first time? What the hell are you talking about?" Saxon demanded. His head pounded as his pulse rose. There was a knot of fear in his stomach. "Jesus, can't you bastards leave me alone?"

"I mean, Mr. Saxon, that we have your score from UCLA," Lee said evenly. "Also your SAT, your grades, and a whole bunch of stuff about you. You'll be glad to know that you haven't managed to pickle your brain. Not enough to matter, anyway. You're still smart. Which is what I had to know before we could talk."

"What the hell is this? You from the police?"

"Hardly." Lee shook his head. "No, Mr. Saxon, not the police." He smiled without humor. "We're looking to hire someone. You've got the right qualifications, provided the booze left you enough brain cells to use your education." He tapped the score sheets. "Apparently it did."

"Hire someone? For what?" Saxon demanded.

"A teaching job."

"But—"

George Lee chuckled.

"Not around here," he said. "Someplace where they never heard of Sherry Northing. Or Bart Saxon, for that matter."

Sherry Northing. Just how much did—

"Who are you people?"

"Does it matter? Anyway, you'll find out if you need to know."

"Teaching job where?"

Lee shook his head.

"You won't have heard of it. The point is, there's this fairly primitive place that needs a science teacher. You were recommended for the job."

"Recommended by who?"

"Hector Sanchez."

"Oh. My star pupil," Saxon said. "Berkeley, then Ph.D. at Cornell—I heard he got a government job—"

"Sort of. He works for the National Academy of Sciences."

"Is that who you're with?"

"Not exactly, but we've worked with them."

"I'm surprised Hector remembers me," Saxon said.

"He does, though. Said you inspired him. Matter of fact, he said if it wasn't for you he'd probably be running drugs in the barrio. Or in prison, or dead. He remembers you well, and he sticks up for you. That's why I came looking for you, to see if you can handle this job."

"Nice of him." Part of it was true. That was during the early part of Saxon's teaching career, the second year he'd had his own classroom. Hector probably would have ended up in the gutter if Saxon hadn't taken an interest in him. It had taken months to get the confidence of a bright—hell, brilliant—barrio kid, get him to believe he could get somewhere through schoolwork, get him—

"Does he know about—"

"About Sherry Northing? I doubt it," Lee said. "I didn't until I came looking for you. Why should he?"

Saxon grimaced. It was true enough, of course. It wasn't really a big story. High school teacher drinks too much, gets seduced by politician's underage daughter, surprised *in flagrante delicto*. Disgraced. Wife leaves him, teacher loses job—it was a big enough story in Black Oaks, at the time anyway.

"No, I don't suppose it would be a big story in Washington," Saxon said. "Not an important story to anyone. Except to me." And to Ann, and Ben, but not anymore. Ben wasn't old enough to understand why Mommy couldn't stand Daddy anymore . . .

"And you don't care?" he asked. "About—"

"Not really," George Lee said. "Saxon, I'll be honest with you. It's not like there's a lot of qualified people looking for this post."

"Why not?"

"Because it's in the middle of nowhere," Lee said. "You might say the end of the world, a very primitive place. And we need somebody fast."

"We?"

"Your country," Lee said. "You'll get the details if you qualify and you want the job. No point in telling you more than you need to know. We need someone to teach science. Your students will be from the ruling class of a very primitive country. Smart but not much education,

some are illiterate even in their local language. If you take
the job, you'll have to learn that language. You'll also have
to buy a lot of equipment and get everything together.
Books, computers, you name it, if you think you'll need it,
buy it and get it packed up for a long trip. Money's not a
problem, but we need somebody fast."

"How fast?"

"If you want the job, you leave in three weeks. And
there's a lot to do first. Fact is, that's the big problem,"
Lee said. "There's just a hell of a lot to do, all kinds of stuff
to buy, damn little time, and we don't know if you can do
it all." He patted the test sheets on the table. "So. We
know you've got the brain cells. But can you stay sober
long enough to get the job done?"

"Probably not," Saxon said. "Not even sure I want to.
You promised me fifty bucks, and a pint of Scotch."

"You'll get them. Look, you take this post, once you get
there, set up shop, get started, you can have all the booze
you want, no problem. Chase skirts, too, and nobody will
worry a lot about how old they are."

"I didn't chase—"

"I don't care," Lee said. "The point is, here's another
chance, if you want it. Bright kids, some of them. Place that
respects teachers. You'll be the only science teacher around.
You can make a difference in their lives." He looked at
something Saxon couldn't see. "And if you blow it, what the
hell, they're no worse off than they were before."

"Thanks for the confidence."

"I'm talking to you, aren't I?" Lee looked Saxon in the
eye. "You haven't given me a lot of reason to have
confidence."

"Okay, I'll give you that one. So what do I have to do?"

"Stay sober for a couple of days," Lee said. "Then ask me."

"Yeah, sure—"

"Well, I'll make it easier," Lee said. "You can stay here." He took the keys out of his raincoat pocket. "There's some food in the kitchen. Here's the fifty bucks I promised. I'll be back tomorrow afternoon. If you're sober, we'll talk." He pointed to the kitchen. "The bottle of Scotch is in there."

# ⇥ CHAPTER TWO ⇤
# A BOTTLE OF SCOTCH

Saxon stared at the bottle. For months, a bottle of Scotch had represented everything he wanted out of life. Or everything he thought he wanted. Or—he looked at it again.

Why?

Well, why not? No one wanted a child-molesting drunk. Not that Sherry had been a child. She sure hadn't looked like one, and the molesting had been a fully cooperative venture. With his pants on. Hers too, although her top was off. He hadn't let her take off anything else. She wasn't a student in his school. And she'd said she was nineteen.

*And you believed her, right?*

Saxon reached towards the bottle, then shook his head.

*I don't know if I believed her or not. I sure wanted to believe her. And damn it all, I was sure she was eighteen at worst. Not fifteen!*

Jailbait. Worse than jailbait. He'd avoided jail. The DA

offered him a deal. Plead guilty to a minor sex offense. It sounded good—

But of course it made him a registered sex offender, and ended any chance he'd have of being a teacher, in California or anywhere else. And the funny part was he could probably have gotten off clean, just not plead guilty to anything, tell them he wanted a jury trial, tough it out. But he hadn't known.

*I should have gotten a good lawyer. But I didn't want a good lawyer, because dammit all, I did it, and I was a teacher, whether she was one of my students or not. That's supposed to* mean *something, and I* damned *well shouldn't have been fooling around with someone her age even if she* was *nineteen! And a good lawyer wouldn't have helped with Ann, anyway. She'd have taken Ben and left no matter what. I think she would.*

But there hadn't been a good lawyer. Sherry didn't look fifteen, but the DA's people told him how she'd be dressed for the trial, sweet sixteen, tiny dabs of makeup—what they didn't tell him was that Sherry had made it clear to the district attorney that when he put her on the stand she wouldn't look fifteen no matter how they dressed her, and she'd let the jury know she didn't *act* fifteen, in court or out, and Bart Saxon was a long way from her first conquest, and wouldn't her city councilman old man have loved that! He'd never have let it come to a trial!

But no one had told him until after the preliminary hearing where he pled guilty. His community service was cleaning trash off the Nimitz Freeway. Ann sold the house and moved east with their son, and he wasn't even sure where she was, and she didn't have to tell him since he was a registered sex offender. But if he made any money, she could have a lot of it. And Bob, good old Bob, the insurance man down the street, got a divorce and moved back east with Ann, and how long had that been—

He reached for the bottle. It felt right. He could feel the warmth of the whiskey, warm in his throat, warm in his stomach—he put the bottle back down, still unopened. Time enough for that tomorrow night. Hear what George Lee had to say. Anyone can stay sober for a day. One day. Get through the day.

✧ ✧ ✧

Lefty O'Doul's was special, a place where, so long as you had decent manners, they'd treat you with dignity. There was Oscar, once a concert musician, now living on a pension. Oscar always dressed for dinner, in a suit that was far too large for him so he pinned it in the back to make it fit a little better. And Sarah, who must have been eighty years old, a retired teacher. She lived on beans and table scraps but once a week she had just enough money to eat at Lefty's, generally on Wednesday night, when there were other teachers and a former professor, all down and out, not as far down as Saxon. But down, forgotten by everyone. People who'd been important once. Or if not important, had pulled their freight, contributed. Been good people who worked hard, and now—

The décor was old-style saloon with a cafeteria-style serving line. Nothing special, nothing fancy, a place to feel at home in. And they were polite to street people.

Wednesday was when Saxon tried to get there, if he'd saved enough and had found a place he could take a bath. He liked the company. They didn't know who he was, but they knew he'd been educated. And they wondered why he was wasting his life and education, but they never asked. Not really.

Today was Thursday, though, and no one Saxon knew was there. He told himself that it didn't really matter, and maybe it didn't, but it would have been nice to have someone to talk to. He went through the cafeteria line and took corned beef and cabbage and boiled potatoes, and a dessert. He thought about beer. One beer wouldn't do any harm. Beer was good. He wouldn't get drunk on one beer. But his decision to be sober the next day had become a determination to prove to himself that he could do it, so he had a Coke instead. The realization that he had a place to sleep, with a bathroom—there had been towels and soap and a razor and a new toothbrush—made him order coffee. He'd have no trouble sleeping, and what if he did? There was a warm, safe room, and a book—the Virginia Woolf biography looked interesting—and a small television if he wanted to watch that.

He had thought he was used to life on the streets. Beg until he had enough money to buy liquor. Drink until he didn't have to think any more. Find a place to sleep, a doorway, or maybe a mission, if he was really hungry or needed a bath. Nothing to look forward to, nothing to regret, no bills to pay. Life on the streets blended one day with the next.

Except Wednesdays, when he'd try to clean up and meet his—not exactly friends, or were they? His fellow denizens of Lefty's on a Wednesday night. Used-up intellectuals. What he might have been if he'd had a couple fewer drinks that night, and spent the next fifty years teaching. Or if he hadn't got home early three days before that night, when he drove up just in time to see Ann rush out of Bob's house, with good old Bob half-dressed in the doorway, and Ann running to get home—

She hadn't seen him. He wasn't even sure of what he'd seen, but suddenly some other things he'd seen but hadn't paid attention to had begun to make sense. Not enough sense to make accusations, nothing to be sure of—but that was reason enough to have a couple of extra drinks there at the party, and—

When he was honest with himself, he knew there'd always been a reason to have a couple of extra drinks. Work too hard. Too many students. Too many papers to grade. Always something. Not that he drank all that much. Not enough that he was drunk. Just a little too much, too often—

This wasn't getting anywhere. Maybe trying to be sober wasn't such a good idea.

He pocketed his leftover roll and butter packet out of habit, then another roll and a slice of bread someone had abandoned at the next table as he left. Outside it was still blustery. The rain had stopped, but there was a cold chill wind. It would be warm in the apartment. He hadn't noticed where the heat came from. Radiator, probably. Maybe electric. But it was warm. The memory made him walk faster.

Just past the Glide Memorial Church he heard footsteps behind him. He scurried on, walking faster, and realized that was a mistake. He was walking like someone who had something to lose. A big mistake. The way to get along was to shuffle, have nothing and be nothing.

There was someone behind him. A few steps to the door. The sex shops on either side of the door were open, maybe—

"Hey, man, got any money?"

Saxon didn't recognize the voice. He tried to ignore the man.

"Hey, bastard, I'm talking to you. You got any money? Gimme some money."

"Shit, I don't got money," Saxon said.

"Well, maybe you got some blood then?"

Saxon turned then. The man wasn't as big as Saxon. He was dressed in a long overcoat, some kind of ragged wool that might have been military surplus. He wore a dirty knit cap. One hand was held low and to his side. Saxon didn't see a knife, but in the dim light he couldn't be sure there wasn't one.

"I told you, I don't got any money," Saxon whined. Better to whine than get in a fight whether the man had a knife or not, but he felt ashamed.

"Sure you got money. I seen you before. You street shit like me. Now you come out of that place there." He pointed to the door between the sex shops. "Then I see you come out of Lefty's. Don't know who you are, but you got money. You stole it, you must've stole it. You ain't no better'n me, share up."

Saxon remembered the man. He'd been at the Glide a couple of times in the soup lines.

"I mean it, I don't want to have to hurt you, now. Don't make me do that, just gimme some of that money you got."

"I won't give you shit," Saxon said. "Get the hell out of here."

"Wrong answer, man—"

"Let be, Dickhead," someone said. "Chill it out, fat boy."

The newcomer was a big Black man named Cal. Cal Haskins, Saxon remembered. He didn't know him well, but a couple of times they'd shared the same doorway, and Haskins hadn't tried to rob him. Once Haskins had shared a cup of coffee. He was about as close to being a friend as anyone was on the streets.

Haskins used a one-handed flip to open a butterfly knife. He didn't hold it menacingly. He just held it, as if it had magically appeared in his hand.

"Cal, you leave me alone now," the man whined. "You got no cause to cut me."

"Sure, I leave you alone, you just get out of here before I stuff your sorry head up your ass," Haskins said.

"I coming back with my homeys, we fix you good."

"You just do that. That's right, just turn around and get the hell gone—" As the man turned away, Haskins kicked his ass. Not hard, more in contempt than to hurt him. And laughed. "Well," Haskins said. He laughed again and folded up the butterfly knife. "Saxon, you all right?"

"Sure. I could have handled it—"

"Sure you could." Haskins turned away.

"Or maybe I couldn't," Saxon said. "Hey, thanks. Hey, Cal, I'm sorry. Thanks, really. Want a cup of coffee?"

Haskins stopped.

"You buying?"

"Better'n that. I'll make some." Saxon fished out the keys Lee had left. "Up here. Come up and get warm."

"Warm? Coffee? Maybe that dickhead was right! You robbed a bank or something?" But he was laughing.

"Come on up and I'll tell you about it," Saxon said.

## ◈═ CHAPTER THREE ═◈
# NATION BUILDING

Haskins looked around the room and whistled. "Man, you got a pension or something?"

"No, this is a perk that comes with a job offer. Have a seat, I'll make some coffee. There's not a lot to eat—" Saxon fished one of the rolls from Lefty's out of his pocket. "But this is clean."

"Good enough. Thanks. What kind of job?"

Saxon filled the kettle and put it on the stove. As he spooned out Taster's Choice into cups he heard Haskins behind him.

"Scotch! Never mind the coffee."

"I'm not opening it," Saxon said, and Haskins frowned.

"That's kind of mean. I saved your ass."

"Yeah, and I'm grateful, but I'm not opening it."

"Hmm. Okay, it's your Scotch, you don't want to share, that's your business."

"Not that at all. I'm not opening it because if I do I'll

drink it, and then I won't get the job." Saxon came to a sudden decision. "Tell you what, you can have it when you leave. The whole bottle. But take it with you. Once it's open, I'll drink it sure as hell."

Haskins went back to the other room and sat at the table.

"Now that's right generous," he said. After a moment he stood and took his overcoat off. His old sweater underneath the coat was patched, and had dirt spots, but it wasn't filthy. "Nice and warm in here," Haskins said. "I axed you before, what kind of job? Must be something, you going to give away a whole bottle of Scotch."

"Teaching," Saxon said. "Some foreign country. Primitive place."

"Well, well," Haskins said. "I used to do that."

Saxon poured boiling water into the cups and brought them into the other room. He set a cup in front of Haskins and sat down.

"You don't believe me, do you?" Haskins asked. There was amusement in his voice.

"I didn't say that."

"You didn't have to. Hell, I wouldn't believe it myself. But I did."

"What subjects did you teach?" Saxon asked.

"Not quite like that," Haskins said. "I was a corporal, part of what the Army called a nation-building team. We taught things like village sanitation, personal hygiene, where to put the crapper." He looked away. "I should have stayed with it."

"Why didn't you?"

"Thought I didn't like the Army," Haskins said as he

returned his gaze Saxon. "Thought it was better outside. Maybe it would have been, but I got strung out."

"You have a habit?"

"Not anymore. Used to, big time."

"How'd you kick it?"

"Glide sent me to rehab. The drug part took." Haskins' eyes fixed on the bottle of Scotch still unopened on the kitchen counter. "What you going to teach?"

"Science, I guess," Saxon said. "It's what I taught in high school before I—well, before. They tell me the place is really primitive, though, so I expect I'll have to teach a lot of basics first."

"Primitive. Africa?"

"Cal, they haven't told me yet."

"What did they tell you?"

"Not a lot." Saxon explained what he knew.

"CIA," Haskins said, when he finished.

"Huh?"

"Has to be, man. Think about it. They know who you are, all about you. They going to hire you, give you money to buy equipment, ship you out in three weeks? Has to be CIA. State Department, anything else, they'd be two years in red tape hiring somebody, another year in buying equipment. Military wouldn't be recruiting people off the streets to begin with. Has to be the Company." Haskins drained his cup. "We worked with them CIA boys in Zaire. Bet that's where this is, Central Africa somewhere. Lots of primitive places there. Has to be Africa."

"Well, it could be."

"Wonder if they need anybody else," Haskins mused.

"Hey—lay off. You'll queer it for me."

"How? They tell you to keep this a secret?"

"No—"

"Then they don't give a shit," Haskins said. "The Company likes things secret, but if they're really worried about it they'll tell you big time, probably watch you too."

"So what are you planning on doing?" Saxon asked.

"Same as you, man. Wait here, leave that bottle sitting there on the counter, and talk to the man when he shows up." Haskins voice dropped. "Prob'ly nothing comes of it, but can't do no harm to ask him about it."

"Ask about what?"

"Goin' with you, man. They need you to teach science, you going to need somebody to teach scut work, else you going to spend all your time teaching about digging wells upstream from the crapper! Man, I been there, I know! Saxon you don't know nothing about how bad it gets, some of those back-ass places, but I do. I've been there. You let me talk to that Dr. Lee."

"Why do you want to do that?" Saxon asked, and Haskins shook his head.

"Saxon, that was the best time of my life! I was doing something. Not shooting people, not shooting up, doing something. Little kids following me around like I was a hero. I was tired as hell, all the time wore out, but I haven't felt that good since. Come on, man, you got to give me a chance!"

"Chance, sure, but—" The one thing you didn't do on the streets was ask why someone was there. They might tell you—many were eager to tell you, or at least tell you a story—but you didn't ask. Better to pick a man's pocket than try to get into his head without invitation. Saxon wondered if he'd made up that phrase or one of the counselors at Glide had said it. But this time was different!

"You never had any other chances?"

Haskins looked at him hard.

"Oh, yeah, man, I had lots of chances. Blew every damn one of them. For a while I told myself the VA was going to put things right for me. Even got me a lawyer, he's still working on it. Then the Glide. And Social Welfare. Always somebody owed me, always looking to collect what I was owed. Nothing worked."

"Never got a break," Saxon said, and Haskins' face tightened.

"Yeah, that's what I told myself, but hell, Bart, I got breaks. Breaks don't do junkies no good. Glide did that much for me, I got rid of the goddam habit. And I knew I'd get a break once I kicked the habit. Well, this looks like it."

✢ ✢ ✢

The bedroom had probably been a closet at one time. The bed was far too small for two people, and the couch was way short for Haskins.

"I'm good on the floor," Haskins said. He found an area near the steam radiator under the window in the main room. "Good right here. Warm."

Saxon worried about that. What was to keep Haskins from taking the computer, anything else, while Saxon was asleep? *And that's stupid, Saxon thought. If he wanted to he could knock me in the head anytime.* But what if Dr. Lee got angry, called off the whole deal because Saxon couldn't keep his mouth shut, had to brag to a friend, not even a friend, a guy he'd met on the street?

*But Cal wants the job more than I do! And if that blows it, well, I'm no worse off than I was this morning. Better, really. I've got a friend now. Sort of. Practically almost.*

✛ ✛ ✛

Haskins was sitting at the table with a cup of coffee when Saxon woke up. The bottle of Scotch was on the kitchen counter, still unopened. Haskins looked cleaner.

"Morning. I'd have got you a newspaper, but I don't have the keys to get back in."

"Newspaper?"

"Man going to interview you, he's going to want to see if you take some interest in your surroundings," Haskins said.

"Sounds reasonable, but how do you know?"

"Told you, I worked with the Company people before. They're big on shrinks. Betcha anything this Dr. Lee is a shrink himself."

"Well, he could be—"

"Lend me the front keys, and a couple of bucks. I'll get the papers and something to eat. I'll be back by the time you get cleaned up."

Saxon hesitated for a moment then laughed at himself. If Haskins wanted to steal from him, he had only to take out that butterfly knife. Saxon took a five-dollar bill from the change he'd got at Lefty's, and laid it and the keys on the table.

✛ ✛ ✛

The headlines were about how Boris Yeltsin was able to get the backing of the Russian military and end the recent putsch against him. The article said that, and the withdrawal of Russian troops from Poland, officially signaled the end of the Russian Empire, which struck Bart as about damned time, given the fact that the Soviet Union had officially ended two years before. There was an article about China conducting a nuclear test, ending what was supposed to be a universal moratorium, and one about the boom in Silicon Valley and a program called Mosaic that allowed people to access some sort of web that connected computers together.

Bart was actually a little surprised how none of it was interesting to him, after so long on the street.

✤ ✤ ✤

George Lee let himself in at two. He nodded greeting to Saxon, then frowned at Haskins.

"How much does he know?" he asked.

"Pretty well what I do," Saxon said. "Something wrong with that?"

"Maybe not. Who are you?"

"Cal Haskins."

"Mind giving me your prints?"

"Naw, I expected that," Haskins said. "Where we have to go?"

"I can do it here." Lee opened his briefcase and took out a small box that he plugged into a port on the desk computer. He lifted a folded down antenna. "Here, you know the drill."

He rolled Haskins' fingers one by one on the transparent plate of the scanner, then sat at the computer and typed rapidly.

"Calvin Haskins," he read a moment later. "Former Corporal, Adjutant General Corps, US Army. Honorable discharge. No known profession. No visible means of support. Nine arrests, one conviction for breaking and entering, sentenced to time served and probation. Three arrests for possession, charges dropped when you entered rehab. Completed rehab four weeks ago."

"That's me," Haskins said. He hesitated. "They left out a couple. I copped a plea to petty theft in Los Angeles, but I didn't serve any time. They booted me, told me to get out of town and never come back. Same thing, sort of, happened in Bakersfield."

"So what are you doing here?" Lee demanded.

"That thing tell you what I did in the Army?"

"Military government. I could probably find more, but why don't you tell me?"

Haskins explained.

"Nation building, they called it," he said when he was done. "I liked doing it, Dr. Lee, I surely did."

Lee eyed him suspiciously.

"Sure you want this? Did Bart tell you he'll be going to a primitive place?"

"No more primitive than parts of the Tenderloin," Haskins said. "What the hell good am I doing now?"

"Good question," Lee said. He gestured towards the fat San Francisco newspaper on the table. "Lot of jobs in there."

"Not so many for me," Haskins said. "Maybe I can be a fry cook. Done that. Done a lot of things. Wash dishes. Done that. Gardening? I liked gardening, but it's harder to find work. Too many Chicanos, Japs, everyone knows about them. How's a Black man gonna find that kind of work around here? Used to work in a nursery. Done a little farm work. None of that around here either." He shrugged. "One of these days maybe I'll go back to Texas. Better chance there. Show me in there something for a Black man down on his luck in San Francisco."

"You tell the tale well," Lee said, and Haskins grinned.

"You know I do. Mostly I don't got a job because I don't want one." Haskins' grin faded, his eyes widened and his nostrils flared. "But I can't stay here. If I stay too long I'll be hooked again. Somebody'll find me dead with a needle in my arm. Them shrinks at the Glide say the only way I'm gonna stay clean is to care about something, something bigger'n myself. The Army gave that to me, I was just too bull headed to see it."

"Do you understand that if you accept this job you cannot leave until we allow it, and that might be a long time?"

"Sure, I figured that."

Lee frowned, then nodded.

"All right. We can use some help, and we don't get many volunteers. One thing. Don't sign on with the notion of ripping us off. We'd really resent that, and it's not worth it. Work with us, help us get all the gear assembled, and if you decide at the last minute not to go, I'll pay you more than you're likely to get for anything you can steal—and you won't have to look over your shoulder for the next year, either."

"Year."

"Or more. Unless you run a long way from here," Lee said. "And we won't ever forget, even if we're not actively looking. You turn up on our screens, we'll squash you."

Haskins grinned knowingly.

"I guess I worked with you guys before," he said. "I know better'n to cross you."

"Who do you think we are?"

"You're the Company," Haskins said.

Lee didn't say anything.

"So just what does this job pay?" Saxon asked.

"Why do you care?" Lee demanded.

"Good point. Maybe I just want to keep score." He hesitated. "Mostly because my ex-wife is entitled to half. For child support."

"You're not going to be anywhere subject to the jurisdiction of US courts," Lee said dryly.

"Maybe not, but I still have obligations to my kid."

"Commendable. Well, your salary would be seventy thousand dollars a year," Lee said. "If we were paying you directly in the United States. We won't be." He looked thoughtful for a moment. "We'll send half that to Mrs. Anderson. The other half will be paid into an offshore bank account you can draw on. Needless to say, you won't be subject to US taxes. We'll also pay you the equivalent of thirty thousand in locally acceptable currency. That's the equivalent of a fortune there."

"And me?" Haskins asked.

"Hadn't thought about it," Lee said.

"Half what he's getting?"

Lee laughed.

"Well, what, then?"

"Thirty thousand local," Lee said. "Still a small fortune, there. I may as well be blunt, there's a certain degree of difficulty in setting up bank accounts. We thought Mr. Saxon might want some means of sending money to his child, so we already took steps to accomplish that. We hadn't counted on you."

"And I ain't in much of a bargaining position," Haskins said. "Okay, thirty grand and saving's up to me. But no taxes."

"That's the deal."

"Done," Haskins said. "Walking around money here? For outfitting?"

"We'll outfit both of you. All right?" Lee looked from Haskins to Saxon and back, and nodded satisfaction. "That's settled. Let's go, then."

"Go?" Saxon asked.

"Go. As I told you, there's a lot of gear to buy. You would be far too conspicuous bringing expensive computer equipment here, not to mention the security problems. You'll work out of Silicon Valley." Lee chuckled. "Where everyone buys computer equipment. If anyone pays attention to you at all, they'll think you're another startup company. Ready to go?"

Saxon and Haskins exchanged glances.

"Sure," Saxon said. "We haven't lost anything here."

"We'll take the computer," Lee said. "The van's downstairs. Get anything else you want. We won't be coming back here."

They took a bottle of milk from the refrigerator, but left the bottle of Scotch on the kitchen counter. If Lee noticed that he didn't say anything.

## ⊰⊱ CHAPTER FOUR ⊰⊱
# NUCLEAR PHYSICS

They drove to San Jose. Not far from the freeway was a major street that had been upper middle class once, gone downhill, and was in the process of regentrification. They turned into a side street of large houses, some large enough to have been called mansions in their prime. About half the houses on the block seemed to be residential. The other half had signs identifying them as commercial offices, but they still looked like houses. Lee parked the Dodge van in the driveway of a two-story house that sported the sign UNIVERSE SOFTWARE AND COMMUNICATIONS.

"This is it," Lee said. He led them up on the porch. Before he could unlock the door, it opened. "And now it's time to meet the third member of your team."

She was small and wiry, vaguely Italian in appearance with brown eyes, dark hair, and small features except for a Romanesque nose too large for the rest of her face. With a smaller nose she might have been beautiful, Saxon thought, but even with the nose she was pretty enough. She wore tan trousers and shirt, both neatly pressed, and had a radio and baton in her wide, black equipment belt. A badge said SECURITY OFFICER, and the nametag above her shirt pocket said SANDORI.

"Lorraine Sandori," Lee said. "We usually call her 'Spirit.' Bart Saxon, meet Spirit. And Cal Haskins."

"Which one's the boss?" Sandori asked. There might or might not have been a smile, and Haskins chuckled.

"Well it sure ain't me. Good to meet you, Officer. I think we met before."

Sandori nodded.

"Where?" Dr. Lee asked.

"Tenderloin," Sandori said. "I rousted him for hustling tourists. One of the crackdowns." She turned to Saxon. "I've seen you before, too. Same places."

Saxon nodded.

"Never busted you, though. So now you're the boss."

Saxon thought about that for a moment.

"If he says I am."

"Okay, that's settled then," Sandori said. This time she did grin. "Gentlemen, may I show you to your rooms?"

✜ ✜ ✜

They each had a room on the second floor. Saxon's was sparsely furnished with a bed, dresser, table, and chair. Haskins' room was similar. All the furniture was used, some very much so, as if this had been a rooming house before Lee rented it. Saxon's room had a private bathroom attached. There was another down the hall, and a third in the tiny servant's suite Sandori had claimed. There were clean towels in the bathroom, and someone had made the beds with clean sheets.

"Housekeeping service comes for two hours every other day," Lee explained. "They get here at eleven sharp. Rooms all right?"

"Sure," Saxon said.

"Good. We'll get started downstairs. You can have ten minutes to unpack."

Saxon grinned to himself. He didn't need ten minutes. He was wearing everything he owned, and so was Haskins.

He tried to remember what he'd seen in the papers about Officer Lorraine Sandori. He didn't often read the papers, but sometimes, so he would have something to talk about Wednesday evenings at Lefty's. It had been something involving a shooting, a gang member with friends in the Mayor's office. Black kid? Saxon couldn't remember. Young kid, sixteen maybe, carrying a gun. There hadn't been any question about the shooting being justified, but there'd been demonstrations even so, as well as threats from the other gang members, promises of retaliation against the whole police department. Some cops complained that their lives weren't safe with her on the force. The Mayor had taken Officer Sandori off the streets, put her in some desk job. It hadn't been all that long ago, but he couldn't remember any more. *Maybe she resigned*, he thought. *I can see how she would. Quit and get a job as security.*

Security for who? CIA? Haskins was sure of it.

There was a knock on his door.

"Time to get started," Sandori said through the door.

✤ ✤ ✤

The old living room was set up as an office, with a computer, two telephones, mostly empty bookcases, and tables with nothing on them. The dining room was furnished with a big formal dining table, shield-backed chairs, and varnished wood sideboards. All the furniture was scarred and battered, but it had been expensive once.

The meeting was in the dining room. Sandori had made coffee in the kitchen. She brought it out and set it on the sideboard, poured herself a cup, and sat down at the table.

Saxon grinned to himself. *She'll make coffee but she's damned if she'll serve it. Okay by me, but Lee doesn't look all that happy about it.*

George Lee waited until Haskins and Saxon had poured their own coffee, then went to the kitchen for a glass of water. He came back to sit at the head of the long table and looked at his watch.

"Four. A little late to get anything done with the electronics places, so we'll start early tomorrow. Tonight after dinner we'll go to Sports Chalet and get you three some new clothes, outdoors gear. Do you have questions?"

"A million of them," Saxon said. "But I'm not sure where to begin. We're going to need stuff, some expensive."

"Let me worry about the expense."

"Sure. But I thought about what I need while we were driving down. There's a lot."

"I know. There are limits, but money isn't our major worry," Lee said. "Shipping is, both volume and weight. I'll have some cargo containers delivered. All your stuff will have to go in them. Two, I think. Three at the most. We'll pack them here."

"I can help with outfitting," Haskins said. "Tell me the climate, I'll get us gear for it."

Lee nodded.

"Glad to hear it. Climate varies. Wet, usually hot, but it can get cold in the mountains."

"Mountains," Haskins said. "Snow?"

"There can be snow."

"Hmm. Now where in Africa—"

"I never said it was Africa," Lee said. "Just think tropical shorelines and high mountains with snow."

"Not too many places like that," Haskins said.

"Mosquito nets? Snakes? Scorpions?" Sandori asked. She wasn't laughing.

"Probably not," George Lee said. "But I never thought about it. I'll have to ask. You keep thinking that way, think about what you'll need."

"I'm not much for the rugged outdoors," Saxon said.

"That's why we brought Ms. Sandori aboard," Lee said. "And Mr. Haskins. Let them worry about that aspect."

"I pretty well have to," Saxon said. He sat in thought for a moment, rubbing his chin, then refocused on Lee.

"Okay. So we're looking at some tight weight and volume limits. Laptop computers, then. Cost more but they're smaller, use less power—"

"By all means."

*Inscrutable Chinee*, Saxon thought. *Well, I'm not sure he's Chinese, but he's inscrutable enough*.

"What about power?"

"There isn't any," Lee said.

"None? Can we at least assume petroleum supplies?"

Lee chuckled.

"Assume nothing. You can take some diesel fuel with you, but not enough to operate beyond a few months. There's oil in the ground, even some bubbling oil pools, but all the refineries have been blown up."

"Blown up. You mean like in a war. Guerrilla action?" Sandori asked.

"Not precisely," Lee said. "That war's long over. But look, the place is primitive. I can't promise you peace and tranquility. There will certainly be bandits, and hell, the government's no better than it should be."

No better than it should be, Saxon thought. The phrase was mildly jarring. Why would a Chinese-American sociologist be using an English lower-middle-class expression? Another question to be answered someday.

"Maybe this is too dangerous," he said.

"Chicken?" Sandori asked, and Haskins chuckled.

"More dangerous than the streets here, man?" He laughed again.

"All right," Saxon said. "The point is made." He turned back to Lee. "But without oil, kerosene, something, we can't run a diesel generator. You already said there's no reliable electric power. What do we run the computers on?"

"Computers don't use much juice." Lee waved dismissively. "Get solar cells and batteries."

"Expensive," Saxon said.

"Labor's cheap there," Sandori said. "Right?"

Lee nodded.

"Man-powered generators, then," she said.

"Yeah!" Haskins said. "I've used those. You need a bicycle to do it right, though. And we take the diesel generator in case there's kerosene."

"You might be able to distill kerosene from sludge oil," Lee said. "Whether it would run a diesel generator I don't know. But in any event manpower and solar cells will do. With batteries. And a bicycle generator, they use those in Vietnam. I'll get all that in the budget. Spirit, you can make some calls about solar-cell suppliers. And windmills. Do they make windmills that would power a computer? How big are they? Find out."

"Now?"

"Sure, now," Lee said. "Look, people, time's short and there's a lot of work to do, and talking about it gets none of it done! You've got an hour before closing time. Use it."

"Okay."

"And tonight, all of you, make lists. What you need. Survival gear. Clothes, toothbrushes—"

"Spare eyeglasses," Haskins said. He looked significantly at Saxon's bifocals. "Captain broke his glasses once, it was two weeks getting new ones."

"It'll be more than two weeks replacing them where we're going," Lee said. "Right. Make a note, get to one of those cut-rate places and have them make you five pairs. Which reminds me. Dental work. Spirit's already started. Bart, we have appointments for you with a local dentist. We'll work Cal in, too. We want to make sure you won't have any dental emergencies."

"I got good teeth," Haskins said. He grinned. "Won't hurt to get them looked at, though. Hey, I like this, it's like the Army."

"Five pairs of glasses," Saxon said. He scribbled on loose-leaf paper. "Speaking of notes, there are some great new electronic gadgets. Make notes with a stylus. Talk to computers and everything."

"You may have all the toys you like, Mr. Saxon. Well, within reason. Particularly if they are small and light and don't use much electric power."

"Good."

"You'll also take books," Lee said. "Textbooks and reference books. Presume the power fails and you have no access to your computers. Assume you will not have access to libraries or book stores, and that the books you take with you may be the only ones you'll ever have."

Saxon looked at him quizzically.

"Just how remote is this place?" he asked, and noticed that Sandori had a thin, knowing smile. Did she know something he didn't?

"It is primitive and remote and communications are difficult," Lee said. "What's the most remote community you can imagine?"

"Upland New Guinea," Saxon said. "Barring that there's no Lost City in the Amazon Basin. Wasn't there some anthropologist killed looking for that? Sometime in this century, at that."

"I don't recall, but you will not go wrong thinking that way," Lee said. "Remote, and both communications and transportation depend on factors we don't always control. Plan for long periods without much contact with civilization."

"Medical support?" Haskins asked. "We'll have that, won't we?"

"You should," Lee said carefully. "But once again, you'll be better off if prepared for minimal support."

"So we take medical manuals. Prescription drugs? Morphine?" Saxon asked.

"Make a list. I'll see what I can do," Lee said. "Medical and surgical manuals, yes."

"Surgical?" Saxon said.

Haskins laughed.

"Do it yourself brain surgery. Be sure to have a good handbook," he said, but Lee wasn't smiling.

"It's happened, you know," he said. "Anything else?"

"Weapons," Haskins said. "I'm supposing you'll have some military units along with us, but do we need personal weapons? 'Cause if we do, with my record, somebody's going to have to buy them for me. Maybe for Mr. Saxon, too."

"Spirit will take care of that," Lee said. "Do you have preferences, Mr. Haskins?"

"I like the old Government Model .45 just fine," Haskins said. "But I expect Saxon would rather have the Beretta nine-millimeter, and I could live with that just to keep the ammunition supplies simple." He grimaced. "Comes to rifles, I'm no great hand with a long gun anyway. Know my way around 'em, but not my thing. Never had a preference, anyway. Army standard is fine by me."

"I think we already have H&K rifles," Lee said. "The G3 in seven-point-six-two-millimeter NATO standard, I believe."

"They'll do. What kind of troops will be with us, anyway?"

"I don't know," Lee said. "But we're not sending you there to fight. You'll be there to teach."

"Fine by me," Haskins said.

Saxon nodded. *Fine by me too*.

❖ ❖ ❖

Saxon unpacked the shopping bags and put his new clothes carefully away in the dresser and closet. There was another box that would go directly into the shipping containers, but he still had plenty of new stuff to wear. It was chosen for function rather than style, although the bush jacket was fashionable enough. It was all expensive, too, Gore-Tex mountain parka, Tilley adventure-cloth pants and shirt and hat, thermal underwear, photographer's vest. All very natty.

Lee hadn't seemed to worry about how much he put on his platinum American Express card. It was all first class, and anything Saxon or Haskins thought they might need had been bought without question, often with spares.

"Weight and volume," Lee had said, so they bought most of their personal equipment from the backpacker section of the store.

Bart Saxon got comfortable in the easy chair and turned on the reading light. He opened a book he had picked up, James Burke's *The Day the Universe Changed*, and began to read. It felt good to be warm and dry and clean, well fed, with a place to sleep; but mostly it felt good to be an intellectual again. Burke's writing was a bit wordy and tedious but made an interesting point about how a change in knowledge dramatically altered human understanding of themselves and the world around . . .

❖ ❖ ❖

Saxon closed the heavy steel doors of the cargo

container with a slam and applied the big padlock. There was a certain finality about locking it up. Three weeks of work, and they were done.

His jaw hurt. They'd found half a dozen cavities, which shouldn't have been a big surprise given the way he'd been treating himself. Now they were all fixed, and he had new toothbrushes, one an electronic thing that ran on rechargeable batteries and did sonic cleaning so he wouldn't get gum disease. They all had them, as well as the usual variety. Each had a backpack of personal gear. Toothbrushes, binoculars, personal radios, eyeglasses, camping equipment, flashlights, guns, all packed into one of the cargo containers. Repair kits for every damned thing, like they were going to the Moon.

Otherwise the big steel containers were jammed full with everything Saxon thought he'd need to teach science to "smart but primitive future leaders." He had laptop computers, batteries, solar cells, books, and hundreds of CD-ROMs each containing the equivalent of a dozen and more books. There was an *Encyclopedia Britannica* as well as several smaller and less complete encyclopedias. These were both in print and on CD-ROM. Another set of CD-ROMs held the classic eleventh-edition *Britannica*; then he'd found a printed copy in a used book store in Silicon Valley and bought that as well. It was bulky, but worth it. That was when they'd decided there would be three containers.

The number of books he could carry was limited, but CD-ROMs were compact, and he had a number of readers. They ought to last a while if he took care of them. He hoped they would, anyway; and on CD-ROM he had nearly every classic of English literature, plus dozens of other literary works in languages Saxon didn't know. Math and science disks, textbooks, illustrated lectures, science demonstrations, Burke's *Connections*, all on CD-ROM. There were also copies of papers like Einstein's that had once changed the world. Engineering texts, the Feynman lectures on freshman physics, the complete Loompanics catalog of "primitive living" titles, five mathematics simulation programs including both Macsyma and Mathematica, computer design programs with expensive math and physics add-ons, a program that claimed to be a complete chemistry lab simulator and another that simulated electronics breadboards. He was short of student laboratory equipment, but there was a pretty complete chemistry research lab with reagents, and five excellent microscopes from small compound wide angle to an extremely powerful microbiology scope.

There was a good telescope, and mirror blanks for making an even larger one. A small machine shop that fitted into a large sample case. All told, he was better equipped than he'd been in the school in Blackhawk. Electric power would be a problem, but they had both manual and diesel generators, and a knockdown windmill, as well as the solar cell collectors. Rechargeable batteries were both heavy and bulky and there weren't enough of them, but he had as many as Lee would allow him. There might not be enough power for a machine shop, but there would sure be enough for his laptop computers.

Saxon waited until Haskins had gone inside, then stopped George Lee on the back porch of the big San Jose house.

"You have to know that a lot of that stuff is over my head," he said. "Look, I taught high school science. I know math, and I could teach college freshman chemistry and physics, but I can't even read Einstein's original papers on relativity! I sure can't teach that!"

"You don't have to."

"Then why do we have all that advanced stuff?" Saxon gestured towards the cargo containers. He'd concentrated on buying equipment and books and software for teaching elementary science, and had been astonished when the higher-level programs began arriving by UPS and Federal Express, first a trickle, then a flood of them, all ordered by George Lee from catalogs he'd gotten by answering ads in *Scientific American* and *Science Digest*.

"Does it hurt to have the information along?" Lee demanded.

"No—"

"Is there anything you need that we're leaving behind to make room for it?"

"No. I guess. I mean we could use more student computers."

"You've got a dozen. That's more than you asked for."

"I hadn't thought it through. We need more. Maybe some of those new digital cameras they're marketing. More laptops . . . "

"All right, how many more laptops do you want?" Lee asked.

"Maybe another dozen? With built-in CD-ROM readers."

"Let's go get them. It'll be a squeeze but we'll get them in."

The salesman at Fry's would be very happy indeed.

"Now?"

"Why not?" Lee asked. "And anything else you need. We're short on time in case you don't remember. Now what else?"

"How about those LCD projectors? And spare copies of some of the CD-ROMs."

"Good. I already put in some spare copies of the ones I thought were most critical. I also threw in a few crates of books. Just in case your power systems don't work."

"Thanks. I mean, there's got to be more I didn't think of, but—"

"Better think harder, then. We'll be leaving soon enough, and it'll be a bit late then. If you don't have it going in, you may never get it. Let me make that clear. If you don't take it with you, you very likely will never have it. So think now."

"All right, I'll give you another list in the morning, but I still can't teach nuclear physics!"

"No one is asking you to teach nuclear physics," Lee said. He seemed very serious.

# ✦═ CHAPTER FIVE ═✦
# POLICE INSPECTOR

It was dusk at the old airstrip somewhere in the hills east of Hollister and west of the San Joaquin Valley. They'd finished their shopping and packing the day before, and slept in until 9:30. At noon trucks had pulled into the driveway of the San Jose house, and work crews had used a small crane to set the cargo containers into the truck beds. That took longer than expected, but eventually the trucks drove away, and Lee hustled Saxon and Haskins and Sandori out of the old house and into the Dodge van.

"Time," he'd said.

They'd driven in silence through the San Jose Valley, stopped at the Round Table in Hollister for pizza. After that they drove south and east of Pinnacles and off into the interior of San Benito County. Now they stood in the clapboard operations building of an airfield that didn't seem to have a control tower or lights or even paved runways. A couple of small aircraft were parked nearby.

Neither looked as if it had flown for years, but the operations shack was attached to a surprisingly large hangar. The hangar was completely closed up, the windows painted over with silvery paint. It seemed far too big for this tiny airstrip. The only other buildings in sight were a farmhouse and barn a mile away on the ridge above the airstrip's valley.

"Why do I get the feeling you aren't telling us everything?" Saxon demanded, and Lee gave him a thin smile.

"Probably because it's true. I've admitted there are things I can't talk about until you're firmly committed to the project and on your way. Last chance, Bart. Spirit. Cal. You can walk out now, take your money—we'll make it four thousand dollars each—and you'll never hear from us again. Otherwise, let's go."

"I'm less worried about the mystery than why there is a mystery," Sandori said, and Lee smiled again.

"If I told you much more, you might identify the place, and that's what our principals can't allow if you're not coming."

"Contras," Haskins said. "Couple of friends tried to get me off to fightin' for the Contras when that was still going on. This is something like that. Right?"

"Close enough," Lee said.

"Are we overthrowing or defending?" Saxon asked, and Lee looked thoughtful.

"A good question," he said after a moment. "Both."

"Can't be both," Haskins said.

"Sure it can," Lee said. "You're to work with the existing government, but what you're doing is going to transform the place, whether they like it or not. There's no way you can bring science and technology to a place like this without turning the whole place upside down. So—both."

"I may like that part," Sandori said.

She wore a print cotton dress, only the second time Saxon had seen her in skirts. Her legs looked sturdy, well-muscled. Well shaved too, he noticed, and was a bit surprised. In three weeks he'd learned very little about her beyond her militant championship of women's rights.

"You may well like that part," George Lee said. "God knows the women can use some education."

"Not just where we're going." Her voice was firm.

"All right, not just there," Lee said. "But it's there you can make a difference. I never saw a place more in need of Women's Liberation. And it's time to decide. Bart. Coming or going?"

"Let's get the guarantees straight," Saxon said. He looked around the operations office. It seemed bare of schedules and papers and the kind of clutter he'd expect. It was clear this airstrip didn't get much business. And what business it did get might not be on the record...

"When do we get home?"

Lee shook his head. "All I can promise is that you'll be at least six years on—over there. At least six years. After that we can negotiate, depending on what you've accomplished. By then you'll have a sizable international bank account in hard currency. More important will be what you've done for yourself locally. You'll know the language, have important positions. In local terms, you'll be rich."

"What does rich mean?" Sandori demanded.

"As we told you. The equivalent of millionaires. With respect from the locals if you've done your jobs."

"What's this equivalent?" Haskins demanded.

"Depends on the currency, of course," Lee said. "The per capita income there is under a hundred bucks a year. Look, did we stint on your budget up to now? Have we broken our word to you in any way?"

"No—"

"We bought you all the equipment you wanted, and some you didn't ask for. And now it's decision time. Bart. Coming with us or going back to the streets?"

"I wouldn't be going back to the streets," Saxon said. "Sober they don't look so good. Not sure what I could do, anyway. Okay, I'm coming. When do we leave?"

"In about ten minutes. Cal?"

"I'll stick with Bart," the Black man said. He straightened noticeably. "Sure."

"Ms. Sandori?"

"Spirit. I'm coming."

"Good. Glad to have you aboard, Spirit. This way—"

There were two uniformed men and a metal detector in the next room. The uniforms were similar to the ones they'd provided Sandori, khaki with private security patches, but they had holstered pistols as well as batons. Lee gestured towards the metal detector.

Sandori stopped, frowned, and produced a Glock pistol from her handbag. Then she hesitated a moment and drew a Beretta from somewhere under her skirt. "What do I do with these?"

"In here." Lee waved and one of the uniformed

guards took a metal camera case from under the counter. It had foam rubber inserts. "You'll get them back," he told her.

She put the pistols in the case and Haskins shrugged and took out a butterfly knife and a Beretta. "These go in there too?"

"Yes," Lee said. "Bart?"

"I don't have any weapons."

"All right, this way." He indicated the door to the hangar.

Saxon noticed that Lee had not gone through the metal detector. He saw Haskins and Sandori exchange looks which told him they'd noticed as well.

✢ ✢ ✢

"What kind of airplane is that?" Haskins demanded. He looked closer. "Jesus Christ. It's—"

"A flying saucer," Sandori said quietly. "I don't believe in flying saucers."

"I would be much disappointed if you did," Dr. Lee said. "We've certainly taken enough trouble to discredit any stories about them."

"But this is one," Saxon said. He studied the dark gray craft that nearly filled the large hangar. It was big, probably larger than a 747 without wings, but that was hard to determine in the dim light. There was little to give size-reference data. It was just—big.

It wasn't really a saucer at all. It was flat on the bottom, and long, an ovoid shape like a football sliced lengthwise below the center line, then slightly flared at the bottom. There weren't any recognizable features. Bulges and distortions in the hull seemed randomly placed, and none of it made any sense. It looked vaguely menacing although Saxon couldn't say why.

Absurdly, it sat on a wheeled carriage with large truck tires. A tractor stood ready to tow it out of the hangar.

"I ought to be a great deal more astonished than I am," Saxon said. "Did you put something in the coffee?"

"No. That would be illegal." Saxon looked at him in puzzlement, but Lee said nothing else, and his expression was serious. Then he gestured with a backhanded wave. An opening appeared in the featureless side of the gray ship, a brightly lit rectangle just in front of them.

"Shall we go aboard?"

"I'm not getting in there!" Haskins protested.

"I am afraid you are," Lee said. He gestured towards the door they had just come through. The two uniformed guards had drawn their weapons and were watching them closely. "The only question is what condition you'll be in when you board. You had your chance to say no. Now it's a bit late."

"Why, for God's sake?" Haskins asked. "'Cause we seen this ship? Ain't nobody gonna believe me. Or Bart neither."

"They might well believe Ms. Sandori," Lee said carefully.

"So—" Haskins stopped himself. "Bart, what the flaming crap do we do?"

"We get aboard. At least I think I will." Saxon turned to Lee. "I take it this assignment is farther away than you intimated?" he said, and Lee smiled.

"You could say that."

"But it's the same job? Science education?"

"Very much so. You know what equipment you bought."

"Where's our gear?" Saxon demanded.

"Already aboard. If you hadn't come we'd at least have that much done. Your weapons and equipment are also aboard, including some you didn't think to get. We had— other consultants—in choosing them. With luck you won't need weapons, but you can't always be lucky."

"And me?" Sandori said. "What's my job, then?"

"The same as before. Security. Protect and assist Mr. Saxon. Try to include women in the education process. I did not exaggerate the primitive nature of the place you are going."

"Now just a damn minute," Sandori said. She looked at Haskins and Saxon. "You're talking about going to another goddam planet—"

Lee nodded.

"Which makes me the only woman in the world. For them. Thanks, but—"

Lee chuckled again. "Wrong. Ms. Sandori, you don't have any choices here, but you won't be the only woman in the world, nor are these the only men. Tran is settled with humans. The culture is primitive, but I assure you quite human."

"What kind of humans?" Haskins demanded. "Black people?"

"I frankly don't know. I believe there may be Moors. Does it matter?" Lee said. "They're certainly human beings. As am I, as you may have noticed."

"You come from there?" Haskins asked.

"Not from where you're going, no. But I was neither

born nor raised on Earth. Now. Please get aboard. You'll be no use to us if you're dead, but if that's what it takes—"

"I don't think he's kidding," Sandori said.

"I'm not, although in fact the necessity will not arise. We have the means to stun you. You won't appreciate the headaches."

Saxon ignored that.

"So how did these humans get to—Tran, you said?"

"Tran, and no more conversation. You'll be well briefed. I guarantee that before you get there, you will know more about Tran's history than anyone at present on the planet. Now get aboard. We're running out of time."

✢ ✢ ✢

They were in a windowless compartment about the size of the San Jose living room office. The walls were plain and featureless except for several large squares that looked as if they might be coverings for something else. Otherwise there was nothing to look at. Saxon felt stirrings of claustrophobia, enough to keep him from talking, or paying attention to Haskins who was saying something Saxon didn't care about. The steel walls seemed to be closing in. Saxon shuddered.

Seven steel airline seats were bolted to the floor. At least they looked like airline seats, but Saxon noticed they'd been modified. They reclined further and there were heavy-duty head rests.

Lee took one of the seats and gestured them into others. The straps were simple, similar to the full restraints airline crews use, and Saxon busied himself fastening them. George Lee settled into his chair, fixed his straps, and promptly went to sleep. A few moments later they felt the ship move as it was towed out of the hangar.

Five minutes went by. There was a feeling of acceleration.

"Whoo," Haskins said. The floor rotated under them. "Uh—"

There were brief periods of acceleration, changes of direction, more accelerations, then a long period of high weight, high enough to discourage conversation. In about an hour the high weight stopped, and there was a brief period of weightlessness. Saxon fought the urge to vomit. Then they were heavy again for another hour or more. To distract himself from the closing in walls, Saxon estimated the accelerations.

*Assume we accelerated, and now we're decelerating*, he thought. About an hour at something like two gravities. Now decelerate—he whistled.

"Moon," he said. "We're going to the Moon."

"Astute," George Lee said, and went back to sleep.

✢ ✢ ✢

A soft tone sounded, and Lee got up.

"Ah. We're here."

"Low gravity," Saxon said. "Definitely the Moon."

"You're calm enough about it," Sandori said.

"Sure. I have to be," Saxon said through his teeth. "No point in being anything else."

"Maybe you feel that way, but I'm ready to freak," Haskins said.

"No you're not," Sandori said.

"Well, maybe not, then."

There was a slight pressure change. A door appeared. Saxon wasn't sure whether it opened or dilated: it was just suddenly there, and Lee led the way through it. Beyond was a rough-walled corridor, then a series of doors that definitely did dilate to open, and finally a carpeted room with tables and chairs, all furniture that had clearly been made on Earth. A Formica-topped counter ran along one wall. It held a Krups cappuccino machine and a Mr. Coffee coffee maker. Cabinets above the counter held cups and other supplies. There was a sink with running water. The fixtures were standard ones you'd see in any home appliance store on Earth. The overhead lights were fluorescent shop lights. Except for the dilating door there was nothing alien in the room.

"Make yourselves at home," Lee said. "The bathroom is through there, press the square button on the wall to open the door. Bart, if you'll come with me—"

"What about us?" Sandori demanded.

"Later. Have some coffee," Lee said. "Don't worry, Bart will be back soon enough, and you'll all be on your way. Inspector Agzaral prefers to talk to him alone first."

"Inspector Agzaral," Sandori said. "Inspector? Police?"

"A policeman, yes," Lee said. "Unlike in San Francisco, inspector is a very high rank in our service. You'll all meet Inspector Agzaral later. Bart, we don't want to keep him waiting."

Saxon followed George Lee through a series of corridors and dilating doors. Each door closed behind them, and Saxon couldn't figure out how Lee got them to open. He certainly wasn't pressing buttons. Saxon tried getting ahead of him to see if the doors opened automatically, but they didn't. If Saxon got there first, the door stayed closed until Lee approached, then it opened without his seeming to do anything. Saxon wondered if he should ask, but decided not to. Watch, wait, learn . . .

Eventually they came to a large office. It held a desk and a large screen that showed Earth from space. There were alien artifacts in plenty, incomprehensible panels with lighted squares, an oddly shaped thing that might have been a clock but had lights blinking in a pattern where there should have been a clock face, strange sculptures of animals that had never lived on Earth. There were also crystal decanters and sherry glasses, an ordinary General Electric wall clock, and other familiar things. The contrast between prosaic and alien was startling.

A tall, thin man dressed in what might have been a robe or a gown sat behind the desk. The gown was rust colored, with insignia and decorations, some, like a stylized comet and sunburst, familiar enough, others incomprehensible. The man stood when Lee ushered Saxon into the room. After a moment he held out his hand. Like Lee he seemed vaguely Oriental in appearance but Saxon couldn't have said why. The head was a bit large for his body, the eyes a bit large for the face, but then the face was elongated rather than round. If he'd said he was an alien, Saxon wouldn't have believed him.

"Agzaral," he said. "Pleased to meet you, Mr. Saxon."

"I—I guess I'm pleased to meet you," Saxon said. Agzaral's hand felt normal enough, strong grip, what Saxon under different circumstances would have called a good handshake. The inspector seemed distracted, as if thinking about things other than Saxon, but at the same time his assured manner gave off a feeling of competence. Saxon thought he might like him.

"I'm probably more pleased to meet you," Agzaral said with a thin smile. "Please be seated. We won't have a great deal of time, and I don't know you well. If you find something I say incomprehensible, you may ask clarification—"

"It's all incomprehensible," Saxon said.

"If so, we've chosen the wrong hero," George Lee said.

"Hero."

"Yes. Or perhaps protagonist," Agzaral said. "You have an epic task, nothing less than saving a civilization. Perhaps a race. I believe hero is none too strong a word, but protagonist will serve if you prefer."

Saxon looked from Lee to Agzaral for signs of humor, but saw none.

"Me?"

"You are the one chosen."

"That's the first problem," Saxon said. "Why me?"

Agzaral made a gesture that might have been a nod of agreement and might have been irritation at a silly question.

"You were recommended."

"By Hector Sanchez," Lee added.

"Hector knows about—" Saxon gestured to take in the alien artifacts, including the large screen showing Earth. It was clear that the clouds and the solar terminator were moving, and this was a real time view. It was now night in California, but the lights of San Francisco and Silicon Valley were clearly visible. "—this?"

"No," Agzaral said. "Dr. Sanchez works with one of our

agents whom he believes to be a supervisor with the Central Intelligence Agency. I offer you the observation that your government's habits of secrecy in matters that need none have been very helpful to us in the past. It was so this time. Dr. Sanchez was told that the CIA needs a science teacher to work in primitive conditions on a project of great national importance which will benefit a primitive society. He volunteered your name instantly as a person extremely well qualified, then expressed doubt that your wife would let you accept the assignment."

"It wasn't hard to discover that your wife's views would no longer be a problem," Lee observed. "Sanchez's recommendation was so enthusiastic that I thought it worthwhile looking farther."

"But still—"

"There are rules on recruiting Earth humans," Agzaral said. "For any purpose, but particularly for off-planet work. The rules are complex, but let us say that your legal situation actually made things much easier for us. You don't need to know more."

"Habits of secrecy," Saxon said.

"Perhaps, but there's also the time factor," Agzaral said. "We're not trying to be secretive in this case. In essence we are not allowed to tell you what you're volunteering for, yet we're supposed to accept only volunteers. This usually translates to 'was it reasonable for you to be sent?' In your case it was. You will learn much more on the journey to Tran."

"Please listen and save questions for later," Lee said. He looked at a small box on the desk in front of them. Lights flashed in a pattern that meant nothing to Saxon, but Agzaral and Lee exchanged looks and nodded. "Inspector Agzaral hasn't a lot of time."

"All right." Saxon settled back in his chair.

"Begin with your remark about secrecy," Agzaral said. "It is a habit of long standing. Only a few of your Earth years ago, my revealing to an Earth human what I am about to tell you would have earned me a painful death. It would do so even now if there were the smallest chance that you would return to relay this information to your government."

"*X-Files*," Saxon said. The new show had been quite a hit among those in the lounge at the Glide. Bart knew many of his fellow street people thought the show was more truth than fiction.

Agzaral frowned, but Lee laughed.

"Close," he said.

"What you've said is that I'll never go home again," Saxon said.

"From what I've learned, you have little reason to want to," Agzaral said, and Saxon nodded.

"I guess that's true. I thought about this on the way. It was pretty clear this was a one-way trip. If I could go back, why hasn't someone already?"

"Some have claimed to," Agzaral said.

"Sure, obvious nut cases—unless you really are into sexual abuses?"

"Hardly," Agzaral said. "So you are not astonished."

"Astonished perhaps, but hardly unhappy. I really don't have anyone left on Earth. And I'd like to teach again. I assume I really am going to teach young humans on an alien planet?"

"You are."

"And my—associates?"

"Same story," Lee said. "You need assistants, and what do they have to go back to?"

"Cal, certainly, but Spirit?"

"She has better reasons than Cal not to return to Earth," Lee said, and Agzaral gestured impatiently.

"What is done is done," he said. "Depend upon it. Neither you nor your companions will ever return to Earth, but the work we have for you is more important than anything you would ever have done on Earth. Accept that, and allow me to continue."

Saxon nodded.

"You said Earth humans," he said. "That means you and Dr. Lee aren't?"

"I was born on Earth," Agzaral said. "Long ago. Dr. Lee was not. We are both human."

"Not born on Earth. In this solar system?"

"No."

Saxon nodded again.

"Interstellar travel. Faster than light?"

"Yes."

"An interstellar civilization, then. How far does it extend?"

Agzaral smiled thinly.

"The answer depends on your definition of civilization. The galaxy contains many of what you would call civilizations."

"The part you run."

"Several hundred light-years," Agzaral said. "The center of the Confederation is more than two hundred light-years from Sol."

"Big. All under one government?"

"It is a Confederation of unequals. Of planets, races, clans, families. Mr. Saxon, I don't mean to insult your intelligence, but the chances that you will ever understand Confederation government and politics are extremely small. I grew up with them, politics is literally my life work, and I understand perhaps a tenth of what I need to know." He waved that away. "Fortunately, understanding the complex politics of a decadent high-tech civilization is no part of your task." Then he grinned as if amused.

"So what's so damn funny?" Saxon demanded.

"It is funny," Agzaral said. "You don't need to understand a decadent high-tech civilization, but you'll certainly need to know a great deal about a low-tech civilization as complex and dynamic and incomprehensible as Renaissance Europe."

"Very much like Renaissance Europe, in fact," Lee said.

"I take it humans run this civilization."

"The primitive one? Of course."

"No, I meant the—galactic civilization. Confederation, you called it. Humans run that?"

"Not precisely," Agzaral said. "There is a sense in which that's true, but not the way you may expect. In your studies of Earth history, did you ever hear of the Janissaries?"

"Heard of, not sure I remember anything about them," Saxon said. "Turkish elite soldiers? Something like that."

"They served the Ottoman Empire, which was Turkish," Agzaral agreed. "But they were not Turkish. They were Christian slaves, Slavs mostly, taken as young children as tribute, rounded up by their Bosnian and

Albanian neighbors who had chosen to convert to Islam and thus avoid having their own children taken as taxes. They generally came from the Balkans, the area recently called Yugoslavia. The important point is they were taken when very young and impressionable and made slaves, not of individuals, but of the Turkish state. They were forcibly converted to Islam and brought up to serve the Empire, and they became fanatics in its service. Indeed, they soon became the elite troops of the Turkish armies, and were also the chief civil servants, department heads, advisors to the Sultan—so you could in fact say they ran the Turkish civilization. But they were its slaves, not its masters."

There was a long silence while Saxon wondered what he was supposed to say. But then, slowly, he began to comprehend.

"You mean that humans in your Confederation are Janissaries?"

"We aren't called that, but yes," Lee said. "We've often wondered where the Turks came up with the idea for the Janissaries. Inspector Agzaral suspects it was from one of his predecessors in the security services."

"How long has this been going on?" Saxon demanded.

"Over five thousand of your years," Agzaral said. "Let me continue. Over time, the Janissaries on Earth became corrupt. They began to have their own agenda, their own goals which were not the same as those of the empire they served." He shrugged. "It was inevitable, I suppose."

"And that's happened here?" Saxon demanded. "What the hell is going on? Are you trying to recruit me into some kind of Galactic human conspiracy against the government?"

Agzaral smiled.

"I believe you may have selected the right person despite my misgivings," he said. "Congratulations, Gregeral."

Lee smiled faintly in reply.

"Of course, it isn't quite that simple." Agzaral said. "'Conspiracy against the government' is too strong a phrase. Neither is it entirely incorrect however." He frowned for a moment, as if in thought. "Think rather that we aid one part of the government against another."

"To what purpose?"

"The advancement of humanity," Lee said.

"A dramatic way to put it, but yes, something like that," Agzaral said. "Our end goals are . . . several, but one of them—perhaps the most essential—is the admission of the human race to the Confederation. As equals, not as a recruiting ground for slaves."

"That's noble enough," Saxon said. "Assuming I can believe you. And your other goals?"

"The *survival* of humanity," Agzaral said flatly.

Saxon looked at him for long, motionless seconds, then shook his head.

"The survival of humanity isn't your 'most essential' goal?" he asked incredulously.

"The inspector didn't say humanity's admission was the most *important* goal, Bart," Lee said quietly. "He said it was the most *essential*; the one without which survival may well become impossible."

"Impossible?! You just said this has been going on for thousands of years!"

"It has," Agzaral said. "And during those millennia we

have seen at least four civilizations and eleven intelligent species exterminated by the Confederation."

Saxon looked at him in horror, and the inspector made the same shrugging gesture.

"In three of those cases, it was human hands which carried out the murders, Mr. Saxon. We obeyed the orders of our masters. It is what we do."

"But . . . but *why*?"

"The Confederation prizes stability above all other things. It is a civilization which has taken thousands upon thousands of years to evolve, the matrix upon which a dozen races, each with the technological capability to destroy worlds, interact in ways which preclude the use of those weapons upon one another. They will allow *nothing* to destabilize that matrix. Anything which seems likely to do so—anything which *may* do so—must be . . . neutralized."

"And—?" Saxon said, looking at him when he paused.

"And certain factions of the Confederacy and of the High Commission are hardening in their belief that their human slaves threaten precisely that destabilization," Agzaral said levelly.

"Why?"

"Because they fear, correctly, that at least some of us would refuse to obey their orders and destroy another civilization, another world . . . if that world were Earth."

"Earth? They want you to destroy Earth?!"

"That decision has not yet been made. It may never be made. But Earth's current rate of progress frightens them, although most of them would reject the use of the verb 'fear.' Yet whatever you may choose to call it, the factions to which I refer have grown progressively more anxious over the last fifty or sixty years of Earth's history. In the past, Earth has been protected. A nature preserve, perhaps, because it is the home of our species and past Confederation policy has been to introduce occasional, carefully metered infusions of 'wild' human genes into their Janissaries. Despite that, there is evidence that the High Commission has, in the past, intervened to enormously reduce—to cull, perhaps—the population of Earth. The last such attempt occurred in your fourteenth century."

"What are you talking about? Nobody attacked Earth in the fourteenth century!"

"No?" Agzaral cocked his head. "You have, perhaps, heard of the Black Death?" Saxon swallowed hard, and Agzaral's hands shrugged again. "The most effective biological weapons are normally those developed from pathogens already present in the environment, Mr. Saxon."

"This Confederation *did* that? To *Earth*?"

"It did," Agzaral said. "This is something that we confirmed from the secret archives only recently. Within the last ten of your years."

"My God," Saxon whispered.

"Not all of the races of the Confederation are equally enamored of stability above all else," Agzaral told him. "Several of the 'younger' members were forcibly compelled to accept the Confederation's policies, the limitations set upon their technology and their own actions, when first they attained interstellar flight. It was one of those races which aided us in confirming the truth of the Black Death. Not out of altruism, of course, but because they hoped that we would join with them in . . . modifying the Confederation's policy, shall we say."

"Why would they hope that if you've been these 'Janissaries' for so long?"

"Because the High Commission used biological weapons to kill a quarter of Earth's population in the Middle Ages, when your entire planet boasted perhaps four hundred and fifty million people, most of whom didn't have even gunpowder. What do you think they might resort to when Earth's population is over five and a half *billion* and it has attained nuclear weapons? Tell me, Mr. Saxon, are you familiar with the term 'dinosaur killer'?"

It was very, very quiet in the inspector's office for several seconds. Saxon stared at the other two men, nausea rolling about in his belly.

"Understand me," Agzaral continued. "I and some of my fellow Janissaries were prepared to aid Earth, if we could, but we saw Tran as a place where humans could continue to grow and develop even if Earth was devastated. Even if the Confederation decided to exterminate all 'wild humans' once and for all. But there were also Janissaries who would *agree* with a decision to destroy Earth. Who see the thousands of years in which we, the human slave-soldiers of the Confederation, have preserved the peace of not billions but trillions upon trillions of sentient beings, as far more important than what might happen upon a single backwater world the vast majority of them have never seen.

"But the factions on the High Commission and in the

Confederation who favor what we might call a final solution to the Earth problem may very well not stop there. There is a reason the High Commission of six hundred of your years ago used biological means and hid it from the Janissaries of their own time."

He paused, and Saxon shook his head.

"What reason?"

"Fear," Agzaral said. "Humans are ubiquitous throughout the Confederation's worlds. They are not allowed to make *policy*, yet there are more humans in more star systems than any other single species, and they man the Confederation's fleets, staff its police forces, administer its bureaucracies, and regulate its commerce. If those humans, or a sizable percentage of them, should turn upon their masters, the consequences could be catastrophic."

"That's good, then. Right? I mean, if they depend on you that heavily, then they have to be more cautious about something that might drive you into rebellion."

"Unless they decide to reduce that dependency by eliminating those upon whom they depend."

"What?" Saxon shook his head again, feeling like a boxer who'd taken one punch too many.

"It's a serious policy proposal among the factions most concerned over potential destabilization, Bart," Lee said quietly. "Exterminate humanity, the same way the Confederation has exterminated other races, and the 'human problem' goes away forever."

Saxon's jaw clenched, and it was Agzaral's turn to shake his head.

"No decisions have been reached yet, Mr. Saxon, and there are factions on the High Commission who would strongly oppose any such policy. I think they would be unlikely to oppose the notion of 'pruning' Earth equally strongly, but some of them definitely *would* oppose that, as well. I personally suspect that some of those considering a 'final solution' are less concerned about the danger humanity might present than they are about eliminating the police forces and regulatory agents who inhibit their actions in the name of the Confederation. From our perspective, however, their motivation matters rather less than their intention."

"Yeah, I can see how you might put it that way," Saxon said bitterly, and Agzaral's hands moved again.

"I told you you would never fully understand Confederation politics, and I certainly have no time to explain their intricacies to you now. But what you *do* need to know is that an entire spectrum of strategies is in motion. The equation is so complex, its solution dependent upon so many variables, that we are forced to play for a hierarchy of possible outcomes, from most favorable to least favorable. And that is where you enter the lists, Mr. Saxon."

"Me? What's *my* part in all this?"

"We need science teachers," Agzaral said. "Most of what Dr. Lee has told you is the exact truth. We need to transform a primitive world into a modern one. Modern not merely by your standards, but by ours."

"What do you mean by primitive?"

"The dominant civilization is at a level comparable to Earth's medieval period," Agzaral said. "With some elements of the Renaissance."

"You want it to move from Renaissance to space travel,"

Saxon said. "No, from Renaissance to *interstellar* travel. And how long to do that?"

"It took five centuries for Earth humans to reach your moon," Agzaral said. "We won't have that long. Our hope is that you and the knowledge you're taking with you can shorten that process considerably."

Saxon frowned.

"Knowledge is one thing. Building an industrial base to *do* something with that knowledge is— But of course you know that."

"We do," Agzaral said. "We do, and that concerns us, but there's nothing more we can do about it."

"I do point out," Lee said, "that Earth went from mostly animal-drawn transportation in World War I to trucks and aircraft in the Second World War. A matter of thirty years. Twenty-five years after that they were on your Moon. Note also the progress of parts of your so-called Third World. With the right knowledge base, industrial development can be quite rapid."

"But what's the point?" Saxon demanded. "You think you could build a bunch of primitives up into something with the firepower to take on this Confederation of yours? The one that's already exterminated a bunch of other species?"

"That is not precisely what we have in mind," Agzaral said dryly.

"Then what *do* you have in mind?"

"At the moment Tran is primitive, even by your standards. If, however, it attains the level of interstellar flight, as a unified world, the Confederation's own rules would require it to extend the possibility of membership in the Confederation to it."

Saxon looked from Agzaral to Lee and back again.

"And there's a reason these antihuman hardliners of yours wouldn't just wipe this place—Tran, did you call it?—off the face of the universe instead of granting it membership?"

"That is where our allies come into play," Agzaral said. "Some of those other races which resent their subordinate positions, or who fear they might someday find themselves in humanity's place, would agitate strongly against any such decision. They would insist that the Confederation honor its own long-standing law, and although they may be constrained by the limitations the Confederation imposed upon them at the time they became members, they are still voting members. They cannot simply be ignored, especially when at least one of the Confederation's oldest races is prepared to stand with them, as well. The outcome would not be a certainty, but that is precisely the nature of our problem. There *are* no certainties."

"I see." Saxon inhaled deeply. "Should I assume that Tran's membership in the Confederation would constitute your best-case scenario?"

"It would constitute *one* of our best-case scenarios. It is always possible that Earth will not be devastated, in which case it will almost certainly attain a qualifying level of technology well before Tran. It is certain, however, that *Earth's* admission to the Confederation would be hedged about with far more restrictions and limitations than any other member race, and the Confederation's long history with Earth would make that more acceptable to the potentially undecided factions on the High Commission.

And Tran also represents our next-to-worst-case scenario: the world upon which our species may survive after it has been wiped out everywhere else in the galaxy."

Agzaral's tone was calm, almost dispassionate, but an icicle ran down Saxon's spine.

"How much support can I expect?" he asked, dreading the response.

"All of our plans require that we have minimal contact with Tran lest we draw the attention of the very factions whose attention we must, at all costs, avoid."

"'Minimal contact,'" Saxon repeated. "I'm getting the impression that I'm about to be very much on my own."

"That's pretty much it," Lee agreed. "It's highly unlikely that we'll be able to provide any additional support after you've reached Tran."

"Great." Saxon sagged back in his chair.

"There is another element in play," Lee said after a moment, frowning slightly. "Another group of Earth humans recently arrived on Tran. A group of mercenary soldiers under a Captain Galloway of the United States Army. Inspector Agzaral permitted them to go to Tran, but they weren't sent by us. We didn't select them and they weren't sent to transform or unify the planet, although Galloway seems to have adopted that mission. Or some of it, at least. He may even accomplish it. He's proven quite capable."

"Wait a minute—wait a minute! If *you* didn't send them, who *did*?"

"They were sent by a race called the Shalnuksis," Agzaral said, "who paid a great deal of money to transport Captain Galloway and his men to Tran in order to grow a highly valuable crop for them. The Shalnuksis are a commercial, trader race, and they expect to earn back their expenses with considerable profit. And while many of the Confederation's races despise them, others admire them, and they have considerable influence with one powerful faction of the government. For historical reasons, they have commercial rights to exploit Tran. For political reasons, they choose not to openly assert those rights, but instead rely on keeping Tran, and its future, a very low-profile issue in Confederate politics so that they can exploit it 'out of sight, out of mind.' This situation has endured for several thousand of your years, and with Earth's development of space travel and the new... uncertainty about humanity's place in Confederation affairs, the most powerful Shalnuksi clan has even less desire for the other governing races to recall the existence of Tran."

"So they sent Galloway to grow this crop—I'm guessing we're talking about something like opium—for them?" Saxon shook his head. "Sounds like a wonderful guy!"

"Captain Galloway had even less choice about accepting his assignment than you did," Agzaral said. "And there is indeed some hope that he will succeed, as Gregeral has just suggested. Moreover, through an accident—well, through a mistake no one could foresee—Galloway may shortly acquire significant additional capabilities. If he *is* successful, we expect you to work with him. On the other hand, he may fail, and while Gregeral is correct about his competence, the odds of his success are not high. Bluntly, Mr. Saxon, at this point you represent a low-profile insurance policy for the possibility—perhaps even the probability—that he will *fail*."

Agzaral hesitated, then went on.

"Insurance or primary, it's important work," he said. "Out there is a planet of humans with no future. And here"—he gestured towards the image of Earth on the screen—"is a planet of humans with a totally unknown and unpredictable future. And in the Confederation is an entire species facing potential destruction. What you do on Tran will certainly change the lives of the people there, but you may also change not only what happens to Earth, but what happens throughout the entire Confederation, as well."

"The fate of humanity rests with me." Saxon tried to say it ironically.

It didn't come out that way.

Agzaral's hands moved in that shrugging gesture yet again, but his eyes were dark as they met Saxon's.

"So!" Saxon said after a long, silent moment. "What do I have to work with?"

"What you've brought," Agzaral said. "Understand that you already know more about the Confederation—and about our plans—than anyone on Tran. For our part, we will do what else we can. That may be a lot if certain plans mature, but as Gregeral has already suggested, it is far more likely that the most important thing we can do for you is to arrange for you to be forgotten. For Tran to vanish in bureaucratic records. We are unlikely to have the means to do much more for you, and possibly nothing at all. To be precise: given a choice between directly aiding you with technology and supplies, and assisting in hiding your existence from the Confederation, we will choose the latter. It's for that reason that we have provided you with as much as we could now."

"Like Einstein's papers," Saxon said.

"Precisely," Lee said. "You may not be able to read them *now*, Bart, but that need not be true for you always. It certainly need not be true of your students, and I've tucked away what you might think of as a scientific Rosetta Stone for you, as well."

Saxon eyed him speculatively, but then Agzaral made a throat-clearing sound and Saxon's gaze returned to him.

"While it would be very tempting to provide additional support," the inspector said, "every ship we send increases the probability that you will be detected."

"What about this other guy? This Army captain? Galloway?"

"We are trying to aid Captain Galloway, but the fact remains that we can do little more for either of you."

"Aid Galloway. You approve of him, then?"

"A difficult question," Agzaral said. "In general, yes. He's proven to be both capable and ethical, and a better teacher than his education would indicate. The fact remains, he and all his men were soldiers, not teachers. It will be part of your task to ascertain Galloway's capabilities and intentions, and to decide whether or not to work with him. Of course, that must remain secret."

Agzaral waved a hand in a different gesture, one that meant nothing to Saxon.

"Remember this," he said. "The official story is that you're being sent to aid Captain Galloway in his work. Your specialized knowledge will help him increase the yields of the cash crops he is growing. This is what your companions will be told, and what you will pretend to believe when speaking with them. For reasons you do not understand you will be set down on the planet at a considerable distance from Galloway. And that is all you know." His voice lowered and became very stern. "This is important, Mr. Saxon. Any conversation you have outside this room, any conversation at any place, no matter how private you may think it, may be monitored by your enemies, and that will continue until you reach Tran. Any conversation at all, at any place."

"But not here?"

"Sometimes here," Lee said. "But not at this moment."

"Enemies. That seems to imply a more . . . immediate threat than you've been discussing to this point."

"I begin to have hopes for you, indeed, Mr. Saxon," Agzaral said with a smile. "And you are correct. As we have already mentioned, the Shalnuksis regard Tran as their personal property. They are not your enemies now, but if they suspect that you are going to Tran for any purpose other than to help Galloway increase his production, they will be. Your official mission is to educate the natives with a view to making them better at farming, in particular at growing the recreational drugs they wish to trade in. Remember that. It's important."

"What happens if these . . . Shalnuksis figure out what I'm really up to?"

"If your cover story is penetrated, you will be killed," Lee said.

"And you?"

Agzaral's smile was thin.

"We've taken suitable precautions for protecting ourselves, but the result of indiscretions on your part will be highly unpleasant for you and for Tran. Believe me, you cannot profit from exploiting what you know, but you can harm yourself and many others in the attempt."

"You don't trust me."

"Clearly untrue," Lee said. "Make it that we trust you, but we still take precautions."

"At this point my head is spinning," Saxon said.

"I would be surprised if it wasn't," Lee said. "But there's one more thing."

"Oh, Jesus!" Saxon looked at him in disbelief. "There's *more*?"

"Of course!" Lee actually chuckled, but then he sobered.

"Tran becomes important to the Shalnuksis at approximately six hundred-year intervals. One of those intervals is upon us, which is why it has also become important to us."

"So these Shalnuksis muck around in its history every six hundred years?" Saxon asked in a resigned tone.

"Exactly," Lee said. "You can study Tran history at your leisure during the journey and see just how thoroughly they have 'mucked around' in it. The short version, however, is that every six hundred years, the Shalnuksis have brought at least one new group of mercenaries to Tran. Sometimes several, and sometimes in considerable numbers. Each group was aided in establishing domination over a suitable area for cultivating crops to produce the drugs Inspector Agzaral mentioned earlier."

"So they brought a different Earth culture every six hundred years? Jesus, that must be one mixed up place."

"At least one culture. Often there was more than one expedition, each from a different Earth culture—and not always at six hundred-year intervals. From time to time certain Tran artifacts have become valuable, and one or another Shalnuksi trader group found the means to send human agents to gather them. The expeditions were then abandoned, as always. The one unbreakable rule is that no human returns from Tran to Earth."

"What, never?"

"No. Never. Not hardly ever, but never," Lee said. He chuckled. "I, too, enjoy English operettas."

*English, not British*, Saxon thought. *I wonder if that means anything*.

"I also enjoy them," Agzaral said. "But our protected time grows short, so let us conclude.

"Tran is, as you put it, a mixed up place. In different areas at different times it has been dominated by Achaean heroes, Scythian archers, Persian cavalry, Roman infantry, Celtic clansmen, Byzantine cataphracts, and others I don't recall offhand. In addition to natural evolution from the Bronze Age slave masters, there have been interactions among all those. And others. Unlike Earth, however, these competing cultures have not been permitted to develop and grow."

"Not permitted?"

"Precisely. The Shalnuksis have seen to it that they do not by eradicating any nonprimitive technological footprint their current expedition may have left."

"Eradicating. How?"

"All Tran cultures have legends of 'skyfire.' Legends based on fact, of course. And those legends also suggest that anything, such as technology, which might threaten the sky gods brings swift and terrible retribution. Thus skyfire also serves as a deterrent to innovation between visitations."

"So who does the bombing? Humans?"

"Sometimes. At least once the Shalnuksis have acted on their own. It depends on the cost."

"Cost. We're talking about thousands of human lives—"

"More," Inspector Agzaral said.

"And they're concerned about *costs*."

"Yes. After all, they are businessmen, and these are only humans, not Ader'at'eel or Shalnuksis. Cost is always important to the Shalnuksis; humans are not. But the cost of doing business on Tran is inevitably high, because the periods in which it has value are so short and the intervals between those periods are so long. Costly as the transport and supply of mercenaries may be, it is still cheaper to bring in fresh agents once every six hundred years—and to eliminate them, if necessary, when their utility is done—than it would be to maintain a presence on the planet during those intervals."

"'Businessmen.'" Saxon snorted bitterly.

"Indeed," Agzaral agreed. "Yet that is one of the factors that may ultimately work in our favor. In approximately twenty years most Shalnuksis will lose immediate interest in Tran, but it will have great commercial value to them again in another six hundred years . . . if it remains outside the Confederation. If it attains Confederate membership, however, they will be unable to exploit it. The average lifespan of the Shalnuksis is about four hundred years. They reach sexual maturity at some thirty Earth years of age, and they have a keen interest in the prosperity of their grandchildren. All of which means that they will also be doing their best to help the rest of the Confederation forget Tran exists in the meantime."

"Well, that's the first good news I've heard yet!"

"Indeed," Agzaral said again. "Yet in order to protect that investment, they will again seek, and almost certainly gain, permission from their government to eradicate Galloway's contaminating influence by bombing the more advanced parts of Tran back into the Bronze Age. That has happened before in Tran's history, and it is, after all, fully in keeping with the Confederation's policy of maintaining the status quo, is it not?"

"Jesus, Mary, and Joseph," Saxon muttered. "You're telling me that not only do I have to modernize this place, I have to do it without anyone noticing?"

"Actually, that's pretty accurate," Lee said.

"But—" Saxon cut himself off. "Okay."

"One way to avoid notice is to hide," Agzaral said. "It's likely—possible, at least—that you'll have that option. We believe there's a government on Tran that will be glad to hide you in exchange for what you can teach. It may be able to do so." He looked at the image of Earth for a moment. "And it may not."

"And this—Captain Galloway? If I hide I can't help him. I take it I'm not really supposed to help him, whatever we all tell Cal and Spirit?"

"It would be better if you can," Agzaral disagreed. "The decision will have to be yours once you reach Tran and have the opportunity to evaluate the situation, however. Our current information is obviously out of date, but it indicates that he has made some good alliances. Yet he's made enemies, as well, which was inevitable. I have some confidence in his abilities and more in his intentions, but no certainties. You may well decide to throw in your lot with him. In any event, we need insurance against his failure."

"But what's his status on Tran?" Saxon asked.

"He is Warlord for the youthful king of a powerful kingdom, and an influential counselor to the chief of a smaller clan group, as well as an ally of one of Tran's more powerful empires. Left to himself, he might well be successful in stimulating an industrial revolution on Tran and ringing in great progress. The problem is that he may not be left alone."

"I thought you wanted him to succeed."

"We do. What we want isn't always of definitive importance, however," Lee said with a thin smile, and Agzaral nodded.

"To put it mildly. Mr. Saxon, the Shalnuksis expect to earn back their expenses with considerable profit, which means that the most important objective now, from our perspective, is that they realize some, but not much, profit from this expedition. If the expedition causes great losses, their desire to maintain Tran as their private preserve, 'off the books,' as I believe you might put it, will be substantially weakened. If it gains great profits, however, they may be tempted to continue surveillance of Tran in order to protect their investment or even to find additional ways in which to exploit it in the intervals between their regular expeditions."

Saxon shook his head in wonder.

"There is another development," Agzaral said. He

spoke briefly in a language that sounded vaguely Asian to Saxon, caught himself, and continued in English. "It is the reason you are being sent now. The Halnu Trader faction of the Shalnuksis decided to send its own expedition to Tran. Their goal was twofold. One was to establish a countervailing claim to Tran for their own clan at the expense of the planet's current owners. The other was to accelerate the imposition of control by mercenaries working for them. Their intention was to significantly increase the area their mercenaries would be able to place under cultivation before the peak growing period arrives.

"However"—the inspector smiled thinly—"they overreached themselves. They recruited a mercenary group that does not meet the rules set for recruitment. As a result I was able to make it possible for the forces they recruited to join those of Captain Galloway, assuming Galloway is clever enough. The combined assets may be enough for him to succeed in establishing what amounts to a planetary government."

"And if he can't?" Saxon asked, and Agzaral made that hand-waving shrug gesture yet again.

"If Galloway is successful, he will find a way to bring you into his group. And if he fails, you still have the resources to transform the planet through education."

"If I'm your last hope, it's a thin reed."

"We know," Agzaral said, and Lee shook his head.

"If we could give you more support, we would," the younger man said. "Unfortunately, there are simply too many things beyond our control, and it would be far too dangerous for us to attempt to force them under control."

"The important point is to outlast the Shalnuksis'

current period of interest," Agzaral said. "Whatever may happen on Earth and in the Confederation, time will be on your side . . . assuming we succeed in our effort to see to it that Tran is forgotten. Hold on long enough, and you automatically win."

"How long is long enough?" Saxon asked.

"Twenty Earth years ought to be enough," Agzaral said. "Not really a long time."

"At the end of which, they're going to bomb every sign of our existence *out* of existence." Saxon shook his head. "Would it be too much to hope that you can at least give us a heads-up about when the hammer is likely to come down?"

"We will certainly tell you what we can—if we can. But it would be wise of you to prepare for a certain amount of destruction on the assumption that you will have no warning at all when the time comes."

"How the hell do you prepare for that?"

"By not being destroyed, of course," Agzaral said. "You hide your capabilities and the progress of the groups you advise so that you will be overlooked in the bombardment. The Shalnuksis have no desire to sterilize the planet. Quite the contrary. Nor will they wish to use nuclear weapons, which are, after all, expensive. Kinetic impacts—meteors if you will—should be sufficient for their purposes, and rocks, unlike nuclear weapons, are cheap. What they want is to so intimidate the population that they equate technological progress with death and destruction. And of course to kill off those who may have learned new technologies. But understand, the locals have survived all of this before. They have some mechanisms, coupled with legends and religious practices, which will help them do so again. But mostly, you hide."

"Hide. Where?"

"We have chosen a civilization," Agzaral said. "You will learn about it on your journey. Or you may choose another. You must understand, our choices are limited, and these conditions in the Confederation are temporary. We must act now, and we will not be able to help you much. That was not our original plan when we approached you, but matters have changed. We had not intended to place such a burden on you, but we do not control the matter." He paused and looked gravely at Saxon. "You are being given a great opportunity as well as a great burden."

"But—"

Saxon stopped himself. Whether these men lied or told the truth was important, but not just now, because nothing he could say would change their actions. Well, one thing. He could quit. But that seemed a sure formula for personal disaster.

Not just personal disaster, if they *were* telling the truth. And there was opportunity in this, as well. He might be important again, not a Tenderloin bum but a man with a mission, an important mission. Something to live for.

"Remember that we will be pursuing two approaches to decrease the probability of a massive bombardment and to buy you as much of the next six hundred years as we may," Agzaral said. "First the political approach: lessen Shalnuksi influence in the High Commission and the Council. That is my task. I have agents working on it. They may be successful. I certainly have hopes, and if they do succeed, the permission for a truly massive bombardment of Tran may not be forthcoming. The second is to buy off the Shalnuksis. Frankly, that one is more likely to succeed, but whether or not it does is largely up to Captain Galloway, although you may well be able to aid him in that regard. We will tell you how. Your cover story contains large elements of truth, and you will have new means to increase agricultural yields beyond those Galloway has introduced. The problem with that approach is that it carries the very real danger of discovery if you help him."

"If we're discovered we'll be bombed?"

"Quite possibly," Agzaral said. "If it becomes known you're teaching science and technology, quite probably." He looked in concentration at the gadgets on his desk. Whatever he saw seemed to satisfy him.

"But there's also the chance that if I help this Galloway I can prevent the bombardment?"

"Yes," Agzaral said. "And I am aware of the dilemma that poses. Fortunately, you won't have to make any immediate decision." He glanced at the instruments on his desk. One flashed an orange light. "We are very nearly out of time. In moments I will hold up my hand. When I do, I will ask you some questions. Your answers will be recorded and are important. Be very careful what you say."

"But—"

"You'll know more later," Lee assured him.

"Sure, but what do I say?"

"The expected answers will be obvious," Agzaral said. "Recall the cover story. You have been recruited to aid in increasing agricultural production. You need not try to hide confusion. It is expected that you will be confused at this stage."

*A test,* Saxon thought. *Just another goddam IQ test.*

"Okay. Sure. But let me get this straight. I'm going to Tran with a lot of equipment and knowledge. More than Galloway has?"

"More knowledge. Not more military strength."

"And you're really hoping I'll go hide rather than help Galloway."

"I am hoping you will make the right choice," Agzaral said. "And I do not know what that will be. Remember, we have concluded that the best thing that can happen to you would be for the Confederation to forget that you and Galloway and the whole world of Tran exist."

"Forget for how long?"

"Until you can build ships of your own, of course," Agzaral said.

The light on the desk turned red and Agzaral held up his hand.

# ⊹⇒ CHAPTER SIX ⇐⊹
# MISSION

The office door opened and Haskins and Sandori came in. Agzaral looked pointedly at Saxon, then at the devices on his desk. Saxon nodded as if he understood.

*And what do I understand? We're being listened to by Agzaral's—superiors? Masters? They've approved our going to Tran to increase production, but nothing else?*

Agzaral stood. His expression was unreadable. If Saxon had been forced to label it, he would have said "formal."

"I am Inspector Agzaral," he said, "and while you have a few choices, I control them all. I have explained those choices to Mr. Saxon, and now to you. If I use terms that you are unfamiliar with do not interrupt until I am finished.

"You will be conducted to a planet settled largely by humans whose current technological level approximates that of Earth's fourteenth or fifteenth century. There are no intelligent native species, although it is possible that had humans not come the centaurs might have developed intelligence in a Galactic Cycle or so."

Saxon frowned. He could guess the meaning of the term. Sandori looked puzzled. Haskins merely looked to Saxon, saw no action was needed, and waited.

"Your mission is to aid in the production of certain native crops," Agzaral said. "There is already an expedition to Tran with this mission, sent there by a race called the Shalnuksis, who are merchants and traders. You should cooperate with that expedition as much as possible. You carry much of the knowledge of Earth, and you may impart any that you believe will aid to increase production. It is important that the Shalnuksis be satisfied with the crops produced. Beyond that you may be able to better the lot of the Tran humans. We would prefer that you do so, although that will not be pleasing to the Shalnuksis." Agzaral looked significantly at Saxon, as if he expected Saxon to understand a hidden signal. "And unfortunately, I cannot give you much better advice."

"We have the knowledge of Earth," Saxon said. "Enough knowledge to transform that place. It's an experiment, introducing that much knowledge into what amounts to a fifteenth-century civilization. A dangerous experiment."

Agzaral nodded.

"Agreed."

"But I can do so?"

"If you believe that sharing that knowledge with those actually charged with raising the crops in question will lead to increased crop production, by all means. That is the primary mission. But once that is accomplished you are not forbidden to be of general help to everyone on the planet."

"So why us? I'm certainly not qualified."

"I doubt anyone on Earth is qualified," Agzaral said. "Not in the sense you meant. You meant 'worthy.'"

"Yes—"

"And the fact that you ask it is one qualification," Agzaral said. "We don't have infinite choices here. We needed someone educated, willing to go, able to go without causing a lot of questions to be asked, intelligent, and not thoroughly arrogant—that does not generate a long list of candidates."

"Now I'm astonished that you found me."

"Accident," Agzaral said.

"Not quite," Dr. Lee said. "Your former student really did lead us to you. We've done business with him before. He believes we're CIA."

"And me?" Haskins asked.

"We wouldn't have come looking for you, but once Mr. Saxon brought you in we found no disqualifications, and some of your past experience may very well prove useful. You were given ample opportunities to quit. You didn't. Not disqualified and didn't quit. End of matter."

"And why am I qualified?" Sandori asked.

"Come now, Ms. Sandori, you yourself believe you are the best-qualified person in this expedition. One of the best qualified on your planet," Lee said.

She looked at him sharply.

"It's true, no?" Lee demanded.

"Do I have to answer?"

"You just did," Agzaral said. "You met our requirements:

no one will miss you. You volunteered. You are competent, and you have a strong desire to change things for what you think is the better—and some practical experience in what happens when you try that. Our opinion of your suitability may not be as high as your own, but we do think you suitable."

"And you don't have many choices," Sandori said.

Agzaral stared at the picture of Earth for a long moment, then turned back to them.

"We've kept your expedition small. You have knowledge, you have enough weapons to defend yourselves, but you don't represent enough force to make much difference in battle.

"As I say, there is already an expedition on Tran. It is composed of Earth mercenaries, and Captain Galloway, its commander, brought enough military power to change Tran's history, although that was certainly not his mission. The Shalnuksis have commercial rights to Tran produce. They intend Galloway's changes to be temporary, and their assessment may be correct. Galloway's power is evaporating. He will never have the industrial base to produce modern ammunition, so he is being forced to build a new power base using locals and what technology he can introduce.

"He has had a surprising impact, not always for the better, but generally so. That will continue."

"So why don't we just go help Galloway?" Sandori asked.

"In fact, the Shalnuksis desire you to do precisely that," Agzaral said. "We cannot, of course, control your actions after you arrive on Tran, but the entire reason they have agreed to sending you there is to assist Captain Galloway. Understand that. You may have a beneficial effect on the planet, but that is definitely secondary."

He regarded them all for a moment, and Saxon nodded.

"All right, I guess that defines our priorities. Where on Tran are we going?"

"We have chosen your landing place," Agzaral said. "It is a Republic, called the city-state of Nikeis."

"Fourteenth-century republics were usually oligarchies," Saxon said.

"And Nikeis is no exception," Agzaral agreed, "but its oligarchy is surprisingly open to new talent. New talent with wealth. You will have wealth as well as knowledge. It shouldn't be that difficult."

"Will Galloway know we're coming?"

"No." Lee shook his head. "There isn't any way to let him know."

"No, there is not," Agzaral agreed. "And there is one other point to keep in mind, Professor Saxon. Should Captain Galloway's expedition fail, the Shalnuksis will expect *you* to produce the crops they desire. You will not have the military means he had, which means you will need local allies to produce them in return for what you can teach them."

"That doesn't sound like you have a huge amount of confidence in this Galloway," Sandori observed.

"I have confidence that he will try very hard to complete his mission," Agzaral told her. "Unfortunately, at last report he wasn't doing so well."

## ✦≈ **CHAPTER SEVEN** ≈✦
# THE LANDING

**One week before the Battle of the Ottarn River**

Bart Saxon stared at the screen. A blue planet, largely water, showed in brilliant colors. He noted exaggerated icecaps at both poles. There were two large continents, one larger than the other, with outlying islands. Saxon focused on the larger continent, the one he'd been told they were going to land on. At this magnification he could see nothing of human works on the planet below, but he studied the geography. There ought to be a big city where those rivers ran together, another somewhere near that obvious mountain pass. The western high plains seemed barren of features and very dusty. Nothing there? It would be amusing to see if he could find cities by choosing what appeared to be good geographical locations for them, then zooming down to find out what was actually there. For now he was content to look at the planet as a whole.

Storms raged across the southern hemisphere. Of course north and south would be arbitrary, but the locals had chosen "north" so that the suns would rise in the east, and most of them lived in the northern hemisphere of the larger continent. Saxon had read that there was also an island culture halfway around the world from the dominant settlement, but little was known about it. Apparently some forgotten Shalnuksi trader had imported a colony of Tonganese Islanders sometime during the First Millennium of the Christian era on Earth.

Whatever the traders had expected, according to the records he'd seen, the result was about what Saxon would have predicted: the islanders had developed a culture very close to what Captain Cook had found in the South Seas. Had this been an experiment in cultural anthropology? That seemed unlike the Shalnuksis, who seldom did anything except for profit, but it was still the most reasonable explanation. It had been much the same with the Steppe cultures brought in and settled on the high western plateaus of the northern continent. They'd been put in place, then abandoned, and if anything had ever been expected of them, it was forgotten.

*So damned much I don't know*, Saxon thought. *And what I don't know can certainly hurt me. Maybe Galloway knows more, but Inspector Agzaral doesn't believe it.*

"It looks wet," Haskins said. "And them ice caps are big. I mean, really big. Looks cold."

"It is mostly cold. Warming, though," Saxon said. "And there's land under much of that ice. If it melts, the seas rise. A lot."

"So what did you decide about Galloway?" Haskins asked. "We're supposed to help him."

"I know," Saxon said. "But the pilots can't find him."

"What?"

"They say they can locate him, but he's not where they expected him to be, and nowhere they can land."

"So what do we do?" Haskins said.

"We can look for Galloway, or we can go camp out in this Nikeis place," Saxon said. "Go there and get settled and then try to hook up with Galloway."

"I'm for that," Sandori said. "If we took a vote that's the way I'd vote it."

"This ain't no democracy," Haskins said.

"Not if you always vote with Saxon, it's not," she agreed.

"Lady, I know who Doctor Lee and that Inspector Agzaral put in charge."

"If we could just hook up with Galloway I'd do that," Saxon said. "But they don't seem to think they can do that. So it's land near one of Galloway's cities, or near Nikeis. Those are the choices, and they're not giving us long to make a choice, either."

"I think I am going to like this Nikeis," Sandori said. "A republic, and we start off rich."

"True. They also speak Italian," Saxon said. "Which you already know."

"We all got crash courses in both the Tran lingua franca and Italian, and you don't know either one of them all that well. At least I know some Italian. Might come in handy."

"Okay, I'll give you that," Saxon conceded. "But I got more hypno sessions in lingua franca than Italian. Okay, language doesn't matter, we just have to learn. Upside, Nikeis is a republic. Spirit knows the language, and maybe something of the customs. Downside?"

"I don't know dick about no boats," Haskins said. "'Scuse me, Miss Spirit."

She grimaced. Haskins seemed to enjoy treating her with exaggerated deference.

"We have a lot of material about boats and navigation," she said. "Some of it may be useful."

"Yeah, if you can learn about boats from books," Haskins said. "And I don't think you can. But what the hell."

"That's a lot of water . . ." Sandori said, looking at the screen again.

"About ninety percent," Saxon said. "Of course Earth is eighty or so. And if you look at the Pacific as one side, just about all the land is on the other. Here a lot of the land is at the poles covered with ice. Less land to live on. You're right, that's a lot of water, and they tell me it's rising. Navies will be important. We'll teach them maritime commerce. Buckminster Fuller always said the maritime interests were the real drivers of civilization."

"If they started off as Venetians, they know more about maritime commerce than you do," Sandori said. She grinned. "You or me."

"You're from Venice?" Haskins asked.

"Grandfather was. Another grandfather from Florence. Mother from Turin."

"Real Italian lady," Haskins said. "Good thing, I think."

There was a buzz. Saxon lifted the communicator handset.

"Hello?"

"Awantshu."

Saxon had no idea what that meant, but the unknown pilots of the ship always said it.

"Good day," he responded.

"Your Colonel Galloway is a very long way from the communicator his employers left with him," the alien voice said. "We have no way of making contact with him."

"So?"

"If you are asking why this is significant—"

"I am."

"Then I tell you that we will not risk this ship by exposing it to Galloway's weapons, so we cannot set you down at his location, nor can we warn anyone that you are coming. You must land on this planet without prior negotiations with the local inhabitants. Choose where you wish us to place you."

"Is this what you agreed with Inspector Agzaral?"

"His Importance employed us for a mission. He cannot require us to risk our ship. We agreed to transport you, and we will do so. Now choose where you wish to be landed. The landing will be recorded, and the record given to His Importance."

"A moment." Saxon told Haskins and Sandori what the alien had said. "And it doesn't sound like we have a lot of time to decide," he said.

"I like Nikeis, of course," Sandori said, and Haskins shrugged.

"I'll go where you decide," he told Saxon. "I sure don't know what's best. But if we have to fight somebody I'd sure rather fight locals than Galloway's mercs!"

"Why would we fight at all?" Saxon asked.

"Maybe I just got a nasty suspicious mind," Haskins said. "Maybe I been on the streets too long. But—"

Sandori smiled thinly.

"Venice was the most civilized place on Earth in its day," she said.

Saxon shook his head slowly. *What the hell do I do? All I know about old Venice is from* La Giaconda, *and it wasn't all that nice a place in that opera. But they treated Othello all right in Verdi's opera. Othello was a mercenary general. So were Cassio and Roderigo. I think. Was that the opera or Shakespeare? I have all that information, but it's in the containers and I can't get at it. Damn all.*

*They're going to set us down somewhere, and nobody knows we're coming. Near one of the places Galloway commands, but not necessarily near him. Or near this Nikeis. I guess if those are the choices I don't have much choice.*

"We're ready to land near Nikeis," Saxon said into the handset. "We'll need to hide the cargo except for what we can carry."

"Yes. We have chosen a place. It will require that you walk seven of your English miles to a road," the pilot said. "The terrain is level and only lightly forested. There is a major road to the north. Is this acceptable?"

"I suppose so." He got nods from the others. Seven miles wasn't far. They had good lightweight camping gear and boots, and they were all in good shape thanks to the ship's gym. "Let's do it, then."

⊹ ⊹ ⊹

It was dark when the ship set them down in a meadow surrounded by woods. Lights flashed as automated systems unloaded the three large cargo containers onto the meadow.

"We sure going to need help moving this stuff very far," Haskins observed. "What do we do, one stay here and watch the stuff? Who hikes, who stays?"

"We can decide in the morning," Saxon said. He raised his voice to shout into the ship. "What do we do now?"

"Awantshu. The road is to your north. It is an east-west road. You cannot have difficulty finding it."

Sandori fingered her compass. It seemed to work all right, north was more or less north.

"I've got a bad feeling about this," she said, and Saxon laughed.

"Lady, you have a bad feeling about everything."

"I suppose. So what do we do now?"

"Wait for morning," Haskins said. "We sure don't want to be thrashing around in the dark in woods we don't know. Come morning we can go look for people."

"Who stays here?" Sandori asked.

"Why should anyone?" Haskins asked. He pounded the heel of his fist against the side of one of the containers. "Plenty solid, good locks. Take hours to get through this, even with a good hacksaw. With what they have it'll take days."

"Yeah, okay," Saxon said. "I sure wish we knew more about what we're doing."

"We've got knowledge and trade goods," Sandori said.

"Sure, if somebody don't just take them," Haskins said.

"Think they would?"

"Officer Sandori, I have no idea," Haskins said. "But why wouldn't they?"

"It's a civilized city-state. They're not barbarians. Besides, they can take stuff, but ideas are a bit harder to get. They won't know how to use anything. We can show them. And it wouldn't be smart to get us too pissed off," Sandori said. She fingered her pistol.

"Yeah," Haskins said. "Of course, they ain't never seen a pistol."

The two of them had argued this a dozen times. Saxon sometimes took one side, sometimes the other, but he didn't know what would happen. If they'd gone to Captain Galloway they'd have a better idea of who they were dealing with. *Too late for that,* Saxon thought. *We can try him later. If we can find him.*

There were mechanical sounds behind them. The ship's hatchways and doors closed.

"Good luck." The voice came from the small communicator box that lay beside Saxon's pack.

"Thank you," Saxon said.

The ship lifted silently, straight up out of the clearing, and was gone in seconds. It was the first time Saxon had been outside it to see it fly.

"Impressive," he muttered. "I wonder how the hell they do that?"

"Beats me," Haskins said. "But you're sure right, it was impressive."

"Some kind of magnetic effect?" Sandori wondered.

"I can't see how that would work, but I can't think of anything else," Saxon said.

"And now we're alone," Sandori said. "And I think I'm just a little scared."

Haskins laughed. "Only a little?"

"Let's get some sleep," Saxon said. "We've got a good three-hour walk in the morning."

"I'll get out the tents," Haskins said. "Two enough, or you want one all to yourself?"

"Two's enough for me," Saxon said. "Heck, one's enough for me."

"Two, please," Sandori said. "And thank you, Cal."

✛ ✛ ✛

The meadow was small. Young trees grew at its edges, and behind them were older trees, nearly all conifers. Earth trees, Saxon realized. A few strange flowers dotted the meadow, but the grass underfoot seemed earthlike, and they could easily have been in California. There was almost no sense of an alien world until a large and strangely marked insect flew past.

"Young growth," Haskins said. "This place was logged out, maybe fifty years ago."

"You can tell that?" Sandori asked. "How?"

"Just can." Haskins looked around. "I did some logging once. Hard work, too hard for me! But look over in the woods there, see that stump? That tree was cut down with a saw. Too even across the top, and trees don't just break over and fall."

"Oh." She looked around nervously.

"Long time ago," Haskins said.

They were in the middle of breakfast. Haskins proved to be skillful with the small Mountain Safety Research stove, and a good cook. Saxon savored the last of the fresh eggs and bacon. He had just finished when the communicator box spoke.

"Mr. Saxon. Awantshu."

"Here!"

"You need not walk to the road. There is a party coming towards you. They have been moving purposefully in your direction for half an hour, and it is clear they know where they are going."

"What should we do?"

"We have no advice," the voice said. "We have delivered you to a place of your choosing."

"How would they have known where to come?"

"Perhaps we were seen. We made no effort to hide," the voice said. "We used lights freely in landing you."

Saxon nodded to himself.

"You said this area wasn't inhabited."

"We saw no signs of inhabitants. In any event they are coming to you. It remains only to observe."

"You'll watch."

"Yes. We are required to report your situation to Inspector Agzaral."

"And if they slaughter us?"

"We will report that to His Importance. Good luck."

"How many are coming?"

"We count seventeen. Nine are mounted. All appear to be armed, and some are in armor."

"A war party?"

"They appear to be escorts to a large wagon train moving eastward along the road. That wagon train has halted. Although we saw no one watching, it is our belief that the landing last night was observed, by them or someone closer. You would have been discovered in any event. Is it not better sooner than later?"

"I suppose so."

"Good luck."

"Wait! Maybe it would be better to move us to another location!"

"We cannot do that. Good luck."

"Why can't you?"

"That was not part of our contract nor is it within our discretion. Good luck."

Saxon shouted at the box but there was nothing else.

"Okay, Boss, so what do we do?" Haskins demanded. "Dig in? Lay out heavy weapons?"

"We don't have any heavy weapons," Saxon said. "And I'd rather not start off with a firefight even if we had them. It won't do you two any harm to get out rifles and take up positions between the containers, but don't shoot unless I tell you."

"Or you aren't able to give any more orders," Sandori said.

"Well, yeah, there's that," Saxon said.

✦ ✦ ✦

The waiting was the hard part. A thousand doubts ran races in Saxon's head. Should they run away, abandon their cargo? That couldn't be intelligent. Without the equipment they had no reason to be here. There was nothing to do but wait.

✦ ✦ ✦

The approaching party made no attempt at concealment. First there was the sound of a trumpet, then a half dozen crossbowmen, led by a fugleman with a banner, emerged from the woods into the clearing. They formed a rough line, broken in the middle, their bows held low in what had to be a deliberately unthreatening pose. When the crossbowmen were set, four horsemen rode through their lines and out into the clearing.

"Ave!" one shouted.

The spokesman had neither helmet nor armor. He wore a dark blue velvet doublet slashed to reveal scarlet silk lining, dark hose that looked like silk, and a black velvet muffin-shaped hat. A sword, thin but shorter than a rapier, hung at his left side. His beard was well trimmed.

*Looks young,* Saxon thought. Under thirty. *Handsome devil.*

"Ave, indeed," Saxon answered.

The man responded with rapid sentences in Italian. Saxon thought he recognized a few words, but no more than that. He stood there, helplessly.

"He says he is Caesare Avanti," Sandori said from behind him. She came up to join him. "He's a Senator in Nikeis, and his uncle is a Councilor. These soldiers are his retainers. We're in the territory of the Most Serene Republic of Nikeis, sometimes known as the New Venetian Republic."

"Hot damn. Did he say what he wants?"

Sandori spoke liquid syllables and got more in answer.

"He asks if we are star men. He says he knows two star men, and we carry weapons that resemble those the star men carry."

"There goes secrecy. Tell him sure, we're star men, and we're here to help them."

Sandori spoke a few words, then nearly collapsed with giggles.

"What in the world?"

"Sorry. Can't help it," she said with a grin. "I said, 'We come in peace. Take me to your leader.'"

✛ ✛ ✛

Caesare Avanti seemed excited. He gawked at the visible gear—nylon tent, mountain stove, canteens and mess kits, backpacks and sleeping bags—and kept glancing at their holstered pistols.

He also kept eyeing Sandori's ankles. She wore camouflage trousers with the bottoms rolled up. Saxon remembered she'd put on boots when they got up, but sometime after the Nikeisians arrived she'd taken off both boots and heavy socks and put on slippers.

"It will take some time to bring sufficient transport for all this," Senator Avanti said. He waved his hand to indicate the cargo containers. "Perhaps you could unpack what equipment you will need and come with us. We will leave men to guard this site, and when the transport column arrives they will bring everything to the seaport city."

Sandori translated into English, then asked him, "Do you understand the value of what is here?"

"Of course not."

"But you will concede that it is great. Senator, who do you trust to guard such a fortune? Every power on this planet will pay to obtain what is here."

"What use will it be?" Avanti asked.

Saxon struggled to understand, and interrupted the translation to say "To whom? Captain Galloway can use anything here." Saxon spoke in what he hoped was the planetary lingua franca, and Avanti nodded in apparent understanding.

"Does he know you are here?"

"He is expecting us." Saxon said. "And does he not have agents in your city?"

"He does. They enjoy the hospitality of the Signory," Avanti said. "As do the Roman agents."

"Those you know of," Sandori said.

"True."

"I think it best to wait," Saxon said. He looked over to where Haskins was standing guard with a battle rifle.

"And we will continue to enjoy the pleasure of your company," Sandori said.

Saxon could have sworn she was batting her eyes at the young Senator.

# PART THREE
# STRANGERS

## ✦✦ CHAPTER ONE ✦✦
# THE SUMMONS

Rick Galloway left Sergeant Walbrook to organize the final evacuation of Armagh and moved north with his guards and staff. They camped at a major crossroad, with branches leading northeast to Taranto, west to Chelm, and north through borderlands into the Five Kingdoms. He planned on sending most of this party west to join Tylara, while he took an escorting force to Taranto to investigate what was happening in Nikeis.

The day's march was satisfactory, and Rick had Warner as his guest at dinner. As they were finishing, there were shouts from the periphery guards. A few moments later Sergeant McCleve came into Rick's command caravan.

"Reporting, Sir," he said, and Rick returned the salute.

"Kind of private, Sir," McCleve said. "Medical report, Sir."

Rick nodded and turned to Warner.

"Guess that's your cue."

"Right, Colonel. I'll go see to my gear."

Rick waited until Warner was gone and he was alone with McCleve, then nodded.

"Have a seat, Sergeant."

"Don't mind if I do."

"Wine?"

"No, Sir, water's okay. Unless you've opened some of the reserves?"

"No."

"Then just water." McCleve watched Rick for a moment and grinned. "Seeing as how surprised you are—"

"Maybe a little." Rick shrugged. "Okay, a lot. Never saw you turn down a drink before."

"You didn't notice, I guess. Been sober for months," McCleve said. "Got that devil licked to the point I can enjoy a glass and not want more. No point in cheap wine, though. I do like the taste of some of the best."

"That's good news, Sergeant." Rick frowned. "You're the closest thing we have to a doctor. Maybe it's time we recognized that."

"Sir?"

"Doctors are usually officers," Rick said. "Perhaps it's time to promote you to captain."

"Not a lot of point to it, is there, Sir?" McCleve said. "Not as if it would put me in a higher pay grade, so to speak. The locals all call me Lord anyway, and why would I care if Warner and Bisso call me 'Sir'?" He grinned. "Of course it might be interesting to have Elliot 'Sir' me, 'specially if we both end up back at the University. Maybe I ought to think on that one again."

"All right. If you have new thoughts on the subject, come see me. Now, do you have a report?"

"Yes, Sir. You asked me to stay behind to examine Publius. I did. From all I can see, it's arthritis, the first stages of leukemia, multiple sclerosis or lupus, Colonel. I'd say lupus, but without a blood count—and we can't do those here—I can't be sure. If it's MS or leukemia, I can't help him."

"Lupus. Is that fatal?"

"Can be. It's an autoimmune disease, Colonel. Tends to be debilitating. Symptoms are a lot like arthritis, only generally much worse, but severe lupus can take out the kidneys or other organs. Attitude counts a lot."

"Is there a treatment?"

"Maybe, but not one I have," McCleve said. "Prednisone is the standard treatment for it back home, and it helps, but the side effects can be nasty. 'Course, we don't *have* any prednisone, though I suppose we could ask the Shalnuksis for some." He shrugged. "Hasn't helped much with anything else, I know, but we sure can't make it here."

"We can always *ask*," Rick agreed with a shrug of his own. "I wouldn't hold my breath waiting, though."

"Yeah, tell me about it. Now if I had some books on lab techniques maybe I could get started figuring out how to produce more of what we need locally, but I don't. Too bad we didn't have a good chemistry set with us in Africa! I've made a passable microscope, but chemistry was never my strong point anyway."

"You seem pretty familiar with lab work," Rick said.

"Sure. I have an MD degree, Colonel." He grinned at

Rick's astonishment. "From Guadalajara University. After I graduated I pretty well drank my way out of getting a license in the US. After a while I joined up as a medic. I'm a lot out of date, but I did have the training."

"Now I'm pretty sure we'll *have* to give you a commission," Rick said, and McCleve snorted in amusement.

"I doubt it matters a lot, but it's okay with me."

"So what's the prognosis with Publius?"

"I left him some aspirin," McCleve said. "Told him about willow bark, too. Willow bark works here just as good as it does on Earth. Damn near as rare, too! But he's got the resources to look for more. And I gave him some mumbo jumbo to keep up his spirits. Attitude's likely to be as important as anything else. If he keeps his spirits up, he's good for ten years anyway, maybe more, but lupus is pretty tricky, Colonel. It can hurt like hell, and bring on fits of depression, and if he gets too discouraged there's lots of ways to go out rather than face it."

"I see." *One more thing to worry about, but nothing I can do*, Rick thought. *Not now, anyway.* "Thanks, Doc."

"Sure." McCleve stood and saluted. "I'll give it some more thought, Colonel, but I can't think of anything else just offhand."

Rick nodded. "Thanks."

⁜ ⁜ ⁜

The crossing was important enough to support a major village. It also held one of Rick's semaphore posts. At dawn the semaphore arms began waving and a runner came to Rick's caravan. Rick heard him shout "Urgent message from the Wanax," and went back to his breakfast.

An hour later he had the message. It was brief:

"To Rick Galloway, Warlord of Drantos, greetings. We advanced on Aachilos. At first we met success, but now we have been defeated. Many star weapons were used against us. The host of the Five Kingdoms pursues us. I do not know their numbers. There are star men serving the Five. I do not know their numbers. Bring all your forces to the Ottarn Fords immediately. Disaster threatens. Bring all forces. You will learn more as you approach the Ottarn. Ganton, Wanax."

It was followed by authentication codes that left no doubt this was a message sent by Ganton.

"But whether he had a dagger to his throat is another matter," Warner said sourly.

"Yah, but what do we do?" Sergeant Major Elliot asked pointedly. "'Send all forces' isn't a command that makes sense, Colonel. How the hell will we feed them all? Send them to face what? And if you strip Chelm what holds back that goddam army sitting in your crop fields? Skipper, this is stupid."

*And Ganton isn't stupid. Or hasn't been.*

"Panic, Top?"

"Looks that way to me," Elliot said. "'Course you know him better than me, Colonel."

"It's a direct order. Sir," Warner said. "If he's looking for a way to get at you, direct disobedience is a pretty good charge."

"I'd say you have a nasty, suspicious mind, if I didn't worry about the same thing myself, Mr. Warner," Elliot said.

"Disobedience to an order that can't be carried out," Rick said. "There's no way we can feed a big army at the

Ottarn. Hell, we damn near stripped the place ourselves. We can get fodder sent in from the local areas, and carry rations, but that's sure going to limit how many troops we can bring."

"Yes, Sir," Warner said. "But it doesn't change a direct order, Colonel."

"No, it doesn't," Rick said. "But we don't know what we're facing, either. How many star weapons? Is this some renegade from our outfit?"

"Who would it be?" Elliot asked. "He said 'many.' We're not missing 'many.' Clavell and Harrison, they're in Nikeis. Maybe Murphy went off his head and joined the enemy, but that don't make sense, and it still doesn't add up to 'many.' Colonel, to the best I can make it we've accounted for everyone we brought here from Earth, and I just named the only ones not dead or directly under our command."

Elliot looked thoughtful.

"Unless Gengrich went rogue again, but if he had we'd have heard." The sergeant major looked around to be certain no one but Warner and Rick could hear him. "And even if we didn't hear, your Lady would, she's got those Children of Vothan watching down there. No. To the best I can make it, this has to be someone new." He looked thoughtful. "Colonel, I'd sure feel better about this if we'd heard anything from our people in Nikeis. I don't much believe in coincidences. Lights in the sky at Nikeis, now Ganton runs into opposition with star weapons."

"Sounds like new players," Rick agreed. "Wonder how many?" He paused to think. "So. Okay. We send mounted forces, and not many of those. We have to sort out who goes north and who goes west from here. Elliot, I'll leave that to you. Sounds like we may need Walbrook and his mortars with us, so get a runner back to him and tell him to hand over the evacuation to Walinski. Then he's to join us as quickly as he can. Get all our noncombatants and supplies and logistics together and have them wait here for Walinski's lot. And tell Walinski to get a wiggle on. Leave anything we can replace. I want him headed west with enough guards to make sure he gets there. The rest of us head north to the summons. That includes Warner and McCleve, I want them with me. Get your book out, Warner, I've got semaphore signals to dictate."

"Aye, aye, Skipper."

"All coded. Signal to Tylara, copy of the Wanax's message and orders. To Mason, leave Tylara a bodyguard. Henderson and Boyd, I think. He's to bring the rest of the mercs to the Ottarn. Particularly Ark and the LMG, and Frick and McQuaid with the Carl Gustav. We don't have many rounds left for that, but bring what we have. It may be needed. Leave the one-oh-six with Tylara; there isn't enough ammunition left for it to be worth much in the field.

"The Musketeer Dragoon Company, I guess. They aren't trained very well, but they may be better than nothing. Bring light cavalry. Reiters, all of them, all of the mounted archers. Bring the mobile supply trains, logistics people. Tell him to use his judgment, but it needs to be fast and self-contained. All mounted, keep the movements secret, and make it as quick as possible. Warner, get that off."

"Yes, Sir—Colonel, that's going to leave your county pretty defenseless against that Fiver army camped there."

"Maybe not. If the enemy doesn't know, it won't matter

at all. Even if they do they'll have to assault fixed positions, and Tylara can handle that. At worst she can hold the castle until I get there." He thought for a moment. "It won't hurt to remind Mason that the Great Guns aren't part of what I consider mobile forces. Leave those big cannon to defend the walls. Make sure that reads like a reminder and not an insult to his intelligence."

"Yes, Sir." Warner nodded and Sergeant Major Elliot chuckled.

"Given them gunners are local militia and you're stripping the county of most everything else, I'd think it would take a direct order to get Lady Tylara to let go of those guns in the first place."

"If even that would do it," Rick said. "Okay, but it never hurts to be explicit, particularly in a semaphore message. What I want to get across is they should keep what it takes to hold Chelm, but the Wanax has directly ordered us to 'bring everything.' That's the way to start the message, with the royal order. She'll catch on quick enough, she's sharper than I am about local politics."

Rick wasn't surprised when neither Warner nor Elliot wanted to comment on that.

"Another thing," Rick said. "I need administration more than guns. Top, I want you to take the civilians and logistics and supplies back to Chelm and start organizing madweed cultivation."

Elliot frowned slightly. *Doesn't like being under Tylara's direct command,* Rick thought. *Well, nothing I can do about that.*

"Sir." Whatever misgivings Elliot felt they didn't make it into his voice. "Do I take Rand?"

"He's one of the best scouts we have. I may need him here to deal with this. I'll send him back to you as soon as I can, but I think I better keep him."

"Sir." Elliot paused. "And Lady Siobhan?"

"Oh God, I forgot she was coming with us!" Rick said. "To marry Major Mason. Only now I'll need Mason here. Take her with you, Sergeant Major. She'll be safer there than anywhere else, and it's the best place for her to wait for Mason anyway. I'll send Tylara a note so she'll expect her."

"You might let Art Mason know she's coming there," Warner said. "Sir."

"Right. You do that. Now, Warner, a message to Drumold. Tell him what's going on. Use his own judgment."

"He's got no reason to come to the Ottarn," Warner said. "Ganton's writ doesn't run in Tamaerthan, and I don't think the little king's going to get any volunteers, either. Took all you could do to get the clans to come up here the first time, and that was before his barons pissed them off. Again."

"I know. Let them know. It's all we can do just now. When you get that drafted I'll add a personal note to my father-in-law."

"What about Nikeis?" Warner asked.

"Has to be put on hold. I'll put together a message to Publius explaining the delay."

"Going to be hard on Harrison and Clavell," Elliot said.

"I know that. Not sure what I can do."

"Diplomatic note to the Doge in Nikeis," Warner said. "We are greatly concerned that we haven't heard from our men in quite some time, and beg that our ally find out for us if some ill has befallen them. All sugar and spice. That's what I'd do, Colonel."

"Sounds good," Elliot said. "Best to stay friends if we can. Let Publius put on the pressure. Least until we know more."

"Right," Rick said. "Do that. And I've had a thought."

"Sir?" Warner asked.

Rick looked around. Only Elliot and Warner were close.

"Tylara may have a way to learn more about the situation."

"The mean little kids," Elliot said. "Yes, Sir, that she may."

Tylara's band of child assassins was a sore subject. For over a year Rick had feared they might be turned on him, and now that things were better between him and Tylara there was still the danger of discovery of the assassins and their victims. *If word gets out,* Rick thought to himself, *we're through. Fortunately, Tylara's changed their mission to observation and protection. Right now intelligence is what I need.*

"I'll write that request myself," Rick said. "Okay, get those messages off. Elliot, sort out the farmers and civilians and escort them to Dravan. Except for your escort, everybody else comes north. Bisso will be senior sergeant with me. Warner, you're my direct staff aide and adjutant. Better get foraging parties going out ahead of us. Forced marches, gentlemen."

## ⊰⊱ CHAPTER TWO ⊰⊱
# THE OTTARN AGAIN

**Twenty days since the Battle of Ottarn River**

The Ottarn encampments were barren, but when Rick's banners came into view, Wanaxxae messengers appeared as if from the ground itself. Rick recognized two royal pages. They were boys about twelve, expensively dressed sons of noblemen who'd wrangled themselves a place in the royal household. Both wore daggers, and one carried a short muzzle-loading rifled flintlock carbine slung over his back. The concept of the Minié ball was catching on throughout Dravan.

*And it will get to the Romans and the Five Kingdoms soon enough*, Rick thought. *Soon enough. How many years until my Tamaerthan archers no longer have an advantage? Or for that matter, our star weapons, when everyone has a rifled musket?*

"That's got to be the Lord Speaker's grandson," Warner

said. "That carbine cost a king's ransom, Colonel. Literally, I'd say."

"Right. I'll be polite."

The boys ran up, one waving maps.

"Greetings, Warlord of Drantos," he shouted. "In the name of the Wanax, you are most welcome."

Warner grinned at Rick.

"Little better reception than you got the last time, Colonel. Ganton must have been worried. Would his message get to you, and more important, would you come? Heh."

"Yeah."

"Still, it must have galled him, having to ask you for help. And so soon."

Rick nodded.

"And that's what worries me. A lot." He signaled for his aides to help him dismount. *Days in the saddle, and I've got piles.* McCleve had made an ointment of lanolin and some local herb that seemed to help a lot, but Rick wished again for an early meeting with the Shalnuksis. They were supposed to be bringing Preparation H.

✣ ✣ ✣

Rick examined the maps with a scowl.

"Okay, so we're here, and the army got ambushed northwest of here, in these hills. The enemy's presumably headed our way. Now where the hell is the king?"

He faced a ring of blank looks.

"Where did he tell you to go once you found me?" Rick demanded.

"His Majesty required that we remain with you. His

Majesty will send for us when we are again needed," the page said. The boy seemed shaken and afraid.

"Tell me about the battle, son."

"I know little, Warlord of Drantos. I rode with the Wanax, as is my duty. We were in what he called 'standard order of march,' which he had learned from you . . ."

Rick nodded. Point, scouts, advance guard, advance party, all mounted, with the king in the advance party. The main body of the army would be behind the king . . .

"The scouts were ahead of us, out of sight over a hill. Suddenly there was shouting, and the sounds of guns. Not Great Guns like our cannon, nor like the muskets." The boy waved his carbine. "Not like this. There was no smoke. It was like your weapons. I have heard the Wanax fire his Browning, and the sounds were like that. And very many."

"Many. How many?" Warner demanded.

"Lord, I do not know. Too many to count. And after that, the scouts and the advanced guard came over the hill fleeing for their lives. The Wanax tried to rally them, but he could not, and soon the panic took even his guards. We rode for our lives."

"Pursuit?" Warner asked. "Anyone chasing you?"

"None I saw, lord."

"And you never saw the enemy?"

"Men fell from their saddles two stadia from the enemy. There was nothing to see."

"Shee-it," Warner said. "That's good shooting."

Rick nodded. Two stadia was over five hundred meters. Against moving targets.

"So what then?" he asked the page.

"We fled until our horses were tired," the boy said. "Then we paused, realizing that none pursued. The Wanax said he must rally the men, without an army he was Wanax no more. Then the Wanax gave me messages, for you and for the semaphore tower. He ordered me to deliver the messages to the semaphore, then come here and wait, for you or for him. I have done so."

"Good lad," Rick said. "And how long ago was that?"

"Lord, there have been thirteen nights since that day."

"Thirteen days. Hell, they could be anywhere," Warner mused, and Rick nodded.

"And you heard nothing more about the Wanax?"

"Nay, Lord, I heard more. You asked if I had seen him. I have not."

"Okay, what did you hear? And who from?"

"Lord Murphy came here yesterday," the page said.

"Murphy! Where is he?"

"He said he would not be far, and you should wait for him," the boy said.

"Holy shit," Bisso said.

✢ ✢ ✢

Murphy rode in at dusk. The horses were lean and thin, and the men gaunt. "Looks like they've done some hard riding," Warner observed.

Rick nodded. Living off the land was never easy, and Murphy's job was to make it harder, burn crops and fields, and always keep moving. It was a job for Westmen, and Rick noted Mad Bear, formerly an enemy, now blood brother to Murphy, seemed to be second-in-command. Hal Roscoe and the other merc whose name Rick couldn't remember were back with the other troops. Three more troops with star weapons, plus Mad Bear's Horse People and Murphy's feudal tenants. There was also a company-sized unit of mounted archers. Useful.

The mounted archers seemed in better shape than Murphy's troops. The rest of Murphy's forces looked more like their renegade Westmen allies than a civilized military force. Thin and hard worn . . . *Except for the centaurs*, Rick thought. *More for them to eat? Makes sense, they eat stuff horses and people can't. But whatever the reason they sure look in better shape than most of the horses. We won't get much service out of those mounts until they've had a season to recuperate and fatten up.*

"Good to see you, Colonel," Murphy said. He gestured, and two young riders rushed up to hold his horse as he dismounted.

Rick nodded to himself. Murphy was a lord of Drantos in his own right, a feudal landholder and guardian to an important ward, as well as a sergeant, brevet to officer, in Rick's mercenary force. Other troops watched Murphy's status carefully. Some resented him, others were envious. All saw in Murphy a clue to their own future.

*Which means I need to be careful with him.*

"Good to see you, My Lord. You've had considerable success. And my thanks for the gifts."

"Was it Akkilas? Sir," Murphy asked.

"We don't know," Rick said. "It may have been."

"Anyway, we got a bigger problem now."

"Yeah. Come have some coffee and tell me about it."

"Coffee. Yeah," Murphy said. "Looking forward to that. Soon as I see to my men. Where do we camp, Colonel?"

✢ ✢ ✢

Murphy sipped coffee and looked up with a grin.

"Now that's what I miss not being a regular with the outfit, Colonel."

Rick considered the implications of that remark, and that Murphy would lead off by making it. Then he shrugged slightly.

"We don't have much, My Lord. And now, Lieutenant Murphy, would you care to tell me what the hell is going on?"

"As best I can. Sir," Murphy said. "We drove into the north, and then started working our way southeast. Towards the Ottarn, where we expected the Wanax. You saw the condition of the horses. Without remounts there wasn't a lot else to do. So we were moving southeast, burning crops and harrying supply parties, when we ran into that group under Akkilas. Or whoever it was. We caught them by surprise, got lucky and killed most of them, including their leader. Someone told me that was Akkilas himself. It looked like maybe the war was over, what with the heir dead and all. So I sent the head and shield to you and started working my way back home. It was slow going, 'cause we'd burned out most anything useful. We'd been at that awhile when there comes a Black Rod Usher."

Rick could hear the capital letters in Murphy's voice.

"A gentleman usher of the Black Rod," Murphy repeated. "He had a summons for me. Two, actually. One a summons to a Great Council meeting at the Ottarn battlefield. I read it over, and it looked like the meeting was already over, probably over before the summons was sent, but by God, Colonel, it was a real royal warrant summoning me to a meeting of the peers of the realm!"

"Hmm," Rick said.

"Yes Sir, hmmm," Murphy said. "So the Black Rod asks, 'Do you accept the summons?' and I point out the meeting is over, and he asks it again, real formal like. 'Lord Murphy Bheroman of Kalstra, do you accept the summons?' he says, so what could I do? I said yes."

"Murph, that pretty well ends any questions about your nobility," Warner mused.

"That's the way I took it, Mr. Warner," Murphy said. "And then he took out the second summons. That ordered me to attend the Wanax in person and named a rendezvous point well on the way to Aachilos. It also said I was to tell no one. Emphatic about that point. Tell no one." Murphy grimaced. "So I headed north again."

"So, Murph," Bisso demanded, "what the hell were you doing taking orders from the Wanax?"

"He had to," Warner said. "Once he accepted that summons, he's part of the peerage. It would be treason not to attend the Wanax in person to swear fealty. And you notice that Black Rod character got Murphy to accept before he pulled the second rabbit out of his hat."

"That's about the size of it, Mr. Warner," Murphy said. "Colonel—Warlord—My Lord—just what the hell do I call you now?"

"Colonel will do," Rick said. "So now that you've told us your new status, what the hell happened? Where is the King?"

"I found the main body of the Fiver army and skirted around that until I got here, and a messenger took me to the Wanax. He's about a day's ride northwest trying to rally the army, or at least round up enough units that it can look like an army," Murphy said. "Day's ride for his people. Four hours for mine."

"Maybe you better start at the beginning."

"I wasn't there for the beginning, Colonel. I was on the way to meet His Majesty in answer to that Black Rod summons when I ran into some mounted archers. Ours. I have them with me. They were trying to get home to Chelm, but they only had a general idea of which way that was. They'd been conscripted by the Wanax for this expedition into the Five Kingdoms. Hadn't liked it much, being turned over to somebody else. They consider themselves part of your household troops, yours and Lady Tylara's, and neither one of you was along. So they were probably pretty ready to run anyway, when they ran into an ambush."

"Ambush," Rick asked with growing interest. "By how many?"

"Don't know, Colonel," Murphy said. "Not many, or a lot, depending on who tells it. You can talk to them yourself, but I doubt you'll get more than I did. They were riding along, scouting ahead of the army, when they came under fire from what I'd figure was fifty rifles."

"Fifty rifles!" Warner exclaimed.

"Jesus H. Christ," Bisso said. "Skipper, that's more'n we have 'less you include the musketeers. Murph, you said rifles, right? Not muskets? Real rifles?"

"Real rifles, Sergeant. Modern firearms. Smokeless ammunition. Not automatic, or anyway they don't fire on automatic. Belgian FNs I'd guess, from the sound and what I could see when I went scouting." He fingered his binoculars. "And whoever the hell they are, they can shoot! Colonel, this was more'n a week ago, and since then I've been trying to get a handle on who we're up against, and I don't have any better idea than I did when we started! I can't get close to them, nobody can get close to them. Hell, Colonel, these guys have got Mad Bear and his Westmen scared!"

"Okay, Murphy," Rick said. "But you must know something more about what we're up against."

"Yes, Sir, it's a whole damn army. The main body's typical Five Kingdom, maybe two thousand lances. The leader's some guy in wolf skins."

"The Honorable Matthias, Priest of Vothan," Rick said. "The High Rexja's Marshal. At a guess, anyway. So you had no trouble getting close to them." Two thousand lances would be about six thousand men, about as large an army as anyone could field given the logistics.

"No Sir, it's just an army of ironheads. They've got some light cavalry scouts, and shortbow camp guard infantry, nothing special. It's their advance party that's killing us."

"Tell us," Rick prompted.

"There's a body of horsemen, medium cavalry, mostly. Couple hundred. They're escorting thirty wagons and a bunch of infantry marching in column. Between fifty and a hundred infantry, all carrying rifles, FNs probably. Look like FNs, but they could be Rhodesian R-1s. That shape, anyway. Pretty distinctive."

Rick nodded.

"About half of them have green jungle cammies and green berets. The rest have khakis, wide-brimmed hats. I think I spotted a couple of officers, khakis and hats. And damn it all, Colonel, that's all I know! It's all I can see at extreme range with binoculars, and you can't get closer to them. Soon as you get anywhere near, they deploy to a prone position and start shooting, and holy shit! They can shoot like—well, like MacAllister, only this is every damn one of them. In that first ambush they killed maybe two hundred men in a couple of minutes. That spooked the rest."

"Might spook anyone," Warner said.

"Hell, they're just mercs," Bisso said. "We want to know more, sneak in at night and look."

"Tried. Lost three men. Best poachers I had, never got a word back," Murphy said.

"Hmm." Bisso looked thoughtful. "That good, eh?"

"Yes, Sergeant, that good," Murphy said.

"So whoever they are, what are they doing?" Rick demanded.

"Colonel, as near as I can tell, they're systematically finishing off every pocket of Ganton's army left in the Five Kingdoms. They're working their way southeast, and they're bringing in supplies in big supply trains, too damn big for me to attack with what I've got. They send out these light cavalry parties and any time they run into resistance they march up this infantry force, and that's all she wrote. And I have to say, I'm spooked, Colonel. I'm afraid to go after their supply trains. What if there are more of those mercs? If there's a hundred in their forward body, who's to say there's not fifty more hidden in one of those supply trains?"

"So the upshot is that a Five Kingdoms army is taking a cakewalk to the Ottarn," Rick said. "And what's to stop them from going on to Armagh and Edron?"

"Nothing I know of," Murphy said. "The Wanax couldn't stop them." He looked around at his colleagues. "And Colonel, I don't think you can either."

# ⊰⊷ CHAPTER THREE ⊷⊱
## SCOUTING

"You wanted to see me, Colonel?"

Rick nodded. Technical Sergeant Harvey Rand had earned his promotion organizing madweed production. The army abandoned the rank shortly after World War II, though the Air Force kept it. Rick had reintroduced it so Rand wouldn't be in the ordinary chain of command, but would still have the authority to get his job done.

But he'd been sent to the madweed fields as a prisoner, to work off a blood debt. He still wore the beard he'd grown in his years of independent service with Gengrich in the south. His clothes were locally made, local copies of the US Army field uniforms he'd lost down south, buttons rather than Velcro and snaps, but the camouflage dye was nearly as good as standard issue on Earth. He still had a Walther PPK, but his other weapons were locally made as well. Nothing fancy. Most of his pay went to compensate the family of the sentry he'd killed while

Rand was part of the breakaway group. Rand's bad luck was that the sentry had had noble family connections.

Rand stood at attention, relaxed, his face calm, a mild expression of curiosity but no more. *Not rebellious*, Rick thought. *And not sullen. He took his punishment a hell of a lot better than I would have.*

*And I need him.*

"At ease. Rand, I've paid off all your debts. You're a free man. As free as any of us, anyway. Your pay's your own from here out. As far as I'm concerned, you're back in the outfit on regular duty. You can keep the rank."

"Thank you, Colonel." Rand spread his feet slightly but stood nearly at attention.

"You don't wonder at what I want in return?"

"I think I've guessed, Sir." He looked directly at Rick. "And you'll tell me whether I ask or not."

Rick noted the suppressed grin. Rand was working hard at being The Good Soldier . . .

"Let's see. Rand, back in Africa you were about the best night scout we had. You still any good?"

"Maybe a little out of practice, Sir, but yeah, I think I'm pretty good. It's not something you forget."

"Right. Okay, you know what I want then. We're up against something new, apparently a new group of mercs from Earth. I need to know how many, and what they're equipped with, and anything else, like who sent them. Take anything and anyone you'll need, and go find out."

"Yes, Sir."

"It may not be easy. Murphy says these troops have Mad Bear and his Westmen spooked."

Rand nodded.

"Means night action, then. The Westmen're as good as me in daytime, but they never were much good at night. I am."

"All right. One more thing. I'd rather have a little information and a live trooper than no information and a dead one. Come back alive, Rand."

"Colonel, I sure as hell intend to obey that order. Right now, I take it?"

"As soon as possible. Murphy's troops have been keeping track of them, you can get there in about three hours."

"Yes, Sir. I'll set out in an hour then, and go in tonight, after the True Sun's gone but before the Stealer sets completely. That's late enough most will be trying to sleep, and I like dusk better than dark for slipping in."

Rand was quiet for a while as he considered the task.

"Jack Beazeley just came in with Murphy's people," Rand said in a manner that didn't sound like a question.

Rick nodded in reply.

"Good. I'll want him to watch my back. I'll need grease paint. And a couple of Mad Bear's people to hold the horses. Nobody better'n them for keeping animals quiet. That ought to do it, if we can do it at all."

"Good enough."

"Skipper, this ain't likely to be easy, if Mad Bear's people can't do it, maybe I can, and maybe I can't."

"I know. Come back alive, Rand."

"You know it, Colonel."

✤ ✤ ✤

Rick was awakened by Sergeant Bisso.

"Rand's back, Colonel."

"He all right?"

"Seems to be. Quiet, though."

"Okay. Orderly room in ten minutes," Rick said. "Secure the area around it. And have some coffee ready."

"Sir."

✢ ✢ ✢

"Gurkhas," Rand said. He looked formidable in his camouflage outfit, leaves fixed to his hair and twigs poking out of his uniform, his face streaked with brown and green paint. "Gurkhas."

"What?"

"Yeah, Colonel, you heard me right. Gurkhas. Fewer'n eighty, more'n thirty. At least three white officers, Brits by their accents, I got close enough to hear them talking but I couldn't quite make out what they were saying."

"They'd have to be Brits with Gurkhas," Bisso said.

"No, Colonel," Warner said. "There are Gurkha regiments in the Indian Army." He frowned. "What I never heard of was any Gurkha mercs. I mean, yeah, they're all mercenaries, but they only hire out to governments. Britain and India."

"Sultan of Brunei," Bisso said. "He had a regiment of Gurkhas with Brit officers. I know, 'cause a buddy thought of hiring out to him once."

Rand looked quietly amused.

"The officers are white," he said. "The troops aren't."

"Rand, you're sure these are Gurkhas?" Rick asked.

"Yes, Sir. I heard them. I know what the language sounds like. And I have pretty good night glasses, I could see them. Short little Indian-looking bastards, big grins, FN rifles, kukri knives, white officers. They're Gurkhas all right, Colonel."

"How close did you get, Harv?" Bisso asked.

"Close enough to see that much," Rand said. "If you mean did I sneak around in their camp, hell no!"

"Don't blame you," Bisso said.

"No wonder my poachers couldn't get close to them," Murphy said. "Colonel, I don't mind tellin' you, this is a little scary."

"Anybody have experience with Gurkhas?" Risk asked.

Headshakes.

"Spent three days on a troop train with one of the Brit Gurkha outfits," Rand said. "That's how I know what they sound like. But mostly I've just heard stories."

"So has everyone else," Bisso said. "Damned scary stories."

"Okay," Rick said. "What do we know for certain about them? Larry?"

Warner struck a lecturer's pose.

"They've been associated with the British Army for over a hundred years. They come from Nepal up in the high Himalayas. Hindu religion. There are at least five tribes they recruit from. Real rugged country, everybody's poor. They serve out their enlistments and go home with their retirement pay, and that's the main support of their villages. There were like ten regiments of them when India got independence. The Indians took on about half, and the Brits kept the rest. I don't know how they get along with the Indian Army, but the Brits have always had a kind of love for them. They served in nearly every war the Brits had after about 1850, and everybody I've talked to says they're the best light infantry in the world."

"So what are they doing here?" Rick demanded. "Freelancers? Did the British government send them?"

"Don't seem likely," Murphy said.

"I've never heard of freelance Gurkhas," Warner said. "They're recruited directly into their regiments, and only the British and Indian governments have recruiting rights. And Murph is right, it's unlikely either the British or Indian governments sent them here."

"Nothing else seems likely either," Rick said. "Well however they got here, they're our problem now. Anyone know a weakness? What spooks them?"

"Skipper, the way I hear it *nothing* spooks them," Bisso said.

"They're not our only problem," Warner said. "They're the toughest part, but are we forgetting there's a whole Five Kingdoms army out there? And our army is scattered. Skipper, I'm not so sure we can handle the Fivers with what we've got."

"He's got a point," Murphy said sourly. "They've been building up with those supply wagons. Is that Matthias any good?"

Rick nodded. "Yes, I think so."

Murphy went on, "So the bottom line is, there's an army out there bigger than ours will be if we can round up everyone. It's commanded by a good man. So far, no big deal, the Colonel's pulled us through much stickier situations than that."

Warner nodded.

"Combined arms," he said. "Use our firepower combined with locals."

"Only this time it's the other guy who can use that trick," Murphy said. "Face it, if Ganton fights this Matthias without us, he's going to lose. And if we fight those Gurkhas we'll probably lose, there being more of them and assuming they got ammo, and why wouldn't they? They haven't had to do much shooting. So the way things stand we lose to the Gurkhas and Ganton loses to the Fivers." He shook his head. "So what do we do about it, Skipper?"

And they were all looking at Rick Galloway.

✣ ✣ ✣

Rick sketched out what he knew of the Gurkhas in a letter to Tylara. It wouldn't be welcome information. Nor would the rest.

"I am summoned to meet with the Wanax. The Black Rod Usher was deferential." Rick briefly considered crossing out the last word and substituting another, but decided that Tylara would have no problems with it in context. "'His Majesty requests that you attend him,' he said, and he was very respectful. We can both remember when he'd use a different tone. I'll go, but I don't know what the heck I'll tell our Wanax. This is a tough situation, and I don't have advice for him. I wish I had you here to advise me. For other things, too. I sure miss you.

"I've heard legends of Gurkha troopers all my life. Probably as much legend as fact, but if half of it is true they're going to be hard to beat. And whatever happens, it can't be a good sign that there's fresh star troops on

Tran. Who sent them? Why to the Five Kingdoms? If the Galactics are taking a hand in this, God help us.

"Then there's the situation in Nikeis. More evidence of Galactic activity. But I've heard nothing on my transceiver and neither has"—he stopped himself before he could write Gwen's name—"anyone else. I await word from our Roman allies who have sent spies in droves to Nikeis, but I can't wait too long. My comrades won't like it if I just write off Clavell and Harrison. Neither will I. And we have to know just what came down from that starship. If you have any way of finding out what's going on in Nikeis, it would be well to do that.

"Everything is a bloody mess." He crossed out the last sentence.

"I love you, I miss you. And the children. Kiss them for me. Be sure Mikhail learns his lessons. He'll have to take my place one day. And we can hope Isobel can marry for love. And that she'll be as happy as we are. And now I am off to see the Wanax. God bless us all. Rick."

He folded up the parchment and sealed it, then dripped on more wax and used his ring to seal it again. This wasn't the kind of thing he wanted to send by semaphore. Some of those operators knew more English than they let on. It wasn't an urgent message, not urgent in that sense. It wouldn't do Tylara a lot of good to get it fast—but it was important that she get it if he didn't come back from his meeting with Ganton.

*I'm not really worried*, he thought. *Not really.*

But he called in a wounded horse archer who was being invalided home with comrades, and charged him to deliver it in person to the Lady Tylara.

*Just in case*, Rick thought. *Just in case.*
*So what now?*
*Well, we can't beat them. And if you can't beat them—*

# ✦═ CHAPTER FOUR ═✦
# BLOODY HELL

Ganton's encampment was small, a field camp with no pretensions of luxury. It was concealed in a hollow a dozen miles from where the leading elements of the Fiver army had made camp. Rick noted the light cavalry patrols and pickets around the camp and nodded approval. The boy king was learning his trade.

*Sanitary arrangements look good, too*, Rick thought. *He's definitely learning.*

This time a page held Rick's stirrup as he dismounted in front of the royal pavilion. Of course it wasn't a pavilion, hardly more than a miner's tent, something that could be struck away in moments at need, but it did have the royal banners. Ganton came to the entrance himself. He was bareheaded, and his armor was dusty. *Doesn't look so regal now.* Rick shook that thought off. *He's still the Wanax.*

"Welcome, Warlord of Drantos," Ganton said formally.

"Welcome, Lord Rick, Eqeta of Chelm. Welcome, Rick Galloway, Colonel of Mercenaries. And welcome, friend. Have I left off anything important?"

Rick couldn't help smiling at that.

"Nothing, Majesty. It's good to see you again."

"I could wish under better circumstances." Ganton gestured towards a table with chairs. One of the chairs had a thick cushion. "I know you do not like to sit on the ground," he said. He gestured towards the cushioned chair. "And you will have had a hard ride. Do you need refreshment?"

"Wine and water, I think," Rick said, and Ganton nodded.

"I guessed as much." He clapped his hands, and a steward brought in a tray with bottles and goblets, set them on the table, and left. Ganton poured water and wine into goblets and indicated that Rick should choose which he preferred. There was a small tray of sugared cakes. Ganton ate one himself.

*All the amenities*, Rick thought. *I still wish Tylara were here. She's on to this court intrigue stuff.*

"As you see, I took your counsel," Ganton said. "I thought to move swiftly to Aachilos before the opposition could rally. The result has not been to my liking."

Rick nodded.

"I offered to come with you."

"You did, and I thought long on that. It was known to all what the Great Council decided, that I should seek to be heir in the Five. Worse strategists than you might see my best chance as an immediate march north. They would be preparing for that, possibly make peace with

Strymon and ask him to command the defense. But if I seemed to dismiss you, perhaps even to be angry with you for the suggestion that we march north, word would go out. Aachilos would not send for Strymon. Word would go to the Green Palace, and Strymon would not keep his forces ready to march. Not having you would be a high price to pay, but deceiving the Five including Strymon would be a reward worth a high price." He shrugged. "So I thought. It has not worked as well as I planned. Yet—had you been with me, would the result be different?"

"I don't know, Majesty."

"It might have been worse. You might have been killed in ambush. Do you know these new star men, My Lord Rick?"

"No, and I had no word of their coming. I know no more of whom they serve than you do. But I do know who they are."

"And?"

Rick sipped at the goblet of wine. *May as well get this over with*.

"On my world they are called Gurkhas, and they are said to be man for man the finest soldiers in the world," Rick said.

"This is no comfort."

"No, Majesty, only truth."

"Can you defeat them? You must defeat them! With them removed we face no more than the Five, and against that force I can make a good retreat and hold my borders. You and I together might do much more than that. But against those—Gurkhas—I can do nothing." He looked up to heaven. "I have no soldiers who will stand and face them. Except you, Lord Rick."

Rick nodded.

"Where is the rest of your army? Scattered?"

"Not so scattered as my enemies believe," Ganton said with a thin smile. "Many units are together and I know where they are. Messages come and go to me even if the units do not always find each other."

"You retained the division structure you used at the Ottarn?"

"I did. Their units are dispersed but each leader knows how to find his own. I can assemble an army in four days' time, Lord Rick, but until those—Gurkhas—are defeated, that would only give them a tempting target. Or so I thought. What advice have you for me?"

"I have to think on it. You say in four days you can have an army again." *Optimistic*, Rick thought. *But it's a number to start with.* "It won't be much longer before the reinforcements I've ordered appear at the Ottarn. With proper handling we can certainly win a defensive battle against the Five. We might indeed do better than that."

"Except that we face more than Matthias and his forces," Ganton said. "I asked once if you could defeat these Gurkhas. You did not answer. I ask again."

Rick shook his head.

"No," he said flatly.

Ganton didn't look surprised.

"Then we are lost."

"Not quite," Rick said. "I can't do it alone, but let's see what you and I can do together."

"You have a plan?"

"Perhaps." *Not so much a plan as a course of action*, Rick thought. *And one I'm going to hate*.

The True Sun had risen a little more than an hour earlier. The wails of the women and children were heart rending. Rick sat upon his horse impassively as he watched the wretched column of villagers form up. There were few men. The Five Kingdoms commanders had summoned the ban and the arrière ban, all the young men and many of the older ones. The women and children might have been able to eke out a miserable existence among the ruined crop fields. Now they wouldn't have even that hope.

*I hate this.*

"Everybody's out," Bisso shouted, and Rick nodded.

"Do it."

Riders with torches rode from house to house. Smoke curled up from each house as they passed. Foragers gathered anything edible including many things Rick wouldn't touch. No one would be living off this land, not now and not this year.

"Move 'em out!" Bisso ordered.

Tamaerthan footguards grimaced horribly and waved their weapons, shouting terrible threats and striking the villagers with small sticks, driving them away from the smoke and flames that had been their homes. The wretched column moved slowly up the dirt track of a road, northward towards the Gurkha encampment.

"Whose house doth burn, must soldier turn," Warner said. "We've brought the Thirty Years War to Tran."

Rick nodded impassively.

"You'll permit me to say I don't like this," Warner said.

"God damn it, none of us like it, Mr. Warner," Bisso said. "The Colonel no more than any of us, can't you see that?"

"Sure," Warner said. "Sorry, Colonel. I'm just glad I don't have to give these orders."

"You ain't got to watch this, Colonel," Bisso said. "We can handle it."

"I know, Sergeant," Rick said. "But if I can order it, I can watch it. Some of it." The scene would be repeated over a twenty-mile radius, everything burned, houses and barns destroyed, animals rounded up to supply Rick's forces, the people turned out and sent northward towards the enemy. "They made a desolation, and called it peace." That was said of the Highlands under William III and the first two Georges of England.

*Now it's my turn, and if we ever take this land how in God's name will we be able to rule it?*

*And if we don't? What the hell do those Gurkhas want? Who sent them? Why?*

*I have to know. Maybe all this is for nothing. But it's all I know to do.*

*And who appointed you God?*

*I don't know. Inspector Agzaral. The Shalnuksis. Skyfire, death and damnation, they are all coming to this planet no matter what I do. Maybe I can make things a little better, maybe I can't, but I have to try.*

The wails were fading out now as the refugees moved northward. The fires of the burning homes and stores and workshops continued to blaze unchecked. The east wind pushed a long plume of smoke across the valley. The desolation was complete here. Time to move on to another village.

Rick mused idly at his desk. It was early afternoon, but he was drowsy after lunch, still sleepy after a bad night. Images of the peasants they'd burned out over the last couple of days haunted his dreams.

*Got to get this settled soon*, he thought. *I can't go on doing this much longer.*

The map on his office table showed his fortified camp: a prosperous farmer's house taken over for headquarters, with palisade and a ditch around it. Somewhere to the southeast would be Ganton's encampment, smaller than Rick's because Ganton was unable to collect all his forces. The Drantos troops had been shaken badly by their encounters with the new star men, and it showed. Legends of their marksmanship floated through Rick's camp, and not even the presence of Rick's star men was enough to reassure his mounted archers and pikemen that they were safe.

"Major Mason has arrived," Haerther announced.

"Good. Send him in," Rick said.

"Colonel," Mason said. He eyed Rick carefully. "I guess you look better than I thought you would."

"Good to see you, too," Rick said. "As always."

"Gurkhas?" Mason asked.

"Yes. How did you know?"

"Everybody knows. Even the locals, they don't know what Gurkhas are, but they know we're facing them and your troops are nervous. That scares the locals. Hell, it scares me! So what do we do? Sir."

Rick shook his head.

"First things first. How are things at home?"

"Better'n you might think," Mason said. "Lady Tylara came in like a tornado, do this, do that, shook everything up. New defense works, entrenchments, more raiding parties, nothing I wasn't doing but she was able to get more enthusiasm out of the locals than I ever could." Mason smiled. "And talking about you all the time! Whatever happened out here, Skipper, I sure like her better this way!"

"Me too, Art. I've got my wife back."

Mason looked serious.

"Damn I'm glad to hear that. You were a mess, Colonel, a pure-dee mess without her. Anyway she comes in like a house afire, and that made it a lot easier when your next messages came."

"You believe she can hold off Ailas?"

"Yes, Sir, I believe she can and then some. It's like she thought she'd have to do it all along. Like she'd had a vision."

*Or information from her private intelligence net*, Rick thought. *No point in bringing that up.*

"Anyway, Colonel, I don't think you need to have any worries about the home front. She maybe can't drive Ailas out, but she can sure hold him where he is—best part is she sees it that way too. Maybe she had something else in mind before you sent for all the troops she could spare?"

"Could be," Rick said. Second-guessing Tylara was an uncertain game at best.

"And thanks for sending Siobhan to me," Mason said. "Even if I did have to leave before she got there."

"Sorry about that, Art. I was prepared to stand you a big wedding, too. Well, time enough for that when we get past this crisis."

"Crisis. Yes, Sir, that's a good word. Crisis. So how do we deal with the Gurkhas?"

"First we isolate them," Rick said. "Make them depend on their supply lines, and then intercept the supplies. However good they are as troopers, they aren't going to be better than us at organization and logistics. They haven't been here long enough."

"Makes sense." Mason nodded. "But from what I heard Gurkhas can live on a handful of rice and rat meat."

"They aren't supermen. And even if they're everything we've always heard, the rest of the Fiver army isn't! So our first move is to be sure the only thing we face is the Gurkhas themselves. No support troops, no allies. Isolate them. We've been burning out everything around them. Now it's time to work on their supplies."

"Yes, Sir?"

"Why haven't we done it before? Is that your question?"

Mason nodded.

"Because nobody wanted to tackle it. Murphy and his troops are spooked, they're afraid there'll be more Gurkhas among the supply trains."

"Are there?" Mason asked.

"Art, I don't know," Rick said. "But if there are, we're defeated anyway. So we have to assume there aren't."

"Assume."

Rick nodded.

"We assume we can win. Because if we can't, then we

can't. But we have to try." *I think we have to try. If we don't, everything we tried to build here is gone. Dammit, I won't give up without a fight!*

"What do you reckon they want?" Mason asked.

"Whoever's in charge of the Gurkhas hasn't offered to talk," Rick said, "and the Fivers made it clear they don't want a parley unless we're ready to surrender." He shrugged. "So we assume we can win, which means we assume this is all of them."

"Assume," Mason said again, and Rick shook his head wryly.

"The Gurkhas and their Brit officers just got here. They can't have been around long, or we'd have heard about them. And that means they can't have a lot of trust in their native allies. Gurkhas have a hell of a reputation back home, but hell, we're doing pretty well in that department here! Bards sing about our battles."

"That they do, Colonel. Especially about you."

"Yep, and for once I'm glad. So put yourself in that Brit officer's place. Would you disperse your men under those circumstances?" When Mason shook his head, Rick nodded. "Exactly. So it's a reasonable assumption he's got them all together, and the only Gurkhas we face are in that one group. And they'll need supplies."

"And if these guys are supplied directly by Galactics?" Mason asked.

"No sign of it. If they are, we lose," Rick said. "It's as simple as that. So we assume they aren't." *Assume we can win, then make the bare minimum assumptions for that to happen. Then plan for the worst, but at least you're prepared for success.*

It sounded good in books. Now he had to live with it.

"There's more, Art."

"Sir?"

Rick took out a folded paper.

"This appeared on my desk this morning," Rick said. "I have no idea how it got here, but it's from Lady Tylara. She gives details that, um, well, no one else would know."

"And it just appeared?" Mason asked.

"Yep."

"From Lady Tylara. Just appeared. Colonel, I think we'd best look into the camp followers."

"I doubt any of the Children of Vothan will be around after delivering a message," Rick said. "I'm convinced that it's genuine. It's also disturbing."

Rick took up the paper.

"It's in English, no code, and short." He began to read aloud. "My Lord Husband, greetings. Isobel has lost her front teeth. New ones are growing. My husband, something is very wrong in Nikeis. I suggest you go there immediately. More news will find you in Taranto. The matter is urgent. I love you. Tylara."

"That's it?" Mason asked.

"That's it."

"More news," Mason said. "In Taranto. More of the mean little kids?"

"That's what I'm guessing," Rick said. Mason had discovered Tylara's childhood assassins and was one of few who knew of them.

"Surprised you haven't started for the coast already."

"How? I couldn't do anything until you got here. Not

sure what I can do now. We can't just cut and run and abandon Ganton to the Gurkhas."

"No Sir, we can't, but I guess you can."

"Think you can handle this, Art?"

"Deal with the Gurkhas? Me? No, Sir, I can't. I reckon you can, but I sure can't."

"So we keep raiding their supply lines. I'll send the best we have to intercept the Gurkha supplies, and we'll give it a few more days," Rick said. "Maybe we'll get a stroke of luck. We're due for one."

✤ ✤ ✤

Tech Sergeant Rand wore an enormous grin.

"Colonel, have I got a present for you!" Before Rick could say anything, Rand thrust a black-colored plastic case at him. "Radio, Colonel. One of theirs. Still works, far as I know. No reason it shouldn't."

Rick's eyes widened and he reached out for it. It was much smaller than the ones they'd lost with Parsons, about five inches tall, with a five-and-a-half-inch flexible antenna. It was too big to fit conveniently into a pocket, but there was a metal clip on the back to hang it on a soldier's webbing. Or maybe not, he thought, looking at it more closely. It wasn't military issue at all. Or he didn't think so, anyway. It was labeled "Kenwood," although he couldn't see a model number anywhere on it.

"They know you have it?" Sergeant Bisso asked.

"Depends on who you mean by 'they,' Sergeant," Rand said. "It's like this, every time we raided one of their supply wagons, them Gurkhas come running. I followed orders and ran away before they could engage, but I wasn't accomplishing much. So I got to moving further up the trail and they still kept coming, so I figured they must have some kind of communication system. Something better than us."

"Good thinking," Rick said.

"Thank you, Sir. So I figured, okay, I can't sneak into the Gurkha camp, but these are just Fivers. So instead of raiding their supply wagons I snuck in and cut the head guy's throat, and sure enough, here this was right next to his bed. So I took it, come back out, and we hit that supply train hard, and nothing. Nobody came to help them."

"Hoo Ha!" Bisso grinned widely. "Rand, you just made my day."

"Mine too," Rick said. "This bears thinking about. They've got communications, a lot better than we have." He turned the radio in his hands and looked back at Rand.

"It was turned off when you found it?"

"Don't know. I didn't fool with it."

Warner came into the tent.

"Heard Rand brought—hey!" Warner caught himself. "Excuse me, Colonel, I forgot my manners."

"We'll overlook that," Rick said. "Know anything about this unit?"

He handed it across and Warner examined it closely.

"Not a lot. Most of it's obvious. On/off switch, push to talk." Warner turned the right hand turret atop the radio and the words "Tac 01" appeared on the rectangular window on its front. He turned the other knob and the window changed to "Tac 02," and then to "Baker."

"Frequency selector," he said unnecessarily. "Don't see a squelch knob, but these are for speaker and mic jacks.

Digital selection, so we're probably looking at at least a hundred possible frequencies or so."

"Kenwood," Bisso said. "Why does that sound familiar?"

"I think RadioShack sold—sells—Kenwood's stuff," Warner replied. "Not their proprietary brand, though. Japanese?"

He handed it back to Rick.

"Push to talk." Rick examined the unit carefully. "Okay, it can't do any harm to turn it on. If they don't know we have it yet, they'll learn soon enough."

"VHF, so it's gonna be line of sight and probably not more than three to four miles range even in flat terrain without more antenna than that, Sir," Warner pointed out. "Won't have much reach from here." He waved his free hand at the wooded hollow in which Rick's command tent was pitched.

"One way to find out, I guess," Rick said and turned the frequency selector back to its original setting. Then he turned the on/off knob to increase the volume. His only reward was a slight hiss.

"Not much static," Warner said. "Why would there be?"

The set squawked.

"Whoa!" Bisso looked at Warner. "Thought you said line of sight?"

"I did." Warner thought for a moment. "They must have a base station—something a lot bigger with a lot higher antenna. They're using it for a crossband repeater."

"Which means all their handhelds have the same range as the base unit," Rick said.

"Yes, Sir. They'll all go through the repeater. That has

to be how they could get enough range to cover their supply wagons over so wide an area. And in such rough terrain, come to that."

The radio squawked again.

"Somebody's talking. What the hell language is that?" Bisso demanded. "Is that Gurkha?"

Rand shook his head. "Sounds like local with a bad accent."

Rick laughed. "That's exactly what it is. Who do we have who knows the northern accents and can speak English?"

"Murphy, but he's not here," Bisso said. "Let me see who I can find."

Eventually they found a Priest of Yatar from the local area. His name was Atanar, and while he didn't speak English, he knew the southern dialects Rick and his men had learned. The radio had fallen silent by the time they brought him in.

"Do you know Lord Father Apelles?" Rick asked.

"I have been presented to His Reverence," Atanar said. "I would hardly be said to know someone of that rank. But His Reverence was most gracious."

*Figures*, Rick thought. *Apelles is a decent sort. Although quick promotion has ruined a lot better men than him.*

The radio squawked again. Atanar listened intently.

"It is heavily accented, and there are words I do not know," he said. "But he is asking for someone named Iztanaster, and seems concerned."

"Probably the supply train leader," Rick said. "Rand, you bring back any prisoners?"

"No, Sir. Sorry. Wasn't sure those Gurkhas wouldn't be coming, so we hit that train fast and hard. Then I ran like hell before anyone could get that radio back. Disarmed everyone not killed and turned them loose."

"Right. Good work." Rick listened to the radio again. "Bloody hell."

"Sir?" Warner asked.

"Just repeating what I heard," Rick said.

"But that's—"

"Precisely." Rick picked up the set and thumbed the push to talk switch. "Hello. Are you there?"

There was a short silence. "Who is this, please?"

"This is Rick Galloway, Colonel of Mercenaries and Warlord of Drantos," Rick said. "With whom do I have the pleasure of speaking?"

"One moment, Sir." There was a pause.

"Good afternoon, Colonel Galloway," a different voice said two or three minutes later. "This is Clyde Baker, one time Major of Her Majesty's Gurkhas. I take it you're responsible for all the starving people coming up the road to my camp?"

"No more than you are," Rick said.

"Well, perhaps so," Baker said. "So, Colonel, what may I do for you?"

"We should discuss that," Rick said. "As well as the return of your radio. And perhaps we have mutual interests."

"That's more than possible," Baker said. "Although I don't think my employers will be pleased by any discovery of mutual interests between us."

"I wouldn't expect them to." *Damn*, Rick thought. *That clipped way of talking is catching.* "But I suspect I know more of the situation, both local and Galactic, than you do. Between us we may know more still."

"Very likely. You propose an exchange of information. A parley."

"Certainly. Flag of truce. Of course neither of us trusts the other."

"Indeed. Unfortunately, we cannot continue this discussion for long, unless perhaps you have a way to recharge that radio unit? What do you propose?"

"Send an English-speaking subordinate under a flag of truce. Have him ride south from your camp on the main road to the Ottarn. I'll have one of my officers meet him about ten kilometers from your camp. They can arrange a time and place for us to meet. And terms."

"Acceptable. Look for Leftenant Cargill in two hours. He will carry a sidearm. His escort will be well behind him. Have your man carry a white banner and leave his escorts behind when they meet. Good day."

✛ ✛ ✛

Rick tried unsuccessfully to hide his relief when Art Mason returned from the parley. Rick fidgeted until Mason joined him at the long table in his command caravan. Rand and Bisso sat opposite Rick.

"Wine," Rick said to his steward. "For all of us, and that will be all."

"Sir." The Tamaerthan scout poured from a clay jug, left the jug on the table, and went out of the tent. Mason sat and looked around. "No Tran locals," Mason observed.

"Not here and not within earshot, Major. I've got Passavopolous out there watching the perimeter," Bisso said.

"Just in case," Rick said. "The locals will be very curious

about what star men say to each other. I expect someone has informed the King already. How did it go?"

"All very correct, Colonel," Mason said. He took his seat at the table. "Not a lot to report, though. They sent an English—well, Scot—subaltern, their idea of someone expendable."

"Art, you are not expendable—"

"I know that, Colonel. I volunteered 'cause I'm as curious as anyone here! Anyway, you'll meet their Major Baker tomorrow, a klick west of where I met Lieutenant Cargill. Tomorrow at True Sun zenith. Truce until then. And no one else is to know about this."

"No one else? Like who?"

"Like the people we work for," Mason said. "Cargill was explicit about that." Mason's voice changed to a bad imitation of a Scots accent. "Major Baker said that 'our employers would not appreciate private conferences among us, don't you agree?' Something like that."

"Man, he's right there," Warner said. "Can you imagine what the little king would say if he knew? Put them Gurkhas with our troops and we can name the next High Rexja right off."

"It would still be a long campaign, now that Matthias is alerted, but I suppose that's true enough." Rick agreed. "Did Cargill say anything like that?"

"No, Sir. Just that we ought to keep these conferences to ourselves."

"You trust them to keep a truce?"

Mason shrugged.

"Don't reckon it matters what I think. I sure wouldn't call off the guards."

"We won't. So. What are they doing here?"

"Damned if I know, Colonel. Cargill wasn't there to give away information. Or swap any, either. All business. Respectful, though. Plenty of 'sirs' after I introduced myself as a major. But he didn't give anything away."

"Begging your pardon, Colonel, but I don't like this parley business much," Sergeant Bisso said.

"Come to that, I don't either," Mason said. "But my orders were to arrange a meeting, and I did that. Don't mean I think the Colonel ought to go to that meeting. I may not be expendable, but I'm more so than the Colonel."

"But you're convinced Cargill is genuine?" Rick asked.

"Genuine how, Sir? He sure seems like a typical Brit officer to me."

"Not a Galactic in disguise?"

"No way I'd know that, Colonel, but I sure didn't get any false vibes from him. You know something we don't, Sir?"

"No." Rick shook his head. "I'm as surprised by all this as you are. Look, there's only one way we're going to find out more, and we all know it. I'll have to meet their commander."

"That you will, Sir, if there's going to be any meeting. Something else," Mason said. "You're to bring identification. Something that proves you're Captain Rick Galloway of the US Army."

Warner eyed Mason quizzically.

"Major, you're saying they know who Colonel Galloway is?"

"Beats me," Art Mason said. "I asked that, but Cargill

wouldn't comment. He just said that Major Baker would discuss matters with Captain Rick Galloway and no one else."

"And he called me 'captain,' not 'colonel'?" Rick asked.

"Yes, Sir. That he did."

"We have to meet him," Rick said. He fingered Tylara's message in his pocket. "But we need to get this over with fast, and that means making them an offer they can't refuse."

He sat thinking for a moment.

"Can Westmen women ride?" he asked.

"Better than most of our men." Mason looked at him quizzically.

"Send a dispatch to Murphy. Tell him to ask Mad Bear to send as many of the young widows and fatherless ladies who've come of age from the lodges of the Silver Wolves as can get here in a day. Tell them to pack their finest traveling clothes, that we may have found men worthy of them."

# ✦══ CHAPTER FIVE ══✦
## PARLEY

Sergeant Walbrook and the mortar crews were ready. The meeting place was in an empty field, the bottom of a shallow bowl overlooked by low hills to both north and south, a kilometer west of the main road to the Ottarn. A small dirt track led east to the main road, but otherwise there was nothing to see. The field had recently been burned over, so there was no cover anywhere. The center of the bowl was well in range of Rick's mortars, and spotters lay at the top of the ridge overlooking the meeting place.

"I don't like it," Art Mason said.

"You don't have to like it," Rick said. "But if they kill me, you make sure their guy doesn't leave there alive either."

"What you want to bet they won't have their heavy weapons zeroed in on that flag?" Sergeant Bisso asked.

"Not a thing, Sergeant," Rick said.

"We don't know they have any heavy weapons," Warner reminded them. "They haven't used any."

"Not yet," Rick said. "But they won't need them, with fifty rifles."

"At that range they'd need to spray and pray," Mason said.

"So we have mortars and the Carl Gustav, and they have rifles. Area weapons on both counts at these ranges," Warner said.

"Mexican standoff," Bisso said. "There's the flag."

A lone rider rode from the north to the middle of the bowl. He carried a white banner on a lance, and after looking around in all directions, moved about twenty yards from where he'd stopped. Then he planted the lance in the ground. There was just enough wind to make the banner flutter. The rider turned and rode back in the direction from which he'd come.

Two mercenaries crawled along the ridge behind Rick. Soft spoken commands guided them as they placed aiming stakes visible to the mortar crews but not to anyone on the other side of the meeting bowl.

"You can bet they'll be doing the same thing on their side of the ridge," Mason said sourly.

The messenger rode over the ridge and vanished. They all waited.

"Here he comes," Warner reported. He pointed to a lone rider coming down the opposite hill.

Rick mounted and rode down the hill alone.

"Good luck, Colonel," Art Mason said softly.

✢ ✢ ✢

Rick clucked his mount to a walk. No point in hurrying

things. He watched, carefully, as the other rider came towards the flag. Closer.

*This would be the time*, Rick thought. There was no sign of activity on the ridge ahead, but from what he'd heard of the Gurkhas there wouldn't be any sign until it was too late. *Fifty rifles at that range would spray down a big area, but if they fired now, they'd get me without hitting their man, and my troops may or may not be good enough to get him.* He felt sweat running down his ribs. *Damn all. I didn't used to be this scared. That's what having your wife back will do to you. Give you something to live for, and you're scared as hell.* He rode on at a walk. *One. Two. Three . . .*

The critical moment passed. The riders closed on the flag. Rick got there first by seconds, and halted.

The approaching rider wore British battle dress, jungle camouflage that stood out in this dusty land, hardly camouflage at all. His unit and rank badges shone. His sidearm—*Good God*, Rick thought, *is that really a Webley revolver?*—was holstered with the flap buttoned. The hat was a brimmed khaki hat with chin cord, clean and crisp like the uniform. Neatly trimmed mustache, no other facial hair. Brown hair combed back under the hat. *Handsome fellow. Midforties, I'd guess.* Looking closer Rick could see that the man's uniform had been pressed.

For a moment Rick felt shabby in his mail armor and tabard.

The man came to a crisp salute, palm out.

"Major Clyde Baker, at your service, Colonel. Shall we dismount?"

Rick returned the salute.

"Rick Galloway. Perhaps we'd be more comfortable mounted."

"As you wish, Sir. First there is the matter of identification."

"Guess I'll dismount after all," Rick said. "Major Baker, just what in the world do you expect me to produce as proof of my identity?" He swung down off his horse and dropped the reins.

Baker dismounted crisply. Rick thought Baker was probably a better rider. He seemed to have an easy confidence, but he held the reins as he stepped towards Rick. Horses trained differently? But Baker couldn't be used to Tran horses unless he'd been here a lot longer than Rick thought he had.

"Sir, I'm not sure what I need for identification. Yet it's important that I establish your identity. Perhaps you'd care to tell me how you got here?"

"Why should I?"

"Colonel, I'm not trying to be coy. There are matters of some importance here, and there's only one man on this planet that I can be frank with. His name is Rick Galloway, one time captain in the United States Army. I believe that man is you, but I must be certain. I know how Captain Galloway got to this planet."

"Do you, now?"

"Your story begins in Africa," Baker said. "On a hill, making a last stand."

Rick frowned in thought.

"Right. We were at the end of our rope when this flying saucer picked us up. We were taken to the Moon, where a police inspector named Agzaral examined us."

Baker nodded when he heard the name.

"You spoke with Agzaral yourself?"

"Yes. Tall, thin faced, wore a kind of gown with badges and honors on it. Like a dashiki. Spoke English but sounded more Brit than American. He offered me the choice of coming here as a mercenary or going somewhere else as what amounted to a welfare case. I chose Tran."

Baker nodded.

"Sir, I'm going to take something out of my pocket. It is not a weapon."

"All right."

Baker reached carefully with his left hand into his right hand breast pocket. He took out what appeared to be a photograph. He looked at it, then at Rick, and his thin smile broke into a wide grin.

"Excellent." He held out his other hand. "I've been looking for you, Colonel Galloway. Had to be sure I'd found the right man."

Rick took his hand. The grip was firm, and Baker seemed almost friendly.

"And why would you be looking for me?"

"I've been told I can trust you." Baker's grin faded. "And I hope to God that's true."

✦ ✦ ✦

"We seem to have a lot to discuss," Rick said. "And this isn't a very good place for it."

"Agreed. If our employers don't know of this meeting yet, I expect they soon will. I forgot to mention it to mine—"

"Somehow it slipped my mind to send a runner to the Wanax, too," Rick said with a thin smile.

"Considering that they're both very likely to hear of this quite soon, it may make both your boss and mine a bit suspicious, don't you agree?"

A warm breeze blew across the valley. It felt good.

"Suspicious is a mild word for it," Rick said. "And they're certain to hear of it within hours. So what do we do now?"

Baker shook his head slowly.

"Inspector Agzaral said you were a decent man and that I could trust you. That I should work with you if the situation warrants. He seems to have some kind of plan that involves both of us. Part of that involves sending you new resources in an indirect manner."

"New troops?"

"I think not, at least none other than us. 'Resources,' he said. They'll involve instructors but not troops." Baker looked narrowly at Rick. "I don't know all the details."

*And you're not telling me what you do know.*

"I see."

"In any event, I don't have much choice," Baker said. "I'm convinced that I must work with you. But I do have the men to think of. They're not very happy with all this."

*And they'll be a lot less happy when they find out I can't get them home,* Rick thought. *Unless they already know that.*

"I wouldn't think they would be. Where do they think they are?"

"The Senior NCO thinks we've been swept up by the gods to fight in their wars," Baker said. "From what Agzaral said that may be as good an explanation as any."

Rick nodded.

"I can think of worse. How did you get caught up in this?"

"Force reduction. We were stationed in Malaysia. Some units were to be disbanded. Budget cuts. Rather than disband units, they chose the most expendable men from each unit to be sent home. I was given the responsibility of getting them there. My orders were to take the men to a beach area to wait for transport by hovercraft. An experimental hovercraft. We waited two days and a large hovercraft of a strange design came in low over the water in the middle of the night. It didn't look like any craft I'd ever seen, but everything else seemed all right, so we went aboard. At which point I was summoned to the bridge."

"Where you were interviewed by aliens," Rick said.

"Not then. There was a man, certainly human, who said he was from the Foreign Office. We were being taken to another ship, and we would go aboard. It was in a hangar, God knows where, somewhere in Malaysia, and we never saw anything but a gangway. Once we were all aboard I met the aliens. They told me we'd been recruited into their service."

"But my God, man, won't you be missed? Fifty Gurkhas and three British officers go missing?"

"Sixty Gurkhas. And, no, I very much doubt we will be," Baker said. "We were expendables and it happened once before, a Gurkha unit being disbanded turning bandit."

"I never heard that."

"And you won't, either. Which is the point, don't you agree? They'll think my lot did the same thing and hush it up instead of asking questions. We weren't far from the opium trade route. Enough jungle in the Golden Triangle to hide a dozen regiments. More than enough demand for good troops at high wages, too. I'm not guessing on this, Colonel. Inspector Agzaral said we were already listed as deserters."

"Was he happy about the situation?"

Baker shook his head.

"You met him. Hard chap to read. But my impression is that he was livid."

"I'd think he would be," Rick said. "I got the impression that the only men the Shalnuksis were allowed to kidnap were men who were doomed already. Your story doesn't match that."

"That's close to what I was told," Baker said. "Apparently there was a disagreement on the matter between this Inspector Agzaral and the aliens. It got pretty tense at one point until Agzaral straightened up and—well, I don't know, Colonel, because it was in a language I never heard before, but it looked to me as if he laid down the law and read them the riot act. They weren't happy about it, that was clear, but neither was he."

Rick tried to imagine the scene, but couldn't.

"On that score, can you describe the aliens you saw?"

"Human sized, long legs. Rugged. Flat faces, nothing much of a nose, hands looked more like gorilla than human. General shape was more like chimpanzees without hair. Nose slit—well it was a little more than a slit, but not a real nose—moved as well as their mouths when they talked. There were three of them sitting at a table."

"Shalnuksis," Rick said. "At least it sounds like them. Including the group of three. They work in trios for some reason. What did they say they wanted?"

"To hire my services to protect their property. Apparently they have claims to this planet, and they face poachers." Baker grinned. "I gather that's you. My mission was to defeat you and turn over whatever you've collected to a ship that will come to find us. After that we would be returned to Earth."

"Did you believe them?"

"At the time, I suppose, but Inspector Agzaral told me flat out that they were liars, and that we will never be returned to Earth. I didn't much care for that, but he made it very clear. We can work for the aliens or not, but nothing we can do will buy us a return ticket. This is a one-way trip.

"Like you, I was given a choice: come here as a mercenary or be taken to some holding planet where I would have no position at all and would wait until they thought of some use for me. That was no choice at all, so I accepted mercenary service on his terms. That was when he told me I did have one choice: I could work with you or against you, but in his opinion you were the one man on this planet I could trust."

"Flattering," Rick said. "Do your men know they're never going home?"

"Not yet. Leftenant Cargill suspects. Leftenant Martins is certain that once we kill you we'll be homeward bound. As to the troopers, they never expected to go home until their service was up. As near as I can tell, they're happy enough not to be dismissed, to still have jobs and expect pensions." Baker gestured expressively. "They're not stupid, Colonel. A bit primitive, but not stupid. They know about space travel, and they know they're not on Earth, but they expect to encounter marvels serving Her Majesty, and this is just another of the technological miracles the English pull off from time to time."

A dry wind came up from the west. Clouds scudded across the sky. Even after his years on Tran the planet didn't seem like Earth. It must have been worse for Baker, and his Hindu Gurkhas.

"But they do expect to go home with pensions."

"Yes."

"That could be a problem. My men all know better. They don't like it, but they understand we're here to stay. What will yours do when they find out?"

"I don't know. It depends on Sergeant Major Tulbahadur Rai, I expect. He's senior NCO. Understand, Colonel, this isn't a regular setup. Many of these men don't know each other. These are the men thought expendable when it came time for a reduction in force. Except for Sergeant Major, he's near retirement age anyway, and chose to take early retirement so a younger man wouldn't be sent home."

"So with the exception of your Sergeant Major, they're not the best men in Her Majesty's Gurkhas?"

"Perhaps not, but I assure you the worst of them is damned good. They'd never have been recruited if they weren't, and their training is thorough." Baker paused. "Before you ask, I was being rotated home on family leave before they gave me this assignment. Martins had family leave to get married, and was anxious to get back to his fiancé. This detail was supposed to get him home two months sooner, and apparently he had friends in the right places to get put on." Baker chuckled. "Some would say it serves him right."

"And Cargill?"

"I'm not sure why Cargill was going home. I never served with him before. Nothing bad in his record that I know of."

"I see. Excuse me a moment." Rick turned away from Baker and raised his left hand to wave, lowered it, then raised it again. "Just letting Major Mason know all's well," Rick said. "What do we do now?"

"That's rather up to you," Baker said.

"Up to me."

"Yes, I think so. After a lot of thought, I've decided that I would rather work with you than against you, Colonel Galloway."

"Under what conditions?" Rick asked.

"Yes, that is rather the question, isn't it? How far can we trust each other? I've been asking myself that since we got to this Godforsaken place." He paused, frowned slightly in thought, and tried to smile. "You have rather a good reputation, you know. Formidable but fair. Honest, keep your word, loyal to your employer. Even the—" Baker broke off and changed to an even thicker northern Tran dialect. "Honorable Matthias agrees."

Baker waved expansively. "Of course our meeting like this is somewhat outside of that," he said in English.

"So we can work together," Rick said. "Of course there's the question of the product you're supposed to take away from me. Your Galactic employers are unlikely to be satisfied with what you can grow, and if I give you much, my own will be unhappy."

Baker hesitated.

"Colonel, can we work together? Will you accept me and my men into your service?"

"What about the Honorable Matthias?"

"He'll have to be told. I have enough shards of honor left that I can't be part of some treacherous plot. I won't turn my coat in the middle of a battle."

"Good. I wouldn't want you to."

"It probably wouldn't work anyway," Baker said. "The Honorable Matthias doesn't much trust me to begin with. When he hears I've been meeting with you he'll believe we're plotting against him."

"There's that. Do you have any other conditions?"

"Only that all of us be treated the same as your other men, Colonel."

"I can agree to that, but with limits. I have fewer troops than you, but we've been here longer. All my men have a status. Not quite noble, but nearly so. All of us are 'star lords,' but some of us are actual lords in our own right. You and your officers and the senior NCO's won't be a problem, but I can't guarantee noble status for every one of your troopers. I'll do what I can, but no guarantees."

"That's all right. Gurkhas are used to being treated a bit differently from white troops. Most of them are amused by it, so long as things are fundamentally fair."

"Fair I can promise. Reasonably fair. But there's still the problem of what we give your Galactic employers. I don't think we'll have enough madweed harvested to satisfy my own Shalnuksis, let alone supply yours."

Baker regarded Rick carefully for a long moment.

"All right. In for a penny—Colonel Galloway, my employers probably won't be coming. Officially we're here on our own."

"And why is this?"

"Inspector Agzaral ruled against the—he called them the Gadnatwen Trader faction—who'd hired me. He was telling them they had no claims on this planet or its products, and they were liable to heavy fines and penalties for kidnapping us, and if they sent unauthorized expeditions to Tran they would be in gross violation of the trade regulations." Baker shrugged. "At least that's what he told me he was telling them. They were certainly livid about it."

"So how did you get here?"

"He made a deal with them. They'd created this problem, Earth humans who could never go home, and they had to contribute to its solution. They'd pay a fine and he wouldn't report them to the Trade Commission. Part of their fine was to transport us and the gear they'd already kitted us up with here, regardless of the convenience or the cost. That was when he told me to use my judgment, but probably my best bet was to trust you. He never explained it in so many words, but I understood all this to mean that neither my kidnapping nor my transport to Tran would ever appear on an official report."

Rick nodded understanding, but he felt bewildered. *So now what is Agzaral up to? But I don't dare ask, not yet anyway. How would he know that the—Gadnatwen faction—would deliver Baker and his troops safely? Did he care? But he must have cared enough to organize this. He must be planning another visit by someone he trusts.*

*Les? That would be useful. Gwen can wheedle some information out of Les. Maybe. I think Agzaral trusts Les.*

"So they brought you here."

"Yes. Just before we landed, one of the aliens attempted to persuade me to serve them," Major Baker continued. "To keep the mission they'd given us, to defeat you and take over your crops, take your place here. He promised rewards and more equipment—Agzaral caught them before they'd finished fitting us up—and hinted that if I killed you and took over he'd be able to take us all back home." Baker cleared his throat. "Load of codswallop, of course. Agzaral was very clear on the matter. Even if Agzaral dropped dead, there was no way home, because that was a policy of the High Council. No groups of wild Earthlings go back, because if we ever got back to Earth there'd be no way to keep it all quiet, and with this many someone would believe us. I pretended to go along with the aliens because I didn't see any choice in the matter."

"How will you communicate with them?"

Baker took a familiar-looking device from his belt pack.

"This apparently works forever. They told me not to worry about power."

Rick nodded.

"We've got one of those ourselves." *Best to keep knowledge of Gwen's personal communicator to myself for now, besides the sets can't seem to communicate with each other, only to starships.* "It's always worked and it never needed recharging. So you expect your Shalnuksi hosts to return?"

"No, Sir, I don't," Baker said. "Inspector Agzaral told me there might be strange offers, but that the Confederation had ways of knowing what ships visit this planet. Of course he could tell me anything he wanted, just as they could, but I rather believed he has that power."

"How did you hook up with the Five Kingdoms?"

"That's where they dropped us. They claimed they were teaching us the only language they had available, so they were sending us where that language was spoken." Baker frowned. His tone changed. "You can understand this, can't you?"

"Not very well. They taught you a fairly thick northern dialect," Rick answered in the speech common within the Five Kingdoms, then snorted. "Must have amused them no end to hand you over to the locals out for my scalp already! It'll just have to do for now. You'll pick up the southern dialects quick enough. So you made a deal with the Five Kingdoms."

"Sort of. They didn't know what to do with us, until this chap in wolfskins showed up. It was Matthias. He didn't appear to be overly surprised to see us. He was enthusiastic about hiring us to go after you. Since I didn't have any other way to find you, we took the job. If you were anywhere near as competent as your reputation makes you, I expected it wouldn't be long before you came up with a way to communicate with me. Wasn't easy avoiding direct confrontation with you and still being useful enough that we had employment if I couldn't negotiate something with you. Last thing I wanted was a blood feud."

"You did a good job there. All right, what's next? You have to go back to your camp to get your gear—"

"No, Sir. Everything we brought from Earth is with us.

The only things we left in camp are replaceable local items. We're ready to come over anytime you say. Now, preferably."

Rick frowned.

"Major, I very much want to believe you, but are you asking me to allow your unit, fully armed, to close with mine?"

Baker laughed.

"Colonel, you have a nasty, suspicious mind."

"The situation calls for a bit of healthy paranoia," Rick said.

"On my part, too," Baker said. "Surely you don't expect me to disarm my men? I have more reason to trust you than you have to trust me, but even so—"

"An interesting impasse," Rick said. "Have you any suggestions?"

"None immediately. Given your locals, you do outnumber us."

*Not by as much as you think.*

"All right. For today we'll march in separate columns and make camp independently." Rick took out a map. "We're here. How soon can you reach this crossroad? It's about ten kilometers."

"Three hours. Another hour to set up camp." Baker studied the sky. "Still an hour of daylight when we've done all that."

"Good. Do that. When you get there, I'll have guides to show you where to camp. What about messing the troops? Any special requirements?"

"We don't eat beef or pork, and not all that much meat of any kind."

"That just the men, or officers too?"

"I enjoy roast beef and ham, but I won't eat them when the troops are present. Neither will the other officers, but that's just courtesy. Gurkhas know British troops will eat anything. They joke about it."

"Local cereals all right?"

"Indeed. Colonel, I'm not worried about your men, but what of Wanax Ganton's troops? Won't they attack us on sight?"

"Or run away," Rick said. "Wanax Ganton finds a different temporary camp every day. It will be within a few kilometers of my camp, and he'll probably have scouts mingling with my forces, but I don't anticipate any problems. Just to be sure, I'll have Captain Lord Arwel join you en route. He'll be carrying my banner." Rick indicated the devices on his tabard. "He'll have a dozen scouts with him. They'll ride ahead, he'll ride with you. You shouldn't encounter any royal forces to begin with, but if you do, I expect that banner carried by a Drantos baron ought to be enough.

"I'll also send ahead to have the evening meal ready for you. Major, you and your officers are invited to dine with me at dusk this evening in the star officers' mess. The fare will probably include stew, and God only knows what kind of meat went into it, but it will be hot. I'll have an officer come to escort you. Meanwhile, I'll send Arwel and some mounted archers as guides. And I have your radio if you need to call me."

"Sounds reasonable. Sir."

"And what will you do when Matthias sends messengers asking where the hell you think you are going?"

"Sir, I will reply that it is no longer his business and send them back to him," Baker said. "And warn him not to follow us, at his peril. I rather think that will be notice enough."

"Right. Major, you mentioned some more resources Agzaral is sending to this planet."

"I did, Colonel." He looked up at the True Sun. "But it's a somewhat . . . lengthy story, and I have more guesses than fact. If I'm to be at your dinner by dusk, I want a bit of time in hand to be sure I'm not late. By your leave, Sir?"

Rick nodded.

"You can tell me tonight at dinner. Godspeed, Major."

# ✦═ CHAPTER SIX ═✦
## ALLIANCES

"Ten-hut!"

Everyone stood as Rick came into the room. It had been the main hall of a reasonably successful farmer, and was too small for the formal harvest-style dining table; but then the table was large for the number of people standing in their places. Rick went to the head of the table, stood a moment, and sat.

"Please be seated," he said.

There were murmurs of thanks, but no one spoke as Rick looked down the polished length of the table. Opposite him on the far end was Major Baker. On the side to Baker's right, Lieutenant Richard Martins sat next to Baker, with Lieutenant Henry Cargill to Martins' right. Senior Warrant Officer Larry Warner sat to Rick's immediate right, then an empty seat reserved for Murphy, then Major Art Mason. Sergeant Bisso stood at the door to supervise the dinner crew, all members of Rick's household guards.

Everyone at the table was armed. Outside, an escort of Gurkha troops was being served freshly baked bread and lentils by young ladies of the Silver Wolf tribe. Rick's guards and a few elders of the tribe watched from close nearby. The main Gurkha encampment was in the far corner of the compound housing Rick's star forces and some of the Tamaerthan and Chelm troops. *And so far, so good,* Rick thought. But there was an air of tension in Rick's dining room that no amount of smiles and military courtesy could dispel.

Rick looked up to catch Sergeant Bisso's eye and nodded satisfaction. The old farmhouse would never look like a military headquarters, but Bisso had found a few touches. The wattle and daub walls had been cleaned and Bisso had managed to find a few tapestries to cover some of the larger areas. They didn't all match, but there was a glass for each person at the table, and the often-mended tablecloth had been freshly washed. No splendor, but no squalor either.

Rick stood.

"As all of you know by now, Major Baker and I met in parley this afternoon. His detachment of Gurkhas was kidnapped along with his officers in circumstances a bit different in detail from ours, but the effect was the same. They were taken to Earth's Moon where they were offered a choice of service with the Shalnuksis or detention as paupers. Major Baker chose to come here. What choices were you given, Major?"

Rick sat. Baker stood for a moment, then said, "We're all tired. Shall we do this seated?"

"Excellent suggestion," Rick said.

"Thank you, Colonel." Baker sat with an expression of relief. "In answer to your question, Inspector Agzaral said that we were to join with you and assist in completing your mission if I deemed that possible. Otherwise we were to act at discretion. His manner was ambiguous, but I thought it clear that he preferred that we join up and assist you. When that proved impossible upon our arrival, I acted in a manner that would not exclude that possibility and awaited developments." He flashed a half grin to everyone at the table. "Needless to say, I was greatly relieved when I discovered you are still alive and willing to talk with us."

Rick nodded.

"And you're here as our guests and potential allies."

"Indeed, Colonel."

"Major Baker, I present my officers," Rick said. "All of you, we tend to informality in the mess. Speak freely if you have questions. Major Mason is my second-in-command. No need to get up, Art. And this is Chief Warrant Officer Warner, who serves as intelligence officer among other duties."

"How do you do, Sir?" Warner said.

"Mr. Warner is also Provost of the University," Rick said. "In fact that's his primary mission, but that got interrupted by the latest wars. I expect he'll be glad to get back there."

"Yes, Sir," Warner said with enthusiasm.

"You've established a university? You're teaching modern, uh, technology to the locals?" Lieutenant Cargill asked. "Sir?"

Rick nodded.

"We are. We rotate officers and specialists to temporary

duty as teachers. The Rector is Gwen Tremaine. From Santa Barbara, California. Lady Gwen has some rather special connections with the human Galactic agents. For example, one is father of her oldest child."

There was a moment of silence as the newcomers digested this.

"That must be quite a story," Major Baker said.

"It is. I'll ask her to tell it to you when you meet. Major Baker, I presume you had no difficulties en route?"

"None, Colonel. Your Captain Lord Arwel met me shortly after we began our march. I confess we had a bit of a language problem, but I think I'm getting the hang of your dialect." Baker looked amused. "As you surmised, Colonel, riders from the Honorable Matthias caught up with us an hour after we began marching southwards. As we'd agreed, I told them my units were no longer in his service, and I would regard any attempt to follow us as a hostile act."

"So did anyone follow?" Warner asked. "Sir."

"Well, yes, Mr. Warner, several of them tried," Baker said. "But we shot their horses out from under them, and that rather discouraged them. Following my lads is never a very good idea. It took a bit to convince my former employers, but they gave up after a while. Fortunately, we didn't have to kill anyone to persuade them."

"So the Fivers know you've changed sides?" Art Mason said.

"I rather expect so, Major."

"That should discourage them from attacking Wanax Ganton's force," Warner said. "Maybe they'll even turn and run."

"Wouldn't count on it," Mason said. "But I reckon it's definitely taken some of the wind out of their sails."

Rick nodded agreement.

"I've got scouts out just to be sure, but we should be safe enough while they digest the new situation."

Sergeant Bisso came in from the kitchen.

"Colonel, shall we begin serving?"

"Yes, thank you, Sergeant." Rick turned to his guests. "I have very limited fare, but there's a good bottle of Hunter's Sherry I brought along in case there was a special occasion. I'd say this qualifies. Sergeant?"

"Sir." Bisso brought in a bottle with a bright yellow label and stood back as the stewards poured, then left the room. When the glasses were filled, Rick looked to Larry Warner.

"Mr. Vice?"

Warner stood. "To new friends."

There were mutters of approval.

"My, that is very good sherry," Lieutenant Martins said. His voice sounded strained. "Very good indeed."

"Something troubling you, Leftenant?" Major Baker asked.

"Well—well, no, Sir—"

"Spit it out," Baker said.

Martins frowned. "Sir—"

"Leftenant Martins, you are not usually so reluctant to speak," Baker said. "Colonel, his problem is that he believes we have only to shoot you down and take over your operations, and the Galactics will permit us to return to Earth. Home by Christmas, if only you weren't in the way."

Martins turned beet red. Sergeant Bisso stood impassively.

"Now, mind you, if I thought that were true," Baker said, "I might be scheming to accomplish it myself. But it's not."

"Not a chance," Larry Warner said. "Excuse me, Colonel."

"Nothing to excuse," Rick said. "If we're all going to work together, the first requirement is that we all understand the situation." Rick looked Richard Martins full in the eye. "Did you get this notion from Inspector Agzaral, or the Shalnuksis?" he asked.

Martins gulped.

"I never had much chance to speak with the Inspector, Sir." He hesitated, then decided. "It was the aliens who told me they'd come back to get us. We should collect whatever you were growing for them—" He looked around for support, got none, and plunged on. "Drugs. A crop of drugs. If we could collect what you were growing and turn it over to them, it would be enough to pay our passage back to Earth."

Baker nodded.

"Henry, were you also told this?"

"Aye." Cargill had a definite Glaswegian accent. "I was, Sir. I didn't believe a word of it."

"Why not?" Rick asked.

"Sir. That policeman made it very clear to begin with. We'll never go home again. And if anyone has ever returned to Earth with a story like this, I never heard it. And I would have; I was always interested in stories about aliens. Besides, if those bawbags get the crops they want, what's their incentive to defy the police and put us back on Earth? A ship coming here for these drugs isn't going to Earth afterwards; there's nae a market there. More likely to dump us out the airlock! We're here, and we've nothing for it but to make the best of it."

"But the troopers—"

"Richard," Major Baker said. "We'll have to cope with what the troopers believe, but right now it's important for us all to understand just where we are."

"Yes, Sir."

"We're not going home," Clyde Baker said. "I wish otherwise, but that's the situation. We have to make the best for ourselves right here. I'm convinced that our best course is to ally with Colonel Galloway. I've told you why; do I need to repeat it?"

"I'd like to hear it," Art Mason said.

Baker smiled.

"Certainly, Major Mason. First, and most important to me, is that Inspector Agzaral told me directly that Captain Galloway was the only man on this planet I could trust."

"Good advice," Mason said.

"And since we arrived here I've heard no reason to doubt that," Baker said. "Colonel, even your enemies speak highly of you. Many speak in awe, even reverence. You seem to be something of a military genius."

"Or damned lucky," Rick said with a laugh.

"I never discount luck. I also know what von Moltke said about luck."

"Comes only to the well prepared," Warner said sotto voce.

"Precisely. The Inspector also told me that the only

Confederate group authorized to visit this planet would be controlled by Colonel Galloway's employers. No one else was coming here. The aliens delivering us were not coming back, and we hadn't met the group who were coming to buy from Colonel Galloway. So I had two facts: I was never going home, and I could trust Colonel Galloway.

"I considered my alternatives. One was to serve the Five Kingdoms as mercenaries. That would put us in competition with Colonel Galloway, but we have three score Gurkhas and the Five Kingdoms are more powerful than your Wanax Ganton, so we might be successful. If we took that course, we would have power so long as our ammunition lasts. After that we're in competition with the locals. I'm not saying we can't learn to use local weapons, or even develop some new ones of our own, but we would never catch up with Colonel Galloway. His forces already have cannon and muskets, in addition to modern weapons—and he has a source of supply for his modern weapons. For that matter, it's clear he has at least some modern heavy weapons, which we do not. Even to get more ammunition for our rifles or the Brens we would first have to defeat Galloway, learn how to grow the crops, make contact with his Galactic buyers, persuade them to do business with us—and do all that while keeping our local employers happy enough that they feed and pay us." Baker looked at Martins with a raised eyebrow. "There are other variants on that course but none presents very attractive prospects, don't you agree?"

"But the aliens who brought us here?" Martins protested. "Even if they won't bring us home, don't we have to worry about them?"

"According to Inspector Agzaral, they won't be coming here at all," Baker said.

"But Sir, why would they want us to—to plunder Colonel Galloway's supply if they're not coming to profit from it?"

Baker looked to Rick.

"I confess I hadn't thought that through," he said.

Rick thought furiously, then shrugged.

"I can think of two reasons. First they may hope Agzaral or his superiors reverse the ruling and give them trade rights. That doesn't get you back to Earth, but it does give them a reason to make you think you can get there.

"Second, clearly they have no love for the Shalnuksi faction that brought us here. Anything that damages a rival. After all, it's not likely anyone would know why you went rogue and kept us from gathering crops."

"Which rules out that alternative," Baker said. "Striking our own deals with the rogue Galactics doesn't seem a very worthwhile idea. I found Inspector Agzaral believable enough, and he was very clear that he wasn't pleased with the people who brought us here."

"People who brought you here," Art Mason said. "And just who would those be?"

Baker spread his hands.

"I suspect I know less about the Galactics than you do, but my surmise is that there's a group authorized to grow and harvest drugs on this planet. That's the group that brought you. There's another that wants to become a part of that trade and they're the ones who brought us here. Thugs seeking to muscle in on the activity? But with enough influence that the Galactic authorities deal with them, if reluctantly. But frankly I was hoping you could tell us more about the situation."

"Aye," Cargill muttered. Martins was silent.

"Another possibility would be to strike out on our own," Baker continued. "Find some local backwater and take it over, become feudal lords in our own right and begin to blend in with the local customs. Properly cared for, our weapons will last a long time, and if we're careful with the ammunition we won't run out very soon. We could probably do that, developing better weapons made with local technology and our own skills."

"Gengrich," Art Mason said.

"I beg your pardon?"

"Gengrich tried that. Led a bunch of mercenaries south to set up their own kingdom. How'd it work, Mr. Warner?"

Larry Warner made a sour face.

"You know damned well how it worked. Granting Major Baker is smarter or luckier than Gengrich, it would still be a near thing whether they got through the first winter. It's primitive out there, Major! Colonel Galloway married into the local leadership, and now we all have status without having to beat up anyone to get it. We don't have to forage, locals do that for us. We don't have to grub around for money to pay for consumables. When we do have to fight, we get credit for the victories. All that no matter what happens with the Galactics. Much better even if we never hear from them again."

"Well summarized, Mr. Warner," Baker said. "The point being that it would be hard to get a better status than Colonel Galloway has already offered us."

Rick nodded.

"There is also what the locals call the Time," Baker said.

"Yeah, there's sure that," Art Mason said. "How much of that do you understand, Major Baker?"

"Not a lot, Major Mason. Clearly less than I ought to know."

Mason looked up the table at Rick.

"Colonel, you're better at explaining this than I am."

"I'll give you the essentials. We can do details later," Rick said. "This appears to be a binary star system with the smaller secondary circling the primary at about the distance from Saturn to the Sun, but in fact there's a third component. Every four hundred or so local years—six hundred Earth years—the third element, a red dwarf, approaches close enough to affect local climate. Ice melts, seas rise, general merry hell with the weather. That's the time when the madweed crops grow. Apparently the crop grown in the twenty years of the Time, the third star's closest approach, is enormously valuable. The Shalnuksis have been sending expeditions to gather and grow 'Tran Natural' every six hundred years or so for at least two or three thousand years. Every time they've come they brought a new military faction from Earth. Greeks, Romans, Scythians, God only knows who else. Which is why this place is a mess! Incidentally, Lieutenant Martins, in all that time none of this ever seems to have seeped into Earth myth and legend, which is a pretty good argument that no one ever got back from here."

"Yes, Sir," Martins said. "But—my fiancé—"

"Your fiancé will marry another or die an old maid,"

Rick said with an edge of compassion. "Sorry to be so blunt, but that's the way it is."

"On the other hand, there are girls here," Warner said. "Some delightful. As a star lord you start with pretty high status."

"Star lord," Cargill repeated. "We're all lairds?"

"We are," Warner said. "Some are loftier than others, but we're all nobles."

"So we're in for a time of troubles," Major Baker said. "I presume you have plans for getting through them?"

"I do," Rick said. He kept his tone confident. "We've allied with Rome, the Wanax Ganton, a maritime republic, and a dominant highland clan. The Roman and Tamaerthan alliances are rock solid."

"But not the Drantos alliance?" Baker asked.

Rick frowned.

"Solid enough. The King resents his dependence on us, but he doesn't have a lot of choices. And my wife is quite solidly in control of the County of Chelm, the single most powerful county of Drantos. Most of my local troops are loyal to Tylara, not the Wanax, and the Tamaerthan archers and pikemen have no ties to Ganton at all. We're pretty solidly established, Major."

"So what's our goal?" Baker asked.

"Long term or immediate?"

"Both. Sir."

"Long term, to be well established enough that we can retire to a secure place. Our children will inherit our weapons. If we've done our job right, they won't need to use them much.

"To do this, we'll need status and land. I have both, in

Chelm and in Tamaerthan, and I hope to gain status in the Roman Empire as well. Relevant to you, I also have an alliance with several clans of Westmen."

"I've heard of those," Cargill said. "Scythians, no?"

"More like Mongols, I'd say," Rick said. "Possibly the same thing."

"Are those the dark-skinned young ladies who are serving my lads dinner this evening?" Baker asked.

"Yes," Rick answered.

"I see," Baker said. "Some of the ladies were quite striking. I'd say some of my lads were quite taken by them."

"The point being that they're very likely distantly related to the Gurkhas. Major Baker, if your troops are interested they'd start with good prospects among my allies in the Silver Wolves tribe."

"Even still, who wants to tell them they're nae going home?" Cargill asked.

"No one, but I'll have to do it," Major Baker said. "As to when, I'll leave that for a council of war to decide."

"It's the Colonel's decision," Art Mason said.

"Well, I don't dispute that," Baker said. "So. The goal is to settle onto our own lands and raise warrior children. Not a loftier ambition?"

"Something like that," Art Mason said. "With status and stability. It's stability we need, and if we go conquering we won't get that. What we want is that not all our kids have to turn soldier. Stability. If we go legitimate there's need here for every kind of professional. And our girls can marry well, they start with a big advantage."

Rick tapped his glass on the table to get attention.

"Major, we went through most of these questions when we first came here. Lieutenant Parsons thought we could all be kings. That didn't work out so well." Rick raised his voice slightly. "Did it, Sergeant Bisso?"

"No, Sir, that it didn't," Bisso said from his place near the door. "Those were bad times, Major Baker."

"I'll tell you about that another time," Rick said. "Meanwhile, our dinner, such as it is, awaits. Sergeant, you may have the service begin, please."

✣ ✣ ✣

Rick waited until the dinner plates were cleared away.

"We have a passable local port," he said then. "Courtesy of Sergeant McCleve, Professor of Medicine at the University."

"Sergeant McCleve?" Lieutenant Martins asked.

"Our medic," Rick said. "He earned his degree from the University of Guadalajara but never received his license. Turns out he's a pretty good doctor and teacher. In any event, I put him full time on learning the rest of his trade."

"And viniculture as well?" Baker asked dryly.

"He didn't need any orders for that," Mason said. "But not to worry. Since Colonel Galloway took charge, McCleve's been a connoisseur, not a drunk. Mostly, anyway."

Bisso's stewards brought in glasses and three bottles of local make.

"Sergeant Lewin is our professor of agriculture at the University and grew the grapes used in the wine," Rick said proudly. "We'll pour our own, Sergeant. Thank you."

"Sir." Bisso waited until the other orderlies had left. "I'll be right outside, Colonel." He left the mess room.

Baker inspected one of the wine bottles.

"Help yourselves, gentlemen," Rick said.

Baker poured himself a glass of the wine, sniffed it, and sipped.

"My, that's quite good," he said. "All right, Colonel, I suppose this is the next step." He stood and saluted. "Colonel Galloway, I accept you as commanding officer. I reserve my allegiance to the Queen, but I accept that I will not be receiving orders from the Crown."

Rick stood and returned the salute. They shook hands. "Thank you. I accept your allegiance." He stood, waiting.

There was a long pause, then Henry Cargill stood. He saluted.

"Colonel Galloway, I accept you as commanding officer, reserving only my allegiance to Major Baker and the Queen."

Rick returned the salute. As Cargill sat, Richard Martins stood.

"Colonel Galloway, I accept you as my commander under the same conditions as Lieutenant Cargill."

Rick returned the salute.

"Thank you." He sat. "Now, Major Baker, you mentioned something about Brens?"

"I did."

Baker sipped more wine, then sat back in his chair.

"We were a travel draft, returning the lads home to be demobilized, not moving to another combat posting, so we were scarcely what one might call fitted up for a mission to an alien planet.

"Our abductors didn't seem to quite understand all that implied. Or perhaps they simply didn't care." He grimaced, and not at the taste of his wine. "They asked me to recommend an equipment list, and I did. I asked for the sky, actually. Didn't get it, or anything like it, of course. And after their run in with Agzaral, they had precious little interest in completing the list. Still, I did get a goodly bit of what I'd asked for. Initially, they planned to equip us with your M-16, but I, ah, objected strenuously, shall we say? It's a better weapon than the L85, which—no offense, Colonel—is a piece of shite, but—"

"Excuse me, but what's an L85 and why should I be offended by your opinion of it?" Rick interrupted quizzically. Baker looked at him for a moment, then snorted.

"Apologies, Sir. I'd forgotten how long you and your chaps have been away."

"One way to put it," Art Mason acknowledged, and he and Warner chuckled.

"The L85 is what's replaced the SLR, which was basically the FAL," Baker said. He arched one eyebrow at Rick, who nodded in understanding. There were a few M-16s among his mercs, although the CIA had armed most of them with the H&K G3 assault rifle, for which he was grateful, but there were a couple of FALs, as well. Both the G3 and the FAL were bigger and heavier than the M-16, but the FAL, especially, was also incredibly rugged. Both of them had a longer effective engagement range than the M-16, and their 7.62-millimeter round was more effective against armored Tran warriors than the M-16's 5.56-millimeter slug.

"I like the FAL, myself," he said. "Why was it replaced?"

"That's why I said 'no offense,'" Baker said with a smile. "The L85's chambered for the same round as your M-16, and it's the second time you Yanks have pushed NATO into standardizing on one of your rounds instead of one of ours!"

"Sorry about that," Rick said with an answering smile and Baker shrugged.

"Actually, the five-point-five-six works quite well at its designed ranges, but we found out in the desert that the L85 Enfield designed to use it still has a few teething problems. Pity, really. I like the layout a lot, but not at the expense of reliability. Besides, my chaps hadn't been upgraded yet. So I insisted on the SLRs they're familiar with, and I think it pissed our 'sponsors' off right royally."

"Why?"

"I'm not positive, but I suspect one reason they preferred the M-16 originally was that they had better local contacts—for creeping around under Agzaral's radar, at any rate—in North America. All the ammunition they supplied to us has US or Canadian head stamps, and almost everything else came from the US, as well. I did manage to hold out for Brens for our light machine guns, but I suspect they only agreed because I argued in favor of ammunition commonality. And they're the South African conversions of the old Mark One.

"At any rate, we've SLRs for all our men, which is probably a very good thing, given our ammunition situation, since it's only semiautomatic. In fact, that's one reason I argued against the M-16. I cannot *believe* the way some troops burn through their ammunition given the chance to fire fully automatic! As I implied earlier, we're very light on anything approaching heavy weapons, however. We have two Brens, but only a total of six replacement barrels. Uses thirty-round rifle magazines, so at least we don't have to worry about belted ammunition. No mortars, no recoilless rifles or rocket launchers. We do have a couple of hundred hand grenades—the L2A2, which is more or less identical to your own M26, I believe—and three Milkor grenade launchers. South African, again," he added as Warner frowned. "Not a bad weapon at all, really. Forty-millimeter revolver launcher with a six-round drum. Unfortunately, we've only about eighty rounds for them, and they're the heaviest firepower our 'employers' provided. I did have my Webley along—personal weapon; belonged to my father—and they deigned to procure three hundred rounds for it. Leftenant Cargill and Leftenant Martins had to make do with American issue, I'm afraid."

"Well, we can always use more forty-five ammo!" Mason observed, but Baker shook his head.

"Sorry, Major. I know you Yanks have always had something of a fetish about the forty-five, but your Army adopted the Beretta nine-millimeter in '85."

"Nine-millimeter?" Mason looked at him in horror.

"'Fraid so, old chap."

"Crap. Almost makes me glad I wasn't there to see it!"

"At any rate, that's pretty much our inventory, weapons wise. Of course, all of the men have their kukris—can't separate a Gurkha from his knife!—but all told, we've only about two hundred rounds of rifle ammunition per man. Well, we've an extra three thousand rounds that I've earmarked for the Brens, as well, but that's only about six minutes of sustained fire for one of them. We're reasonably well kitted out for webbing, rucksacks, that sort of thing. And we do have some medical supplies."

"Medical?" Rick's voice sharpened, and Baker nodded.

"We don't have anything remotely approaching a doctor, but I did lobby hard for a decent dispensary. Didn't get everything I wanted, of course, but we've a fair supply of painkillers, medical supplies like bandages, field dressings, and splints, a decent surgical kit, and quite a lot of antibiotics." He grimaced. "I suspect those were added to the list by Agzaral, actually, and there are rather more of them than I'd requested from our 'employers.' That's one reason I think it was Agzaral; those bastards weren't giving us *anything* they didn't have to after they got caught with their fingers in the biscuit tin."

"McCleve's gonna be happy to hear about *that*, Sir!" Mason said, and Rick nodded.

"Yes, he is. And I promise we'll use them wisely, Major. You wouldn't happen to have added any Preparation H to that would you?"

"Well, yes, Sir. Several dozen tubes, actually. I rather thought it might be needed if we were going to be spending the rest of our lives in saddles."

"You, Major Baker, are a very wise man," Rick said fervently, reminding himself that Rank Hath Its Privileges. He contemplated that blissful thought for several seconds, then shook himself.

"So, anything else?" he asked. "Aside from the radios, that is." He smiled. "We noticed they're not exactly Royal Army issue. More of that inferior American crap?"

"I wouldn't go that far, Colonel," Baker replied with an answering smile. "Though they are civilian issue and American. I wanted army-issue radios, since those are what we're most familiar with and they're just a *tad* harder to break than civilian models. But that wasn't in the cards, either, I'm afraid. They seem solid, though. I believe they're supplied to your firefighters, in fact, so they ought to be fairly tough and resistant to water damage, for example. And they equipped us with a crossband receiver base unit for them—gives us about eighty to a hundred and twenty kilometers' range, depending on terrain and weather. I understand that many of your local emergency services in the States, especially in rural areas, use similar units. I'd be lying if I said I was fully confident in their durability, however, and we have only nine of them. In addition, we did get two RT-320 HF radios, as well, for long-range communications. Unfortunately, they're outside the frequencies of our 'firefighter' units, so they're not mutually compatible."

"What sort of range does your—RT-320, you said?—have?" Rick asked.

"Depending on the antenna, more than two thousand kilometers," Baker replied. "That's with a static antenna using sky-wave communications. Under normal conditions with a two-and-a-half-meter whip antenna, it's good for a ground-wave range of at least forty kilometers."

*Two thousand kilometers? That's right on twelve hundred miles! If Tylara and I each had a radio—*

Rick shook that thought aside—for the moment—and shook his head at Baker.

"All of that sounds good, Major. Obviously, I wish you'd

gotten everything you asked for, but I'm not surprised they didn't fully equip you after Agzaral intervened. And speaking of Agzaral, you mentioned that he had further plans."

## ᐦᐦ CHAPTER SEVEN ᐦᐦ
# PLANS

"They were planning another expedition," Baker said. "One authorized by Inspector Agzaral. It wasn't going to be large, but it would be well equipped, and your employers were paying for it. The notion was to send instructors to assist you so that there would be more product to claim."

"When would they arrive?" Rick asked.

"About the same time we would," Baker said. "Possibly before. Agzaral wasn't certain. Apparently he couldn't obtain the transportation he'd expected to use, and had to rely on someone else. I gather he wasn't entirely happy with what he was stuck with."

"Reinforcements. New equipment," Rick said. "Nothing of the sort's come . . ."

"Those lights off Nikeis—" Warner exclaimed.

Rick looked thoughtful, then nodded.

"I think so. In fact it's pretty clear that's exactly what

happened. Our reinforcements went astray and ended up in Nikeis."

"Sure how I see it, Colonel," Warner said.

Art Mason looked thoughtful.

"So what do we do?" he asked.

"We go get them."

"Uh, begging your pardon Colonel, but Nikeis is an island, and none of us knows crap about naval operations," Mason said and Rick nodded, then grinned.

"But our new comrades are islanders," he said. "It's in their blood."

"Not so sure about that," Baker said. "And I've never seen a ship on this planet. I'd guess they've come to the galley stage?"

"Something like that," Rick agreed. "I don't know a lot about them either. Fortunately the Romans do. They operate a small navy and they have records. I asked Publius to meet us at Taranto, the Roman port city. Of course that was before this dustup, but I expect he'll be there. He's as interested in what's happening in Nikeis as I am."

"So that's our plan?" Lieutenant Martins demanded. "We pack, forced march to the coast, learn about naval operations somehow, and invade this island nation? Do they have a lot of experience with ships? We certainly have none."

"Makes it interesting," Baker said. "Meanwhile, how are we going to integrate our units?"

"We keep them as separate units, of course," Rick said. "None of my people know anything about commanding Gurkhas. You'll stay together as a unit. Of course we'll merge the logistics functions."

"In other words, we turn over our ammunition," Baker said.

"Well, all that the men don't normally carry with them," Rick said.

Baker looked thoughtful for a long moment.

"Very well. Sir. I'll give the orders in the morning."

Martins opened his mouth.

"That will do, Richard," Baker said. "I understand thoroughly. But either we accept this arrangement with Colonel Galloway, or we don't. If we do, being cagey about it won't help. We're already at his mercy."

"Sir?"

Baker pointed to the wine bottles.

"Poison? Of course not, but it was possible. And I note that Sergeant Bisso commands a section of men with automatic weapons. Meanwhile, our men are being charmed by comely women. Do you really think we have had any alternatives since we sat down to this dinner?"

Martins frowned.

"Exactly. Relax and enjoy it, Leftenant. Incidentally, I expect you'll make captain in Colonel Galloway's service long before you would have in the Queen's. Now have another glass of port."

✥ ✥ ✥

There were sounds from outside.

"Sergeant of the Guard! Post Number Two!"

"Main gate," Art Mason muttered. More commotion. Rick tried to keep a calm expression until Bisso came in.

"Armed party approaching, Colonel. Claims to be from Wanax Ganton."

"How many?"

"Maybe five lances," Bisso said. "Give or take a few supernumeraries. You've met the leader. Lord Enipses. He's got a chain of office I've seen before."

Rick frowned the question.

"Looks like the medallion Lady Tylara used to wear."

"Enipses as High Justiciar. Interesting. Make them comfortable, but keep them together," Rick said. "And invite Lord Enipses to come join us, if he pleases. Put it that way, be elaborately polite, Sergeant."

"Sir!"

"And then ask Tech Sergeant Rand to scout around. It's dark out there, might be interesting to know if anyone else knows where our headquarters is."

"Perhaps I should have some of my lads take a look," Major Baker said. "They're passable as night scouts."

Warner suppressed a giggle.

"Do that, Major," Rick said. "But just scouting, please. Right now we have to be very careful about who gets killed."

"I'll do just that." Baker gestured to Cargill to follow and went out.

"Bisso."

"Sir?"

"Make sure Rand knows there'll be Gurkhas prowling around out there. And he's to keep that garrote in his pocket."

"Yes, Sir."

"And now we wait. Be seated, gentlemen. There's still a bit of port left." *And I'm sounding more like Baker every minute . . .*

⁂

A few minutes later a boy came into the dining room. He wore expensive court clothing and had a bronze carbine slung over his back. He stood nervously in front of Rick.

"I come from Wanax Ganton, with a message for the Warlord of Drantos."

"I recognize you, young master Dridos. Speak."

"Lord Enipses, High Justiciar of Drantos, awaits your leave to speak."

Rick frowned.

"Warner, does this make sense to you?" he asked in English.

"No, Sir. It's a new kind of formality from anything I've seen."

"High Justiciar," Rick said. "When Tylara was Justiciar she outranked me except in actual battle. I'm guessing this puts Enipses as top dog, and they sent a page I'd recognize to make sure I believed it."

"Sounds about right to me," Warner said. "You suppose he has orders for you?"

"His own or the King's." Rick turned back to the royal page. "Bid Justiciar Enipses to come in, if it pleases him."

The page bowed and turned slowly, then ran out of the room. A few moments later Enipses, in full mail armor covered by an embroidered tabard, strode in, the page at his side. He wore his chain and medallion conspicuously.

Enipses held his helmet under his left arm, but his face was framed by a mail hood. His expression was stern, almost grim, but his eyes betrayed a touch of fear as he examined the others in the room. He looked directly at Rick.

"At the command of the Wanax the Justiciar of Drantos stands before the Warlord of Drantos."

"You do indeed," Rick said. "Congratulations on what must have been a recent appointment. Tell me, My Lord, why I am so honored at this late hour?"

"His Majesty has received disturbing information," Enipses said. He eyed Lieutenant Martins with suspicion. "That you have been joined by new star lords, some previously in the service of the Five Kingdoms, yet you have made no report to His Majesty about these newcomers."

"As you see, this is all true," Rick said. "As to why it has not yet been reported to the Wanax, it is, like your appointment, a very recent development. There has been neither time nor need."

Enipses opened his mouth to speak, then thought better of it. He swallowed hard.

"My Lord, I would have thought there is a very great need for a report to the Wanax."

"There is. Now," Rick said. "Not previously."

Enipses stood in silence, and Rick took pity on him.

"Until very recently it was not decided what status the new star lords would have," he said. "Now they have entered into my service."

"Your service," Enipses said.

"Yes. Into my service as Colonel of Mercenaries. They have sworn no allegiance to Drantos or its Wanax."

Enipses took a moment to digest this. Then he turned slightly.

"Dridos!"

"Yes, Grand—Yes Lord Justiciar!"

"Bid the gentleman usher to attend us."

The boy darted out, and returned a moment later accompanied by the Black Rod Usher who had summoned Rick to the council on the Ottarn battlefield. He carried his rod of office proudly.

The usher looked to Enipses, then approached Rick and bowed.

"Lord Rick, Warlord of Drantos, the Wanax has bid me say that he both needs and desires your counsel, and therefore summons you to his presence at your earliest convenience."

"Interesting way to put that," Warner said sotto voce.

"Indeed," Rick said. "Our earliest convenience is now. We will all travel together. Major Mason, please assemble a suitable escort of forces to accompany me and Senior Warrant Officer Warner. As senior officer you will command here, with Major Baker as second-in-command."

"I will inform His Majesty," Enipses said.

"No, My Lord, you will not," Rick said. "There's no need. The summons said our earliest convenience. Surely His Majesty will not be astonished if we come immediately, and we travel together." He turned to Art Mason. "I'll thank you to arrange that escort for me. Also, signal Rand to come in, and tell both Rand and Major Baker I'd like a word with them before I go."

Mason nodded.

"I don't like this much," he said in English. "Something odd here."

"Agreed, Art, which is why I need to speak with Rand and Major Baker."

# ⊱ CHAPTER EIGHT ⊰
# AMBUSCADE

Rick's escort consisted of five star lord mercenaries under Sergeant Bisso. All were mounted on horses except Private First Class Passavopolous. Ark rode a mule and carried the light machine gun cradled across his saddle. His shoulders were covered with ammunition belts.

In addition, Captain Lord Arwel, son of a Chelm baron, commanded a group of mounted archers, some Tamaerthan clansmen, others Chelm recruits. They carried short compound bows, and constant practice had made them proficient at using their bows from horseback. They were grouped with half a dozen Tamaerthan infantry archers. The clansmen looked awkward enough when mounted, but they carried longbows and full quivers, and no one observing them on foot doubted their capability.

One more detail, Rick thought. Longbows could be improved by horn backing, but persuading the clansmen to use compound bows in preference to their native simple bows was difficult. Compound bows had a bad habit of delaminating in wet weather, while self bows endured the wet at a cost of stretching bowstrings. On the other hand, it took years to learn to use a big self longbow that had a range anywhere near that of a good compound bow.

*Ah, well,* Rick thought. *One day someone will develop a good foot archer compound weapon that outranges the longbows.* Longbows might be superior to muskets, but skilled longbowmen were much harder to find than competent musketeers. *We better develop it first or the Tamaerthans will be in trouble. Steel bows and wire? How do you make those? But by then we'll all be using rifled muskets anyway. Romans are certainly on their way to using muskets. I wonder what a legionary with a musket will be called . . .*

*Everything's happening at a faster pace. Can I keep up with all this? It's all getting away from me, and I don't have time to think it through. I need someone to think about these changes. Gwen can do that at the University, but she needs Warner, and I need him with me, and—and it's time to get on with this. My mind wanders a lot lately.*

"Where is His Majesty's encampment, My Lord?" Rick asked, turning to Enipses.

"I will lead you there," the new High Justiciar said, then looked back at Rick's escort. "Surely you do not need so many?"

"We aren't that far from the enemy, My Lord," Rick said. "And we've seen suspicious activities, mysterious riders, in these hills. Indeed, my scouts detected someone just outside our perimeter not half an hour ago." Rick frowned sternly. "My Lord Justiciar, surely you've heard that when I returned from my visit with His Majesty just weeks ago, I was set upon by enemies who wished to kill me. I barely survived, and since that time I've always traveled with a sufficient escort."

Enipses scowled, but had nothing to say. The Firestealer had set, and the only light was the grim glow of the Demon Star, just bright enough to cast dim shadows in the gloomy dark. Enipses pointed to the east gate of the camp. The camp path joined an east-going road that was just visible beyond the gate.

"That way," he said.

"Best take this at a walk in this light," Bisso said.

They set out towards the gate, Enipses' escorts ahead of them, Rick's troops bringing up the rear. Warner was strangely silent. Rick frowned, but said nothing. He wondered if Warner had hemorrhoids. An old high school joke surfaced in his thoughts. *We don't have to worry about money. I have piles. True enough for me.*

Maybe for Warner, too. Warner wanted nothing more than to return to teaching. *Well, that's his problem. I've just got my wife back, and I'd like to be home too. We got the Gurkha menace licked. Now what the hell is going on in Nikeis? Get this settled with Ganton and head for the coast, preferably tomorrow. Another long ride.*

They rode out in near silence. Enipses periodically urged haste, but Rick ignored him and kept his horse at a slow walk. The others kept pace with him. When they were a few yards beyond the camp gate, the two young pages and the Black Rod Usher broke loose and rode away at the gallop.

Warner rode up to join Rick.

"No surprise now," he said.

"Not without we shoot them," Passavopolous said. "And I don't reckon anyone wants that."

"No." Rick waved to Art Mason, lowered his arms to his waist, and raised his right arm. He turned back to the mounted party. "We may proceed, My Lord Justiciar."

Behind him an armed party of Gurkha riflemen was silently forming up in camp with Major Baker in their lead. If Enipses noticed he said nothing.

They rode at a slow walk, in near silence, for half an hour until a light showed ahead. An armed party of about twenty approached.

"Who is there?" Enipses' warden rode at point and didn't seem surprised to see others coming.

"Who challenges the Wanax of Drantos?"

Enipses rode forward. "The Lord Justiciar of Drantos brings the Warlord of Drantos into the presence of the Wanax, as instructed."

"Powder dry, lads," Bisso said softly.

"You know it," Passavopolous answered.

The group came forward. Mounted men at arms, mail armor, most armed with crossbows as well as sabers, Rick noted. Bodyguard weapons: fire once, and fight with sword and buckler. Effective enough for a short while, but not so useful against real mounted archers or heavy cavalry.

He didn't recognize any of them. An officer came forward.

"Justiciar! Warlord of Drantos! Greetings in the name of the Wanax! I am Radnos son of Dnestros, third captain of the Royal Guard," he said. "We are sent to conduct you to His Majesty. I have been instructed to be certain that you are the party he summoned. My pardon, Lord Justiciar, Warlord, but those were my orders."

"A reasonable precaution, Captain," Rick said. *But why a captain, even a noble one, and one I don't know at that? There are plenty of nobles with the King. Men I've worked with and have some reason to trust. This is very odd. I need to think about this.*

"The Wanax urges haste, My Lords," Radnos said.

Rick clucked his mount to a slow walk.

They had been moving through relatively open country, but ahead of them were low hills covered with scrub brush. In the dim light of the Demon Star it was impossible to see more than a few yards off the road.

"Good ambush country ahead," Passavopolous said.

"Yeah. Begging the Colonel's pardon, but I don't much like this," Bisso said. "Something funny is going on. I know the Guard captains. All of them. Or I sure thought I did."

"So do I," Rick said in English. He raised his voice. "Captain, I appreciate your concerns, but there's no need for you or any of your men to be behind me. Please stay ahead of my escorts. And where I can see you."

"My Lord."

"I'm certain you heard me. Kindly indulge my whims, Captain," Rick said.

The newcomers formed into a column of threes. They were clearly impatient to ride ahead, but Rick continued at a slow walk.

"Keep a good eye out," Bisso said softly in English as they moved cautiously down the road. "I don't like any of this." The other mercenaries muttered agreement.

There was a chirp from Rick's shoulder bag. He let the others get ahead of him as he took the radio out of the musette bag.

"Galloway."

"Rand, Colonel." Rand's voice was muffled. "Halt your column. Pronto, Sir."

Rick blinked.

"Column," he shouted. "Halt!"

Rick and those with him stopped. Enipses and the others continued ahead for a moment, then Enipses ordered a halt and Rick thumbed the push to talk switch.

"All right, I've done that. Now why? Over."

"Colonel, no more than two stadia ahead of you the road goes along the base of a ten-foot bluff," Rand said. "Over."

Rick pushed the talk button.

"I think I see that. Just barely, it's all dark shadows, no details. Over."

"Yeah, I can just see you," Rand said. "I can't talk loud, hope you can hear me. Colonel, there's about two hundred men in ambush on the high side above the road there, and there's more, don't know how many, taking positions on the low side. They're prone with crossbows loaded and ready. They're waiting for someone to come in range. Probably you."

"Four hundred men."

"Maybe that many, yes, Sir."

"Horses?"

"Not with them. Maybe down the hill, but I haven't seen any."

"Crossbows. Mail armor?"

"Yes, Sir, near as I can see. I haven't tried to get that close, Colonel."

"Any sign of the king? Or anyone we know?"

"Can't tell from this distance even with night glasses. They're hiding out, but some of them are pretty close to the road."

"Right. Good work. Anything behind me?"

"No enemies I saw. Major Baker is bringing up some of his Gurkhas," Rand said. "They're maybe ten minutes behind you. They're scouting more careful than I was, I was trying to stay ahead of you. The Major's channel is labeled 'Baker.' Over."

"Okay. Out for a moment, then. Stand by."

Captain Radnos trotted back to Rick. Enipses came back to join them. "It is never wise to keep a Wanax waiting," Enipses said. "And the pages will surely have told him of our approach."

"They did indeed, My Lord Justiciar," Radnos said. "Warlord, is there some concern?"

"Not sure yet, Captain. I will need a few moments. Please bring your escorts back closer to us."

"My Lord?"

"Indulge me, Captain." Rick turned the frequency turret until the word BAKER appeared in the display window, then thumbed the button. "Baker?"

Silence, then "Baker here, Colonel. I'm moving up to join you. I heard the report from Leftenant Rand."

"Lieutenant?"

"Brevet. I sent Corporal Ranui and five of my troops with Sergeant Rand, and told the corporal to treat Rand like an officer for this mission," Baker said. "Works better.

I'm bringing up thirty of my lads. We'll be in position in a few minutes."

Warner came up to join the other star men.

"This is odd, Skipper," he said.

"You can say that again, Mr. Warner," Bisso muttered.

"Warlord, what is the delay?" Captain Radnos demanded. "His Majesty will be impatient."

"I regret that, but His Majesty will have to endure his impatience," Rick said. "Please bring your men a bit closer. Thank you. Tell me, Captain Radnos, what do you know of an armed body of men concealed beside the road just ahead of us?"

"My Lord?"

Bisso looked to Rick, then made hand signals to the escort. Stand ready. Action expected. There was a loud metallic sound as Passavopolous charged the LMG. The mounted archers spread out slightly as the men muttered to each other. The foot archers dismounted and strung their bows.

"What is this?" Enipses demanded. "Armed men?"

"Lying in wait ahead of us, My Lord Justiciar," Rick said. "On that bluff ahead that overlooks the road. Others on the low side of the road. In ambush. You didn't know?"

"No, of course I did not know—how do you know this?" Enipses demanded.

"I have star ways," Rick said. *And damned good men who can run ahead of a mounted party scouting as they go.* "Captain Radnos, are those your men lying in wait ahead of us?"

"No, Warlord!" Radnos looked around. Four rifles were

not quite aimed at him. The horse archers finished stringing bows and made arrows ready.

Haerther frowned and moved between Rick and Captain Radnos. He held his shield in a ready position, his hand on his sword.

"Bisso," Rick said.

"Sir!"

"Dismount the escort. Form a defensive perimeter. Defend in all directions but heaviest to forward," Rick said in English. He pointed down the road. "About four hundred men with crossbows."

"Sir!" Bisso issued rapid orders. "Dismount and prepare to fight on foot! Horse holders take the mounts to our rear. Expected attack from ahead! Move!"

Rick changed to the Drantos dialect of the Tran language.

"Lord Enipses, I suggest you stay with us, but if you do, you will have no need for your escort. They may join Captain Radnos. There, on the road ahead of us. Captain, you will please have all your men dismount and stand in place. Right there, please, Captain, and at once."

"Warlord—"

"Precisely. The Warlord of Drantos has given you a direct order, on what may be a battlefield, Captain. I expect to be obeyed." Rick pointed to Passavopolous and the light machine gun. "And I have the means to enforce that order if it comes to that. Have your men dismount. Now."

"It is my duty to defend you," Radnos said.

"Thank you, Captain, but for the moment the best thing you can do for me is to dismount all your men and stay just there, in the middle of the road, just ahead of us. Bisso, if anyone tries to ride out of here, cut him down."

"Roger that, Skipper."

"That goes for Lord Enipses' escorts," Rick said. "My Lord Justiciar, we will see that you are safe. Your escorts will join Captain Radnos in forming a forward defensive position in case of need. For the moment it's better that they stay where I can see them. In this light that means close by."

"Warlord Rick, what is this?" Enipses sputtered.

"My Lord Justiciar, there was an ambush set up just ahead of us. Captain Radnos had to pass through it on his way here. Doubtless if he'd sensed any danger he would have warned us, but apparently he didn't. You will forgive me if I rely on my own resources under the circumstances?"

Rick signaled to one of the clansman horse archers.

"Duncan!"

"Yes, My Lord!"

"See to Lord Enipses. Find him a safe place within our defenses. Choose a partner to hold your horses. Your task is to see to the Justiciar's safety. Guard him well and closely."

"With my life, My Lord!" Duncan seized the reins and led Enipses back down the road before the Justiciar could protest.

Passavopolous was conferring with Bisso. They moved to the small ditch to the side of the road. Ark set the gun mount at the lip of the ditch and locked the LMG to it.

"Good field of fire here," Ark said. He didn't add that he also covered Radnos and his men ten paces away. "We got time to dig in, Colonel?"

"Don't know."

Bisso waved the other star men to either side of the machine gun.

"Colonel, just back here behind Ark if you will, Sir."

"My Lords! What are you doing?" Radnos demanded.

"Captain," Rick said. "Let me be blunt. I want you and all of your men where I can see them." He handed the reins of his mount to Haerther. "Get some help," Rick said. "I want you to look after Lord Bisso's mount. And Lord Ark's mule."

"You be careful with Sugarplum," Passavopolous said. "Big as I am there's not many other critters I can ride. Colonel, you got any idea of what we're facing?"

"Maybe nothing," Rick said in English. "But maybe three to four hundred, probably with crossbows. The troops with Radnos may or may not be in on this ambush," Rick said. He changed to the local dialect. "Bisso, make sure the troops understand. No shooting unless you're shot at, not without direct orders, except if Radnos or any of his troops try to get out of here, one warning shot, then cut them down."

"Sir."

Rick selected channel six and thumbed the talk button.

"Rand here."

"Report."

"Nothing different. Bunch of men at arms, crossbows and swords, lying flat on the ground. They were watching the road, now they look upset. There's somebody moving up and down the line like he's giving instructions, but I can't see who it is. Colonel, I don't know how much longer I can hang out here before they see me, but I think long enough. Major Baker's brought up the Gurkhas and he's ready to deploy them. I think he's got in mind surrounding them."

"Surrounding them?"

"Sure seems like it to me, Colonel."

Rick thought about that.

"Galloway out." He changed channels again.

"Baker here."

"Major, what are you doing?"

"Deploying to neutralize the threat, Colonel."

"Do you intend to attack four hundred men with your detachment?"

"Certainly. With your permission, of course."

"Not overreaching?"

"I wouldn't think so. We have complete surprise. My men have good night vision. Our first volleys will take out a hundred or so. I wouldn't expect the others to put up much of a fight after that. I mean, they haven't before."

Rick thought about that for a moment.

"You think these are Drantos troops, then?"

"No data, Colonel, but who else would they be?"

"Part of the Fiver army."

"And how would they know to be here, Colonel?"

"Good question. So you think you can take them."

"I'm quite certain of it."

"Carry on, but do not begin action unless you're attacked. I don't know what we're facing. There's some indication that those men are Drantos nobility, and if they are, every one we kill could be a new blood feud! That's a general instruction, Major, keep the slaughter to a minimum. We not only have to win a battle, we have to live with the consequences. Over."

"Understood, Colonel. I'll get the proper instructions to my troops. One thing, we believe we've spotted their leader."

"I would very much appreciate it if you could take that man alive," Rick said.

"Understood."

"Okay, then. Out." Rick switched the set off and looked around.

*Who the hell are we facing? Could the Wanax be down there? We're nominally in Fiver territory, but I don't know of any Fiver troops in here, and how would they know to lay an ambush for me anyway? Baker's probably right that these are Drantos troops, and we've got to cross a good stretch of Drantos to get to the coast. And God help us if it comes to civil war! Tylara's got enough to worry about with the Fiver army in Chelm, she sure doesn't need Drantos troops ravaging Chelm.*

*Calm*, he thought. *We don't know what we're facing or why. Enipses seems genuinely surprised. Can't tell about Radnos. He could be a good actor. But why? There's no reason Ganton would want us dead. None I can think of. One thing's sure, this took time to organize, must have started just after Enipses set off to see me. Someone knew we'd come this way, and when. Who besides Wanax Ganton?*

"Colonel, I'm sure glad we didn't ride into a trap," Bisso said. "But how the hell did you know about it?"

"I sent Rand out ahead of us," Rick said.

"So that's why we moved so slow," Passavopolous said. "Well, it's a lucky thing you sent him out."

Not precisely luck, Rick thought. Or was it? He looked

around at his small command. The escort had seemed large enough when they left camp, but now it seemed tiny.

Rick's troops were deployed in a circle, most of them in an arc centered on Ark and the LMG, others farther back down the road with the horses. Some of the horses were lying on the ground. Others resisted. Two centaurs were screaming defiance at their handlers. Rick's rear guard was a scene of confusion, but everything else seemed orderly.

Out in front of him it was a different story. Enipses' original escort and the detachment under Radnos were dismounted, but they milled about, some taking a defensive posture, others arguing. All of the horses were standing, but they'd been bunched into groups of five with a horse holder to each group. There was loud cursing.

"Mr. Warner, come with me, please," Rick said. He went back to the center of his perimeter. The Justiciar was seated inside a circle of shields held by clansmen. "Lord Enipses," he said softly.

Enipses stood.

"Warlord, I protest—"

"Another time, My Lord Justiciar," Rick said. "We have no time now. I have a question for you."

Enipses frowned, then nodded.

"There is always time for the proper courtesies, My Lord. Having said that, I will overlook formalities at this time. Yes, My Lord?"

"There are four hundred men, with crossbows, lying in wait less than two stadia up this road," Rick said. "They're concealed and ready. Do you have any reason why I shouldn't kill the lot of them?"

"But who are they?"

"That, My Lord Justiciar, is precisely what I'm trying to find out."

"Surely you do not suspect that I—or that His Majesty—that these are our soldiers?"

"My Lord Justiciar, I suspect nothing. I merely want to be certain that these are enemies, and no one you know about, before I kill them all."

"Warlord, I know nothing of them. Nothing!"

"Thank you. Now how well do you know Captain Radnos?"

"Warlord, I know him not at all."

"He's not part of the Royal Guard?"

"Of course not."

"He said he was."

"I didn't hear him say that. If he says that he puts on airs," Enipses said.

Rick nodded. The Guard were elites, many from noble families, who joined the Guard for family advancement. Enipses would know many of them, and certainly all of their officers.

"Then who the devil is he, and why would the Wanax send him to meet me? And how would he know we were coming here? Would your grandson have told him?"

"Yatar, no!" Enipses looked startled. "My Lord, I—My Lord, please, what is it that you suspect? Is my grandson in danger?"

"What were his orders?" Rick demanded.

"He was to ride quickly to the Wanax and tell him we were coming immediately, so that proper preparations could be made for your welcome."

"Not to alert an ambush," Rick said.

"By Yatar and Christ, Warlord! Why would His Majesty set an ambush for you? How could you suspect such a thing? You were His Majesty's Guardian! He regards you as a father! Lord Rick, have you lost your wits?"

Rick nodded slowly. The old man was sincere enough, and what he said made sense.

"Not Wanax Ganton, then," Rick mused aloud. "So who does want me dead? Someone who commands troops? Who probably commands Captain Radnos?"

Enipses started to speak, then fell silent.

"You thought of someone," Rick said.

"I hope—I hope I have not."

"The name, My Lord."

"No. No, it cannot be him. It cannot. Your pardon, My Lord, but I have no suggestions."

"Colonel, we both know who has to be behind this," Warner said in English.

"I think you're right, but keep it to yourself for now," Rick said.

The handset buzzed.

"Galloway."

"Rand, Colonel. Major Baker is with me. We're deployed. Say the word and we'll take them out."

"Rand, who the hell are those people?"

"No idea, Colonel." Rand's voice was muffled as if he were speaking into his hand. "We're not that close to them. They're kind of on ready alert. They're spooked now that you've dismounted, they were ready for you, but now they're all confused." Rand paused. "Colonel, I'm pretty good, and them Gurkhas may be better, but we're not going to get close to them right now. I mean, maybe we could find one guy off by himself and slit his throat, but that would be taking a lot more chance than I want."

"No, don't do that," Rick said. "You say Baker is with you?"

"Yes, Sir."

"I'll call him direct." He changed channels. "Baker?"

"Still in place, Colonel. I should point out that this is an unstable situation. If we stay here long enough someone's going to see us. Inevitable, I'd say."

*Yeah, I know that,* Rick thought. "Can you give me ten minutes?"

"I'd hate for it to be longer than that."

"Right."

"Colonel, is there some problem here?" Baker asked.

"Local politics," Rick said. "The officer who met me claimed to be part of the Royal Guard, but according to the Lord Justiciar, he isn't. That doesn't mean the rest of these people aren't, though, and the Guards have a lot of younger sons of the aristocracy in their ranks. If any of those ambush troops actually are Royal Guards—or even if they're not, but they're still noble—we're right back to those blood feuds if we kill them. I damned well don't want to be the one who starts shooting."

"Awkward," Baker said.

*And I don't want to admit that I just don't like killing a bunch of people without knowing who they are,* Rick thought. *But I may not have much choice . . .*

"Stand by, Major. I'll be back shortly. Galloway out."

Rick turned to Enipses.

"My Lord Justiciar, I ask you to come with me. I have

instructions for Captain Radnos, and I want you there when I give them."

"Certainly. Warlord, what is happening here?"

"I wish I knew." Rick strode forward to where Ark had set up the light machine gun.

"Captain Radnos, please attend the Lord Justiciar," Rick said. "You won't need your men."

He looks nervous, Rick thought, as Radnos strode towards them. Because he's up to something, or just the situation?

"Captain, you said you were of the Royal Guards."

"I am, Warlord."

"Then why does My Lord Justiciar not know you?"

"Warlord, I am of the Guards assigned to the King's Companion. We have only recently combined with His Majesty's forces," Radnos said, and Enipses nodded in understanding.

"That is true, Warlord."

"Did the Wanax himself send you to conduct me?" Rick demanded.

"No, My Lord. Companion Morrone gave me my orders. But he often speaks in His Majesty's name."

"And where was this?"

"My Lord?"

"Where was Morrone when last you saw him?"

"Just outside the encampment of the Wanax," Radnos said.

"With how many soldiers?"

Radnos frowned.

"Answer, Captain," Enipses snapped.

"Three hundred."

"Armed as you are armed, I presume?" Rick asked.

"Yes, Warlord, mail, crossbows, and swords, mounted on horses. Although Captain Janisos has a centaur."

"So the men hidden along the road ahead are Companion Morrone's Guards," Rick said. "Royal Guardsmen. Presumably loyal to Wanax Ganton. Lying in wait for the Warlord and Justiciar. Tell me, Captain, what do you know of this?"

"Warlord, I know nothing!" Radnos insisted. He turned to Enipses. "Justiciar, you know my family! I am the younger son of the Bheroman Dnestros! I would never be disloyal to the Wanax!"

The Justiciar regarded him coldly, then looked at Rick.

"Warlord, I believe that may be true. He bears a resemblance to the bheroman."

"Now I'm really worried," Warner said softly in English. "Skipper, whose plot is this? Morrone doesn't like you much but he wouldn't kill you without the king's permission. Would he?"

"Easier to get forgiveness than permission," Passavopolous said.

Warner looked thoughtful, then nodded.

"Good point," Rick said, also in English. He turned back to Radnos and Enipses.

"Captain Radnos, how could you have gone past three to four hundred men lying in wait with weapons and not have seen anything?"

"It is not possible, Warlord. There were no men there when I came down that road. One of my tasks was to be certain the road was safe."

"It appears that it isn't safe now. Who followed you from the camp of the Wanax?"

Radnos gulped and turned away.

"So that's how it is," Rick said. "Captain, you say your task was to be certain that road was safe for me and for Lord Enipses?"

"Aye, Warlord."

"Then I suggest you do that."

"Warlord?"

"Take your escort and go ahead of us. You see up ahead there is a ten-foot bluff along the left side of the road. There are men lying in wait on the bluff, and more on the low side of the road. Order them in the name of Warlord and Justiciar to come out and form up in the road."

"And if they refuse my orders?"

"Turn and ride as if Vothan's wolves pursued you, Captain. Get away from there, because we're going to unleash Hell."

## ━━ CHAPTER NINE ━━
# AYO GURKHALI!

Captain Radnos mounted. He shouted commands, and his escorts mounted and formed a column of twos. There was just enough light to show them moving down the road at a slow walk.

"Skipper, what's going on?" Bisso asked. "He sure don't look eager."

"I wouldn't either," Warner said.

"I think Morrone's decided to take matters into his own hands," Rick said.

"He wouldn't do that against the King's orders!" Bisso protested.

"Like hell he wouldn't," Warner said. "Morrone makes no secret of it, he believes the Colonel doesn't kowtow enough to the King and he resents hell out of it. We've all heard stories."

Bisso and Passavopolous grunted agreement.

"Colonel," Bisso said. "Just for the hell of it, would you please get off the skyline?"

"Right." Rick scrambled down into the ditch. "My Lord Enipses, I suggest you join me."

"Surely I am safe enough here," Enipses said. "My Lord, I believe you have lost your senses! There are no traitors here!"

Radnos had almost reached the edge of the embankment. His group halted, and Radnos turned to point back up the road towards Rick.

"The traitor has turned coward!" he shouted. "He is there, above you. We have the numbers, we have the will. Forward lads! For the Wanax and Drantos! Kill the traitor!"

There were shouts. Armed men sprang up from both sides of the road and a dozen crossbow bolts whistled past. Enipses fell clutching at his neck. Two of his escorts dropped to the ground. Rick couldn't tell if they were hit or instinctively diving for cover.

"Get down, you idiots!" Bisso shouted. "Troops, prepare to engage!"

"Haerther!" Rick shouted. "See to the Lord Justiciar!"

Haerther and two clansmen dashed forward to drag Enipses to the safety of the ditch. Another volley of crossbow bolts whistled in and one of the clansmen fell. Enipses was dragged to the shelter of the ditch. Blood flowed from a nasty gash on his face.

"Priest!" Haerther shouted. "Priest of Yatar, the Lord Justiciar is wounded!"

"Look to the front!" Bisso shouted. "Hold your fire until they get closer. Stay down!"

A blue-robed apprentice dashed forward in a deep crouch. He knelt beside Enipses.

"Be careful of him," Rick admonished.

The apprentice looked up. He was a young man, no more than twenty, a recruit from one of the Chelm villages, but it was clear he had already been through some of his priestly training.

"As I would anyone," he said. "I have balm."

Balm. Antiseptic cream laced with blue bread mold. Rick nodded in satisfaction. Much of Tran's bacteria hadn't yet adapted to attack humans, so infection wasn't as universal here as on Earth battlefields, but some common infections had clearly been brought from Earth. Local fungus could be dangerous, but the bread mold penicillin was effective on the Earth bacteria. Blue bread mold and sanitary practices . . .

"Carry on," Rick said.

Bisso was looking down the hill with his binoculars. He raised his battle rifle and fired twice.

"They're not too eager to rush us, Colonel," he said. "But four hundred? May be a near thing if they can get organized. Morrone's a pretty good leader, too. At least he can get men to follow him."

"Right. Ark, stand by."

"Roger that, Colonel. We're pretty low on ammo for this thing."

"Make it count," Bisso said. More crossbow bolts whistled overhead. "Shooting high, and they don't want to close. Maybe it's going to be all right."

"I think we'll know a lot more in a moment," Rick said.

As he spoke an amplified voice cut through the dark.

"Gurkhas, make ready for volley fire! Mark your targets! Take your aim!"

"Who the hell?" Bisso demanded.

"Fire." Thirty rifles went off at once. There were flashes from one side of the road, and Rick thought he saw other flashes farther up. The classic ambush pattern for rifle fire was L-shaped to avoid fratricide.

"Hot damn!" Bisso exclaimed.

"*Ayo Gurkhali!*" The shout came from one side of the road. "*Ayo Gurkhali!*"

"Kind of chills the blood, don't it?" Passavopolous said. "Hah."

"Intended to," Warner said.

"Yes, professor," Bisso answered.

The bullhorn spoke again.

"Make ready to fire in volley! Mark your targets! Take your aim! Fire. Take aim! Fire!"

"*Ayo Gurkhali!*"

"Skipper, what the hell is going on?" Bisso asked.

"I think you're seeing just why we wanted these guys as allies," Warner said. "I'm sure glad they're not after us!"

"You can say that again, Mr. Warner," Passavopolous said. "You can say that again."

There was total confusion near the bluff. Someone was shouting from the road, but Rick couldn't make out who was saying what. The bullhorn spoke again.

"What the hell is the Major saying?" Bisso asked. "Is that Gurkha?"

"No, it's that goddam northern dialect," Warner said. "I think he's trying to tell them to surrender, but they sure won't understand him."

"Oh, crap," Rick said.

"Mark your targets! Take your aim! Fire!"

The rifles spoke again, like one prolonged shot.

"*Ayo Gurkhali!*"

Rick thumbed the handset. "Major?"

"Sir."

"What's the situation?"

"They haven't a clue as to what's happening, Colonel. I think they want to surrender, but I'm having a bit of a problem telling them how to do it."

"Give the bullhorn to Rand for a moment, please. Tell him I'll be talking to him. Out." He changed channels. "Rand, tell those poor bastards to surrender in a language they'll understand. Have them go to the road and lay down their arms. Be sure Major Baker tells his men that. The fewer of those people we kill, the better off we'll all be."

"What about any that run away?"

"Rather have them alive than dead. Be sure the Major knows that."

"Sir."

✛ ✛ ✛

The one-sided battle lasted another ten minutes, but now there were only individual rifle shots, punctuated by the Gurkha battle cry. Once there was a shout of *Ayo Gurkhali!* followed by a blood-curdling scream, then silence.

"No shot," Warner observed.

"Them knives," Bisso said. "Christ, Mr. Warner, this gives me the creeps!"

"They're surrendering, though," Passavopolous said. He pointed towards the road. More than a hundred men stood there with their arms held high. "You know, I haven't seen one of them Gurkha troops tonight. Not one."

"I doubt any of the enemy saw one either," Rick said.

"Son of a bitch. I sure don't want them mad at us, Colonel," Bisso said.

"Nor do I, Sergeant," Rick said. "Nor do I."

✢ ✢ ✢

Rick's handset chirped.

"Galloway."

"Baker here, Colonel. I think you can bring your men down to collect the prisoners now. We've checked and disarmed all the downed troops along the road. Perhaps you should stay back a bit just in case there's one armed sniper left looking just for you, but there's no organized resistance. And until you've got them covered I'd as soon they didn't realize just how few of my lads they're facing. Might give them ideas, don't you know."

*He's amusing himself,* Rick thought. *Well, I'd be proud too.*

"How many prisoners do we have, Major?"

"I'd estimate about two hundred surrendered, and perhaps another seventy-five wounded. I wouldn't expect many of the wounded to survive, unless you're better at treating gunshot wounds to the torso than we are."

"No knife wounds?"

"I'd be surprised if there were. When my lads use their knives the result generally isn't a wound."

"Butcher's bill?"

"None of ours that I know of, Colonel. The surprise was complete."

"Right. We'll be down shortly, then."

"Good—Uh, Colonel, stand by a moment. Yes, Leftenant Rand?" There was a long pause. "Colonel, there's a contingent of horsemen coming up the road towards us. Proceeding cautiously."

"The King's Guards," Rick said. "Coming to see what's going on. Do your very best not to engage them, Major. I'll send someone along to talk to them. Now we'll get moving. Out."

Rick turned to shout. "Mount up! Get ready to go take charge of the prisoners."

He turned to Bisso.

"Get down there and set up to guard a couple of hundred prisoners," he said. "That includes that Captain Radnos they sent and all his men. Put them where you and Ark can cover them. I don't expect any trouble from them but you never know. And there's more troops coming up the road, may be friendlies, may be something else. Set up with cover, but for God's sake don't start shooting! It may be the Wanax."

"Yes, Sir, but wouldn't it serve him right?"

"I don't know, Sergeant. I do know that if we kill the King we'll be hostiles in hostile territory. Remember what that was like when Andre Parsons was leading you?"

"I remember, Colonel. We'll be damned careful."

Duncan came up leading two horses. Rick acknowledged him with a nod and turned to Haerther.

"How is Lord Enipses?"

"Wooden quarrel, sliced his cheek above his mail shirt, My Lord. Baniclos has stitched the wound and applied balm. If the quarrel wasn't poisoned he may be all right."

"I will live, My Lord," Enipses said. A large bandage

held a compress against his left cheek. "Young Baniclos is quite skilled. I no longer bleed."

"Can you ride?"

"I would rather not, My Lord, but I suppose I have little choice."

"Lord Enipses, my scouts report a group of men coming from the direction of the Wanax's camp," Rick said. "I'd presume they're guardsmen. I would not care to see them—or the Wanax!—wander into a battle zone."

"Yatar no!" Enipses struggled to his feet. "Lord Rick— My Lord, just what did happen?" Enipses pleaded.

"As you saw, Captain Radnos ordered an attack on us, and my troops defeated the ambush." He turned to shout. "Duncan, bring Lord Enipses his mount and prepare to accompany him!"

"Your troops," Enipses said. "All those star weapons! And that battle cry. I have never heard that battle cry before."

"It may not be the last time you hear it," Rick said. "Those are my new troops, Lord Enipses. New men from the stars. Be certain that His Majesty understands that. Now ride, while I make certain you will be allowed to pass through on the road." He pressed the transmit button on the radio.

✠ ✠ ✠

Rick's mounted archers herded the prisoners into the clear area where the bluff began. Ark had set up the LMG to cover them, and Bisso stood by with the foot archers and the other star men. Ten minutes later Rick was joined by Major Baker and his Gurkhas. The Gurkha Sergeant Major was grinning like a thief.

"We did well, Colonel, Sir! Did we not?"

"You did well indeed, Sergeant Major." Rick nodded. "Well indeed." He caught Baker's eye and got an approving nod. "Well indeed," Rick repeated.

## ⊹⇒ CHAPTER TEN ⇐⊹
# COMPANION

Everything was happening at once, and everyone needed a decision from Rick.

First things first. Set up a command post. The best place was a wide spot in the road a hundred yards before it went along the bluff. The Gurkhas could cover the area nicely; it was far enough from cover that no one would be sneaking up on him, and close enough to the prisoners that Ark could cover them with the LMG. He summoned his guards to set up a perimeter defense around a headquarters area. There were still more questions than answers, but then Bisso came up with a prisoner.

"Morrone," the sergeant said. "He demanded to see you and when that didn't work he begged. I brought him as soon as I knew who he was."

Wanax Companion Morrone had no helmet. His belt had been removed so that his mail shirt hung awkwardly. Morrone's hands were bound behind him. He ran forward to kneel awkwardly at Rick's feet.

"My Lord. I ask for mercy, not for myself, but for my men. They but followed orders they were certain came from the Wanax."

"You had orders from the Wanax to kill me?" Rick demanded.

"No, My Lord. This was my action and mine alone."

"Then why?"

"Because you bring no good to either the realm or the Wanax," he said defiantly. "I thought that in the past, and I believe it still more now. You settled Westmen on royal lands. You have no proper claim to Chelm save through your wife, and she only as dowager, and yet you gave Chelm lands to the nomads. You are not loyal to the realm. But that is my thought, not that of my men or my sovereign. Kill me, but spare my men."

"Sounds like a good suggestion to me, Colonel," Bisso said.

"I'll consider it." Rick kept his face impassive. "Let's be certain we understand each other. The Wanax didn't order you to attack me. Neither this time nor in the ambush on the road away from his camp last month."

"My Lord, he did not. Both were my actions and mine alone, and I undertook them with my own troops."

"You hate me that much?"

"I do not hate you at all, My Lord. But I think you are a great danger to the realm. So do many of the great lords. You weaken respect for the Wanax even as you increase his power over the peers. You ruin them yet undermine the Crown at the same time, and you will bring skyfire and ruin to Drantos!"

"Other great lords follow you, then. Which ones?"

"None work with me, Lord Rick. I have done this alone. I had hopes of support from the great men of the realm after you were removed, but I asked no one else to aid me in this matter. As to which lords might support me, you would know those as well as I."

"I suppose I do know," Rick said, nodding thoughtfully. "So this is going to be as big a surprise to Ganton as it was to me?"

"It will be, My Lord."

"Get up, Companion. Now. Just what the Sam Hill was your plan?" Rick winced as Morrone got to his feet without assistance. Still strong and still dangerous. And still the king's oldest and closest friend.

Morrone stood defiantly.

"With you dead, the Wanax would be in control again. He could incorporate your troops into his command." He tried to shrug. "Of course the price of that might be my head, and were my acts discovered I expected the Wanax to offer that to your surviving men."

Rick frowned. "Stiff price."

"I was willing." Morrone attempted another shrug. "You have done great things, Lord Rick, but your presence is not a good thing for Drantos. Ganton would never rid himself of your evil presence, so I would do it for him. But I failed."

"Haerther!"

"Sir!"

"Take charge of Lord Companion Morrone. I'll need him shortly, so don't keep him far away. And be careful. He is a strong warrior and a very dangerous man. There are many who would obey him still."

"Armed party approaching," a sentry called. "Small party. They have halted."

"Be alert, lads," Major Baker shouted.

"Officers' Call," Rick shouted. "Officers here. Guards, protect this area."

"Shield wall! Guards, surround the Warlord!" Haerther commanded. "My Lord Companion, come with me." He led Morrone away as the guards swarmed around Rick and stood facing out, shields at ready. Baker and Warner came to join Rick.

"Emissary from the Wanax," a guard officer announced.

"Let him through." Two clansmen stood aside.

The Black Rod Usher looked nervously at the circle of clansmen forming the shield wall around Rick and his command group.

"I come in the name of Ganton, Wanax of Drantos," he said. "His Majesty commands me to conduct you to his presence."

"Not bloody likely," Major Baker muttered.

Rick frowned.

"Colonel, Major Mason will have my ballocks if I let you go anywhere unescorted, and he damned well *ought* to!" Baker protested. "I don't need to remind you that you were a couple of hundred yards from an ambush, do I?"

"Not Ganton's," Rick said.

"So that man Morrone says," Baker said.

"Begging your pardon, Colonel," Bisso said, "but I'm with Major Baker on this. We let you go out there and get killed, and Mason will have our arses, and it won't be nothing we don't deserve, either."

Rick looked to Warner, who nodded back.

"Looks that way to me, too, Colonel."

"My Lord," the usher had stood silent during this interchange, but his unhappiness was obvious, "the Wanax is waiting!"

"Tell His Majesty—"

They were interrupted by a shout. "Make way for the Wanax!"

Ganton strode into the shield circle. He was bareheaded and accompanied by two richly dressed Guardsmen. A clan shieldsman tried to bar his way, but Ganton ignored him and strode past. The Black Rod Usher tried to speak, but Ganton silenced him with a gesture.

"We greet you, Warlord of Drantos," Ganton said. His voice was unwavering and he stood proudly. "It appears we owe you much," he continued. "Not least for the discovery of treachery in my own ranks. And for adding much to our strength."

He looked expectantly at Major Baker, and Rick thought furiously for a moment, then shrugged mentally.

"Majesty, may I present Lord Clyde Baker, Major of Mercenaries, commander of—" Rick hesitated, then plunged on. "Of Galloway's Gurkhas, star lords who have newly joined us."

Ganton hesitated, then extended his hand to Baker.

"Welcome, My Lord," he said. "Am I correct in believing that not long ago your—goorkhas—were in service to the Five Kingdoms? And defeated my army?"

Baker bowed to kiss the king's hand.

"Unfortunately, yes, Majesty," he said in his atrocious northern dialect.

Ganton shook his head in incomprehension.

"Bloody hell, Colonel, how do I talk to him?"

"I understand some English," Ganton said.

"Then let me say you are regrettably correct. My apologies for the misunderstanding."

Rick doubted that Ganton understood all of that, but the King nodded graciously.

"The apology is accepted, My Lord," he said.

There was a disturbance at the edge of the shield wall.

"Let Lord Enipses in," Rick shouted. Enipses and Duncan came into the circle. Enipses looked pale.

"You should rest, Lord Justiciar," Rick said.

"I thought I might be needed," Enipses said, and turned to the Wanax.

"Majesty, it is all true," he said. "We were attacked by command of Captain Radnos. I heard him myself, and shortly afterward I was wounded. When the battle subsided Warlord Rick sent me to find you, but I missed you in the dark. Lord Rick but defended himself. Himself and me, as well, Majesty!"

"Peace, Justiciar," Ganton said. "I have been told that you sought me. Lord Rick, when I heard the sounds of battle I rode quickly with my guards in fear that you were attacked. Your Lord Rand found me and assured me you were unharmed, then brought my party here."

Rick nodded.

"Bisso, where the hell is Rand?" he asked, and Baker cleared his throat.

"Colonel, I sent him with the Gurkhas I'd assigned him to scout the perimeter, just in case we have any more unexpected visitors. He still has his radio."

"Oh, good work." Rick's head buzzed, and suddenly he felt faint. *Damnation, what's happening to me?* He steadied himself by holding Warner's shoulder. *Radios. Not used to having radios. Hell, I'm not used to much of anything now. Baker's a real officer, he knows more about this stuff than I ever will.*

"You all right, Colonel?" Bisso asked.

"Yeah." *Except I don't know what the hell to do now, and I don't dare let anyone know that.*

"May we speak alone, Lord Rick?" Ganton asked.

Rick nodded, and waved to the others.

"Give us a some space, please," he said, and the shield bearers moved outward, extending the perimeter and Rick and Ganton stood alone in the middle of the circle of warriors.

*One thing is damned clear,* Rick thought. *He trusts me. All the troops here are mine. And he came right to me when he heard there was trouble.*

"Lord Rick, do you believe I ordered this attack?" Ganton asked.

*Not a demand,* Rick thought. *More like a plea.*

"No, Majesty, I'm convinced you knew nothing of it. But you do know who led the ambush?"

"I dread the knowledge," Ganton said. "Radnos is Companion Morrone's man. His favorite. His father is a loyal bheroman." Ganton looked ready for tears. "Tell me, my Warlord, was this the act of my oldest friend?"

Rick nodded slowly.

"It was, Majesty. He has confessed it."

"He lives?"

"He does, Majesty. As my prisoner."

"Morrone is my oldest friend," the young king said slowly.

"Are you asking for his life?"

Ganton hesitated.

"I am, My Lord," he said after a moment.

"There are conditions," Rick said.

"My Lord?"

"Many of the Companion's Guardsmen were killed and wounded in this battle," Rick said. "Morrone is responsible for the battle, and thus responsible for all blood debts. All, and without quibble," Rick said. *The last damn thing I need is a bunch of Drantos lords hating me for haggling over the payments.*

"Granted. Eagerly granted. I will make the settlements myself, and extract the costs from Morrone." Ganton made a wry face. "He will easily be able to afford them, I think, thanks to my former generosity."

"There is more," Rick said.

Ganton frowned.

*Best not push this too far*, Rick thought. *I don't want to humiliate him. But this needs to be settled.*

"Majesty, he was also responsible for the ambush on my party after my visit to your camp," Rick said. "They were disguised as troops of the Five, so the question of blood debts never arose, but now we know they, too, were Drantos soldiers, members of the Companion's Guard. Some of those men were killed, as were some of mine, and they too are Companion Morrone's responsibility."

Ganton nodded.

"Of course."

"And finally, Majesty, my shieldsman was gravely

wounded in that attack. He is to have a generous pension, guaranteed by the crown."

"Is that all?" Ganton smiled. "Lord Rick, I have already begun arrangements for that! When I heard that your life was saved by your shield bearer, I ordered that suitable crown land in Chelm be found so it could be granted to him! In my gratitude! Do not be concerned."

*Now that's worth checking on*, Rick thought. *Before or after he started north to Aachilos? After, I'll bet, but it will be interesting to find out.*

"Then I think this matter is settled," Rick said. "I will have Companion Morrone delivered to you this night. He's unharmed, but I must warn you, Majesty, that while I bear him no great ill will, my soldiers may not share my own opinion. It would not be wise for the Lord Companion to encounter them." Rick grinned slightly. "The Lord Companion is a fearsome champion, but my soldiers don't share his views of chivalry."

Ganton fingered his Browning automatic pistol in its ornate holster. He returned Rick's smile.

"I do understand, My Lord."

*That's good*, Rick thought. *But it's one more favor I've done him. You don't make friends by doing favors, you get more friends by* receiving *favors. Which brings me to—*

"Majesty, I have a request of you."

"Name it, My Lord. If it be in my power—"

"It is a great favor I ask. I wish to be relieved of my responsibilities for a time. A short time, I hope."

"What is this?" Ganton demanded.

"Your Majesty should have no problem withdrawing to Drantos," Rick said. "That's a less satisfactory outcome to this campaign than having the Wanax Ganton become High Rexja of the Five Kingdoms. We can all agree to that. But we are now far from Aachilos, and surprise has been lost. The chancellor will have summoned the support of all the Five Kingdoms to his aid, and that will include messages to the Green Palace. If they're smart, they've pardoned Strymon, which means we no longer face the defeated expeditionary army under the Honorable Matthias. Instead, we may soon face the entire host of the Five Kingdoms under its most competent commander, a general familiar with our ways. Without surprise, it would be a long and bloody path to Aachilos."

"Even with your new—Gurkhas—My Lord?"

"Alas, I cannot come with you to Aachilos," Rick said. "And I will need my Gurkhas where I go. That is the favor I must beg of you. Matters have arisen that I must attend to, matters of conflict among the stars. I do not ask this lightly, Majesty."

"What will you do?"

"I must take my forces to Taranto," Rick said. "I sent two of my men to Nikeis. They've vanished, and Nikeis ignores my requests for an explanation. Indeed, the republic has closed its borders. None come or go." Rick's face grew stern. "Majesty, I will have my men returned or avenged."

"Do you need my aid?"

"Thank you, Majesty, but I have more than enough power. What I need is the time."

"And the matter of the stars?"

"Surely your Majesty has heard of strange lights and

odd sightings on the mainland opposite Nikeis," Rick said. He watched Ganton closely, but the King was giving nothing away.

"I've heard very little." Ganton frowned. "And nothing at all from my ministers in Nikeis since the battle when the Nikeisian troops departed in a huff," he said. "Their captain said he was offended by the division of the spoils of battle. I sent a rider after him, and another to Nikeis with my own account, along with an offer to settle the matter on their terms, but I've heard no reply, whether from their captain or from the Doge." Ganton frowned again. "Nikeis and the mainland near it are sealed. No messengers I've sent there have returned. Now you tell me of 'strange lights and odd sightings.' This is news enough to make anyone uneasy, Lord Rick!"

"Majesty, I agree," Rick said. "And that is why I must go there immediately."

"And you must take all your forces, including your new Gurkhas?"

"I fear I must. We know too little of what may be happening in Nikeis for me to take less." Rick paused. *O Lord*, he thought. "My medical corpsmen are all apprentices and priests of the new faith."

"Both my archbishops have warned me Nikeis will not accept the new faith," Ganton said. "Nikeis is Christian and considers everyone else, perhaps even the Romans, pagan or worse. But I think that no reason for alarm. Nikeis has always tolerated all religions. Besides their great cathedral and many churches, there is a Temple of Yatar and a Temple to Vothan in the city of Nikeis! So I'm told. I'm also told there is a Church of Rome and another of the Christians of the South. I know of no church of the Unified Faith as yet, but I think you have no need to fear on that account." Ganton paused. "I can send members of my court, men skilled in diplomacy. I have one, Bheroman Tancius, who has been more than a year among the Signory in Nikeis. Perhaps he can be of help."

"I would welcome his aid, Majesty. He should make haste to my camp, we depart in the morning for Taranto."

"He isn't here. I will send for him immediately, and perhaps he can join you. In Taranto. The Roman city."

And long a thorn in the side to the Drantos rulers, who once claimed the port city and the lands around it. Ganton didn't press the claim, but he had to be aware of it. Rick took a deep breath.

"Publius meets me there."

"Publius. Father of my beloved Wanaxxae. Perhaps I should accompany you."

"I do not think that wise, Majesty. It will be no small task to assemble your army and bring it safely home to Drantos. A task that will require your abilities, I think."

"Perhaps so." Ganton paused for a moment, then asked in a low tone, "Will you return to my service, Eqeta of Chelm?"

*Neatly reminding me of my feudal obligations*, Rick thought. *Clever of him.*

"I remain Your Majesty's loyal servant," Rick said. "As does the Eqetassa, who holds Chelm against a great army. She has need of me when I'm done in Nikeis."

"Done with what? What does this mean? What seek you in Nikeis?" Ganton demanded.

"That's what I mean to find out, Majesty. Yet whatever

else may be true, it's been too long since I heard from my agents in Nikeis. It's time I see to the safety of my men."

"Lights in the sky," Ganton said. "And perhaps new wealth in Nikeis. I need not warn you to be careful in your journey?"

"Be assured that I will be, Majesty." Rick smiled crookedly. "When one knows as little as we do, caution is always wise."

"And few men know less than we do, Lord Rick." Ganton managed an answering smile, but it was brief, and his eyes darkened. "Do you believe the great star lords have visited Nikeis? Have they left gifts of great importance? Must the realm fear attack with star weapons from Nikeis?"

Rick heard the plea in the young king's voice. *He's as daunted by all this as I am. And he can't escape any of it any more than I can.*

"I intend to answer those questions as quickly as I can, Majesty," he said. "In the meantime, nothing that we *do* know will change what you must do now."

Ganton nodded looked at him a moment longer, then nodded.

"Then Christ be with you, Warlord. And with your men in Nikeis."

# PART FOUR
# MARE NOSTRUM

# ❖❖ CHAPTER ONE ❖❖
# PROFESSORE CLAVELL

**Three weeks before the Battle of the Ottarn River**

Gulls cried outside the windows of the Council Hall. A stiff sea breeze brought in a fresh scent of salt and the sea. The high-ceilinged classroom was ornate, decorated by oil paintings of ships and the sea. A large fresco of the Winged Lion of Nikeis dominated one end of the room, and on all four sides elaborate plaster cornices with painted geometric designs topped plastered walls. The desks and chairs were solid and functional, but the table feet were carved into lion paws, and everything shone from new varnish. It was the most elegant classroom Sergeant Lance Clavell had ever seen. Or heard of, for that matter.

The wall behind Clavell's lecture table had been stripped of its decorations, and he pointed to the drawings charcoaled onto the whitewashed surface.

"This is the life cycle of the liver worm," he said. He pointed to one drawing. "If you look into water drawn from cattle fields, you'll see small moving flecks. They're very small, too small for you to make out details, but in fact they're worms, which we call liver flukes. This is what one would look like if it was big enough to see." He tapped the diagram behind him.

"This worm is the cause of many of the diseases found among your cattle. If you allow cattle to drink from water full of cow excrement, you'll always have the liver worms. They can get into people, too, if they drink that water. The worms make both people and cattle sick. The symptoms are about the same for both people and cows, wasting away, no energy, loss of appetite, sometimes blood in the urine or the stool. Cattle or men, it's the same disease."

*Stop a moment. Let them digest that*, he thought. *Okay, now go on.*

"We've asked the star masters we trade with to send us potions that may be effective in treating this, but we don't have any now, so the only way to prevent having the worms inside you is to avoid them. So it's important to learn how this spreads—which is mostly by letting people and cattle deposit their wastes upstream of where they drink."

*Well, they do listen good*, Clavell thought. Twenty-two teenagers, four of them girls, scribbled madly on slate boards. Paper was far too expensive to use for student notes, even for these kids from the ruling families of Nikeis, but the professors at the local college—not really a college, but the closest equivalent Clavell had yet seen on Tran, other than Colonel Galloway's University—

assured him that writing notes helped learning even when the notes were erased the next morning in preparation for another day.

*And it may be true*, Clavell thought. *I think maybe taking notes I never looked at again helped me learn. Can't be sure.* His college days were lost in an alcoholic blur.

He was pretty sure his pupils spent their evenings using their notes to explain what they'd learned to the local professoriate, and the professors were writing books they'd publish later, but that was fine with him. The professors were part of the old aristocracy. The rulers of Nikeis listened to them even if the old farts thought themselves too important to sit for lectures. The word was getting out fast.

The students were mostly from merchant and artisan backgrounds. Maybe. *At least I think that's where they come from. I know some do. But one's the daughter of a high Council member. I don't know what he does when he's not being a politician.*

Clavell shook his head wryly. This city-state republic was complicated, a lot more so than Drantos, where lords were lords and peasants were peasants, and everyone pretty well knew where he stood. Nikeis was different. There weren't any lords. Titles weren't inherited. Most of the power went to the rich nobles—*what the hell is the difference between a noble and a lord? But there is a difference, and everyone here knows it, even if they haven't explained it to me.* Whatever the difference was, it didn't prevent Nikeisian nobles from doing all the crap Drantos nobles did and shoving their noses deep into business and finance, as well. Or from knowing they *were* nobles.

*At least they talk to me.*

Everyone in Nikeis was polite, everyone talked all the time, and half the time they were lying. The problem was, which half?

But that didn't matter much. Colonel Galloway didn't care who learned what his traveling medicine shows taught so long as someone learned the lessons. The word was getting out. Germ theory of disease, infection, microscopic parasites, hygiene, inquire into causes, *look for causes* and don't just accept that whatever happens is God's Will. Ask questions and get answers.

*Enlightenment, Colonel Galloway calls it. Enlighten them. So I do. Which makes me a real professore, even if them local professor guys are too haughty to come to my lectures like they were students.*

Clavell had told the leading physicians of Nikeis about the germ theory of disease and the importance of hygiene. They hadn't argued, but they hadn't agreed either. Instead he was invited to lecture to selected students. Not medical students, because there weren't any medical schools; you got to be a doctor by apprenticing to a doctor. But there were students in something very like an undergraduate college. In theory Clavell was part of that, and attending his classes was part of the curriculum for selected students. Which made him a professor, even if he didn't get invited to many of the college's social functions.

Professor Clavell. Clavell chuckled as he thought what some of his college instructors would have thought of that. Lance Clavell had a football scholarship and spent more time studying linebacker tactics than anything taught in an academic classroom.

He'd spent even more time drinking and smoking pot and generally letting things go to hell until he'd found himself faced with a choice between the army and life on the street. He'd became a gentleman ranker, a college kid in the army, but he could fight and after basic he was in pretty good shape again, so they didn't make him a clerk. Over time he found that the army and booze together worked well enough. He wasn't getting anywhere but there wasn't anywhere he wanted to go. It all worked well enough until that damn flying saucer kidnapped them to Tran. Things started to go to hell then, and he had to start paying attention. Things got better when the troops got back together with Galloway. It could have been a lot worse. Galloway made him a professor . . .

"Professore." One of the students had raised his hand.

Clavell glanced at his seating chart. Fernando Dandolo. Merchant's son. Dressed expensive.

"Yes, young Master Dandolo?"

"We know this wasting sickness, but we never knew the cause. But you've told us you come from another world, yet you know of this worm!"

"Very good, Master Dandolo," Clavell replied. "It is from—the world I come from, and where your forefathers came from."

"Ah. Most thought the wasting sickness a curse, from witches and those who deal with the devil. But we've found that it is sometimes helped by ambulato berry tea," the student said.

"Does it work?"

"Professore, I don't know. It is said to be helpful. At least with people. I didn't know that this was the same wasting sickness that cattle get," Fernando said. His voice had changed, but not all that long ago, and was still high pitched.

"Can you get me some of that tea? And the berries it's made from, of course."

"Yes, Sir, I would be very pleased to do that."

"Thank you."

"It may be costly," Ginarosa Torricelli said. "The plant doesn't grow here."

Clavell didn't have to look up her name on the seating chart. She didn't dress up, but he thought she'd easily be the prettiest girl in the room if she wanted to be. Probably the richest as well, and her father the councilor was said to be in with the Doge. Unlike the other girls in the class, she was a good student, always dead serious. Bigwig or not, her father was always pleasant, but he had a spooky smile that gave Clavell the creeps.

"Where does it grow?" Clavell asked, but no one knew. The consensus was that it probably grew in the southern lands south of the southern Roman provinces. Clavell frowned. He'd been in some of those provinces, and he'd never heard of ambulato berries. Harrison might know something. Clavell took out a notebook and made a very short entry with his ballpoint pen. The skipper would want to know about a cure for liver flukes. It might not work, but it was worth trying.

"I think it must come from the far south. Only the great ocean vessels, the *navi*, ever bring ambulato berries," Fernando said.

"And your father owns two of them," Ginarosa said. There were giggles, but Fernando nodded in agreement.

"Are these worms the same as the—uh—*bacteria* that cause, uh, what you called 'infections' of wounds?"

Lucia Michaeli. He didn't have to look up her name either. She was always curious and often asked questions, but she got distracted when listening to long answers. Her parents were artisans and owned a bronze foundry. Clavell estimated her to be nine years old or so, but those were Tran years. She was probably at least sixteen in Earth years and she wore subtle makeup and dressed like a woman, not a girl. She was obviously quite aware that she was attractive, as well. Clavell wasn't sure why she was in classes at all since it was pretty clear her ambition was to be a cortigiana. Of course all the females in Nikeis who weren't already rich and high up among the ruling families dreamed of being cortigiane. It was an accepted way to power for women.

Almost accepted. There'd been some fuss last week about suppressing whores, and apparently the Council—one of the Councils, anyway, there seemed to be several of them with overlapping powers—had an ongoing debate over whether some of the cortigiane were whores or entertainers. Fernando had tried to explain it to him but Clavell hadn't understood very well. Mostly, though, cortigiane were accepted as necessary and even desirable, as well as very expensive. Which didn't explain why Lucia was in his class. What could a cortigiana learn here that would be useful to her profession? Maybe there was some prestige attached to being educated? Or she could just be naturally curious as well as bright.

Clavell didn't know much about cortigiane. He generally consorted with a much lower class of feminine companions. Whores were legal but taxed and regulated, and Clavell was rich by local standards. Colonel Galloway sent his teams out with pretty good funding if they were going to civilized places, and he hadn't had to spend much because the Signory furnished his quarters free and paid him a stipend to teach.

*I could afford a live-in cortigiana. Maybe I ought to try that. Just for research, of course.*

"Good question, Signorina Michaeli, but it requires more than a simple answer," he said out loud. "It's true that both the liver worm—we call them 'flukes'—and the bacteria that cause infections are tiny animals, but the bacteria are so very much smaller that you'll never see them without magnifying glasses which we don't have. The liver flukes are small, but you can see them if you know what to look for."

*And damn all I wish I knew how to build a microscope! I could show them.*

"There are many kinds of bacteria, and they cause many kinds of sickness. Likewise, there are many small worms that infest humans and our animals. The smallest worm is much larger than the largest bacterium."

A church bell rang the afternoon hour marking the end of his lecture.

"We'll continue this tomorrow," Clavell said. "We'll go through their life cycle, and learn how to prevent these little animals from making you sick and killing you."

"Both the worms and the . . . bacteria?" Lucia asked.

"Yes, of course, both. But tomorrow we look mostly at flukes."

Lucia smiled at Clavell as she left the classroom.

*Flirting practice*, Clavell thought. *Son of a bitch, I'd like a piece of that. Best not. I get enough, this is soft duty. Dunno about her. Artisan class. Not nobility, but rich. Has to be rich or she wouldn't be here. She acts like she's available but you never know about girls like that. That'd be enough for Boyd.* Any encouragement at all was enough for Boyd, which is why he never got sent out on independent duty. *I don't need his reputation! Skipper would never send me out on soft duty like this. And son of a bitch, this is soft duty!*

The other two girls in his class were clearly from wealthy families, and they didn't flirt. If they asked questions they were practical. One of them, Marchesina, was the daughter of a Senator and clearly expected to be married to someone of her own rank. That would probably be the Torricelli girl's future too. Now that was one attractive girl! Her father ranked higher than anyone else's, as far as Clavell knew. She was also the prettiest of the four, even if she didn't act or dress like she knew it, and best not go there . . . Clavell supposed both were in school to learn household management. *So now I'm a home economics teacher! Well, it's still soft duty.*

He waited until the others had left, then gathered up his lecture materials. He'd had a leatherworker make him a messenger bag/briefcase to hold all the stuff, and the fashion was catching on. Half the merchants in Nikeis carried something like that now. Clavell wasn't sure he'd invented the thing, but he hadn't seen anything like it before he got his, and now they were everywhere.

*It's good duty here, but it's time to go back*, he thought. Time and past time.

Giamo Fieschi was waiting for him outside his classroom. Clavell wasn't sure who Giamo was. Obviously he was a son of one of the ruling families, but if he had any titles he hadn't told them to Clavell, and Clavell had noticed that anyone who had anything like a title in Nikeis generally used it. Sometimes Giamo sat in on the classes, but mostly he didn't. He seemed to be the one detailed by the Doge to look after the star lords.

"Ave, Giamo," Clavell said. Everyone spoke some kind of Italian here, but most of the upper class also knew the mainland lingua franca spoken throughout Drantos. Clavell had grown up in a mixed neighborhood and spoke some Italian. *Probably why the Colonel picked me to come here,* he thought. *'Course the Italian I learned is a hell of a lot different from what they speak here! I'd probably have more students if I could lecture in the local brand they speak in Nikeis. Oh, well. I'm picking up some of it.*

Between the mainland lingua franca and his bastardized Italian, Clavell got by. *But just barely,* he thought. *Just kind of languaged out. Never thought I'd learn as many tongues as I know already. Soft duty, except that part. That's hard, but I manage.* Technical words were easy. He just used English, or the older Latin terms if he knew them.

He and Giamo exchanged pleasantries. As usual, they went on quite a while.

"Signor Fieschi," Clavell said after he felt that had gone on long enough, "I must ask. Is my transportation ready? It's very pleasant here, and your hospitality has been far more than generous, but I really must return to Drantos soon."

Clavell had already found out there were few ships for hire in Nikeis. Nothing came into the harbor through the twisting channels of the mud flats and lagoons without permission from the Signory, and there were patrols all around the complex of islands and marshes. Nikeis was known as Queen of the Seas, and they took the title seriously.

"I've already stayed months longer than Colonel Galloway had expected me to." *Not to mention I don't want Colonel Galloway to think I've deserted.*

Giamo looked dismayed.

"We understand that you must leave, and the Signori of the Great Council made a ship ready," Giamo said. "I had hoped to tell you this today, but today there was news from Drantos! Alas, I regret that your ship must now be employed for a different purpose." Giamo seemed excited, not like the suave diplomat he'd been until now.

"News?"

"Alarming news. Grave news. News of war! The Five Kingdoms have invaded Drantos! Even now your Wanax Ganton summons all his allies to resist. The Warlord Rick has been sent to the west to defend against an invasion. He holds his strong points in Chelm, but in the east there has been a great battle. The Companion Morrone was defeated, and the Eqetassa Tylara has been made captive—"

"Holy shit! Damn all! Signor Giamo, I have to go and go now. Now!" *Colonel's going to have my head!*

"Calmly, calmly!" Giamo gestured wildly. "The Eqetassa is safe. She was made prisoner by Strymon, Prince of Ta-Meltemos, and a man of greater honor does not exist. He would never harm her, nor will her ransom be severe."

"Christ be thanked," Clavell said without any trace of humor. Or of hesitation, he realized. *Good to be among fellow Catholics. Well, near enough to Catholics. They have a bishop, and their masses look a lot like what we had when I was a kid, in Latin and everything.* "But that doesn't change the situation! I have to go report to the Colonel."

"We agree," Giamo said. "But there may be difficulties. The Wanax has demanded immediate aid from his allies. It is urgent that we answer the call of our ally, and our forces leave tonight in the only ships available. Without your ship there would be too little transport—even with your ship there's barely enough for what we must send! They depart at once! The Council will explain as much as we can, and requests that you meet with them at the Doge's Palace this evening at twilight." Giamo chuckled. "Surely you can wait that long!"

⁜ ⁜ ⁜

Clavell made his way across the Palazzo San Marco towards the palace they had assigned him. Back in Italy, it would have been the *Piazza* San Marco and "palazzo" would have meant palace, but the Nikeisians used "palazzo" interchangeably for both.

Nikeis was a complex of marshes and islands, the larger islands high enough to have room for houses and palaces well above the high-water marks, others not high above sea level at all. All the islands surrounded a central lagoon, and it was obvious to Clavell that they were the above-water elements of a volcanic caldera. If there'd been any question in his mind, it had vanished the day he hiked to the top of the steep hills which towered above the flatter, sea-level plains of San Giorgio and San Lazzaro. The square he was currently crossing was Palazzo San Marco Inferiore. There was a Palazzo San Marco Maggiore on top of the hill, although only its tallest buildings were visible to anyone approaching by sea. That was because it was actually set into a large, bowl-shaped depression which was clearly an ancient volcanic throat. Clavell didn't think he'd feel very comfortable living permanently on top of a volcano, but these obviously hadn't erupted in a *lot* of centuries. And the broad, shallow bowl offered a lot more building area than one might have thought looking up at that steep-shouldered cone from below.

But Palazzo San Marco Maggiore wasn't much used. The roads up the sides of the cone were steep and winding, and its height placed the palazzo far too high to be convenient to the seaborne trade that was Nikeis' lifeblood . . . at the moment, at least. That was clearly subject to change, however, and there were also markets, and another cathedral, and palaces up there, as well, although none of them seemed important . . . at the moment. The Doge's Palace and government were all down here at sea level.

Everyone reminded him at every possible opportunity what a great honor it was to have been assigned a palace on the main public square. Clavell supposed it was true, but the Palazzo stank all the same. There were too many people, and too damned many birds. Sweepers worked with brooms and buckets, but there were never enough to keep up with the birds and dogs.

Elegant palaces rose all around the three landward sides of the palazzo. Their lower floors held factories, merchants, saloons, and every other form of commerce. Two sides of the brick palazzo were lined with booths where merchants hawked their wares. Clavell was pleased to see cheesecloth covering meat in several of the booths. One butcher had built a glass case to show off perishable foodstuffs resting on ice, and ice cost a hell of a lot here in Nikeis. It was a sure sign that someone was listening to what he said in his lectures and his sessions with the ruling councils. Some of the merchants were learning.

Set in among the merchant booths were cafés with both indoor and outdoor tables where gaily dressed people drank wine and tea and talked in low voices. Clavell could understand why they talked in low voices. It was said that anyone you met—waiter, courtesan, sewage bucket carrier, anyone at all—might be a paid informant for the Signory. When he tried to find out just who the Signory were, he got different answers, but they all added up to being the people who ran Nikeis. There was a council with that name, but the word seemed to mean more than that.

The palazzo was crowded, and Clavell was careful to keep his jacket closed over his .45 Colt. Armor was forbidden in the city, although it was pretty obvious that some of the men in the Palazzo wore fine mail under their fancy robes. Clavell wasn't sure what they'd make of his flak jacket, but he wasn't wearing it. He probably didn't really need the pistol, either, but he felt better with it resting in its shoulder holster. No one he saw was openly armed, but he knew that nearly all the men carried daggers.

Clavell wore the fancy clothes of the Nikeis merchant class, form-fitting hosiery and silk shirt, but when he'd had his outfit made, he'd insisted on a proper coat that he could button up. Nikeis was notorious for its pickpockets. Clavell thought the coat made him look pretty natty, and some others must have agreed because he saw two others dressed almost the same as he was. They were carrying briefcases, too. *Lance Clavell, fashion setter!* He chuckled.

As always he had an uneasy feeling as he crossed the Palazzo. He shrugged it off. It was easy to get spooked here, with all the stories of how the Signory ruled through assassins. All the stories couldn't be true, because there wouldn't be enough people left in Nikeis to run the place if they were. Even so, Clavell avoided crowds and was careful to note who came close to him, and the closer he got to the palace they'd assigned him the better he felt.

A drape in a second-floor window shook momentarily and was still. Servants watching for him to come back. It felt odd to have servants, but he wasn't going to argue. It was the way they did things here, and he had to do the same if he was going to hold up his status as a star lord and the Colonel's representative, didn't he? Sure he did!

He chuckled and shook his head at the familiar thought as he crossed the last few yards of the Palazzo.

*Soft duty, Lance. Soft duty!*

Two liveried footmen opened the big bronze door to his palace as he reached it. Giacomo, his butler, took his briefcase and followed behind him as he went through the marble-floored rooms. Despite the luxury, he suppressed a slight shiver as he stepped into the welcome coolness. All of this would be underwater when the Time fully arrived, and he wondered how much, if any, of this opulent palace would remain when the sea level dropped again. What would it look like, gazing down from the tops of the hills or from the houses perched on their flanks, as the squares, and then the palaces, and then the cathedral disappeared into the rising water? When only the highest roofs, the towers like the one on the Doge's Palace, and the cathedral's spires remained above the waves?

*They know about the Time here,* he thought. *Know more about it than I do, I guess.*

The signs were all around him: high-water marks, nearly fifty feet above the Palazzo, were painted on every building. And Palazzo San Marco Maggiore sat up there nearly unused, on standby . . .

✢ ✢ ✢

Jimmy Harrison was sprawled in a big leather chair at one end of the big room that served as living room, study, and reception room. It was a good room. The whole palace was—well, palatial, Clavell thought. Soft duty.

Harrison hadn't bothered to dress up in local clothes. He still wore his combat uniform, and he waved a glass of beer as Clavell entered. A glass, not a mug or stein. They had real glass workers in Nikeis.

"Got some for you." Harrison waved the glass again.

"Not right now, Clarence."

Harrison sniffed. It was an old joke. Harrison had been named Clarence at birth, but he called himself Jimmy and so did most everyone else, unless they had an urge to tease him.

"Yeah, right now, Sarge," Harrison said. Private Harrison emphasized the title. It hadn't been all that long ago that both of them had been privates. Clavell didn't think Harrison resented his partner's promotion, but it was hard to tell. "We got news. All kinds of news. Hell's a popping over on the mainland."

"I heard some of that. What do you know?"

"Not one whole hell of a lot. Just that the Five Kingdoms have invaded Drantos, there's a big army sitting on the Skipper's lands in Chelm, Lady Tylara's a prisoner of some fag prince, Morrone lost a big battle, and everything is going to shit. The Signory are sending troops to meet Wanax Ganton at the Ottarn River Ford, wherever the hell that is."

"Fag prince? I heard it was Strymon that had her. He's supposed to be big on chivalry."

Harrison stood and carefully put down his own glass of beer so that he could pick up a fresh one. His left hand was missing. He wore a gloved wooden hand today, but sometimes he wore a dull hook, other times a fork thing, and it was amazing how well he could function with just the one hand. He could even shoot. Maybe better than he had before he lost his left hand down south.

"I made that fag part up," he admitted as he carried a pint glass of beer over and held it out to Clavell. "Here. Look, I don't know from chivalry. Not sure I ever heard of this Strymon before, for that matter. But it sure don't sound good over there. You sure we want to go back?"

"Of course I want to go back."

"Maybe you want to think on it."

"Jimmy, what the hell are you getting at?"

"Just this, Sarge. Over here we're important. You more than me, 'cause you have a real knack for this teaching stuff, but we're both pretty big. Got friends, got girls, got some pay..."

"I have some pay," Clavell said. "Damned little."

"Much as we ever got from Galloway. You get paid to teach. I get some ducats for physical and weapons training, some just for telling stories. Between us it's more than the skipper paid us!" He gestured towards the paintings on the walls and the balconied stairs leading up. "We live damned good, Lance. We eat good, better'n we ever did with the Colonel. Got servants. And there's none of this lords and serfs crap, anybody can be anything here—"

"Anybody born rich enough."

"Naw, there's plenty of room at the top for people who start low and get rich. That Torricelli dude, a real big shot, they say he's one of the Council of Ten even, everybody knows he's a prostitute's son who got where he is as an assassin! And you don't get no higher than a Tenner Councilor." Harrison whistled softly. "Assassin. Hell, Lance, you and me, we been killing people for somebody else all our frigging lives! It never got us in the Senate! But it could here."

Clavell took a glug of the beer. *Damn good beer*, he thought. *Not cold, they don't have any way to make cold except to bring in ice from the north, but damn good anyway*. He winced.

"Problem?" Harrison asked.

"No, remembering about why they don't have much brandy here."

"Yeah. Making brandy with lead pipes don't work too well."

*Something else I can teach them*, Clavell thought. *Maybe they know that already, but there's so damned much I can teach. And it's fun. And they learn fast here, too.*

"Councilor Torricelli? You say he's an assassin?"

"It's what I hear." Harrison shrugged.

"His daughter's in my class."

"I'd be damned careful, then. Just when I think I got things figured out here, something new happens. Like I think a chick has loose morals and she don't, and another straitlaced one looks impossible and all of a sudden she's spreading her legs in my bedroom."

"Ever have the Torricelli girl?" Clavell asked.

"Never been near her. She never paid me no mind at all. Anyway, I never wanted to, and besides, come on, Sarge, do I look stupid? Man, you don't want to be alone with that one! Suppose she invites you? What the hell do you do? Say yes, say no, you're dead either way if she don't like the outcome!"

"You think?"

"Yeah, I think, and so should you. You got the hots for that chick?"

Clavell didn't answer.

"Shit. Well, be damned careful! Look, the women here aren't like the ones we met back on the mainland. Complicated, that's what they are. They study it!"

"Yeah, I reckon they do," Clavell mused. "Anyway, she's not likely to make me any offers."

"You do like her."

"Well, she's a bright little thing. Serious."

"Serious. Lance, you mean, like, *serious*? You thinking marriage?"

"Crap, Jimmy, I barely know her and she's half my age. But yeah, I guess I am thinking marriage. Maybe not her, but somebody. Neither of us getting any younger. We're never leaving this planet, time to think about—"

Harrison cackled.

"Come on. Since when have you ever worried about how old a girl was?"

"Like I said we're talking marriage here, a lifelong thing, not just a roll in the hay. Compatibility is important. You never thought about it?"

"Sure. Then I think about the skipper and Lady Tylara, and I know better. Now there you go. Love match, that was, and now they look daggers at each other across the table."

Clavell turned to look out the window that faced east across the Palazzo. Although the Palazzo was lined with buildings on three sides, the east side was bare except for a floating wharf at water's edge. A football field's length across the channel running along the Palazzo's edge there was another island with more fancy buildings, each one of them with a highwater mark.

*It's coming*, Clavell thought. The Palazzo was dry now, but every day there were six inches of water over it at high tide, and the way things were going it would be permanently underwater in a few weeks. As would the first floor of their palace not long after that.

"Jimmy, you saying we ought to desert? Just stay here?"

"I'm saying the Time is coming and they know about that here. Nikeis expects to do pretty well through this big time of troubles," Harrison said. "They're even hiring troops to take advantage of it. They'd hire us! So yeah, we ought to think about staying. We got a good deal here, Lance, and yeah, maybe we got our start as ambassadors or whatever the hell we are. I know that. But now you're so damned useful they'd want you if they'd first found you hiding in the sewers! Yeah, I know where that leaves me, but it's where I always been. Only thing I'm really good for besides telling stories is watching somebody else's back. But Lance, I'm damn good at that! And it's a lot easier to watch your back here than it was back there in Drantos! This is a civilized place, none of that dread lord with a temper crap. It's a damn sight not the U S of A, but it's closer to it than anywhere else we've been on this stupid planet. Keep your nose clean here and you'll stay alive. Face it, wouldn't you rather live like this than back with Colonel Galloway?"

Clavell shuddered. Colonel Galloway didn't usually give any soft duty. One campaign after another, sleep in the field, eat whatever crap they could scrounge. One long damn campaign after another.

"Damn straight I would, but what do you think the Colonel will do when he hears?" he asked, and Harrison shrugged.

"Don't know. What can he do from Drantos or Chelm? But maybe it don't matter. I notice they're in no hurry to let us start back."

"I noticed that too," Clavell said thoughtfully. "And Giamo just told me our ship's got to go to the mainland without us, carrying some expeditionary force so they can honor their alliance with Wanax Ganton. He told me they'll explain the rest at a meeting this evening."

"Going to explain why they're sending their troops but not sending us?" Harrison patted his holstered .45 and chuckled. "We'd be a lot more use to Wanax Ganton than a shipload of Nikeisian troops, and everybody knows it."

"So I should ask them tonight," Clavell said.

"Or maybe you shouldn't," Harrison said with a wink.

✛ ✛ ✛

The Doge's Palace was on the south side of the Palazzo, facing northeast across it, and like everything else in Nikeis it was ornately decorated inside and out. The walls of the entry hall were covered with enormous oil paintings, mostly of ships and the sea. One showed a big naval battle, a hundred galleys jammed together with boarding parties fighting it out on the decks while archers, crossbowmen, or javelin men fired from the forecastles and quarterdecks. Harrison stopped to study it.

Clavell nodded to himself. It never hurt to learn just how the locals fought.

The meeting was in one of the smaller council rooms. It was a lot like the room where Clavell taught his public-health classes, but better decorated, with paintings of young men and women lounging around on a picnic, and one big polished wood table in the center of the room. Nikeis seemed to have dozens of councils. There were Councils and councils, and it wasn't at all clear which Council did what.

When Clavell and Harrison had first arrived—on a hired Nikeisian ship; no one else had been willing to take them there—they'd been presented to what they were told was the Signory in the Grand Hall. The Doge had sat on his high throne and several dozen men of all ages from twenty to ancient had stood in a patterned array in front of him, all in red and blue robes and elaborate hats, while soldiers with halberds had stood against the walls. Ever since then Clavell had been reminded of what an honor it was to meet the Signory, but he'd never been able to find out precisely who those people were or how they got their jobs.

Today there were ten councilors on one side of the big table as Clavell and Harrison were conducted to seats on the other side. Giamo stood against the wall behind Clavell, and after he'd introduced Clavell and Harrison he wasn't talking. Clavell had met some of the councilors before. Others were complete strangers. They were all introduced, but in rapid fire Italian that Clavell didn't really understand.

Their spokesman was Piero Avanti, who was introduced as Councilor Avanti. Clavell reckoned him at about forty-five Earth years old. The others were Senators and councilors. There were three Councilors. The Senators wore fancy hats, and outranked Councilors, but Councilors outranked Senators and dressed any damn way they wanted to. One wore ostentatious finery, but the other two wore very plain and comfortable clothes. Avanti was one of the plainclothes types, with a clean dark wool robe of a good weave but nothing fancy at all about it, and no ornamentation at all except a gold chain.

"Your Excellencies," Clavell said. He'd learned early on not to address these people as "Lords." They didn't believe in lords, or said they didn't, even if sometimes they acted as haughty as lords. "I wish again to thank you for your hospitality."

"We are pleased that it pleases you," Avanti said.

With warmth, Clavell thought. With warmth, like he meant it. *Or like he's a good actor?*

"It has indeed pleased us," he said. "Which makes me regret all the more that we must insist on departing."

"But how will our young people continue their education without you?" one of the councilors asked. "They've learned much of great value. You have saved lives."

"I've taught nearly all I know," Clavell said.

"We would know more," an elderly Senator said. "We have heard that your—Colonel—has taught the smiths of Drantos to make Great Guns, and gunpowder. We have smiths and foundries better than any in Drantos, and we would know more." The tone was friendly and the accent was atrocious, but there was no question of what he meant. "Can you not tell us more of those?"

"Excellencies, we were sent by my master Colonel Rick, Warlord of Drantos, to teach public health and the germ theory of disease." Clavell struggled with the words, which were literal translations of the English but sounded strange in the mainland lingua franca. And they'd be even stranger in Italian. *Piccolo animali.* Little tiny animals. "I've taught what I know to those who will listen, and now I must go teach others."

"But you know of guns and gunpowder," the Senator said.

"Senator del Verme does not ask for secrets," Councilor Avanti said.

"Thank you," Clavell said. *I just bet he doesn't.* "The true word is that I know no secrets. I know about medicine and public health. That's what I know and what I was sent to teach, and I've taught what I know."

"We understand, but we know there is much more to learn," Piero Avanti said. "We would know more of the ways of men among the stars, and of the Time to come. We beg you to stay."

He sounded very earnest.

Clavell frowned slightly. "To be blunt, Signori, there seem to be few interested in what I teach."

"You misunderstand," Avanti said. "You have spoken to our physicians. Perhaps they will learn, perhaps they will not! Learned men do not always wish to be taught! But young people are eager to learn. Your students include representatives from our most important professions and guilds. Already our merchants are adopting practices you recommend. Those who do not—they will learn, too! Signor Clavell, the Most Serene Republic does not make sudden changes! We act slowly, and with care to see that what we do does not destroy the serenity of the Republic. Your theories have spread widely and are daily debated among physicians, merchants, and all those who are important to the Serene Republic." He shrugged. "And you may at any time address the councils of the Signory. You have that opportunity at this moment! What would you have us learn?"

*Crap doodle*, Clavell thought. *Song and dance time.*

"Your Excellencies know about the coming Time of Troubles."

"We have records," Avanti said. "We see the seas rise, and the Demon in the night sky. We know the stories they tell on Terra Firma, but none of us are star lords. Do you now tell us more?"

"It's beyond my knowledge," Clavell said. "But my Colonel knows much more than I do, and he gives that knowledge freely to his friends. He's established a school, which he calls the University. I am authorized," Clavell stumbled over the word. "I am permitted to offer half a score of your people places at the University, where they will learn far more than I can teach them. I know little of the knowledge you seek, of astronomy or chemistry or the making of weapons. I am only a soldier who's gained some medical knowledge, not a scholar. I have no great wisdom. Those at the University know far more and are better teachers."

"Do they teach the secrets of the Great Guns to everyone?" Senator del Verme asked.

"I haven't been at the University," Clavell said. "But my understanding is that there is no secret knowledge. All questions are answered as best they may be."

"To anyone who asks?" Councilor Avanti demanded.

"To all those properly admitted to the University. And I have that power of admission."

"All questions freely answered. An odd concept," Senator del Verme muttered. "Free knowledge?"

"We will eagerly accept your offer," Councilor Avanti said. "We will choose those who should go. Doubtless you will know some of them already. How shall they proceed once chosen?"

"They will need to travel to the Garioch, or perhaps to Edron," Clavell said. "The war will have made this more complex. I'll be told on my return and I'll make certain you know where to send the new students and what credentials they may need."

"This is excellent news," Avanti said, nodding in satisfaction.

"Then we may depart?"

"Was ever there doubt?" Councilor Avanti looked horrified.

"When will our ship be ready?" Clavell asked.

"In due time, Sergeant." Avanti had no problems with that title. "In due time! These are perilous times. Pirates have reappeared in the Inner Sea. There is war on Terra Firma, armies and raiding parties everywhere. The Wanax Ganton marches to the Ottarn River where he will fight a great battle. We are obligated by our treaties to assist him with what we can send." Avanti leaned across the table and regarded Clavell intently. A confidential tone came into his voice. "You do understand that the Serene Republic has very little army of its own? We hire captains, such as yourself—especially such as yourself, and Nikeis is known as a generous employer—when military forces are required. Indeed, citizens of the Serene Republic are forbidden to command more than fifty men, lest their ambitions exceed their due stations. Of course that limit would not apply to you, if you ever entered our service."

Jimmy Harrison chuckled.

"What's this expedition you're sending in our ship?" he asked, and there was a moment of silence, then Avanti laughed softly as if to cover Harrison's rudeness.

"Brother Antonio Moro, one of our warrior monks, leads three dozen brothers of his order and two hundred hired halberdiers," Avanti said. "Those in orders are sometimes exempted from the limits placed on those who are permitted political ambitions. My own nephew goes with them as proveditor."

"Alas, I don't understand that title," Clavell said.

"I do." Harrison turned to Clavell and said in English, "Think a cross between supply officer and commissar."

"Ah. How'd you know?"

"Our butler had that job once," Harrison said.

"Oh." *Which means he's probably still some kind of agent of the Signory. But then maybe everyone is.*

"Could not we go with Brother Antonio?" Clavell asked. *Colonel and the fricken Wanax would expect me to be there with your forces.*

Avanti looked astonished.

"Why, I suppose you can! We had not considered that! We understood that you wished to return to Armagh, and we had not sufficient soldiers to send as escort through a war zone. Yes, you could go with Brother Antonio—"

Senator del Verme cleared his throat.

"Excellency, I regret that the ship departed an hour ago! You urged haste, and I thought that was your wish."

*And that's an interesting little drama*, Clavell thought. *Probably rehearsed, too.*

"It will be sufficient to conduct us to a Roman port," he said. "Rome will escort us to Castle Armagh."

Councilor Avanti nodded, but—

"Indeed," he said. "Alas, that will require an armed galley. The areas near the Roman port of Taranto are not safe. The Romans have attempted to suppress the pirates of that region, but they have been unable to do so. Perhaps you would be safe in a Roman warship and perhaps not, but a Serene Republic ship will be attacked on sight unless it carries marines and projectile weapons—and all of the Serene Republic's warships are on patrol except for the one we had assigned to your use, and—" He shrugged. "In any case you must wait for its return."

There was more diplomatic talk, but it was pretty clear to Clavell that nothing he could say would get him out of the Serene Republic. Not now, and maybe not ever. *Relax and enjoy it,* he thought.

"So," Avanti was saying, "we will know more another time, but perhaps it would be better if Your Excellencies did not attempt to return to your homelands just yet. Think on it! Drantos is invaded by at least two armies from the Five Kingdoms. There have been great battles, and the last one did not go well for Drantos.

"No one in Nikeis knows where your Wanax is, or where your Colonel Galloway might be! His lady was taken. Does he attempt rescue, or does he negotiate ransom? We do not know. We know only that there is war in your lands, all is unsettled, and until we know more, surely it is better to enjoy the hospitality of the Serene Republic?"

"Suits me," Harrison muttered.

"We're pleased to accept," Clavell said. "Until we know more of the situation."

Everyone in the room was smiling.

## ✦═ CHAPTER TWO ═✦
# THE YOUNG LADIES OF NIKEIS

**One week before the Battle of the Ottarn River**

Lucia Michaeli sat staring into the filthy canal. The place stank, but she didn't really notice because it always smelled that way. The small fig tree arbor sheltering her table was high above the canal water, built on stone foundations that served as store rooms, but the water seemed nearer than it had even a month before. *And there's water on the Palazzo San Marco,* Lucia thought. *Professor Clavell says that the water will rise to the high-water marks! In a few years, perhaps less! I live in strange times.*

A waiter brought a pitcher of wine and a glass.

"Will there be anything else, Signorina?"

"Another glass. My friend will join me—ah, there she is."

Lucia felt bold to call the daughter of one of the

Council of Ten a friend, but it was true. Ginarosa
Torricelli had very few friends, because she was shy and
awkward—and everyone was terrified of her father, who
was said to be not only the Doge's favorite assassin, but
well regarded by the entire Signory. To have the favor of
both Doge and the Signory was rare, and Lucia's mother
was suspicious of Ginarosa's friendship. "The great ones
do not make friends for the same reasons you and I do,"
she had told her. Lucia understood the suspicion, but she
was sure that it was unfounded. Ginarosa had very little
guile—and she certainly had few friends. Smart enough
to recognize those currying favor with her father, and
unwilling to be charming for the fun of it. And not
religious enough to become a nun.

*She doesn't dress very well, either*, Lucia thought. *If
she learned how to dress and do her hair properly she'd
be prettier than I am. Her mother should teach her these
things, I don't know why she doesn't. And it's odd that
Ginarosa has so few friends. She's open, she says what she
thinks, no flattery, no little stories—but then if she learned
how to flirt she wouldn't be Ginarosa. She's always
serious, always studying the way things are done. In that
she's like my sister Catarina, but Catarina isn't so much
ignorant of the ways of men as uninterested in them.
Almost intolerant. Ginarosa would know more if she
thought she could . . .*

Lucia smiled as her friend took a seat across from her.
Their arbor was attached to a modest café and looked
down on a small canal, well away from the Grand Canal
and the Palazzo. The True Sun stood high overhead.

"I don't think my father would want me to be here,"

Ginarosa said. She looked around, examining the small canal. High buildings rose on each side, and clotheslines ran across the canal at third-story height. Interesting food smells mingled with the foul odor of the canal. Some large fish rose to make ripples in the dark water. A boy about two years old played in a wooden pen in one corner of the arbor. A peaceful place, not like the bustle of the Palazzo.

"I won't tell him," Lucia said.

"You won't have to," Ginarosa said. "He'll know. He knows everything I do! I think his men follow me."

Lucia frowned. That would be interesting. What kind of men would an assassin send to guard his daughter? *I haven't seen anyone. But he is Council of Ten. He would have the best men—and women?—available, so perhaps it's not surprising at all that I don't see them.*

She leaned her head forward so that her eyes would be hidden from anyone watching, and looked for strangers. No one was obvious, but the path on the other side of the canal was busy, perhaps someone in that group? At the moment the traffic was mostly workmen, many from the Arsenale. The wind shifted momentarily, bringing a whiff of hot pine scent from the factory complex, and Ginarosa wrinkled her nose.

"I smell that a lot lately," she said, and Lucia laughed.

"And I've smelled it all my life! It's part of what they do in foundries!"

"But more in the last year, I think."

Lucia nodded agreement.

"My father has hired more men," she said. "And my brother is on Terra Firma buying charcoal and copper."

"Yes. Why?"

"Why?"

"There have been three ships loaded with copper and tin," Ginarosa said. "At the Arsenale they are building ships and casting bronze fittings and making weapons. Why?"

Lucia shrugged.

"I do believe you know more about my father's business than I do! What a strange thing to wonder about."

"Yes, I suppose it is, but I do wonder," Ginarosa said. "My mother says I may be a boy trapped in a girl's body. They should have sent me to Terra Firma; I'd be a good proveditor."

"I think you would!" Lucia giggled. "Do you feel like a boy?"

"No, no!" Ginarosa laughed. "I can appreciate a well-filled stocking and big shoulders! But mother says I have strange interests."

She and Lucia were both dressed simply, so they might have passed for girls from the local neighborhood, except that Ginarosa wore a jeweled cross that peeked out of her blouse when she leaned forward. Lucia thought no thief would miss seeing that. Could someone already have seen it? But this was broad daylight, in a mercantile area of the city, with many citizens around them. No thief would strike here. And perhaps Ginarosa's father did have men watching her. The thought was comforting, as was the dagger hidden in her sleeve.

Lucia poured wine and they both sipped at their glasses. It had a good taste, sweet and fruity, but Ginarosa grimaced slightly.

"Isn't it good?" Lucia said. There was a plaintive note

in her voice. The wine was the best the shop offered and
it cost more than Lucia had wanted to pay.

"It's very good," Ginarosa said with a smile. "That's the
problem, I like good wine, too much I think. Mother says
I need practice, that it's important to be able to drink too
much wine and still keep your wits, but I have more
experience at that than she knows!"

"Tell me!"

"There's nothing to tell. Three times now Carlo has
gotten me to drink too much."

"And?" Lucia demanded, and Ginarosa smiled thinly.

"There isn't any 'and,'" she said. "I kept my wits. More
important I kept my skirts down."

"Carlo," Lucia mused. "He doesn't notice me."

"Do you want him to?"

"I would but, he's yours."

"Not really." Ginarosa giggled. "He'd like to be.
Actually, that's not it. He only thinks he ought to be and
acts that way. Mother says Carlo's father wants something
from us. I don't know what, probably to be junior
proveditor of the new expedition they're sending to Terra
Firma." She caught herself and looked around the small
arbor. "Don't tell anyone about that. It's secret."

"But you were alone with him, drinking wine with him!
Don't you want him?"

Ginarosa bit the knuckle of her forefinger, looking
pensively out over the canal.

"I don't know what I want," she said at last, still gazing
across the canal. "But I'm pretty sure it's not him."

"But you like boys! Don't you want them to want you?"
Lucia couldn't imagine a situation in which she wouldn't

take some advantage of having a boy fall under her spell. If only she knew how! *And here is Ginarosa, plain Ginarosa, the ugly duckling, who wins and doesn't even care!*

Ginarosa looked back at her and giggled at her tone.

"It doesn't matter what I want, and it doesn't matter how I look, or how I act, or anything," she said. "My father is Council of Ten! Every family in the Signory wants to marry into my family. I could be a pig, a squealing mud-sucking pig, and they'd still want me. They'll find someone for me to marry soon enough. I can wait for that."

"You can? Don't you—well, you know."

Ginarosa giggled nervously.

"Surely. When I'm alone in my room. But I know better than to lose my head with anyone."

"I guess you can keep your wits," Lucia said. "But wasn't he—well, insistent?"

"Surely he was, but he's not a fool. He's afraid of my father. Everyone is."

She shrugged and Lucia nodded. Any sensible man would be afraid of Councilor Torricelli. It must make things even more difficult for poor Ginarosa.

"I've never been alone with a man," she confessed. "I'm trying to learn about men, but I have to do that at balls and parties. There, I told you my secret. Now you tell me yours."

Ginarosa darted a look around, then leaned forward across the table and her voice fell to a near whisper.

"I think I love our star lord teacher," she said.

"Professor Clavell? But he's *old*!"

"Not that old! And he talks to me, looks into my eyes."

Those eyes looked almost dreamy at the moment, and Lucia smiled faintly.

"He looks at my breasts when he talks to *me*," she said. "But, Ginarosa, your mother will never let you marry him! You'd have to live on Terra Firma, and they're all heretics over there! And—really?"

"Really, and yes I know all that," Ginarosa said. "No one else knows, and I don't suppose anyone else ever will know. And I know it's all hopeless, and, and, Lucia I'm so unhappy! I'm smart enough to know I don't have any chance with him, he's a star lord and he probably has a big family back where he lives. Only I don't know if Father will ever let him leave! It's been weeks now since he told the class we were done with lessons, but we're not. And we're not really learning anything new, either."

"He talks to you a lot, though," Lucia said in an encouraging tone. "I think he likes you. But he's certain they'll be leaving soon. Perhaps you can go with him. To this University he told us of."

"You, more likely," Ginarosa said. "I would give anything to go, but I don't think they'll let me do that. They won't let me do anything! Maybe I'll go into the Church, only my father won't let me do that, either. He'd say it would be a big waste, and he'll have some family he wants me to marry into. That's all they see in me, someone to marry so I can give them more influence. As if I knew how! I can't influence anyone!"

Lucia plucked a linen kerchief from her bosom and handed it to her friend.

"You have to learn how," she said. "It's the only power women have."

"I know." Ginarosa dabbed at her eyes with the kerchief. "Lucia, I know a lot of things, but I can't *do* them! Mother says I think too much."

"That may be some of it," Lucia said. *And listen to me, sounding like an old cortigiana!* "But you can learn. It's not hard to get men to do things you want them to do."

"Not hard for you."

"Rosa, it wouldn't be hard for you, if you'd try."

"How do I try?"

"Let's go to your house, and I'll show you."

✢ ✢ ✢

The Palazzo was flooded. That happened regularly now at high tide. The tide was going out now, but even at low tide there would be several inches of water over some of the paving stones. Lucia thought that it wouldn't be long before they would have to move everything up to the upper palazzo. That would be inconvenient.

Lucia and Ginarosa skirted the edge of the water, which did not quite reach the walkways around the Palazzo, and shopkeepers dashed out to display wares. Lucia paused to look at a silk scarf, and glanced back the way they'd come. There was a man back there, one she thought she'd seen before. He'd been in the crowd on the other side of the canal when they were having lunch.

A man, following them. She felt a guilty thrill. Probably one of Gina's household, Lucia thought. A retainer, maybe a soldier. Assassin? Bodyguard? When she looked back again he was gone. Probably just a man with an errand that had nothing to do with them. But it was exciting.

Councilor Torricelli's townhouse was across a small

canal from the Palazzo. Unlike most of the houses around it, there wasn't much decoration, inside or outside. Lucia wondered about that. Most of the Signory tried to impress everyone with their wealth, commissioning statuary and columns and other decoration, but the Torricelli mansion was nearly as plain as Lucia's smaller house.

The front door of the palazzo was open and two messengers raced out as the girls approached. Then a small group came to the door and dashed inside.

"That's Ensign Cornaro!" Ginarosa said. "He went to Terra Firma on Professore Clavell's ship! With Senator Avanti! Now he's back! Lucia, he's Councilor Cornaro's youngest son!"

"What does this mean?" Lucia asked.

"I don't know," Ginarosa said. "Let's go find out!"

She led Lucia around to a servants' entrance, then up back stairs to the second floor where there was a musicians' balcony above the main room. Lucia glanced over the rail. Councilor Torricelli was seated at a desk at the far end of the room. A half dozen men in robes—Lucia recognized two of them as members of the War Council who had visited her father's bronze works—sat nearby. Ensign Cornaro stood in front of the desk, and everyone was looking at him, so that no one looked up at the balcony at all.

Ginarosa put her finger to her lips and indicated a bench where they could sit without being seen.

Lucia sat and held her breath. Spying on a Councilor. One of the Council of Ten! She wondered just how afraid she ought to be. But Ginarosa didn't seem concerned.

"...and the lights came to the ground?" Councilor

Torricelli was saying. "With no sound? How far away were you?"

"We didn't know at the time, but we later discovered that it was six Roman miles, Your Honor."

"So you went there, of course."

"Yes, Your Honor. Senator Avanti insisted that we make haste. He rode on ahead to spy but what he saw caused him to come back and bring the entire party together."

"Senator Avanti abandoned his caravan?" Torricelli's voice was cold enough it frightened Lucia.

"No, Your Honor, he divided the guard and had those who stayed behind form a wagon fort. He also gave orders for a messenger to go to the port and hire more soldiers. Then we set out to see what we might make of those strange lights.

"It was star lords, Your Honor. We found them in a clearing. Our captain had the crossbowmen cock their weapons, but keep them lowered so they wouldn't be threatening, then led us into the clearing. There were two star men and one woman, Your Honor. All were dressed alike, in the manner of the Star Lord Harrison, and all carried weapons. Star weapons, much like those the Signori Harrison and Clavell carry."

"The woman was armed?"

"Yes, Your Honor. The same as the men. Your Honor, she was their spokesman! The men didn't speak our language at all. They know only the trade language of Terra Firma, and that not very well. But the woman speaks our language as well as the trade language. Her accent is strange, but we could understand her. And she was armed as they were."

Ginarosa made cheering gestures and Lucia thought about what this might mean. Armed women. Not carrying daggers in a sleeve, but openly armed. With star weapons! She'd heard that on Terra Firma, in Drantos, the star man commander Rick was married to a contessa, and that the contessa commanded armies and carried a star weapon. Carlo had told her that the weapon was a wedding gift from her star man husband, but he hadn't been very sure of that. Still it made a favorite fantasy, to marry a man who gave her a star weapon on their wedding day.

"She was their spokesman," Councilor Torricelli repeated. There was a frown in his voice. "One of them was her husband?"

"No, Your Honor!"

"You sound very certain of this, Ensign Cornaro."

"Your Honor, I am very certain. We hadn't been there an hour when the signorina made it very clear that she found Senator Avanti a pleasant companion! And the other star men saw this and made no complaint at all. Your Honor, one of the star men was black."

"Black?"

"As black as coal, Your Honor, and very tall. It wasn't paint. His skin was black."

"I've heard there are black men in the far south provinces," someone said.

"Captain Adanante had a black deck crewman at the Battle of Low Strait," another said. "I knew him. He came from the south. He spoke a common language of Terra Firma."

"But this was a star man," Torricelli said. "Ensign, you're certain of this?"

"As certain as I may be, Your Honor. He was armed as the others and treated as an equal. He spoke to the star man leader without ceremony. As did the woman."

"Tell me of this leader," Torricelli said.

"He was tall, yet smaller than the black man, and he spoke softly," the officer said. "He wore spectacles, like a scholar. He spoke pleasantly with Senator Avanti, but mostly through the woman. His name was—" the officer hesitated "—Bart Saxon. A name I've never heard before."

"Saxon? That is a people, I believe," Councilor Celsi said. "But I know not where they abide."

"Signor Saxon was the leader," Ensign Cornaro said. "But he always consulted the others before he came to a decision."

"Why are these star men not with you, Ensign?" Torricelli asked.

"The boxes, Your Honor! There were three huge boxes made of the finest steel, each twenty piede long by half that in width and height! Each side of each box was a single sheet of steel, Your Honor. A single sheet! They are said—Signor Saxon said—they have much of the knowledge of all the star men in there! More weapons, fantastic equipment, but most of all knowledge! Signor Saxon said that with what is in those boxes he can teach us to make the kinds of marvels that star men use! But only he can make use of what is in them. It would be of no value without him."

"Mmmm. And where are those—boxes?" Torricelli asked.

"They are to be brought here. A ship must be rebuilt to carry them one by one, because they are so large.

Senator Avanti is making those arrangements now! I was sent to notify you."

"Thank you, Ensign," Torricelli said, and glanced at his companions. "Do we have more questions? Yes, Councilor?"

"You say that this star woman seemed to find my nephew attractive? And he was not displeased?"

"Yes, Signor."

"And they said openly that they have all the knowledge of the star lords in those boxes?"

"They did, Councilor Avanti. They also made it plain that the knowledge was in a form that would be useless without their interpretation."

"You believed that?" Torricelli asked.

"Your Honor, I neither believe nor disbelieve. I am not familiar with the ways of star lords."

"Nor are any of us," someone said. "Our children know these men Harrison and Clavell better than we do. I never thought that a wise decision, to stay far from them and send only children to listen to them."

"There were good reasons," Torricelli said.

"I notice that your daughter is one of the students."

"As is the daughter of the foundry guild chief, the sons of four merchants, the son—"

"Indeed, Councilor Torricelli," Councilor Avanti said. "I understood the reasoning for not allowing any one of us to spend time alone with those star lords. Knowledge is power indeed. But tell me, does not this news change everything? We will need new policies. This is a matter for all the Signory."

"It is," Torricelli said. "It certainly is. But we must act

quickly. First, we must be certain that all this knowledge comes to us, not to Rome or Drantos!"

There were murmurs of agreement.

"And not to any one of us alone," Councilor Celsi said. "But others may have seen these lights. This must be seen to quickly!"

"Do I note your agreement, Councilor Avanti? Excellent. We are agreed," Torricelli said. "We will now go to the Doge. All of us. And select a commission we can trust to take a company of loyal soldiers to Terra Firma to secure these boxes. I doubt any of us will sleep well until they are secured in the Arsenale!"

"What soldiers do we trust with something so important?" Avanti asked. "I trust my nephew, and his troops are loyal, but everyone might not agree."

"Agree or not, we need our most trustworthy troops!"

"Whom you have sent to the aid of Drantos," Avanti observed dryly, and Torricelli grimaced.

"Yes." He thought for a moment. "Ensign!"

"Aye, your honor?"

"I wish to send a message to Brother Antonio, who was sent to join the Wanax Ganton in honor of our treaty. The message is urgent. How large an escort will be required?"

"Five lances should be sufficient to deal with bandits," the young officer said. "More would attract undue attention."

"Five lances it shall be," Torricelli said. "From the Doge's guard. Choose a suitable detail, a captain of good family who can be trusted with gold and an important message, to leave as soon as possible. My friends, I think it's time that we seek the Doge on an urgent matter. We must compose a message recalling Brother Antonio. And there will be other messages. We must act quickly."

Lucia huddled down on the bench to be sure she was not seen as the signori left the Great Hall. Her friend looked knowingly at her.

"So, Rosa," Lucia said. "This is how you live?"

"It is not always so exciting. Will you come with me?"

"Certainly. Where, Rosa?"

"To tell Star Lord Clavell," Ginarosa whispered, then paused. "Oh, does this mean he'll go away now? But he should know, he should know. Star men. One of them black, and one of them a courtesan! And all the knowledge of the stars to come here to Nikeis!"

Lucia gulped hard.

"But you mustn't tell, Rosa. You mustn't!"

"But he should know—"

"Perhaps. But surely you can wait until we know more. And if your father learns that I overheard—"

Ginarosa looked startled, then grave.

"Yes. I hadn't thought of that. He is no danger to me, but to you—I don't think he is a danger to you, either, but better not to risk it. I will say nothing until we know more. And I'll be careful what I say, even then. Be calm, Lucia, you'll be in no danger. I promise you."

*And I have never seen you in this mode. In control, knowing—truly the daughter of the Counselor Torricelli, composed and calm. Why do you hide this?*

"Thank you. And I must get home . . ."

"Of course. I'll send a servant to see you safely home. And thank you for the wine, friend Lucia."

✢ ✢ ✢

Lance Clavell got through his lecture somehow. The students pretended to be interested even though Clavell had told them all of this before. Today he'd been talking about different kinds of bacteria.

Again.

He gathered his notes as the students left. Not so much left as fled, he thought. *And I can hardly blame them. I don't have much to interest them. Drawings, and I'm a bad artist.* He looked up to see Ginarosa Torricelli standing at his desk. As usual she was dressed rather plainly. *She'd be the prettiest one in the class if she tried,* Clavell thought. *And she's damned well the most interesting one. Belay that thought, Lance, me lad. It could get you killed.* He looked up to be sure the others were gone. She looked nervous. *And if she is, do I want to hear what she has to say? Her father's an assassin . . .*

"Yes, Signorina?"

"Do you know how to use a microscope?" she asked.

*Whoa! Now* that's *nothing I expected!*

"Yes, but how do you know of such things?"

"You mentioned that as the name of the instrument with which we might see small things," the girl said.

"Oh. Did I? I'd forgotten."

"Perhaps this will help," she said, and took a large lens from her bag.

Clavell looked at it: a magnifying glass, circular, perhaps four inches in diameter, with a bronze band and handle. Certainly handmade, by a very patient craftsman.

"Are these common here?"

"No, no, they're rare, and expensive." The girl shook her head. "I don't know how they are crafted, but very few glassworkers have the skill to make one. But is this what you meant by a microscope?"

"No, a microscope requires more than one lens," Clavell said. "In a careful arrangement. But this should be good enough to show the liver flukes."

"Not bacteria, though?"

"No. Why do you ask?"

"I think we have one. Or rather Senator Avanti is bringing in a microscope from the mainland," she said. "I haven't seen it, but he used that name."

"Where would Senator Avanti get a microscope?" Clavell asked, his expression puzzled. *And how the hell would he know what to call it? Maybe she told him.*

Ginarosa smiled.

"I see they didn't tell you," she said. "I thought they hadn't. So I should be afraid to do so, I think."

"No one tells me anything," Clavell said. "Including why I can't go back to my home."

"Do you truly want to leave?" she said. "We must not stay too long, my father's men will be suspicious. Of course what they will suspect will not be conversation." She smiled again and lowered her head.

*Careful, Lance*, Clavell told himself. *This could be big trouble*.

"But we should be safe for a few more minutes," Ginarosa said. "And it isn't I who tempts you," she added quietly. "Professore, you've spoken of this University in Tamaerthan. It seems a wise and learned place. I had thought I wanted nothing more than to go there. Now—"

"Now you don't want to go? Why?" he asked, and she shrugged.

"Perhaps something better is coming here," she said. "I cannot tell you more. Ask my father. They haven't told you anything, that's clear, and I think you should know, but I dare not tell you. And it would be dangerous to tell them the source of your curiosity."

She turned and walked away. Clavell stood staring after her.

## ⊰⊱ CHAPTER THREE ⊰⊱
# INTELLIGENCE

"You wished to speak with me, Professore?" Councilor Torricelli's smile was warm, and his voice pleasant. "Please. Be seated. Will you have wine? Something else, perhaps?"

"Your hospitality is admirable," Lance Clavell said. "Yours"—he gestured to indicate the large reception hall of Torricelli's home—"and your city's as well. Except that there's too much of it."

Torricelli frowned. "What do you mean, Signor?"

"Pardon me for being blunt," Clavell said. "I'm a blunt man. Signor, we've been here many weeks longer than ever we intended. Events happen on the mainland. Rumors are everywhere. You send armies ashore. And when we seek to return to our homes, there's always a good reason why we can't leave. I can't find my Roman allies and their officers have vanished. I can't send messages to my Colonel, and I have none from him although I'm certain he's sent inquiries about me. Signor

Torricelli, the time has come for honesty. Why are we being detained?"

"You find life here unpleasant?" There was a slight edge to Torricelli's voice.

"Of course not. This has been the most pleasant time since we arrived on this godforsaken planet! But Signor, I don't think you appreciate the situation. My Colonel has no doubt made inquiries about my welfare. If he doesn't hear from me soon enough, I don't know what he'll do, but I would hate for there to be some misunderstanding here."

"There will be no misunderstanding," Torricelli said. His manner was polite, but the atmosphere had changed entirely. Clavell sensed danger. Undefined danger, but very real.

"I wouldn't be so certain of that," Clavell said. "My Colonel has many ways, and he is a determined man."

Torricelli smiled thinly.

"Your Colonel is a formidable man," he said. "I understand that he's never lost a battle. But those were all land battles, Professore. I had not heard that Drantos has a navy."

"Signor, for those who can cross between the stars, crossing a few miles of sea should not be difficult."

"You require a ship," Torricelli said simply.

"I do. But I am not my Colonel. I have no instruments to summon ships from the stars."

"And your Colonel does?"

"You will have heard that he sells goods to the starships," Clavell said. Now to use just the right words. "He has means to summon his clients."

"I see. Do you know the means?"

"Like all star things, it is simple. In this case a small box one speaks into. I've seen it, as of course I've seen the starships, but I don't know how either is made. I have no notion of what Colonel Galloway may ask from the starships, but I tell you again, it would be unfortunate for there to be misunderstandings."

"I have a great appreciation for star power," Torricelli said. He shrugged. "However. You demand explanations. What are my alternatives?"

"Signor?"

"I am not master of the Serene Republic. I am leader of perhaps the strongest faction, but that isn't the same thing. The Serene Republic seldom acts without agreement among the Signory, and we don't have that at this moment. Bluntly, Professore, I need more time. The Signory are undecided about the future. Things develop that we do not understand."

"Perhaps I may be of assistance in that understanding. My Colonel most certainly can be."

"I am aware of that, and I thank you for the offer, but the Council has decided that it isn't yet time to have that sort of discussion with the Warlord of Drantos." Torricelli grimaced, as if to disparage that decision, then frowned. "So I required time. How may I gain that time? I prefer that you remain well disposed towards the Serene Republic, else I could have you placed under guard," Torricelli said. "If needs must, I may do that. But you may have friends among my enemies. I could have you held in a dungeon, but that would make you my enemy whereas now you are merely dissatisfied. Or we may both pretend this conversation never took place."

✦ ✦ ✦

"So it's like that, is it?" Jimmy Harrison leaned closer. "So what do we do about it? You sure as hell can't hire a ship now."

"Maybe we could. A fishing boat. Or a grain ship, there's lots of them, and far as I can see everything's for sale in this city. Everything. Hell, Jimmy," Clavell said, "maybe I shouldn't have gone to see him, but I figured we might as well get some of it out in the open. Now we know."

"What do we know?" Harrison asked. "They don't know what to do with us, and the factions don't agree so they can't iron it out. Pretty usual for Nikeis."

"Why can't they agree? We came here to teach sanitation and public health. We've done that. Now why can't we go home?"

Harrison shrugged.

"They want more."

"Like?"

"Well, we know they're interested in gunpowder, and how it's made."

"What little we know we can't talk about," Clavell said.

"So what else do we know? We know there's something weird happening, with that Torricelli girl claiming there's a microscope coming here, and she thinks maybe a university will be established here. A university that teaches star science. Only one way that happens, Sarge."

Clavell frowned the question.

"Another starship, Sarge. What else could it mean?"

"Holy shit. Maybe you're right!"

"Course I'm right," Harrison said. "Surprised you didn't think of it. Your friend Rosa's thought of it. You can be sure her father knows it."

"So there's new star people, and they're not telling us about it," Clavell said slowly, and Harrison nodded sagely.

"Looks that way."

"Think the Skipper knows?"

"If not now, he will." Harrison shrugged. "And the Romans will find out for damned sure. They have spies everywhere."

"So how do we tell the Skipper?"

Harrison shrugged again.

"You choosing sides?" He poured a full glass of white wine.

"What the hell do you mean by that? We're part of Galloway's outfit. We already chose sides."

"Did we? I don't recall being asked about any of this." Harrison kept his voice low as they sat in the center of their large reception hall, ornate, lavishly cushioned chairs close together. "I don't recall being asked about none of it. Yet here we are, whispering in our own house, scared of being overheard by our own servants. Thing is, they *are* our servants. Maybe they answer to Torricelli and his friends, but they make life easy for us. Soft duty, Sarge.

"Now you tell me about loyalty, Sarge. I don't see Bisso and the Ark comin' in the front door to take us home. What I see is that everyone who comes near us could work for Torricelli, and every damn one of them has a dagger."

"So what do we do?"

"We wait, Sarge. Keep our ears open, watch each other's backs, and keep our mouths shut. That's all we can do. Better'n what's happened to the Romans."

"You sure about those stories?"

"No. All I'm sure of is that we never see Roman officers

anymore. Used to be they was at parties with us. Now they're not. Maybe they all went back to Rome, and maybe they're all in dungeons or dead for all I know."

"What else did you hear?"

"Well, there are rumors about dungeons, but Sarge, mostly what I heard was that they was all sent home just about the time we thought we was leaving. Told to pack up and get out, right then, and there wasn't any problem finding them a ship." He shrugged.

"Makes more sense than killin' them," Clavell said. "Rome's got a navy, and there's a lot of Romans. Maybe they'll come looking for us. Cinch they will if the Skipper asks them to. And he will, Jimmy. He will."

"Yeah, probably, and so what? Any way it happens, all we can do is wait."

"Okay, Jimmy. We wait. I won't go storming into Torricelli's place again."

"Good." Harrison looked thoughtful. "Of course, there's nothing stopping you from talking to his daughter. She still gives you a pash?"

Clavell nodded slowly.

"I don't think she knows, though."

"Keep it that way, but talk to her when it's safe. Maybe she'll let something else slip. Just remember, she grew up a Torricelli. She started learning this intrigue stuff about the time she was weaned. You won't learn nothing from her she doesn't want you to know."

"Then what's the point?"

Harrison laughed.

"She's smart Sarge, but she's still a pretty girl, and you ain't all that gone to seed. Maybe what she wants you to know is a bit more than what her old man wants you to know."

Clavell frowned.

"Now you're really talking a dangerous game."

"Maybe. But you know, you could do worse than marry that girl, Sarge. We could both do worse. What if the Skipper can't get us out of here? We still need something."

"He'll come get us!"

"Sure, but just suppose he can't?" Harrison looked thoughtful. "We gotta talk to somebody, I guess. I'll look around."

✢ ✢ ✢

Harrison wore a hook today.

He used it to support one side of a tray with a pitcher of wine and three glasses, and got the tray to the small table without incident. Clavell had offered to carry it, but Harrison had been insistent on doing it himself.

Clavell watched as he set out glasses for Clavell and their guest, then slowly filled them. *Patience*, Clavell thought. *He'll get to the point soon enough.*

The guest was average height for Tran, meaning he was half a head shorter than Clavell. He wore typical middle-class clothing for Nikeis: broadcloth doublet, well-tailored of a good grade of satin, ruffles at sleeve and throat. Hose, probably cotton, fine thread. Not much jewelry. Dagger with a handle wrapped in silver wire just visible under the jacket. The guest waited patiently while Harrison filled his glass.

"Okay," Harrison said then. "Sarge, you remember I told you about a Roman nobleman who was Gingrich's intelligence officer down south. This is him. Meet Marcus

Julius Vinicianus. I saw him in the market the other day, thought I recognized him, so I went out looking for him today."

The Roman stood and bowed.

"Technically I am not a Roman," he said. "At least not by citizenship, which is why I am free to speak with you— although I don't think the Signory will be pleased when they find I've done so."

Clavell stood and returned the bow.

"Have a seat. Okay, why won't they be pleased, and what will they do about it?"

"They'll be displeased because they wish to control everything," Vinicianus said. "They will assume I've told you things they don't wish you to know. As to what they will do, I think nothing. I'm very useful to them, and I have many friends among the Signory. The Council of Ten might well have sent an assassin to prevent my meeting you, but they are very practical people. It will do them no good to stop my mouth after I've told you what I know."

"You haven't told us anything," Clavell protested.

"Ah, but they will assume I have," Vinicianus said. "And of course, you've told me nothing, either. Nor have you paid me."

"Paid. What do you want?" Clavell looked at him narrowly, and the Roman shrugged.

"Good will, mostly. Money is always useful, but I am in no great need at the moment. And I doubt you can tell me anything useful that I don't already know." Vinicianus smiled broadly. "Cease your concerns, Sergeant Clavell. I have no desire to toy with you. As I said, I will settle for good will."

He raised his glass in a toast.

"To new friends." He sipped and set it down. "To begin, I assume you know of the starship."

Clavell shook his head slightly.

"We infer, but we don't know," he said. "They haven't told us anything."

"They probably will, once they learn all they can," Vinicianus said. "The Serene Republic moves slowly in reaching a decision, but when the time comes to act, they can all act as one."

"Damnedest system of government I ever heard of," Clavell said, and Vinicianus shrugged.

"Perhaps. In any event, it is known that a starship landed on Terra Firma, and left behind three star lords. Well, two lords and a lady," he corrected himself. "One of those lords is a black man. I see that does not astonish you, so it must be true, there are many black men among the star lords although we've seen none with your group.

"They also left three very large boxes. By large I mean taller than a man is tall, and perhaps four man-heights by two in plan."

"Son of a bitch! Sounds like shipping containers to me," Harrison said, and Clavell nodded.

"Any idea what's in them?" he asked.

"Wonderful things," Vinicianus said. "All the knowledge of the stars. Books. Weapons. Instruments of science. Wonderful things beyond my abilities to describe." The Roman shrugged. "At least so my agents tell me. I have never been permitted to see the one that has so far been brought to Nikeis. My agents believe none of the boxes have been opened since they arrived here. They remain sealed, locked with starcraft locks. I doubt a Nikeisian thief could open one, but as they've been described to me, a blacksmith could."

"One of them is already in Nikeis?" Clavell asked, and Vinicianus nodded. "Where is it?"

"It rests under guard in the Arsenale," Vinicianus said. "A curious guard, a guard composed of members of many factions. A guard with a rainbow of opinions and loyalties! My agents tell me that the second box will be lodged in Senator Avanti's palazzo, not half a Roman mile from where we sit."

"Avanti's house?"

"Yes. The nephew of Councilor Avanti, the young Senator, was apparently the first person of quality to find the new star people. Unlike the box at the Arsenale, it will be impossible to hide the second box's arrival. It, too, will be guarded, but with this difference, all of those guards will serve either Councilor Avanti or Councilor Torricelli, and one of the guests in that house is the star lady who brought it here.

"He and the lady, whose name is Lorraine Sandori, are said to be lovers." Vinicianus shrugged. "It is certain that she sleeps in the Avanti palazzo, but in which room and with whom is beyond my knowledge at the moment. I should know soon enough, but even more interesting is that the third and last—container—will be brought to Nikeis with the two star lords, a Professore Bart Saxon and Signor Cal Haskins, the black man, as quickly as the ship they have modified to move it can land the second box and return to Terra Firma. After much debate, the Council of Ten has decided to land the last box openly in

Palazzo San Marco while the lords are welcomed by the Doge himself."

Harrison whistled to himself.

"I'd give a heap to have listened in to that debate," he said, and Vinicianus smiled.

"It would seem pointless to hide it," he said. "With all the factions which now guard the Arsenale, the whole city will soon know. I'm surprised you haven't heard of it before now, and all the world will know when the second box lands openly tomorrow." He shrugged.

"All right." Clavell regarded Vinicianus coldly. "Now tell me how you come to be here in the first place?"

The Roman shrugged again.

"As your friend said upon introducing me, I was given the task of securing information for the Star Lord Gengrich during the time when he had his own establishment. When he decided to rejoin Colonel Galloway, there was no more work for me to do there. Moreover, Galloway and the Roman Empire are allies, and while the Imperials would welcome my return, it would not be a welcome I would enjoy, so I looked to other ways and places for my living. The Signory are always in the market for information, so this seemed a logical place to come to." He fingered his fine clothing. "I have not done badly at it."

"Seems to me there was another rumor," Harrison said. "Something about you learning too much, something about Lady Tylara, and you didn't dare fall into Galloway's hands."

Vinicianus shrugged again.

"There are always unpleasant rumors. I dare say that if your Colonel wished me dead, I would be."

"If'n he could find you," Clavell said. "But that's not our problem. I don't have any orders about you, and I don't think anyone else does. Jimmy?"

"Nothing." Harrison shook his head. "Like I said, there was a rumor about Marcus here knowing too much, but hell, there's stories like that about everybody, including Major Mason and Sergeant Major Elliot for that matter. So I guess it's just rumors. Unless you'd care to tell us something?"

"I fear I know no more than you," Vinicianus said. "I've heard many rumors, of course, but I see no point in spreading rumors. I deal in information, not speculation."

"So what did you tell the Signory?" Clavell demanded, and the Roman smiled faintly.

"As much as I had learned from a season of service with your Captain Gengrich," he said. "What they thought most important was the way Captain Gengrich made gunpowder."

"Gunpowder. You already told them?"

"Of course." Vinicianus smiled. "Have you failed to notice that they now collect manure and urine?"

"Sure. I thought that was because they learned about hygiene from me."

The Roman shrugged yet again. It was obviously one of his favorite gestures.

"Perhaps that is part of the reason, but they've built a complex of compost pens on Santa Barbara island, as well, and they convey manure and urine there. That was how Captain Gengrich made saltpeter."

"Saltpeter," Lance Clavell mused. "So that's what they're doing over there!"

"I would assume so. I haven't visited the place, nor would I want to. As to hygiene, you gave away what I could have sold. Ah well. They were eager to pay for other information. About star weapons, and your ways of justice. And, of course, all I knew of the rapidly deteriorating conditions in the south, as the waters rise. Captain Gengrich said the summers will rapidly grow longer and hotter. The Signory seemed eager to learn these things."

"So you ratted out Gengrich," Harrison said.

Vinicianus looked pained.

"What an unpleasant way of putting it," he said. "I do require an income, since I could no longer remain in service to Gengrich. I made no oath to My Lord Arnold, but he remains my friend, and nothing I told the Signory is of any danger to him." He frowned slightly. "Much of what I told them of the coming Time they already knew. They paid me for confirming their knowledge, although not as much. They were particularly interested in the rapid rise of the waters. Already many of their harbor defenses are useless, which is a source of great concern to them."

"So how fast is that water going to rise?" Clavell asked.

Vinicianus frowned.

"It already rises faster than Gengrich supposed it would. I've seen maps in Rome that show the seas engulfing all of the swamplands between Rome and Drantos, but how quickly that will happen I do not know. I would think the Signory would know better than I."

The Roman shrugged, then pointed to the high-water marks painted on the palace next door to them.

"They know how high the water will rise, but apparently not how quickly. I find that puzzling."

"So you told them everything you know."

"Of course. I have my living to make. But nothing I told them endangers Gengrich or your Colonel. Or you."

"Except maybe gunpowder," Harrison said. "And they keep pressing us to tell them how to make it when according to you they already know."

The Roman nodded.

"That's their way. They wish confirmation. It's always their way. I'm astonished that they don't question you daily about what Warlord Rick calls the Great Guns. I would wager it won't be long before they cast such guns. They have at least one foundry capable of doing it."

Clavell nodded.

"The daughter of that foundry owner is in my class. Good student."

"Higher-class citizens always seek new knowledge here. It should be no surprise that they already know the secrets of gunpowder."

"So it would be safe to tell them the formula," Harrison said. "Fifteen to three to two. Mix it, wet it, and corn it. Might be a good idea, Sarge. They'll appreciate knowing. That's the formula you gave them?"

"Precisely so. Those portions, by dry measure."

"And willow charcoal," Harrison said musingly. "Where do you reckon they'll get sulfur?"

Vinicianus shrugged.

"I told them their trade ships and agents should look for springs that smell of rotten eggs. That was what Gengrich did."

"Black powder and alcohol," Clavell muttered. "Used to know a song about that. Never did know where to get sulfur. Well, well." *But I do know better sources of saltpeter, I think. Gull rocks. Bat caves. Maybe there's money in knowing that?* He turned to the Roman. "So why are you telling us all this?"

"I've told you little you won't learn in due course," Vinicianus said. "As I said, I hope to earn your friendship and good will. And perhaps you may need my services another time."

"Need 'em now," Clavell muttered.

"For what purpose?"

"I need to get a message to Colonel Galloway," Clavell said. "You want to earn some good will with the Colonel, let him know all this right away. That we're here and can't leave, not mistreated but we're sure as hell prisoners. Tell him that Nikeis is going big time to make gunpowder. That there's maybe new star people with all kinds of star goods. Get that word to the Colonel, and I guarantee you he'll be grateful."

Vinicianus smiled thinly.

"I'm certain you are right." He looked up to see one of the household children scurry past with a mop and pail. "Your housekeeper's child?"

"How would I know?" Clavell shook his head.

"You don't, but I do," Harrison said. "Her name's Chara. We sort of own her. Orphan kid, as it happens. Nobody knows from where, talks Terra Firma all right but don't speak much Italian, kidnapped on the mainland and brought here by some fisherman who wanted a servant. Grabbed me around the knees when I was walking down by the docks, and begged for a job where they didn't beat her." Harrison shrugged. "So I bought her. Didn't cost much."

"Oh. Well, you done good," Clavell said.

"Yeah, she's worked out all right, works hard," Harrison said. "Cook treats her like one of her kids, and she's getting a little meat on them skinny bones. So tell us, Marcus, can you get a message to the Skipper or not? I'm bettin' you can't, this place is sealed up pretty good."

Vinicianus shrugged.

"It would be difficult and very expensive at this time. Are you certain you wish to make such an attempt? The Signory will expect you to do so, of course, and they will be watching you closely." He shrugged again. "As they will now be watching me, since I do not doubt they know I have been here. Do not think ill of me if I decline the attempt, at least for now. It may be easier in a few days."

He watched Chara the kitchen maid retreat out of sight and smiled softly.

## ❖⟷ CHAPTER FOUR ⟷❖
# CROSSING

**Twelve days since landing**

Bart Saxon watched uneasily as the sailors lashed the cargo container to the reinforced deck of the big ship. There was activity all around him. Longshoremen and deckhands loaded the ship next to them with copper and tin ingots, another ship down the way was being loaded with charcoal. Saxon could see the fires from the charcoal kilns all around the port city.

This was the last of the twenty-foot containers. The first had been safely taken across to Nikeis by Haskins and Sandori while Saxon stayed to watch the other two. Haskins had returned to report it safely across, installed in Senator Avanti's palazzo with Ms. Sandori to watch it, then went back over with the second. Saxon had been surprised to see Haskins return with the ship after shepherding the second cargo container. That left two of the containers in Nikeis with only one star guard.

Of course there was nothing to be done about it. Sandori had sent him, claiming concern about Saxon. Haskins wasn't precisely afraid of Sandori. Intimidated would be a better word, Saxon thought. But it all added up to his coming back to Terra Firma leaving two containers on the island with only Officer Lorraine Sandori to guard them. Saxon frowned at the thought. It wasn't that he didn't trust Sandori, but she'd become increasingly friendly with the young Senator Avanti, and the Senator was understandably curious about the contents of those containers. Moving them was expensive, and Avanti had never lost an opportunity to remind Saxon of that. For all his suspicions, what were the alternatives to cooperation with Avanti and the Serene Republic? Saxon could think of none.

*What the hell can she be planning? Probably nothing. Keeping her options open, not closing off any. That would mean she wouldn't go too far, not just yet. But she's thinking of what she can do on her own. I'm sure of it.*

Those cargo containers were almost certainly the most valuable objects on the planet, but it wasn't clear whether the Nikeisian elites understood that. Sandori certainly did, which probably meant that Senator Avanti did . . . Saxon shook his head in frustration. Saxon had the only keys, but that wasn't anything permanent. The best locks would yield to a sledgehammer.

*And it only takes one dagger in the right place to get the keys away from me*, Saxon thought.

If anyone planned on doing that, it wasn't obvious. The Nikeisian officials they had met were uniformly polite, and their hospitality was exaggerated. They were meticulous about recording every ducat they spent on this operation, but the charges they made didn't seem excessive. From what Saxon could discern, gold was important here—and there was a modest but weighty bag of Krugerrands in this last container, and only Saxon knew about them. It ought to be more than enough if the Nikeis officials were as honest as they protested they were.

*Odd*, Saxon thought, *but they do seem to be honest. Merchant societies often are. Maybe they have to be*.

Honest or not, the Nikeisians were certainly efficient. Within a week of their landing on Tran a sizable expedition of oxen and wagons had appeared in the clearing. The containers were far too large for existing wagons, but in four days new and very large wagons had been built and the containers had been manhandled onto those wagons. Teams of twenty-four oxen had pulled each container over the trail to the main road, then eighteen-oxen teams had pulled them the dozen miles to the sea. Progress had been slow but quite steady, and everything was done professionally. Clerks had noted every expense as they moved from the clearing to the road, then into the fortified harbor city. It added up to an impressive sum in ducats, but when Saxon found what they paid for gold he stopped worrying about it. He could afford this—and Spirit might be paying in something other than coins.

*Not my concern*, Saxon thought. *Or I hope it isn't*.

The journey to the sea had been interesting. This area was obviously a center of industrial activity. Loggers were everywhere. On their first day Saxon saw what looked like an enormous tipi of logs stood on end. Men were plastering the outside of the tipi logs with dirt. Saxon thought hard about what they were doing, but then he saw a similar structure on fire, and realized they were making charcoal. Charcoal would be important in metal refining and forging, and the Nikeis workers seemed to know precisely what they were doing. This wasn't anything they'd learned recently. They passed several more charcoal kilns as they made their way to the sea coast.

*And we almost certainly have ways to improve the charcoal-making process*, Saxon thought. *That's in the books I brought.* The *Britannica* was a gold mine of information about the early technology of the Industrial Revolution. *That alone should be enough to pay the debts we've run up. Charcoal. Black powder. Maybe even nitric acid and guncotton. Smokeless powder. Nitroglycerin . . .* The last thought brought a mischievous grin to Saxon's face. *Dad would be proud . . .*

*We've been well treated. It's been expensive, but all's well so far*, Saxon thought. The Nikeis officials treated them as wealthy visitors. They'd been advanced local currency—ducats, which Saxon remembered from Shakespeare but had never seen before—and a line of credit for food and drink. Every item was written down by a clerk. *But then, damned near everything they do is written down. Damnedest country for record keeping I ever heard of.*

Yes, all was well and they were treated as wealthy and honored guests. But there had never been any discussion of where they were going.

✣ ✣ ✣

The ship was about a hundred and fifty feet long. Saxon paced it off before they boarded. A hundred and fifty feet long and more than forty feet wide amidships, with a high forecastle forward and a narrow poop deck a full deck higher aft. A stubby, sawed off tub. It was fitted to row, but it also had a pair of masts. It bore the name *Queen of Heaven*, and the locals called it a *navis oneraria*. A merchant ship. It hadn't been built for anything as large as a twenty-foot cargo container, but the sailors had made do. The deck had been beefed up with square timbers the size of railroad ties, and the container rode on those amidships, ahead of the mainmast and between the left and right rowing benches. The middle benches on each side had been cut short to make room for the container between them. Saxon could see the raw wood at the edges. The container was lashed down by ropes to both sides as well as fore and aft, and it wasn't going anywhere.

"Actually, it might keep the ship floating," Haskins said. "If it came to that. Them things are pretty watertight."

Saxon shuddered.

"Thanks. Well, two are safe over there, so I guess we're all right. What's it like? On the island?"

"Islands. Lots of them. You keep askin' me that, and I keep telling you, I didn't get far from the docks," Haskins said. "Now Miss Spirit can tell you more, I reckon. She seems to be doing all right with that Senator kid."

"They were getting pretty thick on the trip coming to the harbor," Saxon said. "Are they sleeping together?"

"Don't know for sure, but it wouldn't surprise me none." Haskins shrugged. "They sure spend enough time together. One thing, if'n the women I saw are typical, she's got competition. Some real hot babes in that city. On the other hand, Miss Spirit's likely the thinnest woman on the island."

"The women are fat?"

"Not so much fat, maybe, but sure more rounded out than Miss Spirit," Haskins said. "Lively, too. Not that I saw all that many women around the docks, but there was some. Some real fancy dressed, too, not just the kind of women you expect to see around sailors. Didn't seem to mind what color I was, either." Haskins chuckled. "Miss Spirit wasn't so happy to see them, though. Kept saying she had to find a hairdresser and a dress shop. Real insistent about it."

"That doesn't sound much like her."

"Sure don't, Bart. But that's how she was."

"All right. Now why are you carrying that?" Saxon indicated the H&K battle rifle slung over Haskins' shoulder.

Haskins shrugged again.

"They asked if we had star weapons to protect the ship," he said. "Miss Spirit told them we did, and they wanted me to carry mine." He grinned. "Not like I've ever had to use it. We didn't even do a demonstration, not that it's needed, I think these guys know all about what a rifle like this can do."

"How would they know that?"

"I don't know, Bart, but they sure haven't acted all that curious. Maybe they seen them in action already."

Saxon thought about that for a moment.

"You know, you may be right," he said. "Galloway's been here for years. There's no way these people can make a smokeless powder rifle, but they've got to have heard of them." Saxon looked at the bronze fittings of the ship. There was a forged pump of bronze and iron. No cannon, but once the idea occurred to these people they'd be able to make cannon, he was certain of that.

"If the signori please," Captain Fieschi said. "It is time to depart. The tide will be in our favor."

"Certainly," Saxon said. He let Fieschi lead them up the wide gangway. "Will the weather be favorable?"

Fieschi shrugged.

"Only God knows, Signor Saxon, but we usually have favorable winds and small seas at this time of year. And it is less than two days' voyage at worst."

The gangway led to the main deck. They went aft between two benches of oarsmen.

No chains, Saxon noticed. Apparently the Tran version of the Serene Republic was like Earth's Venice, free oarsmen. Venice, or classical Athens, he thought. A strong man could make a reasonable living as an oarsman. A good one might even become a ship captain.

They climbed a stairway to a poop deck that rose above the main deck to almost the height of the cargo container, so they could look right over the container to the front end of the ship. Rowers were taking their places at the benches. Armed marines stood on the forecastle. There were two devices up there. *Onager. That's the name*, Saxon thought. A small stone-throwing torsion catapult. There was no sign of ammunition for the two onagers, but the marines who stood next to them were apparently the crew for the weapon. They seemed to be doing something, but Saxon couldn't make out what. The entire ship had an air of ordered confusion, with everyone familiar with what had to be done so no one was giving orders. Things just happened.

There were cabins under the poop deck, and they were shown to two of them, presumably officer quarters vacated for Saxon and Haskins.

"Can't complain nohow about the hospitality," Haskins said. "See you up on deck in a minute?"

"Sure." Saxon looked around the cabin.

*Stateroom. They'd call it a stateroom in English*, Saxon thought. *God knows what that is in Italian. I guess cabin will have to do.*

The room was larger than he'd expected. It was stuffy, owing to a complete lack of windows or portholes. A bed was built in against the hull side of the cabin. Saxon noted that it had high sideboards so that he wouldn't fall out if the ship rolled in high seas, and nodded in satisfaction. He expected to be seasick, and he was pleased to see a bucket half filled with seawater set securely into a wooden structure fastened to the bulkhead by his bed. Apparently they thought he might be seasick too.

There was no sign of a bathroom. There had to be something. The ship didn't stink. The maritime crew and the oarsmen had to have some place. The bucket? Maybe more buckets? He could ask Cal.

There were shouts and the sounds of rushing feet. Saxon came out into the hall between cabins and went up the ladder to the deck above. The oarsmen were in their places with the oars raised high, while linesmen cast off and pushed the ship out from the dock with long poles. Once they were away from the dock the oarsmen dipped oars and began to push.

*Push*, Saxon thought. *They're standing and facing the direction we're going. Using their legs. I don't remember reading anything about that. But they sure are.*

He looked back to the shore. The dock was part of a fortified harbor, a walled castle with stone breakwaters extending out to make a small basin. The castle flew banners with the winged lion and battle-axe of Nikeis. Saxon had seen similar banners in books about Venice, except he didn't remember any battle-axe on the Venetian banners.

Hills rose steeply beyond the walls of the port town. Saxon saw logging operations on every hill in sight. As he watched, loggers felled a tall tree near the top of the nearest hill. If they kept up operations at that pace the trees would be gone in no time—but it was pretty obvious that this wasn't any ordinary forest. The trees were too regularly spaced, and mostly the same size. Planted? They must have been planted a long time ago to have gotten so big! And there were charcoal burnings everywhere, giant tipis smoldering away. Other big trees were being dragged down hill. A raft of trees floated near shore.

They moved out past the breakwaters and into the open sea. Not far outside the breakwater a brisk wind came up from the left quarter behind them, and the captain shouted orders. Lateen sails quickly appeared on both masts. Sailors rushed about with lines, everyone moving with precision without more orders. Soon the ship began to move rapidly through the water. The oarsmen, seemingly without orders, brought the oars inboard and secured them, then sprawled on their benches.

*And we're on the way to Nikeis*, Saxon thought. *Now what?*

✣ ✣ ✣

Later in the evening the wind was stronger. There were whitecaps on most of the waves. They had an evil reddish cast in the light of the Demon.

Saxon had little experience on water, and none outside San Francisco Bay. He'd heard of the Beaufort scale for rating the strength of winds, but he didn't know how to use it to rate the strength of this wind. Whitecaps on all the waves, one wave in twenty breaking. Half gale? Fresh breeze? For that matter, would the Beaufort scale work on another planet? He didn't see any reason why it wouldn't, but the thought nagged him. Gravity about the same, but atmospheric density would be different. How different? He couldn't think of a way to measure that. Pressure he could manage if there were any mercury on the planet. How many millimeters high could mercury rise under a good vacuum? Or in strong wind? But the gravity would be a bit different, acceleration wouldn't be thirty-two feet per second per second. But he could measure that and then come up with the local planetary gravity. Drop something and time it? Galileo used inclined planes and balls. That would work. He'd have to do it before his watch stopped working. Get that local g acceleration and it would be the key to a lot.

Maybe he could work that out another way. Use a pendulum—he shook his head to rid himself of the speculations. Time for that sort of thing when they got settled. The formulae would all be in the books.

Whatever the wind strength, the waves didn't look dangerous from the decks of the *Queen of Heaven*, but Saxon thought he would hate to be out in that in a small sailboat. *I'll have to look things up when I get my laptop running. A lot of what I need to know will be in one or another edition of the* Britannica.

That thought brought up another—more of a worry,

than just a "thought," he admitted to himself. He'd made certain he had at least one printed copy of the *Britannica*, and there was hard copy of several other sources, as well. But an awful lot of what he had was only on CD-ROM. CD-ROMs were wonderful, and he had just about every book ever written. There was a whole course on sailing ships on one of them, for example. But they weren't going to do him any good without power. Still, there seemed to be plenty of wind here, so if it held up out at the—islands? archipelago?—there ought to be enough for the windmill to keep the laptops charged. The disassembled windmill and its generator took up more than a quarter of container two. The bicycle generator was in three, this one, along with some laptops and a lot of CD-ROMs. Somewhere in there was an inventory of what was in all the containers, but Saxon hadn't tried to find it since their arrival. Time enough for that when they were settled.

The containers had been sealed back in the clearing where they landed. They'd all agreed that once they had retrieved their personal gear and weapons, they wouldn't reopen the containers until they were settled in Nikeis and all three of them were present.

Sandori had used a melon to demonstrate her pistol to Caesare Avanti. He hadn't seemed surprised. Another reason to think they'd seen star weapons before. But they'd been astonished when Haskins and Saxon had shown the capabilities of their personal radios to communicate without shouting.

"There's a lot more," Sandori had said. But that had been enough to get Avanti moving on bringing in wagons and oxen.

"Keep him guessing," Sandori had said. "Look, these people are mostly merchants. They know knowledge is valuable, and they're sure we know a lot they don't. That makes us valuable."

"Don't hurt that he's a right handsome stud, though," Haskins had answered. That had brought a blush.

*But she's right,* Saxon thought. *We aren't strong enough to just bull our way through. We need to deal with civilized people, and these seem to be just that. But how do I establish contact with Captain Galloway? And do I let them know that I want to?*

Dinner was in a large cabin that served both as the captain's quarters and a wardroom. Saxon was surprised to have an appetite despite the ship's motion. *Maybe I'll get through this without getting sick after all. Maybe.* Captain Fieschi tried to keep a conversation going, but the wind and sea noise and Saxon's inadequacy in Italian made that difficult, and after a while they ate in silence.

The stew was reasonably tasty and the bread quite fresh.

"Baked today?" Saxon asked. Captain Fieschi shrugged.

"Probably in town," Haskins said. "Never saw them bake on board ship. Galley's pretty primitive. Hot water, boiled cereal, and stews, but I never saw any baking."

"So how do I take a pee?" Saxon asked, and Haskins grinned.

"Lee rail, there's a place just for that," he said. "Took me a while to get the hang of it."

"Better show me now," Saxon said. His stomach growled and he tasted bile. "Right now, I guess."

"Sure." Haskins stood and bowed to the captain. Saxon noted that and bowed as well, then followed Haskins out onto the poop deck forward of the stern cabin. Haskins led him down steps to the main deck. Most of the oarsmen were seated in small blanket-covered groups, talking and throwing dice, but a few were stretched out asleep on the deck.

"No chains," Saxon said.

"Nope. All free men," Haskins said. "Some of the professional oarsmen make good money. If anybody has galley slaves it's not the Signory. Just over here, Bart. There's one on each side. You go to the one on the lee side. That's the opposite of the windward side. Just now it's the starboard side, which is on your right when you're looking forward, just in case you don't know."

Saxon nodded.

"Thanks. Starboard and—port?"

Haskins shrugged.

"Port in English, but here it's starboard or something like that, starboard's close enough, and babordo. Babordo means left. We call them starboard and port in English. Starboard and babordo, forward and aft. Those don't change like windward and leeward. Just now leeward's the starboard side."

He pointed to a small opening in the ship's railings where a platform jutted out a couple of feet over the ocean. Ropes and rail posts made it relatively safe and easy to use.

"Thanks, Cal. Hate to do this in winter," Saxon said.

"Maybe them as have cabins use buckets when it's cold out." Haskins shrugged again. "Bart, what the hell are we going to do when we get settled onto that island? I expect it's easier getting to this place than getting away from it."

"We try to find a way to get word to Captain Galloway that we're here and looking for him, I think," Saxon said.

Haskins nodded.

"You agree that it's best to work with Galloway?" Saxon asked.

"Bart, I'm leaving that up to you. Whatever you say is okay with me. You like Galloway, that's fine with me."

"Glad you came?"

"Beats being on the streets," Haskins said. "Feels like I may be some use here. Maybe. Sure better chance of that here than in the Tenderloin."

Saxon considered that and decided that he agreed. He wasn't sure he knew what he was doing, and he hoped to hell Agzaral and Lee hadn't picked the wrong man, but at least he had a purpose now. A purpose and a future, and that was a lot more than he'd had in San Francisco. He nodded to himself and carefully climbed out onto the platform. It was more secure than it looked, but he'd hate to have to use it in stronger seas. He finished his task, and found there was a bucket with a line on it next to the rail opening. He used it to dip up some water and washed his hands.

"Now you wash down the area you used," Haskins said. "They don't know about germs here, I think, but they do know they don't like stink."

"Don't blame them. Cal, I don't know exactly what we do next, or how. What I want to do is find this Galloway, but I don't know how to do that."

"Yeah. We don't have a lot of choices," Haskins said.

"Least this outfit has people and ships to move all our stuff. No sign of anyone trying to steal it, either. They seem friendly enough. Reckon that's Spirit's doing. She's sure one good terms with that Caesare Avanti, and Avanti's daddy is a big cheese over there."

"But you don't know if they're sleeping together?"

"Like I said, if I had to bet, I'd say they were, but I don't know anything. Just everyone's damned friendly. And they don't care that I'm Black. Takes 'em a minute to get used to it, I don't think they ever saw a Black man before, but once they do it's okay. I think I like this place."

✧ ✧ ✧

The boy said something in Italian, realized he was not understood, and switched to the mainland trade language. He strained to keep his voice calm.

"Captain Fieschi wishes to speak with you on deck," he said, and Saxon frowned.

"Now?"

"Yes, Signor, you and the other signor, please."

"Right away," Saxon said. He put his head into the other stateroom. "Cal, we're wanted on deck."

"Roger that."

They went up to the poop deck. Captain Fieschi pointed towards the west, where the True Sun was setting.

"If you look closely, Signor, you will see there are two ships on a course to intercept us."

Saxon brought out his binoculars. He could make out few details. Two ships, galleys, one big triangular sail on each but oars dipping at what Saxon thought was a slow but steady beat.

"Whose?" Saxon asked.

"I do not know. They are not ours," Captain Fieschi said. "What are those marvels?"

"Binoculars. You don't know that word. Lenses? Make things look closer."

Fieschi looked doubtful.

"May I look through them?"

Saxon put the binocular strap around Fieschi's neck.

"Be careful, they break. You look through here, and use this rocker to change the focus—move that back and forth until you see best."

Fieschi looked puzzled at first, then disappointed, then startled.

"I see!" He lowered the binoculars, stared, then raised them again. He did this several times. "Do you have many of these?" he asked.

"Several."

"They will be immensely valuable," Fieschi said. "Now I understand why the Signory were willing to pay so much to lease my ship to convey you safely to Nikeis."

He went back to inspecting the distant ships.

"Who are they?" Saxon asked.

"No insignia on the sails, no flags. I think pirates."

"Pirates," Saxon said. "Are they dangerous? Can they catch us?"

Fieschi shrugged. "Normally I would say no to both questions," he said. "*Queen of Heaven* is well able to defend herself. But with that large—container—on deck, it is not so certain. And we are much slower."

"I see. So what will you do?"

"Try to stay out of their reach, unless you request otherwise," Fieschi said. "Unfortunately, our destination is well known, and altering course to run before the wind would put us downwind of Nikeis. That container is a hamper with the wind off the babordo quarter, but I do not know by how much. I am certain that we will be a great deal slower than they are when trying to climb into the wind."

"And if we can't outrun them?"

"Then we fight, of course." Fieschi shrugged again. "I was hoping you would have weapons to assist in that."

"Cal? You understand what he said?"

"Some of it. Pirates?"

"Right on. We may have to fight. You're going to be better at that than I am."

"Which ain't all that great," Haskins said in English. "I was never much of a rifleman. Qualified with the M-16 all right in basic, so I know what I'm supposed to do. But—"

Fieschi had been listening to them without understanding.

"You can do nothing now?" he asked.

"Good grief no," Haskins said. "How far you reckon they are from us?"

Saxon squinted.

"Couple of miles?"

He took back the binoculars from Captain Fieschi. *They've got some kind of markings in there I can use to find distances, but I don't know how to do that,* he thought. *Principle's easy enough, wish I'd thought to take a lesson or something. Oh, well. He looked again.*

"More like double that, I think," Haskins said. "Too far for me. When it's a couple of hundred yards, let me know."

he frowned. "They likely to have those catapult things? How far can they shoot?"

Saxon struggled with languages but managed to ask Fieschi, then frowned at the answer.

"Sorry, didn't understand."

Fieschi thought and tried again.

"Nine lengths of this ship? But not with much accuracy above three lengths of this ship. That is what we can do with our ballistae. Theirs will not be as strong unless they have captured one of our ships. Or a Roman ship," he added begrudgingly.

"Cal, he says they shoot about four hundred fifty yards max, maybe a hundred and fifty with any accuracy."

Haskins nodded.

"Well, we can shoot farther, but I wouldn't bet on hitting nothing closer than a hundred yards. Maybe not that far. I ain't no marksman, Bart."

"That ought to be good enough," Saxon said. "They don't want to set fire to us, they want to capture us. We let them shoot first. If they don't shoot we let them get close enough you can hit someone. If they still look hostile, then you spray down their poop deck. That ought to do it."

"Yeah," Haskins said. He didn't sound very sure of himself and he glanced back at the unknown ships. "Maybe nothing will come of it. They don't look like they're closing much."

"So does that mean we *can* outrun them?" Saxon asked.

"It may." Captain Fieschi sounded doubtful. "But it may simply be that they choose not to close with us, instead. *Queen of Heaven* is a formidable ship, Signor. Our ballistae crews are well trained. The rowers have weapons and most of them are trained in their use. That is without your star weapons." He indicated Saxon's holstered pistol. "I would not care to be the pirate that attempts to take this ship."

"There are two," Saxon observed.

"Yes, and if they are accustomed to working together that could present problems," Fieschi said. "We will not maneuver well with that container on the deck. Is it your advice that we avoid contact with them?"

*I hadn't thought I was giving advice*, Saxon thought. *Interesting. Was this some kind of council of war?*

"Yes," he said. "If that's possible, we should avoid them."

"I will have the rowers stay ready. If those ships begin to approach we will add their power to the wind."

Saxon had been watching the oncoming ships.

"I think they just slowed the beat," he said. He chanted slowly. "Dip. Pull. Return. Yes, I'm certain they've slowed the pace."

Fieschi stared into the setting sun.

"You are correct. They need the oars to keep up with us, I think. So it would appear their ships *are* slower than *Queen of Heaven,* despite the container. On this heading with this wind."

Dusk came quickly, leaving the evil red glow of the Demon Star.

"I will set three to watch," Fieschi said. "The demon will give enough light to see if they come closer. You may as well go to bed."

*Sure*, Saxon thought. *I'm on an alien world being chased by pirates. No point in losing any sleep over it.*

✦ ✦ ✦

He slept badly until near dawn, then managed to get into a deeper sleep with strange dreams he couldn't quite remember. It was bright outside when he woke. He went up on deck and stared west, then took out his binoculars and searched the horizon.

"They are gone," Fieschi said from behind him.

"Did we outrun them?"

"They did not try to catch us," Fieschi said. "The lookouts tell me they followed until shortly after dawn, then turned to the northwest."

"That's good news."

"Yes, Signor, but it remains disturbing that pirate ships should follow an armed ship of the Serene Republic even for a short time. Their usual concern is to avoid us. I was hired to be the supply ship for a squadron that chases pirates before the Signory leased this ship to transport your—containers—and without that"—he pointed to the big metal box—"and in this wind it would have been no difficulty to catch one of them, close as they approached. They are bolder than I have found them to be in the past."

"Why would that be?" Saxon asked.

"I believe they have heard stories of the great value of our cargo," Fieschi said. "They wish to be sure of our destination, and are now certain we are bound for Nikeis. Signor, I have heard stories that tempt even me! Your lenses—"

"Binoculars."

"Binoculars." The captain said the word again. "Your binoculars alone would be of great value. Imagine being able to examine a ship from far away while they are as yet unaware of any details about *Queen of Heaven*! I have heard of such instruments in the hands of the Warlord Rick, but I never thought to see any. And that weapon your man carries, I presume it is what they call in Drantos a battle rifle. I have heard that it can strike down an enemy far beyond crossbow ranges. And these are but what we can see! The pirates must be tempted by the prospects of such booty!"

"More than you are."

"Of course more than me, Signor. I have a contract with the Serene Republic. My home is in Nikeis. I have traveled to many places, but I would not care to live anywhere else."

*Interesting*, Saxon thought. *Very interesting.*

✢ ✢ ✢

Nikeis was well in sight by midmorning.

Saxon studied the island complex with his binoculars. At first there was nothing to see, just an irregular shape above the sea. As they got closer he could see that Nikeis was bigger than he had expected it to be. There was a lot more than one island. First there was a low stretch of land a few feet above water, no more than a sand bar. It had low wooden buildings and docks. Crews dried nets on some of the sand bars, but there was not much other activity. Beyond that were grassy marshes, and past those was a complex of higher islands. One large island rose no more than twenty feet out of the sea, and was entirely flat. It was covered with grain fields and some barns. Farms, but not houses. Other islands were covered with houses. The main island, irregularly shaped, had a low shelf at sea level then rose steeply to a plateau nearly a hundred feet above the sea. The whole main island seemed to be a single city, and there were palaces and houses on the other islands near it. Further away was another farm island.

Stone forts stood guard on islands near the channel entrances. Saxon examined them curiously. The fortifications were small in area but surrounded by treacherous sandbars. Each fort was several stories high, all built of stone. Otherwise, the marshes and sand bars weren't well developed, but the land on the real islands was either farmland or covered with ornate multistoried buildings with balconies, all painted in bright colors. There were banners and flags everywhere. The True Sun was high overhead. Nearly noon, Saxon thought.

Two small ships, ten oars to each side, came racing out of a channel between two of the stone forts. When they came near, *Queen of Heaven* turned into the wind and Captain Fieschi shouted something to the master of the first boat. They conversed at length, then the two galleys turned and raced away towards the city. They raised bright ribbons to the masthead and looked very festive as they went.

After *Queen of Heaven* turned into the wind, the crew quickly furled the sails as the rowers unlashed their oars. When the oarsmen were ready they steered towards the narrow passage that led into the interior of the island complex. Captain Fieschi stood by the steersman and quietly gave instructions.

The ship moved more slowly under oars, and Saxon frowned as he discovered something else he hadn't realized about ships.

*Funny, I always assumed they'd be faster under oars, but we were actually faster under sail! Not as maneuverable, I'll bet, but faster. And those other boats, those "fusta" Fieschi called them. They're a whole different design. A lot narrower for their length, and I bet they aren't as deep, either. They are faster rowing, too, I'll bet . . . at least until the rowers get worn out.*

He supposed that wasn't the kind of things navies worried about if they had steamships and gas turbines and nuclear power. Something to keep in mind here on Tran, though.

The captain steered them through twisting narrow channels between islands covered with buildings until they came out into a wide lagoon a quarter mile from the main island. Just in the center of the main island was a low plaza.

*Palazzo*, Saxon corrected himself. *Palazzo. And apparently they use the same word for palace? Cheez.*

An ornately dressed group waited for them on the palazzo. A floating wooden platform about two feet high had been built along the water's edge. Much of the paved palazzo itself was under six inches of water, but even so hundreds of people stood in the square, all waiting for them in ankle-deep water, all cheering. Two dozen men and a few women stood on the platform. Saxon scanned the crowd with his binoculars. Sandori and Senator Caesare Avanti stood in the center of the welcoming committee. Everyone seemed to be smiling.

The crowd in the palazzo was definitely happy despite having wet feet, and they continued to cheer loudly as *Queen of Heaven* came closer. Most of those in the palazzo were men, but not all. Of those closer to the platform where the Doge sat, several were couples, generally middle aged to elderly. The women were all well dressed, but they mostly ran to overweight. Most of the women Saxon had seen, both here and on Terra Firma, were definitely full figured. A slender teenaged girl in the first row of those in the palazzo caught his eye. Well dressed, slender waist. She stood out from the crowd.

*Best not go there*, Saxon thought to himself. *I don't know what their version of the Tenderloin looks like, but I bet it looks like a grave.*

The ship's officers shouted orders, and the oarsmen on one side backwatered as the others pulled. The ship turned and was brought slowly alongside the floating dockwork at the edge of the plaza. As they threw lines out and made fast, Saxon saw two men standing near Sandori and Avanti. One of them was dressed more or less like other men of rank in the welcoming party, although there were differences. The other was wearing US Army battle dress. Both wore shoulder-holstered pistols.

## ✣━ CHAPTER FIVE ━✣
# INTRODUCTIONS

Lucia Michaeli hugged herself in excitement as the ship came through the lagoon towards Palazzo San Marco and the floating pier in front of her. No one noticed her excitement. The Palazzo was filled with shouting people, many of them standing in water above their ankles because they couldn't get a place on the welcoming platform. Lucia couldn't remember a time of greater excitement in Nikeis.

She stood next to her father. Mother hadn't felt well enough to come. She was in her fifth month, and it hadn't been a good pregnancy. It wouldn't be, Mother was too old to have another child, but God's will be done. This would be Mother's seventh, and only three still lived: Lucia, her older sister Catarina, and her older brother Andreas.

God's will. Professore Clavell never questioned God's will. Never. But he showed that many plagues people thought to be the will of God were the result of small animals in the water, or of tiny creatures that lived in the blood of fleas, and by avoiding the causes one could avoid the plague. That there was often a way to prevent what everyone knew—had always known—was the will of God. That was disturbing. It was exciting, too, but there was no one to talk to about it, not even the Professore. He would not speak of God, not even of the new Unified Church that rumor said was sweeping Drantos. One story had it that it was the religion of the star men and was prevailing even in Rome. But Professore Clavell would never answer her questions about it. He would talk about medicine and health, and that was very interesting, and sometimes he would talk about other matters which he called "technology"; but he would never discuss God or the human place in God's universe.

When Signora Michaeli declared that she was unable to come to the welcoming ceremony, it was natural that Lucia would go in her place. Her brother Andreas was on Terra Firma contracting for charcoal, and her older sister Catarina was shy, seldom going outside the home except to the foundry. Catarina knew much about the foundry, and charcoal, and the forges, but she had few social skills, and she was afraid of meeting young men. She was two years older than Lucia, almost an old maid, and she would probably be a spinster, or go into the Church. Father despaired of her ever marrying . . .

The crowd kept shouting as the *navi* was rowed across the lagoon. It was easy to see the great box on the deck. *Container*. That was the word Professore Clavell had used after he was told of the first one brought across by the star visitors. No one knew what was in those containers. One had been brought in the dead of night direct to the Arsenale where it was guarded by militia. There were rumors of star visitors welcomed by the Doge and the Signory, but not even Ginarosa Torricelli knew all the story! Not until today.

Andreas' friend Vincente worked in the Arsenale, and he'd told Lucia that the container couldn't be opened, although he wouldn't admit that anyone had tried. It had not been difficult to get Vincente talking, but he hadn't known much. There were said to be locks that could only be opened by the Star Lord Bart, who would come with the last container. Lucia strained to catch a glimpse of the new star lord, but there was too much activity on the ship's deck, and she couldn't make out which one was the star lord.

The ship came closer. The container was larger than she'd imagined, a huge box of painted metal. Ginarosa said that the one in the Arsenale was made of steel.

This would be the third container. There was a second container in Senator Avanti's palazzo! There were many rumors of how it had gotten there, but one thing was certain, the container now stood in Avanti's reception hall. The other news was the star visitors, a black man and a star lady who had come with the first containers. The black man had gone back to Terra Firma, but the star lady lived in Senator Avanti's palazzo! And now she could see the black man, on the quarterdeck of the *Queen of Heaven*! That must be the other star man with him.

Lucia and Ginarosa had tried to see the star woman and the container, but they'd been turned away at the

door when Ginarosa Torricelli tried to call on the Senator.
Lucia chuckled at the memory. It hadn't been easy to get
Ginarosa to do that, even though everyone knew that
Councilor Torricelli would be glad of a marriage into the
Avanti household. It had taken nearly all of Lucia's skill to
persuade her friend to be so bold, and it had done no good
at all. The major domo had been polite—everyone was
polite to la Signorina Ginarosa Torricelli!—but he hadn't
even let them into the reception hall. They'd seen neither
star lady nor container.

Lucia's maid said she'd heard from a cousin in service
to the Avanti family that the star woman lived in the Avanti
house. In a room with a door that connected to the
Senator's bedroom! Thinking about that gave Lucia
strange tingles. Well, not so strange, she thought. Not
now. Familiar, delicious. Lucia knew everything about sex
except what it felt like when consummated. That would
have to wait. Maidenheads brought a high price, and—
she suppressed the thought and looked again at the
container on the incoming *navi*.

Everyone in Nikeis was talking about what might be in
the containers, but Lucia didn't think anyone knew. There
were too many different stories. Still, the stories were
interesting. Secrets. How to make weapons that struck
down enemies from a full Roman mile! How to speak to
someone in another city! Ways to cure diseases! When she
asked Professore Clavell if those things were possible, he
said they were! That in the lands he came from such
things were common! "Technology," "high tech"—those
were words he used, and Lucia was careful to memorize
them. Despite her questions she hadn't learned much

more than that, though. Professore Clavell didn't really know what was in these containers, and Lucia didn't think he really knew how to do all those marvels although she didn't doubt that he'd seen them done. Most people were like that, accepting what they saw without wondering how it came to be. It was surprising that Professore Clavell would be that way, but apparently it was so.

Professore Clavell hadn't talked to the star visitors. Or said he hadn't. He'd even acted surprised to hear that there were star visitors in the city, although everyone in the Rialto knew about them. He had to have known about them. That was puzzling. Professore Clavell kept his own counsel, but he wasn't very good at it. Perhaps he might be in Drantos, but not here in Nikeis where everyone had secrets and learned to keep them.

He knew about the star visitors now! Lucia could see Professore Clavell, a handsome figure in his oddly cut velvet doublet. Good legs, his stockings didn't appear to be padded. Perhaps a bit more at the waist than there ought to be, but not excessive, not like some of the Councilors.

The ship with the star visitors came closer. The other star visitors, that was, for of course Professore Clavell was a star visitor himself, but he had been in Drantos for more than seven crossings of the Firestealer behind the True Sun. Lucia had grown up knowing there were visitors from the stars, but meeting Professore Clavell hadn't been the same as meeting someone just come.

The Signory wanted to know more about the star life, but Lucia didn't think they were learning much. Lucia had learned as much in the classroom as the Signory had learned by all their questioning. Professor Clavell did not keep secrets. He just didn't know that much. So who did know the secrets of what the Professore called "high tech"? Did the black man? Was that the secret of the stars, that only black men knew this high-tech magic? Or perhaps, perhaps . . .

The star lady Lorraine wore a wine-colored gown. She stood close to Senator Avanti, who stood next to his father Councilor Avanti. The star lady looked thin. Perhaps she had hidden charms. And perhaps she knew the high tech, but Lucia didn't think so. If she did, surely the Avanti family would send for someone who knew about foundries. Someone like Lucia, or more likely Catarina, who knew more about foundry operations than even their brother, nearly as much as Father. Someone who could understand. But the Avanti family had not done that . . .

The *navi* was steered alongside the floating dock that was tied to the Palazzo. Lucia knew about such things, because Fernando had told her. Fernando's father owned ships. He was a nice boy, and Lucia liked him, and sometimes she felt sorry for encouraging him when she had no intention of ever being more to him than a friend, but it was well to learn how to make boys do what she wanted. And useful! She'd learned all about ships and docks from Fernando. They'd even gone out into the lagoon on one of his father's ships, Lucia dressed like a boy, but all the sailors knew! That had been exciting. Even her father had smiled as he berated her for doing it. Fernando's father was a Senator, and he might someday become a Councilor. He was not a handsome boy, alas, and he giggled. But he was a useful friend, and Lucia was careful not to encourage him too much, but to keep him as a friend, even to let him hold her hand once. Once only.

Sailors used ropes to pull the ship tight against the padded fenders on the floating dock. A shout went up when they were done, and an ornate gangway was thrust out to the ship. People pushed in front of her, and Lucia couldn't see what happened next, but she knew. The Doge was making the new Star Lord Bart welcome.

That went on for a long time, then the Doge called Senators and Councilors forward. After each was presented he left the platform, so after a while Lucia could see. All three of the new star visitors were up on the platform with Professore Clavell and his companion. There was the black man. Lucia had never seen a black man before. And the Signorina Lorraine, thin, too thin, but she had strong muscled arms, lips very red, attractive wine-colored gown. Lucia envied her painted lips and red cheeks, and wondered if that too was a secret from the stars. The wind whipped up her gown to show her slender ankles from time to time.

Her father took her hand. "Come."

Lucia put on her best smile as her father led her up to the platform. The Doge was seated on his great throne. He nodded greetings to her father as Councilor Fontana presented them to the star lords.

"Signor Fabiano Michaeli, Master within the Metal Forgers Guild," Fontana said.

The star man Bart Saxon extended his hand, and her father shook it. And then, and then—!

"Signor Bart Saxon, may I present my daughter Lucia, who comes in place of her mother who is ill."

Lucia held out her hand, and the Lord Bart took it, and raised it to his lips and kissed it! Lucia's heart pounded.

"Welcome to our most serene city," Lucia said. *And now is the time for all my art*, she thought, but then she realized she was blushing, instead. *Such a handsome man! It was all she could do to contain herself.*

And then Lord Bart looked at her, and smiled.

*I never thought to love*, Lucia told herself. *I never thought to love.*

She was presented to the black star man, and the Signorina Lorraine, but she hardly noticed.

✦ ✦ ✦

Lance Clavell's feet hurt, but at least the ceremonies were finally coming to an end. *Maybe I'll get to sit down sometime today*, he thought and looked sourly at Jimmy Harrison.

Harrison nodded. No need to say anything. Clavell wrinkled his nose and wished for a cigarette. That wouldn't be happening. The nearest tobacco was a long way off . . .

The ceremonies continued. This was one hell of a lot bigger reception than they'd thrown for Clavell and Harrison. *We got presented to the Doge and some nobles in the Palace. They went the whole hog for this guy. That container, that has to be a big part of the reason. So what's in it? Weapons? Books? Both?*

*But at least we finally know what's going on*, Clavell thought.

Three of them. Before the ship arrived they'd been introduced to Lorraine Sandori. They'd been separated before they could say anything important, but they had managed to exchange a few words in English. Clavell wondered if that had been a mistake. The Signory now knew that the star visitors all shared a common language, one that locals had little hope of learning. That might be important. Nothing to be done about it, of course. *I'm not as clever as Harrison*, Clavell thought. *And neither one of us is a patch on the Skipper, but we're all we've got just now.*

*And it might not be important at all. It's easy to get paranoid around here. In this place, you don't suspect there's a plot, you know damned well there are a dozen of them! But you don't know what the plots are, or who can tell you.*

Bart Saxon. Looked like a professor. A real one, Clavell thought. And the way he and Lucia Michaeli looked at each other! Maybe nothing to that, but maybe there was, too. He didn't know Saxon, but Clavell thought the man had looked interested—and Lucia had looked at the star lord in a way Clavell had never seen her look at anyone else. As if she'd lost control of her emotions, and that would be a very strange thing for Lucia the apprentice courtesan to do. Hard to tell, hard to tell.

Of course Lucia was all dolled up. Not unusual for her and certainly to be expected for a big shindig like this. She looked pretty good, too. Young, but a lot of girls her age were already married here. They married young, and childbed fever had a lot to do with that. So many women died in childbirth—and so many kids died in infancy— that they had to start producing babies early.

*One more thing our hygiene lessons are helping with, thank God!* Lance Clavell was prouder of some things than others, and that was a big one. *Yeah, me and Semmelweis! You go, Lance!*

It was going to take a while for custom to catch up with the new reality, though, and young Lucia was definitely of marriable age here in Nikeis. And a lot of families would think it a step up to marry a daughter to a star man, for that matter. Maybe the Michaeli family would think it was better than having her be a courtesan. It would certainly help their foundry business if this Saxon guy knew anything about modern metalworking. Clavell wished *he* knew more about metalworking, but he might as well wish for gold or extra ammunition . . .

The crowds were thinning out now. The Doge got up from his throne and into a sedan chair. No wading across the Palazzo for him! He was carried across the Palazzo towards his palace, his bearers wading in ankle-deep saltwater. The tide was going out now. It was always high tide just after local noon and midnight. *Must be sun tide*, Clavell thought. *This place don't have much of a moon*. He could understand how the sun—or a moon if Tran had a large one—might pull the water up as it passed over. *But why is it high tide on the other side of the world from the sun or moon?* He was sure he'd been told how tides worked, but that was a long time ago and he couldn't remember much of it.

"If you please, Professore," Giamo said as Clavell and Harrison followed the nobles off the platform. "There will be more ceremonies in the Palace."

Harrison grimaced, and Clavell snorted.

"I could do with a little less ceremony," he said in English.

"Me too, man."

Clavell looked over his shoulder toward the unfamiliar voice. Harrison was beside him, but behind them was a Black man in wilderness survival clothes that could only have come from Earth. *Must be Cal Haskins*, Clavell thought, smiling back at him.

"The hospitality of the Serene Republic can get a bit heavy," he said.

"So you're part of the Galloway outfit?" Haskins asked.

"Yes. You know about Colonel Galloway?"

"I know Saxon says we're supposed to find him and help him grow some weed," Haskins said. "Sounded like weed to me, anyway."

"Super weed," Jimmy Harrison said. "But that's close enough. 'Cept the stuff's nasty, a lot nastier to grow than hemp. But yeah, that's one of the things the Skipper does, grows and harvests madweed." *No secret to that*, Clavell thought. *Everyone in Drantos knows it, so the Signory will know it too*.

"So they sent you here to help us?" Harrison continued.

"Something like that," Haskins said. "You reckon anyone here except us speaks English?"

"Pretty sure none of them do," Harrison said. "They tell you where you were going? Before they picked you up, that is." No need to explain who "they" were.

"No, I thought we were headed to Africa for the CIA," Haskins said. "You?"

"Nope. Heh, we were already *in* Africa for the CIA. 'Course we didn't have much choice," Harrison said. "Rather come here than face the Cubans."

"Cubans?" Haskins asked.

"Long story," Harrison said.

*Interesting*, Clavell thought. *He doesn't know how we got here. Maybe his partner does?*

They were well across the Palazzo and almost to the Palace now. They watched as the Doge was carried in, then the nobles followed him inside.

"You reckon we'll ever come out of there once we go in?" Harrison asked.

"What's all that?" Haskins asked. "Something going on I ought to know about?"

"There's always something going on in Nikeis," Clavell said. "And you ought to know all of it, but we can't tell you because we don't know much either. We didn't even know for sure you guys were on the planet until a couple of days ago. Now you say you're here to help the Skipper. Maybe they'll let us talk things over after all the bullshit's finished."

"That'd be nice," Harrison said. He took a deep breath. "Okay, in we go."

✣ ✣ ✣

The ceremonies in the Doge's Palace were finally over, and Bart Saxon was glad enough to leave the Doge's Palace and go to another palazzo, which he understood was where the Signory had put up Clavell and Harrison.

They crossed the city square, escorted by Councilor Torricelli. The tide had gone out during their time in the Palace, and the stones were wet and slippery. Shops were open all around the Palazzo and people sat sipping coffee or what passed for coffee here, more like tea if it was anything like what they'd given Saxon and Haskins during the receptions. Everyone watched as they went by, not even trying to hide where they were looking and some flat-out stared. Their destination was in the second layer of palaces beyond the shops of the square.

Once inside he looked around in curiosity. He decided that the great hall of Sergeant Lance Clavell's palazzo would usually be impressive, but it looked small after the Doge's Palace, which had proven to be huge and ornate inside and out. *Still, this place is large enough*, Saxon thought. *And now it's mine as well as Clavell's. Wonder if he resents that?* He regarded the lavish tapestries and hangings. The Signory were certainly treating them like honored guests. *Now if they'll just leave us alone to talk . . .*

It must have been clear what he was thinking, because Councilor Torricelli bowed and spoke in Italian too rapidly for Saxon to understand. Then he and his retainers departed, leaving the star men alone in the big hall. Men, Saxon thought. Spirit had been gay enough at the reception in the Doge's Palace, but she'd sent her regrets through Senator Avanti when they were invited to accompany Clavell and Harrison.

*Is she a hostage? Or is this a mutiny? Except it wouldn't be mutiny, she doesn't owe me any loyalty, and whatever relationship she has with Senator Avanti sure as hell isn't hostage and captor. Maybe she really is just tired out. It has been a damned long day. But I do wish I knew what was going on in her head. What does she want? Hell, what do I want?*

He looked at the ornate decorations in the big hall and nodded in satisfaction.

"Nice place," he told Lance Clavell. "Sure you don't mind sharing it?"

"I don't own it, and I'm the one that suggested you stay with us." Clavell shrugged. "Of course it was pretty clear Torricelli's people liked the idea. Keep us all together. Easier to guard us. He's got a detachment outside right now."

"Guard is fine," Harrison muttered.

Clavell nodded and lowered his voice.

"Easier to watch us, too. And make no mistake about it, Mr. Saxon, they do watch us. Every damn minute. They won't understand English, but they're good at reading body language. And just be sure, someone's watching us all the time. Including now."

He jerked his head towards the balcony railing above them where half a dozen servants waited for anyone to show a need.

"Why?" Haskins asked, and Harrison laughed.

"Because that's what they do, Cal. That's what they do. Welcome to the Serene Republic."

"Okay, they watch us. Fine by me," Haskins said. "But what's the rules here?"

"Damfino," Harrison said. "Me, I'm just real careful."

"Careful?" Haskins asked. "You mean like with the women?"

"Yeah," Harrison said. "Some of them look available and usually aren't, but some are safe."

"How can you tell?"

Harrison chuckled.

"Cal, they usually make it pretty clear. My rule is, if it's not really clear, then don't. Use common sense."

"Lot of them look real young."

"Well, they marry at ten or eleven here," Harrison said.

*"What?!"* Saxon stared at him, and Harrison burst out laughing.

"Sorry! Sorry, man! Couldn't resist." The merc shook his head and wiped his eyes. "Year's a different length here, remember?"

"Oh, yeah." Saxon shook his head and chuckled. "Got me," he admitted, and did some quick mental math. "So seventeen or eighteen?"

"Closer to sixteen, for a lot of 'em," Harrison said with a shrug.

Marry at sixteen, Saxon thought. Somehow that was disturbing. And did all the young girls look at men like the Michaeli girl had looked at him? She was a beauty. *And they marry at sixteen* . . .

". . . but it's pretty soft duty here, Cal," Harrison was saying. "Be glad you're over here and not having a tour in the madweed fields."

"Madweed. We're here to help you grow madweed," Haskins said. "Don't know much about that, but it's what they said we were here for. Not sure how we can help. One thing at a time, I guess."

"The further you stay from the madweed fields the happier you'll be," Harrison said.

"So what's next?" Clavell asked.

"That's up to Bart," Haskins said. He looked to Saxon. "He's in charge, far as I'm concerned."

Saxon shrugged.

"Still working on what we do down the road, but the next step's pretty clear," he said. "I've asked that they bring

the latest container here. To this house. Spirit says they'll
have it here by morning, it takes a big gang of stevedores
to unload it and bring it across the Palazzo, even on
rollers."

"Think that thing is safe where it is?" Harrison asked.
"Maybe I ought to go down and do some guard duty
around that ship tonight."

"No signs of tampering with either of the two
containers that were already here," Haskins said. "I don't
think they can get into them things without it showing.
Not sure you could stop them if they decided to just break
in . . ."

"No, I'm pretty good but I can't do a point defense
against the whole damn Serene militia," Harrison agreed.

"And standing guard there would certainly be a sign of
distrust," Saxon said. "If you were asking me, I'd say we
have to trust them."

"You mean don't stand guard," Clavell said.

"Yes, that's what I mean."

"Just making it clear," Harrison said. "Okay, what's
next?"

"When we get the container in here I'll show you stuff,
you tell me what we can do with it," Saxon said. "But
mostly we have to let Captain Galloway know we're here."

"That may be hard to do," Harrison said. "The Signory
are nice, polite, generous, but they sure as hell haven't
been letting us send messages. Or leave here. And I'm
guessing that once they see what all's in them boxes of
yours they'll be even less likely to let us go wandering off."

"Colonel Galloway will come get us," Clavell said.

*He sounds damned positive about that*, Saxon thought.

"How?" he asked.

"I don't know," Clavell said. "But he will. The Skipper's pretty smart. He'll hear what's going on. The story about the containers must be spreading all across the planet by now. If he ain't heard it yet, he will. Soon."

"You know, I reckon that's right," Harrison said. "I don't know if Galloway gives a rat's ass about us, but he's for damned sure going to want to know about all that stuff once he hears about it, and you say a lot of people over on the mainland got a look at those containers. He'll find out about them. The Colonel won't know what's in them boxes, but he'll sure as shit figure there's a lot. So yeah, he'll be showing up."

The private sat back for a moment, looking thoughtful as he considered the possibilities.

"So what *is* in those boxes?" he asked then. "Guns and ammo? Sergeant Clavell's student kids told us you say that's not what's in there. Not sure how they know that, but it's what they say. So what *is* in there?"

Saxon went to the side table and poured himself a glass of claret. Everyone drank wine here. It would be easy to get drunk and stay that way. The interesting thing was that the one night he'd had too much of the stuff, it wasn't much fun. *I'd rather have water. Maybe I'm growing up?* That took thinking about, and he hadn't really had time to think on it. The sense of having a mission, of a reason for living, was still growing in him, eating through the stagnation of his year in the Tenderloin. Life was interesting again. Humans, in need of education. In need of Bart Saxon. A scary thought, but nowhere near as scary as living in the Tenderloin for the rest of his life. And nobody on this planet knew about registered sex offenders.

"Whatever they know they got from Miss Spirit, not me," Haskins was saying. The others looked at Saxon, and he nodded in agreement.

"Not from me, either. Had to be Lorraine. Not sure how much they understand of what she told them."

"A lot. My students were asking me about microscopes so I figure there's one of those. So what else did you bring?" Clavell asked impatiently.

"Books and information, mostly. A whole library of books, books about everything. Physics, electronics, biology, you name it. As to equipment, laptop computers, windmill power generator. Bicycle power generator, too. Some radios. Some tools. Scientific instruments. Not much in the way of guns and ammo."

"What's a laptop computer?"

"Just what it sounds like, a personal computer you can carry around with you," Saxon said. "That whole field has advanced a lot since you left Earth."

"I can see that," Clavell said.

"Radios," Harrison said. "The skipper will be damned interested in radios."

"Only handheld units," Haskins said. "Not more'n a few miles' range."

"A few miles is one hell of a lot better than *no miles*," Harrison said with a chuckle.

"Encyclopedia?" Clavell asked, ignoring the byplay.

"Three, including *Britannica*," Saxon said with a nod.

"Industrial Revolution on the half shell," Clavell said, and Saxon laughed.

"Yeah, I suppose it is, once I teach them how to read English."

"Only, from what I hear, the Shalnuksis don't cotton to that idea," Harrison said. "They bomb the shit out of anyplace on the planet that looks like it's developing technology. That's what the skipper used to say. Maybe we better think hard about what you do with that stuff."

"What's that? You say we're not supposed to teach these people?" Haskins frowned. "But that's what the inspector told us they wanted us to do!"

"And Colonel Galloway tells us to be careful what we teach," Harrison said. "We was sent out here to teach and preach about public health, but we're supposed to be careful about technology. Here you bring the whole Industrial Revolution in one package."

"I don't know what to think," Saxon said. "I mean, they sent us with a bunch of useless stuff if they *don't* want me teaching them. But on the other hand, Cal"—he looked at his friend—"he *did* say helping Galloway's the main job. Might not be a bad idea to get his take on all this before we go around starting any scientific revolutions?"

"Hey, like I said, you're the boss, man!" Haskins said with a laugh. "You wanna throw on the brakes, though, you better be telling that Spirit lady. If it ain't already too late. She's telling everyone what a new day this is going to be. Started already, that's for sure."

"We agreed not to open the containers unless we were all present," Saxon said. "And I have the keys."

"And she's got number two in her living room," Haskins said. "And she's anxious to open it."

"Okay, so we all get together and open them up to see

what's inside. Admire the contents," Clavell said. "And then what?"

Saxon shrugged.

"I was recruited to come here and teach science to smart but uneducated kids," he said. "That's what I volunteered to do, anyway. It turns out that the real mission is to help Galloway grow crops for export, but teaching science is what I know how to do, and like I said, if they didn't mean for me to do that, why send all this equipment?"

"Not sure that's what the Skipper'll want you to do," Clavell said, "but what the hell. If you want to teach, you came to the right place. The Serene Republic, that is. There's plenty of students, they all want to know stuff, and nobody's against learning. Not like some places. One town on the mainland, we had to shoot our way out. Turns out the local priest was sure we were sending everyone to hell by teaching hygiene. Disease is God's Will, and it's a mortal sin to prevent it. None of that bullshit here, at least I haven't seen any. Sure none in my classes. Everyone wants to learn."

"Maybe not a fair sample," Harrison muttered.

"Well, no," Clavell said. "But it's who the Signory picked."

"Who are your students?" Saxon asked. He frowned as Haskins poured himself a third glass of wine. Probably no harm in it, but . . . "Who did they send?"

"Mostly younger nobility," Clavell said. "Some upper middle class. Mostly boys, four girls. Everyone here is used to being in school. They all have to take military training, for one thing, and the upper-class kids have schools for that. All the boys. But there's girl schools, too.

That's mostly housekeeping and cooking and home economics, some music, but there's girls in the merchant business too. You met one of the girls in my class when you landed."

"Ah. I remember. Lucia. She's easy to remember."

"Yep. Pretty thing. She wants to be a courtesan."

Saxon frowned, and Clavell laughed.

"Apparently it's not all that frowned on as a profession for middle-class girls here."

"She seemed a bit young."

"I told you, they marry at about sixteen here, and she's actually a little older'n that, I think." Clavell grimaced, recalling his earlier thoughts in the Palazzo. "I think some of that's because their medicine's so primitive. Lose a lot of mothers to childbirth fever. That's getting better since the Colonel started introducing the idea that germs are behind infections. It's going to take a while for the social patterns to change, though, even if the Nikeisians start applying the lessons big-time."

"That young?"

Saxon frowned. Despite the incident with Sherry Northing, he'd never been remotely tempted to fool around with any of his students before disaster struck. He hadn't been blind to how attractive some of them had been, but they'd never attracted *him*. Not until Sherry, and he'd been drunk that night. Drunk and angry and *stupid*. Not only that, he'd genuinely thought she was at least nineteen. Or at least, that was what he'd been telling himself. But that Lucia . . .

*God, maybe I did have a thing for younger girls all along and never realized it! Am I a "dirty old man"?* The thought was more than a little disturbing, especially after all this time. *But I am not going to screw up that way again. It's just—*

"Younger'n that, a lot of them." Clavell's reply to his question pulled him out of his thoughts, for which he was grateful. Or he thought he was, anyway.

"So your students haven't been what you might call a sample of the general population," he said, getting himself safely back to the original thread. "Don't know how I feel about that."

"Way it is." Clavell shrugged. "Oh, not back at the Colonel's University, but here in Nikeis—and just about everywhere else on the planet, for that matter—them as has gets, and them as don't have don't. Can't say I'm crazy about it, either, but things are gonna have to change a lot before we get to what you might call equal opportunity on Tran."

Saxon was about to comment on that when one of the servants rushed in.

"Councilor Torricelli," the servant announced. "His Honor says the matter is urgent and begs immediate audience."

"His daughter is in my class, too," Clavell said. "Okay, Bart, I think we need to meet with the Councilor. You agree?"

*Now what? And just who's in charge? And of whom?* Saxon looked to Clavell and shrugged.

"Bring him in," Clavell said.

Torricelli was red-faced. He spoke rapidly in the mainland trade language, stopping to repeat himself often when Saxon looked confused.

"We have messages from our scouts in the north," he said. "My pardon, Signori. I wish you greetings and good health—"

"Consider the formalities served," Clavell said. "You have urgent news, Councilor?"

"Indeed," Torricelli said, and launched back into his voluble explanation. He spoke far too rapidly for Saxon to follow, but Clavell nodded. Then he turned to Saxon and Haskins.

"He says this comes from a scout patrol ship from up north," he said in English. "There are pirates there and they've joined up with the naval forces of the Five Kingdoms. A fleet is assembling. A large fleet, of pirates and Five Kingdoms ships, acting together. And because of the alliance with Drantos, the Serene Republic is at war with the Five Kingdoms."

Saxon frowned.

"Fivers and pirates," Harrison said. "That can't be good. Ganton's at war with the Five, and Nikeis is an ally of Ganton. Not so close an ally as they used to be, but I bet it gets a lot closer now that the Signori need us."

Torricelli's distress was obvious. He spoke rapidly in Italian, slowing down when Clavell protested. Saxon couldn't understand three consecutive words, but after a while Clavell nodded.

"The Five Kingdoms, a pirate group, and the Grand Duchy of Riccigiona," Clavell translated.

"What the hell is that?" Harrison demanded. "I never heard of it."

"I have, just barely," Clavell said. "Small northern outfit. Trees, mountains, seaport, neutral outfit so they tell me. Used to be neutral, anyway. Councilor Torricelli says they have ships and a trained army. Now they're all in one big alliance, and they're merging their fleets."

Torricelli spoke rapidly again. Clavell nodded.

"There's only one goal such an alliance would seek," he translated.

"And we're it?" Saxon asked, and Clavell nodded yet again, his expression unhappy.

"Looks that way." He listened as Torricelli spoke again, this time not as rapidly. "Five hundred ships. Possibly more," Clavell said.

"That's not good."

"It gets worse," Clavell said. "It gets a lot worse."

"What do you mean?" Saxon demanded.

"I mean that they're scared," Clavell said. "The Signori are scared. Their harbor defenses aren't so good now, what with the water level rising. Once an enemy gets in the lagoon there's not much to stop them from coming right to the main island. I hope you brought some ammo, Bart, because it looks like we're going to need it."

# ⊹⇒ CHAPTER SIX ⇐⊹
## TARANTO

Rick was tired and ached all over. *Just one more day in the saddle*, he thought to himself. His neck and shoulder were acting up as was the pain in his stomach. At least the hemorrhoids were a hell of a lot better, though. *God bless Major Baker, and God bless Preparation H!*

While he was being thankful for things, he was also thankful for proper roads, and this one was up to Roman standards. To save time, they'd bypassed most of the road from the fords of the Ottarn to Armagh and only yesterday regained the road from Armagh to Taranto. The ride was smoother now and so he felt fewer jolts as his horse moved at a walk down the road.

He was listening to a conversation between Warner and Martins to keep his mind off the ride. He could hear an edge of irritation in Warner's voice after answering Martins' latest round of questions about Tran, and he chuckled to himself. Martins reminded Rick of a younger

Warner, the one abducted by a flying saucer from a hilltop in southern Africa over fourteen years ago.

"So why were they sending you guys back home?" Warner asked in a bid to change the subject and head off further interrogation.

"Defense budget cuts," Martins answered. "After the Cold War was over, Parliament was looking about for spots to save money, and they hit on us. A 'peace dividend,' they called it."

"The Cold War is *over*?"

Rick turned around in his saddle. Martins looked very self-conscious with just about every merc staring at him.

"Ah, yes," he said, "the Soviet Union collapsed. After the whole Star Wars thing they just couldn't keep up. The whole Communist empire collapsed in on itself."

"How did a movie cause the Russians to give up?" Warner demanded.

"It wasn't the movie." Martins sounded a bit defensive. "That was the nickname the press used to ridicule a space-based missile defense system proposed by the American President, Ronald Reagan, as infeasible. They used the movie title because they thought the missile defense idea was a joke. Turns out it worked. The Russians went bankrupt trying to keep up."

"Wasn't Ronald Reagan a movie actor?" Mason asked.

"He was also the Governor of California," Rick interrupted. "I guess he got promoted." He looked back at Martins. "So there was no nuclear exchange? No World War Three? No fight in Europe?"

"There were some proxy fights in Central America, Afghanistan, Africa, places like that," Martins answered, then blushed. "Ah, I suppose you chaps would know a bit more about that than I would, at least in the early days." Rick nodded gravely, fighting an urge to smile, and the young Brit went on hastily. "But there was no direct combat between NATO and the Warsaw Pact. There *was* a war after the Cold War came to an end, when Iraq invaded Kuwait and your President Bush and our Prime Minister Thatcher put together a coalition to turn Iraq back out again. Wasn't much of a fight, though. It simply proved the dominance of the West with their smart bombs and laser sights." He shrugged. "As I said, the Soviets just couldn't keep up and the whole Soviet Union went tits up. The West won the Cold War."

"Well hot damn!" Rick exclaimed. "Freedom reigns on good old Earth."

"Hate to interrupt." Baker secured his radio as he rode up. "Scouts report a detachment of Roman cavalry approaching from the other direction."

A little while later the detachment came around a bend, escorted by Tamaerthan mounted archers.

"Second Praetorians," Warner said. "Publius."

The Roman troops were led by an ornately armored tribune, clearly a young man of wealth.

"Hail, Lord Rick, Friend of Caesar and Patrician of Rome!" he shouted. "I am commanded to lead you to the villa we have reserved for your use!"

"Can't fault that for a reception," Major Baker said.

"Publius Caesar begs haste," the tribune added. "There are messages of grave concern."

"Publius Caesar is here?"

"He is, Friend of Caesar. He awaits you."

*Son-of-a-bitch*, Rick thought. *He's taking this pretty seriously. I suppose I shouldn't be surprised.*

"Perhaps you should ride ahead, Colonel?" Baker suggested. "We'll get the troops to quarters."

Rick thought about that for a moment, then nodded.

"Sounds good," he said. "Major Mason will be in command."

Baker saluted. "Of course."

*He sounds cheerful enough*, Rick thought. *And I have every reason to trust him. So why do I worry? But goddammit I worry about everything. If he stops obeying me, I have no way to command his troops. And he could leave any time he feels like it. I hate this.*

"Warner, Bisso, come with me. Haerther, bring my guards. Let's ride." *Twenty damned miles. Thank God for Preparation H!*

⁜ ⁜ ⁜

It was late afternoon by the time they reached their destination.

The walled city of Taranto lay at the head of a bay in the western border territories of the Empire. The harbor with its outlying protection island reminded Rick vaguely of the city of La Paz in Baja California. Taranto was a minor port on the southwestern section of the great bay the Romans called the Inner Sea. The Inner Sea separated the Roman Empire from Drantos and the Five Kingdoms, and Taranto was geographically more a part of Drantos than Rome. Two generations ago Taranto had owed allegiance to Drantos, but during the civil wars the city had looked to Rome for protection and now had been Roman long enough that few cared to dispute Roman ownership.

*And*, Rick thought sourly, *that's* another *border dispute I'll have to settle before it festers*.

The main part of the city stood on a bluff above the waters. The lower city with its dock areas would be drowned as the seas rose in the coming years, but the walled part would stay above the new sea level. When the seas inundated the swamps to the south, Taranto would be separated from Rome by water.

Rick thought about that. Taranto might easily become an important commercial port when the great bay was connected directly to the southern territories. Drantos had never been a maritime power, with no ports or maritime commerce on the Inner Sea, and but little on the southern shore. That would change in the next few years, however. Which meant Taranto might become important and that ownership of the port could easily be a matter of dispute once again. It would be more important to Drantos than to Rome, at least initially, but that too would change. Most of Rome's naval activities operated out of the eastern coast of the Empire, but the new passageway south would make many eastern Roman ports obsolete. So would the rising water levels. Rome would need ports to her west—but on the west coast, not across the new straits. Drantos needed Taranto. Rome didn't, or at least not as badly. Perhaps transfer might be negotiated now, while everyone was friendly and the city's importance was less obvious? One more item to keep in mind.

*And why is it* my *job to think of all this stuff?* he wondered, but there was no one to answer that question.

✣ ✣ ✣

The large villa stood on a steep hill, two hundred feet above the sea which lay half a mile to the east. A stone wall, twenty feet high, ran along the western boundary of the ten-acre property, and the villa itself had an interior garden with fountain and pool surrounded on three sides by a colonnaded porch. The open side of the garden area gave a magnificent view of the harbor and the sea beyond.

The harbor was natural, but it had been improved with sea walls and a breakwater surrounding an inner anchorage, and Rick counted nine ships tied up to docks. Others were anchored offshore. Rick counted again, a total of thirty-nine ships including fishing boats. One of the ships was significantly larger than the others. Three-masted and long and sleekly built, it flew Roman banners, and Rick nodded.

*Flagship,* he thought. *Publius said something about a quinquireme, but that doesn't look like a classical galley to me. More like something from the Battle of Lepanto. Ram's higher up, for one thing. They probably settle things mostly by deck fighting by marines, not in classic ancient-world naval warfare like Salamis. They ram to board, not to stave in the other ship.*

Rick studied the ships in the harbor. The sleek ones were warships. The others—Rick counted seven ships that didn't look like the others. Taller, more rounded, wider and fatter. Bigger for the most part, too, but they seemed to have only a single oardeck each.

*Must be merchant vessels, hold more cargo but slower. What they called "cogs" back home? Of course I'm guessing. Wish I'd read more about medieval naval warfare. The only naval battle I know anything about is*

*Lepanto, and that was gunpowder era. Well,* early *gunpowder, with cannon on galleases, but there was a hell of a lot of hand-to-hand combat on the decks of the galleys. What I don't know could get us all killed . . .*

*And damn all, I am so* sick *of that! It's somebody else's turn to be in charge. Only there isn't anyone.* He felt the mild burning sensation in his stomach that was becoming a constant companion. *Am I getting an ulcer?* Ulcer would explain the pain in his stomach, but what was causing the sharp pains in his left shoulder and neck? *Fatigue? Something a lot worse than an ulcer?* No way to know . . .

Rick sent Warner on an inspection tour while he found the bathroom, and was impressed by its tiled elegance. There was running water, a continuous stream from a tile pipe. It flowed through a waist-high basin, then drained into an attractively designed commode to disappear through the outer wall. The room smelled of soap and oils.

"There is a bath in this villa, Patrician," a male voice said behind him. "Permit me to name myself. I am Appodocius, your body servant for as long as you remain in the Villa San Angelus. My master, Publius, Heir of Caesar, has placed me at your disposal. I am a skilled body servant."

*Wonder what that means,* Rick thought. *Masseur? Catamite?*

"Fires for the bath were lit this morning, so the caldarium and tepidarium will both be ready whenever you desire," Appodocius said.

"Thank you." *A hot bath. Luxury.* Rick turned to look at the newcomer. Appodocius was about thirty. A scar ran from behind his left jaw to disappear into his tunic, and he walked with a limp, but he seemed cheerful enough. Well-muscled, had the bearing of a soldier. *Slave and body servant*, Rick thought. *Publius must have good reason to trust him. Well, when in Rome—*

"Publius, Heir of Caesar, is coming to this villa," Appodocius said. "He will join you as soon as you have rested from your journey. There is important news."

*Important it may be*, Rick thought, *but it's bloody well going to wait an hour while I get cleaned up and use that hot bath!*

⁘ ⁘ ⁘

Rick relaxed in the tepidarium and dreaded leaving it. The shoulder pains were gone, and his stomach felt better than it had for weeks. *Good daydreams, too*, he thought. *Tylara. The kids. Not the nightmares I've had the last year. Get this mess done with and get back to her. Live like a human again. Delegate more. Play with my kids. It's what we all want.*

The reverie was interrupted by a voice from the dressing room.

"Beg pardon, Skipper, but Publius is here."

But first there were more fires to piss on. Rick sat up from the warm water.

"All right, Mr. Warner, I'll get dressed. Is everything satisfactory?"

"And then some, Colonel. House big enough for all the officers, another building big enough to be a barracks and probably has been one, and that big level field outside for a camp. Storerooms with wheat and barley and one room full of potatoes. Small herd of pigs, and some goats. We'll be fine here."

"Nice to be appreciated. You say Publius is here?"

"Yes, Sir, he's in the big hall. Big smile, but something's got him spooked if I'm any judge."

✦ ✦ ✦

Publius Caesar wore armor, a muscled breastplate trimmed with polished bronze, too ornate for the field but it would serve at need, and it was subdued compared to what he wore on state occasions.

"Hail, Friend," Publius said formally. He gestured for the attendants to pour wine.

Rick and Larry Warner raised their hands in salute. Roman etiquette strictly forbade bowing between equals and all free men were in theory equal. Unlike the practices of Drantos and the Five Kingdoms, Roman nobles were supposed to be honored for their abilities, not their birth. Rick had shocked everyone the first time he forgot that. Not a drastic mistake, Rick thought. But an error all the same.

Publius Caesar selected two goblets of wine, drank perfunctorily from one, and passed it to Rick.

"Hail, Friend Publius," Rick said with a nod of thanks as he took it. "You will recall my aide Chief Warrant Officer Larry Warner. Friend Publius, I hadn't expected you to come here yourself."

"Nor had I, but the news is disturbing. You must know at once, and I would be thankful for your thoughts on what this means. I have summoned Tribune Caius Julius to tell you what his *frumentarii* have discovered." He indicated a younger officer in armor who stood respectfully in the doorway, his helmet under his left arm, and Rick nodded acknowledgement. Sheathed sword, not

bound with ribbons. A trusted officer. Most of Publius'
officers were trusted. And two commendation armbands.
A *competent* trusted officer.

"I'm glad to hear any news," Rick said. "First I have
news of my own. We have new star forces. Three score,
with star weapons."

Publius frowned.

"I had heard you had acquired new star forces, but not
so many as that."

*Actually*, Rick thought, *the rumors they told me you
were listening to were that I had hundreds of new
riflemen, which accounted for the big victory over
Morrone, whose forces were now rumored to have been a
thousand and more. Hard to know what Publius really
thinks. But he's beginning to digest the fact that I have
new forces. This has never been an alliance of equals, even
if the Romans are developing tactics for dealing with
pikes, and almost certainly are working on both cannon
and muskets.*

It would be a far less equal alliance now. The sixty
Gurkhas were a significant addition to Rick's force and a
great change in the balance of power—as Ganton had
witnessed. Publius didn't seem overly concerned about
the news. *Good actor, or is he beginning to trust me? Or—*

"We will have need of all those and more, Friend of
Caesar," Publius said. "Begin, Caius Julius."

Rick guessed the tribune's age at about thirty. Like
Publius he wore a muscled breastplate with mail short
sleeves. There were gold decorations, and gold at the
armor's rim, making the intelligence officer gaudier than
Publius. Intelligence advisor to the Son of Caesar would

be a position of some power, so the tribune was very likely from a good family. *I wonder how he was chosen as an intelligence coordinator, and why he's trustworthy? I don't really know a lot about Roman organization policies. I do know their intelligence service is pretty damned good. Except when it comes to Gurkhas . . .*

"Hail, Friend of Caesar," the tribune began. "I have nothing from Nikeis itself, but much from the land they call Terra Firma."

"Nothing from Nikeis itself?"

"We have had no messages from the islands since the Signory closed their borders and expelled our agents. Messages have been sent, but none have been acknowledged, nor have we observed anyone from the island carrying messages to Wanax Ganton."

"And I've received no word from Clavell and Harrison, my agents in Nikeis," Rick said. "No word from them at all, despite repeated messages to the Doge." *Of course you know all that, but I may as well get it on the record.*

Publius nodded gravely.

"Tell us, then, Tribune, what your men have observed," he said.

Rick listened with growing alarm as the tribune described what the Roman spies had learned of the events on the mainland opposite Nikeis. There had been lights in the sky, almost certainly a starship landing. Shortly after those, a wagon train from a nearby forest had come to the port city. It bore three armed star visitors, one a Black man, one a woman. The starship had also left three large boxes of high-quality steel. It had taken eighteen oxen to draw a specially constructed wagon holding one of the boxes along a well-paved road. The Roman accurately described shipping containers.

"These boxes—" the tribune continued.

"We would call them 'containers,'" Rick said. He used the English word for lack of anything better.

"Containers." The tribune repeated the word and nodded. "These *containers* were taken into the port city of Pavino, and from there each was carried, separately, across the straits to Nikeis, each time by the same ship, which is one of their *navibus onerārius*, with decks strengthened and altered to hold the weight of the— container. The first voyage was accompanied by the black man and the star woman. When the black man returned to join his companion, who appears to be the leader of the group, the woman did not accompany him. The black man accompanied the second container to the islands and again returned. Four days ago the last container departed from Pavino accompanied by the two star men and all their gear. They have left nothing on the mainland. We are certain that the destination in each case was Nikeis."

"So Pavino is four days to the north."

"One day at the gallop plus two days by messenger galley," the tribune said. "Our maps show the total distance to be one hundred and seventy Roman miles. Heir of Caesar, our galley was followed by a ship we presume to be of Nikeis, but there was no confrontation. There was an attempt by pirates from the marshes to our north. Four of their vessels attempted to close with us, but we were faster than they."

Publius nodded.

"Recommend a suitable reward for the captain and

crew," he said. "So. In summary there are three large containers and three new star lords, all lodged in the island city of Nikeis."

"We presume so, Heir of Caesar."

"But you know nothing of the content of those containers."

"Heir of Caesar, we do not."

"You were pursued by a Nikeisian ship?" Rick asked.

"Perhaps escorted would be a better word than pursued. By a galley that had all the appearance of a Nikeisian patrol warship," the tribune said. "I saw no flag and we did not investigate. We presumed the information we had was of more importance."

"*Much* more importance, Tribune Caius Julius," Rick agreed with a laugh.

"What did the Nikeisian ship do when the pirates attempted to intercept you?" Publius asked.

"It stood off at a distance and observed. When we pulled away from the pirates the Nikeisian ship followed until dark. We saw nothing of it or the pirates the next morning."

"Might they have rendered aid?" Publius asked. "We are nominally allies of Nikeis."

"I do not know, Heir of Caesar," the tribune said. "They did not run away."

"Who would have won?" Rick asked.

"With the aid of the Nikeisian ship we should have won, but battles are never certain."

Rick nodded.

"Sounds like the Nikeisian captain made a wise decision. Now, what have the Nikeisian representatives told us?"

"Nothing. Neither the local factor nor any of their officials admit any knowledge of these events. I suspect they have not been told. The Serene Republic is often secretive, even to its own officers."

"And there are no messages from my men in Nikeis?"

"None. I have asked," Publius said.

"I'll need to see the local Nikeisian factors," Rick said.

"Certainly, but nothing will come of it," Publius said. "We have watched them closely, and they have received no messages of any kind for weeks."

"No ship has come here from Nikeis?"

Publius looked to the tribune.

"Fishing vessels, Heir of Caesar. Merchantmen. But we saw no written messages, and none of the fisherfolk spoke at any length with the local Nikeisian factor. Truly, all act as if nothing whatever has happened."

"Then I suppose we have to get their attention," Rick said. "Nikeis has much to explain to her allies."

"I think as you do," Publius agreed with a thin smile. "Unfortunately, there is more."

Rick frowned.

"Continue, Tribune, if you please."

"All I have told you is known to the Ganvin pirate nation," the tribune said. He shrugged. "That is what they call themselves now. A nation they are not, but there are many pirates in that alliance. The Ganvin band is the largest, and the others have joined with them in hopes of great gain. They have also joined with the Five Kingdoms, no great naval power, but they do have ships, and trained soldiers. Then there is the matter of the so-called Grand Duchy of Riccigiona."

"I've heard that name, but I know little of it," Rick said.

"Until recently there was little worth knowing," Caius Julius replied. "They are a city-state of traders, tributary to the Five Kingdoms. They have long been trade rivals of Nikeis, but mostly they have been neutrals, keeping peace in the northern reaches of the Inner Sea."

"Keeping peace," Rick said. "Tribune, do you mean literally?"

Caius Julius nodded.

"Their forces are never large, perhaps two score of galleys at most and never more than fifteen hundred soldiers, mostly naval warriors. But they have a good reputation in battle. Pirates prefer to attack Nikeisian or even Roman ships before trying to take a ship with a Riccigionan escort. And now they have joined in alliance with the pirates and the Five Kingdoms.

"The Ganvin band is even now assembling a fleet of more than a hundred galleys, and they have raided towns in the north for slaves, doubtless to be rowers on their ships. This alliance sprang to existence not long after the containers appeared in Pavino. It is not difficult to deduce the goals and destination."

*I don't like the timing,* Rick thought to himself. *This alliance of rivals came together pretty quickly with no warning.*

"You believe they intend to attack Nikeis?" he asked.

"It seems likely." The intelligence officer shrugged. "They know of the containers. That knowledge spread like wildfire among the pirates. No one knows what is *in* them, however. There are rumors of star weapons, but no one actually knows. Yet it is obvious that the containers have great value, and the pirates have cleverly tempted Nikeis in the hopes of provoking them to use those weapons. So far they have not done so. There has been no Skyfire and no Great Guns, no firearms of any kind, have been fired. This has emboldened the pirates and their allies.

"Nikeis has few defenders at this time. We have concluded that the pirates intend to attack Nikeis and take what they can before Nikeis can recall their fleets and hire soldiers."

"The pirates aren't afraid of star weapons?"

"Evidently not," the tribune said. "They know that the containers are defended by only three star lords, one a lady—an armed lady, but a woman none the less." Tribune Caius Julius shrugged. "Three with star weapons are still only three, and can be overwhelmed by numbers. We cannot know the pirates' thoughts, but that is my deduction. They seek to strike quickly and take what they can."

"Clavell and Harrison have battle rifles. The pirates don't know about them?" Rick asked.

"If so I have not learned of it," the tribune said. "Understand, Friend of Caesar, we only know that your agents were alive and well when Nikeis closed the city and expelled the Roman officials under the pretext of a disease outbreak. We do not know if the star lords Clavell and Harrison are free or if they have control of their star weapons. If they do, perhaps the pirates face five star weapons, not three. That is still a very small force with which to face a hundred galleys. Even pirate galleys, and with the addition of the Five Kingdoms and Riccigiona the pirate alliance gains both many more ships and skilled captains."

"How much time do we have?" Rick asked.

The tribune spread his hands. "I would say not long at all."

"So." Publius stood. "I have sent word to Rome, and sent messengers to all Roman ship commanders, summoning them to the defense of Nikeis, but I do not think any will arrive in time to be of use. We cannot fight a hundred galleys with the forces in this city. Can you?"

"A hundred galleys? Possibly. Warner?"

"It could be close, but we've got the Gurkhas."

"Precisely," Rick said. "What will Nikeis do?"

Publius shrugged.

"We only recently learned of the Ganvin coalition," he said. "I doubt the Signory learned much earlier than my *frumentarii*. Nikeis has never maintained large fleets and armies in home waters, and the major part of their fleet is in the far south or on the eastern coast of Rome. They have always depended on divisions among their enemies, and on hiring mercenaries to defend them at need, and that has served them well enough. Until recently the pirates were divided into bands with nothing in common save greed and enmity against the Five Kingdoms. Now that the Five Kingdoms have joined with the pirates and the Grand Duchy the situation is very different. Given time Nikeis could assemble enough force to withstand a hundred warships and more, but if the pirate bands bring a full hundred galleys quickly I would not think Nikeis able to resist." He shrugged again. "Such a force could not hold Nikeis indefinitely, but I think the city might well be sacked. Of course, I am no expert in war at sea."

*Neither am I*, Rick thought. He started to say that, and thought better of it.

"How did this team of rivals become an alliance so quickly?"

"Wild stories about what is in those iron boxes abound. It would appear greed has provided a sufficient common interest."

*The timing still seems wrong*, Rick thought to himself. *This seems to have come together too quickly.*

"Do we know how large a fleet Nikeis can assemble?" Rick asked.

"No more than a score of warships of any size whatever," Tribune Caius Julius said. "They boast the ability to build ships in a day. Whether that is true or not I do not know, but I have never seen it done, and I doubt the ability of new crew aboard a new ship." The tribune shrugged. "I have no new information, but my conclusion is that we have more ships than Nikeis at this moment."

✛ ✛ ✛

The dining room table in Rick's villa was too low, and despite two woolen cushions the chair was too hard, but it was more comfortable than the benches his officers had to make do with.

Rick explained the situation to those officers after dinner.

"The upshot is that we have to get their attention in Nikeis, but the main priority is to keep these damned pirates from sacking the place. Please, somebody tell me he knows about galley warfare!"

No one spoke.

"I was afraid of that. Well, I don't either. And we have to learn fast."

"The Romans will know something," Warner said. "They've got warships down there in the harbor. Ask them."

"And let them know how little we know," Major Baker said. "Perhaps not our best plan."

"They'll know we're lubbers anyway, Sir," Lieutenant Martins said. "Sailors always do."

"Leftenant Martins has some yachting experience," Major Baker said. "He's the closest thing to a sailor we have, I'm afraid."

"They'll find out soon enough," Rick agreed. "But let's start with what we do know before we let on to our Roman friends just what lubbers we are. How are we going to defeat a hundred galleys?"

"Logistics," Warner said. "The trick to galley warfare is feeding the rowers. They eat a lot, and you have to carry it with you. Water, too, you can't carry more than a few days' water. A hundred men, maybe a hundred fifty with marines, a gallon a day bare minimum, leave out the weight of the jars and it's still a lot of water to carry. They can't keep that fleet together very long."

"A hundred men at a gallon a day. Eight hundred pounds a day," Major Baker said. "Do we know the cargo capacity of a galley? I wouldn't suppose eight hundred pounds is all that much."

Warner looked at him with an irritated frown.

"But Mr. Warner isn't that far off," Lieutenant Martins said. "I don't claim to be an expert on galley warfare, but I know galleys have a shallow draft with a low freeboard. They're essentially oversized rowboats which—"

"Excuse me, Lieutenant," Art Mason said, "but that doesn't sound like the galleys down there in the harbor. That quinquireme of the Romans, it looks a lot bigger than that."

Martins paused, looking chagrined, and Rick saw Warner smile. The warrant officer started to speak, but Rick intervened quickly.

"The lieutenant was describing classical galleys," he said. "Like the ones Athens used. But you're right, Art. Tran galleys are bigger and heavier than that." He looked at Martins. "I know it was already getting dark by the time you got here, Lieutenant. I recommend that tomorrow morning you take a look at the ships in the harbor. What the Romans call a quinquireme is what Nikeis calls a great galley, I think, and I'm not sure how they classify these things. 'Quinquireme' suggests something with five oardecks to me, but far as I could tell through my binoculars, the one in the harbor here only has three. So left to my own devices, I'd call it a trireme . . . which the Romans don't. So there's something else going on here, and I don't have a clue what. I do remember that Polybius and Pliny wrote a lot about different sizes of galley and used numbers to differentiate. There were fives and sixes—all the way up to *nines* in at least one account I read—but there's no damned way someone stuck nine banks of oars onto a galley! So I think we'd better figure it out. I'd like to do that a bit discreetly though—as in without admitting to the world that we don't have a clue about how it works."

"Of course, Colonel," Martins said just a little stiffly. "I'm afraid I know very little of the history from that period."

"Don't feel too bad, because there hasn't been a day here on Tran when I didn't wish I knew more about *some* period of history! If I recall correctly, the classic Venetian galley was basically the ultimate refinement of what you're describing, and it eventually evolved into something called a 'galleas' that was supposed to be more seaworthy and big enough to carry guns. Tran doesn't have guns—well, didn't until we arrived—but I expect some of the same considerations might have played into evolving a heavier design. Not as heavy as the galleases the Venetians took to Lepanto, though. If I remember, they were heavy enough they had to be towed by a couple of regular galleys if the wind dropped, and these don't."

"I think you're probably right about that, Skipper," Warner said. "On the other hand, I expect a lot of the pirate galleys we're talking about would be almost exactly like the ones Lieutenant Martins is describing." He shrugged. "They're going to be interested in raiding and plundering, not supporting a mercantile empire. For that, you need speed and maneuverability more than you need brute fighting power."

"Good point, Mr. Warner. A very good point," Rick agreed with a smile, and nodded to Martins. "Continue, please, Lieutenant."

"Yes, Sir." Martins paused a moment longer, as if collecting his thoughts, then resumed. "What the Colonel has just called a classic galley can carry a couple days' supplies, but that's about all. They are designed to stay near the coast, they don't usually go far from land, so they can normally afford to sacrifice carrying capacity in favor of that speed and maneuverability Mr. Warner mentioned.

This pirate fleet's larger ships might carry additional stores, but they'd still have to transfer those stores on shore to feed the rest of their force. So we should have a very good idea where they are coming from."

"A hundred ships," Rick said. "With a hundred and fifty men each. Probably more like a hundred and seventy to two hundred on the great galleys, but most of them will be the pirates you and Lieutenant Martins are talking about. So a hundred and fifty's probably a pretty good average number. Call it fifteen thousand men, between them. That's a hell of a fighting force."

"Half that would be a large force," Lieutenant Cargill said. "If they'll fight, but perhaps they'll nae be keen to face our rifles? Still, I'd nae like a standing battle with those odds."

"Colonel, you said the pirates are raiding for slaves. Slaves aren't going to fight for the people who just enslaved them!" Mason said.

"Or not all of them," Lieutenant Martins said. "Some might, you know. Vikings sometimes added slaves to their crews."

"Didn't know that," Warner said. "Call it ten thousand fighting men, then. That's still a lot."

"Half that is still a lot," Martins said, and Warner nodded in agreement.

"But no guns," he said. "Bows, we don't know how good, but there'll be some. No guns, but crossbows which are pretty near as good as muskets. I noticed there's catapults on the forecastles of the Roman ships in the harbor. And weapon racks around the masts. Figure the pirates for the same thing. I'd guess the typical battle is you shoot catapults and arrows, then try to ram so you can get aboard the other guy's ship."

"No corvus," Lieutenant Cargill said. "At least none I've seen."

Several of the others looked at the young Scot in surprise, and he shrugged.

"Saw it once on a BBC historical presentation," he said, and someone laughed.

"Well, it's a good point," Warner said, "but I'm not surprised we haven't seen any. The Romans used to beat Carthage in naval battles with the corvus—"

"Larry, I didn't see any BBC specials," Art Mason said. "I don't know what the hell a corvus is."

"Oh. Sorry, Major. The early Roman Republic was a land power, splendid armies but no navy at all. The story is that when the Romans realized they'd have to fight Carthage on the seas, they built dry land mockups of ships and used those to train soldiers to row while they were building a fleet. When they got ships, they didn't know how to fight at sea—it takes a lot of training to use the kind of ramming tactics the Greeks used, and they didn't have it—so they put a big gangplank up forward with an enormous spike. Get close to the other guy, drop the corvus. Means 'crow,' that spiked gangplank looked like a crow's beak, maybe. Anyway, drop the corvus. The spike goes in the other guy's deck. Now your marines swarm across and it's like a land battle. The Carthaginians might have been better sailors, but the Romans were better *soldiers*, so they cleaned the Carthaginians' clocks. Rome won all the big naval battles. Only thing was, the corvus was so heavy and destabilizing that any time there was a storm they'd lose just about all the ships that had one. So they gave it up."

"Oh. Thanks," Mason said, and Warner laughed slightly.

"I never quite understood that, but it's for sure that the Romans gave up the corvus. The point is that it's a good idea but not one we want until we're really desperate, and we haven't got time to rebuild the ships anyway! But look, the way they fight here, it's got to be ram and board. They don't have guns."

"They've got bows," Rick said.

"Damned big arbalests on the Roman ship," Cargill said.

"I'd think twenty of my lads with their rifles would be more than a match for any kind of galley," Major Baker said. "Just keep the engagement at range."

"If we can get them to go aboard a rowboat," Martins said. "Not sure they'll like that."

"Aye, that may be a problem," Cargill said. "They're nae keen on boats."

"So far morale is fair," Baker said. "They still think this is a mission, and they're happy enough that they won't be disbanded and sent home. But they still think they'll get home eventually, of course."

"Sergeant Major suspects something is wrong," Martins said. "He was due for retirement, and now he's off on a mission in a very strange place. He knows this isn't Earth."

"I expect they all know that," Rick said. "You tell me they aren't fools. They knew it the first time they saw a centaur, if not earlier."

"Yes," Baker said. "They know. So far they haven't

made any great point about it, but they will when we don't tell them when they get to go home."

"The word is getting around," Martins said. "That we don't expect to go home again, so why should anyone else? That hasn't entirely sunk in yet, but it will."

"Will they fight for us?" Rick asked.

"You saw them do it," Baker said.

"I did indeed, Major Baker. Can you get them on the boats?"

"Sergeant Major can," Baker said. "And he'll do it. More out of habit than anything else, I expect, but he'll do it. So far the Gurkhas are loyal, at least to the Queen, if not to us. No guarantees on what happens when they find we're not the Queen's men anymore."

"We'll have to get them aboard," Rick said. "It's our only way of defeating superior numbers. On water anyway."

"What we need is cannon," Warner said. "Get me a good bronze foundry and some time and I can make naval cannon."

They all looked at him.

"Well it may take some experimentation, but yes, I can do it," Warner said. "So could you, if you'd try. There are foundries in Chelm, and some good ones around Edron, too, but the Romans have the best foundries from what I can tell. Wouldn't surprise me if we find out the Romans have built a couple of cannon. They'll sure be experimenting with them."

"Edron's going to be an island," Rick mused. "Possibly within a year, certainly within ten. For a short while it will mean forests near the sea. Foundries already there. Not hard to build shipyards."

"Your pardon, Sir, but that's all wishes for the future," Major Baker said. "Steam engines wouldn't hurt as long as we're wishing."

Rick nodded.

"Yes, sorry, I got ahead of myself. We'll have to develop both, I think. Naval cannon and steam engines. Wood at first, but it won't be long until we're making ironclads."

"Your best powder mills are near Armagh," Mason said. "Maybe we should think about putting a garrison there while we still can." He shook his head sadly. "We just about abandoned the place, now we have to get back there. Maybe things are better with Ganton now."

"They are," Rick said. "Thanks particularly to Major Baker and his merry men. Who should I put in charge there?"

"Left to me, I'd put Elliot there," Art Mason said. "He can't be happy being under Lady Tylara's eye. Hell, let him choose a bodyguard and go back, they're used to him being in charge."

More goddam decisions.

"Make it happen, Art. Use the semaphore."

"Yessir."

*Abandon Armagh. Get to Chelm, then go right back to Armagh. Monkey motion. That's how Elliot will see it,* Rick thought. *Maybe he'll be used to it. Anyway, it'll have to do.*

"We'll need Armagh if we're going to build industries," he said. "And shipyards. Time to start looking for another base, just in case."

"Cannon, steam engines, powder mills," Warner mused. "Paddle-wheelers first, I think. Then sidewheelers. Propellers are better, but I don't know much about designing them. Except that it's a hell of a lot harder to get it right than most people think."

"Warner, maybe we need to secure Armagh, but we're not going to develop cannon and oceangoing sidewheelers in the next couple of weeks!" Art Mason said. "And from what I'm getting, that's about how long we've got."

"Yes, Sir," Warner said. "Sorry. We won't have them in weeks, but I'll bet you anything you like that in well under five years naval battles will be fought with cannon and steam. And ironclads in under ten years. Probably a lot less. But given the present situation, Major Baker's right, isn't he? All we have to do is get twenty riflemen a hundred yards from an enemy galley and they can put it out of action pretty fast."

"Assuming there's no storm, our men aren't seasick, and for that matter, that we can find the bloody enemy," Baker said.

"We don't have to find them," Rick said. "We just have to keep them from sacking Nikeis."

"Which may solve the problem of how we get the Serene Republic's attention," Warner said. "They've got to have heard about this upcoming pirate raid."

"And if they haven't, we can certainly tell them," Major Baker said.

"A hundred yards may not be enough," Mason said. "I've seen them arbalests at work."

"I share your concern and Major Baker's," Martins said. "As much as I respect our troops, they are not Marine Commandos. Our strategies should not be overly reliant upon rifle fire, particularly on the water. Fortunately, we have other capabilities at hand which can enhance the Roman fleet."

He paused, and Rick looked at him speculatively.

"And those capabilities would be—?" he invited after a moment.

"Galleys are designed to fight primarily to the front," Martins said. "They usually have a ram on the front, often the arbalests we've seen, a place for the marines, grapnels, a boarding ramp, on Earth maybe a corvus. All of their combat power is forward. The sides are for the oars, the stern for command and steering. The sides or the stern of a galley are very vulnerable. If you can flank them, their numbers become irrelevant, in fact a liability. Within reason, at least."

Rick leaned back, gazing at him with pursed lips.

"And how do we gain that flank? I tend to suspect they'd be at least as aware as we are of what a bad idea it would be for them to let us do that."

"If what we've seen on land holds at sea, we have significant advantages they can't match, Sir. We have radios, backed up by your semaphore, and signaling rockets. We have binoculars and we have compasses. Those should give us significant advantages in maneuvering for position."

"We're talking considerable odds. You'll have to be decisive at the point of contact, even if you catch them on the flank."

"Yes, Sir. That's where our firepower can come in handy."

✛ ✛ ✛

When the conference ended, Major Baker waited until the others were gone.

"A word with you, Sir."

"Yes?"

"Risky business, putting my lads onto boats. None of us know a thing about sailing. Martins has a little yachting experience, but not much. We'll have to trust the boat crews to know what they're doing. Sure you want to do that?"

"No, I'm not sure at all," Rick said. *And I'm not sure how much to trust Martins, either, but he's onto something.* "But we can't let these newcomers and their containers fall into the hands of pirates! Particularly if they're the instructors you said Agzaral was sending."

"I'd think that less dangerous than letting any knowledge from Earth loose unsupervised in Nikeis. Or anywhere else for that matter."

"Now there's an interesting thought," Rick said. "Actually, that's likely to happen no matter what we do. Once they know it can be done, the Nikeisians will probably develop technology nearly as fast as we can. They can sure do more with the technology than Dràntos. Closest thing to a free society on the planet."

"You know this?"

"No, of course I don't know this," Rick said. "Guessing from the reports I had from Clavell." *And what I remember of the Venetian Republic, and how it fascinated the Framers, but this isn't the time to talk about constitutions.* Not now, but someday...

"Your free society may just have your men in a dungeon, you know," Baker said. "Are you certain you aren't romanticizing? Freedom, liberty, Yankee Doodle—Beg your pardon, Colonel, but I've seen Yanks do that before."

Rick frowned, then grinned.

"You may be right. And my first concern is my troops."

"As is mine," Clyde Baker said. No smile. He seemed very serious, and Rick nodded slowly.

"We both have the same problem. Tell me, Major, do you enjoy power?"

"I enjoy order," Baker said. "It's why I chose to be a professional soldier. Can't say I never thought of having a run for Parliament after retirement." He smiled thinly. "Not such a good idea now. No Parliament, and not much prospect of retirement."

"Mamelukes," Rick said, and Baker frowned.

"I've heard the word," he said. "Egyptian soldiers, weren't they? Napoleon defeated them. Can't say I know anything else about them."

"They were slave soldiers," Rick said. "In Egypt, yes, but all over the Middle East."

"Like the Janissaries?"

"Yes. Only in Egypt the Mamelukes took over. Threw out the local government, set up their own—and decided to stay slave soldiers. They were mostly from the Caucuses, Circassia, and they bought more Circassian slaves. Trained them well. Mastered their military skills. Napoleon said one Mameluke could defeat a half dozen Frenchmen, possibly more. Professional soldiers. Elected their own officers. Promoted on merit—they were all slaves, you see."

"And they ruled the whole country?" Baker looked thoughtful.

"They sort of supervised it. Appointed civil governments and left them alone unless they got too far out of line, in which case they threw them out and put in new ones. Worked for a couple of centuries, and they pretty well avoided a lot of the civil wars the rest of the world was going through. Lasted until Napoleon brought in the French army."

"And that's us?" Baker said.

"One model, I suppose."

Baker looked thoughtful.

"Indeed. Is this what you contemplate? Someone has to be in charge. Have you ambitions to be Caesar?"

"No. Not sure what I want, but my ambition is to retire to Chelm and raise my children. That takes peace and we're not going to have any of that. Not right now, anyway."

"That won't ever work," Baker said.

Rick frowned.

"Pardon my bluntness, Colonel, but this is important. Whoever controls that knowledge will pretty well direct this planet's progress."

"Possibly. Knowledge spreads fast, you know. It's very hard to keep secrets. A few years, perhaps, but once something is known to be possible, it gets out fast. I'm sure the Romans are hard at work on gunpowder, for example. They know the formula by now, and they have foundries. I'd bet they're forging cannon, and I wouldn't be astonished if they have experimental harquebus formations already! Knowledge can outrun conquest."

"Renaissance," Baker said. "Yes, Sir, I understand that. But doesn't that give us a certain responsibility? At least to try to ensure some sort of order?"

"Yes, I suppose so," Rick said. *I hate it, but he's right. Damn all.*

"Which brings us to the key question," Baker said. His voice lost all the bantering tone and became very serious. "I pledged loyalty to you, and I meant it. Still do. I didn't commit to any council of officers."

"Even if you're on it? You certainly would be."

"I'd expect to be. At the moment my status is simple. I'm a mercenary hired out to you. You play the political games, and it's complicated by your status in this Chelm place wherever that is, but in effect you're a mercenary who's hired out to Drantos. All of which is very well, but where do we stand with the Galactics who brought us here?"

"For the moment I'm growing their damned crops and selling to them," Rick said.

"Colonel, you're making things pretty damned complicated if that's your simple goal!"

Rick went over to the side table and poured two glasses of the local port wine. Port. It couldn't be Port, there wasn't any Portugal here, but this was a lot like what he used to call Port . . .

Rick shook his head and handed the handblown glass of wine to Baker.

"Cheers. You're right, of course. I assume that in twenty years or so the Shalnuksi traders will lose interest in Tran. They always have. About twenty years and they're gone, sometimes bombing the hell out of the place on the way out, sometimes not. I don't have any control over that. Agzaral may have plans, in fact I'm sure of it, and last I heard he wasn't for bombing this place, but he's made me no promises. His plans change, too. He let you come here, and that sure didn't fit the situation he described to me."

"Of course, he has plans," Clyde Baker said. "He was quite explicit about my best choice being to work with you."

"Or he could simply be working to concentrate his targets," Rick said and Baker frowned.

"Do you believe that?"

"No. Thinking back to my interviews with Agzaral, he was always acting as if we were being recorded and he couldn't be straight, but he'd like to be." Rick shrugged. "Of course, he'd act that way if he were a villain, too. Gwen—that's Gwen Tremaine—got to know one of the human Galactics pretty well—"

"Had a child by one of them, I believe you said."

"Yes. She doesn't talk about it a lot, but she's clearly fond of Les. The pilot who seduced her and abandoned her on this dump. And from everything I can infer, the human Galactics don't have any ill will towards anyone on Tran, star men or natives." Rick shrugged. "Major, it's beyond me. Gwen wanted to go native and hide, but she seems to have changed her mind about that. Whether that's because of something she learned from Les or just a change of mind I don't know, but she's got three kids to look out for, and she's not trying to hide any longer."

"Will he warn her if they're coming with bombs?" Baker asked.

"I'm quite sure he will if he can."

"How long will we have?"

Rick shook his head slowly.

"Major, I don't know. From what I can get out of Tran history, we have a good ten years and probably more. I've been working on that assumption. I've also assumed that it's contingent on our being worth our keep, so I've worked pretty hard to gather a good harvest of madweed. We've got quite a lot for the next trade, which ought to happen in the next few months, possibly sooner. Another reason to get things settled here!"

"And then?" Baker prompted.

"My goal's clear enough. I'm hoping to have some control left after the Galactics leave and we're on our own. Since I'm not immortal and I have no way of knowing if my kids will be any use, what's left? I'm responsible to my men, Major Baker. You don't like a council of officers much, and neither do I, but what are our alternatives?"

Baker nodded.

"Timocracy, I think Plato called it. I don't see anything better coming, and there's no urgency in decision. Unless you get yourself killed," Baker said carefully. "That would produce a messy situation."

"I'll try not to."

"Good. So what's our plan, Colonel?"

Rick shook his head, trying not to show his dismay.

"No immediate details. Keep pissing on fires until we have some time for real plans. Some things are damned obvious. We have to secure those containers. Time enough to dispose of them when we know what's in them! I doubt they're empty, but all I can do is guess what they've brought. Or why the Galactics let any technology get through at all. Maybe the Earth guys who brought them will know. But first we have to get possession! When we've done that it will be time to sell more dope to the Shalnuksis. I've got plenty enough to keep them happy. So we meet the Shalnuksi traders, and with luck we'll learn something from that. Then there's a Five Kingdoms army sitting on my land that's got to be chased out of there—"

"Assuming it doesn't just melt away now," Baker said. "Your friend Ganton had the Five Kingdoms people scared enough there was talk of recalling that army. That was before my lads put Ganton on the run, but I rather doubt they feel very secure now that we've changed sides. And your musketeers and pikemen may not be much of a threat to my lads, but they're sure a match for the locals. And then some. I wouldn't be much concerned about chasing that army out of your backyard. I expect your wife is well on the way to doing it now."

*Interesting,* Rick thought. *I suppose he's been talking with Mason about Chelm and Tylara.* He poured each of them another glass of port.

"Not unlikely, actually," he said. "Which makes one less problem to worry about. But we still have to deal with the Five Kingdoms. Southern refugees will be coming in floods, and we'll have to settle some of them on the Fivers. Then we'll still have problems with Westmen, more could start coming down the passes." He drank a big swallow.

"Since you seem to be playing matchmaker, perhaps I should learn more about these Westmen."

"As you've seen, Westmen are Oriental in appearance," Rick said. "I don't know the culture they came from, or when, but ethnically they look to me to be the nearest thing to Gurkhas I've seen. Primitive culture, polytheists."

"That could be interesting."

"The tribes I'm allied with have a settlement west of

Chelm," Rick said. "You'll meet more of them, if we get past this crisis."

"No lack of work," Baker said, raising his glass in salute. "That can't be all bad news! Cheer up, Colonel. If I come up with a better plan I'll tell you, but I'm not unhappy with my decision."

# CHAPTER SEVEN

"Colonel, Major Baker's here," Bisso said, and Rick looked up from his desk with a stab of irritation. They were scheduled to meet with Publius' fleetmaster tomorrow morning and they'd probably be sailing from Taranto by afternoon, or the next day, at latest. Finding a moment to write Tylara something longer than a semaphore message was always difficult, and he doubted he'd have another opportunity before they sailed.

"And did the Major say *why* he's here?" he asked, laying down his pen.

"No, Sir. Just that he'd 'appreciate a moment of your time.'" Bisso shrugged. "He was real polite, Sir, but I think he thinks whatever it's about, it's important."

"I see. In that case, you'd better send him in."

"Lieutenant Martins is with him."

"In that case, you'd better send both of them in."

"Yes, Sir."

The sergeant disappeared. A moment later, he returned with Baker and Martins.

"Gentlemen," Rick greeted them without rising, then pointed at a pair of backless Roman chairs. "Sit. Tell me what this is about."

"Of course, Colonel," Baker said. The Brits settled onto the chairs, and the major glanced at the writing desk.

"First, I apologize for interrupting you," he said, "but there's a point we haven't had the opportunity yet to discuss."

"What sort of point?" Rick asked. *God, I hope he's not coming up with some reservation about accepting my command at this late date! He seemed happy enough last night, but—*

"Let me begin by spreading a few well-deserved compliments," Baker said, smiling as if he'd read Rick's mind. "I've been thinking about our conversation, and in the process, about how much you and your men have already accomplished here, Colonel. And you've done bloody well—even better than I'd thought. Better, if you'll forgive me for saying this, than I would ever have anticipated out of a lad straight out of you Yanks' college ROTC." He shook his head, his eyes very level. "The situation you got thrown into, first in Angola and especially here on Tran, is mind-boggling. The fact that you've not only survived but created the support base you have, is . . . well, let's just say that I doubt very many men in your position could have done either. Certainly your Andre Parsons didn't!"

Rick's eyes narrowed. But—

"I appreciate the testimonial, Major," he said dryly. "How well deserved it is would be a judgment call, of course. I seem to sense a 'but' lurking in there somewhere, though."

"Because there is one, Sir," Baker said levelly. "I meant it when I said you've done bloody well, but it's always possible to do better, and it seems to me that you're a bit thin on what one might call the staff functions."

"I see."

Rick leaned back in his chair, regarding the two British officers, then shrugged.

"That depends in part on what you mean by 'staff functions,'" he said. "Obviously, I had to build pretty much from scratch. I was the S-2 in Africa, but there weren't a lot of intelligence sources here, initially. We didn't have an operations officer, or a logistics officer, or a plans officer—Hell, Parsons and I were the only two officers who made it to Tran! I've filled most of those billets, functionally, at least, but I've had to play it by ear more than I would've liked. I would love to have some of the field manuals my ROTC classes had! In fact, I've requested them. But the Shalnuksis don't seem to think about that sort of thing."

It was Baker's turn to sit back with an expression that looked a lot like relief, Rick thought.

"Colonel," the major said after a moment, "I'm more reassured than I can say to hear what you've just said, for two reasons. First, it confirms my observation that while you may be a bloody amateur, if you'll pardon the term, you're an extraordinarily competent bloody amateur." He smiled crookedly. "And, second, it suggests that you'll take the suggestion I'm about to make in the spirit in which it's offered."

Rick said nothing, simply gazing at him steadily, and Baker nodded to Martins.

"Get out your little book, Richard," he said.

"Yes, Sir."

Martins reached into a pocket on the front of his field jacket and pulled out a small olive-green binder. The Velcro-fastened cover bore the stencil COMMANDERS BATTLE BOOK, and he leaned forward to place it on the corner of the desk.

Rick looked down at it, then raised his eyebrows as he looked back at Baker.

"Is this what I think it is?"

"I believe it might be called a step in that direction, Colonel," Baker said with a slight smile. "It's rather a fetish object for our junior officers, but a useful one."

There was a tearing sound as Rick opened the cover and read the title page. TACTICAL AIDE MEMOIRE, it said, and he flipped to the table of contents, ran his eyes down the neat column of subject listings, then turned through the clear-plastic-coated pages. Finally, he looked back up at Baker.

"I would have killed for this," he said quietly, one hand resting on page 1-13-1, the template headed SQUADRON/COMPANY GROUP ORDERS, BREACHING AND OBSTACLE CROSSING.

"As it happens, we have three copies of it," Major Baker said, "and also as it happens, Leftenant Martins is very good with it."

"I've been trying to develop a general staff from scratch

ever since we got here," Rick said. "With this as a model," he tapped the binder with his forefinger, "we might just be able to develop a real one."

"Colonel," Baker's tone was very serious, "I can't begin to tell you how happy it makes me to hear you say that."

"Major, there's a line from a Clint Eastwood movie that was released a few years before my adventures in Africa that I think applies here. He said, 'A man has to know his limitations.' Trust me"—he tapped the binder again—"more than a decade on Tran ensures that he does."

⚜ ⚜ ⚜

Fleetmaster Gaius Junius wore armor and decorations like any other senior Roman army officer, but his boots had no hobnails, and he wore no spurs. Rick was told that Junius ranked as a legate, and while it wasn't common, officers did go from naval to land commands, but Junius had spent his entire career as a naval commander.

The harbor headquarters building was called the Praetorium but it had a distinctly naval atmosphere, although Rick would have found it difficult to say why he had that impression. It was built of limestone on the typical Roman model, apparently replacing whatever had served when Taranto had been unambiguously a part of the Kingdom of Drantos. Many of the harbor buildings more closely resembled the gothic styles favored in Drantos, but the Praetorium was purely Roman, atrium surrounded by pillared open hallways and small rooms on two sides, leading to a grander building across the atrium from the gate.

A map of the Inner Sea had been painted on a large

table in the meeting room of the Praetorium. Rick studied it with satisfaction.

"This is accurate?" he asked.

"As nearly so as we can make it," Junius said. The admiral seemed pleased that Publius was attending the meeting and asking his advice. It was clear that Junius thought the Navy sadly neglected and looked forward to the opportunity to convince Caesar of the importance of maritime matters.

Rick traced the labyrinthine passages through the complex of small islands and marshes that guarded Nikeis.

"Not an easy place to get into."

"Not if you have to fight your way in," Fleetmaster Junius said. "Of course we've never had to do that. They remain allies, for the record."

"For the record," Rick said.

"They need our help," Junius said. "If they had time they could put together enough force to resist this pirate alliance, but they don't have time, Friend of Caesar. I believe there will be enough pirates to overwhelm the Nikeisian defenders."

"We can't allow that," Rick said.

"Can we defeat the pirates?" Publius asked.

"Heir of Caesar, I don't know," the Roman admiral said. "With what I can take to Nikeis now, I think not, even with the favor of God. Unless Warlord Rick brings great power."

"We have great power," Rick said. "And we believe we can defeat any enemies, on land or on the sea, but we have little experience fighting on the sea. What I need is some enemies to practice on."

Publius looked at him quizzically.

"It cannot be difficult to find enemies. I have seldom found it so, at least."

"No, but what I need are enemy *warships*," Rick said. He looked up to Junius. "Are there any nearby?"

"Some pirates here," Junius said. He pointed to a small delta of swamp and islands some sixty miles to the north of the port. "They're clever. If we send the fleet, they disperse among the swamps and hide. If we send a single ship, they come together in such strength that we dare not risk battle. They raid the coasts of Drantos and the Five Kingdoms."

"They must be a small threat indeed," Rick said. "I've heard nothing of them. As Warlord I would know of any real danger to the realm."

The Roman officer shrugged.

"There are few of them in these southern waters, and the local villages have organized a defense, so perhaps they never become a concern of the Wanax. Our merchants avoid the area by crossing to the Roman shore before going north to Nikeis, so it's been of little concern to us. But those will be the closest pirate ships I know of."

"How many?" Rick asked.

"Never many." Junius shook his head. "Perhaps five galleys remain. There had been more, but patrols report that some of them recently went northward. From the reports of the *frumentarii*, it may be that they've joined the pirate coalition."

"Five," Rick mused. "Sounds about right. If we send three merchant ships will they fight?"

"It is likely. They would expect to win."

Rick nodded.

"That's what I want them to expect. Fleetmaster, we'll need three merchant ships. Each will carry an officer and twenty of my men with their weapons. They'll sail past the swamp while we follow at a distance with the rest of the fleet. We'll go clean out that pirate nest on our way to Nikeis. May as well do something useful while we learn how to fight at sea."

⁘ ⁘ ⁘

There were twenty-two ships in the expedition. Five were merchant craft carrying cargo to Nikeis. The rest were Roman warships, all smaller than the flagship the Romans called a "quinquireme" and everyone else on the planet called a great galley. Several of them, which the Romans called "triremes," were simply smaller quinquiremes with only two masts, not three. The remainder were "liburnians," which were basically Martins' and Warner's "classic galleys," lighter, with only a single rower on each oar and—for the most part—only one mast each.

Fleetmaster Junius chose three of the merchant ships as decoys. Their masters weren't pleased to have their vessels commandeered, but they didn't care to argue when they found they were negotiating with Publius Caesar.

"You will be paid," Publius had told them flatly. His frown had shown that he was concerned about where he would find the money, but he didn't say that.

Rick left the details to Major Baker and his officers. Each merchant ship would carry twenty Gurkhas, an officer, a few Roman marines, and one of their nine radios, while their base radio remained aboard the quinquireme, where it would be safest. The soldiers aboard the merchant ships would remain hidden until the pirates had committed to action. It was the best plan anyone could think of, and Rick approved.

"Risking a lot, here," Baker said carefully. "Lose one of these decoy ships and you've lost a lot. Lose them all—"

"I know," Rick said. "Which is why we'll be just over the horizon behind you with the rest of the fleet. And why you'll be bloody careful."

"Aye, aye, Sir." Baker chuckled. "Well, we can sound like sailors, anyway." His expression belied his tone. Baker was worried.

"Yeah. I'll be glad enough to get this over with. You're Jellicoe," Rick said.

Baker looked puzzled.

"British admiral at the Battle of Jutland in World War I," Rick said. "Churchill called him the only man who could lose the war in an afternoon."

"Well, perhaps," Baker said. "Of course, you're not risking anything you had before you met me."

"Should I? I can come along with you—"

"No, Sir, that wasn't what I meant. Anyway, I don't expect any problems. We outrange them by a lot. It should be a piece of cake."

"Maybe I *should* come with you," Rick said. "I have to learn how this naval warfare stuff works—"

"With respect, Colonel, you don't," Baker said. "Your man Warner was right. There isn't likely to be more than one more major naval battle with the kinds of ships and weapons that exist now. Once we defeat this pirate coalition and the secret about gunpowder and cannon gets out throughout the planet, the whole nature of war at sea—land too!—is going to change. We'll have a hell of a job keeping up!

"Colonel, you have enough to worry about without having to learn naval tactics that will be obsolete in a couple of years. Leave that nonsense to me and the Romans. What you'd best be worrying about is what happens after we finish off these pirates."

✣ ✣ ✣

They set out at dawn. The three merchant ships went northward along the shore, and when they were barely in sight over the horizon, Rick followed with the Roman fleet, standing just out of sight from the land and keeping the merchant ships barely visible.

*If the plan works*, Rick thought. *It should work. Need to watch the weather of course. And it's important to know what we can do at sea.*

After some thought, Publius had decided to join Rick and his staff on the flagship *Ferox*, and they had been introduced to Captain Pilinius, Fleetmaster Junius' flag captain, as they came aboard. He was a cheerful man in his thirties, a seasoned professional seaman who didn't seem much impressed by all the visiting dignitaries. He was clearly a bit embarrassed at the lack of accommodations for his powerful guests, however. *Ferox* was a large, multidecked vessel, but she was also packed like an Earth sardine can, and there was very little cabin space to go around.

Rick had been surprised to discover that none of *Ferox*'s oarsmen sat on its upper deck. Or, rather, that the ship *had* an upper deck, which served as a sort of roof for the rowers, rather than an open oar pit. From an offhand remark Pilinius had let fall, *Ferox* was "cataphract built," which suggested that the "roof" was intended as armor, a feature designed to protect the rowers from missile fire. That made a lot of sense, and it also provided a much larger fighting platform for marines.

The mystery of the numbers had been solved as well . . . probably.

The quinquireme had three banks of oars on each side, which—logically—should have made it a *tri*reme, as far as Rick was concerned. The triremes, on the other hand, had only *two* banks of oars on each side, which should have made them *bi*remes. Or that was what he'd thought. In fact, the ships' designations were derived from the number of rowers, not the number of oars. A trireme had two men on each upper oar and one on each lower oar, so three of them were stacked vertically in what Pilinius called a "file." The quinquireme was a bit longer and did have a few more oars in each bank, but it had two rowers on each oar in the upper two banks and only one on each oar in the lower bank, which produced files of five men each.

A solid upper deck might protect the rowers, but it couldn't do much for ventilation, which Risk suspected had to be a vital consideration when it came to how long and how hard your crew could row, so there were several smaller hatches on the raised forecastle and quarter deck where wind scoops could be rigged. In addition, much of the ship's midships deck consisted of a single huge hatch which could be opened to provide air to the oarsmen. The hatch could be closed and battened down in sections;

when fully open, it was over fifty feet long and eight or
nine feet wide. There was no sign of chains, and each
rower had a short sword racked at his elbow where it
would be readily available yet out of his way while he
rowed.

*Ferox* was bigger than he'd expected, as well. The
upper deck was just over a hundred and fifty feet long,
and its beam was about sixteen feet at the waterline. It
was closer to thirty-five at the upper deck level, though,
because the oarsmen sat in a box that was built out from
the hull on either side. In some ways, it reminded him of
the way US Navy aircraft carriers' hanger decks
broadened their hulls. The edge of the upper deck was
about nine feet above the waterline, although the sturdy,
solid bulwarks—obviously intended to serve as protection
against incoming arrows and crossbow bolts—increased
its total freeboard to about fourteen feet. There were
nettings on the bulwarks where the crew stowed its rolled-
up hammocks each morning. That would increase their
ability to absorb incoming fire, although Rick didn't
remember ever reading about the Roman navy of Earth
doing that sort of thing.

*Sailing ships did that during the Age of Sail, I think.
Did the Romans even issue hammocks, though? Wonder
if Warner has a clue about that one?*

The ship also had two large torsion catapults or
ballistae, like enormous crossbows, on the forecastle and
a trio of arrow throwers spaced out along each bulwark
amidships. Each arrow thrower consisted of a gimbal-
mounted, trough-like firing tray that could be loaded with
six enormous arrows. They were actually closer to fletched

javelins than anything Rick would have called an arrow, and they were fired using a single, torsion-driven striker that was cranked back with a windlass and then released to strike the butts of all six arrows with enormous force.

The arrow throwers were primarily close-in, antipersonnel weapons designed for a scattergun effect, but the ballistae on the forecastle were quite another matter. Large spear-like bolts, much heavier than the arrows of their little brothers mounted on the bulwarks, were laid out near each of them, and their torsion bands, like those of the arrow throwers, were wrapped in a waterproofing made of well-oiled parchment. They could also fire other types of projectiles, and a supply of stones, each of which probably weighed forty or fifty pounds, rested in boxes nearby. They were remarkably uniform in size and shape, and Rick reminded himself that early cannonballs had also been made of shaped stone. There was also a rack of clay pots—empty, at the moment—clearly of a size to be launched by the catapults, and a dozen Roman marines were stationed on the forecastle to operate the artillery. They were dressed in cloth tunics and there were no hobnails on their boots, but the other differences from the standard Roman army uniform were minor.

All in all, Rick thought, *Ferox* was a formidable fighting machine, and its crew was much larger than he'd estimated. According to Pilinius, the quinquireme carried three hundred rowers, seventy marines, and twenty-five deck crew to run the rigging.

*I just hope the Fivers and the Riccigionans don't have a lot like it! I doubt the Five Kingdoms do, but Riccigiona may be an entirely different kettle of fish. It sounds like*

*the Duchy's got itself a professional navy, like Rome and
Nikeis, and that could be bad.*

The visitors were conducted to the quarterdeck.
Pilinius made certain they were all safely in their assigned
places and out of the way before he began to shout
commands. Signal flags rose up lines on the masts.
Landsmen cast off the harbor lines and the oarsmen
shipped oars. The burly oarmaster raised his hammers,
and at a signal from the captain began to beat out a pace
on a big wooden block as the squadron began filing out of
the harbor.

Once into the open sea, Pilinius set the big lateen sails
on each mast and the rowers ran their oars back inboard.
They moved more rapidly under sail, and once they were
well underway, Rick went below to the battery-operated
repeater set Baker had brought to Tran. The antenna had
been mounted well up on *Ferox's* mainmast, connected to
the set by coaxial cable, and he picked up the microphone
and pushed the talk button.

"Test. Rabbit One, this is Big Mamma. Over."

"Rabbit One here. Given that there are nine radios on
this planet it's not likely I'd be anyone else, is it, Sir? I hear
you well. Over."

"Good. We have communications. Over."

"We're making the expected pace," Baker said. "The
plan calls for us to be in sight of the swamp before noon
tomorrow, and I expect that will happen. We'll anchor
offshore at dusk tonight, as planned. With this wind I
presume the anchors will hold. Captain Oranato is a
fussbudget, but he appears competent enough. Over."

"The lookouts at masthead can make you out at the

horizon," Rick said. "We're keeping pace with you. The fleet is right behind us. Yell if you need help. And keep a close watch tonight! Over."

"I'll do just that, Sir. But I don't think we'll have any problems. Over."

"Any issues with the crew? Mr. Warner working out all right? Over."

"No problems with troops. Not with Oranato, not with mine," Baker said. "Baker out."

"It is true, then," Publius said when Rick came back on deck. "You have ways to speak to your men at great distances. You did not have such in our previous battles."

"No. The equipment was brought here by Major Baker."

Publius nodded, frowning thoughtfully.

"Will there—is there more of this magic in the containers?"

"There may be," Rick said. *And he's a pretty smart bird. He knows how valuable all this stuff is. And the ship is his.* Rick was glad of the weight of his Colt .45 in its shoulder holster. And that Bisso and Rand would stand watch outside his cabin.

Of course, now wasn't the dangerous time. The dangerous time would be after they'd defeated the main pirate fleet. Both Rome and Nikeis needed his help now, but when that threat was removed . . . And it was probably not a good idea to count one's battles before they were won. One fight at a time. On the best reckoning they'd be outnumbered by more than two to one in a naval battle with the pirate alliance, and it might be as high as five to one. That might not make any difference, since the pirate fleet wouldn't have guns, but it was still something to worry about.

† † †

They anchored at dusk.

Rick estimated they were less than a mile from shore. The land to the west was flat, but marshes began just to the north. The wind was from the northeast, an onshore wind, but it was very light, and no one seemed concerned. The anchor held nicely, at least.

Rick's binoculars indicated that some of the land was cultivated but he saw no one. Probably fear of pirates and slavers. They would farm in large parties rather than individually, with lookouts to watch for incoming sails. It might even have been the sight of his fleet that drove everyone inland. Probably was, now that he thought about it.

This stretch of coast was nominally under the governance of an Eqeta who was seldom seen, and who managed to trim between Rome as an ally and Drantos as sovereign without rendering much assistance or tribute to either.

"Could the Eqeta actually be in alliance with the pirates?" Rick asked, and Fleetmaster Junius shrugged.

"We have little to do with this shore," he admitted. "Rome has little commerce with the Five Kingdoms to the north, and when we do go there, we go by way of Nikeis. Nikeis commands the Inner Sea."

"Nikeis may claim to," Publius said. "But the pirates clearly have a rival claim of some strength."

Rick nodded silently. A hundred ships was a considerable claim.

Dinner was cold, mostly bread, and there was little

further conversation. Rick had no desire to betray his utter lack of knowledge about naval warfare, and his attempts to draw more information from Fleetmaster Junius were received politely but without much encouragement. Rick went to bed early. They'd found him a small cabin with a hammock. It wasn't comfortable, and it took a long time to get to sleep. His stomach growled and more than once in the night he winced in pain.

Rick kept thinking about his conversation with Baker. Like it or not, the history of this planet was going to change radically, thanks to whatever was in those containers. The only religious war he knew of on Tran was the one with the Defenders of the old faith led by Phrados the Prophet. Before that there was no record or memory of one—none that anyone remembered, anyway; there had to have been at least minor squabbles, given human nature—so they hadn't had Reformation and Counter-Reformation. Maybe they wouldn't. The only major religions were pagans and Christians, and the new Unified Church was absorbing one of the major pagan powers into something like a Christian church, largely because Rick and his star men seemed to accept Christianity. Religion was strong here: there were many histories of divine intervention and skyfire every six hundred years or so. No wonder they believed in God and gods. But wouldn't that change with the spread of science and scientific method?

He fell into a fitful sleep and dreamed that someone was shouting that Great Pan was dead.

✢ ✢ ✢

Rick woke before dawn and wandered down to the galley, where there was a fire in a large ceramic stove. A cook obligingly put on a kettle to boil, and after a cup of mint tea that would have to serve, since he hadn't brought any of his precious coffee on board, Rick climbed up the rope ladder at the ship's mainmast and took out his binoculars. It was shortly before the rise of the True Sun. As the glow in the east grew brighter Rick could just make out Baker's little fleet on the northern horizon. He watched until he saw all three ships turn away on a northwesterly heading.

"They're getting under way," he called down.

"My thanks, Patrician," Captain Pilinius yelled back. Rick was taken aback for a moment; he was still getting used to his new Roman title.

Pilinius shouted orders, and the sailors raised the big iron-and-wood anchor. The other ships of the fleet did the same. Sails were set, and they moved steadily northward, careful to keep Baker's fleet just at the horizon as seen from up the mast while Mason, Bisso, and Rand took turns climbing up to observe with binoculars.

At noon the radio gave a message alert.

✢ ✢ ✢

Larry Warner perched on a tiny platform halfway up the mast of the tubby merchant vessel *Sagitta*.

*Sagitta my ass*, he thought, gazing through his binoculars. *Damned hard to think of anything less like an "arrow" than this tub!*

The *navis oneraria* was on the small size for its type, about the size of one of the Roman triremes, and that meant its masts were on the short side, too. Which was just as well, since it meant he'd fall a shorter distance before he splattered on the deck. It also meant he couldn't see as far as he could have from a greater height, but he was just fine with that.

His current roost could hardly be called a crow's nest, but that was the only term he had for it. Down below there was no sign of the Gurkha troops, although Major Baker stood on the quarterdeck. From close enough he would look a bit strange in his battle dress, but there wasn't any chance of that. The pirates wouldn't have telescopes.

*Not yet*, Warner thought. *But once the idea gets loose . . .*

He scanned the horizon to the east, then northeast. He'd seen nothing since they got underway just after dawn, but they were headed northwest—well, more like northwest-by west he supposed, if he was going to be all nautical about it—with the wind out of the northeast. That meant it was coming in almost broad on their beam, which he thought he recalled was supposed to be the best point of sailing. Or was that with the wind on the quarter? It didn't seem to matter much, either way, because they weren't setting any speed records, even with the lateen sails set on both of the ship's stubby masts. They could probably have gotten more speed out of the ship by rowing, but Warner had been surprised to discover how seldom oars were actually used. Merchant ships like *Sagitta* used them only to maneuver in and out of harbor, or in a dead calm, and they were slower than hell when they did. War galleys were a lot faster under oars than merchant ships—had a lot to do with their hull forms, he thought; they were much longer in proportion to their beams. But even they almost invariably cruised under sail and stripped down to their oars only when a fight was imminent or they needed to move against the wind. All of which meant that if anything dangerous was around, it would probably be coming from upwind.

He scanned again, this time to the southeast. He could just make out the sails of the trailing fleet, and he turned back to the north.

*Bait, that's what we are*, he thought, and a line from *Pogo* came unwanted. "Once you been bait, you ain't much good for anything else." For some reason that hit him hard. Because they were a long way from Earth, and he'd never see a *Pogo* cartoon again, he realized glumly. Then he grinned.

*Too bad I can't draw. I could do my own. If I need to miss something from Earth, a cartoon possum shouldn't be all that high on the list.*

He scanned eastward, then north again. Then—Hah! Something there, but a lot farther *west* than he'd expected. He focused in to be sure of what he was seeing, then called down to Major Baker.

"Sail ho. Two of them, actually. Sails just in sight, hull down, almost dead north*west* of us."

"Only two?"

"So far that's all I can see, Sir."

"Right. Keep watching." Baker turned to Captain Oranato and tried to say "Enemy in sight" in the common Tran trade parlance, but Oranato's expression showed that Baker's northern accent had defeated him.

More sails crept into view, and Warner called down again, in English then repeated his message in the local language.

"Five sails in sight now! Bearing north-northwest. They

look to be headed east-southeast, not straight for us. There's another. Six. Six so far, all on the same course."

"Right," Baker shouted. "Corporal Wakaina, take Mr. Warner's place on the mast! Warner, I'd rather have you down here, in case we need to give information to Captain Oranato."

Warner grinned.

"Yes, Sir. Coming right down."

As soon as he was on deck, a Gurkha trooper with binoculars clambered up the mast to replace him.

"I assume they're trying to catch us, Mr. Warner?" Baker asked.

"They're northwest of us, Sir," Warner said to Baker in English, then translated for Captain Oranato. "Maybe six miles away, and steering a bit south of due east. They look to be heading about as close to the wind as they can under sail."

"Not quite a reciprocal of our course," Baker murmured, rubbing his chin. Then his eyes narrowed. "They're sweeping around to get upwind of us," he said. "Of course, they can see us. Ask Captain Oranato what he would normally do in this situation."

Oranato must have understood without translation, because he was already speaking—rapidly, and with wide gestures.

"Basically, he'd get the hell out of here," Warner translated. "This is a merchant ship, after all. Usually, he'd turn southeast, directly away from them, or southwest to put the wind straight behind us, and run for it. But southwest's straight into the swamps from here. So under the circumstances, he'd turn *north*east, as close to the

wind as he can sail—close-hauled, I think they call that—
and try to get out to sea. Get away from the swamps and
get some maneuvering room to dodge them."

"Hmm. So at some point we ought to do that. How
soon will they be sure we've seen them?"

"Anytime now, I'd think." Warner shrugged. "They
can't know about binoculars, but even so . . ."

"Precisely. So the one thing we don't want is for them to
think we want them to catch us. Mr. Warner, ask Captain
Oranato to run off to the northeast, but slowly, as if there's
something wrong with his ship." He thumbed the radio.
"All Rabbits, this is Rabbit One. Enemy in sight. We will
turn northeast as if running away. Keep station on us and
close to a hundred meters behind, please. Acknowledge.
Over."

The radio squawked twice in acknowledgment and he
shifted channels.

"Big Mama, enemy in sight," he said. "Repeat enemy
in sight. Six sails, I repeat, six sails in sight. I believe they
have seen us. They are trying to close with us. I will signal
when engagement is near. Over."

"Nothing else to report?" The radio flattened tones, but
Rick sounded anxious, and Baker grinned at Warner.

"Not a thing, Sir," he said. "Out."

The wind was light, so Captain Oranato chose to tack
through it under oars rather than wear ship. They cast off
the sheets to spill wind from the sails, the oarsmen pulled
the bow through the wind, and the deck crew reset the
sails on both masts. The canvas filled, and they began
moving faster, headed east-northeast, away from the shore
with the wind coming in from port and well forward of

the beam. Warner was astounded by how close to the wind their lateen sails could come, but Captain Oranato left the men on the oars to help the canvas along. It took several minutes for Baker to persuade him to at least slow the oarsmen's stroke.

"Excellent," the major said then. "Now to let the Colonel know." He selected a channel and thumbed the radio again. "Big Mama this is Rabbit One. Over."

"Big Mama here. Is all well, Major Baker? Over."

"Well, we now have seven sails closing. There doesn't seem to be a great deal of doubt about their intention; they turned to pursue as soon as we altered course. We're steering to east-northeast, as if running from them, but we're not at full stroke. They're definitely pirates, not great galleys—single-masted, the lot of them—so we have more sail area than they do, but they're also built for speed. We aren't, and they have the wind from a more favorable angle. Captain Oranato estimates they should catch us up in a couple of hours. Over."

"What do you want us to do? Over."

"Sir, mostly we need you to stay out of sight if we expect to lure these chaps out where we can get at them. I'd rather fight them at sea than try to thread our way through marshes and swamps. Over."

"We didn't expect seven. Does that worry you? Over."

"No, Colonel, it doesn't worry me at all. Over."

A short pause.

"All right. We'll stay out of sight. Be careful, Major. Over."

"That I will, Sir. That I will. Out."

✦ ✦ ✦

The wind came up stronger an hour later, and some of the Gurkha troopers looked a bit green as the ship pitched. Baker went down to the main deck to be sure they weren't in distress, but came back up to the poop deck in good spirits.

"Nothing wrong that a chance to fight won't cure," he said, and thumbed the radio again. "All Rabbits, this is Rabbit One. Ask your skippers to stand by for maneuver, it's time to go catch those buggers while we have enough daylight to work in. Acknowledge, Rabbit Two. Over."

"Martins here. Acknowledged. Stand by one." There was a pause. "Skipper says they'll want to wear ship rather than tack in this wind, Sir."

"What the hell does that mean?"

"We're headed east-northeast, the wind is from *north*-northeast, and the pirates are west-northwest of us, Sir," Martins said. "To tack we'd turn to port and put the bow through the wind. He's not going to do that. He's going to turn to starboard—turn right—so the stern goes through the wind. Then he'll turn right some more to get on the new course towards them."

Baker frowned, then looked at Warner.

"Did you understand that?" he demanded.

"Yes, Sir."

"Good. Explain it to Captain Oranato. Then you can have a go at explaining it to Leftenant Cargill, if you will. I'll just listen in to be certain you get all the fiddly bits right for him."

Warner grinned.

"Of course, Sir," he said, and his grin grew wider.

✣ ✣ ✣

It took half an hour to accomplish the maneuver. By the time they were headed for the enemy fleet, the two lead pirates had lowered their sails and were barely a kilometer away. Their oars moved gracefully in full sweep, and they were closing fast on Baker's ship. The Roman marines, dressed as merchant sailors, gathered on the forecastle, readying the ballista which had been hidden under a tarpaulin. They were careful to not look very professional while they did, and the Gurkha riflemen stayed out of sight, clustered just forward of the oarsmen. Their rifles were still cased and they lay back on the deck, hands clasped behind their heads, chattering among themselves as the fleets closed.

Captain Oranato shouted orders, and his sailors began hauling in the lateen sail to the big yardarm, then lowered the yard until it rested on supports. The oarmaster increased the pace of his hammering, and the oar strokes became more rapid. The two lead pirates slowed their forward pace.

"Got too far ahead of their pack," Baker observed. "They'll pay for that."

"Bit surprised they don't just turn and head back until their friends catch up," Warner said. "They're faster than we are, and if the three ships I was chasing suddenly turned on me, I think I'd start wondering if something was going on that I didn't know about."

"We're merchant ships; they're warships. Well, pirate ships, at any rate." Baker shrugged. "They're certain to have bigger crews than any merchant vessel, as well, but we do outnumber them three-to-two. Probably think we've decided our best chance is to try to overwhelm them before their friends arrive, but I doubt they're overly concerned about the outcome."

"Likely the best ships they have, too," Warner said. He scanned the approaching ships. "They're crawling with armed men, Major. They think they're ready for us."

"I'm sure they do." Baker nodded with an unpleasant smile. "But whatever they're ready for, it's not us."

The ships drew closer together and Baker took out a whistle and sounded it for attention. The Gurkhas looked in his direction, and he pointed at the oncoming pirates.

"All right, lads! Make ready for volley fire!" he ordered, and the Gurkhas uncased their rifles. Warner glanced at the other two ships and their riflemen were doing the same.

The pirates came steadily closer.

*Duck and cover? Or stand here like I'm brave?* Warner thought.

The Roman marines had their artillery ready, a spear-sized bolt in the catapult and a dozen cocked crossbows to support it, but they remained seated on the forecastle while the Gurkhas knelt on one knee behind the ship's bulwarks. Warner could see archers on the pirate ships, and he and Baker and Warner were the only people—which meant targets—visible to them at the moment. Not a pleasant thought.

"They're upwind of us," he said nervously.

"Bit out of range for arrows, surely." Baker sounded infuriatingly serene as he studied the lead pirate through his binoculars.

"Closing, closing…make ready to fire," he said conversationally to his men. "We will fire in volley at one hundred meters range. Your aim point is the forecastle of the lead ship. Take your aim—now!" The Gurkhas rose higher on their knees, swinging their rifles over the top of the bulwark, as Baker put one hand on the mast while he felt the timing of the ship's roll. A moment passed, and then—

"In volley, *fire!*"

The twenty rifles crashed in what seemed like one long shot.

"Change your aim point to the oardeck!" Baker shouted. As he did, there were two more volleys, one from each of the other *navibus onerārius* in their flotilla, and suddenly the forecastles of both approaching pirate ships were littered with bodies.

"No archers standing!" Warner reported, and Baker bared his teeth.

"Piece of cake," he said, and turned back to his men. "New aim point, change targets! The port oardeck is your aim point! Take your aim, in volley, *fire!*"

The rifles crashed again, and Baker paused to assess the damage.

They were nearly abreast of the pirate ship thirty yards to their port. Most of the oars were unmanned, and there seemed to be chaos on the enemy ship.

"Good enough. New aim point. Change your aim point to the steersman. First section, make ready. First section only, fire at will."

There were several shots with no effect, then the enemy steersman doubled over. Warner heard cheers. Then the Roman officer on the forecastle shouted orders, and an arbalest bolt penetrated the pirate ship just aft of the mast. There were more cheers, although Warner didn't think they had hit anyone, and the Roman officer pointed to his firepots.

"No, dammit!" Warner shouted. "We want that ship, Centurion! Not a burned hulk."

They passed the pirate ship at a distance of twenty yards. Someone had taken the steersman's place, and shouted orders could be heard. A few pirates had bows, but the Gurkhas were both faster and more accurate. As they swept past there was more individual rifle fire, and again the pirate ship had no steersman.

"Now, Mr. Warner," Baker called. "Let's see about that fellow."

He pointed at a third pirate ship, a thousand yards or so behind the two leaders, that was suddenly backing oars as their quarry turned on them.

Warner shouted to Captain Oranato, who grinned widely and gave orders to the steersman. The oarsmen on the deck below were cheering.

Warner looked southeast. A dozen sails had appeared over the horizon, and he touched Baker's sleeve and pointed.

"Colonel's coming up."

"Yes, we'll let him deal with those two." Baker raised his voice. "Stand by to engage," he said, then thumbed his radio to the general channel. "All units, this is Rabbit One. We'll cripple the third enemy and see if we can catch any more of them. Once we've hit this next ship, leave these for the main fleet to deal with. We will then engage the next three pirate ships in line. I note that the trailing ships have slowed their pace, I believe they may try to run away. Acknowledge. Over."

"Rabbit Two, aye, aye," Martins said. "Well done, Skipper! Over."

"Rabbit Three, aye, aye. Over," Cargill said.

The third pirate ship tried to turn away at the last moment, but its captain had left his decision too late, and Warner cheered as *Sagitta* bore down on the galley.

"We'll rake him, by God!" Baker shouted. He grinned at Warner. "Well, that's what they say in the Hornblower novels. Make ready for volley fire. Your aim point is low on the steering deck. Keep it low. Stand by . . . take aim. In volley, fire!"

Five minutes later the third pirate's sail fell.

"The rest of them are running away," Warner said. "They've seen the fleet, I think."

"Or what happened to their companions," Baker said. He shrugged. "Either way, we aren't going to catch them. They're pulling away from us now." He frowned. "Waste of ammunition to fire on them at this range. All right, Sergeant Major, you can have the lads put their weapons away. This job is pretty well done." He thumbed the talk button. "Mission accomplished, Colonel. What's next?"

"Stand off until we bring up the fleet," Rick said. "We'll get things—uh—ship shape. Then we'll take the fleet to call on Nikeis." Rick's chuckle came through on the radio. "After you transfer back to *Ferox*, we can send your merchant captain on ahead to tell them what he just saw."

## ✦═ CHAPTER EIGHT ═✦
# MEETINGS AT SEA

Nikeis lay ahead to the north, bright in the noon of the True Sun. A blustery wind out of the northeast raised whitecaps and the Roman quinquireme tossed unpleasantly as the oarsmen kept it stationary against the wind. Rick stamped impatiently as a smaller boat approached the fleet from the channel entrance to the Nikeis harbors.

Captain Pilinius scanned the approaching boat with Rick's binoculars.

"Galliot," he said. "Not a threat."

The Roman reluctantly gave the binoculars back to Rick, as careful as Rick was in removing the strap from around his neck and using both hands to hold the optics. His expression was close to pure envy.

"I expect that's just the point," Rick said. "They want us to know they're no threat. I'm sure Captain Oranato's put the fear of God into Their Serenities or whatever the hell they call them."

"The Signory," Warner said helpfully. "Colonel, I expect your very polite letter saying that you expected to be met by Clavell and Harrison as well as their officials probably scared them more. I liked the tone you used."

He turned his own binoculars onto the southern entrance to the Nikeis island complex a mile to their north.

After a moment Rick did the same. The channel entrance was guarded by twin stone fortresses, each over fifty feet high, standing over a complex of walls and low wooden houses. The channel turned sharply right a hundred feet past the entrance forts, winding its way through mud flats punctuated with other tower fortresses until it reached the main island complex. About two miles from here, Rick thought. A mile of mud flats, and those odd-shaped towers.

He'd been told the northern entrance to the Nikeis complex was more open and less easily guarded, but he couldn't see that because of the city itself.

No city walls. The main defense of the city would be on water. If a hostile army landed there would be street fighting, and whoever won, it would be bloody. He began visualizing an invasion of ten thousand troops. How many could Nikeis turn out to oppose the invaders? Where would they make a stand? The upslopes of the main islands' steeply sloped spines would be hell on an attacker, but everything of value lay on the flats below them, and— aside from the population, at least—it couldn't be moved. If they didn't want their entire city looted or burned, that meant fighting on the low ground.

He scanned the island complex. The southern entrance

channels seemed to be protected by tower forts, but it was hard to tell which of those forts was manned, or what they would be manned with. Not cannon. Not yet, but now that Nikeisian troops had seen the Great Guns in battle, it couldn't be long before Nikeis had some too.

Presumably there would be chains across the harbor entrances, but Rick saw no signs of them. Probably they were lowered now. But aside from raising the chains, just how did Nikeis intend to defend itself against an invading fleet?

And the tide was coming in. Even as Rick watched some of the mud flats vanished under water. It was difficult to estimate the depth, but it seemed evident there must be new, unguarded channels to the city itself. Defense of that harbor would be complicated.

The inner lagoon and its central island complex were no more than twenty miles square, and probably a good bit less, with the higher island system an irregular blob some three to four miles wide. Rick frowned. Ten thousand men might very well take the city, and hold it if organized resistance collapsed. But first they'd have to get ashore onto the actual city islands.

"Hail," someone called from the oncoming galliot.

"Looks like Clavell and Harrison, Colonel," Warner said. "I think they took your suggestion seriously."

"As they should have. Who's that with them?"

"Black man," Warner said. "In what looks like civilian survival gear. Earth man, I'd say. And three official-looking guys in robes and fancy hats. Signory, for sure. Damned if I know about any Black men, Skipper."

"There were rumors of a Black star man," Rick

muttered. "Well, we'll know soon enough. Bring up Major Mason and Major Baker, and ask Major Baker to stand twenty of his Gurkhas armed at attention along the stern rail. Might help if we have to negotiate."

⁜ ⁜ ⁜

Clavell and Harrison were brought aboard by Roman marines, then led aft to the quarterdeck where Rick waited. They were not alone. The Black man and three expensively robed Nikeis officials followed them at a discreet distance and stood on the main deck as Clavell and Harrison climbed the stairs—ladder, Rick told himself—to the quarterdeck where Rick waited. Baker and twenty Gurkhas stood at attention along the stern rail with bayoneted rifles at order. They looked uncomfortable on the pitching quinquireme, but that only made them look more grimly dangerous, and Rick suppressed a grin.

*Just what I wanted. The Signory must have heard what those rifles can do.*

Clavell and Harrison obviously hadn't suffered at the hands of the Nikeisian Signory. They were both clean and looked to have been well fed, Harrison perhaps more than was good for him. *Clean clothes and a steady gait*, Rick thought. *I doubt I'll be hearing any complaints.*

Clavell wore what Rick would call local finery. Harrison wore star clothes, camouflage battle dress. Both had .45 Colt pistols in shoulder holsters, and in addition Harrison had an H&K battle rifle slung over his right shoulder. When they reached the quarterdeck they snapped to attention and saluted.

"Sergeant Clavell and Private Harrison reporting, Sir!" Rick returned the salute.

"Welcome aboard. It's been a while since we heard from you."

"Yes, Sir. I sent you reports, but I reckon they didn't get through," Clavell said.

*Cheerful enough*, Rick thought. *No sign of discomfort. Glad to see us. Not sure Harrison is, but Clavell's all right. He's looking for orders, doesn't have schemes of his own. Of course I'm guessing.*

"Get through or get out, Sergeant?"

"Don't reckon they got out, Colonel," Clavell said. "I don't think the Signory have been letting my messages get out. I expect they still have them all."

"I'll ask," Rick said. "Were you mistreated? Imprisoned?"

"No Sir," Clavell said. "Only complaint I have is not being able to get messages in or out. Well, that and the fact they lied to me about not having a ship available to get us home before you locked up with the Fivers. They were making *damned* sure nothing they wanted to sit on was gonna get to you any earlier than they could help. 'Side from that, Colonel, we were treated like royalty."

Rick nodded satisfaction. "I'll get your full report later. At ease, men. Good to see you again, Harrison."

"Glad to be back with the outfit," Harrison said.

*Sure you are*, Rick thought. *Sure you are*. Harrison had a wife and children at Armagh. They'd been moved to Chelm when Rick withdrew the mercenaries from Armagh, but Harrison wouldn't know that. And didn't seem to care. Still— "Your family was well, the last time I saw them," Rick said. "I moved them to Chelm for safety, but they ought to be on the way back to Armagh by now."

"Safety? Sir?" Harrison frowned.

"There was a bit of a flap when the Five Kingdoms marched south, but that's all settled now. Armagh is safe, and so is your family."

"Thank you, Sir." Harrison nodded, his expression unreadable.

*So that's that?* Rick thought. *I don't know enough about my troops. Are they divorced? Is Harrison keeping a mistress? I don't know much about his wife—southern girl, no family came up with her that I know of. Don't know how many kids, either. Elliot would know.*

"Begging your pardon, Colonel, but who the hell are those?" Harrison asked, pointing at Major Baker and his Gurkhas.

"Reinforcements," Rick said. "We're short on time just now. Mr. Warner will bring you up to date as soon as we get a chance." Rick nodded towards the Black man who stood with the robed Nikeis officials. "Sergeant, who have you brought with you?" he asked, and noted that Clavell looked to Harrison before answering. *Not sure which is the real leader, here,* Rick thought. "Should we invite him up?"

"Yes, Sir." Clavell said. "Sir, he's from Earth."

"Recently from Earth?"

"Yes, Sir, couple of weeks here, he reckons maybe three months in travel. There's three of them. Colonel, there's so damned much, this place, everything happening—"

"I know, Sergeant," Rick said. "Anything I have to know before I meet him?"

"Not that I know, Colonel. He seems a pretty straight-up guy to me."

"Good. Ask him to join us."

Clavell nodded.

"Yes Sir." He turned towards the mid deck and waved, and the Black man came up onto the quarterdeck. "Colonel, this is Cal Haskins. From San Francisco," Clavell said. "Cal, Colonel Galloway."

"An Earthman, I see." Rick extended his hand. "And what brings you here, Mr. Haskins?"

Cal Haskins' grip was firm, and he looked Rick directly in the eye as he shook his head with a faint smile.

"Corporal Haskins, US Army, as was, but that's a long story, Colonel. Sure you got time to hear it all? Them Gurkhas look a bit seasick."

"You know about the Gurkhas?" Rick demanded.

"Not a thing, Colonel. Seen Gurkha uniforms before, and the Major is clear Brit, easy to see that, and after the stories about brown star men and the pirates it wasn't hard to figure. Easy to see they don't like being on this boat, too."

Rick nodded; Haskins had a point.

"Major Baker, you can have your men stand at ease. Or sit down, if they prefer."

"Sir." Baker gave quiet orders. The Gurkha troops sat cross-legged, their backs to the bulwark.

"No, we don't have a lot of time at all," Rick said, turning back to Haskins.

Clavell nodded vigorously.

"That's what that merchant captain said. Shouted it out to everyone in the Palazzo. Pirate fleet coming, he said. Same as what the Nikeisian scout patrols say. Big pirate fleet coming, a hundred ships, maybe more. Two hundred. Maybe five hundred. Gathering in the mainland harbors, getting ready to sail against Nikeis. Pirates, Riccigiona, and Five Kingdom regulars coming to kill us all, coming soon, soon. We'd heard some of that before, but that guy you sent in made sure everybody in the Palazzo heard. Like he didn't trust the Signory to tell everyone. He also said you were coming, with a Roman fleet and star weapons to help Nikeis, and that got cheers, I can tell you."

*That worked*, Rick thought, exchanging a smile with Warner. It had been Warner's idea to send ahead the merchant captain of the ship Major Baker had used to destroy the pirate vessels.

"So they already knew the pirates were coming. How many do they expect?" Rick demanded.

"Don't know, Sir. The Councilors"—Clavell waved at the robed Nikeis officials still on the mid deck—"would know better. One said five hundred ships the other night, but nobody believes that. But a lot, enough to scare them. Never saw the Signory act so fast. They're launching every reserve ship they've got. More ships than crews, they're rounding up clerks and factory workers to be rowers, calling up the militia as marines. Damnedest stir you ever saw, Sir. Whole city's like an ant hill! And they sure acted glad to hear you were coming to help them. Should I bring them up so you can ask them direct, Colonel?"

"In a few moments," Rick said. He eyed the Black man. "I don't think they can begrudge me a few minutes to get your reports. Hell, it's their fault I don't know things already! Mr. Haskins, give me the short version of what you're doing here," Rick said.

"Cal will do just fine, Colonel. I'm here to help Mr.

Saxon set up a school. Least that's what the CIA man told us back in the Tenderloin."

"CIA?"

"Well, a Doctor Lee. Turns out he wasn't CIA, but that's what we thought he was. Said he was recruiting a teacher for a science school, Colonel. That was Mr. Saxon. The teacher he was recruiting, that is. Doctor Lee recruited him for a primitive place a long way off, and when I heard about it, I asked them to let me come along. Used to be I was a corporal in a nation-building outfit, and I hadn't had much of a gig in a while. Sounded like something I could do. I thought I'd be going to Africa, but it turned out to be further away than that. Time I found that out, it was too late to turn back."

"Too late?"

"That's how they put it. They didn't give us no choices."

"So you and Saxon were tricked into coming here?"

"Pretty well. Damn well."

"You don't seem too shook up about it," Warner said, and Haskins grimaced.

"Not now, maybe. Maybe I got over it. But I didn't like it."

"You tried to resist coming once you knew it would take you off the Earth?" Rick asked.

"Damn straight, Colonel, for all the good that did. Once we saw the ship we were supposed to get into was a flying saucer, they didn't give us no way out. Next thing we knew we was on the Moon, and a policeman was telling us we didn't have any choices, we had to earn our keep, go out to help Captain Galloway with his crop 'cause we was never going home."

"A policeman." Rick frowned. "Did you get his name?"

"Inspector Agzaral," Cal Haskins said firmly.

"And he sent you here to assist me? He named me?"

"That he did. Go help Captain Galloway grow his crops, that's what we were told to do," Haskins said. "Didn't understand everything and some of it sounded plain fishy, but that's what they told me. We're here to help you grow more crops by setting up a school. Mr. Saxon will know more than me. Ask him when we get ashore."

"Why isn't he out here?"

The ship pitched as a rogue wave came through the steady chop and Haskins gripped the quarterdeck rail.

"Bart gets seasick," he said. "And, maybe, he didn't exactly trust the Signory Council guys. Thought somebody ought to stay back an' watch Miss Spirit and the cargo. Damn valuable stuff, that cargo."

"Cargo. Shipping containers?"

"Yes, Sir, three of them, with a lot of stuff we bought on CIA credit cards."

"What kind of stuff?"

"High-tech stuff. Books, CD-ROMs, computers, windmill generators, all kinds of stuff."

"Evidently this is going to take some time to straighten out," Rick said, and Clavell nodded vigorously.

"You know it, Colonel," he said.

"And we don't have much time. All right, Sergeant Clavell, is there anything else I need to know before we bring the Nikeisian people into the conversation? How safe are things in Nikeis?"

"I don't know, Colonel. You need to know a lot, and we ain't got time to tell it all just now. Main thing is that

Nikeis is run by factions, and right now the two main factions are run by Councilor Torricelli—that's the one on your left there—and Councilor Avanti. Avanti's son was the one that found Cal and Bart Saxon and Ms. Lorraine Sandori. Torricelli and Avanti right now between them have control of three cargo containers full of electronics and books and God knows what else."

"Guns?" Art Mason demanded.

"Don't know, Major," Clavell said. "Saxon says not many, information mostly, not weapons. And tools. Lots of tools. But Torricelli has troops, and Avanti has troops, and the Doge has troops, and some of the other councilors have troops, and everybody's got ships, and they're all working together to fix up a fleet and train the militia to defend the place from these pirates, and nobody's really in command! Not the Doge, not the Councilors, nobody. But while nobody's really in charge, those guys give orders most will follow. So right now they're the two most powerful men in Nikeis," Clavell finished breathlessly. "They thought they was doing you a big honor coming out to meet you. And I don't think it's too wise to keep them waiting too long. They're acting friendly, but they're damned proud types."

Rick nodded thoughtfully, then smiled thinly.

"Come over here," Rick said. "You too, Harrison." He gathered the three men into an embrace. "Warner, get in on this. Overjoyed to see our men again. Put your heart into it. You too, Art, Major Baker. Big dancing huddle circle! Look overjoyed." He led them in a circular dance.

*Used to do that in football*, Rick thought. *Not that I played much. But they did, and it looks good.*

"Right," Baker said tonelessly.

They all joined in an exuberant welcome leaving Haskins outside the circle, then Rick opened a place on his left and invited him into the welcoming ring.

"How long do we keep this up, Sir?" Harrison asked sourly.

"Long enough to make them think it's some kind of custom," Rick said. "That ought to do it. Break. Back on your dignity. Can't hurt to leave 'em a bit confused."

They broke the circle and stood back.

"Okay, Clavell, invite them up. Look like we're glad to see them."

"Yes, Sir. One thing, Colonel. Don't get the idea you're a better actor than them. Plots and stories and that sort of thing is the way they run this city, and these are the best they've got."

Rick nodded.

*Well, I've given them a good excuse not to be mad at us unless they want to be*, he thought. *The real question is, do I care? I have my men back. I need this Saxon guy, and those containers, but do I need anything else from this place? Of course that's what they'll be thinking, too.*

"Powder dry," he said distinctly. Warner looked startled. Mason and Baker nodded in understanding.

Clavell went down to the mid deck and escorted the robed figures up to the quarterdeck.

"Colonel Galloway, I have the honor to present Councilor Torricelli, Councilor Avanti, and Senator del Verme. The Senator was recently appointed Admiral of the Home Waters. Signory, I present Colonel Galloway, Colonel of Star Lords and Warlord of Drantos."

Clavell spoke in halting Italian, then translated into English, and Rick bowed to each of the Nikeis dignitaries in turn.

"It is my pleasure," he said. "We have much to discuss, and little time."

He studied the three men as Clavell translated. The others hung back, willing to let Torricelli speak for them all. They all had the same look, trying to be friendly, maybe afraid they wouldn't get that message across. They kept glancing at the twenty armed Gurkhas at the stern rail. The Gurkhas were seated but they gave the impression of being at attention. Not happy with the ship's motion, but they sat like statues, their bayoneted rifles stiffly upright with their butts on the deck. The Nikeisians seemed fascinated by those rifles . . . and by the big kukri knives at their belts. Rick had no doubt the merchant captain had described their effectiveness against the pirate ships, and their power had probably grown in the telling.

Torricelli nodded gravely.

"Warlord of Drantos, we greet you in the name of the Doge and the people of the Most Serene Republic. As you say, there is much to discuss and little time, and this is hardly the proper place. Allow me to invite you to the Palace where we have proper records and maps, and we can make more meaningful plans."

"We've brought twenty ships and crews," Rick said. "And their weapons." He indicated the Gurkhas at the stern rail. "They will need berthing and shore quarters."

"This is even now being arranged. Do you have more forces coming?"

"Perhaps, but the timing is critical. We should plan to win with the forces we have."

"That will be few enough against what we believe is coming."

"Which is what?"

"Hundreds of ships from the Gavin pirates, Five Kingdoms, and Riccigiona."

"What is Nikeis' relationship with the Grand Duchy?"

"They have long been our rivals and they are now allied with the Five Kingdoms."

"Do you know of any reason they would sail against you now?"

"Only that they've heard of the great boxes and wish to have them for themselves. Their joining this armada is troubling to us, as their crews are almost as well trained as our own."

"So I've heard." Rick smiled slightly. "Your Captain Oranato will have told you of the effectiveness of our weapons."

Torricelli's expression was impassive.

"We can but hope," he said. "We should make haste. There is little time. Shall we proceed?"

*Sure*, Rick thought. *And how do I know we'll come back out of there? Clavell and Harrison didn't. But I already decided this, I'm going in.*

"I will be pleased to accompany you to the city," he said. "I will summon the fleet when Fleetmaster Junius and Tribune Alantamius have examined the arrangements made for their accommodation." Rick indicated the Roman naval officer. "Major Mason, you'll be in command here: I'll leave Private Harrison with you to brief the Fleet

Admiral and the other Roman commanders. Mr. Haskins, will you remain with them? I'm sure you'll have a lot to tell them. Thank you. Now, Mr. Warner, you and sergeants Clavell and Bisso will come with me."

Rick bowed to the Nikeisian officials.

"I will come with you on your ship, gentlemen. These Roman staff officers will accompany me to see to our berthing arrangements. Time is short, Excellencies, and I believe it's time to get on with it."

"Colonel—" Art Mason looked horrified.

"It's all right, Major," Rick said in English. "I don't think it's a trap, but just in case I'm leaving you with the firepower to do something about it, and Harrison to tell you who to do it to. I don't know what these guys are planning, but they're not likely to do anything until we've dealt with those pirates."

"Sure of that, Colonel?" Major Baker asked.

"Reasonably sure," Rick said. "Not so sure I'll risk His Nibs until we know more. And there's no need to let them suspect that His Nibs is with us, either."

"We need you more than we need—" Rick held up his hand. "Than we need His Nibs," Baker finished, and Mason nodded vigorously.

"Colonel, at least let me send some bodyguards."

Rick shook his head. "I have my pistol, and Warner has his—"

Mason's snort showed what he thought of Warner's skills as a bodyguard.

"More won't help," Rick said. "Harrison and Clavell were there for months without any problems."

"You're just a little more important than Lance and

Jimmy," Mason said. "Colonel, I'd feel better coming with you."

"I would too, Art, but leaving Major Baker to command without knowing much of the local situation is a bit much to ask of him."

"Then take me with a section of my lads," Baker said.

"Trust," Rick said. "We'll need to show some, and this is as good a way as any. They're not going to jump me while that pirate fleet's coming to burn the whole place out!"

"Yes, Sir," Baker said. "Even so I'll feel better when we're all together again."

"Me too. But I won't be any use until I find out just what the hell is going on," Rick said.

"Well, the Nikeisian situation is complicated," Warner began, but Rick cut him off.

"The devil with the Nikeisian situation. Ever read Sabatini? Typical Renaissance-flavored Tran politics. Nikeis I understand. What I can't figure out is what Agzaral thinks he's doing!"

"Oh," Warner said.

"Precisely." Rick turned to the Nikeisian officials. "If Your Honors will lead the way . . . "

# ✦ CHAPTER NINE ✦
## PALACES

When they were aboard the Nikeisian communications ship, Rick cut short Councilor Avanti's attempts to explain why Clavell and Harrison had been incommunicado.

"There's no need to explain," he said. "I understand that you thought it was necessary."

"Then it is of no concern?" Torricelli asked.

"It's of no concern for the present. Now, if you'll excuse me, I need to confer with my agent." Rick bowed.

"Of course," Torricelli said. He even managed a tight-lipped smile.

"Colonel, he looks fit to chew nails," Clavell said, when Rick had drawn him and the other star lords off to the leeward side of the quarterdeck.

"Will that matter? He knows damned well that I must feel the same way."

Clavell shrugged.

"Colonel, far as I can tell, these guys don't let how

they feel interfere with what they have to do. This is the damnedest place for nothing being what it seems, but so far they've got the job done. And they damned well need help."

"So tell me what you know, Sergeant."

"Not a lot. We was set to come home when the story came in about the Five Kingdoms invading Drantos, but before we could get on the ship news came in about lights in the sky over on the mainland, and after that everything closed up really tight. They kicked all the Romans out—I think they jailed some of them, but I don't know that for sure. Maybe Vinicianus knows—"

"Vinicianus? He's here?"

"Sure is, Colonel. I was hoping to use him to get a message to you, but I guess he didn't manage that."

"I see. Sorry. Go on. You may have sent reports, but I haven't received any in quite a while."

"I wrote reports, Colonel. But the only way I could send them was to give them to the Signory to send for me, and maybe they never got around to doing that."

"You wrote in English, of course."

"Mostly English. I put in some stuff I didn't mind the Signory knowing, like how smart my students were and how peaceful the place was—it was peaceful, Colonel— stuff like that in the language they use here. I even put some in Italian, not that I speak much Italian. I was hoping that if I said enough good stuff about them they'd want to send it on to you."

"Good thinking."

"Maybe, but I guess it didn't work."

They were interrupted by shouted orders as the crew

raised the large lateen sail. The ship got underway, heeling hard over as it began the tack northward, and the Roman fleet drew together behind them. Rick saw the flash of red cloaks as Publius emerged on the flagship's deck. He was dressed in the standard clothing of a Roman high officer, and at this distance wasn't recognizable as the Heir of Caesar. Of course, when he went ashore someone would know him, but Publius had wanted to remain anonymous as long as possible.

*He doesn't trust them,* Rick thought. *Come to that, neither do I, but what does Publius have in mind?*

*Trust. None of us trust each other much.* It wasn't likely that Publius would be stupid enough to move against Major Baker in the hopes of gaining command over the Gurkhas. More likely, he would make an offer of friendship—not an attempt to bribe Baker away from loyalty to Rick, but more of general friendship. *Like he did earlier, only that offer was to me and the target was Wanax Ganton. From the little I know of Baker, he'll probably act interested and then tell me about it later. Or I hope so. I've got too many balls in the air. And I can't let my mind wander like this.*

He listened as Clavell continued to report.

"Anyway, they shut this place down tighter'n a drum, right about the time your wife was captured by Prince Strymon. Then the containers started coming."

"Containers."

"Three of them, Colonel. Standard shipping containers, maybe twenty feet by eight by eight high. I haven't seen what's in them yet, but Bart Saxon tells me they're full of everything he could think of that he might need to teach high technology."

The ship began to move rapidly through the water.

"What kind of 'everything'?" Rick asked.

"Books. Bicycle generator. Windmill. Encyclopedia. Microscopes. Things he calls laptop computers. I never heard of them before, but Saxon says the damn things can calculate. And they have these disk things with books on them, all kinds of books. Hundreds of books."

"And Torricelli and company control those containers."

"It's complicated, Colonel, but that's about the size of it. They're all locked, and Saxon has the only keys. I reckon the Signory could bash their way into them, but not without us knowing they did it. One's in the Arsenale, and that one they control completely. Another's in Avanti's palazzo, but Ms. Lorraine Sandori lives there with it. Earth woman. Speaks good modern Italian, good enough to get along with the Signory. From San Francisco—used to be a SFPD cop. She's supposed to be subordinate to Mr. Saxon, but she don't hardly act like she is. Anyway, she's with that container, and I leave it to you to decide whether it's safe or not. The third one's in Saxon's palace— well, my palace, too, since they put him in with Jimmy and me. Unless they moved it in the last couple of hours—and I don't think so—Saxon controls it. But the Signory sure as hell have enough troops to take it away from him if they want to. He's got a pistol, but I don't think he knows much about using it."

"Have they threatened him? Tried to steal anything?"

"Not a thing, Colonel. Like I told you, they've been nice as pie. It's the way they are. I don't trust them very far, but usually when they make a promise they keep it. Just be careful of the wording if you agree to anything."

*Sounds even more like the Venetian Republic*, Rick thought. *At least as much as I can remember of it*. Which was mostly derived from historical novels. *One by Poul Anderson, another by Sabatini. Both pretty careful authors. And a biography of Casanova . . .*

"Okay. Enough for now. I'll go below to exchange pleasantries with the councilors."

*And when we get ashore I'm going to need some time alone with this Bart Saxon. Maybe he knows what Agzaral thinks he's doing. I sure don't.*

He looked up to see that the ship was moving much faster than he had expected.

*Won't be long. Which means that when those pirates get here, we won't have a lot of warning after they're sighted.*

His stomach turned over again, and the ache in his right hip had come back. His piles hurt. He made his way gingerly to the main cabin below the quarterdeck and took a seat at the main table, his head in his hands.

*What the hell am I doing here?*

✢ ✢ ✢

They landed at the main square, and Rick was intrigued by the similarity to Piazza San Marco in Venice. Columns, pillars, relief work over the Doge's Palace. Even pigeons, on the parts of the square that were dry.

*A diversified flock. How many did they bring here from Earth? Maybe there are records.*

A boarded walkway two feet above the cobblestones led to a dry area almost two hundred feet from the floating dock. There were differences from the Venice Rick had visited on Earth, but not startlingly so. Men sat at tables outside the shops around the square and huddled over to talk business. Couples sat and gazed at each other. They were dressed differently from modern Italians, of course. The biggest difference from old Venice was the steep hillside above the western edge of the square. It led to the plateau in the center of the island, and the slope was covered with palaces and more humble structures all the way to the top. There would still be a city here when the waters rose.

More than a dozen men waited at the elaborate doorway to the Doge's Palace. Most were elderly, with elaborate robes and gaudy hats. Rick was led inside, and everyone seemed to talk at once.

Most of the ceremonies were conducted in Italian and incomprehensible, but Rick understood he'd been introduced to the Doge and the Signory, and that they were all concerned about the coming pirates, whose arrival was expected at any moment. A hundred and fifty warships of pirates, Riccigiona, and the Five Kingdoms were on their way and could Lord Rick aid his ally in resisting them?

The question was asked more than a dozen times; but when Rick asked what the Signory could promise in their own defense, the answers were ambiguous. There were ships in the harbor and more were being launched. Crews were being recruited. The number of experienced crews was small, and much of the trained militia was still deployed in Terra Firma. The Signory had serious doubts about the city's ability to defend itself against such a large invading army. But of course God was merciful, and Nikeis had always enjoyed the favor of heaven, and would

Rick forgive them for not sending his ambassadors home sooner, the need of the city was great and Harrison and Clavell were so useful, and—

*First things first*, Rick thought.

"If Your Honors expect me to aid in the city's defense, I first need to know what we have to defend with. Precisely how many ships, and in what condition. And they must be put under my command."

That brought an explosion of comments. Rick waited a moment, then held up his hand.

"Enough! Signores, what do you expect here? There can be only one commander, and you cannot command my ships and weapons!"

"True, Warlord of Drantos," Councilor Torricelli said. "And it is true that your fame is great. Perhaps the bards have neglected to sing of your prowess on the seas?"

Rick waited a moment, then smiled.

"I have none." He smiled more widely. "I need none. Your Captain Oranato will have told you of the effectiveness of some of my weapons. I have others. As to experience with the seas, my fleet is Roman and commanded by an admiral of Rome. A logical commander, and one none of you can be ashamed of obeying."

The Signory whispered together for a few moments. Then Torricelli returned to Rick.

"We have six great galleys and twelve *galee sottili*"— those were the equivalent of the Roman triremes, Rick knew; the actual translation was "thin galleys"—"with experienced crews," he said. "A dozen more *galee sottili* crewed by militia. Twelve *fusta* with reasonable crews, too old to fight but able to row. We count twenty first-class ships in your Roman fleet. Twenty galleys and four *navibus,* which I assume carry supplies. Add all this together, and we have less than half the number that threatens us. The tides will be high, and there will be many approaches to the city at high tide. Their battle lines will be longer than ours, and our flanks will be exposed."

"A reasonable assessment," Rick said. "You believe the *navibus onerārius* of no account?"

"They defend themselves well," Torricelli said.

"Perhaps ours can do more than mere defense. With star weapons aboard they can hold flanks securely even though they cannot maneuver. Councilor, I'm led to believe that ship-for-ship your fleet is a match for equal numbers of Romans. Is this true?"

"It is as God wills, but certainly our experienced crews will be the equal or better of any ships on the Inner Sea."

"And you count twenty first-class ships with experienced crews?"

Torricelli looked grave.

"Perhaps some are better than others," he said. "I would certainly count twelve, including all of our great galleys, as the equals of any ship in the world."

*Leaving eight not quite so good*, Rick thought. *It's better than it could have been.*

"The Romans share your opinion of the worth of your best ships and crews," he said. "They also believe that each Roman ship can best any ship in the pirate fleet, as can any of your better ships. So we have thirty galleys, each the equal of any pirate, another dozen as a reserve to finish off crippled enemies, and my four *navibus onerārius.*"

"Against at least a hundred, and I have heard counts as

high as four times that number," Senator del Verme said. "Those seem long odds."

The room fell silent. Everyone was listening as Rick spoke.

"It will be enough. We will win this battle. It may come to fighting in the streets, but perhaps we can stop them before they can land in the city. We won't have an easy victory, but we will win. Your soldiers saw the Battle of the Ottarn. I have more star forces here than we had there."

"We are reassured by your confidence, but—" Torricelli let his voice trail off.

"Remain reassured," Rick said. "We'll examine details later, but I believe our star weapons will be sufficient to compensate for numbers. We will aid in your defense."

Torricelli's relief was obvious.

"There is much to plan," he said.

"There is," Rick agreed. "We can discuss our order of battle later, when the Roman admiral is present. For now, we require berthing space for the Roman fleet and lodging and supplies for our men. Roman sailors and my own troops, star lords, and my guardsmen. And my Gurkhas, sixty in number."

"We know little of goorkhas," young Senator Avanti said. He paused, looked to his father and to Councilor Torricelli, then said in a rush, "Are these the star men who defeated the armies of Drantos and put Wanax Ganton to flight?"

The older Signory looked away. A few put on expressions of disapproval at the rudeness.

*But no one said anything. No one rebuked him,* Rick thought, and gave the young man a cold smile.

"I would be very careful about what conclusions you

draw from earlier times," he said. "It's true that the Gurkhas were at one time in the service of the Five Kingdoms against Drantos. Now they serve me. Make no mistake; these are my loyal troops, and their power is great on land or sea, as you may already have heard."

"As you say," Torricelli said. "Warlord, we are making arrangements for your fleet and your men now. Let us discuss what you will need."

Rick nodded satisfaction.

"Rice," he said. "My Gurkhas prefer rice to wheat and barley. If you have no rice, potatoes will be a poor substitute but better than wheat."

"We will see what is available, Warlord. What else will you require?"

✣ ✣ ✣

Rick left the logistics negotiations to his staff, primarily Tribune Alantamius of the Roman fleet, who seemed to be an expert on naval logistics. There didn't appear to be any problems, and by midafternoon, Alantamius and the Roman quartermasters reported satisfaction.

A large anchorage area had been set aside in the inner lagoon, and a nearby island with docks was already being partly evacuated to provide space for the crews. From the smiles on the Roman officers' faces, the provisions and quarters would be more than satisfactory, and there was more than enough room for the twenty Roman warships and the six merchant ships in the designated anchorage.

"They have found forty bushels of rice in a trader's warehouse, Sir," Alantamius said with satisfaction. "That should be enough for your Gurkhas for twenty days, perhaps more. As well, there is ample wheat and barley and rye. The Nikeisian officials understand these matters well, not like some of the barbarians we've dealt with."

*And they're hardly barbarians,* Rick thought. *Interesting that you class them as such. Or did I misunderstand? At least you didn't say anything about* other *barbarians.*

He turned to Torricelli, who stood impassively, although Rick was fairly certain the Councilor had understood the patrician officer's remark.

"My thanks, Councilor. The accommodations are more than adequate. I will summon the fleet."

"Write your orders," Torricelli said. "A *fusta* will deliver them."

"Send your *fusta* with pilots to lead them in," Rick said. "I need write no orders."

"But—"

"I will, however, require a high place to stand. The top of your bell tower will suffice. Please lead me there."

Torricelli stood for a moment in puzzlement, then led them to a corner of the palace and indicated a steep circular stairway.

"It is many stairs to the top," he said.

"Yeah," Rick told him. He started up the stairway, followed by Warner, Alantamius, and Rick's household card. After a moment, Torricelli climbed up after them.

It was a steep and gloomy climb, and it went on far longer than Rick had expected. He felt like he had climbed eight stories before he reached the first balcony, and he felt short of breath when he reached the windowed landing where a balcony ran right around the top of the stairs. The stairway stopped there, but there were ladders going up from there to the bells.

Rick estimated that they were about eighty feet above the Palazzo, and the view from the upper balcony was all he'd expected. He could see the entire inner lagoon, and across the other islands and mud flats to the Roman fleet where it maintained station. Rick estimated that the fleet was about a mile and a half to the south of the channel. He scanned about with his binoculars, more to catch his breath than for any information, then unhooked the radio from his belt.

He smiled when the light came on. Officially, its batteries were supposed to be good for at least twelve hours, but he never felt truly confident of that. *Because I know how far we are from the nearest RadioShack? Bit hard to get any more of 'em!*

"Fleet, this is Galloway," he said in English. "Over." When there was no answer, he said it again, using the Tran mainland language. "Fleet, this is Galloway, this is Galloway, Galloway, Galloway. Over."

Slight static, then English.

"Mason here, Colonel. All's well. Over."

"You've got a home," Rick said. "They're sending a boat with pilots. Have the admiral follow them in. You'll all anchor in the same place. Actually, most of you won't anchor; there are berths and buoys. But you get the idea. The pilots will show you where to park. Let the Roman officers handle the safety of the ships. You look to the shore quarters and supplies. Over."

"Aye, aye, Skipper. Anything new on the pirates? Over."

"Maybe tonight, but a night attack isn't expected. Possibly at dawn. Over."

"I take it they're friendly in Nikeis? Over."

"Trying hard to be, anyway. Not too sure of themselves, but they're not likely to try anything hostile. They need us too much. Powder dry, of course. Have the star weapons in waterproofing but ready to take out at need. That's all the star weapons, including the Gurkhas' rifles. Relaxed but ready, that's the status. Over."

"And the Musketeers? Over."

"Bayonets only. Don't even think about issuing ammo aboard ship. They can guard the barracks areas when you get shore quarters, but we don't need any accidental discharges aboard ship! For that matter, I want the gunpowder barrels ashore ASAP. Over."

"Understood. Powder dry, weapons dry and out of sight. Muskets okay ashore, and get all the gunpowder off the ships. And we're to follow the pilot ship to the anchorage and make fast. Over."

"Affirmative. Follow him into the inner harbor. One of us will be there to show you your shore mess areas and quarters. There are supplies and local cooks and I saw plenty of fuel. Tell the captains there will be hot meals tonight, but I want half the crews to sleep aboard ship, and everyone ready to get underway in less than an hour if we spot that pirate fleet coming. We don't know what's coming next, so no more than half the crew off any ship at one time, and everyone—and I mean everyone—is on alert status. Troops can come ashore, but ready to get back aboard if there's an enemy sighted. Over."

Rick lifted his binoculars again and smiled in approval. The Roman flagship was already hoisting signal flags, and there was activity on the other ships.

"Art, I'm in their bell tower. You can see it—the big

square tower on the southeast corner of the palace. Palace, that's the highest building in the city, right down at water's edge and seven stories tall, with the tower running up higher. See it? Over."

"Got it. Can't quite make you out. Over."

"Wave something bright, Mr. Warner," Rick ordered.

"I see something," Mason said. "Okay, I got your location. Over."

"Good. I'll be watching from up here, just to be sure they're leading you where they said they would. Come in single file with decent intervals, just in case the channel isn't as open as they tell me it is. I'd hate to have more than one ship run aground. Over."

"So we don't trust them? Over."

"Trust, sure, but powder dry, Art. They need us, and they need our weapons, and I don't think they're stupid. Far from it. So I doubt they think they can use our gear without us, but you never know. Powder dry. Over."

"Aye, aye, Colonel. One more thing. Do we try to hide His Nibs? Over."

"Only until you get to the anchorage and he goes ashore," Rick said. "Someone's sure to recognize him, so we may as well make as much as we can out of his being here. Ask him to go ashore in full regalia. That ought to amuse him. Over."

"Think he'll like that?" Mason asked. Then, "There's the pilot ship coming. Time to get started. Over."

"Right. Keep someone listening for the signal. I'm turning my radio to standby to save battery life. That's it for me."

"Roger that. Mason out."

Rick turned to Torricelli.

"Your pilot *fusta* has arrived, and my fleet is prepared to follow him to their berths."

"And you were speaking with your ships. From here," Torricelli said in wonder. "I had heard of this capability, but I have never seen it. And it is not magic?"

"Not magic. Only star technology—*technia*?"

"As are those binoculars." Torricelli pronounced the unfamiliar word almost perfectly.

"Yes. Would you care to look?"

"Thank you." Torricelli put the strap over his head before taking hold of the field glasses, then looked through them while adjusting the focus.

*Either he's used binoculars before, or Captain Oranato described how in enough detail that he doesn't need directions*, Rick thought. *Oranato's probably giving lessons in using binoculars. To who? The whole Senate? Another thing to remember. They learn fast and they spread the knowledge.*

"One more thing, Councilor," Rick said. "The Roman commander here is Publius Caesar."

"Publius? The heir?" Torricelli lowered the binoculars abruptly and looked at him, and he nodded. "But, My Lord, we've made no preparations to receive such an important person! No one told—"

Larry Warner harrumphed.

"Publius Caesar is the heir to the Roman Imperium, so designated by Marselius Caesar," he said. "A very important man, but perhaps not so much greater than the Warlord of Drantos."

He chuckled. Torricelli's look was pure annoyance.

"All is well, Councilor," Rick said. "Publius Caesar asked that we keep his presence here in confidence and has only now decided to reveal himself. He won't expect more welcome than you can provide on this notice. Councilor, I have little knowledge of the relations between Nikeis and Rome."

"We have long been friends and allies," Torricelli said a bit stiffly, and Rick caught Warner's broad wink from behind the Nikeisian's back.

"We have had visits from members of the previous Imperial family," Torricelli continued. "Once a nephew to Flaminius the Scholar. But none so high as the heir, and only ambassadors since Flaminius Caesar was overthrown."

Rick noted the distaste in Torricelli's tone. Rebellion was not revered in Nikeis.

✣ ✣ ✣

Rick watched from the tower until the fleet had formed a single file with more than a hundred feet between ships. Two of the smaller triremes led, then the quinquireme flagship, then the *navibus onerārius*. The rest of the fleet came behind. Rick watched for a moment, but there was nothing to see, and certainly nothing he could do from here if anything went wrong. It would take time to bring the entire fleet into the inner harbor and make fast, so he checked the standby status of his radio receiver, then turned impatiently to Torricelli.

"That's underway, Councilor. Now if you please, I would like to meet your other guests. The star people."

"Of course." Torricelli led the way down the narrow stairs to the Palace, then across the broad Palazzo. The crowd in the Palazzo cleared a path for Rick and the Councilors without being told. They watched attentively as their chiefs went past, and then spoke among themselves. No one bowed. Very polite, Rick thought. Not subservient, perhaps not obedient, but polite. They crossed the Palazzo to a five-story palace with ornate bronze doors. Liveried servants swung the doors open as they approached.

"Welcome to my place, Skipper," Clavell said, leading the way in. "We got Mr. Saxon holed up in here. And something you'll want to see. Come in, come in."

"Palatial, Sergeant," Rick said.

"Yes, Sir."

Clavell led them from the reception hall to another and larger room.

The palace's great hall was large, ornate, and dominated by the big shipping container. A man stood next to the container. He was dressed in dark slacks and a fine-weave blue cotton shirt, all very much Earthlike, as were his spectacles and wristwatch. *Early to midthirties*, Rick decided. *And he looks like a high school teacher*.

The other man examined Rick coolly.

*Doesn't seem nervous*, Rick thought. *I would be. Make that I am, actually. Just what's he doing here? But first, what does he think he's doing here, which may not be quite the same thing*.

"I'm Bart Saxon," the man said. "You'll be Captain Galloway. Colonel Galloway, I guess it is now."

They shook hands.

"I was sent here to find you," Saxon continued.

*Well, that answers one question*, Rick thought.

"Sent?"

"By Inspector Agzaral. My mission is to help you grow more crops. A lot more."

Rick nodded and drew Saxon aside so that they were alone.

"The inspector assigned you that mission?"

"Yes."

"And all this?" Rick indicated the cargo container.

"Technology training aids," Saxon said. "Books and information, mostly. There are three of these containers."

"That's more equipment than everything else they've sent me since I've been here combined. All three containers have the same cargoes?"

"Not identical." Saxon shook his head. "But it's all related to the mission. There are two bicycle-driven generators in this one. The other two have a diesel generator and a windmill, respectively. But all three have at least a hand generator and some laptop computers, and most of the basic CD-ROMs."

*He acts as if I know what he's talking about*, Rick thought.

"What are CD-ROMs? I gather laptop computers are desktop computers made portable, but I don't recall CD-ROMs."

Saxon gave him a wry look.

"Sorry. There've been developments in computers and computer science since your departure—"

Rick nodded.

"—and they've probably been more rapid than you think. Certainly faster than I expected. Computers are smaller and faster, and CD-ROMs are a means of storing

data on a computer disk"—he held his hands to indicate
a circle about five inches in diameter—"that can store
many volumes of text. The entire *Encyclopaedia
Britannica* is on disks in a box no larger than a shoebox.
Colonel, I have the equivalent of a technical library for
any major university on those disks."

"Which can only be read by the computers. How many
of those do you have?"

"Dozens."

"And you have all the basic books and equipment for
teaching science and technology up to university level?"

"I hope so. Colonel, I was a high school science teacher.
They gave me two weeks to get everything I was going to
take with me to a place they said was primitive and a long
way away. I got everything I could think of that was
available in San Jose, and it's easily enough to get a good
start on college physics and chemistry. I have reference
works for everything else. Some shop equipment. You give
me some bright kids and a couple of years of peace and
quiet, we'll see what happens."

"Weapons? Ammunition?"

"Not much. Personal arms and a few boxes of
ammunition."

"Enough to win a fight but not a battle."

"Close to the way Inspector Agzaral put it. Wouldn't be
a very big fight, either. I'm not here to fight. Inspector
Agzaral made that clear."

"Agzaral again. And you were recruited for this?
Tricked into coming off-planet?"

Saxon chuckled and blushed slightly.

"I wasn't hard to trick, Colonel. It wasn't like I was

doing anything important to be tricked out of. But, yes, they told me I'd be teaching bright but educationally backward kids. I guessed Africa, or possibly somewhere in South Asia. So did Cal. Neither of us had a clue about going off Earth—I wouldn't have believed them if they'd told me that's what they wanted! Until I saw the craft they wanted me to get into, anyway. And after I saw the ship, it was too late to turn back."

"You said you weren't doing anything important. Were you in danger? Threatened by anyone?"

"No, I wasn't. I was living on the streets, Colonel. It's a long story as to why. I was as down and out as anyone could be, but no, I wasn't in any acute danger. More like chronic—I couldn't have gone on that way a lot longer. I was finished, with nowhere to go, and no use to anyone. Then I was recruited to go to a faraway place to teach influential kids, and that's what I signed up for. I jumped at the chance. It was pretty clear I'd be away a good while, but I thought I was coming back."

Rick nodded. *What the hell is this? I thought I had Agzaral's rules figured out; they couldn't abduct people who weren't already in mortal danger. That's clearly not true. Wasn't true for Gwen, either, or the Gurkhas, come to that. What else don't I know? I need to talk this over with Gwen. Maybe she has a clue. No one else will. But we've got more immediate problems here.*

"And what's your status with Nikeis?"

"We're debtors," Saxon said.

"How's that?"

"Meals, lodging, transportation from the mainland. We owe for all that. They advanced us the costs, and now we owe them a lot of money. I should have more than enough in gold coins to pay that off, but nobody's given me a final bill, so I can't be certain. And I don't know exactly what my Krugerrands are worth. This is a very commercial society, Colonel."

"So I gathered. If it comes to more than you have, I can come up with it. But no one disputes your ownership of the containers?"

"Not sure," Saxon said. "No one has so far, anyway. Maybe none of the Signory do. Not so sure about Spirit. Spirit—that's what we call Ms. Lorrain Sandori. SFPD officer. She's supposed to be an assistant, like Cal, but since we got here, she hasn't been acting like a subordinate. More like a partner."

"And she has control of one of the containers?" Rick asked.

"Two, actually. One's in Senator Avanti's palazzo. She lives there. The other's in the Arsenale, guarded by Avanti's troops, and I don't even know how to find the Arsenale, much less get anything out of it."

"Does she think she owns them?" Rick asked in a lowered voice, and Saxon gestured helplessly.

"She's sure got possession. I don't know what she thinks, Colonel. I don't know what she wants, either. I doubt she does. I have the keys. Not that that will keep anyone out if they don't mind showing they bashed their way in."

"I heard hints of a romantic involvement with Senator Avanti. True?"

"It looks that way." Saxon shrugged. "She's staying at his palazzo, and I'm told her bedroom adjoins his.

Colonel, I never knew her until after we were recruited, I never got close to her, and she hasn't told me very much since we arrived here. I have no idea what she thinks she's doing, but she's well aware that Inspector Agzaral expects us to assist you in increasing your crop yields. I heard him tell her that."

"Why do I get the impression that there's more to this story than you're telling me?" Rick asked, and Saxon frowned.

"Why would you think that?"

"Because, Mr. Saxon, Inspector Agzaral is the most devious man I ever met, but he's certainly no fool. If the purpose of sending you here is to increase the crop harvest, this isn't the way to do it, and he has to know that."

"Colonel Galloway—"

"We don't have time for this discussion now, Mr. Saxon, but you're not likely to have much effect on fundamental technology here in less than a decade."

"Fertilizer, cultivation—"

"Sure, although you might be surprised at how much they already know here. And I've had some success with iron plows. But really, all the immediate effect you'll have could have been gotten by sending me a couple of good books on agricultural techniques. You certainly don't have to teach college physics!"

Rick's voice had risen high enough to attract the attention of Warner and Rick's other companions. They looked at him quizzically.

"Stand easy," Rick told them, and lowered his voice, trying to look normal. "Mr. Saxon, just what is your real mission here?"

"Just what I said. To assist you. And to teach basic chemistry and physics."

"Of the two, which is more important?" Rick pressed, and Saxon frowned.

"I never thought about that," he said, and Rick nodded. *No point in pushing it*, he decided. *The answer's obvious, anyway. They brought the wrong equipment for the education mission to be secondary.*

"And Agzaral had no direct message for me?"

"None he told me about. Colonel, he wasn't sure you'd still be operational. The last report he got was that you weren't doing so well, but he had hopes. He said something about your acquiring some additional resources through a mistake. He didn't tell me how that would happen, but I got the impression it was something he lucked into."

"I see." *That would be the Gurkhas. Maybe.* "And he wasn't unhappy about that? About my getting additional resources?"

"Just the opposite. He seemed pleased. So did his cohort. Cohort, assistant, colleague—they never told me his status. The human not born on Earth who recruited me."

"His name wasn't Les, was it?"

"Not that I know. I heard of a human named Les. A pilot. But I never met him."

"Tell me about this 'cohort.'"

"Nothing to tell. Educated, posed as a professor without any problem. Called himself Doctor Lee. Looked to be of Eurasian ancestry. Nothing special."

"And he recruited you to teach technology?"

"That was while he was pretending to be CIA and that that was the only mission, but yes."

"And after you found out that was bunk?"

"My exact orders were to find out how you were doing, and help you if you were at all successful," Saxon said. "All three of us were given that instruction. We're supposed to aid you in growing crops for the Shalnuksis. To help you."

"Help me?"

"Yes, Sir. Help you increase your crop yields. He was very specific about that. The whole point of my coming here was to increase crop yields."

"And if you got here and found out I was dead, or a failure?"

"Nothing specific. Colonel, it's a little odd. He stressed that he didn't know how you were doing, but I was never given much instruction on what to do if you were failing. Just help you and help increase crop yields."

*Odd? Damn right it's "odd"! There's a message in there, if I could figure it out*, Rick thought. *Or I think there is.*

"But to institute the science classes, as well?"

"Yes."

"I see." *My ass I see. There's something you aren't telling me, even though it's damned obvious.* "You weren't cautioned against spreading technology to the locals? No restrictions?"

"None they told me about."

"Renaissance," Rick said. "Renaissance, Enlightenment, Reformation and Counter-Reformation, Industrial Revolution. All rolled into one package, and you're that package. You do understand that?"

He looked into Saxon's eyes, and the other man nodded slowly.

"Maybe I hadn't thought it through quite that far, but, yes. Of course you're right."

"So we're going to boil the pot," Rick said. "Any suggestions on how to keep the lid on?"

"I—"

They were interrupted as someone knocked loudly at the door. Two men in the Torricelli livery rushed in spouting excited Italian. They spoke far too rapidly for Rick to understand, but then Torricelli turned to him and spoke in the mainland polyglot.

"The pirate fleet has been sighted. Over one hundred ships, all apparently fully manned. They were gathering in a harbor two days to the northwest. They may already be underway."

## ✦═ CHAPTER TEN ═✦
# BATTLE PLANS

"Ten-*hut!*" Master Sergeant Bisso said crisply. He wore new stripes, sewn by a local seamstress. Rick had decided some promotions were in order to make his command structure a little clearer.

Rick strode into the meeting room, formerly the great hall of the shoreside palace overlooking the berthing area of his fleet. The Roman high command had been invited to the Doge's Palace, to receive a welcome suitable for the Heir of Caesar.

*And we're here on San Giorgio Island*, Rick thought. *Could take that as a snub, if I really wanted to, but what the hell. The opportunity's too good to miss.*

He glanced out a window as he headed for the long table at one end of the big room. Unlike the main island, San Giorgio had little high ground. When the sea rose, the island's highest point would be no more than a few feet above water level. All of the buildings on it were made of stone, though, and looked as if they might be stable even when their foundations and lower floors were underwater.

*If the ocean doesn't rise higher than the indicated high-water marks, this will still be a city, with canals rather than streets.*

"As you were," he said as he reached his waiting chair at the table and sat. He looked around the room as other people took their seats. *Nobody here but us star lords. Wait, someone's missing . . .*

"Where's Ms. Spirit?" he demanded.

"She was invited, Colonel," Warner said.

"How?"

Warner nodded to Harrison, who stood.

"Colonel, me and Cal Haskins went over to the palazzo she's staying in. I took the paper myself, and I put it in her hands myself. She was very nice about it. She said Senator Avanti would see that she got here safely and offered us lunch."

Rick turned to Haskins.

"She say anything to you?" he asked.

"Not one blessed thing, Colonel," the Black man said.

*Have to think about that later*, Rick told himself, then turned to Major Mason.

"Glad to see you all made it in safely. Any problems?"

"None, Colonel," Art Mason said. "Other than that I smell some panic. Nikeisian types running around saying the pirates are coming, maybe in hours."

"Don't doubt it," Rick said. "And I'm sure some of our own people wonder why we're sitting around in a meeting instead of running around ourselves. Well, we're in a meeting because I want to be sure while the Romans are busy that we all understand the situation. We have a few hours to plan. If you want to know something or you have anything to offer, speak up! I don't want the Romans to doubt that we know what we're doing when the time comes to lay out our official plan. Even if we know better."

There was subdued laughter.

"When does the balloon go up?" Mason asked.

"The pirates are certainly coming, maybe outside the harbor entrance by dawn," Rick said, "but they won't be inside before morning. I'd guess noon tomorrow, assuming they're smart enough to want to hit us at high water. We plan for that, anyway.

"So." He turned his attention to the entire group. "We don't have long before we have to start meeting with the Romans and the Nikeisian fleet people, and I think we'll be better off if we get our story straight before we bring in outsiders."

"Considering how little we know about naval warfare, that's a splendid idea," Baker said, and Rick nodded to him and Lieutenant Martins.

"None of us are experts in a naval fight, so it's fortunate we have a training aid, courtesy of our British friends. Major?"

He looked at Baker, who nodded back.

"Yes, Sir. Leftenant Martins, please come forward."

The young lieutenant stood and walked to the front. His first two steps were uncertain as all eyes turned to him, but uncertainty vanished into the camouflage of a stiff, upright boarding-school posture. He sat in a chair next to Rick, maintaining the same upright posture, and drew the same binder he'd handed Rick in Taranto from his pocket. He placed it on the table next to the map of Nikeis and the bay, flipped through a few of the pages, then drew a grease pencil and a rag from the same pocket and looked at Rick.

"Colonel," he said, and Rick nodded for him to proceed.

"Sir," Martins continued, "I understand the mission is to retain control of the containers at all costs."

"It would also help if we could get them back to the mainland," Rick observed, and Martins nodded, jotting grease penciled notes into the field manual.

"So our essential tasks include defending the containers," Major Baker took the cue, "and the ships to carry them back. Specifically the ship Nikeis modified to move them here."

"We'll have to keep a fleet in being to guard those ships," Art Mason chimed in.

"So for the moment, we need to defend Nikeis," Jimmy Harrison said.

"Why not just take the contents of the containers and leave?" Martins asked in a neutral tone. "We could leave the empty containers behind."

Clavell and Harrison looked sour, and Saxon blinked in shock. The room was silent for a moment, then several people murmured in approval.

"The Romans have an alliance with Nikeis," Warner said. "I don't know Publius as well as you do, Skipper, but I doubt it would sit well with him if we just cut and run. And those are his ships. He'd have to come with us."

"Agreed," Rick replied. "We might or might not be able

to square it with him, but abandoning one ally is hardly the way to cement an alliance with another."

"And for that matter," Mason interjected, "is Taranto that much easier to defend than Nikeis? Here we have the Nikeisian militia. On the mainland we wouldn't."

*Of course, on the mainland we wouldn't have to* leave *Saxon's goodies in Taranto, either,* Rick thought. *I doubt the pirates would care to follow us too far inland! Probably better not to mention that, though.*

"Tactically, cutting and running might appear to be a better option," he said out loud. "Strategically, though, the consequences of abandoning an ally would be bad. Besides, we'd have to fight our way out; the Signory won't let go of those containers easily."

"Very well, I'll list maintaining alliances as a mission constraint," Martins said, jotting more notes. "Any changes in our tactical situation since we were given this mission?"

Someone chuckled and most of the room smiled at the tension-relieving absurdity of the question.

"We have a better idea of when the enemy will arrive and a better estimate of their forces," Baker said. "And a better estimate of friendly forces. But the mission remains the same."

"So our mission statement is as follows," Martins read from his notes. "Defend the cargo containers, defend Nikeis, maintain our alliances, and retain the means to move the containers to Taranto in the face of an enemy fleet."

"That's good enough for now," Rick agreed.

"So, factors to consider," Martins said. "Enemy forces.

It's estimated we face over one hundred ships and fifteen thousand men from at least three nations."

*Yeah,* Rick thought. *And I still don't know how this coalition came together so fast. Does someone else have radios? Are we all just pawns in some galactic game?*

"Like I said before, some of the men on those ships are slaves," Warner pointed out. "They'll be less likely to fight."

*And what the hell am I supposed to do about* them, *damn it? They* sure as hell didn't choose to get involved in this.

"Friendly forces?" Martins said.

"The galleys and those harbor boats—the *fustas* they told us about," Rick replied. "Ashore, they have about five hundred professional halberdiers and crossbowmen. The halberdier regiment we saw at the Battle of Ottarn is in Pavino, which is good and bad. We could use them here, but there's always the chance the armada could take Pavino as a staging base if we don't hold it. So that leaves us with the rest: irregular forces and militia formations."

"Yes, Sir, they do have militia," Harrison said. "That's every man in the city. They all have some weapons, even the boys. Spears, mostly. They drill every month—some months girls join the boys and practice fire drill with buckets. Other months it's military drill with spears, a few shields, but mostly spears. In theory, we're talking up to fifteen, maybe twenty, thousand. Can't say I've been much impressed, but you never know."

"Probably fair, Colonel," Clavell said. "But they *do* know the city a lot better than we do and probably a lot better than any pirate."

"A valid point," Martins acknowledged. "And we have the Roman ships and the galleys we captured en route."

"Plus a thousand Roman soldiers, plus eighty-odd star lords, counting the Gurkhas," Mason added. "And two hundred musketeers, a hundred Tamaerthan archers, and the Colonel's personal guard."

Martins nodded and kept writing.

"Relative Capabilities," he said. "The pirates certainly have numerical superiority, especially if the militia doesn't stand its ground."

"True," Baker said, "but their force is as much a polyglot improvisation as ours is, and much larger. Controlling it will be a serious challenge, particularly if a goodly portion of it are pirates. Discipline will be suspect, at the least."

"How will that affect how they organize to fight?" Mason asked. "For that matter, how do galleys *usually* fight?"

Jimmy Harrison stood, and Rick nodded to him.

"I think I can offer something on that," Harrison said. "Most of what I know I saw on the big paintings in the Doge's Palazzo. I was studying them while Lance was teaching, Colonel. Some of those paintings get into a lot of detail, and every one of them makes it plain, naval battles are like land battles. They get close and swarm in. Try to ram, lots of crossbows and bows as they close, but mostly they try to board. In a swarm, Colonel. Then it's close-in fighting. Smaller ships bring up reinforcements when the original forces get thin, and then it's a race, who can throw in the most troops to take over the ship. After that, it's on to the next one."

"Sounds like a mass cavalry battle," Mason offered. "But once engaged, forces are even harder to recall."

"In this case, the sea and the wind have a major effect, as well," Martins added.

"And leadership will have to be in the front." Mason nodded. "No radios."

"What about our own forces?" Rick asked. *Need to watch the pace. Hard to balance getting the right inputs from everyone without getting stuck in rabbit holes and wasting what little time we have.*

"To start," Baker said, "our forces may be thrown together, but each element has a well-established chain of command, assuming we don't mix them. Further, we have the benefit of the motivation of survival rather than greed."

"And we know one thing," Larry Warner said. "Sir."

"What's that?"

"We have as much experience as anyone on this planet on using massed rifle fire against a galley," Warner pointed out, and Major Baker nodded with a chuckle.

"I should have brought that up myself. Good point, Mr. Warner."

"Noted," Rick said. "And the effect was decisive."

"Until we run out of ammo," Bisso muttered.

"Will they stand against that kind of firepower?" Warner asked.

"Chancy to rely on their *not* standing," Lieutenant Martins said.

"I agree with you, Lieutenant," Rick said. "The one thing we can't risk is being overrun, land or sea. The pirates don't know what they're facing, so rifle fire will be a surprise to them. But until that happens, they have no reason to be overly cautious about attacking. And in any event, they have to know their biggest advantage is numbers. Assuming they have any intelligence at all, they'll try to swarm us. No reason not to."

"We've got other weapons," Warner continued. "We have the LMG, the Brens, and the Carl Gustav. Mortars, too, if they get ashore."

"Might not want to use mortars inside the city," Rick observed.

"No, Sir," Warner agreed. "But it'd be best of all if we kept them from ever getting there. And one hit from the recoilless, and a ship will be out of it."

"Probably," Mason qualified. Warner looked at him, and Mason shrugged. "Taking a hit from Carl Gustav would have to be a major psychological shock, Larry. But it's a lot smaller than one-oh-five and these ships are built pretty tough. Sure, hit them in the right place, and they're out of it, but that could be easier said than done. If we had any Willie Peter left for the recoilless, I'd be more confident of taking them out with a single hit. White phosphorus has that effect on a wooden ship, and no way in hell to put out. But unless you hit 'em center of mass, and preferably below the waterline, you could probably blow lots of bits and pieces off without actually knocking them out."

"And, again, only until we run out of ammunition," Martins pointed out. "We're still evaluating what we have to work with. Until we've done that, we can't properly develop possible courses of action, and we certainly shouldn't be choosing one at this point."

"But—"

"Larry," Rick intervened. *We don't need Warner and Martins butting heads at this point. Need to get Larry thinking about a task; strategy and tactics aren't his thing.* "I'm confident that between you and Mr. Saxon you can come up with some additional surprises. Mr. Saxon, do you have any magic in those containers you can whip up in the next few hours?"

Saxon had been trying to hide in the background, and he seemed embarrassed at having been brought into the foreground, instead.

"Well, we have some diesel fuel in the containers," he said, quietly at first. "It's supposed to be for the generator." His voice became more forceful as his thoughts solidified. "And some white gas for our cooking stove . . . If we can find some strong alcohol and bottles, I can combine it with tar from the Arsenale to make some Molotov cocktails."

"Sargent Clavell," Rick said. "You mentioned the Nikeisians were experimenting with gunpowder. I think it's time they put some of their cards on the table. We're going to need all they have if this is going to work."

"Colonel," there was a note of caution in Warner's voice, "we don't know what the quality of their powder's going to be like, and we don't have time to test. Could foul our muskets."

"Noted." Rick nodded. "I don't intend to use it for our guns. I do intend to make some surprises for the invaders."

Rick turned back to Clavell and Harrison.

"Remember when you traded with the Nikeisians for that shipment of bird guano for the University?"

"Who could forget?" Clavell grimaced. "Tons of bird crap that smelled to high heaven, but it turned out to be great fertilizer."

"Do they still have any?"

"I'm sure they do, but why?"

"Mr. Saxon, do you think you can do anything with bird guano and tar?"

"Yes, I do," Saxon said with a smile. He paused and thought for a moment. "The results won't be as explosive as refined petroleum, but it would make for a pretty good firebomb. And, like I said, we have some diesel fuel if you want real explosives."

"Larry," Rick said, "work with Mr. Saxon to get as many of those cocktails and bombs together as possible. Sergeant Clavell, get with the provisioners the Nikeisians have assigned to us. Make sure Mr. Warner and Mr. Saxon get whatever they need. These firebombs and explosives might just be the edge we need."

"Colonel," Warner pointed out, "the Nikeisians are certainly going to be able to copy us."

"It's a risk we have to take," Rick replied, then turned back to the rest of the group.

"What else? How about nonfirepower things?" he asked and saw Baker nod in agreement.

"We're defending an island fortress," Mason said. "That's a pretty fair advantage."

"Unfortunately, those fortresses and mud-flat defenses are going to be less effective than they might've been," Rick pointed out. "You'd think they'd have at least chains across the canals into the lagoon, but I haven't seen any sign of them. And the forts on the approaches don't seem to have been well maintained." He shook his head. "I'm wondering if there may have been a bit of 'the wooden walls of Athens' in their thinking."

"May have been, Sir," Mason said. "But Lance was telling me about what all they've got built up on top of those hills. Sounds to me like we could probably evac most of the civilians and pack 'em in up there. That'd at least get them out from underfoot and make moving our troops around the flats a lot easier."

"Another good point." Rick nodded. "Of course, there's still the little problem of how we *hold* the flats."

"I think we can be confident in the discipline of the Roman forces as well as our own," Baker said. "Other than motivation for defending themselves, I can't speak for the Nikeisian forces."

"The Romans have a pretty healthy respect for Nikeisian ships," Rick replied.

"And we have some nonkinetic capabilities which can enable our allies," Martins offered.

"Go on."

"We have watches for timekeeping, and compasses which seem to work even here on an alien planet, so—"

"There has to be a magnetic field for life to exist," Warner put in. Rick gave him a "not now" look, then nodded for Martins to continue.

"The bell tower on the Doge's Palazzo gives us an advantage in height of eye for command-and-control," the lieutenant said. "We also have binoculars, radios, signalmen, and signaling rockets."

"The top of the bell tower's about a hundred feet above sea level. What does that make the visual horizon?" Rick asked, thinking about the view from its top. Judging distances could be hard enough under any circumstances; with only a featureless stretch of seawater, it got even more difficult, and he wanted a harder number if they were going to incorporate it into their planning.

Martins pulled out a pocket calculator and punched numbers.

"Approximately twenty-one and a half kilometers to the horizon, Sir," he said. "Thirteen and a half miles."

"There's an even higher tower available," Clavell offered. "It's up in the upper city, off the Palazzo San Marco Maggiore. Has to be over two hundred feet above sea level. Probably closer to three."

"Make that twenty-eight kilometers—seventeen and a half miles," Martins said. "Thirty-five kilometers, at three hundred feet. And with the three-twenty mounted that high, we could bloody well send a signal back to the mainland. Can't do that with the handhelds, though, because they're outside its frequencies. But even the civilian base repeater ought to give us a good hundred fifty kilometers from that height. Certainly enough for our tactical needs, at least."

"How high are most ships' lookouts?" Mason asked.

"Maybe . . . sixty or seventy feet, max," Harrison said.

"So that would be just over fifteen kilometers," Martins said.

"Which means the Colonel would be able to see twice as far as the enemy commander," Baker observed, and Rick glanced at him. *You guys are maneuvering me into a box, probably with good reason*, he thought.

"Okay," he said out loud, "what's next?"

"It's not just the land and the sea," Baker said. "It's the interface between them. Tricky place to be."

The major's eyes were looking up and to the left, as if he were remembering something vividly.

*There's a story there*, Rick thought. *Okay, I'll bite.*

"Tell me about it."

"When a fleet conducts an amphibious landing, it's at its most vulnerable," Baker replied. "Out to sea, it can maneuver, but once it puts troops ashore, it loses that maneuverability."

"Weren't you at Port San Carlos, Sir?" Martins asked.

"Back in 1982." Baker nodded, and looked at Rick. "Argentina captured several of our islands in the South Atlantic, the Falklands, and we sent a naval task force to take them back. At some point, we had to put troops ashore to remove the Argentines. The fleet was able to fight pretty well when we had room to maneuver, but once we assaulted a port in the middle of the main island, Port San Carlos, the fleet was essentially stuck in place, unable to maneuver while we reinforced and supported the troops ashore. We called it Bomb Alley. The Argie Air Force knew exactly where to find us and concentrated their effort on the ships sustaining the landing. The troopships in particular. Fortunately, they made some mistakes and we were successful. I was with another Gurkha regiment at the time."

*Argentina and Great Britain?* Rick thought. *Wonder what else has happened since we got abducted. Have we really been gone for fourteen years?* He recalled the conversation between Martins and Warner about the collapse of the Soviet Union. *In the end, the United States won the Cold War. So much has changed, both on Earth and here on Tran.*

"The point is," Baker continued, "that our opponents are coming to us, and they'll have a real challenge when they cross that frontier. Think of it as crossing a river or a moat, but immensely thornier."

"And they'll have to make multiple river crossings in this case," Mason observed, pointing to the map on the table. "If we can maintain control of the inner lagoon, they'll be on foot and channeled to the bridges. It would be like fighting from the outer courtyard to the inner keep in a motte and bailey fortress."

"Good point," Rick said. "Let's take the analogy further. If the outer lagoon is the castle wall, we need the containers in a keep."

"So we need to get the other two containers to San Marco," Mason said. "Be even better if we could get them to the upper palazzo."

"Not enough time to move them up that slope," Baker objected.

"You want to make walls with them, Colonel?" Mason asked.

"Yes. This building looks as if it would burn. Stone walls, but all this paneling and tapestry is flammable. And there was plenty of flammable material in the Doge's Palace. Mr. Saxon, how fireproof are these containers?"

"Colonel, I have no idea," Saxon said, shaking his head, "but I'd sure hate to try that experiment."

"I would, too, and we have no idea what the pirates can do by way of pyrotechnics. The Romans throw fire pots, so we have to assume the pirates can do the same, and if they can, and they hit a palace that isn't fireproof, we could lose anything inside it. We know the containers are made of a good steel, though, so they can be a part of the fortification, and I think they'd be safe against a couple of hits with fire pots in the open. They don't have to stand up to firearms, and the rise in sea level means we'll have plenty of water nearby. Anyone disagree?"

"They might have Greek fire," Warner said. "Water doesn't put it out."

"What does?"

"Sand, maybe. And dirt. But it may have its own oxidant—"

"All right, Mr. Warner. Work with Sergeant Clavell to appoint a fire squad and have them gather equipment to fight that kind of fire. Anyone else? Can we hold the Doge's Palace?"

Harrison shrugged.

"I'd sure try," he said. "It's built like a fortress anyway. Put the containers out in front of it like a wall, rifleman between them, musketeers in a block—Colonel, none of these pirates have ever been in a firefight before. I doubt they'll stand more'n one or two volleys."

"I don't know about muskets, but I shouldn't think they would stand up to massed rifle fire any better than Ganton's army did when we first encountered it," Baker said. "Which is to say not at all. At the same time, Colonel, whatever we do, understand that we have no more than two hundred rounds per man. And not every round will kill an enemy."

"Plus, our Gurkhas can't be in two places at one time," Rick noted. "Let's move on. What's next on your checklist, Lieutenant?"

"Time and—" Martins began, then paused as Cal Haskins raised a hand.

"Yes, Mr. Haskins?" Rick said.

"Colonel, I understand about getting the containers outside buildings that could burn," Haskins replied, "and I understand the pirates don't have guns. But these containers' walls ain't all that thick."

"Oh. How thick *are* they?"

"Sides are twelve or fourteen-gauge," Haskins replied. "Call it a tenth of an inch, max." He shrugged. "Plenty to take care of occasional bangs and dings, but I dunno how well it'd hold up to heavy damage."

"Crap, Skipper." Mason grimaced. "That's only about half as thick as a Drantos breastplate!"

"And a heavy crossbow bolt can penetrate one of those if it hits just right—or just wrong, depending on your viewpoint," Rick acknowledged.

"Yes, Sir. So can a pile-headed arrow from a longbow, but at least any of them should be on our side."

"One or two hits like that probably wouldn't do catastrophic damage," Saxon said. "They'd have to hit hard enough to punch all the way through and then hit something critical inside. But I can't guarantee that wouldn't happen. And even if it didn't damage anything, it would break the weather seal and let a lot of moisture in. I don't think exposure to saltwater would do the contents any good."

"And if we place them in the open in the Palazzo San Marco, they'll be in standing water at high tide," Baker said thoughtfully. "Punch a few holes, flood them—"

He shrugged, and Rick nodded. *Damn, they're right.*

*Of course, those containers are what the pirates are here to grab. They probably wouldn't want to wreck them any more than we would. But accidents happen.*

"All right," he said after a moment. "I still don't want them anywhere something could burn down on top of them, but we obviously don't want them anywhere else where they're likely to be damaged. What about this? We haul them into the Palazzo San Marco and put them directly in front of the Doge's Palace. That gets them out of the open and away from fire hazards. Then we throw up breastworks in front of them for our actual fighting positions. God knows there are plenty of paving stones here in the city and I'll bet they've got a whole stack of timbers in the Arsenale, and we've got a lot of hands that can pile them where we need them."

"If the pirates figure out where they are, they'll act like a magnet," Warner pointed out.

"Might not be a bad thing," Mason replied. Rick looked at him, and he shrugged. "Anything that channels them into predictable approaches has to help us, Sir."

"So long as it doesn't attract overwhelming strength," Baker said, nodding in approval.

"All right," Rick nodded back, and returned his gaze to Martins. "You were saying the next item was?"

"Time and Space," Martins replied.

"Like I said, we expect them to arrive around noon tomorrow."

Mason stood.

"Colonel, you're not concerned about a night attack?" he asked, and Rick grinned.

"Major Mason, that's the same thing I asked the

Nikeisian admiral, that Senator del Verme. He said he hoped they'd be stupid enough to try a night attack, but the difficulties of getting around the lagoon are pretty well known among mariners. No pirate's going to try that at night. They'll attack in daylight, probably at high tide, which is just after the noon of the True Sun. Yes, I know, overconfidence is the key to defeat. Del Verme knows that, too. He has picket ships out searching, just in case. We'll have warning if the pirate fleet gets close enough to be a danger."

Mason sat, but Baker frowned, and Rick looked at him. "Major?"

"How far out are his pickets, Colonel?"

"He doesn't have an unlimited supply of ships," Rick replied. "He knows the pirates' probable approach bearing, and he's put an advanced screen about thirty miles out on that bearing. The ships in it are spread pretty thin, but he has an inner picket line fifteen miles out that's a lot thicker."

"Then I suggest we reinforce the inner picket with some of the Roman triremes and equip them with some of your signal rockets. A lookout on that tower Sergeant Clavell mentioned should be able to see rockets at least eighteen or nineteen miles out to sea once they've gained some altitude."

Martins flipped a few pages in his book, looked at a conversion chart, did some quick math, and spoke up.

"If the pirates are making five knots, which is generous, and the outer picket spots them and relays through the inner picket, we should have at least six or seven hours of warning," he said.

"You and Mason work that out with Junius. If he balks, let me know and I'll talk to Publius. What's next?"

"Surprise." Martins looked up and realized that hadn't come out right. "Gaining and employing the element of surprise," he clarified.

"Okay, let's go with the obvious question." Rick looked around the room. "Do they know we're here?"

"There were survivors from our engagement with the pirates near the swamps," Baker replied.

"And if the reason they're coming here was lights in the sky, it stands to reason the local star men are going to show up," Warner added. "But they won't know exactly where we are."

"Actually, they'll know we have the same problems as they do, and galleys don't normally sail beyond sight of land," Martins replied.

"You've mentioned that before," Rick said. "Your point?"

"My point is that they're unlikely to expect *us* to do that, either, Sir," Martins said. "But we can see a much greater distance from the towers here in the city than they can from a masthead lookout, and we have radios. We could position the Romans where the enemy doesn't expect them to be and still maintain command and control."

"Maybe," Warner said. Rick—and Martins—looked at him, and he shrugged. "I'm sure we can, within limits, Colonel. But Lieutenant Martins just pointed out that five knots is a generous speed estimate for one of these ships. If we put the Romans too far out, will they be able to intercept the pirates short of the city?"

Martins looked a bit chagrined, but Rick nodded.

"Valid points for us to keep in mind," he acknowledged. "Let's move on."

"Logistics," Martins said.

"We're good for food and water, so long as we don't lose the island," Mason said. "What we don't have is any extra ammunition for the star weapons or gunpowder for the muskets, unless we want to use Nikeis powder."

"Our opposition has a much more difficult situation," Martins said. "Colonel, your report is that they're coming from a port two days away. Unless they try and take Pavino or another harbor, and according to Captain Pilinius, their galleys don't have as much endurance as Roman ships do. They'll need water, probably even food, and Nikeis is the only place to get them. So they're in a make-or-break scenario."

"And if the wind doesn't work for them and they have to row all night, their rowers are probably going to be tired when they get here, too." Rick nodded. "Hell of a roll of the dice."

"If they do take another port to stage through, we'd gain more time," Martins pointed out. "Probably at least a week. We could do a lot with a week."

"That's quite a dilemma," Baker mused. "Take the ports and gain a base of operations or charge straight in. The smart play would be to acquire the forward base first, but only if they were confident they could hold their alliance together."

"We'll assume the Signory intel is accurate and post the pickets," Rick said.

"Well, that rather brings up another point, Colonel," Martins said. "Weather."

"Go," Rick replied.

"The winds were picking up as we approached the city," the lieutenant said, "and they're out of the northeast, not the west, which is the prevailing wind direction at this latitude. There were a few whitecaps, as well, and I saw red skies when the secondary star rose this forenoon."

"'Red sky at morning, sailor take warning,'" Warner quoted. "Yeah, that seems to hold true here, as well."

"So I expect heavy weather is headed our way," Martins continued. "The current winds are from the northeast. If the enemy fleet comes from the north, they'll be at least partly upwind of the islands and being blown down on the city. Again, another make-or-break condition for them."

"And for us," Rick said. "We can't move until that storm passes if you're right, but at least we have a safe harbor." He grimaced. "All right, file that as a consideration. What about the pirates' possible courses of action?"

"Without the Romans or the Nikeisians' input, we're mostly guessing," Baker said.

"Corporal Harrison seems to have a pretty good idea of how ships fight around here," Rick replied. "And as Lieutenant Martins just pointed out, we know their ships don't have a lot of endurance, so it's pretty obvious they can't blockade us unless they capture a nearby port. So they have to make an assault or withdraw."

"Their limits of command -and -control give them only two viable options, really," Martins offered.

"Which are?"

"Their most likely course of action is a multi-echelon deep assault directly into the main channel on the north side of the islands. Just as Corporal Harrison said. The other approach would be to deploy a very broad line, with fewer echelons, to envelop the islands and find another way—or ways—in."

"Okay, what are ours?"

"Fight them at sea," Warner said. "Turn *Ferox* into a battlecruiser. Put a platoon of Gurkhas aboard. Add the LMG and Frick with the Carl Gustav. Keep it light—no cargo, minimum food and water, and strip out most of the Roman marines. She can outrun just about anything she sees and outfight anything fast enough to catch her. We send that out and see what the pirates do. We put Major Baker's Brens aboard the *navibus onerārius* and they become ships-of-the-line. Assume three Gurkha ships, including *Ferox*, twenty troopers and an officer in each. That's three battleships. Nothing they have can touch them. Add Tamaerthan archers to two other ships, makes two cruisers. Six ships-of-the-line."

"So long as they have ammunition," Baker observed. "Damn thin battle line, Colonel."

"Thin, but powerful," Warner argued.

"If nothing goes wrong," Bisso muttered. "Damn thin, if you ask me, Sir."

"You don't like this, Master Sergeant," Rick said.

"No, Sir, and that's a fact. If you ask me, we forget the damn naval battle. Get those containers and all our people into one place and defend that with all we've got."

"Bisso, that's going to be hard on Nikeis," Clavell protested.

"No harder than if we go out there to fight at sea and they get past us. I don't think Mr. Warner's plan can guarantee they won't."

Warner frowned, then shrugged.

"No guarantees," he admitted. "In fact, some of them are sure to get past us."

*And not your decision,* Rick thought. *Hell's bells, I wasn't even the captain of the track team, and now my decisions could get everyone here killed. Maybe the whole flipping planet. I can't even run. I'm on an island!*

"One thing about Master Sergeant Bisso's plan," Harrison said. "We get all those containers together in front of the Doge's Palace, we're holding Palazzo San Marco. That's the center of town. Gives us the most defensive depth we're going to find."

"What else?" Rick asked, and looked directly at Baker. *You and Martins have something in mind,* he thought, *and it's about damn time you came out with it.*

"Envelopment." Baker stood and gestured at the map. "We send the Roman squadron out the sea, to the east, just as soon as we see the pirate fleet. Then they tack due north to get upwind of the enemy. You guide them from the tower, to keep them out of the pirates' sight the whole way. When the pirates are engaged with the lagoon's outer defenses, the Romans hit them in the flank. Shortly after that, a Nikeisian squadron comes in from the west, snakes its way around the mud flats, and engages them on that side."

"Cannae?" Rick mused.

"Precisely."

"Colonel, what's Cannae?" Bisso asked.

"Cannae was a battle on Earth," Rick replied. "Ancient Rome and Carthage were at war, and Hannibal, the Carthaginian general, knew the Romans intended to smash through his army. So he placed a force in front of them to draw them in and had those troops give ground during the fighting. With the Roman attention focused on advancing, he was able to surround them on both sides. When he hit them in the flanks, the Roman legionnaires were compressed together so badly that men died standing up. The whole Roman force was massacred." He turned back to Baker. "We'd have to put a force in front of them to draw them in."

"I rather think the containers will draw them in nicely, in a strategic sense," Baker pointed out with a thin smile. "Tactically, we put the second Nikeisian squadron in a line defending the main channel. The *fustas* ambush those that make it inside the perimeter. Meanwhile, our troops fight off those that make it as far as the square."

*Who have you been talking to?* Rick wondered.

"The key," Baker continued, "is to let sailors be sailors and soldiers be soldiers. At the same time, reinforcing the Romans with the Carl Gustav, the machine guns, and a few volunteer riflemen would make the squadron very effective when the force flanks the enemy."

*Junius or Publius*, Rick decided. *Probably both*.

"Mr. Saxon's petrol bombs and firebombs would be most effective in the hands of a force upwind of the enemy," Martins offered, and Rick swallowed an ignoble urge to glare at both of them.

*This was a setup all along. A game of "manage the amateur." But damn it, they're probably right.*

"Okay, I'm not going to spend a lot of time arguing the advantages and disadvantages of each approach." He nodded to Warner. "It's too soon to try experimenting with building a battle line." He nodded to Bisso. "And there are too many of them to fight them all on land. We'll go with the Cannae approach. It has the advantage that if we lose the fleet, we can still fight a land battle with most of our forces intact. The Romans get a detachment of riflemen and the Gustav, but the machine guns—and the mortars—stay ashore. Just one question: what happens if the pirate fleet goes with a broad battle line? It'll be hard to keep the Roman squadron out of sight but still close enough to arrive in time."

"In that case," Martins responded, "the enemy fleet's left wing will be equal in number to the Roman squadron and, at a minimum, the enemy commander will be on the horns of a dilemma."

*Now I'm* certain *they've been talking with the Romans.*

"Radios and command structure," Rick said. "We have nine radios, five shoulder mics, the HF units, one hand charger, and Mr. Saxon's generator. We'll need a radio talker, signal corpsmen, and a team of mercs with Admiral del Verme and the same with Fleetmaster Junius—both of them get shoulder mics. Major Baker will have his own radio, as will Major Mason, and the Sergeant Major. Give one to Sergeant Walbrook with the mortars, and the repeater and the charger will go in the tower with me. Lieutenant Cargill, make setting that up and rigging the antenna your first priority; I *don't* want any of us losing comms. That leaves three handhelds. Once we've had time to coordinate with the militia about the best defensive positions outside the Palazzo itself, we'll see about distributing them were they'll do the best for overall coordination. Lieutenant Martins, please work out some simple signals for the rockets with Master Sergeant Bisso."

"We have half a dozen radios of our own," Saxon put in. Rick looked at him, and he shrugged. "They're in the container at the Arsenale right now. I think they're pretty similar to the ones you have."

"Then we dig those out as soon as possible and find out if they'll mesh with yours, Major," Rick told Baker. "The farther we can extend our radio net, the better."

"Of course, Sir. Another job for Leftenant Cargill."

"Art, please dismiss the troops, but I want to have a word with the officers, Mr. Saxon, and Mr. Haskins. Oh, Sergeant Clavell and Corporal Harrison, would you please remain behind, as well?"

Major Mason nodded to Master Sergeant Bisso.

"Ten-Hut!"

Everyone rose.

"Dismissed."

The noncommissioned officers silently left the room. Master Sergeant Bisso conspicuously remained behind, guarding the door.

❖ ❖ ❖

"Major Baker," Rick began as the door closed, "I'd like to talk about a subject not in your templates. Treachery."

Martins glanced towards Baker and blushed a little at the sound of that last word, Rick noted. *Well, we'll deal with that later.*

"I'm concerned about Miss Spirit's absence and the potential for trouble after the battle, assuming we win," he continued, and looked at Saxon. "Why is she here on Tran?"

Saxon shrugged.

"Doctor Lee, back when he was still pretending to be CIA, said she'd help with security. I mean, she'd been a cop. Colonel, I have the same opinion as Cal. I never understood why she wanted to come—well, to go to Africa or wherever it was they were sending us. Or why they recruited her. And she didn't make much of a fuss about it when we found out this wasn't a CIA operation after all, that we'd never come home again. I had her figured for a feminist, but when we got here, the first thing she did was flirt with the Senator."

He shrugged again.

"But she can operate any of the equipment you brought?"

"Sure. None of it's that complicated, Colonel. She knows enough to get the manuals on screen, and after that it would be simple enough."

*As if I understood a word of that*, Rick thought.

"So, if the Signory gets a container, they can use what's in it?"

"If she helps, yes, Sir," Saxon said, and Haskins nodded. "She has some kind of education," Saxon continued, "and she was a San Francisco detective—"

"Uniform, Bart," Haskins said.

"Okay, uniform not detective, but still she'd have had to pass an exam to get that far. I'd say she can make use of anything we have."

"And if we use up all our ammo on the pirates, what keeps her and the Signory from taking whatever they want?" Harrison asked.

"You have any reason to think they'll try, Jimmy?" Bisso asked.

"Not really," Harrison replied. "They been decent enough so far, but you never know what people will do if the prize is big enough. And them containers are about the biggest prize on this planet and the Signory know it."

"For the record," Sergeant Clavell said, "they treated Jimmy and me just fine."

"'For the record,'" Rick repeated. "For the record, the Signory kidnapped you and held you incommunicado until I turned up with a fleet and demanded they turn you loose. I'm not exactly thrilled with the way they've acted since Mr. Saxon and his containers arrived, Sergeant. Still, Nikeis did send troops to the Ottarn, and they've been honest enough in their dealings with us since we got here. But you yourself warned me this is a place full of plots."

"And assassins," Mason added. "So what do we do about it? I mean other than keep our powder dry?"

"I don't know yet," Rick said. "You'll think of something, Art."

Mason grumbled something inaudible, and Rick smiled.

"All right," he continued. "Mostly I just want to be sure we're all on the same page where the . . . call them the 'undercurrents' are concerned."

He looked around the circle of faces until everyone had nodded, then turned back to Saxon.

"The first priority is to get all three containers to the Doge's Palace. Mr. Saxon, your job will be to negotiate with the Signory to get all three of your containers together and carried to San Marco's. Work with Major Baker on where to place them. And we'll need some local talent to bring in workmen and materials for the breastworks."

"Wagon Box Fight," Mason said.

"Or Jan Zizka," Warner said. "Only you've got a lot better weapons."

"Who or what is Jan Zizka?" Haskins asked.

"He was a Czech general in the early fourteen hundreds," Rick replied. "He used armored wagons as a sort of tank with muskets and small cannons. He'd set his wagons in a circle at critical positions, forcing his enemies to come to him and break their teeth. Except that *our* wagons are going to be behind the front line."

"Colonel," Mason asked, "who tells the Signory that we want all those containers?"

"Start with Clavell. He can blame it on Mr. Saxon, and when that sets them off, you can blame it on me."

"Maybe better to start with you?"

"No. The containers belong to Mr. Saxon, so he should be the one directing the Signory on their disposition. No point in confusing them. Besides, I want to emphasize the fact that he owns them—*all* of them—and that he means to go right on owning them."

"And if they won't let go?" Bisso growled.

"Clavell, try to be nice, but they don't have any choice on this. Bisso, use what you have to to make that point. We need those containers."

"I don't suppose you mean that," Bart Saxon said. "About who owns what, I mean. When the battle's over."

Rick frowned.

"Mr. Saxon, do you have some objection to what we're doing here?"

"No, Colonel, I don't. Not really. And there has to be a commander, and that's most certainly you, not me. Apologies. I shouldn't have said anything."

"No harm done," Rick replied. "After you work out the movement of the containers, I'd appreciate it if you'd get to work on those incendiaries. Please work with Mr. Warner. He's developed a few tricks of his own over the years we've been here."

Saxon nodded, and Rick turned his attention to the others.

"I'll set up my command post in the upper city's bell tower. McAllister will be with me. Once the sea battle gets close enough, he'll take out as many steersmen as he can. Warner and Martins, you'll be my liaison with the Roman squadron. I don't want *Ferox* tied down in any melees. Hit them and move on. Don't stay for a fight. The riflemen are there just to make sure you don't get boarded. I'm sure Fleetmaster Junius will know what to do.

"Frick and McQuaid will take the recoilless on the *Ferox*, Art. Find a squad of volunteer mercs to go with them so we don't lose it. Master Sergeant Bisso, your post will be in the Doge's Palace off the lower square coordinating with the militia and the musketeers in the buildings flanking the square. The archers will be a mobile formation; I'll leave them with you to deploy where they're most needed. We'll leave the rest of the city to the Signory's militia, but we'll stiffen them with small teams of mercs.

"Major Baker, you and your men will defend the containers. Your orders are to hold them at all costs and against anyone."

✢ ✢ ✢

Major Clyde Baker and his lieutenants stepped out of the headquarters palace on the way to rejoin their company. As they reached the courtyard, Baker paused and looked around to ensure no one could overhear them.

"Is it just me, or did Colonel Galloway appear a bit distracted?" he asked.

"Yes, Sir," Martins agreed. "I think he knows about our conversation with the Romans."

"Couldn't be helped, I'm afraid. This isn't the first time I've had to maneuver an American commander into doing the right thing by coordinating with the other coalition partners beforehand. Only in this case, this Yank is quite a bit smarter than those Yanks were. Most of them were so arrogant and stupid it wasn't all that difficult to simply lead them about by the nose."

"Major, I didn't expect it to be so easy when you said you wanted to guide him subtly," Martins replied. "After all the legends we heard in the Five Kingdoms about the great Warlord Rick, I expected him to be..." The lieutenant shook his head. "I don't know. More assertive, perhaps?"

"Richard, you need to give the man a bit more credit. He wouldn't be alive by now if he wasn't at least as good as others give him credit for being. More than that, he's wise enough—and willing—to solicit advice and information. Once he's listened though, he doesn't muck about in deciding or putting things into motion, either. We gave him a good plan, and he recognized that and accepted it, even after years of making it all up on his own as he goes along."

Baker paused and looked up. Stars were starting to

show as the light from the primary star faded, and his voice was soft as he continued.

"I expect he's tired as hell—suffering battle fatigue. Wouldn't you be tired after fighting for fourteen years straight on a primitive and savage planet? But that man's brain *works*, and he's thinking about a strategy that goes far beyond fighting over these little islands. He bloody well doesn't need his elbow joggled while he does that, either. So we do our part to help him here on the ground, because at the end of the day, what happens to us and this entire damned planet depends on him."

He looked at the two lieutenants, and they nodded, expressions sober.

"Yes, Sir," Martins said, and Baker nodded back.

"That said, though," he said, "perhaps I should have another talk with Publius."

## ⊱ CHAPTER ELEVEN ⊰
# TURN OUT THE WATCH

The fist pounding on the front door woke Lucia Michaeli.

It wasn't late, only a couple of hours after the Firestealer had set, so she drew on a robe and went to find out what the racket was about. The downstairs part of the house was still partly lighted with oil lamps, and she heard her father and Professore Clavell shouting. Professore Clavell stood in the doorway. Her father, still dressed, had answered the door himself, which was an unusual thing for him to do. And the servant standing behind him held the old battle ax that had hung on the front room wall all of Lucia's life.

There were armed men outside the door—a mixed group of Nikeis workmen and soldiers. Professore Clavell's companion, the star man Harrison, with a hook instead of a hand. A dozen of the Doge's halberdiers. A senator stood with them, and—she put her hand to her mouth. Bart Saxon was there. And Ginarosa Torricelli, roughly dressed as if for traveling, stood very near Professore Clavell. What was she doing out there?

"We need workmen," Clavell was shouting to her father. "Timbers, nails, men, carpenters—anyone who can help build defenses at Palazzo San Marco. I'm told that many of those we need work for you. This is by the order of the Doge and the Signory." He gestured to indicate Ginarosa, who held up a signet ring. "It's all approved."

"It is by order of my father," Ginarosa added, waving the ring. "He is meeting with the Doge. I represent him."

"I don't question that, Ginarosa, but all the timbers will be in the Arsenale," Lucia's father replied. "And all the carpenters will be there or at their homes, not here! I have no men here."

"We know. We're going to the Arsenale now," Ginarosa said. "There's something else there we must have. We stopped here to ask you to gather all the men you can find and take them to Palazzo San Marco."

Ginarosa stepped up to the doorway. She looked very serious, but she turned her head slightly to grin at Lucia before she smoothed her expression and turned back to Lucia's father.

"Signore Michaeli, what we ask is that you designate the men we'll need. You are empowered by the Council of Ten to exempt all you designate from their duties with the watch and the militia. You are yourself exempted, but you are ordered to accompany us to the Arsenale, then to Palazzo San Marco where we prepare our defenses."

There were other shouts outside now, and Lucia ran to look out the window to the street. There was a militia officer with an escort of citizens with spear and shield, accompanied by apprentices carrying short spears—or drums. Lucia recognized the younger brother of one of her friends from Professore Clavell's classes. Plutarco. His father was a wealthy goldsmith. Now Plutarco and four other youthful drummers marched to the middle of the street, beating a tattoo, while criers shouted.

"Turn out the watch! Turn out the militia! All those with arms, turn out in arms. Turn out to defend the city! To arms, to arms! Gather in the palazzos! Report to your officers! Turn out the watch! Turn out the ban! Turn out, turn out!"

"The pirates are here!" her father shouted. "Lucia, Lucia, hide—"

"Hold," Ginarosa said impatiently. "The pirates won't be here before daylight, if then. We prepare our defenses, but we have little enough time to do that. Now come with us—"

"Most of my workmen are at the Arsenale. Many sleep there now as we launch ships."

"Yes, yes. We go to the Arsenale at once," Ginarosa insisted impatiently. "There's little time. Come with us."

"Ah, but wait! There are work crews not at the Arsenale," her father said. "Guido Facione and his sons and nephews. One of our best carpenter crews. They'll be swept up with the band and the watch. You need workmen?"

"Yes, at San Marco's, to aid in constructing defenses," Ginarosa repeated, and Lucia's father turned back into the house.

"Lucia!" he shouted. Then he saw her. "Lucia, get dressed. You must go to the house of Facione and tell him that he and all his work crew are summoned to Palazzo San Marco with their tools. Say that they're excused from the watch and the ban by order of the Council of Ten. Hurry, and wear traveling clothes. Do not disguise yourself; you must be recognized so all will believe you speak for me." He turned to his valet. "Marco, you'll accompany Lucia on her errand. If anyone tries to interfere, say you have the orders of Councilor Torricelli. Lucia, hurry!"

"Yes, Father!"

Lucia rushed up to her room. Her older sister's door was open and Catarina was up, as well.

"I heard," she said, throwing on her clothes haphazardly.

"Where you going?" Lucia demanded.

"To the Arsenale!" Catarina shouted and ran out of her room and down the stairs.

Dressed like a servant girl, Lucia thought. She wasn't surprised that her older sister was going to the Arsenale. Catarina practically lived there anyway. She knew more about bronze and iron casting than anyone else Lucia knew—almost as much as their father and far more than their brother. It was nearly unheard of for a woman to manage a trade or be accepted into a guild, but there was talk of allowing Catarina to have guild status. Their brother wasn't interested. He worked as a salesman, as a factor, as a procurer and trader, and he was very good at that. He spoke four languages and could read and write them all. He would be a good proveditor, but he had little interest in the work at the foundry and probably didn't know the formula for bronze, or how to add the charcoal to iron to make steel. Catarina knew all that and more, and the workmen respected her.

Lucia selected her own clothes with care. Time was short, but it was important she not look like a servant. She chose a thin linen skirt, elegant enough with a few beads and careful embroidery, but light in weight—a skirt she could run in if she had to. Thin cotton hose and her walking shoes with low heels and ankle straps so they wouldn't fall off. They didn't show off her trim ankles very well, but it would be dark out, and the cobblestones were rough. She dressed as swiftly as she could without showing that she'd dressed in haste, then went downstairs.

Marco Salata waited patiently by the front door.

"I have a lantern, Signorina," the valet said. "But I don't know the way to the house of Guido Facione."

"I do."

She looked around. There was no one else in the entry hall but older servants and women.

"Lucia!"

It was her mother, calling from the top of the stairs. She was dressed in nightclothes without a robe, and her voice was thin and strained.

"You shouldn't be out of bed! Maria, put Mother back to bed. Immediately!" Lucia commanded.

"In due time," Signora Michaeli said. "What do you intend, girl?"

"As Father commanded. I will summon Facione and take him to Palazzo San Marco," Lucia said carefully.

"Take. You will go with him. To what purpose? They don't need women for the work they must do there."

"I'll find ways to be useful."

Her mother frowned, then nodded.

"No doubt ways that will be noticed by the star men," she said, and Lucia looked up, startled.

"Do you think I haven't seen you since you met the star men?" her mother asked. "Be off with you. I would rather you here than your brother, but the militia will defend this house if it needs defense. And if they don't, God's will be done."

Lucia stood dumbfounded.

"Now be off, girl!"

"Be safe, Mother." Lucia turned to Marco. "This way."

✢ ✢ ✢

Some of the local militia fell in behind as Lucia hurried through the streets to the house of Facione. Someone had passed the word that she spoke for the Council of Ten, even for the Doge, and the militia officers followed her for want of other orders. Soon more than two score hurried in her wake. All of them were young, inexperienced. Probably of no use in defense of the city, but perhaps useful in whatever the star men needed constructed in the Palazzo San Marco. She took a guilty pleasure in having such a large escort, but—

She halted the ragtag column and eyed it critically, then spied Pietro, a boy not much older than she but far more richly dressed. His father, she remembered, was a senator.

"Pietro!"

"Signorina?"

"Are you in charge of these men?"

He looked around blankly, then back at her.

"I see no one of higher rank, Lucia."

"Then command them for me. I have orders from the

Council of Ten. You will assist me. Now get them into some order so that we don't look like a band of robbers!"

The boy—*he really isn't a lot older than I am*, Lucia thought—looked around in bewilderment. Then he drew himself into a military stance.

"Attention!" he shouted. "Form two files! Follow me in a column of two! Signorina, where are we going?"

"To the house of my father's foreman, where we gather workmen and tools, then we take them to the Palazzo San Marco to aid the Professore and his star man companion." She spoke loudly enough for the others to hear her, and she kept her voice serious and, she hoped, commanding, as if she expected to be obeyed. Pietro nodded, and the others arranged themselves into two straight lines behind him.

Lucia nodded and set off with fresh determination. Before they'd gone a block, at least ten others had fallen in behind her column. She smiled in satisfaction, and her smile widened as more added themselves to it. It wasn't much of a fighting force, but it was all hers.

✦ ✦ ✦

Lucia watched with pride as her workmen constructed the fortress in front of Palazzo San Marco. The three steel containers—the best steel Lucia had ever seen—stood squarely in front of the palace, about fifteen yards apart, raised on timbers which would keep them above water even when high tide flooded the square and well back from the fortifications taking form before them. Teams of men pried up paving stones, levering them out of the Palazzo's pavement, for other men—supervised by her father, Guido Facione, and their workmen—to heap in a shoulder-high barricade reinforced with massive, seasoned timbers from the Arsenale. Wherever possible, the timbers were protected by fireproof bronze sheets, also brought down from the Arsenale with the container that had been there.

And that had been a fight! Even the star woman had opposed it! And Lucia had heard that much of the Signory had argued against placing all the containers in one place. The Warlord Rick had insisted, and one of the boys said he'd brought men with star weapons when he went to confront the Signory. That must have been a great scene, and Lucia would have given much to have seen it.

But now the containers stood in their row, behind the stout parapets. Vats of water and buckets of sand stood ready to control fires, and still more men had used some of the precious gunpowder to demolish much of one of the smaller palaces. Not just for additional stone for the fortifications, either. Lucia had heard one of the star men talking about "fields of fire," as well. It was astonishing how quickly men could work when a pirate fleet was at the door, she thought.

"Good job, I'd say."

Professore Clavell had come up behind her. He didn't look like a professore now. He was dressed in the same odd-colored clothing Lord Harrison always wore, and although his vest didn't look much like armor, the rumor was that it would stop arrows or even spears as well as bronze would. Perhaps better, even though it looked like cloth that was flexible, not like metal at all. He carried what he called his battle rifle and wore another star weapon in a scabbard under his left arm. He also had a very wicked looking dagger, not locally made. In fact, it was unlike anything Lucia had ever seen, and it fascinated her. It would require very good steel, a lot of charcoal hammered into the blade, but her father could sell daggers like that to half the Signory.

"Your classmate, the Councilor's daughter—"

"Ginarosa Torricelli," Lucia said, a bit puzzled by the Professore's difficulty recalling his own student's name.

"Yes, that's her. She was at the Arsenale when we went up to get the container that was there. Very helpful she was. There were some who didn't want us to take it, including your sister, but Ginarosa seemed to have a lot of people behind her when she said she supported us. And she was waving her father's ring, like it gave her a lot of power."

"It would, with her father's men," Lucia said. "Rosa can be very determined when she's sure she's right."

"Yeah, I saw that. So did Mr. Saxon."

"The star man?" She tried not to let her face show her emotions, but it was hard to be calm. "Do you know him well?"

"Not very. But he's pretty smart. He was here earlier. After we retrieved the last container from the Senator's house, he went inside one of them and brought out some things to help us fight the pirates."

"Yes." Lucia was annoyed. The star man was here, but she'd been so busy gathering and encouraging the workers that she hadn't seen him! Now—

"Professore, do you know where he's gone?"

"Last I saw he was heading to our palace to make weapons."

"Oh. And Ginarosa? Signorina Torricelli?"

"Haven't seen her since we brought the containers here," Professor Clavell said with a frown. He looked away, glancing around the Palazzo as if searching for her.

"Where is the safest place to be when the fighting begins?" Lucia asked.

"Right here," the Professore said. "Well, in the Palace there, where arrows can't hit you."

"But— Won't the pirates be coming here?"

"Eventually, Signorina. We hope to kill a lot of them here."

"But there are so many! Or so people say. What if you can't kill enough of them?" she asked, and Professore Clavell looked serious.

"Then nobody in the city is safe," he said. "We're evacuating—moving—as many citizens to the upper city as we can. They should be safe there, at least for now. But if we lose down here, they won't be safe for long. Maybe a few can hide, but—"

"Yes," Lucia said. "Yes, I understand. Thank you, Professore. I will go seek my friend and be sure she stays here, also. I'll put her in the Palace. Now where do you want me?"

"You? You can't fight—"

"Do not be so sure of that, Professore. And whether I can fight or not, I can help put out fires. My father's men obey me, or did you not notice?"

"We all did," Clavell said. Lucia couldn't be sure, but she thought star man was sincere, not mocking her.

"And Ginarosa's father's men will all be with her. And she's my best friend."

"It will be very dangerous here when the fighting begins..." The Professore looked thoughtful.

"And you just told me that no place is safe if we lose this battle." She shrugged. "Perhaps we can help win it."

"Maybe you can," Clavell replied, still deep in thought, then looked into the distance. "Hey, isn't that your sister?"

Lucia looked in astonishment. It was Catarina, walking side by side and chattering with one of the star men who had arrived with the coronel. *What was his name again? Ah, yes Warner!* Lucia remembered hearing that he was a learned man who Lord Rick trusted and turned to for advice.

✤ ✤ ✤

Lance Clavell watched Warrant Officer Larry Warner approach.

Clavell envied Warner's advancement and obvious connection to the Colonel, but he didn't resent it. Warner always seemed a little embarrassed about being promoted over his peers and rarely pulled rank, even if he did have a habit of lecturing. Besides, by all accounts Warner was working his tail off at the University when he wasn't pulled back into uniform. No soft duty for him.

At the moment, Warner's head was bent as he talked with the young lady walking beside him. Clavell had seen Catarina Michaeli on only a few, rare occasions. In fact, he'd seen more of her this evening than he had in all his previous time in Nikeis. Catarina was normally very shy and quickly disappeared after introductions. In fact, he'd heard she was a bit of a recluse who haunted the Arsenale and the family foundry. But tonight, she seemed enthralled by some tale Warner was spinning about a balloon ride.

A group of workers followed them, pulling carts full of barrels and other supplies.

"Mr. Warner," Clavell said in greeting as he saluted.

"Sergeant Clavell," Warner replied with a smile.

"Last I saw you," Clavell said in English, "I thought Signorina Catarina was going to eat you alive. She seemed pretty pissed off that we stole her work crews to move the containers. Then we kept them to build fortifications!"

"Good thing Signorina Torricelli was there to intervene," Warner replied in the same language. "Otherwise, I probably wouldn't be here talking to you. But once Catarina heard my name, she suddenly started asking questions about my balloon rides and how it worked."

Clavell hid a smile and nodded seriously.

"What's in the carts?" he asked, shifting back to the local language.

"Oh, almost forgot. Catarina and her crew were very helpful in gathering together barrels of tar and other things. Including this."

Warner motioned to one of several carts loaded down with barrels. A workmen lifted the lid from one of the barrels, and Clavell smelled the strong scent of guano.

"God, seagull crap!" He shook his head. "If you're looking for Saxon, he's in my place, making bombs. Came by here to grab a copy of *The Anarchist Cookbook*, among other things."

"Really?" Warner chuckled. "Man, could we have used that earlier! Lots of good stuff in there to make things go boom. Speaking of which, were you able to get the Signory to give up some of their gunpowder?"

"Yeah." Clavell grimaced wryly. "I got it. And after taking the containers and asking for everything else the Colonel sent me after, they started to wonder if I was going to ask for the gold in their teeth."

"They do realize all of this is to help defend them, right?"

"Sure. You didn't expect them not to squeal about it anyway, did you?"

"Not so much," Warner acknowledged with a smile. "Wanna bet they don't have spies watching to see what we do with it all so they can copy us later?"

"Thanks, no," Clavell said dryly.

"Alrighty, then," Warner said. "I'm going to go join Professore Saxon in the bomb factory."

"Try not to blow it up," Clavell said, as he saluted again. "I kind of like the place."

"We'll do our best."

Warner headed off, still talking with Catarina Michaeli, and Clavell noticed Lucia trailing along behind.

# ✥≍ CHAPTER TWELVE ≍✥
## BEST LAID PLANS

The Roman quinquireme *Ferox* worked its way eastward from the South Channel, followed by the rest of the Roman squadron. The wind out of the northeast was brisk, strong enough already to raise whitecaps and blow occasional spray across the decks, and it was clearly strengthening. The channel was twisty and not well marked, winding between mud flats, many of them underwater now, which made progress slow. The True Sun was barely above the horizon, and it was difficult to see channel markers in the dawn light. Most of the markers had been removed, anyway, to make life difficult for the invaders.

*Which also makes things tough for allied captains who don't know the channel, of course,* Larry Warner thought. *Can't have everything, I guess.*

They'd headed out in the predawn gloom when one of the rocket-equipped picket ships signaled that it had spotted sails on the horizon. Now they were leaving the lee of the taller islands which surrounded the inner lagoon, headed for a breakwater which marked a safe channel exit from the *outer* lagoon, and the leadsman on the leeward relief platform cast a line forward. Warner stood braced against the mainmast while he mentally translated the leadsman's calls.

"No bottom," he chanted monotonously. Then "Fondo. Bottom at mark three. Bassofondo."

Mark three, Warner thought. Three fathoms. Nikeis still used the original fathom—a bit over five feet; the distance of a man's outstretched arms—brought to Tran by the transplanted Romans. The Brits, taller than ancient Romans, used a six-foot fathom, but as far as Warner knew, the almost-five-and-a-half-foot fathom was standard on Tran, so three fathoms was fifteen feet. Actually, a little more than sixteen. Less than three real fathoms, though. They'd strayed out of the channel, and the water was shoaling, but they hadn't run aground. Close, though. Not much water under the bottom here, he thought, and looked aft.

Captain Pilinius wore his Roman army tunic, with neither armor and helmet nor marks of rank, but that hardly mattered. Everyone on the ship knew he was its master as he stood snarling at the Nikeisian pilot at the starboard steering oar, aft on the quarterdeck. Fleetmaster Junius stood talking to Lieutenant Martins on the babordo side, and Warner remembered some discussion about pecking order seniority and who was supposed to be upwind of whom, but—

"Fondo. Mark three!"

*Shallow, yeah*, Warner thought. *But from Pilinius' expression, I think we're pretty far outside the channel, and it shouldn't be this deep here. Not good. Not good at all.*

He looked up the mast.

"Hang on good!" he shouted. "Water's shoaling. Hang on in case we hit bottom. See anything?"

"Not a thing, Mr. Warner," Private Trevor Manners called down from the small platform just above the hoist block for the lateen sail. "Not a thing."

*At least he didn't remind me it's been all of five minutes since the last time I asked*, Warner thought.

The ship pitched badly, and he looked up at Manners in alarm. But the private seemed to be secure enough, so he turned and peered into the wind, instead. The whitecaps even here in the outer lagoon seemed bad enough to him, but the wide entrance through the breakwater was ahead. Some of the high seas came through into the lagoon, and beyond the breakwater, the waves were higher still, many of them with whitecaps and a few of them breaking. Quite a few of those waves were breaking *across* the breakwater, too, despite the fact that they were still hours away from high tide, and he tried to remember the exact language of the Beaufort scale.

*Large waves begin to form; the white foam crests are more extensive everywhere; probably some spray. That seems to be happening out there. Beaufort scale six, I think. Next step up is a near gale ... and it may not stop there. Wonderful.*

A gale would be a serious blow for ships this size. In fact, the oarsmen were already working hard to send *Ferox* forward with the wind off the port bow, and the quinquireme didn't seem to care for it, even here inside the breakwater. They weren't going to be setting any speed records once they got outside it, either.

*Martins called it "bracing weather,"* Warner thought, and tried not to think about being seasick. *If you don't admit you're seasick it's better,* he told himself firmly. *What the hell am I doing out here?*

Well, if nothing else, this would make him and Martins the two officers with the most sea experience. And Martins was no engineer; he didn't even have a college degree.

*With my experience, I should be put in charge of experimenting with the new navy we'll be building with the stuff in those containers. Admiral Warner. Commodore, anyway. Chief of BuShips! Guns, steam engines—learn about armor and ironclads . . .*

*Of course, first I have to live through* this, he thought wryly.

The shoulder mic clipped to his field jacket epaulet chirped twice. The radio itself was tucked securely inside his jacket to protect it from the salt spray, and he pressed the talk button on the shoulder unit.

"Hunter One. Over."

He released the button.

"Mason," the radio said. "We may have a sighting on the horizon. Don't sound any alarms yet; we're not sure. The light's still pretty crappy. I've got McAllister going up to the top of the tower to confirm. All's well? Over."

"So far, so good. Pilinius hates having a pilot aboard and insists on repeating every instruction so no goddamn Nikeisian buzzard lion is giving orders to his helmsmen, but he looks happy enough. Major, if we're facing action,

I need to tell them pretty quick. We're coming to the breakwater. Over."

"I can see that. Sea looks rough," Mason replied. "But it's going to be a while until they close. Over."

"You're right. It's not like these things are speedboats. Over."

"How are you doing? Over."

"It's rough. We've already got spray coming across the bow and down the ship. And that's here in the lagoon. Out there, I make it Beaufort six, and I think it's getting stronger. Stiff breeze, Beaufort scale says. Next step up is a half gale, and we'll have that in a few hours. Maybe sooner. I think it's too risky to go outside the breakwater. Especially if we have to fight. Over."

"That decision is in the hands of the sailors, I'm afraid. Over."

"Yeah, I figured that. It sounds like they're spoiling for a fight. Over."

*Let sailors be sailors*, Warner remembered Baker saying. *And soldiers be soldiers. Turns out that limey bastard Martins speaks Latin. Learned it in some fancy boarding school in England taught by Benedictine monks. Walked the Colonel right into that one. Might as well have had Publius in on the planning session from the start.*

"You all right out there?" Mason asked. "You're expected to live through this. Acknowledge. Over."

"Acknowledged," Warner said. "One order I'm damned happy with. But the oarsmen don't look too scared, and they're pulling us just fine. Captain Pilinius looks like he's having fun, so far at least." *Of course, he's got that damned*

*Roman stiff upper lip, doesn't he?* "We're all right. In here." He thought about turning the ship broadside on to the seas out beyond the breakwater and shuddered. "We're already being blown all over the place even in here, though. Martins says it's because these ships have no keels, so we get blown downwind. Have to install dagger boards, real rudders or something..."

Warner let go of the transmit button as he drifted deeper into thought. But his ruminations were quickly dispersed when he heard Mason's voice.

"Any danger of your running aground? Over."

"No. In fact, the markers don't mean a lot, because we can sail outside the channel. And if a ship this big can do that, I bet any of the pirates can, except maybe the *navibus onerārius*. They might still have too much draft. I think it's storm surge. I wouldn't expect the outer breakwaters or mud flats to channel the pirates. Over."

"Let me get this straight. You say the water's deep enough that the pirates can just come straight in? Over."

"Not sure, Major, but I know damned well we got outside the channel a couple of times, and *we* didn't run aground. How far that goes, I don't know. I do know the pilot seemed surprised. Over."

"I'll tell the Colonel," Mason said. "Thanks. Anything else? Over."

"Nothing from my end, but how's McAllister doing?" Warner tried to keep his voice calm. It was bad enough heading into a land battle, but out at sea was worse. No way to run away. "Over."

"Mac's up the ladder. Got to the top. Hang on a sec—Okay, it's official. Sails on the horizon. Stand by for the

count. First count. More than ten. Bearing, dead north of
the tower. At least ten sail dead north of my location in
the bell tower. Over."

"That's a couple of hours sooner than we planned on.
Over."

"Yeah. Either the outer picket ships missed them or
they're moving faster than we'd assumed. And the
visibility's not great. Over."

"Roger that. I'll spread the word. Out for a while."

Warner released the button, then cupped his hands
and shouted up the mast.

"Major Mason says sails on the horizon. Dead north
from the tower. That'll be north-northeast of us. Off to
the left. Course, the islands may still be in the way from
here."

"Aye, aye," Manners called down. "But I don't see a
damn thing."

"Keep an eye out. I'm going aft to tell Captain Pilinius."

Warner kept both hands on the safety line that
stretched from the mast to the steering oars as he made
his way aft. He thought clinging to it made him look like
a lubber, but he'd noticed that most of the Roman sailors
did the same thing. All of them held the safety line with
at least one hand, anyway, and no wonder. Going
overboard here would likely be the end.

*Looks be damned.* He walked himself aft, holding the
line in both hands until he got to the quarterdeck ladder.
There were safety lines on it, too. He pulled himself up.

"Hail, Praefectus Pilinius!"

"Hail, Praefectus Warner," the captain replied, and
Warner tapped the radio.

"Those in the bell tower have seen ships to the north. More than ten, possibly many more than that. We see none from the masthead yet—"

The Nikeisian pilot spoke sharply. Publius answered, and they both spoke rapidly, too quickly for Warner to follow. Then the pilot raised one hand and pointed. They turned to follow his pointing finger as a red ball went up the top flagstaff of the bell tower. When it reached the top, it broke out in an enormous double-tailed red streamer and the pilot shouted.

"Enemy in sight," Captain Pilinius said.

⋇ ⋇ ⋇

"Don't like it that the water's so deep already," Art Mason said quietly over the radio to Sergeant Major Bisso. "Over."

"Me neither," Bisso replied. "We're gonna have to fight right here in the city in the end, whatever else happens. Over."

"Always knew we would," Mason said. "Trick is to do as little of that as we can get away with. And at least the radios give us a lot more flex to fix things when the shit hits the fan. Wish we'd had these earlier! Over."

"Me, too." Bisso replied. "Only wish I didn't think we're gonna *need* 'em. Over."

"You got that right, Harry. You got that right. Out."

⋇ ⋇ ⋇

Warner crossed the quarterdeck carefully towards Fleetmaster Junius and Martins. The Colonel had told him to keep as close an eye on Martins as the Romans.

The lieutenant was taking a sighting with his compass, and then drew a line with his pencil on a map. *Actually, it's a chart*, Warner corrected himself. *It has sounding marks on it*.

Martins looked up again, then looked at the bell tower with his binoculars and consulted a chart in his "memoire." Then he manipulated the calipers in his left hand and drew a range arc.

*Must be measuring the angle between the ground and the tower with the reticule in the binos to determine range.*

The Brit did the same thing with a couple of other features while Junius watched with great interest.

"Should we be doing that?" Warner asked in English.

"I'd like us to be able to return," Martins replied, still focused on his work.

"Yeah, but we can still see the tower, and we have the pilot. I imagine the Nikeisians and Romans have been finding their way back for quite a while now. Besides, I'm not sure the Colonel will be happy you're showing the Romans another advanced technique."

"I understand that," Martins said, "but the tower and the pilot may not always be there, and we have no GPS."

"GPS?"

"Sorry. Satellite navigation system put up after you left Earth." Martins' voice was quiet enough Warner had trouble hearing it through the sound of wind and wave as the younger man thought for a moment. "It's been a while since I've done this, so I'm out of practice. I can't speak to the accuracy of my work. I'd need a proper alidade and a sextant for that. Better than nothing, though."

"Praefecti?" Junius asked. His tone was polite but made it clear that he considered their use of English a bit rude.

He'd addressed both of them with the same rank, Warner noticed, but with deference towards Martins.

"I beg your pardon, Fleetmaster," Martins replied in Latin. "I was explaining to Praefectus Warner what I was doing. I suspect he'll soon be able to build even better tools than I currently possess to make it possible for all of our allies' ships to sail well outside sight of land."

"We already do that," Junius replied, and smiled slightly at Martins' expression. "We do try to stay in sight of land in waters we don't know, but that's why any experienced captain keeps his sailing journal."

"Sailing journal?" Martins repeated.

"The record of currents and winds." Junius gave a Roman-style shrug. "An experienced captain, sailing in waters he knows, should make landfall within fifteen miles"—those would be Roman miles, Warner thought, so a tad under sixteen and a half statute miles . . . not that it mattered—"of his destination even if he's sailed the entire way out of sight of land."

"Really?" Martins seemed a bit taken aback, and Junius smiled at him.

"I'm sure your star magic will be very useful in finding our way back this time, Praefectus," he said in an encouraging tone. "After all, wind and wave are far more confused today."

*What was that in the planning session about "galleys don't normally sail beyond sight of land?"* Warner thought, suppressing what he knew was a rather unworthy temptation to ask the question aloud. *And damned if Junius didn't enjoy that! Gotta be sweet when somebody from Tran gets to one-up a star lord!*

"Funny you didn't mention you spoke Latin to the Colonel," he said out loud, this time again in English.

"I remember telling my tutor Latin was a dead language," Martins replied in Latin. "It seems I was in error. Good thing we both learned Latin in secondary school."

*Smart ass*, Larry thought. *I've been here since before you were able to shave, kid.*

He suppressed the temptation to say *that* out loud, too, and grabbed the quarterdeck rail, instead. *Ferox's* motion was sharper as they neared the breakwater. The bow rose harder and faster, then fell back with a sharpness he felt in his legs and spine, and he fought to suppress his stomach's rising queasiness.

He looked away from the waves, concentrating on the bundles at the short ladder up onto the forecastle. At least two lines lashed the Carl Gustav in its weatherproofing to the back of the ladder. Next to it, under the break of the forecastle, a waterproof box contained the recoilless' shells. As long as the ship was afloat it should be all right, he thought. McQuaid, Frick, and the others "volunteered" for the mission were another matter. They didn't look so good.

"Guys, make sure your safety lines are fast!" he shouted in English, then looked around for the other containers. One held the Molotov cocktails, another firebombs, and both were secured as thoroughly as the recoilless and its ammunition.

*Good*, he thought to himself. *Not enough of those. Don't want to lose any of them.*

✣ ✣ ✣

Rick was out of breath by the time he got to the bell tower's observation landing. The stairs stopped there. If he wanted to go higher, he'd have to climb ladders, and he wasn't tempted. If he couldn't see it from here, he wasn't going to see it. Besides, the base radio had been emplaced here, with its antenna farther up, atop the tower and connected to the set by coaxial cable. One of Saxon's bicycle generators had been set up beside it, just in case.

He stepped off the landing towards Art Mason.

"How close are they?" he asked in English, and Mason turned quickly.

"Didn't hear you coming, Colonel. Nearest enemy's maybe sixteen, seventeen miles out. All that wind and spray isn't helping visibility, but there's lots of sails, Sir. Best I can estimate, there's at least eighty or ninety of them, so far. Maybe more; it's all mixed up out there, and they're not all together. Their fleet's strung out for miles. Bunch of ten or a dozen about a mile ahead of the main body, and it looks like some of 'em are still coming over the horizon. Figure they'll be here in three, maybe four hours. Seas are high, wind's high." He shook his head. "They'll be coming straight in, I think. No way for them to maneuver. It's going to be a rush."

"Pretty much like we expected," Rick said.

"Worse, Colonel." Mason shook his head again. "Sir, Mr. Warner says the water's a lot deeper out there than anyone expected."

"But they know the seas rise—" Rick frowned.

"Yes, Sir. Maybe it's the storm. Or maybe some know it and some don't. Clavell says this is the damnedest place for keeping secrets. I don't know, Colonel, but I don't think the outer harbor defenses are worth a damn. A lot of the mud flats have disappeared. I think they'll just come straight in. It don't even look like they have any choice in the matter. I doubt they could get back home in these seas. I think they have to attack, and hope they're lucky getting past the shoals."

Rick nodded.

"Which means they don't have any choice but to use their best tactic. Rush us hell for leather. Maybe this Cannae wasn't such a bad idea."

*Assuming the Romans can maneuver better than the pirates can, anyway*, he thought while projecting as much confidence as he could.

"Well, if the pirates don't kill us, maybe the storm can, Sir."

"That's a cheery thought," Rick replied. "Pass the word for Admiral Stigliano to get the northern squadron ready. And check with Walbrook. Make sure he's ready to move with the mortars."

"Yes, Sir."

As Mason began passing orders, Rick picked up his binoculars and looked through them at the Nikeisian squadron anchored in the inner lagoon near the northern channel. Lying to anchor had allowed the crews to stay rested and fresh, which would give them an edge over the pirates. As he watched, Admiral Piero Stigliano received his signal and there was a flurry of activity on the fifteen assigned ships as they prepared to get underway.

Rick shifted his gaze north to the outer lagoon. At first he was disoriented and uncertain what he was looking at, because features he'd expected to see were no longer visible. Many of the low-lying islands that made up the barrier for the outer lagoon were now awash; the mud flats that made up the rest were nowhere to be seen, although angry white water churned across them.

And the rising tide still had a long way to go . . .

"Looks like Stigliano's going to have to fight in what's left of the outer lagoon," Mason said as he looked in the same direction with his own binoculars. "The seas have really risen."

"I had the same thought," Rick replied. "And if there's this much storm surge now, we're really in for it when it hits."

"Don't like the look of the sky to the north, either," Mason said, and Rick nodded grimly. Visibility was deteriorating as the wind continued to rise. Whitecaps were everywhere, with foam beginning to blow in long streaks, and the clouds rolling in on the wind were dark, angry looking, and moving fast.

"I don't care for it much myself," he said.

"I don't think we should've sent the team with the Roman squadron," Mason said. "I don't see how Frick's going to hit anything with the Carl Gustav from a pitching ship in those seas, and the team with him's going to be wasting ammo if they use their rifles. Especially if it gets worse."

"You're right, but think. It could've been worse. We could have gone with that battlecruiser idea."

"Do you want to recall the squadron?"

Rick chewed on his inner lip for a moment, then shook his head.

"No, we have to figure Pilinius and the others know what they're doing. Leave it up to Junius."

*I sure as hell* hope *they know what they're doing, anyway! Besides, what do I do if they ignore a recall order? Publius obviously wants a naval victory. I have to wonder how much he's willing to risk betting on the weather to get it, but that's clearly what he wants. And since they're his ships, it's entirely possible they'd do what he wants instead of what I want. What's that old saying about never giving an order you know won't be obeyed?*

They heard the sound of hobnailed boots on the steps behind them and turned.

"Hail, Friend of Caesar," Tribune Caius Julius said from the stairs as he came up to join them.

"Hail, friend, Tribune of Rome," Rick replied in his rough Latin as he smiled. *Can't get away from you guys.* "I'm glad you're here."

"Publius asked that I assist you in any way I can."

*I bet he did.*

✢ ✢ ✢

Rick watched the Nikeisian squadron deploy and felt his stomach knot as they filed slowly through the main channel in a line. The channel ran between two islands— Isola di Lido and Isola di San Lazzaro—which were part of the ring surrounding the inner lagoon, a bit higher than the boundary islands of the outer lagoon, and he shifted his gaze up and to the north to see another line of ships heading south towards what remained of the outer lagoon. The seas outside the lagoon were too high for oars, and angry surf boiled white over the semisubmerged outer islands. There was more and more spray as the waves pounded home, boiling in confused white sheets across the submerged mud flats and the outer breakwater. Despite that, the oncoming galleys, at least half of them great galleys, held a remarkably straight line as they leaned to the wind under double-reefed, tight-bellied lateen sails.

*Who* are *those guys?* Rick wondered. *They've got to be professionals.*

"What am I looking at?" he asked Caius Julius, offering him the binoculars. The Tribune peered through them for a moment, then lowered them with a grimace.

"Those are the galleys of the Grand Duchy of Riccigiona."

"Looks like they're leading with some of their best troops to soften us up," Rick said.

"Indeed they are," Caius Julius agreed.

"Which means they could be the only ones who could hold the formation in the storm. Probably that as much as any deliberate planning, Colonel," Mason added.

Rick nodded as he recovered his binoculars. Then he put the strap around his neck and watched through them in fascination as the enemy squadron passed over what had been the boundary of the outer lagoon. They pitched wildly in the shallow, turbulent water, but they held their course and, nearly simultaneously, lowered the spars of their lateen sails, secured them for battle, and thrust out their oars once again in the less tumultuous seas of the lagoon.

*That took guts*, he thought. *They must have realized the mud flats were submerged, but until they actually crossed them, they couldn't be sure by how much. They sure as hell weren't going to be able to stop if it turned out to be too shallow! These people are good.*

He lowered his gaze towards the Nikeisian squadron as that thought ran through them, and his jaw tightened.

*A couple of those ships have green crews. If they don't get out of that column, things aren't going to go well.*

The channel broadened as it approached the wider lagoon, and the Nikeisian squadron began breaking out of the column. The first two ships altered course by forty-five degrees—the first to the left, and the second to the right. The others fanned out behind them, with the ships in trail alternating to follow the two guides. When the last two ships had fallen into place, they all altered course directly north, facing the enemy in a formation like a huge, inverted V, with four of Nikeis' eight great galleons at the refused apex of the wedge.

They'd gotten into formation just in time, and the forwardmost ships started trading fire with the enemy, using their bow-mounted ballistas. The Nikeisian missiles fell short and to the left, driven off true by the winds. The Riccigionan squadron had the wind at their backs, but few of the large quarrels hit their targets on either side. Not surprisingly, given the roughness of the seas even within the lagoon. Ships in both squadrons started to retract their oars as they surged towards one another, and their marines exchanged crossbow and javelin fire.

Rick watched the outermost Nikeisian ships at the right end of the line pivot sharply inward towards the nearest enemy ship. Their prow-mounted rams screeched across the enemy ship's metal-clad bow, then skittered across its wooden sides. The rams had too little angle or momentum to penetrate the hull, but the impact did slow all three of them. Grapnels flew, and the three ships surged together, weapons waving at the point of contact.

More ships slammed together at the other end of the line, but it took the enemies in the center longer to close and the Duchy ships concentrated their fire on the center Nikeisian great galley. Marines fell on its deck, and the Nikeisian rowers were slow in retracting their sweeps in what might have been a sign of inexperience. An enemy galley—one of the faster, more maneuverable *galee sottili*, swerved at the last moment and sped down the Nikeisian's side. Oars shattered as its prow sliced through them, the inboard ends of the long sweeps became furious demons, crushing bone and flesh, and the attacker slipped through the gap it had opened in the Nikeisian line. Grapnels flew at it from either side, but too late to catch it, and it sped off down the channel.

Behind it, both squadrons slammed together into a gigantic raft of floating wood, metal, and fighting men. Marines surged across the bulwarks in a deadly melee. Despite how tightly they were locked together, the ships heaved and rolled against one another, timbers screaming as they grated together, and some men lost their footing. The lucky ones fell back onto their own ships. Others fell into the sea or were crushed between the grinding hulls.

Rowers surged up from their benches, boiling up through the hatches with weapons in hand, piling in behind their marines, and it was all close-range, hand-to-hand butchery. Rick had seen it on far too many battlefields since arriving on Tran, but not like this. Not compressed into such a small area. Not on a heaving, rolling wooden perch in the middle of a spray-lashed sea. And the fact that it was so far away, so distant even through the binoculars, only made it worse somehow.

There was nothing wrong with the Duchy crews' courage, but the three-to-one odds on the outer wings quickly worked in Nikeis' favor. The opposing great galleys locked together in the center, but the Nikeisian *galee sottili* had been loaded with extra drafts of militia to support their marines. They added their weight to the onslaught sweeping inward from the wings, and though the Riccigionan marines fought frantically to hold the bulwarks, their lines cracked in too many places. Nikeisian marines swarmed through the gaps, engaging the rowers trying to reinforce them, and Nikeisian rowers followed, spreading out, taking the Riccigionan defenders from the rear.

The defense crumpled quickly, the outermost Duchy ships fell, and the victorious Nikeisian marines prepared to sweep down the rest of the line while the angry wind drove the entire, rafted mass back onto the channel mouth.

✢ ✢ ✢

Captain Gulian Foscari tried to hide his nervousness as his ship, *Corona*, threaded its way towards the heart of Nikeis. He stood beside Terenzio Rambaldo, *Corona's* first lieutenant, on the quarterdeck, his gaze flicking back and forth between the leadsman on the bow and the windows and balconies of the buildings flanking the channel. That gaze was spending more time on the buildings, actually. The leadsman would tell him if there was a chain or other obstruction in the channel, but crossbow bolts or arrows could fall from any opening in the buildings above them with no warning. There was not a Nikeisian in sight—no doubt they had pulled as many of their women and children as they could up the hills and out of harm's way—but he was sure the defenders would show themselves soon enough, and when they did . . .

The sounds of battle receded as his crew maneuvered expertly through another twist in the channel. Now, safely in the lee of the taller islands, the water was far calmer and it seemed almost silent compared to the blowing wind and tumultuous waves through which they'd sailed throughout the night. It wasn't silent, of course; not with that same wind still muscling its way through the buildings about them, but it was close enough he could actually hear the creak of the hull.

"Our spies were right," Rambaldo said quietly. "Nikeis has neglected its defenses. Perhaps we've already seen the best they have to offer."

"Perhaps," Foscari replied. "I don't intend to rely on that, but our cousins' tightfisted nature may have been their undoing. I do know they were making offers to hire experienced crews very recently."

"It's too late to hire *us*," Rambaldo said with a grin.

"Very true."

Foscari had been there when the Captain General of the Riccigionan fleet discussed the offer from the High Chancellor of the Five Kingdoms. He'd never seen so much gold and silver before, and over and above that, the High Chancellor had promised that the Five Kingdoms would waive all tribute for the next two years if the Grand Duke joined the armada to take Nikeis. That would have been tempting enough, but the promise of loot from the star lord boxes had been even more tempting. That kind of prize could bring a lifetime of luxuries!

Still, a small suspicion had been planted in Foscari's mind that day, and it had grown far stronger now that they were actually here in Nikeis. The gold, the offer, and the details about the boxes and their destination had all arrived in the Grand Duchy well before any rumors of the sky lights had arrived by way of ships coming from Nikeis. Or from anywhere else in the Inland Sea, for that matter. So how had the Five Kingdoms known about them so much sooner than anyone else?

*I fear the hands of the sky demons are behind this message from Issardos*, he thought now, and too many legends warned of the price which always accompanied the sky demons' aid.

They rounded another bend and *Corona* emerged from the channel's shadows into the relative brightness of the inner lagoon. The first outriders of the storm clouds which had pursued the fleet throughout the night stretched overhead, but the visibility was far greater than it had been.

"There!" Rambaldo cried. "There they are—just like he said it would be!"

The first lieutenant was pointing at three preposterously large, oddly shaped boxes lined up before the Doge's Palace on the far side of a half-flooded square. They were painted blue, with dark and strange letterings of different sizes and in different colors scattered across them. Between them and the edge of the square was a head-high barricade, built roughly and in obvious haste out of paving stones, timbers, and what looked like stone taken from demolished buildings. The one thing Foscari *couldn't* see were any defenders.

"Take us in closer," he said. "But slowly! Let's not get deep enough for any nasty surprises while we're all alone."

Rambaldo looked mulish for a moment, but then his own common sense reasserted itself and he nodded before he turned back to the helmsman.

*Corona* sidled cautiously towards the square in the eerie quiet, broken only by the sound of the wind buffeting the buildings all about them, and *still* there was no one to be seen. Crewmen and officers grinned at each other with greedy delight, but there was an edge of disquiet in those grins.

"Maybe they all ran away," Rambaldo said nervously.

"Maybe, but—"

A sharp slapping sound, like a fist against a jaw, interrupted Foscari's response. The steersman went up on his toes, hands flying to his chest, and a spray of blood erupted between his shoulder blades. A single explosive crack of thunder sounded an instant later, and the steersman fell to the deck.

Then Rambaldo's jaw disintegrated in a pink cloud, followed by the same thunderclap. The ship veered off course. The sound of a whistle rang out from behind the waiting barricade, and dark-faced men with strange hats appeared along it.

Someone barked orders in an unknown language, in a voice louder than any Foscari had ever heard. Then the thunder crackled again, far closer and twenty times as loud. Something struck him. He fell to the deck, clutching his own chest, and saw the blood erupting between his fingers. He realized the quarterdeck was covered in bodies. And the forecastle. Bodies like his. Someone was screaming. No, a lot of men were screaming.

It was hard to breathe, and he closed his eyes to rest.

✢ ✢ ✢

The *fustas* swarmed the drifting galley and Rick watched Roman legionnaires and Nikeisian halberdiers storm across its bulwarks. The stunned rowers were overwhelmed before they could even rise from their benches.

"That was excellent, Mac," Rick said. "Pass the word to everyone on the net—well done!"

He returned his gaze to the fight outside the northern channel as Mason keyed the microphone, and his smile faded. The Nikeisian marines had closed in on the last two Riccigionan ships in the center of the line, coming at the defenders from three directions at once. The Riccigionans were clearly doomed, but they stubbornly refused to yield.

"Ah, hell!" Rick snarled as he raised his binoculars to the turbulent seas beyond the outer lagoon and saw the reason they were being so stubborn.

At least a score of additional galleys, the standard of the Five Kingdoms starched stiff as steel at their mastheads by the ever-stronger wind, came storming towards the churning water of the outer barrier. They heeled dangerously as they rode the gale, but they weren't slowing, and even more ships followed astern of them. The Nikeisian squadron was out of time. Even if the city's marines managed to end the fight before the Five

Kingdoms galleys arrived, the defending ships couldn't possibly cut themselves free of the rafted mass and redeploy in time to meet them.

Admiral Stigliano must have reached the same conclusion. The interlocked Nikeisian and Riccigionan galleys had been driven back on the mouth of the channel, and as Rick watched, the Nikeisian crews not actively fighting scrambled to drop anchors and grapnels into the water from as many ships as possible while others lashed them as tightly together as they could. They stretched across the channel, almost directly between the twin fortresses on Lido and San Lazzaro, like a huge, wooden boom. But it was a boom made of ships and men.

*Cork in a bottle*, he thought, and his heart sank. It wasn't a surprise, really. It had always been a possibility—indeed, a probability—that something just like this would happen. *That's why you put Walbrook where you did*. He watched the Nikeisians turning their ships into their city's outer bulwark, knowing it meant most of them would die, and something inside him quailed from the order he knew he would almost certainly have to give.

"Publius says he's going to commandeer the galley they just captured as his new command ship," Mason reported.

"You're kidding me!" Rick lowered his binoculars to look at the major in disbelief.

"Says the *fusta* crews will run the deck. His security team will make sure the rowers stay put, and his legionnaires will be the marines."

"Oh, crap!" Rick shook his head. "Tell him to keep his ass—I mean, kindly *ask* him to at least stay in the inner lagoon."

"Yes, Sir."

*And what the hell do I do if he gets himself killed?* Rick wondered, turning back to the fight in the channel.

⁜ ⁜ ⁜

The shoulder mic chirped.

Warner could barely hear it through the crashing roar of sea and wind, and he was tempted to not answer it. He was too busy hugging the mainmast like a sodden bear while he waged a grim rearguard action against his nausea. Maybe if he just went ahead and threw up he'd feel better afterward?

They'd been sailing for five hours, and he'd had enough rolling and pitching to last a lifetime. Especially after what he'd endured when they changed tack an hour earlier. He'd had to abandon his spot by the mast as the deck crew adjusted the sail, and he'd huddled with the other mercenaries as the steering oar was put hard over.

Martins had explained—with what Warner personally considered appalling cheerfulness—that they'd have to wear ship rather than tack.

"Why?" Warner had asked, and Martins had shrugged. "These galleys' lateen sails are handier for coming about—turning upwind to change tack—than a square-rigger would be without a proper jib." Warner nodded in impatient understanding, and Martins shrugged. "But handier or no, Captain Pilinius doesn't want to risk it in this lot." The Brit waved a hand at the tumult raging around them. "Turning downwind will take longer, because he'll have farther to turn, but it lets him use the wind instead of fighting it. And we're far less likely to get caught and thrown aback facing straight into it."

"Sounds good to me," Warner had said fervently, wiping spray from his face.

Of course, that had been before Pilinius actually did it.

If working with the wind was supposed to be safer and easier, Larry Warner never wanted to be aboard a ship that did it the *hard* way. *Ferox* had rolled madly, heaving in protest, and unless Warner was badly mistaken, she'd damn near capsized in the process. Huge clouds of spray had burst up over the angular shape of her oar box and water had broken green and angry across her decks, washing as high as his knees as he'd clung to the forecastle ladder with white knuckles. It had flooded the upper deck completely until the ship came reluctantly back upright and it fountained from the scuppers. Even Pilinius had lost his air of studied calm as he volleyed orders and threw his own weight against the steering oar.

Still, they'd made it. Somehow.

*And I am* so *never going to sea again*, Warner thought.

The rest of the squadron had made it around, as well, and changed formation in the process. *Ferox* led the port—*babordo*, he reminded himself—column of ten ships to leeward, while *Fides*, one of the triremes, led the windward column, followed by ten more galleys. The wind was even stronger than it had been, with spray flying everywhere and waves rolling up on the starboard quarter like moving, foam-topped mountains. Some of them were considerably higher than *Ferox*'s fourteen-foot freeboard, and the quartering sea added a nasty corkscrew effect to the galley's motion. He didn't like to think about what it must be like aboard the smaller triremes and liburnians.

The shoulder mic chirped again, and this time the sound pulled him up out of his misery to press the button.

"Hunter One, over."

"I was getting a little worried there," Major Mason said. "Thought the radio had gone dead. Over."

"Radio's fine. I'm not so great. Over."

"How bad? Over."

"Damned if I know," Warner said frankly. "I'm more'n a little seasick, and I think Pilinius and Junius"—*and that prick Martins*—"are a lot more worried than they were when we set out. Wind's really picking up. Over."

"Well, I have a little news to take your mind off of that. The bad guys are earlier and moving faster than we'd expected. They're more scattered, too. Their main body's still coming into sight from the bell tower, but it's pretty damned ragged and we're watching a squadron north-northeast of you, heading your way. It's the farthest east of the lot—so far at least. Don't see how they could actually have sighted you yet, though. Most probably just got separated from the rest and now they're steering for Nikeis, but it looks like your courses are going to intersect short of the main body. Over."

"How many? Over."

"I make it a dozen. They're too far away to see their pennants, but there's at least one great galley in there and they're maintaining a line formation, so they're probably not pirates. Best guess, Five Kingdoms. Over."

"Roger. Out."

Warner released the talk button and detached himself from the mast, not without regrets, to make his cautious way aft to the quarterdeck.

"Hail, Fleetmaster," he half-shouted across the angry wind. It came out a little strangled sounding as he fought not to vomit.

"Hail, Praefectus Warner," Junius replied.

"The tower tells me there's an enemy squadron of a dozen galleys north-northeast of us, headed our way."

Martins consulted his compass, then scowled and pointed upwind.

"Bad luck," he said. "They'll have the weather gauge on us."

"If we don't see them yet, then they don't see us," Junius said. It was his turn to scowl.

"Tower says they're in a line formation with at least one great galley, probably not pirates."

"If they're maintaining formation in this weather instead of scattering, they're regular navy ships," Junius agreed. He picked up a leather speaking trumpet from a bulwark rack and raised it in *Fides'* direction.

"Enemy squadron spotted upwind," he bawled through it, somehow making himself heard despite the weather. Warner thought it must be some kind of trick professional seamen learned. "Stand by to detach your division and engage. We will continue as planned."

✛ ✛ ✛

The next wave of attacking galleys swept across the outer lagoon and charged down on the rafted Nikeisian squadron blocking the North Channel. The rising wind clearly left them little option but to make for the closest passage to the inner lagoon, and arrows flew from the moored Nikeisian galleys to greet them. One of the attacking *galee sottili* must have lost its steersman, because it swerved wildly and broached across the waves surging over the submerged breakwater. For a moment, Rick thought it was going fully over, but it managed not to capsize...just in time to be rammed squarely amidships by a following galley.

The rammed galley rolled completely up on its side as the other ship slammed into it, and he saw men spill into the angry waves. Very few of them seemed to surface again.

The ship which had hit it found itself in almost equally dire straits. There'd been no time to reduce sail before it struck, and the impact had snapped its masts. Both of them went over the side in a tangled, thrashing knot of wreckage. The galley itself ripped its ram out of its sister, completing the fatal gash, as the fallen top-hamper dragged it around. The fallen spars were a sea anchor, holding it broadside to the waves. It rolled madly, and axes flashed as its crew hewed desperately at the shrouds tethering it to the wreckage.

But the rest of the oncoming galleys carried through. They surged down on the defenders, sails billowing madly as they let their sheets fly to spill the furious wind from their sails just before they struck. There were only two or three great galleys in this wave, but they were accompanied by far too many lighter ships. Some of them buried their rams in the anchored ships; most of them crashed home without actually ramming, and more grapnels flew as they made fast. More boarders boiled up, swarming across the bulwarks, coming to grips with the already depleted Nikeisian marines and rowers. The defenders had been given precious time to reorganize and station themselves as advantageously as possible, but they were going to be badly outnumbered, and still more enemy galleys were coming up fast. Weapons slashed and stabbed, and something far darker and redder than seawater splashed across the jammed galleys' decks.

One of the attacking galleys jammed itself into a gap at the extreme right end of the Nikeisian line, and more grapnels flew—this time from the shore. As Rick watched, an avalanche of Nikeisian militiamen swarmed over its decks, hacking and chopping, then raced down the line to reinforce the squadron's depleted crews.

His heart rose as he realized they'd be able to support Stigliano after all. Maybe if they could do the same thing at the *other* end of the line, Stigliano could hold his ground despite the odds!

"Some of them are gonna find other channels, Sir," Mason said, and Rick lowered his binoculars again as he turned to face the major and raised both eyebrows.

"Most of 'em still seem to be headed for North Channel," Mason said, answering the unvoiced question. "Probably because it's the main way in from that part of the lagoon. But some of them are managing to avoid all that." He jerked his head at the growing logjam of galleys. "Mostly because of how scattered they got on the way here, I think. They aren't coming in together—not tightly, anyway—and some of them are taking advantage of that."

"How?"

"They're peeling off to stay clear of the main action. Maybe they're just trying to get into the lee of the islands, or maybe they've got somebody onboard who knows the local waters. Hell, Sir, maybe they're just getting lucky!

But we've got at least a couple of dozen veering off, especially to the west, and that means they're headed towards some of the other channels. Gonna have some leakers, Sir."

"From the west?" Rick turned, peering through his glasses, but the buildings on the islands the Nikeisians called Lido and Cannaregio blocked his view.

"What the spotters are reporting, Sir," Mason said, and shrugged. "Don't see how they *could* come at us from the east in this weather, really. The surf's really bad on that side of the outer lagoon right now." He shook his head. "No, Sir, they're trying to get around to the west. Come at us from the leeward side of the main islands. Might even be able to row from that side."

"Crap. What do we have covering the West Channel?"

"Aside from Admiral del Verme's squadron, you mean?" Rick nodded a bit impatiently, and Mason puffed his lips unhappily. "Not much from our side, Sir. Three or four firebomb parties at the narrower spots, but that's about it."

"Damn. How much cover do our firebombers have?"

"Not a ton, Sir," Mason said grimly. "Got militia on all of them, but most of the steadier troops are clustered at the fortresses. Our guys are three or four blocks farther west than that. I don't know how steady *their* militia's going to be if the bad guys try coming ashore short of the inner lagoon. And if they flank the firebombers' positions it'll get ugly."

Rick thought furiously for a moment, then grimaced.

"All right. We're just going to have to hope most of them don't think about stopping early, but we damned well can't count on it. Put Rand on it. Tell him he can have half the reserve archers and a platoon of musketeers, but we need to get somebody in there. And tell him to take one of the radios!"

"Yes, Sir!" Mason acknowledged, and Rick heard him passing urgent orders over the radio as he turned back to the battle for North Channel.

⁜ ⁜ ⁜

"Sail to windward!"

It was difficult to hear the lookouts through the din of wind and wave, but a chain of a half dozen seamen passed the word to *Ferox*'s quarterdeck.

"At least ten sail on the starboard quarter! Coming down on us fast!"

"Sooner than I expected," Fleetmaster Junius said grimly, then shrugged. "I understand Lord Rick is fond of saying no plan survives when the enemy arrives, Praefectus Warner?"

"He is," Warner agreed. No point mentioning that the Colonel had cribbed it from von Moltke.

"A warrior of great wisdom, Lord Rick," Junius said, and reached for his speaking trumpet again.

*And there goes half our strength*, Warner thought as the windward squadron altered course to intercept the oncoming galleys. *That leaves ten ships to take on something like eighty. I sure hope all of our weapons work. Can't swim home, that's for sure*.

⁜ ⁜ ⁜

"Bad news, Bart."

"What? You mean *more* bad news, right?" Bart Saxon asked, looking up at Cal Haskins as the ex-corporal strode into the great hall which had become his bombmaker's workshop.

"Just got the word from Clavell." Haskins looked grim. "At least some of the bastards are avoiding the traffic jam in the North Channel. Dunno where else they're likely to go, but Clavell says there's at least three or four ways in."

"Crap!"

"What is it, Lord Bart?" a voice asked. Saxon turned his head and met Lucia Michaeli's anxious eyes. Obviously she'd understood Haskins' tone even if she hadn't understood the English.

"Some of the pirates are likely to—" He paused, wondering how to say "bypass" in the trade dialect, then shrugged. "Some of the pirates are likely to come a different way."

"Not down the Canale del Nord?"

She didn't sound very surprised, Saxon thought. For that matter, she sounded a lot calmer than he felt, too. Then again, she'd already surprised him more than once tonight. She and her sister—and Ginarosa Torricelli—had all made themselves very useful while he and Warner were concocting their jury-rigged incendiaries and explosives. He'd been a little leery about that, given the possibility of accidents, but Lucia had only rolled her eyes at his tentative objections and then gone right back to work.

"Exactly," he said now. "They may come another way."

"If they avoid the Canale del Nord, someone is likely to come down the Canale Gottardo Capponi," she said in the trade dialect. "There are three—no, four—channels they might use to reach the inner lagoon from the north, but Canale Gottardo Capponi is the closest to the main channel. It's the one between Isola di Cannaregio and Isola di Lido, just west of the Canale del Nord."

"Surely someone is guarding the Canale Got— Gotter—whatever," Saxon said reassuringly.

"Are they?" She shook her head, her expression more anxious than ever. "I'm not certain of that. I know they're guarding the Canale Occidentale—the West Channel— but usually, Gottardo Capponi is too shallow for war galleys. It's broad enough, but not deep enough for anything but the local fishing boats. It isn't a place someone would normally think to guard, but with the water as deep as it is . . ."

She turned away and began snapping orders in Italian. Saxon couldn't understand a word she said, but her militiamen clearly could. They headed for the pyramid of wooden chests in the center of the great hall where the reserve incendiaries had been packed so that they could be transported to wherever they might be needed.

"What are they doing?" he demanded.

"We are going to defend the canal," she told him.

"No! You can't!"

"It is *our* city," she told him defiantly.

"But—"

She only turned away, still spouting commands at the militiamen, and they formed up with four of the reserve chests and headed for the door.

Saxon looked around, searching for one of Galloway's men. But he and Haskins were the only "star lords" in sight. There was just the two of them and—

*Oh, no*, he told himself. *You are not going to do this.*

*Especially not after Galloway ordered you to keep your ass out of the line of fire! You're a frigging* schoolteacher, *not a soldier! But if you can't stop her, then what—?*

"Wait," he said.

"There's no time!" she said impatiently. "Besides, I *am* going!"

"That's not what I meant," he heard someone else say with his voice. "I meant I'm coming with you."

⁂

"Oh, shit," Art Mason said, and Rick turned quickly in his direction.

"What?"

"Looks like those 'leakers' are arriving sooner'n we expected, Sir," Mason replied, lowering his binoculars. "And looks like there's more of them, too."

The major pointed northwest. Rick raised his own glasses to peer in the indicated direction, and his jaw tightened as he saw mastheads clearing the flank of Isola di Cannaregio, headed straight for the West Channel.

There were a lot of them.

He turned back to the southwest where Admiral Otero del Verme's second Nikeisian squadron held position. His galleys were sheltered from the worst of the wind by the bulk of the main island itself, but the seas were rough enough even there that just holding station had to be exhausting to their rowers, and it was getting worse. That was bound to affect their combat effectiveness when he finally committed them. The longer he waited, the worse that would get, and the timing had already gone south on them. The pirates had gotten here well before they were expected, and the Romans wouldn't be able to attack for at least another hour or hour and a half. Even then, they were likely to be at only half strength. And if he waited long enough to send them in simultaneously, the way they'd planned—

"Hell with it," he said out loud. "Signal Admiral del Verme to move up now. He's got to block the West Channel between Cannaregio and San Giorgio."

"Going to be rough on them if they have to go in without the Romans, Sir."

"I know that! But we can't let them flank the North Channel."

"No, Sir," Mason acknowledged, and Rick heard him passing urgent orders as he turned back to the still raging battle for North Channel.

A half dozen additional galleys had crashed into the ship raft, throwing still more men into the fight while he was speaking with Mason. Even with reinforcements from both flanking fortresses, the Nikeisian line was driven back across the spray- and blood-slick decks by sheer weight of numbers. Worse, other enemy galleys had run ashore on San Lazzaro and Lido, pouring men onto the islands. Every man sent from the fortresses to support Stigliano's galleys was one less they'd have for their own defense.

✢ ✢ ✢

"Go back to the Palace!" Bart Saxon said sharply. "Let me take care of this!"

"No." Lucia Michaeli glared at him.

"You found us the right spot. Now the rest of us can handle it, and I want you out of here!"

"No!" she shot back even more sharply.

"It's going to get dangerous!"

"I know that," she said. "Whose city do you think this is?"

"Damn it, if something happens to you—"

"And what if something happens to *you*?! You're—Professore Clavell says you're important to Lord Rick's plans."

"But—"

"'Scuse me, Bart," Cal Haskins said, "but I think you two're gonna have to settle this later. Look."

Saxon shot Lucia one more exasperated glance, then turned to where Haskins stood beside one of the windows. Like Saxon, he had his H&K slung over his shoulder. *Unlike* Saxon, who'd fired no more than forty or fifty rounds with the weapon before they left Earth, Haskins also looked like he knew how to use it. Now he pointed out and down, and Saxon swallowed a curse.

Lucia had picked their current position because it was four streets north of one of the three drawbridges which crossed the canal. All of them had been lowered, blocking any galley, but they were only made of wood, and the militia guarding them were spread dangerously thin. Most of the manpower on Isola di Lido had been stationed along its northern and eastern shoreline, where the real threat had been anticipated. That was why Lucia had insisted that they had to be north of the northernmost drawbridge. Once the enemy saw the bridges, they'd know they had to send men ashore to clear the way.

"But if we sink them first, use *them* to block the channel, the bridges won't matter!" she'd said fiercely, and he'd been forced to agree with her logic. Which made him feel no better now that they had proof her worries had been well founded.

The galley threading its way down the Canale Gottardo Capponi flew a standard he didn't recognize. It wasn't Roman or Nikeisian, anyway. And a second galley had rounded the bend just north of their present position behind it.

"Five Kingdoms," a soprano said at his elbow, and he turned to glare at Lucia.

"Well, it *is*!" she told him pertly, then turned and threw a stream of Italian at "her" militiamen. It was far too rapid for Saxon to understand a word of it, but the militiamen immediately opened the chests they'd brought with them.

"God*damn* it," he snarled, and Haskins glanced at him. "This is no place for a damned *kid*, Cal!"

"Don't disagree, but some of the others ain't that much older'n she is, man. And they ain't listening to her like she was just a 'kid.' 'Sides, at least she can tell 'em what to do in their own language, which is more'n you or *I* can do!"

✠ ✠ ✠

"Praise Vothan," Eurydamus of Tiryns said as *Thunderbolt* eased her way along the shadowed channel. Waves slapped loudly even here, but the solid bulk of the Nikeisian buildings flanking it on either side were a blessed barrier to the brutal wind roaring down the length of the Great Gulf.

"Aye, I'm thinking he had a lot to do with it," Scamandius, his first lieutenant, agreed. "Him and the Thunderer."

"And our turncoat," Eurydamus murmured, cutting his eyes at the man standing beside *Thunderbolt*'s steersman.

Polidoro Scarcello wasn't a Riccigionan. He was a native Nikeisian.

"He cost enough," Scamandius said sourly, then shrugged. "And worth every silver of it. I never would have expected there to be enough water in here, even with the Demon Star."

"A lot of things are changing thanks to the Demon," Eurydamus replied, never taking his eye from the leadsman at the bow.

There was enough water under *Thunderbolt*'s keel right *now*, but there was no promise things would stay that way, and none of the great galleys or *navibus onerārius* could possibly have come this way. He looked over his shoulder at the next galley in line behind *Thunderbolt* with a crooked smile that mixed grudging respect with amusement. Captain Anaxilaus was an excellent seaman, and Eurydamus was fairly certain Anaxilaus hadn't "just happened" to fall behind in the squadron's mad scramble to claw its way into the canal. If someone ran aground in here, it wasn't going to be *him*, and—

A blur of movement at the corner of his eye snatched his attention back to his own ship as something plummeted from above. It trailed a thin line of smoke behind it, and he heard the sharp shattering sound of pottery or glass as it slammed into the deck three feet from him.

His eyes were still widening in alarm when the spray of flame splashed across his legs. He cried out, leaping away from it, beating frantically at the liquid fire clinging to him as it gnawed his flesh, and someone else cried out in alarm as a second plummeting object smashed into the deck, right beside the main hatch. Liquid fire poured over the hatch coaming onto the babordo rowing bench, and alarm turned to anguish as half a dozen men were engulfed in sudden flame. More of the burning liquid spilled hungrily down the hatch, and *Thunderbolt* veered to starboard as the rowers leapt away from the inferno.

✣ ✣ ✣

"*Yes!*" Lucia's shriek of triumph was as fierce as any eagle's as the firebombs smashed home on the leading galley.

She'd insisted on lighting the first one herself, and she'd watched it all the way down to the galley's quarterdeck. It helped that the ship had been almost directly below their fourth-floor perch, but the canal was so narrow they could probably lob the gunpowder bombs—they were a little lighter than the firebombs— clear across it if they had to.

That was Bart Saxon's first thought. His second was that he hadn't really let himself think about what he was making as he constructed the incendiaries. The shrieks of agony and the thickening columns of smoke-shot flame filled him with a crawling horror. Those men down there had come here to plunder Nikeis, and he doubted they would have cared very much how many people they massacred in the process. But they were still human beings, and he was the one who'd built the weapon which had set them afire like so many logs.

He looked away, fighting an urge to vomit, and saw Lucia's profile as she snapped more orders in rapid Italian, pointing at the second ship swinging to starboard in an effort to get around their first victim. If she felt any trace of his own repugnance, there was no sign of it in that fierce, focused young face.

✤ ✤ ✤

"Quickly, Marco! Quickly!"

"Yes, Signorina!" Marco Salata acknowledged. If her father's valet had any reservations about handling the star men's infernal devices he clearly had no intention of showing it.

"Valerico! Your throwing arm is stronger than mine," he said, and the young militiaman stepped up beside him. Valerico's expression showed considerably more trepidation, but he accepted the gunpowder bomb and held it gingerly while Marco opened the slide on the lantern.

"We want to hit the other galley, Valerico." Lucia remembered to smile encouragingly at him. "And we want to do it *quickly*. If we can sink two or three of them it will block the entire canal!"

"I understand, Signorina." Valerico nodded, his eyes widening as Marco lit the fuse from the lantern's flame.

Lucia turned back to the window and grimaced in frustration.

"Move!" she barked, and slammed a pointy elbow into Lord Bart's ribs.

The star man shook his head, like a man waking up, and then stepped quickly aside as he saw the sputtering fuse.

"Now, Valerico!" she commanded.

✤ ✤ ✤

"Hard a starboard!" Anaxilaus of Edron shouted. "*Harder*, damn you!"

The steersman leaned hard on the steering oar and *Sea Harvest* swerved, but *Thunderbolt* was lurching to the right, as well, and Anaxilaus swore vilely. It was going to be close, and if *Thunderbolt*'s ram caught them . . .

*Damned rat trap of a channel!* he thought viciously. *No room to dodge. And what in the gods' name did they* hit *her with?!*

It wasn't the *pyrkagiá* galleys flung at their foes. It was too liquid for that, and burned with a darker smoke, but it also spread even more fiercely. Firefighting parties were reaching for the buckets of sand kept available to smother *pyrkagiá* hits, but the flaming liquid had already found its way below decks through the central hatchway. If *Sea Harvest* collided with Eurydamus' ship they'd become a single holocaust.

"Watch the windows!" he heard Polykleitos, *Sea Harvest*'s captain of archers, shouting. "Watch the—"

It was a smaller, more compact whatever-it-was this time, Anaxilaus thought. One of his marines tried to catch it and throw it overboard, but it slipped past him and thudded squarely down the huge central hatch.

*Had to open it, didn't you?* he thought. *Just like Eurydamus.*

That hatch had been battened firmly down when the sea began making up on the way here, but it had trapped the rowers in a dark, wet, noisome prison as seawater forced its way in through the oarports. They'd needed fresh air, and he'd needed to be able to get them on deck as quickly as possible when the time came, so as soon as he'd gotten *Sea Harvest* into the canal's calmer waters, he'd ordered it opened. Well, at least everyone aboard knew what had happened to *Thunderbolt*, so his crew undoubtedly had the sand buckets ready.

"There!" someone shouted, and he heard bowstrings twang.

He was turning towards the sound when the gunpowder charge exploded between his ship's decks.

⁜ ⁜ ⁜

"*Valerico!*" Lucia cried.

The militiaman stumbled backward, eyes enormous in a suddenly pale face as his hands clutched at the arrow buried in his chest. Marco caught the younger man, and Lucia felt her stomach knot as the valet eased him to the floor in a crimson rush of blood. An explosion cracked outside the window, not as loud as she'd expected, somehow, as she went to her knees beside him.

"Signorina?" he gasped, reaching one bloody hand towards her. She clasped it in both of hers, feeling the hot, slick wetness, watching the terrible red tide spread beneath him.

"Yes, Valerico," she said, bending over him.

"Did I—did I—?"

"You did well, Valerico." She moved her right hand to his forehead, stroking back the hair. "You did *well*."

"G-Good," he said, but his voice faltered as pain twisted his face. "Tell my . . . tell my father I did—"

His voice died and the hand gripping hers so fiercely relaxed suddenly.

"I will, Valerico," she whispered, bending over him. She kissed his forehead. "I will."

She closed her eyes against the burn of tears, fighting them with all her strength, until she felt someone touch the side of her face. Her eyes flared open then, and she found herself looking into Lord Bart's eyes. They were dark behind the lenses of his spectacles.

"He's gone," the star man said in his atrociously accented trade dialect. "I'm sorry."

Her mouth trembled, but she would not show weakness in front of Lord Bart. She would *not*! She—

A tear escaped her, sliding down her cheek, and he brushed it away with a thumb.

"I'm sorry," he repeated. "But we need you right now."

He drew her back to her feet, then tucked one arm around her and drew her towards the window. It felt good, that arm, and she let herself lean against him.

✛ ✛ ✛

"Curse them!" Captain Thalysios snarled.

He knew what had to have struck *Sea Harvest*, although he'd never seen the star men's "gunpowder" weapons actually used. He also knew where it had come from, and he glared up at the windows above the canal.

The explosion aboard *Sea Harvest* had come at the worst possible moment, and she'd staggered sideways, colliding with *Thunderbolt*. The two of them—both burning—were jammed together, blocking the canal. The channel was wide enough his own *Spatha* could have squeezed past, but not without taking fire herself. They had to get those blazing wrecks as far to one side of the canal as they could, but no one could get close enough without coming into range of those windows. Especially not if the defenders had been smart enough to spread through several of the buildings.

Two more galleys came around the bend behind him

and backed oars heavily to avoid collision. That was all they would have needed!

He glared up at those deadly windows, then raised his speaking trumpet as he turned towards the galleys astern of *Spatha*.

✛ ✛ ✛

Another bucket of filthy water went over the leeward bulwark. And then another.

Another.

Warner stood on the quarterdeck, watching a bucket line of marines bail *Ferox*'s bilges. Green water swept across her deck more and more often, and still more of it was spurting past the leather stoppers on the oarports. At first, the deck crew had managed to control the flooding by taking turns cranking an Archimedes screw pump. But that was no longer enough, and Pilinius had ordered one end of the main hatch opened so that the marines could help bail. Warner wouldn't have cared to be one of the marines standing on the ladder and passing those buckets up through the hatch.

*If this picks up any more, we're going to be swamped,* he thought. *When we get back, I'll have to build them a piston pump. Oh wait, a venturi flow tube on the stern with a check valve. Yeah, as long as we're moving, the flow of water will draw fluid out of the bilge.*

The one good thing he could say about fear of drowning was that it helped keep his mind off being seasick, at least until the ship went down.

The shoulder mic chirped twice and he pressed the transmit button.

"This is Hunter One. Over."

"Looks like it's time for you to start your run," Art Mason said over the radio. "If you alter course now, you should be able to get on their flank as they pass. Over."

Warner looked up as Martins and Junius stepped closer to hear Mason.

"Roger," he said. "What course? Over."

"Hard to say—they're really scattered. And we see some really big *navibus onerārius* inbound with them. Over."

"*That* doesn't sound good," Warner said. "Nobody mentioned anything like that to us. Over."

"Noticed that, did you?" Mason replied dryly. "But they're out there, and they're three-masted, probably bigger'n *Ferox*. The Colonel figures they're probably troopships. Which means our *troop* estimates were probably low, too. Anyway, they're here and it looks like they're being escorted by some more of those Duchy ships. Any transports you can keep from landing their troops would be a really good thing. Hold one."

There was a brief pause, then Mason's voice returned.

"Head southwest for now. Over."

"Roger, southwest. Can you see what happened to our other ships? Over."

"Yeah, they're engaging the other squadron upwind of you. Looks like some of the ships are in a big raft fight, and at least one of the other guys has gone down. Not sure that was our doing. Poor bastard might just have capsized. And—oh! Somebody's on fire big time! Think someone just used a cocktail . . ."

"That can't be good," Martins said. "The wind's in the wrong direction. That'll blow back on friendly ships."

"Someone make a mistake?" Warner wondered out loud.

"Maybe. Could've been out of desperation."

Warner looked into the wind, scanning the horizon. He thought he saw a smudge of smoke where he'd last seen friendly mastheads, but in this wind, that had to be his imagination.

"Whoever it is, he's not going to make it. Over," Mason said.

"Gotcha. We'll be changing course shortly. Over."

Warner released the transmit button and looked at Junius.

"The Colonel says to steer southwest. He wants us to go for the *navibus onerārius*, but we'll probably have to fight our way through some of their galleys first."

Junius nodded and beckoned to Pilinius.

"Steer southwest," he ordered, and Pilinius nodded in turn and began bawling orders.

A red flag went to the top of *Ferox*'s mizzenmast as the deck crew sprang to the braces. Pilinius waited a moment longer, for the rest of the squadron to see the signal, then nodded curtly to the three men on the helm. The steering oar went over, the waiting crewmen trimmed the sails, and *Ferox* surged around. The other galleys followed suit, maneuvering to form a wedge formation with the flagship at its apex.

The ride was easier now, although it was still a hell of a lot rougher than Warner might have preferred. The wind was almost directly astern, no longer coming in from the quarter, and the violent corkscrew rolling motion had eased considerably. The seas were as mountainous as ever, but the galley's stern castle was six or seven feet higher than the midships bulwark. That meant waves were no longer sweeping the main deck, and the marines abandoned their buckets in favor of weapons.

✛ ✛ ✛

"Hot work!" Admiral Ottone del Verme shouted to his flag captain.

"Too hot!" Captain Forcucci shouted back, and del Verme nodded in grim agreement.

The timing had gone to hell—not too surprising, with the way the weather had turned. Del Verme had never expected it to be this bad, and it was getting worse as the wind came howling down the funnel of the Inland Sea. Even here in the islands' lee, the seas were high enough to make rowing both difficult and exhausting. He preferred to not even think about what it must be like for the Roman squadron. And anybody who failed to make it into a safe anchorage in the next half dozen hours or so was unlikely to ever see port again.

Not that that was likely to be a pressing problem for his own command.

His squadron had intercepted the enemy just short of the entrance to the Canale Occidentale, but they were badly outnumbered, and still more attackers were clawing their way towards the channel mouth. Some were actually coming up from the southwest, using the islands' wind shadow to fight their way upwind towards del Verme's squadron. He suspected that most of them were more concerned with finding shelter from the mounting storm than with attacking him. Unfortunately, he was in their way, and this was no weather for a maneuvering battle where he might have avoided them. Even if that hadn't been true, sheer weight of numbers had already forced him back into the Canale Occidentale, and at least a dozen enemy galleys had run ashore on Isola di Cannaregio. He wasn't certain they'd done it on purpose, but whether by intent or accident, they'd gotten their marines and rowers onto the island. He hoped the militia could hold them, but he was far from certain of that, as well.

Meanwhile, he had problems of his own. The great galleys at the center of his line had thrown back every assault with relative ease—so far—and the star man-designed firebombs had burned five Riccigionan galleys which had come too close to the seawall on the southern edge of the channel. That had bought him precious time, but the attackers were getting their own infantry ashore on the northwestern shore of San Giorgio, as well as Cannaregio. The firebomb throwers had been driven back, and that had cleared the full width of the channel for the enemy to come at him. Two thirds of his galleys were already locked in combat with half their number of Riccigionan and Five Kingdoms galleys, and twice that many fresh enemies were charging in on them.

It would appear they had actually *under*estimated their enemies' numbers. He hadn't thought that was possible.

"It's time to block the channel," he told Forcucci. The captain looked at him for a moment, then drew a deep breath and nodded.

"*Si, Ammiraglio*," he said.

The captain began shouting orders, and *Pugnale*, Del Verme's great galley flagship, thrust forward into the melee raging in the channel mouth. The other disengaged galleys accompanied *Pugnale*, smashing their way into the tangle to create yet another channel-blocking raft.

"Tell Lord Rick we are going to anchor," he said to the star man at his elbow. He gestured at the southernmost of his galleys, hard up against Isola di San Giorgio. A mass of militiamen gathered on the canalside quay, catching the galley's mooring lines and making them fast.

"Tell him I believe we can stand our ground as long as *Sangue* is able to hold her position and the militia can continue to reinforce my crews."

"Yes, Sir," Corporal Franklin O'Reilly said, reaching for the device—the "microphone"—fastened to his right shoulder.

"And then, Lord Franklin, I believe it will be time for you to go ashore."

"Admiral, my orders—"

"I know your orders," del Verme interrupted. "I'm sure Lord Rick can see us from the bell tower, however, and there are no more complicated orders for him to pass us. We hold here, or we die." He shrugged. "Very simple. But they're getting men onto the islands, even if we hold the channels, and you and your men's star weapons will be more useful defending the Palazzo San Marco than here. Go now, while the bridges from San Giorgio are still in our hands."

"Admiral, without the radio, you won't know when—"

"I know," del Verme interrupted once more. "It doesn't matter. Go!"

The star man looked at him for a moment, and then, to del Verme's surprise, he straightened his shoulders and gave the admiral a star man salute. He returned it in the

Nikeisian style, and their eyes held for a moment. Then O'Reilly said something to his fellow star men and they turned to race across the entangled ships while del Verme's crews began lashing the raft together.

✣ ✣ ✣

Enemy ships continued to pour into the outer lagoon. Half of them went directly to the rafted ships clogging the throat of the North Channel. Most of the others were driven by the wind towards the western side of the archipelago. A lot of them found shelter of a sort in the pocket where the fishing boat channel between the islands of Cannaregio and Lido entered the outer lagoon. Rick couldn't see most of the channel because of the buildings clustered along its sides, but he could see its exit into the inner lagoon. The good news was that the canal was obviously too shallow for the pocketed galleys to get through it. The bad news was that their crews had go somewhere, and the radios confirmed that hundreds— probably thousands, really—of men were swarming ashore on the western shore of Lido and the northeastern shore of Cannaregio.

A few had attempted to circle around east of the ship raft in the main channel, but none of them had made it. They'd been driven onto shoals or beaten to death against the seawall, but he could see hundreds of enemy troops swarming ashore on Isola di San Lazzaro, the island on the east side of the North Channel, as well.

"Message from Lieutenant Cargill, Colonel," Mason said, and Rick lowered his binoculars to look at him. Cargill and Rick's own Corporal Stratton commanded the ten Gurkhas and the single Bren gun which had been deployed to San Lazzaro. "He says they can't hold their ground much longer. The militia's fighting better'n we expected, really, but their losses are rising and they're beginning to waver, even with star weapon support."

"Damn."

Rick raised his binoculars again, his jaw tight. If Cargill was forced back from San Lazzaro, they'd lose the ability to reinforce the Nikeisians fighting to hold the ship raft. And with no influx of replacements, the raft's defenders wouldn't last long.

*God, I hope to hell Cargill can hold*, he thought grimly. *If we lose control of the raft . . .*

He turned and looked to the west. At least there was less pressure on the militia supporting del Verme's squadron and it seemed to be standing firm. As long as it did, del Verme could probably look after himself.

He turned his gaze back to the north and found himself wishing, not for the first time, that he knew Cargill and Martins better. They were so damned young. How good *was* their judgment, really?

*Guess it's always come down to this in the end. It all depends on some goddamned lieutenant's judgment call out at the sharp edge. Doesn't seem to matter whether it's me in Angola or Cargill on Tran. And I've got no option but to hope he knows what he's doing.*

"Tell Cargill to use his own judgment," he said, never lowering the binoculars. "Tell him we can't reinforce him. He's to hold as long as he can and then get the hell out."

"Yes, Sir."

"And then," Rick turned his head to meet Mason's eyes,

"tell Walbrook I think we're going to need him on the North Channel first."

⊹ ⊹ ⊹

Captain Thalysios trotted stealthily through the winding alley, trying not to wince at the unholy racket of the marines behind him. Apparently, none of them had ever heard of the word "quiet," he thought disgustedly. At least the wind howling around the city's roofs should drown it out. Mostly.

Over a dozen galleys—and, more importantly, one of the troop-laden *navibus onerārius*—had made landfall on Isola di Lido. Most of the attackers were headed east, towards the fortress guarding the western side of the Canale del Nord. If they could storm the fortress, they could swarm the mass of galleys blocking the channel from the west. Thalysios was certain that other attackers had made their way ashore on San Lazzaro to attack the other end of the ship raft, as well. But he and his men had headed in the opposite direction.

The Nikeisians had spent years planning their city's defenses. They had to know that any attack would focus on the entrances to the main channels, and they would have deployed their own troops to protect the most probable lines of approach from those points. But there'd been no galleys protecting Canale Gottardo Capponi, and so far as Thalysios could tell, he'd gotten his men ashore undetected. For that matter, they'd covered three blocks without seeing a single soul, far less an enemy soldier. It looked as if the Nikeisians truly had discounted any threat by way of the fishing boat channel and deployed their fighting power elsewhere. Aside from the devils who'd burned *Thunderbolt* and *Sea Harvest*, at least.

Thalysios hoped Polidoro Scarcello's payment would do him some good in hell, because the Nikeisian would never have the chance to spend it in this world. As far as the captain knew, no more than a quarter of Eurydamus' crew had made it ashore, and Scarcello hadn't been among them. But so far, all of his information had proved accurate, and according to the turncoat, only three drawbridges crossed the canal. No doubt all of them had been lowered, if only to facilitate the defenders' own movements. That also neatly blocked the canal for any of the attackers' galleys, however, and at least some troops must have been posted to protect them. That was why they'd planned on landing marines to seize control of them from the beginning. Until whoever had dropped those fiery missiles intervened, at any rate. As long as they were in a position to burn any galley that passed below their perch, no one could get by them to attack the bridges. And if they could sink one or two more ships at the same spot, the bridges wouldn't matter. The wrecks would block the channel quite nicely.

Unless, of course, someone prevented the bastards from dropping any more fire.

✣ ✣ ✣

"What do you figure they're up to now, Bart?" Cal Haskins asked in a low voice.

He and Saxon stood well to one side of another window—not the one they'd dropped their incendiaries from—peering down at the choppy waters of the canal. The first angry drops of rain drummed on the roof above them and the wind sounded stronger than ever, but the canal seemed almost placid by contrast. Except for the two galleys still burning below them.

"Damned if I know," Saxon muttered back, plucking at his rifle's sling. "I think there's still room for them to sneak past the wrecks if they're careful. For that matter, I'm not sure the wrecks are on the bottom. They might be able to push them out of the way, if they're still floating. I don't understand why they aren't at least trying!"

"Probably don't want to cross Miss Lucia's path!" Haskins snorted. He shook his head admiringly. "That's a nasty girlfriend you got there, Bart!"

"She's not my girlfriend!" Saxon snapped, darting an angry look at his friend.

"Hey, man! No need t' bite my head off! I'm just calling it the way I see it. Girl's got an eye for you."

"She's only a kid," Saxon muttered, reminding himself that Haskins didn't know about Sherry Northland.

"Mighty gutsy one, though," Haskins said, bending closer to the window. Unlike Saxon, whose H&K was slung, the ex-corporal held his at the ready, although he was careful to keep his finger off the trigger. "And that's why we ain't seen any more ships down there. No way they're gonna risk what she's waitin' to do to them!"

And that, Saxon had to admit, was no more than the truth. In fact, that was what had him worried. He doubted the bad guys were just going to turn around and go home, so what were they up to?

*Damn, I wish I'd thought to bring a radio!*

He grimaced. All the radios had been pooled, and he'd been so worried about trying to keep Lucia from doing something stupid that he'd done something stupid all of his own. Not only had he forgotten to ask for a radio back, he hadn't even told anyone where they were going!

*I'm* a teacher, *not a soldier, damn it*! he told himself, but that wasn't an excuse. Not a good enough one, anyway. And—

⁜ ⁜ ⁜

Lucia stood beside Marco, trying not to look at Valerico's body. She'd never seen so much blood, and it was her fault for bringing him here.

*Maybe it is*, she thought, *but I have my duty as much as anyone else! I may not be big and strong enough to swing a halberd, but I have a* mind *that works, and Professore Clavell always said minds are far more dangerous than mere* weapons!

She smiled at that thought, despite her own terror and her grief for Valerico, because she'd been right! She'd been right about the Canale Gottardo Capponi, and Lord Bart knew she had! She'd seen the way he'd looked at her, earlier. It had sent a thrill of excitement through her, and she wondered why he hadn't said anything to her about it. She was of marrying age, after all, and if her father wasn't a senator, his position at the Arsenale was one of the most important in all of Nikeis! She had always heard that the star men were scandalously oblivious to birth and wealth, yet Lord Bart had refused to say a single word despite the invitation in her own eyes. Any boy she'd ever known would have been butter in her hands, but not Lord Bart!

Still, she knew she had impressed him. That was good. That was something she could build on. And he was so much handsomer than Professore Clavell or Professore Harrison! Surely, if she charted her course with care—

✢ ✢ ✢

Thalysios had known it was the right building when he saw the three militiamen in the street. They had been very young, little more than boys, and now they would never grow older, because they had allowed their attention to be drawn to the battle sounds riding the angry wind from the northeast. Only one of them had seen Thalysios' men coming, and he'd seen them too late to save himself or his companions.

Or to raise the alarm.

Now the captain led the way up the stairs, sword in hand. In truth, he would have preferred to let someone else have the honor of the lead, especially since half a dozen of the men behind him were armed with crossbows. But after listening to them in the streets, he trusted none of them to pick a way up a wooden staircase without waking the dead. So he eased his way upward, testing each stair tread carefully, hoping none of those crossbowmen had itchy fingers, and pointing out the stairs that creaked to the marines following in his wake.

At least so far none of them had managed to trip and roll all the way to the bottom in a clatter of armor and weapons, praise Vothan!

He reached the top and paused, waiting. A dozen marines gathered on either side of him, packing the narrow hallway, and he nodded to them, then drew a deep breath, laid one hand on the door latch, and lowered his shoulder.

✢ ✢ ✢

*"Lord Bart!"*

Wood splintered, and Saxon heard Lucia scream his name.

He twisted around, jaw dropping as a burly man in breastplate and helmet came crashing through the door with a drawn sword. Lucia and Marco were closest to the door, and Marco charged the intruder with the short battle ax he'd brought along. But the armored warrior evaded the valet almost negligently, and Marco went up on his toes as two inches of bloody steel emerged from his back.

Saxon's hands fumbled, caught between trying to unsling his rifle or reaching for the Beretta under his left arm, and more men appeared, crowding through the doorway, trying to get past their leader as he yanked his sword from Marco's body. One of them held a crossbow, and Saxon saw it come up and level and knew he was about to die.

*"No!"* a young voice screamed, and Lucia Michaeli flung herself at the crossbowmen with a dagger in her hand.

The crossbow's string snapped, and Bart Saxon's universe froze as the steel-headed quarrel punched through Lucia's body in a terrifying spray of blood. The man who'd killed Marco punched her in the head with one gauntleted fist while he twisted away from her thrusting dagger, and her head flew back with a sickening crack.

She plunged to the floor, and even as she fell someone drove a shoulder into Saxon, thrusting him out of the way, and the room filled with thunder.

✢ ✢ ✢

Thalysios recovered his blade and charged forward just as the men on the far side of the room turned towards him. Both wore strange garments unlike any Thalysios had ever seen. One of them was tall and fair skinned; the other was even bigger and his skin was the darkest Thalysios had ever seen.

He had time to register that, and then he saw the weapon in the black-skinned man's hands.

*Star men! They're* star men, *and that's a star weap—!*

⁂

Haskins hammered the doorway with fire. Splinters—and blood—flew as the 7.92-millimeter slugs chewed into the intruders at a range of less than thirty feet. He heard screams and walked his fire along the wall in both directions, stitching the wood paneling—and anyone on the other side of it—with holes in short, controlled bursts. There were more screams from the hallway, and he lunged forward, dropping the H&K to hang across his chest from the sling, while his right hand reached into a jacket pocket.

*Bastards*, he thought, stepping over Marco's body, trying not to think about Lucia. *Goddamned* bastards*! Well, I* got *something for your worthless asses!*

He'd somehow failed to mention to Saxon that he'd "borrowed" a couple of the Gurkhas' precious hand grenades. Now one of them came out of his pocket, he yanked the ring free, released the arming spoon, heaved it down the stairwell, and ducked back into the room.

"Fire in the hole!" he shouted. The Nikeisians only looked at him uncomprehendingly, and he jabbed a finger at the floor.

*"Down—now!"* he barked, and they flung themselves prone just before the grenade detonated.

✢ ✢ ✢

"Lucia! Lucia!"

Saxon was on his knees beside her, ripping at her gown frantically while the blood pooled. He bared the wound, and his gorge rose.

Her eyes slitted open, huge and dark in a face that was far too pale, and her mouth twisted in pain.

"Lucia!"

"I . . . I am sorry, Lord Bart," she whispered. "I didn't—"

"Hush. Hush!" He shook his head fiercely. "You've got nothing to be sorry for!"

"But . . . I wanted . . . you to like m . . . "

Her eyes drifted shut, her voice trailed off, and he realized blood was trickling from her scalp, as well. Not very much—he told himself that and tried to believe he wasn't lying—but that brutal punch must have opened a gash in her scalp. He clenched his jaw, hands fumbling at the emergency dressing Colonel Galloway had insisted every one of the "star men" had to take with him, but he couldn't get it open and she was bleeding to death!

*Stupid, useless, gutless—*

The bitter self-condemnation rolled through his brain. He should never have let her come! He should have *made* her go back once they got here! And if he hadn't frozen, stood there like some spineless idiot, she'd never have been hurt! It was all his fault, and if Cal hadn't been here, they'd *all* be dead!

"Hey, now," Haskins said, and Saxon turned his head

to see the other man on one knee beside him, fitting a fresh magazine into his rifle. "Could be a hell of a lot worse, Bart."

*"Worse?!"* he blurted. "She's bleeding to death!"

"So get some pressure on it!" Haskins snapped, rifle back up to cover the doorway, and Saxon shook himself. He finished ripping open the dressing and pressed it to the ugly groove the crossbow bolt had torn through the left side of Lucia's torso. The trough looked terrifyingly deep to him, but at least the dressing was big enough to cover it, and he leaned on it, pressing as hard as he could.

"That's better, man," Haskins said, eyes still on the doorway. "Now listen to me, Bart. She ain't gonna bleed out if we can keep pressure on that. Didn't cut no arteries, and it may be ugly, but it don't look like it hit her clean, either. Or maybe her ribs turned it some. Anyway, it didn't go through her guts, and that's good, man. That's good! We get her back, and the Colonel's medics'll have a good chance of pulling her through. We just gotta get her there, you with me?"

Saxon nodded dumbly, not trusting his own voice, and cloth tore as one of the militiamen knelt on his other side, shredding a tunic to provide strips to bind the dressing in place.

"We gotta move," Haskins went on. "Bastards know where we are, there's likely a hell of a lot more of them than there are of us, and neither one of us got a lot of ammo. So we can't stay here."

"No, we can't," Saxon acknowledged. "But how do we move her?"

"Don't got time to make a stretcher," Haskins said as Saxon finished tying the bandage in place. "Wish we did, 'cause it'd be a lot better for her. But we're just gonna have to carry her."

"I'll do it," Saxon said.

"No, man." Haskins shook his head, his expression almost gentle. "We only got the two rifles, and ain't none of these locals know how to use one. I'm gonna need you with me, Bart."

"But—"

"Pardon, Lord Bart." It was the militiaman who'd helped him bandage Lucia, speaking the trade dialect. "It would be my honor to carry the signorina so that you and Lord Cal can fight."

The Nikeisian couldn't have understood Haskins' English, Saxon reflected, but it would appear he was no idiot. Saxon didn't know how much use he'd be with his H&K—God knew he hadn't been much use yet! But . . .

"Be careful with her!" he said fiercely in the same dialect, and felt his eyes burn.

"As if she were my own sister," the young man replied, and Saxon gave him a choppy nod. Then he looked back at Haskins and unslung his own rifle.

"All right," he grated. "Let's get her the hell out of here."

✢ ✢ ✢

"Oh, shit!"

"What's wrong, Sir?" Art Mason asked, bringing up his own binoculars and peering in the same direction as Rick.

"Look between Cannaregio and Lido. Where the fishing channel comes out."

"Oh, hell," Mason grunted, and Rick nodded.

"Guess it wasn't that shallow after all," he said grimly, watching the first enemy galley slide out into the inner lagoon.

"We knew the surge was piling water up everywhere. Guess it was piling it up in there, too." Mason shook his head. "Shoulda thought of it, Sir. Sorry."

"Not like you're the only one who didn't think about it. I wonder what the hell took them so long?"

"No telling, but whatever it was, it's not slowing them up anymore," Mason observed as a second galley emerged. Then a third nosed out of the shadows.

"Warn Bisso and Baker they've got incoming. I just hope Publius is smart enough to not try and take these bastards on all by himself!"

"He's Roman, but he ain't an idiot, Sir," Mason said as he turned to the radio.

Rick's grunt was noncommittal. The way this was going, it might not matter what Publius decided to do.

He looked back to the north. The ship raft was still there, but the fortress on Lido must have fallen, because Riccigionan and Five Kingdoms soldiers were fighting their way onto the western end of the raft. More and more galleys—and at least one of the *navibus onerārius*—had crashed directly into it, as well. Men funneled over the new arrivals' bows, and the defenders retreated sullenly, pulling back towards San Lazzaro. From the looks of things, the fortress on that island was still in Nikeisian hands, but for how much longer?

*And now that they're leaking around the flank, your whole plan may be about to go belly up. What the hell made you think you could handle something like this?!*

✤ ✤ ✤

"You ready, Bart?" Cal Haskins asked as quietly as he could through the sound of wind, rain, and—now—thunder.

"Yeah," Saxon muttered, hoping he didn't sound as scared as he felt. The two of them crouched in an alley, peering out through the rainy gloom.

"So far, so good, man." Haskins' teeth were almost shockingly white when he smiled. "And from the sounda things, the militia's still holding."

"Yeah." Saxon tried to put a little enthusiasm into his tone this time, and the truth was that they had done well, so far.

The surprise of encountering star weapons—and the devastating effect of Haskins' grenade in the crowded stairwell—had panicked the group which had attacked their initial position. Its survivors had fled back the way they'd come, abandoning even their own wounded, and Saxon didn't blame them. Haskins had killed or wounded at least a dozen of them in the hallway, and Saxon hadn't even tried to count the bodies on his way down the stairs. Some of them had still been alive, groaning—or screaming—with pain, and he'd been torn between a desire to finish them off for what they'd done to Lucia and Marco and a sense of horror at leaving them to live or die in such agony on their own.

Haskins had pushed them hard as soon as he was confident the bad guys hadn't left anyone in the street outside their building. He'd sent them scurrying towards the southernmost bridge between Lido and Cannaregio on the theory that it would be the last the attackers reached.

Saxon understood his logic, but that didn't mean he'd liked the way their pace had to jar Lucia. She seemed to be drifting in and out of consciousness, and he didn't know how much of that drift stemmed from the wound in her side and how much from the punch to her head. Concussion. *Another* thing to worry about! But young Aristeo Mangione, the militiaman who'd offered to carry her, was a big fellow by Tran standards, with strong arms and powerful shoulders, and he was absolutely as gentle with her as he could be. In fact, every one of their surviving Nikeisians seemed to regard Lucia as a combination battle standard and kid sister, which said a hell of a lot about her personality.

And Haskins had been right to push them hard. They *had* gotten to the southernmost drawbridge before anyone had attacked its sentries, but it was obvious they hadn't had many minutes to spare. Despite the rain, at least some of the buildings behind them were on fire, adding their own lurid glare to the plunging raindrops, and they'd come damned close to being fired upon by one of the militia crossbowmen guarding the bridge before they could identify themselves.

They'd raced across it, hurried along by the sound of approaching battle. It was coming from more than one direction, too, and Saxon's heart had sunk as he realized the enemy was already ashore on Cannaregio in strength. More attackers were sweeping down both sides of the

Canale Gottardo Capponi, as well. It was obvious that the other bridge guards weren't slowing them down very much, and he'd said as much to the teenaged ensign commanding the twenty-man bridge detail. The boy might have been young, but he wasn't indecisive. He wasn't an idiot, either. He'd ordered his men to cut the lift ropes and smash the windlasses at each end of the bridge, then joined their party.

The damage to the hoisting gear would probably slow the invaders down, but Saxon doubted it would slow them very much. They were professional sailors, and that meant they had to be adept at rapid repairs to rigging and masts. It wouldn't take them long to rerig the windlasses and raise the bridge to let their ships past it. On the other hand, the sentries had been far too few in numbers to prevent the bridge's capture, so it made far more sense to cripple it as badly as possible and then hightail it.

The militiamen had been a welcome reinforcement to their own party, and they knew this part of the city better than anyone else in their original group. They'd guided the star men quickly through back ways, and he'd felt his heart rising as they moved steadily towards safety.

And now this.

"How many, you think?" he asked.

"Probably look like more'n there really are," Haskins said. "Call it thirty, maybe."

"Thirty," Saxon repeated, and swallowed hard.

"Might be a few more," Haskins said thoughtfully, then flashed another of those shocking smiles. "Other hand, they don't know we're here, and they sure as hell don't expect no assault rifles!"

"Gotcha." Saxon swallowed again, hoping he wasn't about to vomit, and doublechecked the safety on his rifle.

*Wish to hell I'd fired this thing more*, he thought grimly. *And I hope to hell Cal stays clear, because God knows where I'm going to be spraying bullets!*

*Short bursts*, he reminded himself. The H&K had no three-round burst setting; it was single shots or full auto, with nothing in between. *Short bursts on auto. Don't just hold the damned trigger back or you'll empty the mag in like two seconds. Then where the hell will you be?*

He closed his eyes for a moment and drew a deep breath, hoping Ensign Cardinale really understood the plan, then snorted. Of course Cardinale understood! Wasn't like it was real complicated, was it?

"Get set," Haskins said softly, and Saxon's eyes popped open again. The enemy troops were closer, moving cautiously down the street. They seemed to be paying more attention to the windows and balconies above them than they were to street level, but they were obviously scouts, looking for a way to get around the flank of the militia holding the northern bank of the West Channel. And according to Ensign Cardinale, they were between Saxon's group and the militia's position in the Palazzo Santa Lucretia.

He shouldered his rifle, looking across its sights at the men who were about to become targets.

*Cal's right. Only way home is through them. God, don't puke. Don't puke!*

"Now!" Haskins snapped, and squeezed his trigger.

The muzzle flash was unbelievably brilliant in the dimness, and Saxon realized *he* was firing, too. He felt the recoil, the vibration. His own muzzle flash blinded him, but he knew where the enemy was, and he squeezed the trigger again and again, burning through the thirty-round magazine. He probably wasn't hitting anything—a part of him hoped to God that he wasn't!—but as Cal had explained, that wasn't the real point. The *point* was to take the other side completely by surprise and panic them the same way they'd panicked the survivors of the first attack.

"*Charge!*" Haskins bellowed, and Saxon remembered to jerk his index finger out of the trigger guard as Cardinale and the militia stormed past the two riflemen, halberds and spears lowered.

"On your feet, Bart!" A powerful hand dragged him up off his knees. "Gotta stay close behind them boys! Might need us!"

Saxon nodded and lurched to his feet. He took one more second to be sure Mangione and Lucia were close behind him, then started jogging rapidly down the street behind the whooping militiamen.

✥ ✥ ✥

Warner was actually starting to feel better. It wasn't because the weather had improved, though. Darkness was falling, the overcast had turned into boiling dark clouds and lashing rain, and the wind was stronger than ever. Worse, it was shifting farther towards the north.

He held a stay, peering up into the rain and the spray, and damned if *lightning* wasn't starting to flicker out there in the storm!

*Well, that's all the hell we needed*, he reflected, and glanced across the quarterdeck at Fleetmaster Junius and Captain Pilinius.

From the looks of things, all that airy confidence before they set out had started to wear pretty thin. They were Romans, of course, so they weren't going to admit it, but it showed in the tautness of their shoulders and their focused expressions. Martins' British sangfroid had started to fray around the edges a little, too.

*Serves the bastards right*, Warner thought. *Hell! I've been scared shitless ever since we started on this!*

And despite all that, he really did feel better. Talk about perverse.

*Maybe I've got my sea legs. More likely it's the adrenaline and fear kicking in.*

The reason for that adrenaline was closing with them rapidly.

The lookouts had spotted the masts of the big ships Mason had told them to find twenty minutes earlier. It was just as well that they had, because one of the quinquireme's wilder rolls had slammed Warner into the bulwark hard enough he was pretty sure he'd cracked at least one rib. It hurt like hell, even through his flak jacket, but that was the least of it, because his radio had gone dead, too, so no one from the bell tower could have corrected their course if they'd missed their target. Unfortunately, they'd obviously been spotted in return, and a line of galleys was closing on them from starboard, angling towards them on an intercept course while the *navibus onerārius* angled away.

*At least we're bigger'n any of them*, he thought.

They were all *galee sottili*, although a couple of them looked bigger than any of the Roman triremes. None of them would be able to match *Ferox*'s size and fighting power. Not individually. But that wouldn't matter if someone ripped out the quinquireme's guts on a ram.

The seas were too high for anyone to row, so both sides were under sail, which was unusual for naval combat on Tran, to say the very least. In theory, it ought to favor the longer-ranged riflemen and, especially, the recoilless; in practice, he was less certain it would work out that way. The ship's motion, even with the wind from almost directly astern, was far more violent than he'd anticipated when he suggested turning *Ferox* into a battleship. It wasn't too terrible at the moment, but the *navibus onerārius'* course change to evade them meant they'd have to alter their own course across the wind to catch them. They'd be right back to that gut-twisting corkscrew roll when that happened, and even Rudolf Frick would have a hell of a time scoring hits with the Carl Gustav. For that matter, aimed rifle fire was going to be far less accurate. And that assumed they survived what the sea had in store for them.

*Damn. Wish I'd spent some time inventing lifejackets! Oh, well. No point worrying about that until I don't get killed by the galleys.*

"Was this the way you envisioned it?" he said in Martins' ear, raising his voice to be heard over the crashing of wind and wave. The Brit looked at him for a moment, then shook his head.

"No," he admitted. "From all I'd heard"—his eyes cut briefly in the direction of Junius and Pilinius—"it shouldn't have been this violent at this time of year. The ship's motion is far worse than I'd anticipated."

*Well, at least he owned up,* Warner thought with

grudging respect. *Don't know if he realizes he just pretty much admitted he and Baker were running around behind the Colonel's back, but that's for later.*

"Yeah, well, my battlecruiser idea doesn't look like working out all that well, either," he said, and surprised himself with a grin. Martins smiled back, but then the smile faded.

"What worries me most," the younger man said, turning his eyes back to the oncoming enemy, "is what happens once we're past these chaps."

"Changing course across the wind again?"

"Won't be quite that bad. We should take the wind almost dead on the starboard quarter again, not from broad abeam. Not too worried that we'll broach or anything of that sort."

"Then what *are* you worried about?"

"Your last report was that the lead elements were assaulting the islands?" Martins asked a bit obliquely.

"Yeah," Warner replied.

"Well, I'm rather afraid we may be doing the same shortly."

"What do you mean?"

"I mean that the way this lot"—he waved the hand that wasn't clutching a safety line at the clouds where fresh lightning had just made an appearance—"is continuing to worsen, I very much doubt we'll have any choice but to run downwind to Nikeis ourselves."

"There are at least seventy more galleys out there," Warner pointed out. "Probably more, from what Mason's already told us."

"And I'm fairly certain that almost all of them will have

made it at least as far as the outer lagoon by the time we arrive," Martins replied with a nod. "Sounds a bit dicey, doesn't it?"

"That's one way to put it," Warner growled. He gazed at the oncoming galleys, then shrugged and made his way to the quarterdeck rail and gripped it securely with both hands.

"Frick!" he shouted to the mercs huddled on the main deck at the stairs to the forecastle. No one seemed to notice. *"Frick!"*

This time one of the Roman seamen heard him and tugged on one of the other mercs' sleeve. The merc turned, and the seaman pointed to Warner.

*"Frick!"* Warner bellowed, even louder, and the merc poked the recoilless gunner until he turned and looked in Warner's direction.

"Time to break out the Carl Gustav and the rifles!" Warner shouted, holding up his own rifle case to reinforce the point. Frick looked at him for a moment, then nodded and began passing orders to the men around him while Warner turned back to Junius.

"Please excuse me, Fleetmaster," he said. "I'm going forward to join the others."

"Is that wise?" Martins asked. Warner looked at him, and the young lieutenant shrugged. "My orders were to keep an eye on you. I don't wish to sound callous, but at the University, you're worth more than a hundred of those men."

"We're not at the University, and those are not only my men, they're my friends. It was my idea to bring them out here."

"Ours, actually. And they're my men, as well."

"And unlike me, you know your ass from your elbow where ships are concerned." Warner looked up into the gloom, felt the wind-lashed rain running down his face, then looked back at Martins. "Stay here where you can do some good and might just get us back."

Martins gazed back at him for a moment, then saluted with the palm of his hand facing forward and the tips of his fingers touching his forehead in the British manner.

"*Vade ad Deum.*"

Warner returned the salute in the American fashion.

✦ ✦ ✦

"What do you think you're doing here?!" Admiral del Verme demanded.

"Trying to get back to San Marco," Bart Saxon said wearily.

"You could have been killed!"

"Signorina Michaeli almost *was*." Saxon's tone was as bitter as it was harsh, and del Verme paused in midtirade. Then he shook himself.

"Then we must get all of you out back to Lord Rick," he said.

For the moment, his men were in firm control of the galleys jammed into the West Channel. They'd actually expanded the obstruction a bit, taking possession of half a dozen more pirate galleys which had rammed into it. Most of those galleys' previous owners were floating facedown in the wind-lashed channel while their ships buttressed the defenders' barricade. But del Verme was under no illusions. The lunatic star men and their small party had been forced to fight their way through the enemy strength gathering on Cannaregio. It was only a matter of time—and not much of it—before the militia defending the Palazzo Santa Lucretia at the northern end of his line were overwhelmed. When that happened, when the enemy could come at him from the north, as well as from the sea . . .

"Captain Forcucci, see that Lord Bart and Lord Cal are provided with a guide. Detail another twenty marines to escort them. And find a stretcher for Signorina Michaeli."

✢ ✢ ✢

"I hope you're ready, Frick," Warner said as he finished knotting the safety line around his waist.

All of the mercs and their Roman assistants were on individual lines now to free up their hands. For that matter, he'd tied a line through the shoulder sling of his rifle, as well. In fact, *all* of the star weapons had been similarly secured. Warner didn't think Colonel Galloway would really rather lose one of his men than that man's weapons, but he didn't want to find out the hard way that he was wrong about that.

"Ready as I'm gonna get," Sergeant Rudolf Frick replied in less than enthusiastic tones.

Even with the wind almost directly astern, the ship pitched hard. It might not be the jarring corkscrew motion they'd experienced earlier, but the bow still rose steeply as *Ferox* climbed each mountainous wave, then dove like a homesick elevator as the galley tobogganed down into its trough. It was hard to tell which was thicker, the spray or the rain, but all of them were soaked, cold, and miserable.

Frick had taken a knee on the foredeck, resting the barrel of the recoilless rifle on the bulwark of the starboard side. Now he looked over his shoulder and scowled at one of the Roman marines.

"Get *down* the ladder, damn it!" he snapped. "Unless you like burns, anyway!"

The marine standing halfway down the ladder in question looked surprised, but then he'd never actually seen the Carl Gustav fired. He stood a moment longer, then shrugged and dropped back down to the main deck, and Frick looked around again before he returned his attention to the galleys driving steadily closer.

Warner wondered if part of the sergeant's ire at the marine had actually been directed at him. Frick was definitely in two minds about firing his beloved weapon from the deck of a wooden ship. The back blast which the marine had never seen was spectacular. The Gustav wasn't a rocket launcher, like an old-style bazooka. Instead, it was like a conventional artillery piece with a rocket venturi glued to its ass. It ejected enough of its propellant in a rocket-like blast to offset the recoil of firing an 84-millimeter round down range at up to 840 feet per second, and that produced a danger zone thirty meters deep in which any unfortunate would be severely burned. In fact, it was hazardous to be anywhere within seventy-five meters of the recoilless rifle's venturi, and the US Army had limited a Carl Gustav gunner to only six practice shots a day in order to protect him against the cumulative blast and shock effect of firing what was basically a sawed-off howitzer from his shoulder.

Frick had been less than enthusiastic about the

potential incendiary effect of that enormous cloud of superheated gases. Even fired at a ninety-degree angle perpendicular to the galley's centerline, the backblast would extend clear across the deck and slam into the solid wooden bulkhead on the opposite side. That would probably deflect quite a lot of it back in Frick's direction, even if it didn't actually set the ship on fire. And *Ferox* was less than fifty meters in length. If Frick had to fire at a less acute angle, the blast could blanket almost the entire length of the main deck.

*Probably a good thing we're all so goddamn wet*, Warner reflected now. A bucket brigade had been told off to keep the deck around Frick well soaked with water, but mother nature had kindly taken on that responsibility.

"Clear," Private McQuaid, Frick's loader, told him. McQuaid knelt beside him, on the opposite side of the weapon. That wasn't his normal position in combat, but it was the best they could do on the galley's constricted deck.

"Damn well better keep it that way," Frick growled, putting his eye back to the recoilless rifle's sights. The nearest galley was barely eight hundred yards away and the ships were closing at a combined speed of around eight or nine knots, which gave him three or four minutes, at the most. Under normal conditions, the Carl Gustav could fire six rounds in a minute, but a wildly pitching galley in the middle of a rainstorm weren't exactly normal conditions.

"Fire in the hole!" Frick shouted.

*KABOOM!*

The volume and violence of the Carl Gustav's discharge had to be experienced to be believed. It jarred Warner to the marrow of his bones as the 84-millimeter projectile screamed out of the muzzle.

And vanished into the side of the wave barely sixty yards from *Ferox*.

The white fountain when it exploded was impressive, even under the current sea conditions. It was also completely useless.

"Damn it!" Frick bellowed through the ringing in Warner's ears. He felt as if someone had just hit him in the back of the head with a huge, hot hammer, and he shook his head to clear it.

"Reloading!" McQuaid yelled as he pulled another round from the waterproof container. He turned the venturi lock to open the hinged breach, slid the new round into the rifle barrel, closed the breach, smacked Frick lightly on the back of the head, and dropped back down beside him.

"Ready!"

"Fire in the hole!"

*KABOOM!*

Another white fountain announced another miss, and Warner shook his head again, anxiously, as the lead galley swept closer. The rest of the enemy squadron followed behind, and if *Ferox* collided with any of them, they were probably doomed. Even assuming the gale didn't simply sink both ships outright, they'd find themselves in a fight for their lives against the enemy's marines. And if any of the other enemy galleys were able to add their weight to the fray . . .

"Frick," he said, trying to speak clearly but calmly while McQuaid reloaded again, "you have to fire as the bow starts to come up. Stop and feel the waves flow forward. There's a rhythm to it. Time your shots as the bow rides *up* on the wave."

"Warner, the only wave I'm feeling is a constant one of nausea. So what say *you* take the shot?"

"We don't have time, and you're the best on that thing. Tell you what. You draw a bead on the bastard's bow and tell me when you're ready to fire. Then just hold your position. Just wait until *I* tell you to fire based on our movement. Don't try to adjust your aim or follow the target, it's not gonna move all that far before I give you the word."

"Okay, Zen master. You got it."

"Ready," McQuaid said, back beside Frick at the bulwark.

"And . . . I'm set," Frick announced.

Warner looked aft as a wave overtook the stern. He didn't look at Frick or the target—only the wave as it lifted the stern up and the bow dipped. The wave swept forward, and the bow rose. For a moment, the ship was almost level again, but then the bow started to rise.

"Fire!"

The recoilless boomed again, battering him with the brutal, fiery shockwave, backflash blindingly bright in the gathering dark, and he wheeled back forward as the round screamed out of the tube.

The oncoming ship's foredeck exploded. Marines who'd assembled on it were hurled into the air and over the side. The four-pound high-explosive warhead had hit well above the waterline, penetrated the planking, and detonated inside the galley's forecastle. Warner was disappointed that it hadn't simply blasted the ship's bow wide open, but then its foremast buckled as the blast sheared it off between decks. It smashed down across the forecastle with terrible force, driven by the power of its wind-filled sail, and crushed a half dozen marines and seamen who'd survived the shell's explosion.

That wasn't all it did. It toppled over the side, still fastened to the ship by the rigging, and the galley staggered, swinging round to the sudden, enormous drag. The next wave crashed across it in a solid sheet of green and white fury, and more men were hurled over the side. The galley rolled in anguish as the saltwater swept over it, and its mainmast followed the foremast over the side.

It was done for, Warner realized. Even if it survived, it was out of the fight, but its next astern was coming on fast.

"Next one!" he shouted.

*Thud*. McQuaid dropped a round on the pitching deck.

"Crap!" McQuaid grabbed for it but missed as it rolled aft.

"Take it easy, Dougie," Frick said. "Let that one go. Get another."

The marine the gunner had yelled at earlier poked his head up for a moment, saw the shell rolling towards him, and caught the six-and-a-half-pound round as it tipped over the edge of the forecastle. He cradled it safely against his chest, winked at McQuaid, and then dropped back down into the forecastle's blast shadow.

McQuaid made himself slow down as he pulled another round from the case and loaded it. A bolt from the new leader's ballista vanished tracelessly into a wave fifty yards from *Ferox*'s bow.

"Ready!" he snapped.

"Set!" Frick confirmed a moment later, and Warner looked aft again. This time, the wave set was confused. He couldn't find the rhythm.

"I'm *set*, Zen master!" Frick said pointedly as the first crossbow bolts began whistling in their direction.

There! The wave was overtaking the stern. Now at the mast. The bow was rising, and—

"Fire!"

*KABOOM!*

The recoilless roared, but this time, the round struck even higher on the target's side. The explosion ripped a jagged gash in the bulwark and the combination of the blast and the savage spray of splinters killed or wounded most of the men actually on the galley's forecastle, but structural damage was minimal.

Warner cursed, remembering Art Mason's warning that even the Carl Gustav would require direct hits to cripple something the size of a Tran war galley. He started to say something, then made himself bite his tongue as McQuaid reloaded yet again.

"Ready!"

"Set!"

Warner swallowed. The enemy galley's captain had altered course. He was steering straight for *Ferox*, probably to close and ram before he went the same way as his leader, and Frick's point of aim had moved farther forward as the gunner tracked his target. The backblast was going to go farther aft this time. And if this shot didn't stop the galley, it was going to get through to them.

He looked aft, watching the waves. Timing it. And—

"*Fire!*"

This time the muzzle blast and the sound of the explosion were almost simultaneous, and he wheeled back to see the round smash into the galley's hull, thirty feet aft of the ram and no more than a foot or two above its normal waterline. It blew a gaping hole in the shattered planking, and the wounded galley staggered as greedy water poured into it. It fell off as *Ferox* forged past it, so close he could hear the screams of pain and terror.

*Poor bastards. They're as good as dead in this weather. And if we do the same thing to those troop ships . . .*

Disgust filled him, melding with the nausea he'd fought all day, and he vomited over the side of the ship.

# ✦⚊ CHAPTER THIRTEEN ⚊✦
# GALLOWAY'S LAST STAND

Lance Clavell's radio chirped, and he unhooked it from his webbing and raised it to his ear. He hadn't been assigned a radio, originally, but that was before Saxon had mentioned the additional handhelds in the cargo containers. They weren't identical to the firefighter radios Baker's "employers" had provided to the Brits, and they were probably a lot more fragile, but they were close enough to tie in to the radio net, and Clavell had been glad to get one.

"Clavell here. Over," he said, releasing the transmit button.

"Get your people ready," Art Mason said over the radio. "You've got incoming. Over."

"Understood. Over."

Clavell rehooked the radio carefully, a bit surprised by how steady his hand was, then raised his voice.

"All right!" he told the musketeers he'd been assigned.

"Lord Rick says at least some of the enemy are headed our way! Remember your orders!"

He heard other voices shouting the same warning in Italian as Bisso passed the word from his central position in the Doge's Palace, and he leaned out the open palace window, looking across the Palazzo San Marco towards the inner lagoon.

The rain and dim light made it impossible to make out any details about the galley fight in the North Channel, even with binoculars, but the ship raft seemed to be holding, so where—?

He swung the binoculars to his left, and his jaw tightened as he saw the galleys emerging from the inner end of the fishing boat channel.

*Thought that was supposed to be too shallow,* he thought grimly. *Surprise, surprise! Wonder what else is going to bite us on the ass before this is over? For damned sure* something *is!*

The galleys weren't charging forward as soon as they cleared the channel, either. Instead, they were forming up, damn it.

*Bastards are too frigging smart to come in one at a time. They're going to try to swamp us with a mass attack, instead.*

He lowered the binoculars and looked at the Palazzo itself.

Only the northernmost, lowest section of the big square had been covered in seawater when the last container arrived, but that had been days ago. Today, the water had climbed much higher up the Palazzo's shallow slope. Shallow waves ran in across it to break against the defensive barricade, and the water was up to the calves of the men huddled behind it. More waves lapped ankle deep even across the lower steps of the Doge's Palace, and the dim afternoon light was growing dimmer as a storm-shot evening came on quickly. The pelting rain was cold, the wind blew it almost directly into the defenders' faces, and despite his current perch inside the palace on the west edge of the square, Lance Clavell couldn't remember the last time he'd been colder, wetter, or more miserable.

*On the other hand*, he thought, watching the water wash across the paving stones between him and the invisible edge of the square, *it's one hell of a killing ground. Just as long as everyone remembers their assigned sectors. Last thing we need is friendly fire casualties!*

He'd made that point, repeatedly, to the two platoons of Chelm musketeers under his command. All of the musketeers, not just the ones assigned to him, had been positioned carefully along the barricade and in the buildings to either side. Those on the barricade were supported by halberd-armed militia and two platoons of the Doge's guard. More of the Doge's men were stationed inside the Palace with Sergeant Major Bisso. Additional musketeers covered the Palace's windows. Clavell was less than confident about the priming of the men on the barricade, but the muskets in the buildings should be sheltered from the driving rain.

And then there were Major Baker and his Gurkhas, positioned along the center of the barricade.

If the rain bothered them, they gave no sign of it. They sat calmly on the firing step behind the barricade, sipping hot tea from their canteen cups. As Clavell watched, a

Nikeisian emerged from one of the palaces fronting on the square and splashed across with a steaming pot to refresh their tea, and he tried to imagine something more quintessentially British.

Passavopolous and his Tran-born loader were with them, along with one of the Brits' Bren guns. Passavopolous was trying to make jokes with the Gurkhas. Clavell doubted they understood a word he was saying, but they smiled politely, anyway.

*Guess you'll be finding out how well it all works in about, oh, twenty minutes*, he thought, turning back to watch a solid wave of at least a dozen galleys begin rowing steadily across the lagoon towards him. *You spent all damned day telling people everything was under control and that it'd all work out fine in the end. Hope to hell you were right!*

"Professore! Professore!"

Clavell wheeled to find Ginarosa Torricelli standing up to her knees in the water as she tugged on his sleeve. She looked far more like a bedraggled rat than a Councilor's daughter, yet she and her child militiamen had made themselves astoundingly useful. They'd been assigned to firefighting duties, originally, but the pounding rain had made bucket brigades superfluous. So they'd become scouts, message runners, and guides, instead. They knew the city's streets better than anyone else, and they'd become a different sort of fire brigade, leading flying squads of mercs and Tamaerthan archers, like Jimmy Harrison's, to critical spots. In fact, Ginarosa had been with Jimmy, the last Clavell heard, although Jimmy had made a point of sending her to the rear with "important messages" whenever he thought he could get away with it.

Too bad she was too damned stubborn to *stay* there, damn it!

Clavell doubted Ginarosa's father knew everything his daughter had been up to, and he didn't expect Councilor Torricelli to be delighted when he found out. For that matter, *Clavell* wished the girl would just stay put in his palace where he'd stashed Lucia Michaeli and Bart Saxon for safekeeping. If something happened to her—

"What?" he asked.

"Lord Bart and Lord Cal are back," she replied, "and Lucia has been wounded!"

"Back?" Clavell stared at her. "Back from *where*?"

"They had gone to defend the Canale Gottardo Capponi. Did no one tell you? They were forced to retreat, but they reached Lord Jimmy and he told me to guide them to the Palazzo."

"No, they *didn't* tell me they were going!" *And the Colonel will have my* ass *if anything happens to Saxon, damn it! What the hell was he* thinking?

"You said Signorina Michaeli's been wounded? How badly?"

"I don't know. But Lord Bart told me they need a *medico*, and I thought—"

She gestured at the radio clipped to his webbing, and he grimaced in understanding. Saxon might be idiotic enough to traipse off to "defend" the canal with a sixteen-year-old girl, but at least Ginarosa had her wits about her, and he nodded to her in approval.

"I'll pass the word," he assured her, "but I think a lot

of people are going to need medics. We'll do what we can, I promise, but I don't know how quickly they can get to her. Where is she now?"

"Lord Bart carried her back to your palace."

"She's probably as safe there as she'd be anywhere else. Now you get yourself inside to keep her company!"

"Of course, Professore," she replied, and he unhooked the radio as she waded away from him.

*Yeah,* sure *you'll stay where it's safe,* he thought bitterly, and pressed the transmit button.

"Major Mason, this is Clavell. Over."

"Whatcha got? Over," Mason replied.

"Major," Clavell said, watching the galleys slide steadily closer, "you're not gonna believe what Saxon and Haskins have been up to."

✦ ✦ ✦

"They did *what*?"

Rick stared at Mason, and the major shrugged.

"That's what Clavell says. Says the Michaeli girl got hurt pretty bad, too."

Rick shook his head in disbelief, wondering what lunacy had afflicted Saxon. If Rick had been forced to pick one man on Tran they couldn't afford to lose, Saxon would have to be pretty damn high on the list.

"Gotta say, Sir, that crazy as they were, they could be the reason we didn't have galleys coming through the fishing channel a lot sooner."

"Maybe, but if it was a choice between not plugging the channel and risking Saxon, I'd have voted for not plugging the channel. And it's sure as hell open now, anyway."

"Yeah," Mason agreed.

They stood gazing down at the inner lagoon, and neither of them liked what they saw. Fighting raged all across the arc from San Giorgio to San Lazzaro, and the defense was losing ground. The defenders of the northern ship raft were retreating towards its eastern end, anchored where the fortress on San Lazzaro still held. Cargill and his Gurkhas had retreated into the Fortezza di San Lazzaro instead of falling back to Isola di San Matteo, the way they'd been supposed to, which might well be the only reason that fortress hadn't already fallen. But it had also deprived the bridges from San Lazzaro to San Matteo of the firepower which had been meant to hold them. And it meant that if the fortress *did* fall, Rick lost Cargill and his men, as well.

He bit his lip as he thought about *all* of the men fighting and dying out there. The men *he* was responsible for, God help him, but also the men on the other side. He was so *sick* of the slaughter. Of the knowledge that each battle he won only promised that he'd be available to fight the next one.

And that he only had to lose *one* to lose it all.

"At least it looks like Baker was right about command and control on the other side," he said out loud. "If they were able to coordinate, those galleys would be heading down to hit del Verme from behind and open the West Channel for their great galleys and some of the *navibus onerārius* troop ships. And then we *would* be screwed."

"Small blessings, Sir," Mason replied, then chuckled harshly. "I'll take whatever we can get, though!"

"You and me both, Art. You and me both."

Rick thought for a moment longer, then inhaled deeply.

"What does Bisso have in reserve? Mercs and musketeers, I mean."

"He's got Brentano's team, Sir. No musketeers or archers." Mason grimaced. "I'm thinking he's gonna need Brent's boys right where they are in a couple of minutes."

"Maybe he is, but tell him to send them to San Matteo anyway. We need Brentano on the bridges if Cargill's locked up on San Lazzaro."

"Yes, Sir."

Rick looked back at the North Channel and his mouth tightened. The pirates might not be organized enough to attack del Verme's back, but they didn't have to, either. The increasingly heavy rain and oncoming darkness made it difficult to be certain from here, but it sure as hell looked like the attackers were starting to clear a way through the western end of the North Channel's ship raft, closest to Lido Island. As inextricably as the pounding seas had jammed those ships together, it was going to take them a while, but "a while" wasn't the same thing as forever.

*Getting close to time for Walbrook*, he thought grimly. *And I don't have any dice left to throw after that.*

⊹ ⊹ ⊹

"Oh, shit!" Larry Warner snarled as Sergeant Frick toppled back with a crossbow bolt clear through the bony part of his shoulder. He thudded to the deck . . . and the recoilless rifle tipped over the side.

Even if Frick lived, which was far from certain given the state of medicine here on Tran, he'd be crippled for life. Douglas McQuaid grabbed the gunner as he curled up in agony and dragged him into the shelter of the bulwark while more crossbow bolts slashed overhead or buried themselves in the ship's planking.

The security line on the Carl Gustav jerked taut, and the same marine who'd caught the loose round earlier leapt to heave the star weapon back aboard. He got it as high as the top of the bulwark, then grabbed it by the venturi lock and pulled it the rest of the way to safety. Warner heard him shout in triumph—and then another crossbow bolt took him between the shoulder blades and he slammed to the deck.

Warner put his head up from where he crouched against the inside of the bulwark himself and his stomach clenched.

They'd managed to cripple two of the troop laden *navibus onerārius* with the recoilless, despite the wild seas. It had cost them another six rounds of precious ammunition, though, even with him trying to time the ship's motion for Frick. One of the troop ships had gone down completely, and Warner didn't like to think about how many men must have drowned in the process. The second one had been hit right on the waterline and looked like it was going, too, and they'd put at least eight or nine enemy galleys out of action with a combination of the recoilless and firebombs. But getting in close enough to attack the transports had been costly. They'd lost three of the Roman galleys, including one of the triremes with a six-man section of Gurkhas aboard, cutting their way through the escorting galleys. Worse, the seven remaining Romans were trapped inside the pirate formation now, with fire coming from three directions and at least ten pirate galleys in hot pursuit and closing fast from astern, and Martins had been right about both the force of the wind and the options its direction offered.

*We are* so *fucked*, Warner thought as he ducked back down and peered aft.

Captain Pilinius was down. Whether he was wounded or dead was more than Warner knew, but he'd been hauled below by the flagship's surgeon and it was Martins standing next to the steersman now, while Junius conned the ship. All seven of the remaining galleys, including *Ferox*, showed signs of damage, and the rest of the fleetmaster's winnowed squadron formed a ragged wedge on either side of his flagship as the brutal wind drove them helplessly south.

Warner left McQuaid to do what he could for Frick while he himself clawed his way aft along the safety lines. A dozen bodies lay sprawled along the main deck, marked down by enemy archers and crossbowmen despite the rain and the spray, but Warner reached the quarterdeck unharmed.

So far, at least.

"Frick's down!" he shouted to Martins through the tumult, and the British lieutenant gave him a choppy nod.

"Saw it!" he shouted back. "Anyone else we can put on it?"

"McQuaid, but I think he's going to be more useful shooting boarders with a rifle than trying to hit anybody else with the recoilless with the ship bouncing around like this."

Martins looked as if he were going to argue for a

moment, but then he looked at the pirate galleys closing in from either side and astern and nodded.

"Seems probable," he acknowledged, with a grimace.

"Are we in as much shit as I think we are?" Warner asked.

"Probably." Martins actually managed a smile. "Only one place we can go now, old man." He pointed ahead to where the entrance to the North Channel was coming up fast.

"Fantastic." Warner felt his shoulders slump, then forced his spine to straighten. "What? About fifteen minutes?" he asked.

"Closer to twenty, I should say. Always assuming none of these other buggers catch us up, first. I'm afraid they're likely to overhaul *Fulminis*, at least, before we get there."

Warner glanced back at the squadron's rearmost liburnian, grunted in acknowledgment, and stepped closer to Junius.

"Fleetmaster, I think—"

Junius was turning towards him when the crossbow bolt tore through the fleetmaster's throat. He went down, choking and gurgling on his own blood, and three of the Roman crewmen bent over him.

"Oh, crap!"

Warner went down on one knee as well, but the Roman's eyes, staring sightlessly up into the rain, told him all he needed to know, and he stood again, clinging to a safety line.

"*Now* what?" he asked, looking at Martins. "Who's in command now?"

"Technically, one of the other captains, I suppose," the

lieutenant said. "Don't really see how we can pass command, though. It's a matter of staying in formation and following the flagship at this point. Which means, I'm afraid, that *you're* in command, Mr. Warner."

Warner felt his heart sink, although it was hard to see how even his inheriting command could make things any worse. He swiped rain from his face and turned to peer forward again. He couldn't make out a lot of detail, but—

"Is that gunfire on San Lazzaro?" he demanded.

Martins squinted his eyes, trying to shade them from the rain with one hand. He stared hard into the dimness for a second or two, then nodded once.

"I believe it is," he said.

"Then that means the fort's still holding," Warner said. "It doesn't look like the one on Lido is still in our hands, either. I say if we're going to be forced into all that crap, we do it as close to friends as we can."

"By all means!" Martins actually smiled at him. "For that matter, I don't suppose our chaps would be dreadfully disappointed if we turned up to reinforce them, either!"

✦ ✦ ✦

"Still nothing from Warner?" Rick asked.

"No, Sir." Mason shook his head. "May just mean his radio got wet or the batteries went. Could be a lot of reasons."

"Including the possibility that it's at the bottom of the Inland Sea with him," Rick said harshly.

Mason started to speak, then closed his mouth and simply nodded.

*I shouldn't have sent him out there*, Rick thought. *I*

knew *I shouldn't have! He's too damned important. And
he's my friend, goddamn it!*

A part of him desperately wanted to blame Baker and
Martins—and Publius—for the decision, but he knew
whose it had been in the end.

*And they were right. If we were going to stop them
short of the city, enveloping them in the outer lagoon was
the best way. But it didn't stop them short of the city.
They've got Cannaregio, Lido, most of San Lazzaro, and
more galleys are still piling on from the north. Looks like
two or three more of the big troop transports, too. Jesus,
did we underestimate how big they were!*

"Should I tell Walbrook to light them up?" Mason asked.

Rick bit his lip, staring down at the inner lagoon as the
first wave of galleys through the Canale Gottardo
Capponi suddenly accelerated, surging towards the
Palazzo San Marco. He wanted to say yes. Wanted it so
badly he could taste it.

"Any more word on those transports?" he asked
instead.

Lieutenant Cargill had spotted the late arriving quartet
of *navibus onerārius* from the fortress on San Lazzaro
when Rick had been unable to see them in the worsening
visibility. That was another worry. If this crap closed in
much further, his observation post atop the bell tower
would become useless. Hell, it already *was*, mostly! So
what did he do when he couldn't see *anything*?

The troopships had been escorted by what Rick hoped
to God were the last stragglers of the galleys. Their
hundred-galley estimate had obviously been low. *Badly*
low, in fact, and if the new *navibus onerārius* were fully

loaded with troops, their original estimate of enemy strength had been even farther off the mark than their galley count. And he needed to know where those troops were headed.

"No, Sir. Last report said they haven't committed yet."

*Of course they haven't. But, damn it, the weather's not going to let them stand off much longer. They're more seaworthy than the galleys*—the high-sided square-riggers were far better suited to stormy seas then the low-slung galleys—*but they still have to find some place to call home pretty damn soon. And once I use Walbrook, I lose the shock effect. At least I'm not going to need him on the West Channel, too. But if I turn him loose before the transports commit . . .*

The first wave of galleys swept across what had been the Palazzo's seawall and grounded on its paved surface, and musket fire sputtered from the barricade and flanking palaces as hundreds of men boiled over the galleys' sides and stormed forward through the water. Dozens of the attackers went down, but dozens more took their place, and a second wave of galleys was right behind them.

*We're at the breaking point. If we can hold San Marco, beat them back there, and then relieve the pressure from the North Channel, we've got a chance. But only if we can take out the rest of those goddamn troopships. If they put another five or six thousand men ashore in the wrong place at the wrong time, it'll all go south. And this time, there's no retreat. We lose it here, and it's over. Not just for Nikeis but for everything Tylara and I ever hoped to accomplish.*

*And it's all on me.*

"No," he heard himself say, eyes on the Riccigionan and Five Kingdoms marines and seamen storming towards the barricade. "Not yet. Contact Cargill again. Ask about the transports."

✥ ✥ ✥

Lance Clavell stood just inside the palace that flanked the barricade, watching the galleys drive towards the palazzo. He couldn't hear McAllister's rifle through the storm, but he saw two or three steersmen go down to mark the sniper's presence. It wasn't enough to stop them. It wasn't even enough to slow them down, and the galleys shuddered as their keels grated on the square's paving. Men leapt over the sides, splashed into the water, and turned to charge the barricade.

"*Ready!*" Bisso's booming voice could be heard over both the radio and the bullhorn he'd acquired from Baker, and the Gurkha riflemen rose and leveled their rifles across the parapet.

"Ready!" Clavell repeated to his own musketeers in the palace.

"*Fire!*" Bisso shouted.

"Fire!" Clavell barked.

The Gurkhas' first salvo was a single, explosive crack of sound. Individual, deliberate shots followed, but Clavell couldn't hear them through the roar of his own musketeers' first volley. Choking powder smoke filled the palace. Empty muskets were handed back for reloading; fresh ones were passed forward. He heard another sharp, extended volley from the Gurkhas, and at least some of the muskets out there on the barricade were firing as well, despite the rain.

"Ready!" he said, then paused for a three count. "*Fire!*"

Minié balls and rifle bullets swept furrows of death through the charging attackers. He heard wailing screams in the interval between volleys, but they came on. It was conquer or die for them; they certainly couldn't retreat from Nikeis with the storm roaring down upon them. Besides, they could see the containers they'd come to loot right in front of the Doge's Palace, taunting them.

*"Fire!"*

Another deadly volley ripped through them, and Nikeisians rose on either side of the Gurkhas. Spears and halberds crossed the parapet, thrusting and chopping. Combat swirled madly, crashing up against the barricade. Some of the attackers tried to rip away paving stones or timbers to find a way through it while others lunged up it, some of them climbing mounds of their own dead and wounded to get at the defenders.

Sheer weight of numbers was coming across it, Clavell thought as his musketeers poured fire into the attack wave's flank. They were coming across, and—

Passavopolous and the Bren gunner stood, threw their weapons' bipods onto the prepared positions, and opened fire. They swept a torrent of bullets across the massed attackers, beginning in the middle and moving towards the flanks, and the entire front rank crumpled under its fury. Then two more Gurkhas popped upright with the Milkor revolver grenade launchers Baker had described. The launchers coughed, lofting forty-millimeter grenades far back into the attackers. They spat their deadly missiles in timed fire, and the explosions came with metronome precision.

The combination of machine-gun fire and grenades, on

top of rifles and muskets, was too much. Hundreds of the attackers were down, turning the water around them crimson, and the survivors fell back, took shelter between and behind their beached galleys while they waited for the next wave to reinforce them.

✢ ✢ ✢

"I thought they were getting all the way to the fort before they grounded!" Rick said, watching the first wave of attackers recoil. "Damned storm surge!"

"Not quite," Mason said.

Rick heard McAllister's rifle cracking and thought about telling him to cease fire. Good as the private was, he couldn't pick off enough individual targets in that mass of men to make much difference. But then he shrugged. It wasn't going to *hurt* anything, either.

"Sir, you better take a look at the second wave," Mason said, and Rick raised his binoculars, then swore.

"Well, we know where at least some of the transports went," Mason said grimly, and Rick nodded.

The first wave of galleys had gone in with only their own crews aboard. Maybe they'd thought that would be enough to clear the square, or maybe they'd expected all along that the first wave's grounded ships would simply provide cover for the second wave when it poured *its* men ashore. He didn't know about that, but every one of the galleys in that second wave rode low in the water, heavily overloaded with scores of extra men. As Mason had suggested, they had to have come from transport ships that had gotten through to Lido or Cannaregio.

"Should I order Walbrook to support the Palazzo?" Mason asked.

Rick hovered on the brink of saying yes, but he didn't. He looked down at that tidal wave of ships and men sweeping towards Palazzo San Marco, and he didn't.

"I think they can hold a little longer," he said instead, harshly, wondering if he really did, feeling the consequences of his decision waiting for him. "Pass the word to get ready with the firebombs, but I'm not giving away Walbrook yet. Not till I know where those other damned troopships are."

He didn't look at Mason. He was afraid of what he might have seen in the major's expression.

"Anything from Cargill?" he demanded.

"Not yet, Sir."

Rick nodded curtly and watched the tidal wave surge onward.

✣ ✣ ✣

"Hold on!" Richard Martins shouted, and Warner braced himself as *Ferox* drove down on a Riccigionan galley like a five-hundred-ton battering ram.

The Riccigionans hadn't seen them until the last moment. Probably because they'd been too focused on fighting their own way towards Isola di San Lazzaro. Someone finally *had* spotted them, though, and he saw marines and sailors racing towards their target from other ships.

"*Let fly!*" Martins screamed and the seamen at the sheets loosed them. The sails blew out from the yards, horizontal and cracking like canvas thunder as they spilled their wind. And then *Ferox*'s ram smashed squarely into Martins' chosen victim. The shock of impact knocked dozens of Romans from their feet, but—

"*Now!*" Warner bellowed, coming back to his feet on the forecastle with the other mercs.

A crossbow quarrel struck his flak vest with sledgehammer force, but it didn't penetrate, and rifles crackled. Dozens of defenders went down, but it was the sheer shock of taking fire from star weapons that was truly decisive. The Riccigionans knew there were star men in the city; they hadn't expected to encounter them aboard a Roman quinquireme coming at them out of the gale, and surprise flashed over into panic. They fell back, abandoning their own ship's bulwarks, and Warner and the mercs stepped aside as *Ferox*'s marines charged past them. The rowers were right on the marines' heels. They couldn't possibly hold their own ship against the weight of numbers the pirates and their allies could bring to bear. Their only hope was to abandon the quinquireme, cut their way along the ship raft to the fortress on San Lazzaro.

One of the surviving triremes slammed into the ship beside the one *Ferox* had rammed in a thunder of shattering oaken timbers, and its marines and the squadron's second section of Gurkhas vaulted from its forecastle to join the flagship's crew aboard the ship raft. Another struck home on the quinquireme's other side, and a pair of liburnians slammed into the sterns of their consorts, their crews using the abandoned galleys as bridges.

Warner leapt across to the raft himself, looking around through the rain and the wind while thunder bellowed like overhead demons and the mass of ships groaned in agony as the pounding seas slammed them into one another.

They had a firm bridgehead, but the pirates were recovering from their initial shock. More than that, a half dozen enemy galleys were about to crash in right behind them. They couldn't afford to let the other side do the same thing to them, and he pointed to the left.

"That's where we're going!" he screamed through the tumult. *"Now let's go!"*

A hungry, baying cheer went up from the marines, and they charged.

✣ ✣ ✣

A *third* wave of equally heavily laden galleys swept up behind the first two. Thousands of men boiled up out of them, and Rick shuddered as he remembered the slaughter at the Grand Battery at the Battle of Vis. Passavopolous was in the middle of this bloody madness, too, hammering away with his machine gun, but at least this time his M60 wasn't alone. Baker's Bren gun stuttered and flamed alongside him, and the Gurkhas' rifles crackled in aimed fire.

Waves of dead and wounded piled up on the flooded square, mounding above the water like gory islands, and musket fire ripped into the attackers from the palaces on the flanks. But that huge mass of men continued to surge forward, and crossbowmen and archers stood on the beached galleys' forecastles, firing back despite the pounding rain. Their rate of fire was far lower, especially for the crossbows, but there were hundreds of them. The ballistae fired even more slowly, but when they hit, it was with devastating power, and defenders started going down, despite the parapet's protection.

It was pure, undiluted carnage, concentrated into a

tiny pocket in time and space, and he was the one who'd engineered that killing ground. *He* was the one who'd decided to stand and fight, and he'd brought every single one of his men—and Baker's, and Publius' Romans—to this right along with him. And while they fought and bled and died, he stood up here on his godlike perch *watching* them.

Disgust filled him, and he wanted to vomit, but he didn't. Instead, he stood there and listened to someone else speaking with his voice.

"Warn Bisso they're going to flank him," that someone else said as the fourth and final echelon of galleys peeled off, circling San Marco, looking for somewhere else to put their men ashore.

"Yes, Sir. Not gonna be able to pull too much off the fort to do anything about it, though."

"Then we'll just have to relieve the pressure. It's time for the firebombs."

✤ ✤ ✤

Clavell shifted his musketeers' fire to the missile troops on the beached ships' bows. Ark, the Bren gunner, and the Gurkhas would just have to deal with the frontal assault. At least while their ammo lasted.

Smoke jetted from the windows of the palace across from his position as the musketeers on that side of the square poured volleys into the carnage. Battle rifle fire crackled from his own palace, and he found himself praying that Ginarosa and Lucia and the other kids were safe.

He shouted encouragement, steadying the men, keeping their fire coordinated. Even rifled muskets depended more on volume—on crushing volleys, delivered in a single devastating blow—than on accuracy, and they couldn't afford—

"Oh, shit!" he muttered as the next wave of galleys spread out instead of driving straight in. The bastards were circling, looking for another way in, and with everybody pinned down defending the fort...

Some of the galleys disappeared from view, but he watched one ship take advantage of the high water and drive straight into one of the palaces that normally stood fifteen yards back from the waterfront. It struck between a pair of ground floor windows, the ram drove through the supporting stonework, and marines shoved a boarding ramp through the gap and poured into it.

"Breach on the main island, east side of Palazzo San Marco!" he barked into the radio. *Second Platoon's going to have some close-quarters fighting.*

A red rocket roared up from Colonel Galloway's belltower command post.

"Wagon Box under attack." Mason's voice on the radio underlined the rocket's meaning. "Time for the firebombs. Watch where you put those things—we have friendlies in contact."

Something thumped on the roof above Clavell's head, and a bright, sparkling flame soared through the rain and wind. His eyes tracked the firebomb's fuse as other ballistas fired from other roofs, lacing the air with streaks of fire. They rose in glittering arcs, curving as the wind whipped them, harmless looking as they flew.

They seemed to hang for a moment as they reached the top of their trajectories. Then they swooped downward ... and exploded in midair.

Liquid fire cascaded from the heavens, falling across beached galleys and the men around them in a torrent of flame. Saxon's additions to Nikeis' version of Greek fire had produced an incendiary as viscous as napalm and men shrieked as they burned alive. Others simply collapsed where they stood, unable to breathe, and still others ran screaming, wrapped in clinging fire, and plunged into the lagoon.

Clavell looked away from the carnage.

*God,* please *make them break and run! Haven't we killed enough here* yet?!

✧ ✧ ✧

Corporal Jimmy Harrison stood in the window of a building that overlooked one of the two massive stone bridges between Isola di San Marco and Isola di San Giorgio. A militia formation armed with spears and shields guarded the San Marco end of the bridge below him, but they didn't hold the *other* end.

He hadn't expected San Giorgio to hold when the attackers began sweeping down from Lido and Cannaregio, but the western two thirds or so of it had. Only a few pirate and Five Kingdoms galleys had landed south of the West Channel, and the militia and the squad of mercs Admiral del Verme had sent ashore had held them in check while del Verme himself continued to hold the ship bridge that blocked the channel.

That hadn't kept parties of invaders—some a few dozen men strong, but some much larger—from getting past the defenders and circling towards San Marco. Still, that would have been handleable, if not for the galleys which had snuck in through the fishing channel and landed on the inner, eastern side of San Giorgio. The troops they'd put ashore were far better organized than the ones who'd beached south of the West Channel, and they'd been working their way inland for a couple of hours now. But they'd stayed away from del Verme's defensive lines; instead, they'd moved steadily south, *away* from the West Channel, because their objectives were the bridges that would let them flank the defenses around the Palazzo.

Harrison and Private Ezekiel Goodman were supposed to keep them from getting there.

And this was the last spot where they could do it.

He scanned the windows of a townhouse on the San Giorgio side of the canal, and his eyes narrowed as he spotted a couple of crossbowmen creeping out onto a balcony that overlooked the bridge below him. He braced his rifle on the back of the chair he'd positioned to use as a rest—the loss of his left hand made it difficult to hold a steady aim firing without one—and drew a bead on one of them. He squeezed the trigger, the rifle slammed his shoulder with a familiar recoil, and his target fell. The other crossbowman fled back the way he'd come, and Harrison snarled in triumph.

But the crossbowmen hadn't been alone. A knot of men armed with swords and axes rushed out onto the bridge in what had obviously been intended as a coordinated attack.

Goodman waited calmly, then picked off two men in the front rank as they got to the midpoint of the bridge. The momentum of the charge broke as more men tripped over the fallen leaders, and the handful of Nikeisian crossbowmen in the guard force took out several more. The survivors retreated—wisely, in Harrison's opinion. Even if they'd made it across the bridge, the militiamen waiting for them were the survivors of the militia who'd teamed up with Harrison and Goodman even before the enemy broke into the inner lagoon. They'd acquired a lot of experience the hard way in the last seven or eight hours, and they would have eaten those bozos for breakfast.

They'd started out all the way over on the other side of San Giorgio, but they'd quickly realized the attackers were headed for the bridges. Harrison had radioed it in and asked for reinforcements. He hadn't been surprised by the order to stop them, but it had been accompanied by the unhappy news that the forty Tamaerthan archers they already had were all they were getting. That was enough, combined with the two mercs' rifles and the scratch-built force of militia they'd picked up along the way, to hold a solid stopper almost anywhere. But that was the problem. They could hold *a* solid stopper; they couldn't hold two of them, and the attackers kept filtering around them.

They'd almost been cut off a couple of times, but the Girl Scouts had saved them. He doubted that Ginarosa Torricelli would have been very happy if she'd known where the term came from, but she'd adopted it as a badge of honor when Harrison started using it to describe her youthful followers, and they'd been lifesavers. Literally. They knew this city better than anyone else, and they'd spotted oncoming enemy troops repeatedly, well before they got close, giving the militia—and Harrison's team—time to evacuate as many as they could when they pulled back through the deserted streets to their next position. Nor was that the Girl Scouts' only contribution.

"Signorina," he'd said severely, the second time he came across a clutch of enemy troops with stab wounds in their backs and slit throats, "this isn't what we need you to be doing! You—all of you—are our eyes and ears. Our sense of direction. You know this city, and we don't. We *need* you. *Please* don't take chances like that!"

Ginarosa hadn't said a word, but her icy gaze suggested that she'd learned a little something from her father. He'd glared back, but his best glare had bounced right off her, and there'd been no hope that any of "her" militia would argue with her. They not only obeyed and trusted her, they clearly *feared* her, as well.

But at least he had her safely bottled up behind him on *this* side of the canal now, and he meant to keep her that way. The last thing he wanted was for the most deadly assassin in Nikeis to blame him for getting his daughter killed on his watch! Besides, he liked the girl. When she wasn't scaring the shit out of him, anyway.

Of course, that still left the little matter of holding the bridges.

Another wave of ships swept into the inner lagoon. There weren't many of them this time, and they didn't head straight for the Palazzo.

"They're rowing hard," Harrison said.

"Spreading out, too," Goodman said. "Looks like they're not following the others to the square."

"Don't blame 'em," Harrison replied. "But you're right. And that one's headed *our* way."

"I'll be a centaur's uncle. What're they doing? Ain't no channels for 'em here!"

One of the ships had broken off from the others and headed straight for them.

"If they don't turn, they're gonna run aground," Goodman said.

"I think that may be what they've got in mind—ram a building and jam their ship crosswise in the canal between us and San Giorgio. They come ashore on this end, flank the militia, and the ship turns into a bridge for the bastards on the other side of the canal. If they get away with it, we'll be flanked again."

"Incoming!"

They took cover as a volley of crossbow bolts, javelins, and darts came raining down.

"Damn!" Harrison cursed. "Whoever's in command over there is pretty good. The bastard moved up more missile troops while he figured we'd be distracted by those ships. And it frigging worked!"

Their surviving archers returned fire, but they had too few arrows to waste on blind fire. They had to pick their shots, and unlike crossbowmen, they couldn't shoot from a prone position. That meant exposing themselves in their window positions, and they were unable to suppress the fire coming at the bridge guards. More sailed across the canal, and the militia ducked down behind their shields. Those shields were big enough to give them decent cover against crossbow bolts and javelins, but the fire pinned them down while the incoming galley swept closer. White water curled back from its prow, and its oar blades flashed in the glare of the galleys burning along the edge of Palazzo San Marco as the stroke quickened.

Harrison reached into his rucksack with his remaining hand and pulled out a bottle with a rag stopper. He held it up and shook the viscous, ugly mixture inside for good luck.

"The wind's in our face," Goodman said. "You'll never hit that ship from here. And I don't think one Molotov cocktail's going to stop it, anyway."

"You're right, I can't hit it from here. But I can from the middle of the bridge, and I ain't gonna hit it with *one* cocktail. Hold this!"

He put the bottle against the side of the rucksack and Goodman held it while he looped the rucksack's shoulder strap around it and cinched it tight, fastening the bottle to it. There were four more Molotov cocktails inside it.

"I don't think those Fivers on the other side are going to let you cross," Goodman said.

"Don't plan on asking permission."

"They'll kill your ass, Jimmy!"

"Nah." Harrison grinned. "Mama always said I was born to be hung."

"Let me do it," Goodman pled. "You can't carry your rifle and the cocktails at the same time!"

"You don't have the arm for it, Zeke. 'Sides, I need you up here covering me. You can shoot a hell of a lot better with two hands than I can with one. Now grab that shield and strap it to my arm."

"You're a damned fool, Jimmy," Goodman said as he strapped the shield to Harrison's handless arm. "Since when did you start taking risks for other people?"

"Let's just say I've gotten attached to the place. I owe 'em something, and I guess it's time to pay up."

Goodman shook his head as he finished strapping the shield in place. Then the two of them sprinted down the stairs and over to the street-level door nearest the bridge. They crouched, just inside the doorway, and Harrison squinted down at the canal. The galley was getting close, and he looked at Goodman.

"Still got your Zippo? Good. Light me up!"

Goodman lit the rag of the bottle tied to the outside of the rucksack.

"Back in a sec," Harrison said with another grin. "Cover me."

"Covering fire!" Goodman barked to the archers and militia, and Harrison flung himself to his feet and dashed out the door.

Goodman blazed away with his rifle and their archers and a squad of Nikeisian crossbowmen joined in.

Harrison darted from stanchion to stanchion, crouched behind the outsized shield, as he ran up the slope of the arching bridge. Crossbow bolts and javelins rained down from at least three buildings on the San Giorgio side of the canal. They weren't all that accurate, probably because of the fire coming from his own people, and they could only fire at him from directly in front, but there were a lot of them, and he felt repeated shocks, like rain on a skylight, as they pelted his shield.

He reached the crest of the bridge and crouched, and his right arm came up like a softball pitcher in the bottom of the seventh inning. The rucksack soared upward, trailing smoke from the burning rag, arcing through the rain and wind howl towards the incoming galley. But the throw had brought him out from behind the shield. Before he could raise it again, a javelin struck him in the chest and a thrown stone slammed into his head.

Goodman watched the rucksack and knew Harrison had been right—he could never have made that throw. In fact, as he watched its arc, he was afraid Harrison had thrown it *too* hard, that it was going to overshoot. But the wind slowed it as it reached the top of its trajectory, and he realized Harrison had allowed for that nearly perfectly. The rucksack plummeted almost vertically and hit on the forward edge of the galley's main hatch.

The outer bottle shattered in a fierce bloom of fire, but then the rucksack toppled over the edge, down onto the middle oardeck . . . and the cocktails inside it went up in a massive fireball that flung liquid flame everywhere.

Some of that fire, especially from the initial cocktail, splashed over marines and crossbowmen gathered on the galley's deck, but the true horror came from below decks. Shrieking rowers, covered in clinging flame, clawed their way up through the hatch that was itself a seething inferno. They screamed their way to the bulwarks, flung themselves desperately into the canal in a vain effort to extinguish themselves, and the shrieks of those still trapped below sounded like souls in hell.

Smoke billowed into the wind-sick night, oars flailed in wild confusion, then hung motionless as they were abandoned, and the galley faltered. It turned broadside to the canal and grounded heavily well short of its intended point.

"Jimmy!" Goodman screamed. *"Jimmy!"*

Harrison didn't move, and Goodman slammed his fist into the floor.

"Damn it!"

He stared at his friend for a moment, then shook himself.

"Cover me!" he barked and rose into a crouch. He started through the door, but a voice stopped him.

"Do not worry," it said, and Goodman's head snapped up. The voice was Ginarosa Torricelli's, and it was extraordinarily calm as she crouched on the other side of the doorway, ignoring the crossbow bolts whistling through it. Her eyes met his, and she twitched her head in the direction of the bridge. He followed the gesture with his eyes and saw a team of militia file out into the open and form a shield wall.

"He is one of ours," Ginarosa said. "My men will bring him home."

✤ ✤ ✤

"McQuaid!" Larry Warner bellowed. "*McQuaid!*"

"Here!"

McQuaid appeared at his elbow as if by magic. The half dozen Roman marines told off to guard the priceless Carl Gustav were right behind him, and Warner gave a choppy nod of satisfaction.

"Look!" he said, pointing out into the gathering darkness. "There's two more *navibus onerārius* out there. Can you take them out?"

"If I had any ammo," McQuaid said bitterly. "Still got the tube, but we lost the ammo chest on that last jump forward. Think at least one of the Romans drowned trying to save it. We're dry."

"Well that's not good." Warner grinned mirthlessly. "Because I think they've seen our muzzle flashes and they're headed this way."

"Shit." McQuaid watched the two big transports for a second, then nodded. "Sure as hell looks that way," he said.

Warner looked around. For the moment, the Romans and mercs held a section of the ship raft. They'd managed to bring along all their wounded—so far, at least—and no one on the other side seemed disposed to threaten their current perimeter. Thanks to the battle rifles, no doubt. He found himself wishing they'd had at least one of the machine guns, as well, but wishes weren't going to change anything.

*Problem is we can't stay here*, he thought grimly. *Whoever's running those transports must have figured out we're pinned down, and he has to have enough manpower to overrun everything we've got left, especially if his buddies chime in from Lido. So we've got maybe twenty minutes before they come down on top of us and it's over.*

It was funny, in a way. He'd been scared to death a hundred times since they'd arrived on Tran. This time, he was pretty sure they weren't going to make it, and he wasn't scared at all.

The wet deck heaved under his feet, driven by the pounding seas. The outermost ships were little more than splintered wreckage, battered and swamped by the angry waves but they were so tightly jammed only a handful of them had actually sunk. The sea was nothing if not patient, though, and those same waves were beginning to batter the raft apart. It wasn't going to happen anytime soon, but it *was* going to happen.

Not that they could stay where they were long enough for that to become a problem for *them*.

He looked to the east. Occasional flashes of rifle fire and the stuttering glare of one of the Bren guns still came from the fortress walls, but there were at least several hundred enemies on the galleys between him and the island. He looked back north. The *navibus onerārius* were closer, bearing down on them. Maybe their captains hadn't actually realized there were star men trapped on the ship raft. Maybe the storm was simply bad enough that it was driving them into the raft. In the end, it didn't much matter, though.

He turned and waved to Martins, and the lieutenant jogged over to him, his rifle slung over his shoulder and the surviving Gurkhas—all four of them—at his heels.

"We're screwed," Warner said. "Another fifteen or twenty minutes, and those bastards"—he pointed at the transports—"are gonna be right on top of us. So that's how long we've got."

"Got for what?" Martins asked.

"Got to cut our way through to San Lazzaro." Warner shook his head. "I'm down to my last mag. You?"

"Afraid I'm empty," Martins said. "Aside from *this*, that is." He touched his holstered Beretta, then twitched his head at the Gurkhas. "My lads are just about down to their bayonets, too."

"Well, that's probably about where we all are." Warner looked around again, then shrugged. "At least it's a simple proposition. What you might call a binary solution set."

"One way to put it." Martins surprised him with a smile, then beckoned to the marines carrying the recoilless. "Here," he said in Latin, unslinging his bayoneted rifle. "I imagine you can use this."

"Yes, Praefectus." One of them gave him a Roman salute and took the weapon from him.

"I suppose we should be going," Martins said. "Wouldn't do to be late to the party!"

"Are *all* Brits lunatics?" Warner asked, checking his rifle.

"Probably, a bit," Martins replied. Then extended his right hand. "I'm sorry we didn't have longer to get to know one another, but it's been an honor."

"Don't go all fatalistic on me," Warner growled, but he gripped the hand firmly.

"Wouldn't dream of it." Martins released his hand, drew his Beretta, and snapped the safety lever down. "Last man to the fort buys the beer!"

✣ ✣ ✣

"Baker here." The clipped British voice sounded preposterously calm. "Over."

"Galloway," Rick said into the microphone, staring out into the flame-shot, stormy madness. Half the beached galleys continued to blaze, despite the rain, washing the building fronts in waves of lurid light, but between the storm and the oncoming night, that was about all he could see. "I need an assessment, Major. Visibility's going completely to hell, and I can't see much from here. What's your status? Over."

"I believe the situation is in hand, Colonel," Baker replied. "My lads are short of ammunition, we have only six more magazines for the Bren, and your Passavopolous is down to his last two belts, but the firebombs and the flanking fire have done for them, for the moment at least,

I believe. They seem more concerned about covering in place behind the unburned galleys than they are about trying to advance. Can't say how long they'll stay that way, especially if more of their friends get around our flanks, but absent some major change in the situation, I believe we're secure here. I shouldn't like to see a fresh lot coming at us, though. Over."

"Understood."

Baker's last sentence had been more than a little pointed, Rick thought, and with good cause. The major knew their estimate of the enemy's strength had been disastrously low, and for all his ever-so-British understated calm, he had to be aware of how tightly stretched the defense was.

"I think del Verme's going to hold in the West Channel," Rick continued, "but we've lost control of Lido and Cannaregio completely, and the other side seems to have most of San Lazzaro. We believe the fortress is still holding out—largely because of your Lieutenant Cargill, I suspect—but they're starting to press hard on the bridges between San Lazzaro and San Mateo. So far, San Mateo itself seems solid, though. So does Santa Cecilia and most of San Giorgio. Over."

"And Admiral Stigliano? Over."

"He's dead," Rick said harshly. "What's left of his crews and marines were falling back on San Lazzaro, last we heard. Over."

"The Roman squadron? Over."

"No damned idea," Rick said even more harshly. "Haven't heard a word from Warner or anyone else since we ordered them to attack the transports. Over."

Baker was silent for a moment, and Rick heard more musket volleys. They weren't firing into the killing ground where so many bodies washed in the bloody water, so they had to be engaging galleys which had peeled off to either side.

"Colonel," the major said finally, "I don't think they have another frontal assault on the wagon fort left in them, and we've retaken the two palaces they seized on the southeast side of the square. All of the flanking attacks I know about were launched by single galleys, without support, and we have all of them pinned down. I expect there are some we *don't* know about, but the Nikeisian militia are covering the eastern side of the island and I'm pulling together a reserve of musketeers and halberdiers under your Clavell to serve as a fire brigade. If it isn't needed for that, it will be available to begin pinching out their lodgments one at a time. In my opinion, I can hold San Marco as long as they aren't able to bring a significant force of fresh troops into the fight against us. Over."

Rick nodded and closed his eyes for a moment, listening to the fury of the storm mingling with the fury of combat. San Marco, San Giorgio, and Santa Cecilia were the three largest islands of Nikeis, with the largest populations. If they managed to hold there, they could retake the smaller islands one at a time. But only if they held there.

*And they won't hold if the bad guys clear a way through that mess in the North Channel. Last we heard from Cargill, those last transports were still managing to stand off. If they get inside the lagoon, work their way around Baker, hit him with that "significant force of fresh troops," it's over. Hell, it may be over anyway!*

"Understood," he said again, finally. "Galloway, out."

He handed the microphone back to Mason.

"It's time, Art," he said.

"Sir, there's probably still friendlies out there in the channel."

"I know!" Rick snapped, then shook his head. "Sorry, Art," he said wearily, "but I *do* know. And it doesn't matter. We can't see what the hell is going on out there, we've lost touch with Cargill, and there's no way we're holding that raft in the end. For all we know, they're already cutting a way through it for those damned transports! But at least if they are, they're also concentrated in one spot, and that's what we need. So we hit them now and hope they take the hint, or we're done."

Mason looked at him, and Rick wondered if he looked as used up as he felt.

*I wasn't this exhausted at the Ottarn or Vis, he thought, and I haven't fired a single shot. Does Art realize that I'm done, whatever else happens? And maybe I feel so exhausted because I am so sick and tired of all this. The killing, the dying, the playing God! I'm done. Whatever happens tonight, I'm done. I can't do this anymore.*

"Pass the word to Walbrook," he said.

"Yes, Sir."

✦ ✦ ✦

Sergeant Chester Walbrook's radio chirped, and he snatched it from his webbing and pressed the transmit button.

"Backstop, over," he said.

"The Colonel says to do it," Art Mason said. "Over."

"About damned time!" Walbrook growled. He and his crews had stood by uselessly for hours, waiting for a moment that might never come while other men fought and died without them. "North Channel? Over."

"North Channel," Mason confirmed. "Over."

"Understood. Backstop, out."

Walbrook replaced the radio and turned to his gun chiefs.

"Our turn now," he said with grim satisfaction.

✦ ✦ ✦

Rick stood looking to the north. The rain, the dark, and the wind-shredded smoke were too dense now for him to see any gun flashes even if Cargill's squad was still alive. Were they? And *was* the fort still holding? Maybe it was. Maybe the men in it would even live now, he thought distantly. Of course, they might not, too. Probably wouldn't. *Nobody* lived once the great Captain General Rick came along. Besides—

Something flashed on the northern tip of the Isola di Sant'Andrea, the island between San Mateo and Santa Cecilia. And then, a second later, a blazing white sun seared its way across the night.

✦ ✦ ✦

"Yatar!"

Captain Agesilaus staggered back as the terrible light blasted into his eyes, blinding him. It came at the worst possible moment, just as he was preparing to lay *Summer Dawn* alongside that grinding, twisting mass of wreckage.

It was the last thing he wanted to do. He loved his ship, one of the biggest *navibus onerārius* of the entire Five Kingdoms, and now he was going to murder her. The waves would beat her to death against the rafted mass of galleys as surely as against any rocky coast, but it didn't matter. He'd fought wind and sea with every skill, every trick, learned in thirty years afloat, but he was out of tricks and the sea always won in the end. He'd even tried anchoring, only to have the anchor drag. He either put her alongside that reef of broken galleys and got the two thousand miserable, seasick troops packed into her hold onto it—if he could—or else she went down anyway and took all of them with her.

But *this*!

It had to be another star weapon, but what was it supposed to *do*?!

✦ ✦ ✦

The magnesium candle swung wildly across the night as the wind drove its parachute back towards the center of the inner lagoon. The heavy rain reduced its effectiveness, but its light still poured down across the stormy water like some sudden dawn, and the storm-battered raft of ships across the North Channel appeared out of the darkness.

Rick had his binoculars up, waiting, and his nostrils flared as he saw the tangle of galleys aswarm with men. They *were* cutting a way through the western end of the raft, he realized, and there had to be several thousand of them, either on the raft itself or on the galleys and transports waiting to pour into the inner lagoon as soon the way was clear.

*Good luck with* that, *you bastards*, he thought bitterly, and bared his teeth as something plunged into the water short of the raft and exploded.

Of all the weapons on Tran, the ones whose ammunition he'd hoarded most fanatically were Chester Walbrook's three mortars. He'd even managed to convince the Shalnuksis to replenish his ammunition supply, although like everything else, they'd provided nowhere near as much of it as he'd asked for. That was one reason he hadn't used them yet today.

Of course, there was another reason, as well.

✣ ✣ ✣

"Short!" Walbrook said, peering through his binoculars. "Up fifty!"

*CHONK!*

Another mortar bomb wailed its way through the storm. It plunged into the water and exploded. It was short of the galleys, too . . . but not by as much.

✣ ✣ ✣

"Oh, *shit!*" Larry Warner shouted as the flare blazed overhead. He knew exactly what it meant, and the Colonel couldn't have a clue that Warner and the Romans were still on the ship raft.

They were still a hundred yards, at least, from the fortress at the eastern end of the line, working their way steadily towards it and there were far too many Fivers and Riccigionans between them and safety. But it was also the only place to go . . . and they'd just run out of time for steady, methodical advances.

He tossed his empty rifle to an astonished Roman sailor, who caught it despite his surprise. Then he drew his fighting knife with his left hand and his .45 with his right and shoved up beside Martins.

"All right, you bastards!" he bellowed to the surviving mercs and Romans. *"Follow me!"*

✢ ✢ ✢

"Up twenty!" Sergeant Walbrook snapped, and tapped his toe impatiently while Private Jeff Balaika, the gunner on the number one tube adjusted the elevation wheel again. The gunners on the other two tubes followed suit, putting all three pieces on the same elevation. Once they found the range—

"Set!" Balaika announced.

"Fire!" Walbrook barked, and Balaika's assistant gunner—one of the Colonel's Chelm volunteers who Walbrook had personally trained—dropped another round down the tube.

*CHONK!*

Walbrook peered through his binoculars, cursing the rain and the wind as they drove his illuminating round across the night. Technically, it was supposed to give him seventy-five seconds of light, but that number hadn't been calculated for conditions like this. They didn't have many of them, though, and—

"Yes!"

✢ ✢ ✢

Captain Agesilaus was still trying to grasp what was happening when Walbrook's fourth 81-millimeter high-explosive round landed on *Summer Dawn's* quarterdeck.

✢ ✢ ✢

The explosion flashed with the brightness of a direct hit, and Walbrook snarled in satisfaction.

"All right, lay it to them!" he snapped, and his number-two tube coughed.

Then the number three.

✦ ✦ ✦

Rick watched as the mortar bombs came storming down the heavens. They might have run out of white phosphorus for the Carl Gustav, but not for the mortars. Two of Walbrook's mortars dropped HE onto the ship raft; the third fired WP, and the savage, inextinguishable incendiary blazed despite the rain and the waves and the spray while the high-explosive shattered timbers and men with equal abandon.

Their ammunition supply might be limited, but their enemies had obligingly packed several thousand men into a concentrated target in the middle of the water with nowhere to go, and the mortar bombs ripped into them mercilessly. Walbrook walked his fire along the raft, maiming and killing, burning men alive, and Rick Galloway lowered his binoculars and looked away.

# CHAPTER FOURTEEN

# "ONE MORE SUCH VICTORY AND WE ARE UNDONE."

Bart Saxon sat beside the bed, gazing out the window, and tried to come to grips with it all.

It wasn't easy.

*God, I'm a* teacher, *not a soldier. Wonder how many times I'm going to have to think that over the next few years? Please, God. If You're listening—if You exist—don't let me ever see anything like this again. Please.*

He wouldn't have made it without Cal, he thought. He'd been so far out of his depth, so lost...

*Never had a friend like him before,* he thought. *Never had a brother, either. Now I've got both. So I guess some good comes out of just about anything.*

He looked down from the window on a harbor clogged with floating bodies. So *many* bodies. Tran's aquatic predators and scavengers had penetrated the inner lagoon, and every so often one of those bodies—or a part of one of them—disappeared in a swirl of water.

It was low tide, and burned out galleys lay beached in Palazzo San Marco, surrounded by still more bodies, heaped in windrows where wave and tide had piled them. Working parties of prisoners, guarded by Nikeisian militia, many of them walking wounded, worked to collect the dead men. There were far too many of them to treat with anything like decorum or respect, nor was there anywhere to bury so many. Nikeis normally cremated its dead, but there was neither wood nor time for that, either. The working parties simply loaded them onto barges to be towed out beyond the outer lagoon and dumped over the side in weighted nets.

Some of Nikeis had burned, as well, despite its stone construction and the driving rain. At least the storm had blown itself out, leaving beautiful blue skies and white clouds, a gentle breeze, that only made the ghastly carnage even worse by contrast.

He couldn't see the North Channel from here. Even if he could have, distance would have blurred the details, and he was just as happy about that. The murderous mortar barrage had broken the attack's back, but at the cost of enormous casualties. Not all of them had been pirates or Riccigionans or Fivers, either. No one really knew how many men had died out there. Saxon doubted anyone ever *would* know. But it had to be in the thousands. Just thinking about it was enough to make him shiver, but the timing had been brilliant. The terror and, above all, the *suddenness*, of the savage onslaught when the battle had seemed all but won, had been utterly decisive. The fight had run out of the attackers like water, and they'd surrendered in droves as soon as they were promised their lives by the victors.

Thousands of them had been killed and more thousands wounded, and Nikeis and Colonel Galloway's men and allies didn't begin to have enough medical capacity to deal with that many casualties. Even if they'd had the manpower, a lot of men who might have made it back on Earth wouldn't make it here. That much was obvious. And all the medics and the priests could do was drug those men into merciful unconsciousness and keep them there.

*And while you're feeling sorry for them, what about all the Nikeisians they killed, Bart?*

His mouth tightened. Civilian casualties had actually been amazingly low, given the intensity of the carnage. It helped that there'd never been any fighting on Isola di Sant'Andrea or Isola di Santa Cecilia and very little on Isola di San Marco, beyond the Palazzo itself and the flanking palaces. Something like seventy-five percent of Nikeis' people had lived on those three islands—and San Giorgio—and as many civilians as possible had been evacuated to the upper town before the attack, as well. North Channel had always been the most likely point of attack. That was how Galloway had known where to position his mortars.

But however light *civilian* casualties had been, the militia and the city's ship crews had paid a savage price . . . and even "amazingly low" was cold comfort to the families who had lost loved ones. Or who'd almost lost them, even if they hadn't known they *were* "loved ones."

He turned back from the window at that thought. A part of him thought he ought to be out there, helping to cope with the carnage. But he didn't have the skills they needed. He would have been just one more strong back, and he had—

The girl—no, the *young woman*—in the bed beside the window stirred. Her eyes opened, a bit unfocused and confused. She blinked, and a hand rose to her forehead. Then she turned her head on the pillow.

"Lord Bart?" she murmured.

"Yeah." He smiled. "It's me."

"What—?" She blinked again.

"You have a concussion—what your people call a *nebbia mentale*." He hoped he'd pronounced that correctly. "Lord McCleve says you'll be fine." Actually McCleve had said she *ought* to be fine, but damned if he was going to tell her that. "You're just going to have to rest. You may have to take it easy for a long time, but you'll be fine, Lucia."

She started to stir, then stopped with a mouth-twisting gasp of pain. The hand from her forehead flew to her side, and her eyes widened.

"Oh, yeah. That, too." He quirked a smile at her and touched the side of her face with his own hand. "You got your fool self shot with a crossbow saving my hide."

She lay very still, and not just because of the pain, staring at him, and he stroked her face.

"Things are different here from the way they are back on Earth," he told her, picking his way through the conclusion he'd wrestled his way to while she lay unconscious. "Someday I'll tell you about some of the ways that's true. But back on Earth, someone your age would still be considered a child."

"I am ten years old...almost!" she said. "I am of

marrying age! I've had my courses for—"

She broke off, face coloring, and he laughed softly.

"Trust me, Lucia. No one who saw you going for an armored soldier twice your size armed with only a dagger will ever think of you as 'a child' again. *I* certainly won't."

She looked at him, rebellious eyes trying to focus, then reached up to the hand on her face:

"Do you mean—?"

"I don't know exactly what I mean," he told her. "I only know the two of us have to figure out what we feel." Her expression tightened, and he shook his head quickly. "I know what I think I feel, Lucia, and I think I know what *you* think you feel." *God, what a lot of "thinks" to cram into one sentence! She's going to think I'm an idiot.* "But we've only known each other for a few weeks, and I'm from an entirely different world. We need to be sure you aren't, well—"

"*Infatuato*?" she suggested, and laughed, despite the pain in her head and side, and his expression. "Oh, Lord Bart! I have seen much of that already in my life. Much of it directed at me! It is not what I feel when I look at you."

"Well, maybe it isn't." He smiled wryly, reminding himself that Lucia Michaeli had been training as a courtesan long before he crossed her horizon. "But it's important for *me* to be sure of that, Lucia. And to go slowly with this. It's important to me in a lot of ways and for a lot of reasons. Do you understand?"

"No," she told him, but she smiled as she said it. "I do not understand. I do not *want* to understand. But I am, of course, far too dutiful to argue with my future husband about it."

"*Dutiful?*" It was his turn to laugh out loud. "Signorina Michaeli, I suspect that you are neither dutiful nor very *truthful*, unless it suits your purposes!"

"No," she said again. "But I *pretend* very well, Lord Bart."

✣ ✣ ✣

"No, Heir of Caesar," the young Tamaerthan said firmly. "I regret that Lord Rick is not yet available."

Haerther met Publius' eyes levelly, with all of a Tamaerthan's refusal to kowtow to Rome. But there was more than reflex defiance in those eyes this morning, Publius saw. There was worry and a fierce protectiveness.

"I understand," he said, and saw something very like surprise join all the other emotions in Haerther's eyes when he chose not to press matters. "Inform him, when he is available, that I think it is urgent he and I speak."

"Of course, Heir of Caesar. May I tell him what it is you wish to speak of?"

"Many things," Publius said. "None of them so vital that I need disturb his rest when he has borne so much for all of us."

Haerther's eyes flared wide at that, and then he bowed deeply.

"I will tell him your very words, Heir of Caesar," he promised.

Publius nodded in reply, then turned and left the palace the Doge had assigned to Rick with Caius Julius at his side. As they stepped into the courtyard, Publius glanced casually about. No one was in close proximity.

"I think it is time I spoke with Major Baker once more," he said softly. "Discreetly, of course, Tribune."

"Of course, Heir of Caesar," Caius Julius murmured.

✢ ✢ ✢

Wind howled over a rain-lashed sea where mountainous waves pounded a disintegrating raft of galleys. He stood on one of those galleys, flayed by the wind, battered and soaked by the rain, and all about him men fought and cursed, bled and died. And killed.

Blood was everywhere, hot and steaming in the rain. Men screamed, writhing in agony, begging for their mothers—for *anyone*—to stop the pain. Crossbow bolts, javelins, swords and axes sheared and bit in brutal butchery, but no weapon came near him. No, *he* was inviolate. He walked through that horrific maelstrom untouched and untouchable. It was only *other* men who bled and died. Who lay on those blood-soaked, rain-lashed decks, trying to hold intestines inside opened bellies. Who raised frail, pitiful hands against the deathblow before it ended their lives.

But if he could not be touched, he could hear. He could hear the screams, the wet sounds of edged steel in human flesh. He could hear the wind howl, the waves crash, the clash of weapons, the crackle of rifle and pistol fire. He could hear the sudden explosions of mortar rounds, coming silently out of the night to detonate like hell's own hatred while men blew apart in bloody ruin or plunged shrieking into the angry sea as white phosphorus consumed them.

And he could hear the voices screaming *his* name. He could—

He jerked awake and his own strangled cry of horror echoed in his ears.

He sat up slowly in the comfortable bed and looked around the airy, sun-shot bedchamber. Elegant furniture and beautiful mosaics surrounded him. The open window's curtains flapped gently on the breeze, and he heard the peaceful coo of pigeons and the distant cries of gulls and other seabirds through it.

And none of it could drown those other sounds, because *those* sounds came from deep inside him and the knowledge of what he had done.

He swung his legs over the side of the bed and looked at the bottle of McCleve's best on the bedside table. His stomach heaved. There'd been three of those bottles, once. He'd emptied one of them before he finally passed out. He thought he remembered dropping another, as well. Remembered the half-full bottle shattering on the stone floor. There was no sign of either of them. Haerther, no doubt. Or Mason. Probably both, since they'd managed to get him into bed, too.

*Still covering for me,* he thought, bending over, burying his face in his hands. *God help me, even after* this, *they're still covering for me.*

He drew a deep breath and forced himself to stand. His head pounded, and something had crawled into his mouth and died there, but he made himself walk across to the window. Light-sensitive eyes squinted as he pulled back the curtain, looked out over the inner lagoon.

His belly twisted with threatened nausea as he saw the fresh proof of his handiwork. Dozens of boats moved across the laughing blue water, crews with bandannas tied over their mouths and noses heaving bodies out of its embrace. And those gulls whose cries had wakened him wheeled in circles above them . . . or landed on the drifting corpses to peck and tear at dead men's flesh.

He dropped the curtain and wheeled away from the window, eyes shut once more. Tylara. He needed Tylara. He needed—

*I need to go home*, he told himself flatly. *I need to admit*—finally—*how fucking far out of my depth I am. This isn't me. It's not who I am. Not who I can be anymore.* His eyes burned. *They can't put this on me anymore. I can't put it on* myself. *Because I'll screw it up. An entire goddammed planet! And . . . I'll . . . screw . . . it . . . up.*

Just as he'd screwed up here.

*We should have just emptied the damned containers and left. The Nikeisians could have told the Fivers and the Riccigionans we were gone—could have let them look for themselves! But, no, we had to*—I *had to—stand and fight, didn't* I? *And I underestimated the numbers, and I underestimated the goddamn weather, and I overestimated how frigging brilliant "Captain General Rick" is, and I got*—God, *how many?—people killed.*

*Including my friend.*

He bent his head again, and this time the tears came as he remembered Richard Martins, standing in front of him, left arm in a bloody sling with a hand he might never use again. There'd been tears in Martins' eyes, too, as he stood in the torchlit darkness with the fading storm still raging behind him.

"I'm sorry, Colonel," the young man had said, his public school reserve nowhere to be seen. "God, I'm so sorry. None of us would have made it without him. We tried— we *tried*. But—"

His voice had broken, and Rick had shaken his head.

"Not your fault," he'd heard himself say. "It happens. And it was my call. *My* fault."

"Colonel, you couldn't have known!" Martins had protested. "There was no way we could have told you. And if you hadn't—"

"I can tell myself that just as well as you can, Lieutenant." His voice had been harsher. "It may even be true. But *I* still killed him; you didn't."

Martins had started to say something more, then closed his mouth at an almost imperceptible headshake from Clyde Baker. Rick had pretended he hadn't seen it.

"Colonel," Baker had said, "you've been on your feet for close to twenty-four hours. Get some rest."

"A hell of a lot of other people have been on their feet even longer!" Rick had snapped, glaring at the Brit.

"Indeed." Baker had looked back levelly. "But rather fewer of them will need to make the decisions you will. Leave this bit to us."

*And so you came up here and you got so drunk you don't even remember them putting you to bed,* he thought scathingly. *You got drunk because of how desperately you didn't want to think of Larry out there on those goddammed galleys when you ordered Walbrook to open fire.*

He made himself straighten, look around for clothes, ignore the siren song of the bottle. There were no closets, neither his armor nor his rifle were anywhere in evidence, but his holstered .45 lay beside the bottle on the bedside table. For one long, terrible instant, his fingers longed to curl around the grip, but he made himself turn away from that, too. He couldn't do it to Tylara or the kids.

He finally admitted he had no option and rang the bell. A moment later, the door opened.

"Yes, My Lord?" Haerther said, no sign of contempt in his clear eyes.

"I need to dress," Rick said. "And then I suppose I need something to eat."

✛ ✛ ✛

"Forgive me, Lord Rick, but the Heir of Caesar is here."

"I see." Rick pinched the bridge of his nose, then sighed. Haerther had told him about Publius' earlier visit, even told him what Publius had said, but he'd shoved that thought down. Not until after he'd eaten, he'd told himself. It could wait until then. Of course, he'd only picked at his breakfast, but he actually felt a bit better, physically, at least. Until he thought about facing Publius, anyway.

*Can't put it off forever*, he thought. *Besides, you might as well tell him and get it over with.*

"Ask him to join me," he said, waving at the dining chamber.

"He is not alone, My Lord," Haerther said. "Lord Bart and Major Baker are with him."

Rick's eyebrows rose as he felt an actual stir of curiosity. He stepped on it firmly. It wasn't his job anymore.

"Very well. In that case, ask all of them to join me."

"Yes, My Lord."

The door opened again, moments later, and Publius, Baker, and Saxon came through it.

"Hail, Heir of Caesar," Rick said, standing to greet them.

"Hail . . . friend," Publius replied. Rick's eyes narrowed at the unusual familiarity, but he let it pass as he turned to the other two.

"Major. Mr. Saxon," he said.

"Colonel," Baker responded for both of them.

"Sit," Rick invited, waving at the chairs Haerther had found, and sat back down himself as they settled. "I'm glad you came this morning," he lied. "There are things I need to say to you. To all of you."

"I thought there might be," Publius said. "But first, I believe Lord Bart has something to say to *you*."

"Oh?" Rick looked at Saxon.

"Yes, Colonel." There was something different about Saxon, Rick realized. He seemed . . . almost buoyant, despite all the death and destruction about them. For a moment, at least; then his expression sobered and he leaned forward slightly. "You asked me why I'm really here," he said. "It's time I told you."

"Mr. Saxon—"

"No, Colonel." Saxon cut him off. "This is important. You need to hear it. And I might as well admit that Publius already got some of it out of me."

Rick looked quickly at the Roman, but Publius only gazed back with a bland expression. Somehow, Rick found it easy to believe the Heir of Caesar had gotten Saxon to talk. But *Rick* didn't want to hear it. He was so *tired* of secrets, and secret missions that other people thought up and left him to carry out, however many people he had to kill along the way. And yet . . .

"All right, Mr. Saxon," he sighed. "Go ahead."

"Thank you, Colonel," Saxon said. "We *are* here to

assist you in crop production for the Shalnuksis. That's true. But you were right to be suspicious, because it's also a cover story. I was told that if the real mission was revealed to the wrong people, I and a whole lot of people would be killed and the planet might be bombed back into the Stone Age. Or worse. But the truth is, my assignment's a contradiction. I'm supposed to educate the local population, but to hide it from the Galactics. Agzaral will do what he can to prevent the bombardment, but he couldn't promise anything. He did tell me the Shalnuksis can be bribed and they'd rather not sterilize the planet because of the costs involved—and because they'd lose the madweed, of course. But I was also told I was an insurance policy in case you failed, particularly because Agzaral thought you weren't doing very well when he sent us out."

"Okay, that's your assignment." Rick leaned forward, his interest sharpening almost despite himself. "But I still don't understand why Agzaral went to all this effort to send you here. From my perspective, he took an incredible risk to send you, the others, and the containers. Every single thing Les ever said to Gwen and me was about how important it was that we *hide* any tech advances here on Tran. That he and Agzaral and their friends saw us as a backstop for Earth but that anything we did had to be done by stealth. Had to be hidden, at least until the Shalnuksis leave. And now he sends *you* here with three frigging container loads of high tech? What you brought may—hell, probably *will*—launch the Thirty Years War, the French Revolution, and both world wars all at the same time! And if we don't kill each *other* off, the Shalnuksis will sure as hell do it for us if they figure out what you've got out there! Why the hell should he decide to take that chance?"

"Colonel, I wasn't there when they sent you out. I don't doubt hiding was the plan then. But that was fourteen years ago, and Agzaral's thinking seems to have changed in the meantime."

"Why?" Rick asked bluntly.

"Because all of humanity is at risk now," Saxon replied equally bluntly, and Rick shoved back in his chair in shock.

"You mean here and on Earth."

"No, Sir. I mean *everywhere*."

Rick darted a quick look at Publius, but the Roman appeared extraordinarily calm, and Rick looked back at Saxon.

"Explain that."

"Agzaral didn't have time to tell me everything," Saxon said, and Rick snorted harshly as he remembered his own conversations with the inspector. "But he did tell me there's some sort of quiet rebellion among the humans in the Galactic Confederation. Earth's technology advances are worrying the High Commission even more, and a lot of the humans serving the Confederation—Agzaral called them 'Janissaries'—think the Commission is hardening on bombing Earth back into the Stone Age . . . at least. Apparently, the faction on the Commission that wants to solve the 'wild human problem' once and for all is gaining momentum, and that means the Janissaries who don't want that to happen are making plans to try to stop it by force, if they have to."

"Jesus." Rick looked back and forth between Publius

and Baker, then back at Saxon. "You're talking some kind of rebellion?"

"I don't know," Saxon admitted. "I just know Agzaral seemed both excited and scared by the possibilities. But I don't think he has a choice anymore. He says there's a section in the Confederation, one that's gaining strength, that thinks *all* humans are too dangerous, too disturbing to their status quo, to keep around. That the High Council may just decide to exterminate all of us to put an end to all the arguing. But that's his worst-case scenario, and he's the kind who plays the game on a lot of levels. In his worst-case scenario, we—us, here on Tran—are his last ditch effort to keep the species alive if it does turn into a rebellion and the Confederation decides to wipe out all of 'its' humans at the same time it blasts Earth. But in his *best*-case scenario, we're the trump card that changes humans from slaves to voting members of the Confederation."

"By acquiring interstellar flight on our own," Rick said, and Saxon looked a bit surprised. But he also nodded.

"Yes, Sir."

"That much we already knew, courtesy of Les." Rick shrugged. "I don't know how likely it is, but Gwen and Tylara and I have been playing for that from the beginning, and with six hundred years between Shalnuksi visits—"

"I think Inspector Agzaral is afraid we may not have six hundred years," Saxon interrupted. Rick looked at him, and it was Saxon's turn to shrug. "Nobody outside the High Commission knows what the timetable for any decision about Earth really is, but Agzaral says there are indications that the timing is closing in. We might be talking about decades, or a few centuries—I get the impression the Confederation isn't exactly what you might call flexible—but it's also possible it could happen tomorrow. He wants us ready to claim membership in the Confederation as soon as possible, but that's not the same thing as wanting us to actually *assert* that claim."

*Damn all twisty-minded interstellar Machiavellians to hell*, Rick thought, rubbing one eyebrow.

"He wants us—what? Lurking in the wings? An ace up his sleeve that he can play if things go south with the High Commission or this human rebellion you're talking about heats up?"

"Something like that. He says there are more humans than any other single species out there, because we do so many jobs for the Galactics. I think he wants those humans—all humans—to eventually be free and equals in the Confederation."

"Which means developing interstellar flight here on Tran." Rick shook his head in disbelief. "In time to do any good on this accelerating timetable of his?" He laughed incredulously. "What makes him think we can do that? Hell, I've barely kept our heads above water for the last fourteen years!"

"He says he and his . . . accomplices have placed references in the library of scientific material we brought from Earth to be a breadcrumb trail that will eventually enable us to build starships of our own. A lot sooner than we could do it *on* our own." He shrugged. "That's one of the things *I'm* supposed to be kicking off, God help me."

"Who else knows about that?"

"Out there?" Saxon waved at the ceiling and the stars beyond it. "I don't have any idea. Here on Tran? Cal and Spirit may suspect, but Agzaral and Lee told them only the cover story."

"Then I suppose you've just become the most important man on the planet. Maybe in the whole damned universe."

"No, Sir. I haven't." Saxon looked at him levelly. "You have."

"No," Rick said flatly.

"Colonel, listen to me." Saxon leaned towards him. "It's not just spaceflight. Agzaral says the only chance for a successful entry into the Confederation is if the planet is united."

"United. *Politically* united?" Rick barked a hard, bitter caw of a laugh. "Jesus, now he wants to turn us into Mamelukes!"

"Mamelukes?" Publius repeated the strange word carefully, and Rick jerked an angry, exhausted nod.

"Mamelukes," he said, recalling a conversation—at least a century ago—in Taranto with Major Baker. "You heard the word Agzaral used—Janissaries?" he asked, and Publius nodded. "Well, Janissaries were slave soldiers back on Earth. They were more than just soldiers, eventually—bureaucrats and ministers of the emperor they served—but they were still slaves.

"Only then there were the Mamelukes. They were slaves, too, but they evolved into a powerful military caste, and eventually, they wound up ruling vast empires of their own. They were still technically slaves, but they were also noblemen and even emperors in their own right, and the system they created lasted for over a thousand years. That's what Agzaral has in mind. And he needs us to unify Tran politically to pull it off."

Rick shook his head, thinking about all the warring rival factions. It had taken everything he had, and cost more than he could stand, just to survive. And now Agzaral wanted him to *unify* the frigging planet?

"I'm afraid so," Saxon said. "They won't even consider membership for a planet—for a star system—that doesn't have a unified, single government that can speak for it. And that the Confederation can lay down terms for membership to."

"I don't care." Rick's voice was even flatter. "I'm done."

"No, Lord Rick," Publius said, speaking for the first time since Saxon had begun. "You are not."

"The hell I'm not!" Rick glared at him, then jabbed an angry forefinger at the window and the bodies beyond it. "I'm through, Publius. Through! Let somebody else do all the killing. I've spent fourteen goddamned years just trying to keep my feet under me, keep the people I care about alive, and I just proved I'm not really very *good* at that, am I?"

He heard the quiver in his own voice, but he didn't care.

"I'll get you back to the Empire. Hell, I'll keep the University going, give Mr. Saxon here a place to hang his hat while he invents interstellar flight! But that's it. I came to this world with over thirty men—*my* men! I think about thirteen of them are still alive. That's not a very good proportion, and I will be *damned* if I get the rest of them killed!"

"You have no choice." Publius' voice was almost compassionate.

Almost.

"While I was raised a Christian," the Roman continued, "I was also forced to study Greek and Roman legends. I recall the details of the Titanomacy and Prometheus only too well. You star lords are the Titans. And that one"— Publius pointed at Saxon—"is Prometheus. He brings the fire, the knowledge of the gods."

"As I recall, things didn't go well for Prometheus."

"Yes, he suffered. But eventually he was freed by Hercules, during one of his twelve labors."

"I don't like where this is going."

"I know that. But it changes nothing."

"I'm not Hercules!" Rick snapped. "And I'm tired. I'm tired of always having to watch my back. I'm tired of fighting every goddamned time I turn around. I'm tired of seeing people I care about die. And I'm tired of being the one who decides who lives and who dies when half the damned time I'm *guessing* about what I'm doing! So, no, I'm *not* Hercules. I'm Cincinnatus." He laughed mirthlessly. "Except I can't even do *that* right, can I? I can't just retire to my farm, because half the lords in Drantos want me dead and my farm is full of madweed. But I can damned well stay on it, defend what *I* care about, and let the rest of the world, the rest of the *galaxy*, take care of itself for a change!"

"You can play the part of Achilles and hide in your tent, if you desire. For a time," Publius said. "But not forever, my friend. Achilles retired from battle because he was full of pride, but you have little of that. Far less than I, for example. No, in your case it is doubt and despair that drive you like the Furies. You have just won one of the greatest battles in the history of Tran, and possibly the most *important* one ever fought here. But it means little to you. You say you are tired? I believe that. Yet even though we are very different men, you and I, I can recognize what is truly consuming you, and it is not just fatigue of the body. Your *soul* is weary. Perhaps that is because you are a better man than I. I do not know about that, but this I do know: Bishop Polycarp would agree that there are prices to be paid for giving in to the sin of despair."

"Worse than the ones I've already paid?" Rick asked bitterly.

"I think . . . yes," Publius said softly. "You can hide in your tent for a time, but while you do that someone else—someone like Major Baker, or Major Mason, or I, will be forced to become Patroclus. We will die trying to do what only you can do, and then you will be compelled to step forward anyway, knowing that we did."

Rick stared at him, his heart like a stone, and Publius shook his head.

"No man can outrun his fate, even if he has the feet of Mercury, and this *is* your fate. It may be hard, but it is yours. Your men followed you here willingly. The people of Nikeis looked to you to save them, and my legionnaires were inspired to fight and die at your side. None of them were here to fight because of this man or what is in those boxes. They were here to fight alongside the man who, will he or won't he, must become—has *already* become—the Warlord of Tran, not simply Drantos, to free us from the capriciousness of false gods."

The Roman shook his head again, holding Rick's gaze.

"I think, my friend, that perhaps you are the only man on Tran who has not already realized that. Or perhaps I should say who has not already *accepted* that. The rest of us have known for years."

"He's right, Colonel," Baker said, speaking for the first time. Rick glanced at him, and the Brit shrugged. "I'm a soldier, Colonel. All I ever wanted to be, all I ever expected to be. All I ever *trained* to be. You aren't, but what you are is something more important than that. You're a *commander*. You're not thinking about battles, Colonel Galloway. You're thinking about *wars*, and about what comes *after* the wars, and I could never have built the alliances, the relationships, you have. You think you aren't up to the job?" It was Baker's turn to bark a laugh. "For a bloody 'amateur,' you just performed *brilliantly*. You may not see that, but I damned well do. If you aren't up to the job, then nobody else *is*, and this isn't the sort of task we can leave to someone who isn't up to its weight. No matter how unfair to you that may be. I'll be your military commander, if that will take some of that weight off you. Your Major Mason and I, we'll command in the field, go where you need us, do what must be done. But we can't do the rest of your job. The only one who can do it is you."

Rick looked back and forth between him and Publius.

"How long has this conspiracy of yours been in the works, Publius?"

"You planted the germ of the idea on the day you told my father of the coming Time and he realized how you must have arrived on Tran. Then there were the ancient texts and their warnings. These new arrivals"—he waved one hand at Baker and Saxon—"have only accelerated our plans, Lord Rick. They have not changed them."

"What plans?"

"We are at war with the gods. Or perhaps it would be more accurate to say that they are at war with *us*, and have been for millennia. We know that Rome will be one of the first targets should the skyfire fall again—perhaps the second one, after you. Yet legends hold that when men unite, when they stand together, sometimes they can defeat even gods. I do not understand all of the changes Lord Bart has described to me, but I do not need to. The changes of the Time alone will be terrible enough. All I need to know is that what the sky demons propose to do to us will be even worse. To survive that—to have any hope of surviving that—we must stand together. And my father realized from the very beginning that only someone from outside our squabbles and our historic rivalries and hatreds can unite us. We must stand together . . ."

"'Or we shall certainly hang separately . . .'" Rick murmured.

"*Quid est?*"

"A group of men said something like that on Earth over two hundred years ago. They also said 'give me liberty or give me death,' and they banded together to free a new country from what was probably the most powerful military in the world. That country is where I was born. Now I've learned that after we were brought to Tran, that same nation won a half-century conflict—what we called a Cold War—against another powerful nation that spat on the very idea of individual liberty. Major Baker here told me about a leader who stood up to what he called an evil empire . . . and won."

"I do not know if we can do the same," Publius said. "I suspect the odds we face are worse than the ones he faced. But I also think we have no choice other than to try, and you are the only one everyone—Rome, Drantos, Nikeis, even the Five, in the fullness of time—will agree to follow. It will not be easy, and some of us will follow only if we are compelled to, but we *will* follow. So the only question is whether or not you will *lead* us."

Rick looked at the other three. Quiet wrapped itself about the chamber, perfected and not interrupted by the distant murmur of voices, street traffic, and seabirds, and he felt the weight crushing down upon him.

*I'm not Hercules*, he thought. *I'm Atlas, with the entire damned world on my back. And in the end, whatever else happens, I'll be Rodin's Caryatid, crushed under its weight. And do I have the right to take Tylara there with me? Or will I find out she's been in agreement with Publius and Marselius from the beginning?*

"I'll . . . think about it," he told them finally. "That's all I'll promise, all I *can* promise. But . . . I'll think about it."

⁕ ⁕ ⁕

"Your pardon, Lord Rick," Haerther said, "but it is time."

"I know," Rick sighed, and straightened from where he stood, leaning against the window frame, looking down on the harbor and the wreckage of battle. The familiar weight of chain mail and flak vest pressed down upon him like a shadow of the greater burden waiting for him to take it up.

He absently patted the butt of his holstered .45, lips

quirking as he considered how Art Mason would react if he'd dared to leave the weapon behind. He turned from the window, and Haerther examined him critically. The squire reached out and adjusted the strap of Rick's shoulder holster, then nodded in satisfaction and opened the chamber door for him.

*I don't want to do this*, Rick thought. *But I have to. Whatever I finally decide about . . . anything else, I have to do this.*

He stepped through the door into the borrowed palace's great hall and paused as Publius turned to face him. A dozen others were also present—Art Mason, Clyde Baker, Caius Julius, Publius' bodyguard—but Publius reached out to clasp forearms with him in the Roman fashion.

"Hail Rick, Friend of Caesar and defender of the alliance," he said. "I thought we should see to our wounded together."

"I agree," Rick said, and the two of them walked out of the palace, surrounded by the others, and across the square to the larger structure which had been converted into Sergeant McCleve's field hospital. One of the acolytes of the new United Church who served as medical corpsmen met them at the door.

"Greetings, Lord Rick. Hail, Heir of Caesar." The acolyte bowed to both of them. "I regret that Lord McCleve is in surgery. He will join you as soon as he may. In the meantime, he has asked me to be your escort."

"Thank you," Rick murmured, and the acolyte beckoned for them to follow him into a large hall which had been converted into a ward.

Rick stopped beside the bed nearest the door. The Roman legionnaire in it attempted to rise when he saw Rick and Publius.

"As you were," Rick said gently. "You've earned your rest."

He noticed that the young soldier's right arm was heavily bandaged and splinted.

"How are you?" he asked.

"Well enough," the Roman replied. His eyes were heavy and his words slurred a bit. "I hope your doctor McCleve can save my arm. It was crushed in the fighting in the North Channel."

Rick's mouth tightened as he realized this youngster had been with Warner on the ship raft. He started to say something about that, then stopped himself as he saw the soldier's eyes droop before he fought them back open again.

*Painkillers. Maybe the madweed-derived one*, he thought.

"If anyone can save your arm, Doc McCleve can," he said instead.

"If not, I know it will be restored on the last day. I only hope I can remain in service to the Alliance."

Rick could actually hear the capitalization of "Alliance" in the legionnaire's voice. *I'm standing here with Publius, and the kid says* Alliance, *not Rome. Is Publius right about all this crap? God help me, is he right?*

The continued their tour of the ward. Nikeisian militia, Tamaerthan warriors, Roman soldiers, even mercs lay side by side. Those who were conscious seemed genuinely pleased and enheartened at the thought that Rick and

Publius had come to visit them. Yet Rick was even more aware of the stretcher bearers who passed them periodically, taking still figures with blanket-covered faces out or bringing recently triaged patients in. Everywhere, acolytes were busy treating the wounded. Some prayed with those who needed help, but too many prayed quietly with those who would soon be taken outside.

Eventually, they moved from the common ward to the private rooms. Rick stepped into the first one and paused as he saw Sergeant McCleve. The doctor was bent over the bed, but he straightened at Rick and Publius' entrance, and Rick saw Jimmy Harrison lying in it, unconscious.

"Sorry, Colonel," McCleve said. "When I got out of surgery, they told me you were headed this way, so I figured I'd come ahead and check in on Jimmy while I waited for you here."

"How's he doing?" Rick asked.

"Not good. He's got a bad bruise on his chest from a javelin, but his vest stopped that. It's the only reason he's still alive. But what has me worried is the bruising to his *brain*, not his chest. According to Goodman and Signorina Torricelli, they hit him with a damned brick, and I believe it. If he'd been wearing a helmet instead of just a damned *beret*, maybe—" The medic cut himself off and shrugged. "I'm pretty sure he's got a depressed skull fracture, but without x-rays I can't tell how bad it really is, and I don't like how long he's been unconscious."

"Is he going to make it?"

"I don't know. He's in a coma. I can keep him alive with IV fluids and other techniques, but the longer he's comatose, the more likely we are to see something like pneumonia set in, and that could be the real killer. We're in better shape for antibiotics than we were before Major Baker and Mr. Saxon got here, but we've also got one hell of a lot more wounded to spread them between. And even if he doesn't get pneumonia, I don't know what mental capacity he'll have after taking a hit like that. He *could* be fine, but—"

The doctor shrugged again and Rick nodded.

*Tran's a rough place to have a mental disability*, he thought. *If he does, what will his wife and kids do when they find out? I'll have to make sure he gets a pension that's tied to him but still takes care of them if he dies. Will angels sing for Jimmy?*

"Do your best, Doc. Anything you need—anything— you tell me or Major Mason."

"Yes, Sir."

Rick laid a hand lightly on Harrison's lax shoulder. Then he turned and headed for the next room on his list.

✢ ✢ ✢

An hour or so later, Rick descended the stairs from the hospital's upper floor with Publius. He'd been a little surprised when the Roman walked every step of the way with him. He didn't normally think of Publius as a fountain of humanity, yet the heir to the Roman throne had shown another side as they visited the wounded. Perhaps it was simply a case of his playing the part he knew was demanded of a military commander, but Rick thought it went deeper than that.

*A sense of obligation, at least*, he decided. *Maybe even genuine compassion. That's a quality I never associated with him before! But maybe there's more to him than I thought. I've always known he's smart, but until he and Baker and Saxon dropped that damned conspiracy on me, I hadn't really thought about how much he worries about his responsibilities, not just his position. Of course, protecting the position sort of requires the discharge of the responsibilities, I guess.*

He smiled at that thought, amused despite his exhaustion and the decision looming before him, as they crossed the main ward again, headed for the exit.

Baker and Mason had excused themselves to attend to their duties some time before, and Rick envied them. He didn't doubt they really were as busy as a pair of one-armed paper hangers. God knew he'd dropped enough of the responsibility for dealing with the battle's aftermath on the two of them! But in many ways, he would have preferred to be dealing with those himself. At least it would have kept him busy...and spared him from this face-to-face confrontation with the human cost of his decisions.

They reached the door, and Rick paused. Bart Saxon stood just inside the door, waiting for them. Rick raised an eyebrow at him, but Publius had obviously expected the other star man's presence. The Roman only waved for Rick to precede both of them out the door, so he stepped through it—and froze.

"Tennnn-*hut!*" Master Sergeant Bisso bellowed, and Rick heard hundreds of boots slam together.

Mason, Baker, Martins, and young Cargill stood in a row just outside the door, and assembled on the quay beyond them were hundreds—thousands—of men. It

looked as if everyone not currently on guard duty was
there. Mercenaries, Gurkhas, Drantos musketeers,
Tamaerthan archers, Roman legionnaires, Nikeisian
militia—all of them, in orderly ranks. And beyond them,
the surviving sailors and marines of the Roman and
Nikeisian galleys.

"Preeeeeeeesent, *Arms!*"

Weapons and hands rose as every one of those
assembled men saluted, each nation in its own fashion. A
combined band of drummers and trumpeters played an
inspired, if rough, flourish, and a Nikeisian militia
drummer boy kept time with the other drummers in the
band.

*I'm going to get Mason for this*, Rick thought, but he
realized he was smiling as he returned the salute.

Then the music stopped. A Roman centurion—Rick
remembered he was first spear of Publius' cohort, stepped
forward and extended his right hand high in the air, palm
forward.

"*Ave! Ave*, Galloway Imperator!" He shouted. "Hail,
Imperator!"

Rick's smile disappeared.

*My God. This has to be Publius' doing or was it the*
*troops' idea?* He darted a look at Publius, but the Roman
only looked back levelly. *Either way, he damned well*
*knew about it. Christ, what do I do now?*

He remembered the day Roman legionnaires had
proclaimed Ganton Imperator on another field of battle.
It wasn't the same as emperor, but only one who'd been
proclaimed Imperator could claim the purple.

"*Ave*, Imperator!" the cry thundered up, not a single

centurion now, but the massed voice of the entire formation, and he knew. It *was* the troops' idea. It was coming from the men he'd lead into the holocaust. It was coming from *them*, and he felt the terrifying future roaring towards him, like the storm which had ravaged Nikeis, and knew now that he couldn't avoid it.

Fear of that future ripped through him, but not *just* fear. Not in the face of those voices. Because there was too much pride. Not in himself, but in *them*, and if they could give so much, if they could *die* because he led them, then he had no choice but *to* lead them, wherever that journey took all of them in the end.

"*Ave, Galloway. Ave!*"

The cry went up not just from the troops, but from every window and balcony that overlooked the quay. Rick stood there, eyes burning, his face a stone, as he felt that weight settling upon his shoulders and prayed for the strength to bear it.

"*AVE*, GALLOWAY!"

"Bring this world together, my friend," he heard Publius say through the rhythmically shouting voices.

"GALLOWAY, IMPERATOR!"

"Free the stars," Saxon said from his other side, and Rick Galloway raised his head, nostrils flaring, as the cry rang through the city.

"*AVE! AVE, GALLOWAY IMPERATOR!*"